# Mistress of Shadows

# Mistress of Shadows

AMMIE COME HOME
THE DARK ON THE OTHER SIDE
PRINCE OF DARKNESS

## BY BARBARA MICHAELS

Mystery Guild
Garden City, New York

# Contents

# Mistress of Shadows

# Introduction

I MUST HAVE BEEN ABOUT TEN YEARS OLD WHEN I DISCOVERED Bram Stoker's *Dracula*. It was a gray, rainy day, and I distinctly remember following my mother around the house with the book clutched in my perspiring hand. I couldn't stand being alone in a shadowy room with *Dracula*.

I used to boast that I had read every ghost and horror story ever written, but that no longer holds true. The modern variety is too grisly for me. The degeneration (as I view it) of the genre is due in large part to film and television, with their only too vivid special effects. Blood spurts, body parts fly around, faces disintegrate. In an effort to match or surpass the visual grisliness, most modern horror novels have long loving descriptions of mutilation, rape, and torture. This does not inspire terror in me, only disgust. Dracula never wasted blood.

*Ammie Come Home* was the first ghost story I wrote, and I followed the classic tradition. For me the supernatural has its rules, as strict as those that apply in the real world. A haunting should have a reason—revenge, guilt, unexpiated sin, a task left undone. I'm particularly fond of motives that lie in the past. In order to free themselves from the ghostly terror the victims must employ the same methods of investigation that are used in a detective story or in historical research.

I wrote most of *Ammie* late at night, after my children had gone unwillingly to bed, and I don't mind admitting I looked over my shoulder quite a lot. The house, isolated and large, was very quiet; the room in which I worked had too many doors and windows. I had a wonderful time.

Having found a voice, as the modern jargon has it, I went on writing the sort of book I liked to read. I continued my collection of so-called true ghost stories; my library now includes an entire section of them, from studies of medieval witchcraft to the journals of the Society for Psychic Research. The former category, including Murray's *Witch Cult in Western Europe*, gave me the inspiration for *Prince of Darkness*. There are no ghosts in that book; it deals with evil which, though contemporary in nature, has its roots in the past. *The Dark on the Other Side* represents a third sub-category. At the end the reader is left to make up his/her own mind about the nature of the terror. Was it supernatural, or the creation of a paranoid mind, intent on power? I particular enjoy writing books like this, because I have to create an ambiguous plot, in which every incident can be interpreted in two different ways. The skeptic, one of the major characters, triumphantly produces a rational explanation for everything that had happened, only to be confounded by one small fact that leaves his common-sense structure shaken. I don't mind admitting this technique was inspired by one of my favorite writers, John Dickson Carr, who used a variant of it brilliantly in *The Burning Court*.

The classic novel of the supernatural seems to be out of fashion. No one would like to see it revived more than I. How many times can a person reread *Dracula*?

Barbara Mertz
(a.k.a. Barbara Michaels and Elizabeth Peters)

# Ammie, Come Home

# Chapter

## 1

BY FIVE O'CLOCK IT WAS ALMOST DARK, WHICH WAS NOT SUR-prising, since the month was November; but Ruth kept glancing uneasily toward the windows at the far end of the room. It was a warm, handsome room, furnished in the style of a past century, with furniture whose present value would have astonished the original owners. Only the big overstuffed sofas, which faced one another before the fireplace, were relatively modern. Their ivory brocade upholstery fitted the blue-and-white color scheme, which had been based upon the delicate Wedgwood plaques set in the mantel. A cheerful fire burned on the hearth, sending sparks dancing from the crystal glasses on the coffee table and turning the sherry in the cut-glass decanter the color of melted copper. Since her niece had come to stay with her, Ruth had set out glasses and wine every evening. It was a pleasant ritual, which they both enjoyed even when it was followed by nothing more elegant than hamburgers. But tonight Sara was late.

The darkening windows blossomed yellow as the street-lights went on; and Ruth rose to draw the curtains. She lingered at the window, one hand absently stroking the pale blue satin. Sara's class had been over at three thirty. . . .

And, Ruth reminded herself sternly, Sara was twenty years old. When she agreed to board her niece while the girl attended the Foreign Service Institute at a local university, she had not guaranteed full-time baby-sitting. Sara, of course, considered herself an adult. However, to Ruth her niece still had the touching, terrifying illusion of personal invulnerability which is an unmistakable attribute of youth. And the streets of Washington—even of this ultrafashionable section—were not completely safe after dark.

Even at the dying time of year, with a bleak dusk lowering, the view from Ruth's window retained some of the famous charm of Georgetown, a charm based on formal architecture and the awareness of age. Nowadays that antique grace was rather self-conscious; after decades of neglect, the eighteenth-century houses of the old town had become fashionable again, and now they had the sleek, smug look born of painstaking restoration and a lot of money.

The houses across the street had been built in the early 1800's. The dignified Georgian facades, ornamented by well-proportioned dormers and handsome fanlights, abutted directly on the street, with little or no yard area in front. Behind them were the gardens for which the town was famous, hidden from passersby and walled off from the sight of near neighbors. Now only the tops of leafless trees could be seen.

The atmosphere was somewhat marred by the line of cars, parked bumper to bumper and, for the most part, illegally. Parking was one of Georgetown's most acrimoniously debated problems, not unusual in a city which had grown like Topsy before the advent of the automobile. The vehicles that moved along the street had turned on their headlights, and Ruth peered nervously toward the corner, and the bus stop. Still no sign of Sara. Ruth muttered something mildly profane under her breath and then shook her head with a self-conscious smile. The mother-hen instinct was all the stronger for having been delayed.

## II

Ruth was in her mid-forties. She had always been small, and still kept her trim figure, but since she refused to "do things" to her graying hair, or indulge in any of the other fads demanded of women by an age which makes such a fetish of youth, her more modish friends referred to her pityingly as "well-preserved." She bought her clothes at the same elegant little Georgetown boutique which she had patronized for fifteen years, and wore precisely the same size she had worn at the first. The suit she was wearing was a new purchase: a soft tweedy mixture of pink and blue, with a shell-pink, high-necked sweater. As a business-woman she clung to the tradition of suits, but as a feminine per-son she liked the pastels which set off her blue eyes and gilt hair, now fading pleasantly from gold to silver.

Standing at the tall window, she shivered despite the suit jacket. This part of the room was always too cold; even the heavy, lined drapes did not seem to keep out tendrils of chilly air, and the room was too long and narrow for the single fire-place halfway along its long wall. Ruth wondered idly how her ancestors had stood the cold in the days before central heating. They were tougher in the good old days, she thought—tougher in every way, less sentimental and more realistic. None of them would have stood jittering and biting their nails over a child who was a few minutes late. Of course, in those days a well-bred young woman wouldn't be out at dusk without a chaperone.

As Ruth was about to abandon her vigil a car slowed. It hov-ered uncertainly for a few minutes and then darted, like the strange insect it resembled, into a narrow space by a fireplug. Ruth leaned forward, forgetting that she could be seen quite clearly in the lighted window so near the street. Since there was hardly any subject which interested her less than that of auto-mobiles, she was unable to identify the make of this one, except that she thought it "foreign."

The near door opened; and a tangle of arms and legs emerged and resolved itself into the tall figure of her niece. Ruth smiled, partly in relief and partly because the sight of Sara trying to get her long legs and miniskirts out of a very small car always amused her. Her smile broadened as she got a good look at Sara's costume. Usually the girl was still in bed when Ruth left for work in the morning; Sara was a junior and had learned the fine art of arranging classes so that they did not interfere unduly with social activities or sleep; and every evening Ruth awaited her niece's appearance with anticipation and mild alarm. Every new outfit seemed to her the absolute end, the extreme beyond which it would be impossible to go. And each time she found she was mistaken.

Sara had one arm filled with books. With the other hand she swept the long black hair out of her face in a gesture that had proved the biggest single irritant to her long-suffering but silent aunt. The hair was absolutely straight. Ruth had never caught

Sara ironing it, but she suspected the worst. At least the hair covered the girl's ears and throat and shoulders, serving some of the functions of the hat and scarf which Sara refused to wear; part of the time it also kept her nose and chin warm.

The flowing locks presumably compensated for the lack of covering on Sara's lower extremities. This evening she was wearing the long black boots which had been her most recent acquisition, but there was a gap of some six inches between their tops and the bottom of Sara's skirt. The gap was filled, but not covered, by black mesh stockings, which displayed a good deal of Sara between the half-inch meshes.

Sara's present costume was especially amusing when Ruth recalled her first sight of the girl, that morning in early September. Sara had stepped out of the taxi wearing a neat linen suit, nylon stockings, alligator pumps, and—incredibly—a hat and gloves. Ruth hadn't seen the suit or the hat or the gloves since. In retrospect Ruth couldn't help feeling a bit flattered, not so much by Sara's effort to be conventional for her—since she suspected that Sara's mother had had a good deal to do with that—but by Sara's assumption that she need not continue to be conventional.

Sara leaned down to address the driver through the window. The hair fell over her face again. Ruth forgot her twitching fingers in her curiosity. This was not one of her niece's usual escorts. Sara was apparently inviting him to come in, for the car door opened and a man stepped into the street. He narrowly missed being annihilated by a Volkswagen which skidded by him, but he seemed to be accustomed to this, as, indeed, are most Washingtonians.

Ruth's first impression was neutral. He was a big man, tall and broad-shouldered, but his most outstanding feature, visible even in the dimmish streetlight, was his hair. Its brilliant carroty red seemed untouched by gray. Yet Ruth knew he was not young; there was something about the way he stood and moved. . . .

He turned, in a brusque, sudden movement, and stared at the house. Ruth dropped the drape and stepped back. The sudden lift and turn of his head had been as direct as a touch. And what a fool she was, to stand gaping out at the street like a gossipy suburban housewife—or a Victorian guardian, checking up on her ward. She was blushing—an endearing habit which even fifteen years in the civil service had not eliminated—when she went to open the door. She had been told that she looked charming when she blushed; the rosy color gave vivacity to her pallor and delicate bone structure. Therefore she was slightly annoyed when the eyes of the man who stood outside her door slid blankly over her and focused on something beyond.

"Good God Almighty," he said.

Ruth's first, neutral impression was succeeded by one of profound distaste.

She glanced over her shoulder.

"I'm so glad you like it," she said frostily. "Won't you come in and have a better look? The wind is a bit chilly."

"This is Professor MacDougal, Ruth," Sara said, with the familiar sweep of hand across brow. "He was nice enough to drive me home. My aunt, Mrs. Bennett, Professor."

"Putting his worst foot forward, as usual," said Professor MacDougal, displaying a set of predatory looking teeth. His attention was now fully upon her, and Ruth wasn't sure she liked it. He was much bigger than she had realized—well over six feet and bulkily, thickly built. His national ancestry was written across his face, but it was not the Irish stereotype, which is more caricature than actuality; it was the sort of face one sees in old Irish portraits, combining dreamer and soldier. The hair was not pure red after all. It had plenty of gray, iron-colored rather than silver. The skin of his cheeks and chin was just beginning to loosen. He must be fifty, Ruth thought, but he does have rather a nice smile. . . .

"I'm sorry, Mrs. Bennett," he went on. "That was a hell of a way to address a strange lady, wasn't it? Particularly when you have just returned the lady's young niece. But I like good architecture, and that's a remarkable staircase. Smaller than the one at Octagon House, but equally fine."

"Come in," Ruth said.

"I am in. Want me to go back out and start all over?"

For a moment Ruth gaped at him, feeling as if she were on a boat in bad weather, with the deck slipping out from under her feet. Then something came to her rescue—for days she mistakenly identified it as her sense of humor. She said smilingly, "Never mind, the damage is done. What on earth do you teach, Professor?"

"Anthropology."

"Of course."

"Of course," he repeated gravely. "The abrupt, uncivilized manners, the profane speech, the weatherbeaten look. . . ."

"Not at all," Ruth said, trying to keep some grasp of the conversation. "Sara has mentioned you often. She enjoys your course so much. It was good of you to bring her home."

"She stayed to help me sort some papers. But it wasn't out of my way. I had nothing in particular to do this evening."

"Then you must have a glass of sherry—or something else, if you'd rather—before you go back out into that wind."

He accepted sherry, somewhat to Ruth's surprise; it seemed an inadequate beverage for someone so boisterously masculine, and a beer stein was more suited to his big hand than the fragile, fine-stemmed glass. He sat down on the sofa and relaxed, with a sigh which was an unconscious tribute to the restful charm of the room.

"Nice. Very nice. . . . The hanging stair is the *pièce de résistance,* though. Was the designer old Thornton himself?"

"The man who did the Capitol? So tradition says, but it can't be proved."

"In my salad days—about four wars back—I thought I wanted to be an architect. I took the Georgetown House tour, along with the social climbers and the gushing old ladies, but I never saw this house. I'd have remembered the stairs."

"Oh, then you're a native? They are rare in Washington, and rarer in Georgetown."

"I don't live here anymore," he said briefly.

"But you may recall why this house wasn't on display. The previous owner was an eccentric old lady, a genuine Georgetown personality. She used to say she didn't want the vulgar rabble tracking dust on her rugs and gaping at her possessions."

"That's right, I remember now—though I never heard her reasons expressed quite so forcibly and unflatteringly. Am I right in assuming that you bought the house furnished? You couldn't have collected this furniture and all the bric-a-brac, in your short lifetime."

"Your general assumption is correct," Ruth said, ignoring the blatant attempt at flattery. "But I didn't buy the house. Old Miss Campbell was my second cousin. She left it to me."

"I didn't know she had any living relatives. It's beginning to come back to me now—wasn't she the last of the descendants of the original builder?"

"Yes, she was. This is one of the few houses which has never been restored because it was never neglected; much of the furniture has stood in its present location for a hundred and fifty years. I'm a member of a collateral line. Actually, Miss Campbell's father disowned my grandmother, about a thousand years ago."

"How did you ever captivate the old lady?" MacDougal ran one finger along the scalloped rim of the table beside him. He had big, brown hands with thick fingers, but his touch was as delicate as a musician's.

"Darned if I know. When I came to Washington years ago I called on her, just as a matter of courtesy. I wasn't even interested in the house, as I was going through my Swedish modern phase at the time. But I knew that all her near relatives were dead, and I thought the poor old soul might be lonely. I couldn't have been more wrong! She had a tongue like an adder, and she employed it freely, believe me. If I hadn't been so well brought up I'd have walked out after the first five minutes. But I did adore the house; it was the first time I'd ever seen a place like this. Even now my interest is completely uneducated; I don't have time to study architecture or antiques, I just enjoy them. I was absolutely astounded last year, when Cousin Hattie's lawyer wrote to tell me that she had left the house to me."

"Maybe you were the only relative she knew personally. And she probably had a strong sense of family, like so many of these vinegary old virgins."

"I suppose so. I always felt guilty, because I didn't even know she had died. Her lawyer said she insisted on a private funeral, but if I had only read the newspapers. . . ."

"People our age haven't yet taken to studying the obituaries," MacDougal said dryly. "Why should you feel guilty? She wanted it that way. She isn't going to haunt you. Or does she?"

"Does who do what?" asked Sara, coming in with a tray. Ruth blinked, and managed to keep her face straight. Professor MacDougal was getting what she and Sara, in their sillier moments, referred to as "the full treatment"—smoked oysters, nuts (without peanuts), and hot cheese puffs (frozen).

"Does old Miss Campbell haunt your aunt. Thanks, Sara, that looks good." MacDougal helped himself liberally to oysters; and cast a disparaging eye over Sara's costume. "But I must say that, while I am generally in favor of the clothes you girls are wearing of late, in this room you look as incongruous as a headhunter in Versailles."

"I share your aesthetic reaction," Ruth said with a smile. "But I can't picture Sara in ruffles and crinolines."

"People just aren't impressed by this sort of thing any more," Sara said scornfully. "In fact it's terrible—sherry, antiques and all that junk—while only a few blocks away . . ."

"That sort of contrast is the most banal cliché of them all," MacDougal said; and to Ruth's surprise Sara took the reprimand meekly.

"Yes, sir. But a cliché isn't necessarily untrue, is it?"

"No, dear, and I'd like to have everybody happy and equal too. In the meantime, I'm just going to go on wallowing in my sinful bourgeois pleasures, such as sherry and antiques. Aren't you at all susceptible to the charm of this place? It's your family too, isn't it?"

"I suppose so," Sara said indifferently. "My mother is Ruth's sister, so that makes me Cousin Hattie's—what? Fourteenth cousin once removed? See how silly it sounds? Why should I have any more feeling for Cousin Hattie than I do for Hairy Joe, who plays a great guitar down at Dupont Circle?"

"All men are brothers," said MacDougal sweetly.

"Yes, damn it!"

"Sara—" Ruth began.

"That's okay," MacDougal said calmly. "I shouldn't bait the girl. I can't help it, though. I get a sadistic thrill out of poking the right buttons and seeing them jump. They equate squalor and soulfulness; but, as a matter of fact, Joe plays lousy guitar."

"Oh, I'm not defending the Flower Children," Sara said, in a worldly voice. "Some of them are pretty silly. But at least they're thinking about the important problems, even if what they think is wrong. Whereas the Georgetown mentality—I'll tell you what typifies it for me. The story about the governess who used to make her charges blow out their candles at ten o'clock sharp, and then, after she died, all the lights in her former room would go out at that hour, by themselves. Empty traditions, pointless sentimentality—"

"You did read a book about Georgetown, I see," Ruth said, refilling glasses.

"The one and only. Honest to God, it turned my stomach! So much sweetness and light, and such big fat lies."

"Come now," MacDougal said, grinning.

"You know what I mean. According to that book all the gentlemen and ladies of Old Georgetown were kind, noble philanthropists. Just look at their pictures! Tight-lipped, hawk-nosed, grim old holy terrors! Never a mention of scandal, crime, disgrace—why, you know that in two hundred years this town must have seen a lot of violence. But the books never mention it—dear me, no!"

"One of the things I hate about the younger generation," said MacDougal sadly, "is its bitter cynicism."

"I expect you see a good deal of it, don't you?" Ruth said.

"God, yes; they depress me utterly. You wouldn't consider cheering me after a hard day of late adolescents by having dinner with me, I suppose?"

"We'd love to," Sara said enthusiastically.

"Not you," MacDougal told her. "Just your aunt. You're old enough to scramble an egg for yourself." He added parenthetically, "You have to be blunt with them, they don't understand subtlety."

Ruth studied the topaz shimmer of the wine in her glass. She had only had three small glasses of sherry, not nearly enough to account for the pleasant glow that warmed her. And, after all, he was a professor—such a respectable occupation, she mocked herself silently.

"Thank you," she said aloud, keeping it deliberately formal. "I'd enjoy that. But I've got to be in early."

She knew (and how odd that she should know) that this last qualification would amuse him. It did; his mouth quirked and his eyebrows went up. Sara's reaction was worse. After the first start of surprise she beamed at Ruth like a fond mother sending a daughter out on her first date.

## III

They dined at a French restaurant in Georgetown, not far from the house. The decor was self-consciously and expensively provincial, with brass warming pans festooning the walls, two giant fireplaces, and capped and aproned waitresses. The gloom was almost impenetrable. According to MacDougal this was an unsuccessful attempt to conceal the inadequacy of the cooking.

"I'm no gourmet," he explained, eating with calm satisfaction. "I know enough to know when cooking is bad, but I don't really care. But I'm sorry, for your sake, that I made a poor choice. I don't know my way around town too well."

"I suppose you're gone a great deal," Ruth said, abandoning the onion soup as a lost cause. "And Washington does change a lot, in a short space of time."

"True, to both. I spent last year in Africa, just got back this fall. Maybe that's why I can't afford to be critical about cooking. Compared to what I ate for ten months, this is *cordon bleu* quality."

"What do you do in Africa?" Ruth studied, in some dismay, the omelette which had been placed before her—her usual order when she wasn't sure of the chef. Bad as the light was, it was obvious that the brownish roll on her plate had been sadly mistreated.

"Study Black Magic."

"Oh, really. What is that you're eating?"

"Stew. On the menu it goes by the name of *boeuf bour-guignon,* but it's stew. Don't eat the omelette, if it offends you that much. Fill up on bread, and let me regale you with tales of raising the devil."

"I thought you were joking."

"No, no. Turns out I'm one of the world's foremost authorities on magic and superstition. Don't tell me you've never heard of me?"

He grinned at her and took an enormous bite of stew.

"I'm sorry . . ."

"Can't you tell when someone is kidding you? Have more wine; that's one thing that infernal chef can't mangle."

"Thanks. But how did you ever get interested in such a . . . such a—"

"Crazy subject? Well, you might say I walked into it—on my first field trip, to a village in central Africa where the natives were dying of a curse."

His voice was matter-of-fact, but Ruth saw him cock an eye at her over his wineglass. She decided perversely that she, for one, was not going to jump when he pushed the right buttons.

"Really?" she said politely.

"Terrible woman! Are you robbing me of my sensation?" MacDougal beamed at her. "I'm serious, though. They were, literally and actually, dying because their witch doctor had gotten annoyed and put a curse on them." His face was sober now, his eyes darkened. "They were amiable savages," he said. "Shy and timid as rabbits. I used up all my little stock of first-aid supplies trying to cure them, before the truth dawned on me."

"What did you do when you did learn the truth?" Ruth asked.

"What? Why, I—er—persuaded the shaman not to interfere with my activities. Then I took the curse off."

"Now you are joking."

"No, I'm not. In my youth, in addition to wanting to be an architect—and a fireman, a cowboy, a spy, and a garbage man—I aspired, for a brief period, to be a stage magician. I produced a few snakes out of people's ears, sang songs, did a dance . . ."

He shrugged. Ruth studied him thoughtfully and decided that, despite his bland smile, he was perfectly serious.

"I didn't know such things could happen," she said.

" 'Sticks and stones may break my bones, but names will never hurt me'? That's false, even in our so-called rational society. Names do hurt. The wrong names, applied to a disturbed child, may lead to murder years later. And in a culture where the power of the word is accepted, a curse can kill. It killed eight people in that Rhodesian village."

"I think they want to close," Ruth said, with an uneasy glance at the waiter, who stood in an attitude of conspicuous patience against the wall. "Shall we . . ."

"All right." His smile broadened as he looked at her across the candle flame. "You don't like to talk about it, do you? Why not?"

"Why, because it violates . . ."

"Reason and logic? No, that's not why it bugs you."

"What are you, some kind of psychologist too?"

"In my business I have to be. The phenomena we label 'supernatural' are products of the crazy, mixed-up human mind, and that's all they are."

He held her coat for her, and Ruth put on her gloves. As they went to the door she said, "You're right, the subject does distress me. Silly. . . . But I'm darned if I intend to let you dig into my subconscious to explain why I feel that way." Through his chuckle she added, more lightly, "Anyhow, if poor old Cousin Hattie's ghost does appear, I'll know who to send for."

"Damn it, you're missing the point! I don't believe in ghosts any more than you do; if Cousin Hattie turns up, you'll have to call in a priest or a medium. The things I study are perfectly natural—"

"All right, all right. Sorry."

It took only five minutes to reach the house. They were both silent as the car passed smoothly along the empty streets. Mac-Dougal stopped in front of the house. Instead of getting out and opening her door he shifted sideways and faced her. Ruth was not aware of having moved in any significant manner, but after a moment MacDougal's expression changed and he leaned back, away from her.

"I won't ask if I may come in," he said casually. "I might be tempted. . . . And I wouldn't want to shock Sara."

"She wouldn't be shocked," Ruth said; her smile was only slightly forced. "Only sweetly amused."

"That would be worse. Good night, Ruth."

# Chapter

## 2

THE KITCHEN WAS WARM AND BRIGHT, AND FILLED WITH THE
smell of perking coffee. Ruth was buttering toast when the
sound of footsteps made her drop the knife.

"Goodness, you startled me," she exclaimed, as her niece
entered. "What are you doing up at this hour? It isn't even light
outside."

"I couldn't get back to sleep." Sara yawned till Ruth's jaws
ached in sympathy. "Here, let me do that."

"You're still half asleep. Sit down and have some coffee.
Unless you want to go back to bed. . . ."

Sara shook her head and slumped into a chair by the table.
Her green velvet robe brushed the floor and had full sleeves
trimmed with lace. It was obviously one of the contributions of
her doting mother, but instead of making her look young and
innocent, the rich dark sheen of the material and the medieval
sweep of the style gave her a magnificently anachronistic appearance, like something produced by a Spanish court painter
of the sixteenth century. The girl's skin was smoothly olive; her
black hair, braided into a thick tail for bed, gleamed like polished metal.

With a glance at the clock Ruth poured herself another cup
of coffee. It was still early. She always allowed herself ample
time in the morning.

"Want some toast?"

"No, thanks." The phrase was broken by another gigantic
yawn.

"Come now; you don't need to diet, and if you haven't had enough sleep you must eat." Without waiting for a reply Ruth put two slices of bread into the toaster and gave Sara the plate she had prepared for herself. By the time she got back to the table with fresh toast, Sara was biting appreciatively into the golden triangles.

"Good," she said, and gave her aunt a smile. "Sorry, Ruth. I've got a nerve, I ought to be getting your breakfast."

"I don't know why you should." Ruth returned the smile. What a pretty child she was! The long dark lashes were so thick that they made her eyes look enormous, even when they were heavy with sleep; they had the smudgy sultriness which expensive eye-makeup kits are supposed to produce, and seldom do.

The toast and coffee revived Sara to such an extent that she got up and began scrambling eggs.

"I love this kitchen," she said, stirring.

Ruth cast a complacent glance over her shining kitchen. It looked charming, particularly in contrast to the bleak gray dawn that was breaking outside. The stainless steel of the counter stove, wall oven, and double sinks was as modern as the spotless white door of the refrigerator; but the cabinets had been done in maple, with hammered iron hinges and handles, and the one papered wall had an old-fashioned print of peasants haying, which had been copied from an old French original. The bright red of the workers' shirts and the golden sheaves of grain gave the kitchen a gaiety which was augmented by warm red-brown tile on the floor. Ruth's inherited collection of teapots, in all materials and colors, occupied shelves in a glass-fronted corner cupboard.

"The refrigerator ought to be brown, though," Sara said.

"I don't like colored refrigerators," Ruth said absently. They had been through this dialogue several times; it had the pleasant monotony of routine now. "They're decadent."

"Like colored toilet paper," Sara agreed, and they both laughed.

"I could tell just by looking at this room that you chose the decorations," Sara went on. "Was it so bad when you inherited the house?"

"You should have seen it! I suppose Cousin Hattie had been living on boiled eggs for forty years. She didn't care for new-fangled inventions."

"It must have been ghastly."

"Some of the furnishings were museum pieces. One of those enormous, black, wood-burning ranges—I don't suppose you've ever seen them. Of course, hers hadn't been used for years, since there was no point in firing up such a monster for one person. She cooked on a kerosene stove with a single burner—terribly dangerous, those things are. It's a wonder she didn't burn the house down."

"How about an egg?" Sara brought the pan, copper-bottomed and steaming, to the table and waved it invitingly under Ruth's nose.

"Dear child, I've had one breakfast!"

"It's cold outside. And you don't need to worry about getting fat." Sara put a puffy yellow spoonful on Ruth's plate. "You aren't going to be late, are you?"

"No, that's all right. How about you? When is your first class?"

"Not till eleven. That dull diplomatic history course. But I think I'll go in early and work at the library."

"Or have coffee with what's-his-name," Ruth said dryly.

"Bruce. You know perfectly well what his name is; you're just trying to deny the fact that he exists."

"You sound like your friend Dr. MacDougal," Ruth said. "What time *did* you get in last night?"

"None of your business. As for Bruce, I don't have any mental blocks about him. He simply doesn't interest me, one way or the other. But you know what your mother would say about him."

"He's not as bad as Alan was," Sara said wickedly.

"Never having seen Alan, I can't say. Your mother's description was pretty ghastly, but I'm willing to allow for exaggeration. People do exaggerate," she added, realizing that she had just violated the united front of the older generation, "when they are worried about someone they love."

"That was just Mother being silly. I hadn't the faintest intention of marrying Alan."

"Maybe that's what she was worried about."

Sara chuckled; she had a delicious laugh, soft and throaty and contagious, which brought out dimples in both cheeks.

"Ruth, you're marvelous, you really are. I admire your loyalty to Mother—after all, she is your sister. But don't you think her attitude toward sex is positively medieval?"

"That's a subject on which I am not an authority."

"What, sex?"

"Your mother's attitude toward it. Don't be impertinent."

Her tone was light, but Sara had a sensitivity for nuances which was rare, Ruth thought, in a girl of her age. She changed the subject.

"Alan was just a temporary aberration," she explained airily. "A manifestation of adolescent rebellion on my part. If Mother hadn't howled about him so constantly I would have dropped him long before."

And that, Ruth suspected, was probably true. How many times had she had to bite back the words of advice that popped into her mind when she heard Helen make some maddeningly wrong statement to Sara or one of the boys, some red flag to their bullish emotions. Yes, she reminded herself sardonically, spinster aunts always did know better than parents. And, whatever her mother's minor errors, Sara was a credit to the family—charming, bright, well-mannered, pretty. Then Ruth's smile faded slightly as she studied the girl's face. Pretty, yes, healthy. . . . This morning there was a change. Something was wrong. What?

". . . the fact that he never washed," Sara was saying. "It wasn't that he couldn't, you know; he lived at home and his parents had an absolutely gorgeous mansion in Shaker Heights, five bathrooms, no less. It was a matter of principle."

"I never could understand the principle which is expressed by a cultivated filth," Ruth murmured, only half following the conversation. She was still trying to pin down that elusive sense of wrongness in Sara's face.

"Well, you know, protesting how terrible the world is."

"Adding one more stench to the world doesn't improve it, surely?"

"Ruth, you're hopeless," Sara said, with a burst of laughter. "At least you must admit Bruce is immaculate. It's the beard you can't accept."

"It's not so much the beard as my suspicion that he pastes it on. He isn't old enough to have a beard like Philip of Spain's. Sara, do you feel all right?"

"Sure, I feel fine. A little tired, that's all."

"You said you couldn't get back to sleep. What woke you?"

Sara's eyes dropped. She picked up her fork and began pushing golden fragments of egg around her plate.

"My conscience, probably. I do have to go to the library. There are midterms coming up."

"Well, all right. . . . There is some flu going around and you look a little shadowy under the eyes."

"After all those eggs can you suspect me of flu? No, dear, leave those dishes, you know that's my job. I don't have to go for another hour. Want me to make spaghetti tonight?"

"Fine. You make good spaghetti."

"I should, it's the only thing I can cook, besides eggs." And then, as Ruth collected purse and gloves and started toward the door, she said, "Ruth."

"What?"

"Don't those people behind us have a dog, or cat, or something?"

"The Owens have a Weimaraner, and someone in back owns a Siamese cat. I've seen the dog exploring the shrubbery once or twice."

"Weimaraner? Oh, that ghosty-looking gray dog with the red eyes. What's its name?"

"I haven't the faintest idea. Why do you ask?"

"Oh, no reason." The hesitation, the sidelong look, were so unlike Sara that Ruth felt a resurgence of her concern. The girl sensed this; she smiled, and said quickly,

"It sounds so silly. But that was what woke me, someone out in back calling, in the middle of the night. I assumed some cherished pet didn't come home for dinner."

"Calling what?" Ruth said sharply.

"Oh, damn, that's why I didn't want to tell you; I knew you'd start thinking about homicidal maniacs and peeping toms." Her tone added, "All 'grown-ups' do." Aloud she continued, "It wasn't like that at all, it was just someone calling an animal, or a child. I couldn't imagine that children would be wandering around at four A.M., so I figured it must have been a missing pet. I used to yell that way for our old tom-kitty when his mating instinct got too much for him."

"I hope you didn't make enough noise to wake up all the neighbors. I'll have to speak to Mr. Owens."

"No, don't do that; it was a soft, sort of crooning voice, really. I hope they find poor Sam," she added. "He's a spooky-looking beast, but he was very friendly last time I talked to him through the fence."

Halfway out the door, Ruth turned.

"Sam? The dog's name is Wolfgang von Eschenbach, or some such absurdity."

"It must have been the missing cat, then," Sara said calmly. "I didn't absolutely catch the name, but it surely wasn't Wolfgang etcetera. It was Sammie, or something like that. 'Come home, come home'—that's what the voice kept saying—'Sammie, come home.' "

## II

"The name," said the voice at the other end of the wire, "is Pat MacDougal."

"Impossible," Ruth said involuntarily.

"I admit it's a funny name. Sounds like a cartoon character. But it happens to be my name."

"You silly fool," said Ruth; and blushed scarlet as her secretary looked up in surprise. "I meant, how did you find me?"

"Called Sara and asked her where you worked. The Department of Agriculture has a very efficient information service. What the hell are you doing at the Department of Agriculture—counting apples?"

"Something like that."

"Sounds like a dull occupation for a woman of your talents."

"How do you know—" Ruth began, and stopped herself just in time. "I'm sorry, but I *am* busy today. Can I call you back later?"

"No. Later I'll be at your place, providing, of course, that it's okay with you."

"Well, it's not okay!"

"Wait a minute, wait a minute. Let's start all over again. I don't know why you have this effect on me," said the voice irritably. "I'm generally considered very suave. Mrs. Bennett, my mother is having one of those impromptu dinner parties for which I gather she is famous in Washington. I wouldn't know; she is the main reason why I took up anthropology as a profession. But this time I'm stuck. She asked me to bring a dinner partner, and last night, in the fascination of your company, I forgot to ask you. I know it's damned short notice, but that's my mother's fault, not mine. She does this sort of thing."

"I'm sorry," Ruth began, and then the meaning of what he had said finally penetrated. "Your mother. . . . She isn't Mrs. Jackson MacDougal?"

"Yes, she is." The voice was defensive.

"Well! I don't know. . . ."

"Damn it, Ruth, you've got to help me out. I can't hurt the old lady's feelings, but those characters she collects drive me nuts. Please?"

"Characters? You mean the most famous conductor in Europe, that Russian ballet dancer who defected, the man who wrote that terrible book, the woman who predicted—"

"Yeah, people like that. I don't know who she's got on tonight. Look, you seem to have heard of her, so you know it's not my fault, this last minute business. She does it all the time—and gets away with it, which is even more fantastic. Please?"

"All right. Thank you."

"Thank *you*." There was a gusty sigh of relief from the other end. "Seven thirty?"

"Come around at six thirty for a drink," Ruth said "I suspect I'll need it."

"We both will, but not for the reason you're thinking. Hell's bells, darling, it's just a dull party. Bless you."

"Uh—Pat. What shall I—"

The hollow silence on the other end of the wire told her it was too late. She hung up and turned to find her mascaraed miniskirted secretary regarding her with open-mouthed admiration.

"Gee," said her secretary. "Mrs. Jackson MacDougal!"

# III

"Who's she?" Sara asked.

"Only the most famous hostess in Washington. Invitations to her parties are more highly regarded than invitations to the White House."

"Is that why you came home early?" Sara demanded incredulously.

"Yes, and that's why we are out right now, to get me something decent to wear. Darn, it still is cold. Unusual for this time of year."

"You Washingtonians always say that." Sara clutched her black leather jacket around her as a strong gust threatened to pull it off. Her black hair lifted, lashed by the wind like something out of a witches' sabbath. "Well, really, Ruth, I'm surprised at you. All this effort for some snobbish old society biddy."

"Darling, she isn't like that. Her husband—good heavens, Pat's father—was Ambassador to England; the family is not only terribly rich, but intellectual, cultivated. She doesn't invite the 'in' crowd, only people she thinks will be interesting. That's why her invitations are so hard to come by."

"Hmmm," said Sara, unconvinced. "Well, my dear aunt, whatever your motives, it is obvious that you must do us credit. So where are we going first?"

"First and last," said Ruth, rounding the corner onto Wisconsin rather more briskly than she had intended. "Heavens, the wind simply roars down this street! We're going to Lili's."

"But you always buy your clothes there." Sara clutched a handful of hair in a vain attempt to keep it out of her eyes. "Let's prowl, we've plenty of time. I do love the Georgetown shops."

Ruth liked them too, so their progress was slow, despite the lashing wind that blew down Wisconsin's curving slope as through a tunnel. The tartans in the Scottish import shop held them for ten minutes; it was hard to believe that those wild blends of color—purple, yellow and black, olive and pale green with a scarlet thread, turquoise and orange-red and indigo—were genuine clan patterns and not the improvisations of a mad Italian designer. The mad designers, Italian and otherwise, were represented in other shops which had names like "Whimsique," and "the place," with no capital letters. Ruth found this distressing and said so, but Sara laughed, loitering before a window framed in enormous orange and purple linoleum flowers and filled with such useful items as an Indian water pipe and a bird cage six feet high, of gilded bamboo trimmed with fake rubies and sapphires.

At the Wine and Cheese shop they stopped to buy cocktail snacks and some of Ruth's favorite hock. Then there was a Mexican shop, where Sara yearned over a bright red, wildly pleated dress embroidered all over the yoke and sleeves with black-and-gold birds; and an Indian shop, where Ruth remarked that, one day, she would like to see Sara in a sari, preferably that white one trimmed in gold. Then they decided that they really had to start thinking about a dress for Ruth, and passed nobly by the candle shop and the little gallery and the jeweler's that specialized in antique pieces. By this time, strangely enough, they were blocks from Lili's.

Sara stopped in front of a window.

"Look, Ruth. What a darling dress!"

It was a sheath of rainbow iridescence, with long sleeves, a demure high neck, and practically no skirt.

"This doesn't look like my sort of place," Ruth remarked meekly.

"Let's go in anyhow."

The store was small and thickly carpeted, with its stock discreetly tucked away on racks along the walls and only two isolated models in the middle of the floor. The salesladies, elegant young women who looked like college girls, smiled graciously at the new customers and returned to their conversation.

"That's it," said Sara, advancing purposefully on a dress which stood in solitary splendor in the center of the shop. "I saw it the other day, and I thought of it right away when you said you wanted something dressy but not actually formal."

Ruth eyed the creation dubiously. It was one of the new "romantic" styles—a full velvet skirt belted tightly at the waist with a wide, soft belt, and a white organdy top with long sleeves and a cascade of crisp ruffles down the front.

"It would look lovely on you," she began.

"No, no, it's not my style at all," Sara said. "I'm too long-legged for this new length—midi, they call it."

"An ugly name for an unbecoming length," Ruth said, and ran a finger along the fall of ruffles. They sprang briskly back into shape as if they had been starched.

"Try it on, anyhow. You can't tell unless you do."

When they left the shop with a large parcel in hand, Sara insisted on treating them both to coffee at a local espresso bar. Sipping a liquid which had been referred to as a cappuccino, Ruth did not mention that it bore no resemblance to the drink of the same name which she had enjoyed in Florence four years earlier. She was moved, however, to comment on the price of the coffee and on the decor; the furniture was starkly, uncomfortably modern and the walls were hung with original paintings, in the manner of a gallery. Half the inhabitants of Georgetown painted; the other half bought the paintings.

"I thought these places would be cheaper," Ruth explained. "Like—for students."

"That's right, get with that slang," Sara grinned. "Some students are pretty rich these days. Haven't you ever been in one of these places before?"

"No."

"See what a good influence I am. Two new establishments in one day. I'll have to take you to a discothèque. And you claim to be an old Georgetonian. Or is it Georgetownian?"

"Georgetown is changing," Ruth said dryly. "But I guess people do stay in well-worn tracks. Unfortunately you don't realize you're in a rut until it's too late to climb out of it. You are a good influence, Sara. I'm enjoying having you with me."

"Thanks. I'm enjoying being with you."

They smiled at one another rather self-consciously. Then Ruth glanced at her watch and gave an exclamation.

"We'd better hurry, or I'll be late getting dressed."

"You need shoes," Sara said, slipping into her coat. "No—you have those low-heeled pumps with the big buckles, that's just the thing. Black stockings—"

"Certainly not," Ruth said firmly.

"I've got some I'll lend you."

The total effect—buckled shoes, black stockings, and ruffles—made Ruth self-conscious until she saw Pat MacDougal's face. However, he said nothing, beyond a polite compliment, and Ruth thought she understood why; Sara's smile was too maternal to be encouraged.

"Cook both those lamb chops," she told her niece. "No cheating with T.V. dinners. You need something solid."

"Well, actually, I thought," said Sara, trying to look as if the idea had just occurred to her, "that I might ask Bruce over to eat your chop. If you don't mind?"

Ruth had laid down the ground rules about guests when Sara first came to stay with her, and this was perfectly in order. She heard herself agreeing to the proposal with unusual warmth. She was in too much of a hurry to try to analyze why she was glad to have someone with Sara that evening; a dim discomfort, something connected with the morning, hovered on the edge of her consciousness and then was forgotten, as Pat drew her toward the door.

# IV

Ruth knew the MacDougal home by sight; it was one of the famous mansions of Georgetown, and if she had had no other reason for accepting Pat's invitation, a chance to see the house would have been excuse enough. Now well within the borders of the Georgetown area, it had been a suburban estate when the little town on the Potomac was first founded. The original George Town, as its present inhabitants often pointed out, was a cosmopolitan town, with academies and jewelers and slaves, when the new capital was still a muddy swamp. Representatives of the young nation had to be scolded by the President into taking up residence in the city named for him, and it was with reluctance that they abandoned the amenities of the town named after another, less popular George.

The men who had built the house named it, with more candor than modesty, Barton's Pride. It had long since passed out of the hands of the Barton family; but it still stood as it had stood then, on a knoll surrounded by tall oaks, and it occupied an entire city block, a distinction which few of the original mansions could still claim. The driveway was a superb, sweeping circle; Pat's little Jaguar roared up it with a defiant blast of its exhaust.

After Pat had helped her out of the car Ruth stood for a moment gazing at the magnificent proportions of the facade, now blazing with lights which made the bricks glow rose-pink. The vines which in summer softened the formal Georgian lines fluttered like tattered curtains, the last reddening leaves flying in the wind. Shallow stairs led up to the beautiful doorway with its fanlight and side windows.

The hall was as large as Ruth's drawing room. The immense chandelier, whose crystal drops chimed delicately with the breeze of their entrance, had surely been taken from a Loire chateau. The rug was an acre of muted cream and blue and rose; Ruth had seen its like on museum walls, but never on a floor before. A superb staircase swept up and divided, framing a circular window. On either side of the hall were fireplaces; wood crackled and orange-and-gold flames leaped inside them. Ruth waited until the butler had turned away with their coats. Then she said out of the corner of her mouth, "And you had the nerve to admire my shack."

"Oh, I admire this place," Pat admitted. "The way I admire the Louvre."

"But you don't live here?"

"People don't live in places like this. They perform, as on a stage. Wait till you see Mother in action; you'll understand what I mean."

He took her elbow and turned her toward the wide doors on the left; but before they reached them the panels flew back and Mrs. Jackson MacDougal erupted through them, arms outstretched, face beaming. Ruth gaped.

Washington's most famous hostess was a shimmer of silver: massed diamonds on her high-piled white hair, blazing from her fat little hands and plump throat; and silver, too, in the incredible garment that swathed her from throat to floor and billowed out like a tent as she came flying toward them. A silver lamé caftan, Ruth thought, and stifled a gasp of laughter. Above the ample folds Mrs. MacDougal's much photographed face—superbly, uniquely, magnificently homely—rose like a gargoyle from a cathedral roof.

She threw herself on her tall son, and for one unforgettable moment Ruth saw his rugged face and flaming head swathed in sweeping folds of silver.

"Horrible man, why don't you come more often?" Mrs. MacDougal demanded. "Who's this? Mrs. Bennett? How do you do, very nice, very nice indeed. Much more suitable than the last one. But you only brought her to annoy me. I knew that. Didn't work, did it?"

Pat returned her grin. For a moment the two faces were uncannily alike.

"Not any of my tricks work with you. You were so sweet to that ghastly female that she got the wrong idea. Pursued me for weeks. I had to leave the country to get away from her. Not," he added hastily to Ruth, "because of my brains and good looks, mind you."

"Why should any woman require more?" Ruth asked, since

the conversation seemed to be taking that tone. The old lady gave a peal of appreciative laughter and linked arms with Ruth, displacing her flowing silver sleeve and baring another yard or two of diamonds running up her arm.

"That's right, put him in his place. I never trained him properly. Come in and meet the others. Just a small group; Pat won't come if I have more than a dozen people."

The dozen included the usual lions, a pride of them—so many that their individual distinctions were lost in the general aura of fame. Ruth recognized a much-pursued young senator from a western state and a tall, melancholy man who was the musical half of Broadway's most famous musical comedy team. Ruth's hostess monopolized her, leaving the rest of the guests to fend for themselves; her tactics were so blatant that, in any other woman, Ruth would have recognized them immediately. But she could not believe at first that this descendant of millionaire aristocrats was trying to do her son's courting for him.

"But, Mrs. MacDougal," she protested, after a particularly obvious ploy, "I don't think . . ."

"You think I'm a fantastic old bitch," said her hostess calmly. "I am, it's true, but I'm quite serious about Pat; I'd like him to settle down. It sounds absurd, doesn't it, for a man of his age? He was married before, you know. So were you, I gather."

"He died," Ruth said, stunned into candor by the old lady's sledgehammer tactics. "In the war."

"World War Two? Yes . . . we adults still say '*the* war,' don't we? Pat's wife didn't die; she divorced him. She was a dreadful woman, but I could see her point. He kept dashing off to the jungles of Africa or the deserts of Australia. What fun is that? But it's high time he tried again. He can't go gallivanting around in the wilds much longer; he's getting old. Those places aren't safe."

Ruth's inclination to laugh was quenched by Mrs. MacDougal's expression. It was one she knew well, having seen it so often on her sister's face. Apparently the maternal instinct did not die, even in an eighty-year-old mother for her middle-aged son. Ruth did not find the emotion amusing; rather, it was frightening in its single-minded intensity.

During dinner Ruth watched Pat's expression become increasingly grimmer as the meal went on, through course after superb course. The food certainly could not be the cause of his discontent; Ruth wondered if it might be his dinner partner, who seemed never to stop talking. She was a tall, thin woman, so fair as to be almost anemic looking, with ash blond hair arranged in a peculiarly old-fashioned mass of braids, coils, and ringlets. If Mrs. MacDougal had not been present to dim all lesser lights, the woman's costume might have seemed eccentric: smoke-gray draperies of chiffon which floated dangerously near candle flames and wine glasses whenever she lifted her hands, which she did often, in studiedly flowing gestures.

As soon as the meal was over and the company was being led into the "small drawing room" for coffee, Pat sought Ruth out.

"Let's get out of here," he muttered. "That shameless old—"

The epithet, which presumably applied to his mother, was cut off just in time by the appearance of that matron, who advanced upon him with a purposeful stride.

"Oh, no, you don't, Patrick James," she said severely.

"Mother, you know I hate that nonsense!"

"I know, and I can't imagine why, you dabble in much nastier and less likely subjects all the time. You've never seen Nada, she's the latest rage, and I *insist* you stay. You can't be so rude to Mrs. Bennett, if you won't consider me."

"Oh, all right."

"What on earth is this all about?" Ruth whispered, as they followed Mrs. MacDougal's triumphantly billowing skirts into the drawing room.

"Didn't you recognize that bloodless bean pole I was stuck with at dinner? Another of the old harridan's tricks, she knows I hate people like that. . . . She's the latest thing in the rich spiritualist circles. A medium."

"I've never attended a séance," Ruth said sedately. "It should be interesting."

"It won't be. These babes don't know any of the good tricks. Someday I'll show you a Hottentot shaman at work. They are masters at crowd psychology."

Despite his jeers, Pat behaved himself very well. Ruth suspected that he was professionally interested after all; just before the lights went out she caught a change of expression that reminded her of her boss's face when a particularly complicated problem arose.

The spirits, Mrs. MacDougal explained, were sensitive to light. That was why most séances were held in semidarkness. It was not—this, with an intent stare at her son, who responded with a bland smile—it was not intended to conceal fraud. No such question could arise with Madame Nada in any case, for that lady was a mental medium and did not indulge in the vulgar demonstrations with tambourines, trumpets, and ectoplasmic hands which were so popular with so-called physical mediums.

Throughout the lecture Madame Nada sat with folded hands, smiling faintly. Only her eyes moved. But they contradicted her studied air of repose as well as her pastel blandness; they were small, dark brown, and piercing, and they darted ceaselessly around the circle of spectators, taking in every detail.

When the lights went out there was a general murmur compounded of nervous giggles, sighs, and one loud yawn, whose source Ruth immediately identified. They were holding hands, since this increased the sympathetic vibrations. On Ruth's right was Mrs. MacDougal. Her fat hand was surprisingly cool and dry, and felt pleasantly like that of a chubby little girl—a little girl wearing lots of dime-store jewelry, which scratched the palm. Ruth thought, "All diamonds are paste in the dark," and realized, with a grin which she hastily suppressed for fear of damaging the vibrations, that she was a little bit drunk. The wine at dinner had flowed freely and it had all been too good to pass over.

The boy on Ruth's left was perspiring, and she wondered whether it was a natural weakness or a bad case of nerves. According to Mrs. MacDougal he had just opened a new psychedelic shop on Wisconsin Avenue, which sold posters of the Beatles in various incredible costumes, luminous pinups of Indian mystics, and atrociously made handcrafted leather sandals.

As her eyes adjusted Ruth realized that the room was not entirely dark; the glow from the fireplace made it possible to see shapes, and glinted redly off objects such as Mrs. MacDougal's diamonds and the silver fillet the medium wore in her hair. After a long silence, broken once by a giggle, and a concerted shussshing sound directed against the giggler, Ruth felt herself getting drowsy. Warmth and firelight and a little bit too much wine. . . . What a disgrace it would be, she thought comfortably, if she fell off the chair.

The medium's voice made them all jump. It was slow and soft, drawling the words. Accent and tone had changed, but the voice was still recognizably Madame Nada's. The words were strikingly commonplace.

"Good evenin', ladies and gentlemen."

"Good evening, Maybelle," Mrs. MacDougal said in a bright, social tone. "How are you this evening?"

"Very well, thank you kindly. But we're always well here, you know."

"Yes, dear, I know. Maybelle is Madame Nada's control," Mrs. MacDougal explained, in a piercing whisper. "A gently bred young Southern girl. Poor child, she was raped by a Yankee soldier during the War Between the States. But she has no hatred now."

"Love," said the mellifluous voice of Maybelle. The shaggy young man on Ruth's left stirred uneasily. "Only love and sunshine and peace, here."

"Do you have any messages tonight, dear?" Mrs. MacDougal asked.

"Jes' a few. Strange. . . ." The girl's voice sounded puzzled. "There's somethin' holdin' back. . . . A hostile thought. . . ."

Someone across the circle—Ruth was sure it was Pat—coughed suggestively, and Madame Nada's voice hardened momentarily.

"But I'll try. Some of them want so badly to come through, to help. . . . There's someone here who wants to speak to—a lady?—yes, a lady in the room. I can't get the name. . . . The first letter seems to be a G."

There was an audible gasp from someone in the listening circle. The voice went droning on.

"G-R-A— That's the name of the lady. Is there a lady named Grace?"

"Yes, yes," squealed an excited voice.

"Grace, darling, it's Daddy." The medium's voice changed; it was a man's now, deep but shaky, as if with age. "Remember the party? The birthday party, and the pink dress?"

"Oh, my goodness," gasped the invisible Grace.

There was further conversation about the party—Grace's sixth birthday party, said Daddy, and Grace enthusiastically agreed. However, this was fairly dull for the rest of the group, who shared neither Grace's memories nor her susceptibility to suggestion, and before long Daddy was supplanted by a new voice, which described itself as that of an Indian chief named

Wamasook, who had lived on the site now occupied by the house, "in the days before the white men came to rob us of our land." Wamasook spoke excellent English. He described his beautiful Indian sweetheart, who had leaped from the Rock of Dumbarton after he was killed in battle, and added that one of the settlers had buried a hoard of gold coins in the well before his tribe was attacked. Since there was now no trace of a well anywhere on the grounds, and since Wamasook's knowledge of the modern geography of the site was somewhat vague, this hint did not arouse much interest among the auditors.

The next visitor from beyond announced himself in a thick Scottish accent as "George," and was promptly identified by Mrs. MacDougal as George Barton, the builder of the house. He remarked that the regions where he was presently living were filled with sunlight and flowers and love. Shortly thereafter Maybelle announced abruptly that Madame Nada was tired.

The lights went on. Ruth almost burst out laughing when she saw Pat; he looked so smug, not only at the confirmation of his predictions, but at his own admirable self-control. Mrs. MacDougal also saw and interpreted his expression. Her voice, as she addressed the medium, had something of the tone of a lady complaining to her dressmaker about the fit of a gown.

"Well, Nada, I'm afraid this was not one of our better demonstrations."

The medium, who was rubbing her eyes and yawning, like someone just awakened from sleep, looked surprised.

"Indeed? I am sorry to hear that. Did not Maybelle come through?"

"Yes, but the messages weren't very—significant."

"But I got a marvelous message from Daddy," said Grace, a well-upholstered elderly lady with a black velvet ribbon around her sagging throat. "All about flowers, and love—"

"And sunshine," said Pat, unable to control himself any longer. "Not very characteristic conversation from your daddy, Grace, if the tales I hear about the old shark are true."

"Pat, you bad boy, you know people change when they pass on. What use would it all be otherwise?"

"What, indeed?" said Pat charmingly.

His mother gave him a furious look.

"I am so sorry it was not successful," said the medium

smoothly. Ruth was reminded of something. . . . Cream? No, olive oil.

"Antagonistic influences, I suppose," Mrs. MacDougal said coldly. The medium gave her a quick, wary look.

"Possibly. Possibly it is simply the house. You know, Mrs. MacDougal, that some places lack the proper atmosphere."

Later, looking back on it, Ruth was never able to understand how it had happened. Surely she hadn't been that drunk! And certainly she was not particularly intrigued by the séance, which had seemed to her both dull and embarrassing. Not even in the light of those events which were now close upon her was she willing to admit another explanation. . . . No, there was no reason, except her loose tongue, which frequently got her into trouble, and some vague idea of being gracious to her hostess, who was visibly vexed with the medium's performance.

When they left the house, with Mrs. MacDougal's enthusiastic thanks ringing in their ears, Ruth was meekly silent. She expected an explosion from Pat; his grim forbearance, which lasted all the way home, was in its way even more uncomfortable.

"Won't you come in?" she asked, when the car had stopped. He nodded.

"I'll give you moral support while you break the news to Sara."

"She'll probably be delighted."

"I expect you're right. What made you do such a thing?"

"I thought it might be fun," said Ruth.

"You're a liar." His long arm swept out and caught her by the shoulders, pulling her to him in a quick, casual embrace. She was relieved to hear him chuckling. "You sure there wasn't a touch of 'screw Pat' in your mind? Excuse the language; I'm trying to clean it up for you, but it's damned hard."

"If you mean what I think you mean, the answer is No. I'm too old for such adolescent jokes. And," she added, moving, "far too old for necking in the front seat of a car."

"It's these damned bucket seats." He released her, and began the complicated operation of extracting his bulk from the little car. "These kids must be contortionists. I've always wondered how they manage to—"

The rest of the sentence was lost as he came around to open her door.

When they entered the hall Ruth heard the voices in the living room, and a jolt of unreasonable irritation struck her. She had forgotten Sara's guest, or had assumed that he would have left. She had smoothed her face into a smile by the time she walked into the living room, there was really no reason why she should let the boy irritate her so.

He rose at once. He had beautiful manners, almost too courteous, as if he were mocking the standards of the society he despised, or considered them so contemptible that they were not worth fighting. His clothes were almost, but never quite, too, too much; an occasional ruffle on a shirt, or a flowery waistcoat, or a pair of trousers that fitted his lean hips and long legs almost, but not quite, too tightly. At least his clothes were well tailored and beautifully kept. His hair was long enough to curl under at the neck; the beard was a neat sort of beard, dark and short and trimmed, with tongues of hair outlining the jaw and the lines between nose and lips—the sort of beard worn by Mephistopheles, or a sixteenth-century Spanish nobleman. As he stood beside Sara, his dark face and Sara's olive beauty and sleek black hair made them look like two young members of the old Spanish royal house—except that none of the Hapsburgs had ever been so handsome.

Sara's flushed cheeks might have been the result of the fire's warmth, but a curve still lingered in the shape of her mouth that made Ruth fairly sure of what she and Bruce had been doing. Then Ruth remembered, joltingly, those few moments in the car out in front, and she decided to forget the whole thing.

Pat greeted the younger man with the ease of old acquaintance.

"Haven't seen you on campus lately. Still protesting?"

"Always, inevitably."

Even his voice, Ruth thought irritably, sounded affected. It was a mellow baritone, but the pronunciation was overprecise and emphatic.

"What's the latest?" Pat asked interestedly. "Segregation, the draft, Vietnam—"

"You didn't get my latest petition?"

Bruce bared his teeth in a gesture that was not even intended to resemble a smile. As he probably knew, the dental effect was heightened by the frame of beard around his mouth.

"I get so many of them," Pat said apologetically.

It was an outrageous remark, and Ruth expected, not an explosion—Bruce was abnormally well controlled for such a passionate defender of causes—but a snarl. Instead, the boy's grin turned into a genuine laugh.

"You know what terrifies me?" he demanded. "The thought that I may end up just like you."

"You almost certainly will."

"I know. That's why it terrifies me."

"Okay, pax. Come into my office next week, and we'll fight some more."

"Yes, let's not argue here," Ruth said firmly. "What are you two drinking? Thanks, no; I don't think I could face vodka in any form at this hour. Pat, would you like brandy?"

"What I really would like," said Pat, "is a cup of tea."

"You constantly amaze me. So would I."

"I'll get it," Sara said. She went out, with Bruce following.

"Now," Pat said, when the tea finally made its appearance; it had taken quite some time. "Tell Sara what you've done."

"Good heavens, you make me sound like a murderer. I've invited a few people to dinner next week, that's all. Mrs. MacDougal and a friend of hers."

"The friend's name," said Pat, "being Madame Nada."

Bruce leaned forward, elbows on his knees, black eyes mocking.

"I didn't know you were interested in spiritualism, Mrs. Bennett."

"I'm not. It was just one of those things."

"A séance!" Sara's eyes danced with amusement. "Aunt Ruth, are we going to have a séance?"

"Yes," Ruth said, sighing. "She thinks this house probably reeks with the right atmosphere."

"But it's tremendous fun," Sara exclaimed. "More fun than Spin the Bottle."

"A parlor game? Is that how you think of it?"

"Sure. Although . . . I've used the Ouija board, and I must admit . . ."

"Involuntary movements," Pat said shortly.

"But I wasn't pushing the board, and I'm sure nobody else was."

"That's what they all say."

Bruce's eyes darted from Sara, flushed and erect on the

edge of the couch, to Pat's sour face. Ruth sensed that he was inclined to agree with Pat, but he hated to pass up the chance of an argument.

"I agree that the Ouija board is probably explicable in terms of natural laws," he said pontifically. "But many of the problems of the paranormal have not been properly explored. Take Rhine—"

"You take him. Unscientific and inadequately controlled."

"What are you talking about?" Ruth demanded.

"Dr. Rhine's experiments in telepathy, E. S. P., he calls it. He uses decks of special cards and tries to get a person sitting in one room to send mental images of the cards to a person in another room, who writes down the impressions he gets. It doesn't work. Despite all the juggling with the results."

"The statistical methods," Bruce began hotly; he was now involved in the argument for its own sake.

"Neither you nor I would be capable of judging that aspect. But I know that the controls are inadequate. There are too many ways of faking, deliberate or unconscious. Ask any stage magician."

His eyes glowing, Bruce expertly shifted ground.

"All new scientific discoveries are mocked when they first appear. Take hypnotism—"

"The favorite example of the apologists for spiritualism. Take alchemy, astrology, and the secret of the Great Pyramid. Still pure superstition, all of 'em."

"Boys, boys," Ruth interrupted. "I think either one of you would argue about whether or not the sun is going to rise tomorrow—on either side of the question. Help me decide how I'm going to arrange this ludicrous affair. I haven't even thought about the guest list. How many people does one need for a good séance?"

"The four of us and two guests," Sara counted aloud. "That's six. Do we need more?"

Bruce shot Ruth a quizzical glance. It was so well done that she had no choice but to say, as graciously as she could, "Of course we'll expect you, Bruce. A week from tonight, Friday the tenth."

"Thank you, Mrs. Bennett, I'm looking forward to it," Bruce recited. And then spoiled the effect by adding, with a malicious movement of his lips, "I think you're going to need a skeptic."

"Skeptics I've got," Ruth said wryly.

"Pat's no skeptic, he's the Grand Inquisitor. Burn 'em at the stake, that's his motto. And you—"

"Yes?" This was one of the things she most disliked about the younger generation in general and Bruce in particular—their habit of cheap, pseudopsychological analysis.

"You are fastidious. You dislike the whole idea, not because it's irrational but because it's distasteful."

"Well," Ruth said, surprised, "I guess you're right."

"Sara still hasn't quite given up believing in Santa Claus," Bruce went on. The look he gave Sara was meant to be casually amused, but Ruth caught a glimpse of his eyes, and their expression made her catch her breath. "She's still receptive to wonderment. Trailing clouds of glory. . . ."

"Oh, come on!" Sara was definitely not flattered. Either she had not seen that betraying look or she was too inexperienced to know what it meant.

"So," Bruce concluded, with a sweeping gesture that mocked all of them as well as himself, "I'm your only genuine open mind, completely without prejudice and able to evaluate the evidence."

"There won't be much evidence, I'm afraid. Tonight's performance was pretty sad."

"You caught that, at any rate," Pat said grumpily.

"Oh, yes, it was all very obvious. I was disappointed. I thought she would do better."

"She can, given time for preparation. I told you about Mother's impromptu parties. But I'll wager that in a week Madame Nada will have done a discreet but ample amount of research on you and this house. She will be filled up to here with history—everything she can dig out of the Georgetown guidebooks."

"She'll run into trouble there," Ruth said. "There isn't much about this place in the guidebooks."

"Not even the builder's name, building history, that sort of thing?"

"Oh, well, his name was Campbell, like Cousin Hattie's. Daniel, or was it Abediah? But he wasn't much of a public figure, not like the Bealls and the Stodderts and the really famous Georgetown families."

"Really? Well, that's good."

"Why?"

"Don't you see, Mrs. Bennett?" Bruce was so interested he forgot his affected accent. "The less she can find out from public records, the easier it is to check her sources. If she should come up with something that really isn't in print—"

"Oh, I'll bet she'll come up with something," Pat said.

"Well, I'll spend some time reading up on the house," Bruce said eagerly. "If she slips, I'll catch it."

"Where does the performance take place?" Pat asked, swallowing a yawn.

"We'll need a table, I suppose," Ruth said. "A biggish one. Ten or twelve people. . . ."

"How about the dining-room table?" Sara suggested.

"Over the crumbs and coffee cups? No, dear; you and I will be doing the catering, and I've no intention of scuttling to and fro with trays and sponges in front of guests."

"Then it will have to be in here."

"Yes. We could move these couches farther apart, and sit in front of the fire."

"I think you'll find," Pat said dryly, "that Madame will prefer to be a little farther away from the firelight."

"It's a problem, isn't it?" Bruce began pacing the room, examining it as if he had never seen it before. "I can see why you put the couches in front of the fire, it makes a nice grouping. And the bookshelves at the far end of the room suggest a kind of library corner, looking out over the garden. But the room has an awkward shape. You're losing about a third of your space at this end, next to the street."

"I know, it is awkward. I tried rearranging the furniture, but it wouldn't let itself be moved." The statement, which she had meant as a light comment, sounded unexpectedly alarming. "I mean," she added hastily, "this was the best arrangement; it had been this way for years."

Pat was becoming interested. He walked down the length of the room to the front windows.

"One thing you've got," he said, "if nothing else—an ideal setup for our ghost-raising session. This table in front of the window is round; move it back a couple of feet so we can get chairs all around it, and—"

He was standing with his back to the others, facing the window and the table, on which his hands rested lightly. With the last word his voice broke, and he suddenly bent forward over the table, head bowed and shoulders hunched.

Ruth leaped to her feet.

"Pat!"

"What?" He turned, smiling, and Ruth's nightmare vision of a heart attack faded. "Frog in my throat. A monster. Guess I talk too much."

"Was that all? I thought you were having a fit."

"No, no, I'm fine. Yes, this would do admirably. But you ought to have these windows caulked. The draft is enough to freeze your bones."

"I did have them caulked. It's just a cold spot, that's all. Too cold for your mother, perhaps."

"No," he said slowly. "This is ideal."

"He's right," Sara agreed. "Ruth, maybe an electric heater. . . ."

"We'll worry about that later." Pat produced another yawn. "Come on, Bruce, I'll give you a lift home."

He lingered in the hall for a moment after Bruce had, reluctantly, gone on out to the car.

"I wish you'd call this off, Ruth," he said, in a voice pitched low enough so that Sara, clearing away cups in the next room, did not hear.

"My dear—why?"

"It's too much for you, too much fuss."

"Don't be silly, I don't mean to try to imitate your mother's style of entertaining. It will be very simple."

"I wish you wouldn't," he repeated, in an oddly flat voice.

"Pat, you look so— Are you sure you didn't have a pain just now?"

"No, damn it, I told you I feel fine! Sorry. . . . I guess I am tired; I didn't mean to yell at you. Good night."

Ruth helped to clear the living room, bade Sara good night, and sat down for a final cigarette in front of the dying fire.

She was worried about Pat. Her father had had that same gray pallor, after his first heart attack. Pat was no longer a young man.

And she? Half her life was over, more than half. . . . And what had she to show for it? An old house which was too large, really, for a single person; a pretty, casual niece who would be gone in another year or two, after she finished college—who

would then send a Christmas card and a birthday card every
year, with dutiful messages. Yes, Sara would send the cards; she
was a thoughtful child.

She loved Sara. Drowsing in the dimming light, she realized
that she loved Sara more than was safe or comfortable, with
something of that fierce parental love which had always frightened her in others. But Sara didn't love her. Sara would be embarrassed, probably, at the very idea. In the old days it had been
right and proper to love one's parents, and God; today the tall
candid-eyed young cynics kept their love for erring mankind
and their unfortunate brothers; or, occasionally, for their mates.
Well, she had tried that too. Never happy, even at its most intense peak of longing, it had turned all too soon into misery so
abject that she still felt the echoes of it in her bones, like an incurable, recurrent sickness. Misery, and love and sickness. . . .

I know what's wrong with me, she thought hazily. I'm
falling asleep. . . .


# V

Ruth dreamed that she was lying on the sofa facing the fireplace, as she actually was. Sara stood before her, and that, too,
was as it might have been. But only the girl's face was clear; the
rest of her body and clothing was dim as a landscape seen
through fog that shifts and thickens and disperses, giving tanta-
lizing and misleading hints of what the mist conceals. She saw
Sara's face as clearly as if it were illumined by spotlights; and
here the imitation of reality ended. Ruth had never seen on anyone's face, let alone that of her pretty niece, a look like the one
that disfigured the dream girl's features, and she hoped she
never would. The eyes were so distended that the whites
showed all around the pupils. The complexion, against Sara's
black-brown hair, looked gray as ash, and the pale lips were
parted in a gasp of terror.

Ruth was so frightened that, even in her sleep, she tried to
move. She could not, and recognized that, too, as a common
dream symptom. Almost she welcomed the bodily paralysis as
a confirmation of the fact that she was really dreaming.

Then the shadow came. It was formless at first, but she
knew it had actual form that was somehow concealed from her.

All she could see was its size and its menace, and as it loomed
up against the dream shape of her niece, Sara's mouth opened
in a scream that was all the more pitiable for being silent. The
effect of that soundless shriek was so bad that Ruth woke. And
then she entered the worst part of the nightmare.

She lay, as she had seen herself in the dream, on the couch
that faced the fireplace. Now she could make out the glow of the
fading coals—but vaguely, as if she saw them through air satu-
rated with smoke. The table lamp behind the couch was on,
casting a dim but adequate light over the whole scene. She felt
the roughness of the brocade covering the couch against her
cheek, and the stiffness of her cramped muscles. All these sen-
sory impressions proved that she was indeed awake. Sara's
dream image had, of course, disappeared.

The shadow had not.

It hovered between her and the fire—dark, heavy gray,
smoke-thick and smoke-dark, it was the medium which dulled
the crimson coals into tiny sparks. It had no form, but the form
was coming, struggling to shape itself, so that the thick, sluggish coils of twilight-dark twisted and moved. . . .

Then, as she struggled frantically against the paralysis that
still held her, deliverance came, in the form of a sound which, if
not personally familiar, was at least recognizable as something
from the waking world. A voice, dulled by distance and thick
glass panes into a mournful echo, calling. . . .

"Come home, come home . . . Sammie . . . come home. . . ."

With an effort that felt as if it must wrench her bones out of
their sockets, Ruth swung her feet to the floor and sat up.

And woke, finally and genuinely.

For, of course, the last sequence had been only an extension
of the original dream. It was common enough, to dream of waking. Ruth told herself that, but when she raised her hand to her
forehead she found that the roots of her hair were soaked with
perspiration.

She pushed the damp hair back from her face, drew a long
shaken breath, and reached for a cigarette. Half shyly she
glanced out of the corner of her eye at the fire. It was almost
dead—only a faint reddish glow remained—but it was fading
normally with no greasy pall of dead air to obscure it. Ruth let
out the breath she had not known she was holding. When she

struck the match, her fingers were hardly shaking. But—good heavens, that had been a nasty one!

She wondered what Pat would say about the origins of the nightmare—or Bruce, with his cocky assurance. The last thought brought a faint smile to her lips. No doubt Bruce's interpretation would be shatteringly Freudian.

She finished her cigarette and stood up, conscious of a cowardly disinclination to turn her back on the fireplace—a sentiment which she conquered at once. But she went up the stairs rather briskly, and she left the light on in the living room.

As she drifted off to sleep she found herself listening for a repetition of the call that had roused her. But she heard nothing more. Her room was in the front of the house, and the call seemed to come from the garden side, where Sara's room faced. Sammie certainly picked unsalubrious weather for prowling, she thought drowsily, and then—her last conscious thought before sleep claimed her—funny name for a cat. . . .

# Chapter

## 3

WASHINGTONIANS TAKE A PERVERSE PRIDE IN THE PERVERSITY of their weather, refusing to admit that it is, in this respect, like weather anywhere. Ruth had been a resident long enough to feel a sense of personal achievement when Sunday dawned fair and warm after a week of Alaskan cold. Sara had been out until all hours the night before, with the unavoidable Bruce, but she made her appearance at an early breakfast looking as dewy-eyed and rested as a baby. Ruth thought, "Ah, youth," but did not say it, and waved the girl off to a picnic at Great Falls without mentioning that it was not really quite warm enough for shorts. If she had legs like that, she told herself, she would display them too. And the shorts weren't much shorter, in fact, than the skirts the girls were wearing.

Before indulging in a second cup of coffee she tidied up the kitchen, deriving housewifely satisfaction from the look of shining steel and gleaming porcelain. Then she settled down with *The New York Times.*

The kitchen had been built at the tail end of the house, as kitchens of old houses were in that semitropical climate, so that cooking heat and odors would not permeate the rest of the house. The breakfast bay, where Ruth was sitting, had been added in a later century so that the inhabitants could enjoy the view of the walled garden, with its backdrop of firs and magnolias. They glowed greenly in the morning sunlight, and the birds, enjoying the warmth, were out in full voice.

Ruth struggled nobly with the reports of disaster—national,

personal, and international—for half an hour, and then threw
the paper aside as a particularly penetrating avian shriek
reached her ears. Probably just a jay complaining about some
private tribulation or fancied affront. . . . But perhaps a passing
cat was bothering the birds. She really ought to go out and see.

It took only minutes to change her robe for slacks and
sweater, and to run a comb through her short fair curls. When
she got outside she realized that Sara was right; it really was too
warm for wool clothing. The sun fell like soft intangible fingers
on her hands and face. Standing in the middle of the flagged
terrace, she threw out her arms and lifted her face in a sudden
transport of sheer well-being. It was a wonderful day on which
to be alive.

The garden was large for a city house, but then that was one
of the features of Georgetown that its inhabitants prized most
highly. The house had been built at the very edge of the long
narrow lot, so that there was no front yard at all, only an
areaway. All the land was in back, and it was fenced high on
three sides. Georgetowners lacked the jovial conviviality of
suburbanites; they liked their privacy, and did not take offense
at others' enjoying theirs. Ruth scarcely knew her neighbors,
and there were no gates or doors connecting the yards.

The boards of the fence needed painting, but their ugliness
was masked by shrubs and bushes. All but the box and holly
were bare now; the lilac and forsythia had lost most of their
leaves in the windstorm of the past week, and the ones remaining were sere and yellowing. But Ruth eyed their straggling
contours fondly. She had moved into the house the preceding
spring, and one memory that would be imprinted forever on her
brain was the sight of the garden when she first saw it, with the
great heaps of forsythia like sprawling yellow fountains, sending out sprays so bright as to seem luminous. Cousin Hattie had
not been able to afford a full-time gardener in her last years,
and her part-time boy had spent his efforts on the grass and the
roses and let the gnarled old lilacs and other bushes grow as nature decreed. The results had been beautiful.

After the forsythia faded, then came the dogwood—pale
rose and white stars against the olive green of the firs—and the
gorgeous flaming masses of the azaleas, rose-pink fuschia and
salmon, and white like a spotless drift of snow. There had been
lily of the valley in the moist shadows of the pines, and violets

thrust green fingers into every possible corner, penetrating the chinks in the brickwork of the patio invading the rose beds. The lilac, perfuming the whole outdoors, and spirea, and flowering quince. . . .

Ruth had never been much of a nature lover; she had not consciously wanted a garden while she lived in the apartment on Massachusetts Avenue. She had not known how much she missed one until she walked through the back door of Aunt Hattie's house and saw the forsythia blaze out like little fallen suns.

She stooped to pick up some bits of scrap paper, blown in from the street, and then decided to get her gloves and tools and go at the garden. It was too splendid a day to stay indoors.

Trailing the rake, she went back to see how the roses had withstood the wind. They usually bloomed beautifully well into November, so she had not cut them back; the cold spell had taken her by surprise. On the first blustery night she and Sara had dragged in the wrought-iron table and chairs which stood in warm weather under the big oak in the center of the yard. Its spreading branches had been like sunset during October. Now most of the crimson leaves were on the ground under the tree. That would be the next job, after she had checked the roses.

They were in a sheltered spot, and had not suffered so badly as she feared. Colored confetti flakes of petals spattered the ground—pink and white and crimson so dark it was almost black—but several buds still lifted brave heads, and Ruth decided to leave them just in case the warm weather held. She knew she would never make a gardener; it gave her a physical pang to cut the roses back, as if she were amputating legs off birds, though she knew it had to be done.

Some of the buds could be cut; she would gather them before she went in. She was stooping over the bushes when a squawk of outrage erupted above her head and something went scuttling and scraping along the trunk of the fir tree. A big jay swooped out of the green branches, yelling indignantly, and sat down in the topmost branches of the oak, where it swayed and scolded like an animated blue flower.

Ruth looked up and was rewarded by the sight of a face, triangular and furry, peering calmly down at her from the foliage, like the famous disembodied head of the Cheshire cat. She recognized the cat from earlier visits, and yielded to an impulse born of exuberance and the springlike weather.

"Sammie, aren't you ashamed! Chasing birds is not nice."

Sammie gave her a contemptuous blink and vanished, not in stages like the fictitious cat, but all at once. The scraping noise began again, accompanied by quaking branches, and then a sleek tan-and-brown form leaped the last twenty feet to land on its feet not far from Ruth's. The cat immediately rolled over on its rear end and began to clean its tail with frantic energy.

"You're a pretty thing," Ruth said admiringly, and the cat paused, uncannily, to give her a glimpse of two eyes as blue as the back feathers of the jay before it resumed its washing. Its royal self-possession left Ruth amused and absurdly out of countenance. She was familiar with Mr. Eliot's advice on addressing cats, though she had never had occasion to put it into practice. Now, however, it appeared that she had been presumptuous.

"Oh, cat," she began, following the authority, and then jumped as a voice boomed out.

"Bad girl! So that's where you've gotten to!"

For a wild second Ruth was sure the voice, from a source not immediately apparent, was addressing her. She looked around, and, as she saw the face from which the voice had issued, suspended moonlike upon the top of the back fence, she realized that it had been addressing the animal. The face she raised was pink with amusement, and the face on the fence responded with a beam of obvious admiration.

"Good morning, good morning, my dear Mrs. Bennett! I must apologize for our bad child. Is she annoying you?"

"Not at all. She's a beauty, isn't she?"

"Well, we—yes, we think so. Mrs. DeVoto and I. Please feel quite free, however, to evict her if she becomes churlish. Though members of that breed rarely do so. Patronizing, contemptuous, even downright insulting; but never losing the true aristocratic demeanor."

"I'm sure," Ruth murmured. Mr. DeVoto, she recalled, was a retired official of the Department of State. He had something to do with protocol. He was a nice little man, though; he had swept off his genteel golf cap at the sight of her, and his bald head gleamed pinkly in the sunlight.

"Well, Mrs. Bennett," he went on, "if you are sure that our feline friend does not disturb you, perhaps I will not venture to climb over your fence in order to retrieve her."

"Oh, I'll enjoy her company. But if you want her back I'll be delighted to hand her to you."

"That would hardly be feasible, I fear, though I do thank you for offering so kindly. Kai Lung does not care to be handled except by intimates. Not that she would—er—scratch." Mr. DeVeto's voice sank, as if he were mentioning something faintly obscene. "Dear me, no. She would simply evade your hand if you tried to touch her."

"Yes," Ruth said absently. The bush on the end might be pruned; there seemed to be dead wood there. . . . Then, belatedly, she realized what the man had said, and she exclaimed, "Kai Lung! Isn't her name Sammie?"

"Sammie? Good heavens—gracious me—why, no. She is a female cat, to begin with."

"No wonder she wouldn't speak to me," Ruth said, smiling. "I've not only been familiar, I've been wrong."

"Why would you think her name was Sammie?" Mr. DeVoto was clearly aghast at the very idea.

"Just that I heard someone calling, at night, and I assumed he was calling a pet. There's no reason why I should have thought it was—er—Kai Lung, except that she's the only cat I've seen about, and I know the dog on the south side has another name."

"I can assure you I have not been calling. Good gracious, Mrs. Bennett, I hope you do not think that I would be so thoughtless as to—"

"Of course not. It must be some other cat, or dog, owner."

"I cannot imagine who." Mr. DeVeto's chin sank out of sight as he prepared to retire. "There are no other pets in this block, except for that unattractive beast next door. Well, Mrs. Bennett, it has been most pleasant chatting with you. Perhaps you might join us one evening for a glass of sherry."

"That would be nice."

"My wife will telephone you, then. In the meantime, I do hope you enjoy your gardening."

He lifted the hat he had been holding and replaced it on his head with such perfect timing that, for a second, it seemed to sit suspended on top of the fence as the face below sank out of sight. Ruth allowed herself a broad grin as soon as the face had disappeared, but it was a friendly sort of grin. He really was a nice little man.

She did enjoy her gardening, and she had quite a heap of leaves to show for her efforts when she finished. She had another cup of coffee sitting on the bench built around the oak, and Kai Lung sat beside her and condescended to sample the cream. Then she wound herself into a ball and went to sleep in the sun, and Ruth went back to clipping dead roses. It was a very pleasant day. There was no reason at all why, as she prepared to go in, Ruth should find herself speculating on the identity of the elusive creature named Sammie, and wondering whether he had, in fact, ever come home.

# II

The weather held all that week, providing conversation for hundreds of dinner parties. On Friday afternoon Ruth left work early and took a cab home; she was perspiring slightly as she came in the front door, and was not really looking forward to cleaning house and cooking a meal. The first thing she heard was the sound of the vacuum cleaner. In the living room she found Sara, wearing an apron which completely covered her brief skirt, putting the finishing touches on a room which shone with wax and elbow grease.

"Well, that's the pleasantest sight I've seen all day," Ruth exclaimed, as her niece, seeing her enter, switched off the vacuum. "My dear girl, how nice of you!"

"You didn't think I was going to let you do all this by yourself, did you? I don't have any Friday afternoon classes."

"But it's finished; I couldn't have done better myself. All we need now are the flowers. I brought some home with me, they're in the hall."

"What kind?"

"Some carnations and the inevitable chrysanthemums, I'm afraid, but I found some beauties. That lovely bronze. This is a hybrid, with gold and copper streaks."

"I like mums." Sara wound the cord around the cleaner and shoved it towards the door. "What shall I put them in, the blue Delft pots?"

"That would be good. The white ones can go in the copper vases, and the carnations in the silver. There ought to be a few roses left; I'd planned those for the dining room."

"They've been gotten. Take a look."

Ruth pushed open the sliding doors across the hall from the drawing room, and exclaimed with pleasure. The dining room was a dark room, abutting on the neighboring house so closely that that side had been left without windows. Instead of running the full length of the house like the drawing room, it was backed by a high old-fashioned butler's pantry and the kitchen; hence its only outside light came from the street windows, which were kept curtained because they were so close to the sidewalk. The wall sconces and the chandelier had been electrified, and they gave a warm, rich light. The furniture was heavy and dark. Sara had polished it till it reflected objects, and Ruth had mended the worn spots in the exquisite petit point covering the chairs. The table was already set, with Ruth's best damask and silver and crystal; the beautiful old Delft in the corner cupboard, with its scalloped border, had been washed, and the tall silver candlesticks held bayberry candles whose faded green matched the muted shade of the walls.

"Everything is perfect," Ruth said gratefully. "There's nothing for me to do."

"Except the cooking!"

"Yes, I'd better start the rolls. They'll have to rise twice."

"It's such a job. Why didn't you get frozen rolls?"

"The secret of good cooking," Ruth said didactically, "is to stick to what you can do well, but use no substitutes. I can't handle elaborate meals; they require too many hands at the last minute, and I really don't enjoy cooking all that much anyhow. A roast is easy to prepare, but this one I've got is a roast of roasts; I bullied it out of that French butcher on Wisconsin, and paid a week's grocery money for it. The salad is my own invention, but it's very simple—every fresh vegetable I can find goes into it, plus eggs. You'd be surprised how impressive it looks. So the rolls have to be handmade, those frozen ones taste like cardboard and would spoil the total effect."

"I see your point. You know what I'd cook, don't you?"

"Spaghetti," Ruth said.

"How did you ever guess?"

"Well, I used to serve it myself when I started housekeeping. It has the advantage of being honestly peasanty, but I can't serve Mrs. Jackson MacDougal spaghetti. Not that she wouldn't eat it with perfect aplomb."

"What's she like?"

"She's a darling. You'll like her."

They stood for a moment in silence, their arms lightly touching as they surveyed the room to make sure no touch had been omitted. It was a good moment. Ruth was to remember it later, with a sharp pang of loss.

## III

The guests were due at seven thirty. At six Ruth went downstairs to do the last-minute kitchen work which could not be put off any later if she wanted time to dress. The hors d'oeuvres needed to be made, the drink tray set up, the rolls kneaded and shaped—a dozen little odds and ends, time-consuming and annoying, which every hostess knows.

She had done her hair, but her person was attired in mules and a garment unattractively known as a duster. She had just plunged both hands up to the wrists in dough when the doorbell rang. She said "damn," and wondered who on earth it could be. Sara was dressing and was probably unfit for society at the moment. She would have to answer the door herself.

Snatching up a paper towel she stamped into the hall and flung the door open, prepared to give a short shrift to any luckless newspaper boy or lost tourist. One glance and she started to slam it shut.

"Go away! Go away and come back in an hour. Of all the outrageous—"

Pat had thoughtfully inserted one large foot in the door. Now he shoved.

"I'm not a guest, I'm a waiter. Open up."

She had very little choice. He kicked the door shut behind him and headed for the kitchen, without further comment. Ruth trailed along, too curious now to be angry. But if the parcel he carried contained food or wine, she was prepared to rage.

Pat deposited his bundle on the counter and unfolded it.

"My favorite bottle opener, my best carving knife, and," he held up the white material which had contained the other items, "my apron. What needs doing?"

"But you—you. . . . Words," said Ruth honestly, "fail me."

"This last minute stuff is the worst part of the party. I'm try-

ing to demonstrate," he said, with a sidelong glance, "that men
are useful things to have around the house. What have we here?
Bread or something? Well, I'll leave that to you. What are we
drinking? Where do you keep the gin?"

Twenty minutes later Ruth was shaping the last of the rolls
while Pat put a shaker of martinis in the refrigerate and swept
the kitchen with a comprehensive glance.

"All set, I think. I'll light the fire now, while you change."

"Just a second, till I finish these."

He came up behind her and stood watching, and gradually
Ruth's movement slowed. She had expected this sooner or later
and had not been sure how she would handle it—or how she
wanted to handle it. What she had not anticipated was the mindless lassitude that gripped her at the first touch of his hands.

"Relax," he said, into her ear. "I don't want flour all over
my brand new jacket."

Leaning back against him, she heard his quick breathing,
felt his hands move from her waist to her breasts. His lips slid
down her cheek, seeking her mouth; without conscious volition
she turned her face to meet his. So. . . . Those particular nerve
endings were not atrophied after all. Through the years she had
sought—perhaps unconsciously, perhaps not—partners who
did not arouse the deadened emotions, and had told herself that
they were gone for good. Now, wherever his hands and lips had
touched she felt stripped, not only of clothing but of skin, as if
the skillful fingers manipulated the nerves themselves.

For several long unmeasured seconds her consciousness
hung suspended on a single pivot of pleasure; then the automatic defenses, never so long defied, snapped into place. She
stiffened and moved; and he released her at once, stepping
back, hands touching her waist only to balance her.

Staring dizzily at her own hands, Ruth saw a pathetic
squeezed lump clenched between taut fingers. Automatically
she began to pat it into shape.

"What happened?" he asked quietly. His breathing was
slower but still uneven.

"Nothing. I . . . squashed my roll, didn't I?"

"Do you find me that repulsive?"

"Oh, Pat—no." She turned to face him, hands eloquent;
with the beginning of a smile he fended off her floury fingers.

"I thought the first reaction was too good. Well, I guess this isn't the time or place to go into the matter. Remove your tempting person from my presence and I'll try to behave myself the rest of the evening. We'll pretend nothing happened."

It was no use pretending; every time her eyes met his she remembered, with her entire body. As Sara deftly removed the plates and served cherries jubilee, Ruth's eyes went back to the magnet that had drawn them all evening, and found his eyes waiting and alight.

When they moved into the drawing room Ruth shook herself mentally. It was high time she paid more attention to her guests, especially now that the main event of the evening was coming up. She had invited a couple from the office, amiable nonentities whose personalities would not be obtrusive, and Sara had added two school friends whose faces, then and forever after, remained pink blurs in Ruth's memory.

Madame Nada, decked in swirling black chiffon for the occasion, led the way into the room. She had already seen and approved the arrangements, but their previous occupation of the drawing room had been confined to the couches near the fire. Now, as the medium approached the table, she suddenly stopped short, her hand outstretched in the act of seeking a chair. Ruth heard her gasp sharply.

"Is something wrong?" she asked, moving to Madame Nada's side. The other guests, chatting and relaxed after a good meal, were not paying much attention. Ruth was the only one who saw the medium's face, and she felt as if she were seeing its true shape for the first time. Genuine surprise and a shadow of some other, less innocuous emotion, had stripped away the mask temporarily.

"It is so cold," said Madame Nada.

"I know, there always seems to be a draft at this end of the room. If it's too bad—"

"Draft?" The close-set brown eyes, still wide with shock, met hers.

"Are we ready?" Mrs. MacDougal asked crisply, at Ruth's elbow. She had changed her personality with her costume, and was wearing a soft dressmaker suit that looked like a thousand dollars, which was probably its approximate price.

"I don't know." Ruth turned impulsively. "It is so chilly at this end of the room. Will it be uncomfortable for you? We could move the table. . . ."

"Heavens, no. Pat told me about the draft—that's why I wore a suit. It seems quite comfortable to me. Where shall we sit?"

Ruth glanced inquiringly at the medium, who replied with a slight shrug and a smile. The mask was back in place.

When they were all seated, Ruth glanced around the table. The scene had an odd distinctness. Colors seemed more vivid, faces sharply cut and memorable. She was struck with a feeling that she ought to remember every detail.

The medium sat with her back to the windows, whose drapes were pulled shut. Ruth's co-worker, Jack Simmons, sat on Madame Nada's right, and Ruth had been directed to the place on the medium's other side. Next to her sat Sara, looking especially vivid and alert; her eyes sparkled with anticipation, rich color stained her cheeks, and her olive complexion was set off by the clear yellow wool of her dress. Bruce sat almost directly opposite her. He had been on his best behavior all evening, except for indicating by his very silence that he found the conversation incredibly dull. As his eyes met Ruth's passing glance, he inclined his head slightly, and his beard twitched. Ruth's glance moved on. Mary Simmons, solemn and self-conscious, her reddened housewife's hands clasped on the table; Pat. That was enough, just. . . . Pat.

"We begin," said Madame Nada suddenly.

# IV

Afterward Ruth wondered whether she would have been conscious of that atmosphere if her more delicate senses, those beyond the normal five, had not been preoccupied. A quiver of uneasiness penetrated even that most consuming of all self-interests; for when the lights went out, and the groping hands fumbled and linked, something touched her in the darkness, something impalpable that brushed and passed on; and a long shiver shook her bare arm.

At first the session was not notably different from the other meeting a week earlier. Ruth was conscious of the usual distractions, the annoying little itches which could not be scratched, the intensification of sounds with the loss of sight. The room was quite dark; the heavy drapes cut off all light from the street and the back of the couch shielded the glow of the fire, which had been allowed to die down to a bed of coals.

The medium's breathing deepened and slowed and steadied—the preliminary, as Ruth had been told, to what is called the trance state. Her fingers were linked around the medium's wrist, so she was immediately aware of the moment at which the Madame Nada went into her trance, body relaxed and hands limp.

"A name," the medium droned. "Ann. Something . . . Ann. Mary?"

There was a stir around the table.

"Can she hear us?" It was Bruce's voice.

"No," Mrs. MacDougal answered softly. "Not unless we addressed her directly. She's in light trance now, speaking with her own voice, of impressions she is getting. Later she'll go into deep trance and other personalities will speak through her."

"Mary," the medium interrupted. "Wants to sing. Not doing . . . party. . . ."

Ruth felt Sara's hand contract, and knew she was about to giggle. She squeezed, warningly. However much she shared Sara's feelings, she could not mock her guests.

"Who is Mary?" Mrs. MacDougal asked.

"Pretty! Mary, Mary, quite contrary. That's what Papa calls her."

"Can you describe her?"

"Oh, pretty. . . . Yellow hair. Old-fashioned: long curls. That's funny. . . ."

"Describe her clothing."

"Such pretty, flowery stuff . . . little sprigs, pink flowers. Kerchief around her neck, elbow sleeves. . . ."

Mary Simmons, whose hobby was American costume, gave an involuntary squeak of recognition. The medium, seeming not to hear, swept on.

"A man, too, he's with her. She calls him Papa. Wears long blue coat, brass buttons. Funny whiskers, long, bushy . . . gray. Close the door, close the door, don't let the damned Yankees in!"

The last sentence boomed out, startlingly, in a deep baritone voice, rough with simulated anger. Sara jumped; Ruth, who had done some reading during the past week, squeezed her hand again.

"She's in deep trance now," Mrs. MacDougal whispered.
"Who are you?" she asked aloud.

"Henry. Damn' Yankees, let 'em die. Bolt the door!"

"Henry who?"

"Henry" snorted; he did sound just like a choleric old gentleman.

"Campbell, of course. Henry W. Campbell. My house, damn it; damn' bluecoats can't come in."

"Why don't you want them to come in?" Mrs. MacDougal asked.

"Wait." The voice changed. It was no longer a man's voice; but it was so distorted by some strong emotion that Ruth could not identify it as Madame Nada's. The words sounded strained, as if each one had to be forced through a resisting substance. "No, no. . . . No . . . can . . . not. . . ."

The limp hand flexed so roughly that it pulled loose from Ruth's grasp. The medium's breathing quickened.

"Nada. Listen to me, Nada. Wake up. Wake up. . . . Lights, someone."

The circle broke. Lights flared, leaving everyone blinking. Ruth saw Mrs. MacDougal bending over the medium, holding her shoulders and speaking in a soothing voice.

"All right now?" she asked.

"Yes, yes." The medium straightened and brushed back a lock of hair that had fallen over her forehead. "What happened?"

"An intrusive entity," Mrs. MacDougal said solemnly.

"Strong," the medium muttered. "Strong and. . . ."

She shook herself like a dog coming out of the water.

"Did we get anything of interest?" she asked.

"Oh, yes, splendid. Mrs. Bennett, you know something of the history of the house. Can you verify the incident?"

Put fair and squarely on the spot, Ruth stammered, "Of course the house did belong to the Campbells. I don't recall the name of the man who owned it during the Civil War, but—"

"Yes, it was certainly the War Between the States," Mrs. Mac-Dougal agreed. "Was Mr. Campbell a Southern sympathizer?"

From across the table Bruce said smoothly,

"May I, Mrs. Bennett? Not only was Campbell a rebel at heart—not uncommon in Georgetown—but the incident suggested did occur. When the Union Army fled after the battle of—First Bull Run, I think it was—the wounded, exhausted men streamed back into the city over the bridge at Georgetown. Many of them collapsed on the steps of the houses, and Mr. Campbell ordered his door locked and barred against them."

He waited just long enough for the gasps of amazement to be heard. Then he added gently,

"It's all described in *Old Georgetown Stories.*"

The medium was too accustomed to skepticism to show anger, if she felt any. She gave Bruce a sweet smile and said indifferently, "I have never read that book."

"Does the book describe the old man?" Mrs. MacDougal demanded.

"No. But a blue coat and brass buttons aren't unusual."

"What about Mary Ann?"

"I haven't the faintest idea whether or not Henry had a daughter of that name," Bruce said cheerfully. "I doubt if it would be possible to find out."

"That's why it is impossible to convince you skeptics," Mrs. MacDougal said in exasperation. "If you do find verification, you claim the medium could have looked up the information; if you don't find it, you claim it can't be verified."

Bruce gave her a look in which amusement and respect were mingled.

"You're quite right," he said courteously. "It's hard luck, isn't it?"

"Hmmmph." Mrs. MacDougal turned away from him. "Let's try again, Nada, it's still early. Perhaps we can get something which will convince this young man."

"I don't know. . . ." the medium said slowly.

"Come, it's too good a chance to miss. You went quite quickly into deep trance; obviously the atmosphere here is very sympathetic."

The medium was silent. Ruth, next to her, thought she looked more bloodlessly anemic than ever.

"Perhaps Madame Nada is tired," she said, with no other motive than sympathy. "I understand the trance state can be tiring."

"Yes, it is tiring," the medium said. "But that is not why I am afraid—I mean to say, why I am reluctant—"

"No, you mean afraid," Bruce interrupted, staring at the woman. "What are you afraid of?"

Ruth turned toward the boy with a disapproving frown— and realized that he was right. Madame Nada was frightened, badly frightened and, at the same time, excited. Somehow her fear was more convincing than any manifestation she could have produced. Ruth began, "If you feel that way—"

But her gentle voice was drowned out by a booming "Nonsense!" from Mrs. MacDougal; and after a searching glance at her patroness, the medium shrugged.

"Very well. But I have warned."

"We must all concentrate on pure thoughts," Mrs. MacDougal urged. "Perhaps if we sang a hymn—"

"Oh, no," Ruth said involuntarily. The medium gave her a bleak smile.

"I think not. Just—let us begin."

## V

The medium sank into trance at once, deeply, frighteningly, almost as if she had been dragged under the surface of consciousness by a force she could not resist. The wrist Ruth held went limp, as before; but Ruth shivered as she felt the undisciplined pulse racing wildly under her fingers.

"Names," the droning voice began. "Mary Ann, Henry, a Frank . . . someone named Hilda."

"Go on," breathed Mrs. MacDougal.

"I see two women. One young, one older. Gray hair. Or is it powder? The quarrel, the girl is crying. Poor Mary!"

Ruth relaxed. This was the same sort of vague talk they had heard before, unconvincing because it could be tailored to fit almost any event. Relieved of her anxiety, her mind began to wander, only half-hearing the medium's descriptions and recitations of names which might apply to anyone on earth, or no one. Something about an Indian in a feathered headdress . . . a hanging man . . . a little white dog. That reminded her of the elusive Sammie, and she was speculating idly on his identity when, as if the memory had been a cue, the terror began.

It came slowly and slyly, like a trickle of dirty water through a crack. A voice, the voice of no one in the circle, began to mutter. It sounded, at first, like a recording played at too low a speed—a dull, forced drone of sound, with no words distinguishable. Then it grew louder, and words began to be heard. But still the mechanical impression was there, as if something were being pushed and squeezed through the wrong sort of machine.

The medium had gone rigid. Her thin wrist was no longer lax; it pulled and pounded against Ruth's fingers. Madame Nada had good cause for alarm; for she, of all the people in the room, knew that the muttering horror of a voice did not come from her own throat. She, and one other. Ruth knew that the sound originated, not from her right-hand side, but from her left. From Sara.

The others, of course, assumed that Madame Nada was producing this voice, as she had produced the others. Yet there was a qualitative difference in this sound, and they all felt it. The room became absolutely still. The cold suddenly seemed intense; Ruth had to clench her teeth together to keep them from chattering.

The muttering, mumbling monologue seemed to go on and on; but in actuality the whole business could not have lasted more than thirty seconds, and the voice had forced out no more than six articulate words, before the medium's strained nerves erupted in a hair-raising scream. It broke the horrified paralysis of the others; there were sounds of chairs being pushed back, cries and questions. The lights flashed on. Ruth had a wild, vivid glimpse of Bruce, his hand still on the light switch, his body braced against the wall, his face paper white as he stared at her. . . . No, not at her. At Sara, beside her. *He knew.* Somehow, he knew.

Making the greatest effort of her life, Ruth turned her head to stare at the thing that sat beside her—quietly now, demurely, head bent and hands still. The features were the same—the narrow nose and flowing black hair, the quiet mouth. The physical identity only intensified the terror; for she knew, with a certainty that defied the senses, that when Sara turned her head, something that was no longer Sara would look back at her through Sara's eyes.

# Chapter

## 4

THAT NIGHT, FOR THE FIRST TIME IN FORTY YEARS, RUTH LEFT a night light burning when she went to bed. But whenever she closed her eyes a face took shape against the darkness—the familiar, unrecognizable face that had been superimposed on Sara's face for one impossible moment.

From a social point of view the evening could not be called a success, ending as it did with the demoralization of most of the guests and the complete collapse of one of them. Madame Nada had fainted dead away, falling so ungracefully and painfully that even the skeptics knew it was a genuine faint. When she recovered she could think of only one thing—getting out of the house as quickly as possible. Mrs. MacDougal's car took her home, and Pat felt he had to escort the excited women. The other guests made their excuses like people fleeing a house of death. Séances were only fun when they were artificial.

It was clear to Ruth that none of them really knew what had happened; they were simply reacting to an atmosphere as intense as it was unpleasant. The medium was a true sensitive, in that she had felt the unpleasantness more keenly, but she was no more equipped to cope with genuine horror than were the others.

Bruce would have lingered; but Ruth sent him packing. His presence was not the one she wanted, and, in fact, she was not sure that she wanted anyone. She preferred to be alone with Sara.

For Sara it was, once again; no doubt about that. When Ruth turned shrinkingly back to her niece, after administering first aid to Madame Nada, the illusion (if it had been an illusion) was gone. Sara's voice, Sara's expression—the indefinable, essential Sara-ness—were back.

Ruth was left in bed with two equally unpleasant theories for company. The room was comfortably warm, the blankets fleecy, the brushed nylon of her nightgown soft against her recumbent body; but from time to time she shivered with an ungovernable chill.

What is it that defines an individual? Not the body, the color of hair and eyes, the shape of the face, for these may alter with accident or illness, and they do, inevitably, alter with the one unavoidable illness, old age. Opinions and beliefs, the products of the thinking brain, also change; the bright young idealist may become a cynical supporter of bigotry in old age.

So what is it, she wondered, that makes a man or woman, distinctly himself, different from all others? Give that quality a name—personality—though the name itself is meaningless; it may be what some call the immortal soul or it may be simply a cluster of traits, inherited and acquired. Character, soul, spirit, individuality . . . the turn of the head, the expression of the eyes, the responses to pain, fear, love.

When she was little, Ruth had thought of herself—the real Ruth—as a little homunculus living inside her head, busily manipulating the muscles that moved the puppet of her body, arranging the thoughts that animated her brain by day, sorting and selecting her dreams at night. She wondered now whence she had derived this image; surely there was something like it in one of Louisa May Alcott's books. . . . Or perhaps it was an idea which would occur to any sensitive child—the little soul living inside the brain, looking out through the eyes.

Tonight something had looked out of Sara's brain, through Sara's eyes, that was not Sara.

Ruth twisted uncomfortably between sheets which were already wrinkled and hot. The incredibility of her fancies was even more apparent when she put them into concrete images.

In a way, the alternative was less difficult. It was simply that she, Ruth Bennett, was suffering from hallucinations. That she was able to entertain, even for a moment, the wild hypothesis of

Sara's differentness, indicated that her own mind had slipped considerably from normal standards.

People who are losing their minds, they say, do not doubt their sanity. Ruth suspected that this consoling thought would not be supported by a psychologist. Heaven knew she had enough doubts. But at the basis of all her queries lay one damning fact: that it was easier for her to believe in her mad idea of possession than in her own madness.

Morning is often a revelation in itself. When Ruth woke from a brief, but deep, sleep, she could hardly believe in the dark visions of the night. Sunlight poured in through the window and the mockingbirds who had made a nest in the chimney discussed their plans for the day. Downstairs she heard movement, and Sara's voice, an untrained but sweet contralto, singing "Where Have All the Flowers Gone?" Smells floated enticingly up the stair—coffee, bacon, toast.

Saturday was cleaning day. Since Sara arrived Ruth had gladly abandoned the never-ending search for reliable help. She and Sara could go over the entire house in four hours, and leave every bit of glass sparkling and every chair leg polished. If there was the slightest shadow on Sara's soul it was invisible. She sang like a bird and worked like a demon and, after lunch, went dashing off to keep a shopping appointment with a girl friend. Ruth's decision had been made without conscious debate; not for anything in the world would she have mentioned her fears to Sara. She decided that she would call her doctor for a checkup, just to be on the safe side. But Monday would be time enough; Saturday morning was always busy for Dr. Peterson. There was no hurry.

## II

She met It again that night, walking in the hall. Sara was barefoot, but the old, uneven boards creaked. Ruth came awake as a soldier in a battle zone jerks out of sleep, alert and fully conscious. She knew instantly what was standing outside her door; and knew, as well, the futility of her former attempts at reason.

The hardest thing she had ever had to do was to get out of bed and go to meet it.

## III

"She always wears bedroom slippers," Ruth said. "Ever since she got a splinter in her foot last fall."

Suddenly, without meaning to, she began to cry. Pat, whose face had assumed a deepening expression of concern, slid over and put his arms around her. When the first storm of tears subsided he said quietly, "I don't blame you for being upset, Ruth. But you've got to tell me the rest. What happened after you went out into the hall?"

"I'm sorry." Ruth sniffed, and took a deep breath. "I know I'm not. . . . It was bright moonlight last night; the light came flooding in through the circular window on the landing. It— Sara—" She faltered, seeing his lips tighten at the slip, and then went doggedly on. "She was standing there, on the landing, looking like something out of Mrs. Radcliffe; she always wears nightgowns, not pajamas, and her winter ones are long and high-necked because the house gets cold at night. . . . Sorry again. I'm fighting away from it, aren't I?"

All he said was, "You're doing fine, go on."

"What I'm trying to give you is the picture—a girl in a long pale gown, with her black hair falling over her shoulders. Wraithlike, pale-faced in the moonlight. Her eyes were wide open. . . . No, I can see what you're thinking, but that wasn't it; she was not sleepwalking. My roommate used to walk in her sleep and I know the look. This—Sara—was awake. It was awake, Pat, wide awake; and *it was not Sara.*"

"You're giving me your impressions. You are not describing what happened. We'll worry about subjective sensations after you explain how you got those marks on your face."

"I must look awful," Ruth said drearily.

"You have what is popularly known as a shiner. Plus a couple of scratches on your cheek. How did you explain them to Sara?"

"I didn't. I yelled through the door, told her I had a headache and didn't want to be disturbed. Finally she went out. As soon as she left the house I called you."

"She was—Sara—again this morning?"

"Yes. She offered to get breakfast, call the doctor. She was awfully sweet. . . ."

"All right," he said, as her voice began to quaver. "You've told me everything but the main thing. Sara hit you, didn't she?"

"Yes."

Pat pointed a long finger at the glass on the table beside Ruth. "Finish your medicine. I know this is a hell of an hour for sherry, but you need a stimulant. Why did she hit you?"

Ruth made a face; for a moment she felt sure that the wine would be the last straw for her churning stomach. Then the warmth spread, and her icy hands relaxed a bit.

"Let me try to be coherent. I saw her standing there in the moonlight. After a minute I spoke to her. She didn't answer. I said, 'Sara, are you ill? What's wrong?' She started. She said—"

"Exact words, if you can remember them."

"Good God, I wish I could forget them! She said the same thing she said at the séance. She said it twice. 'Not dead. Not dead.' Then a sort of sigh, and—I think—the word 'please.' She kept repeating that, faster and faster, till the words ran together. . . . She was screaming by then, Pat; in the middle of it, I thought I caught something that sounded like 'the General.' But I wasn't really listening. I felt I had to make her be quiet. It was when I touched her that she—flailed out with both arms. Honestly, I don't think she meant to hurt me; I'm not even sure she knew who I was."

"Probably not."

"Pat, you know Sara. You know she wouldn't ever—"

"Dear heart, is that what worries you?" He smiled, for the first time since he had entered the house; but the lines on forehead and cheek did not disappear. "I don't think our nice Sara has turned into a homicidal maniac, no. Finish your story before I start lecturing. How the hell did you calm her? She's twice your size, and a healthy young animal."

"I didn't. She almost knocked me out with that blow in the face, but she overbalanced herself. Her foot slipped. When she fell, she must have hit her head. I dragged her back to bed. I probably shouldn't have moved her, but . . . well, I did. She passed from unconsciousness into normal sleep without waking, and when I was sure she was asleep, I went to bed myself."

"I'll bet you were ready for it. Okay. I get the picture."

Ruth drew a long breath.

"I just want to know one thing. Who's crazy—me or Sara?"

"Neither of you is crazy," he said violently. "Don't use that stupid goddamn word."

"I'm sorry. . . ."

"So am I. I'm a hell of a therapist, aren't I. Have another drink. Let's both have another drink."

Ruth took the glass he handed her. In the morning sunlight the light liquid shone like tawny gold.

"Don't think I'm not grateful," she said. "But if you would just tell me, without mincing words. . . ."

"I intend to." He drained his glass in one movement of his wrist. "Dismiss, first of all, the notion that you imagined all this. Such things have happened; people with certain types of mental illness have even inflicted injuries on themselves in order to substantiate a fantastic theory. But not you. This thing happened. So we are faced with the only other possibility. Sara is the one who is mentally disturbed. You're probably right in saying that she didn't know you. Now at this point that's absolutely all I can say; I haven't seen the girl. Something is bugging her, some anxiety; I could guess at the obvious possibilities, but I see no future in doing so."

"Oh, God. What am I going to tell her mother?"

"Nothing, yet. Ruth, you're too intelligent to go into a tizzy at the mention of mental illness; this may not turn out to be anything serious. Let's wait and see before we start screaming."

"But what shall I do?"

"First, you will go and get dressed." He lifted his hand as she started to speak, and solemnly ticked off the points on his fingers. "Next we will go out to lunch and get some food in that queasy stomach of yours. Forget about your black eye, the waiter will think I slugged you, that's all, and he'll admire me greatly. Then we will come back here and wait for Sara. When do you expect her home?"

"Five, or thereabouts. But Pat—"

"I want to talk to her," Pat said quietly. "That's all, just talk. Maybe then we can determine whether she needs a neurologist or a psychiatrist or a gynecologist, or just a good swift kick in the pants."

"But—"

"Theorizing without sufficient data is the most futile of all occupations, Ruth. Wasn't it Sherlock Holmes who said that? It applies to practically everything in life. Now go up and get some clothes on."

Ruth went. After her hysterical plea for help, she could hardly refuse to follow his advice. She wondered, as she dressed, what weird combination of motives had prompted her to call him instead of the family doctor. Some of them were reasonably obvious. Others. . . .

She examined the image in her mirror. It looked abnormally normal, all things considered; trim and tailored in a powder-blue suit, silvery hair serene; carefully applied makeup had even diminished the bruise around her eye.

Others. . . . Her uncontrolled thoughts ran on. Other motives might be in doubt. But one was clear. She had instinctively summoned Pat because he was an expert on the subject that haunted her—literally and terribly. Despite what seemed to her a series of betraying admissions, he had not sensed her true fears—because, she thought bitterly, no sane person would ever conceive of such things. He believed that she had called out to him because she needed him, not as a professional, but as a man.

## IV

The sunset was splendidly ominous—indigo and purple clouds rimmed with gold against a pale, clear green sky. The leafless branches of the big oak stood out black against the glory; their complex patterns had an austere mathematical beauty.

Ruth had reached the stage of irrational nervousness when the slightest phenomenon seems prophetic. When the wine-glass, one of an old, cherished set, slipped from her hand and shattered musically on the coffee table, she bit her lip so hard that it bled.

Pat bent to collect the pieces. Then they heard the front door open.

Sara was—Sara. But she was not alone. Ruth recognized Bruce's affected speech with mingled exasperation and relief. One could hardly speak candidly to the girl in his presence. On the other hand, it was good to know that Bruce had been with her. Especially with night drawing in.

Now why, she wondered, did I think of that?

Pat's greeting to Sara was, on the surface, casual and without innuendoes. Sherry was offered and accepted; the two young people sat down; Bruce suggested a fire, and was graciously permitted to build one. The darkness fell with winter rapidity, and they sat by the light of the leaping flames and talked about nothing.

Ruth was silent; light conversation seemed impossible. The devil that Pat had exorcised by the simple fact of refusing to see its possibility slid slyly back, hovering in the gathering shadows. Yet whenever she looked at Sara her brain staggered at the incongruity of it all. Miniskirts and long black leather boots do not suit the supernatural.

As the minutes wore on Ruth felt the tension mounting. Her own silence fed it; so did Bruce's uncharacteristically monosyllabic speech. He sat on the edge of his chair and never took his eyes off Sara. The girl was nervous too; she moved too much, twitching at her skirt, stroking the leather of her boots. She had developed a slight stammer, the first time Ruth had ever noticed any such trait.

"It's dark," Ruth said suddenly. "Let's have some light."

Pat's hand caught her arm as she started to rise. He alone seemed unaffected by the strain.

"The firelight is pleasant," he said. "Leave it."

The words, with their bland assumption of authority, would have irritated Ruth at any other time. Now the sudden need that had sent her groping for light closed in upon her. She sank back onto the couch, not because of Pat's grip, but because her knees would no longer hold her erect. Could no one else feel It? It was coming. It was all around. It was cold and darkness; It fed on darkness. If this went on. . . .

"I understand you haven't been sleeping too well lately," Pat said to Sara.

"No, Pat, don't," Ruth said. "This isn't the time—"

"Of course it is; you're letting this worry you far too much. There's no reason to be shy about it. Everybody has problems at one time or another—nervous strain, overwork. . . ."

"What the hell are you talking about?" Bruce demanded.

"I mean just what I say. Sara has been sleepwalking. That's a sign of nerves, a signal we can't ignore."

"Stop it," Ruth said urgently. "Pat, this is all wrong, can't you feel. . . ." Her voice died, only to rise again in a gasp of terror. Sara was sitting on the edge of the couch nearest the fire. The red light gave auburn gleams to her dark hair, and lit the curve of cheek and chin with a diabolical flush. She had not moved nor uttered a word; but her pose had altered, indefinably but unmistakably.

In the silence that followed Ruth's intake of breath they could all hear the girl breathing in short shallow gasps. The firelight caught the glow of her eyes as they moved. Groping wildly Ruth found Pat's hand and clung to it. She was conscious of a bizarre feeling of relief. He saw it too. The rigidity of his muscles, unresponsive for once to her touch, told of his reaction more graphically than speech. But the reaction that cut Ruth to the quick was Bruce's. He made one small movement, quickly controlled; but she knew enough to recognize it, even from its abortive beginning—the instinctive flight of flexed fingers to his forehead.

"Sara," Pat said softly.

No response. Only that shallow, panicky panting of breath.

"Sara, are you in pain? Tell me what hurts. I can help."

No sound, no movement. Pat freed his hand from Ruth's grasp. He leaned forward as if to touch Sara's arm.

"Don't be afraid. Everything is going to be—"

She flinched away from him, shrinking into the corner of the couch. Pat withdrew his hand.

"You hear me, don't you?"

"I—hear."

The voice was normal enough in tone and pitch; the only thing wrong with it was that it was not Sara's voice.

Even in those two words there was a noticeable difference in inflection. The "I" sound was softer, and there was something about the final "r" that struck oddly on the listening ears.

"You do hear me?" Pat repeated. His voice was soft, but insistent.

"Yes. But I don't know—"

"You don't know what?"

"Who you are."

Pat's arm shot out in a savage silent gesture aimed at Bruce, just in time to keep him in his place. His voice did not lose its even, gentle inflection.

"I'm Pat, Sara. Professor MacDougal. You're taking my course, remember? And doing some typing for me."

"What is—typ-ing?"

"It's a kind of—never mind. You know your name, don't you?"

"Know . . . name. Sara." There was a brief pause; the figure huddled on the couch rolled its eyes, and Ruth felt her hands turn cold. "You called . . . her . . . Sara."

It was too much for Bruce. With a muffled curse he dived, not for Sara, but for the light switch. The chandelier blazed into life, blinding the three who sat by the fire. Ruth's hands flew up to shield her eyes; Pat swore; and Sara, after one muffled cry, turned the color of typewriter paper and fell forward. Pat recovered himself just barely in time to catch her.

"Goddamn it all to hell," he said, kneeling with Sara held across his shoulder like an awkward, long-legged doll; the black boots sprawled pathetically across the rug. "Goddamn you, you young bastard, what the hell did you do that for? Get over here and give me a hand."

"Oh, Pat, don't yell at him; I was about ready to do it myself." Ruth's cheeks were wet with tears of nervous strain. She dropped onto the floor and touched Sara's head. "Is she—"

"Just fainted. Bruce!"

"I'll take her." Bruce held out his arms.

"You'll take her feet. Try not to joggle her. I don't want her to wake up."

At the foot of the stairs Pat handed his part of the burden over to Bruce and let the boy carry her to her room. When Ruth tried to follow them, he held her back.

"Stay with her, Bruce," he called softly. "If she starts to wake, let me know instantly. No, Ruth, you can't do a thing. Come back here."

He took her with him, to the telephone on its little table behind the stairs. When he was about halfway through dialing Ruth woke up. She snatched at his hand.

"Whom are you calling?"

"Whom do you think?"

"Put that telephone down! Pat, you've got to tell me—"

They were both speaking in sharp whispers, their faces only inches apart.

"I'm calling a doctor," Pat said. He was pale; the session had shaken him severely. "If I had realized that matters were this serious—"

"But I told you—"

"It's different when you actually see it." Pat was silent for a moment, staring with creased brows at the telephone. "And I hoped my hunch was wrong. Damn it all—it need not have been this, not from your description. It is comparatively rare. . . ."

"What? What is rare?" With an effort that left her shaking Ruth kept her voice from rising. "What doctor are you planning to call, Pat?"

"A friend of mine. He's a fine guy, one of the best."

"It's after five. He won't be in his office."

"I'm calling him at home."

"But he won't see her till morning anyhow. Can't we—"

"He'll see her tonight—now. Face it, Ruth. I know you love the girl—"

"Yes," Ruth said blankly. "Yes. I do."

"Then you've got to keep your wits about you. This isn't incurable, they've had excellent results with other cases."

"What cases? For God's sake, Pat—"

"He'll want her in the hospital at once, I'm sure," Pat said. "You could go up and pack a bag. . . ."

"Hospital," Ruth pressed her hands to her cheeks. "What hospital? St. Elizabeth's. That's what you mean, isn't it? An insane asylum!"

He caught her by the shoulders and shook her.

"Stop that! St. Elizabeth's is not an insane asylum; it is a hospital for the mentally ill. I thought you were an educated modern woman! Next thing you'll be doing is muttering prayers and making signs against the evil eye! Anyhow, I don't mean St. Elizabeth's. I do mean, and let's get it straight, the psychiatric ward of whatever hospital Jim practices at. Sibley, probably. Ruth, darling. . . ." His voice softened. "After this is over we'll come back and get good and drunk—absolutely stoned. Right now you must be calm or we'll all start screaming. And what good do you think that will do Sara?"

"All right. All right. What is wrong with her?"

He studied her face for a moment; then, as if satisfied, he nodded and let her go.

"Ruth, I'm only an amateur. But the symptoms are so obvious. . . . What you described last night might have been somnambulism—sleepwalking, as a result of some severe nervous

strain. But tonight. . . . She really didn't know me, Ruth; she
was not putting me on. But the most betraying sign was a single
word. She referred to herself as 'her.' 'You call her Sara,' she
said."

"Amnesia?"

"Well, it's related, if I understand the problem correctly. But
this is more than simple amnesia. We talked to someone tonight
who thinks she is not Sara. Ruth, did you ever read a book or
see a movie called *The Three Faces of Eve?* Or maybe Shirley
Jackson's novel, *The Bird's Nest?"*

"Oh, no," Ruth whispered.

"I'm afraid it's oh, yes. I may be wrong. But it looks to me
like multiple personality. What they used to call schizophrenia."

Standing in the hall, with electric lights blazing and telephone near her hand, Ruth knew that she was only half a step
away from the cave, and that the gadgetry of the modern world
was a thin skin covering emotions that had not altered in centuries. The terms were scientific; the thing they described
struck her with the same chill that had struck her primitive ancestors when another word was mentioned.

"Good girl," Pat said, mistaking her frozen horror for acceptance. "I'll call Jim now."

"Oh, no," said another voice. "No, you won't."

They looked up to see Bruce's saturnine beard waving at
them. He descended the last few steps.

"You stupid fool," Pat exclaimed. "Get back up there. If she
wakes. . . ."

"She won't be any worse off, with what you're planning.
Cool it, Pat; she's asleep; she won't wake up for a while. And
when she does, it will be here, in her own bed—not in some
goddamn ward with a lot of nuts and a bunch of headshrinkers
probing into her subconscious."

Pat's face turned dark red. He rolled his eyes heavenward
and started counting aloud. After "four" his color began to
subside.

"Eight, nine, ten. All right, Bruce, I am not going to knock
your front teeth out, as was my first impulse. I will listen to you
first, before I knock them out. But make it fast. I'm not feeling
awfully calm right now."

"Neither am I." Bruce faced him. Feet apart, hands
clenched, he looked like a boxer braced for a blow—except for

his face, which was pinched and haggard. He stood in silent thought for several seconds; it was clear that he was choosing his words with care.

"Are you sure of your diagnosis?" he asked.

"Of course not. How arrogant do you think I am?"

"I don't mean the diagnosis of multiple personality. On the face of it, it's a reasonable hypothesis. I'm questioning your general assumption, Dr. MacDougal, not your specific diagnosis. How do you know that this is mental illness?"

Pat was too puzzled to be angry. His brows drew together in an introspective frown.

"How could it be physical? It's not delirium, there's no fever, no—"

"I don't mean that."

"What the hell do you mean?"

Bruce hesitated. Ruth noticed that the scant area of skin that showed on his cheeks was darker than usual. The boy was blushing.

"What I'm suggesting may seem unorthodox," he said at last. "But if you'll try to look at this with an open mind you'll see that there is another possibility, which fits the observed facts even better than your theory of multiple personality."

"Better? What?"

Bruce looked as if he were about to choke. And then, all at once, Ruth knew what he was going to say before he said it.

"Possession."

# Chapter
## 5

"POSSESSION?" PAT REPEATED. HIS VOICE WAS CALMLY, MILDLY curious. "Possession. . . . You do mean what I think you mean— evil spirits? That sort of thing?"

"Yes." Bruce's face was bright red from the hair on his chin to the hair on his forehead. But his eyes did not waver.

"All right. Go on."

"You mean you believe—"

"I think," Pat said, with precision, "that you are insane or joking. I'll give you the benefit of the doubt and assume it is the former. You are, of course, a crypto-Christian—"

"I haven't been to mass for five years," Bruce said in out-raged tones, as if he had been accused of fraud or burglary.

"Excuse *me*. I meant that your youthful training, though consciously denied, still affects you. Damn it, boy, you're poaching on my preserves! I know all about the superstition of possession; it's an ancient, widespread delusion among primi-tive peoples."

"There is still a ritual for exorcism in the church," Bruce said.

"A ritual dating from one of the most superstitious eras of human history. How many pathetic women were burned, tor-tured, maimed, because their credulous acquaintances believed they were possessed by the Devil? We know now that these symptoms—if they ever existed, except in the imaginations of vicious neighbors of the accused—were those of mental disor-ders, schizophrenia among them. Superstition is my field,

Bruce; do you suppose I've neglected the richest source of all—
the history of the Christian church?"

"I won't argue religion with you," Bruce said. His color was
still high, but argument was his meat and drink. "I'll even admit, for the sake of the discussion, that the Christian faith is
based on centuries of superstition. My contention is that your
modern science of psychiatry is just as irrational—just as much
a matter of superstitious faith."

The tension in the dimly lit hall was almost audible, like a
high keening. When a log dropped in the fireplace in the next
room, all of them started. Pat turned back to his opponent with
narrowed eyes.

"This is no time to quibble."

"There won't be another time." Bruce's embarrassed flush
had gone; his skin was as pale as ivory against the sharp black
lines of his beard. "If you do what you plan to do, she'll lose—"

"Her immortal soul?"

"You could call it that. . . ."

"Show me a soul, Bruce."

The color—excitement, not embarrassment now—blazed
up in Bruce's cheeks.

"Show me a subconscious mind!"

"That's not the same thing!"

"God, yes, it's the same thing! Just once try to break
through your thick crust of adult dullness and see what I'm trying to get at! I'm not insisting on the possession idea. All I'm
saying is that it is as reasonable a theory now, for us, as your
theory of multiple personality. We're hypnotized, in our age, by
the mumbo jumbo of psychiatry just as the men of the Middle
Ages were hypnotized by witchcraft. We've less material proof
of our faith than they had of theirs! That's what it comes down
to in the end, a matter of faith. You ask me to take the word of
Freud and Jung. I don't see why their opinions should carry
more weight than those of Thomas Aquinas and St. Paul—and
Martin Luther, if it comes to that!"

"You reason like a Jesuit," Pat said coldly. "But doesn't it
seem in bad taste to you to debate about Sara's sanity?"

"For Christ's sake!" Bruce brought his clenched fists down
on the balustrade with a force that drove the blood from them.
"I care more about Sara's sanity than I do about some abstract

problem in debate! Why doesn't she deserve the same amount of intellectual effort I give to a problem in logic?"

"This isn't a problem in logic! This is—"

"Wait a minute," Ruth said. She had not spoken in so long that her voice sounded cracked and rusty. Both men turned to stare at her. "You're wrong, Pat. So am I. Isn't this what they accuse us of, the young people—of refusing to keep an open mind? You haven't even asked him why he thinks. . . . I can't say it. I don't even understand what it means."

Hands still clenched on the stair rail, Bruce studied her in openmouthed amazement. Then understanding dawned.

"So that's it," he said slowly. "You felt it too."

"Yes," Ruth said. "If you mean—"

"The Other-ness. The occupation of Sara's body by a force—personality, soul, spirit—that is not Sara. That's possession, Mrs. Bennett. That's what I mean."

"Dear God," Pat muttered. "Ruth—"

"No." She moved back, rejecting his outstretched hand and everything it implied. "Are all three of us mad, Pat? Bruce, and I, and Sara?"

"Not mad, just unbearably distressed and distracted. Damn you, Bruce—"

"At least listen to me!" Bruce glanced up the stairs. There was no sound from Sara's room. "Just give me a chance! I'm not insisting that this is it, Pat. I'm only asking you to consider it as you would any other hypothesis."

"Give me your evidence, then." Pat was livid with anger, but he had his face and voice under control.

"First point—the reaction, not only of myself, but of Mrs. Bennett. Hunches are almost always rationally based; they are value judgments made by the subconscious mind—see, I'm giving you your damned subconscious mind—on the basis of evidence the conscious mind doesn't see. Mrs. Bennett—"

"Ruth."

"Ruth and I are more emotionally involved with Sara than you are. We are more sensitive to her, more able to notice discrepancies. And both of us felt the same thing, and at the same time. Right, Ruth?"

"At the séance. You saw it too."

"Not 'saw,' 'felt.' " Bruce's eyes went dark with memory. "I felt it clear on the other side of the table. And I'll frankly admit it made me feel sick."

"The medium knew too," Ruth exclaimed. "She was terrified."

"Your interpretation of the medium's emotions is not evidence," Pat said flatly.

"How about my emotions?"

"Ah, Ruth—now—"

"And the fact that Bruce and I felt the same?"

"You find now that you felt the same. You're infecting one another. Don't you see—I'm not denying the—the Other-ness, if you choose to call it that. Good God, it's the basis of my own theory."

Bruce rubbed his hands together nervously.

"And Sara's reference to herself, in this last seizure, in the third person?"

"The alternate personalities in this type of psychosis regard one another as different entities," Pat said relentlessly. "Reference to the others as 'she,' or by various nicknames, is common."

Ruth felt herself weakening. He seemed to have an answer for everything. And the proposition he supported had, in a sense, greater hope for Sara's eventual cure than any other; she could not have said why she fought it so strongly, or why she had instinctively supported Bruce's incredible idea. Now her eyes turned to him with a silent plea, and the boy straightened.

"It just so happens that I've read about several of these cases of multiple personality," he said disarmingly.

"I might have known." Under other circumstances the expression on Pat's mouth might have turned into a smile.

"In the first place," Bruce said, "these types aren't homicidal, or dangerous."

"Have you happened to notice Ruth's face?"

Bruce's glance flickered over to Ruth; his knowledge was so intuitively complete that it surprised her to recall that he knew nothing of the previous night's events.

"Sara did that?"

"It was an accident."

"Tell me."

Ruth told the grim little story again. Bruce did not seem disturbed by its ending; what really interested him were the words that Sara had uttered, and he made Ruth repeat them several times. Then he nodded.

"I agree. The attack on you was impersonal. She didn't even know who you were, any more than she knew Pat tonight."

"That will be poor comfort," Pat said, "if she pushes Ruth down the stairs next time, and breaks her neck."

"And it will be poor comfort to me," Bruce said softly, "if your psychiatrist friend sends Sara off the deep end into real psychosis. No, wait a minute, Pat. Remember the Beauchamp case, where four separate and distinct personalities were involved, in one woman? One of these, the "Sally" personality, was almost certainly *produced* by the hypnotic suggestion of the doctor who was handling the case. In another case there were *seven* different personalities which emerged—how, I wonder, and with what help from the inexpert probing of the doctor? Oh, sure, some of these cases were cured—if you can call a random fusion of disparate personalities a cure. My God, Pat, don't your doctor friends scare you just a little bit? They're so damned smug, so sure of themselves—just dig around in the patient's childhood till the probe hits the right little trauma— then, spoing! the pieces all snap back together again!"

"Bruce, I'm not claiming this is simple. Or easy." Pat rubbed his hand across his jaw as if trying to relax tight muscles. His eyes were hooded and sad. "I don't like the situation any better than you do."

"Then listen to me!" Bruce flung his hands wide in a gesture that would have looked theatrical if it had not been so passionately sincere. "Just listen and try to think! Pat, I tell you I know these cases, and this is not like the others! The things Sara has said, and the way she has behaved, do not fit the classic patterns of multiple personality. Nor can I blandly ignore, as you do whenever you strike evidence that doesn't suit your theory, the reactions of other people. Look, I'll make you a proposition. Give me forty-eight hours. Two days. Nothing serious can happen in two days, even if you're right."

"Two days for what?"

"For me to convince you that I'm right." Bruce's eyes blazed. "I have a feeling that we've only seen the beginning of this, Pat. If the situation hasn't changed within two days, I'll give in."

"This is the craziest proposition—!"

"But you have no choice," Ruth said calmly. "Because, when you come right down to it, I'm the one who has to decide. Aren't I?"

Pat's eyes met hers.

"I could telephone her mother," he said.

"You do, and you'll never enter this house again."

"Damn it, Ruth—"

"I mean it."

Bruce remained silent, with the tact of an expert strategist. He did not so much as bat an eye when Pat, breathing heavily through his nose, said, "All right, I'll give in. Not because I like it. Because I have no choice. But I agree only on one condition. I'm moving in. And I'm staying till this is settled. I'll cancel my classes."

"Good idea," Bruce said coolly. "That makes two of us."

And Ruth said, as calmly as if she were welcoming invited guests, "I'm sorry we have only one extra room. But it has twin beds. I'll call work tomorrow and tell them I've got the flu."


## II


They sat around the kitchen table eating pizza. Three of them were eating; Ruth regarded the red-and-yellow circle in front of her with faint repulsion.

"I can't believe you've never eaten pizza," Bruce said. "Where've you been all these years?"

Ruth poked the rubbery red circle with a fork.

"Are you sure it's edible?" she asked dubiously.

The burst of laughter was a little too loud. In the bright, modern warmth of the kitchen they were all able to pretend, but not very successfully, or for very long.

"You didn't want to go out," Pat said. "And nobody feels much like cooking."

The silence fell like fog, wet and clammy.

"Pat, you promised—" Bruce began.

"That I'd give you two days. I'll do more; I'll actively coop- erate with anything you suggest doing. I just want to know how Sara feels about this."

Two of them, at least, had been trying not to look at Sara,

who sat next to Bruce, her eyes still a bit foggy with sleep, her hand openly holding his. But with the other hand she was feeding herself pizza with the healthy appetite of a young woman.

"As I said before," Bruce remarked, with strained patience, "she has the best right of anyone to know what we're doing."

The argument at the foot of the stairs had not ended with Pat's capitulation. He had protested vigorously when Bruce proposed waking Sara, and it had taken further threats from Ruth to overrule him.

"I'll heat some coffee," Ruth said, abandoning her pizza.

She had not felt like cooking dinner; but there was a sort of comfort now in handling the smooth aluminum of the coffeepot, fiddling with the handles on the stove. The familiar charm of the kitchen seemed like a painting on gauze, that wavered oddly in the breeze of unreason, and might at any moment blow away completely, displaying something the senses could not endure.

Ruth poured the coffee, and no one commented on how badly her hands were shaking.

"Let's take it into the living room," she said.

"No." Bruce caught at Sara's sleeve as she started to rise. "I don't—well, let's say I don't like that room."

"Ah." Pat wriggled around so that he was sitting sideways in his chair. He lifted one foot, raising the ankle on the other knee, and slumped, comfortably. "It is your contention, then, that the living room is a focus of the—er—trouble?"

Bruce gave him a sharp glance; but the older man's manner was irreproachable.

"I'm cooperating," he explained, answering Bruce's look.

"Hmmm. Thanks. I don't know what my contention is. That's half the trouble. But the room is abnormally cold. And that was where this—thing—"

"Are you afraid of your own terms? Possession. By what, if I may ask?"

Bruce stiffened.

"Sara ought to have some ideas about that," he said.

"Well, Sara?" Pat said. "I suspect that you were not—"

"No leading the witness," said Bruce; the words were meant to be mildly humorous, but the tone definitely was not. After a moment, Pat nodded.

"Sorry. Sara?"

"You say something happened at the séance?" Sara looked at Bruce. "I don't remember that. Nor the time I walked in my sleep, the night Ruth fell and hurt herself."

Bruce's eyes caught Ruth's, with a command as clear as words. He had not, then, told the girl everything. Ruth nodded slightly. Out of the corner of her eye she saw that Pat was looking smug, and wondered why.

Sara went on, "But tonight was different."

"You were aware of what was going on?" Pat asked. Ruth wondered if other people could read his face as easily as she could. He was now as crestfallen as he had formerly been smug.

"I sure was. Want me to describe it? I'm not sure I can. . . ."

"If it upsets you, darling," Ruth began.

"Tell it anyhow," said Bruce.

"All right." She gave him a look of such blind trust that Ruth's heart contracted painfully. "You know the feeling, when you're waiting for something that you know will be very painful or unhappy? Like an operation; or somebody is going to die. Something you can't get out of, but that you know you are going to hate. You can't breathe. You keep gasping, but the air won't go down into your lungs. You can hear your own heart thudding, so hard it seems to be banging into your ribs. Your hands perspire. You want to run away, but you can't, it won't do any good, the thing you're afraid of will happen anyhow."

The worst part of the description, for Ruth, was that Sara was not trying to be terrifying, but simply to give facts.

"The feeling was like that," Sara said. "But this time—there was no reason for it. Do you understand? I wasn't afraid of any *thing*. I was just afraid. And that's the worst fear of all, the fear of nothing."

Now Bruce's face was troubled, Pat's confident. Apparently the sensation the girl was describing had meaning to them, though it had none for Ruth.

"Then it came," Sara went on. "It—filled me up. Like water pouring into a pitcher. Pat, I could hear you when you were talking to me—but I couldn't answer. I heard somebody, something else, talking. And I couldn't speak or move a muscle."

"That's all?" Bruce said, after a rather painful moment.

"Yes, it went away, and I fainted, I guess. It's so hard to describe. . . . Did you ever wear clothes that were too tight? Shoes that pinched? That was how—it—felt. Something didn't quite—fit."

Somehow that was the worst description yet. Ruth's mouth went dry; Pat's face was disturbed.

"All right," he said. "Relax, Sara. You were aware of an invasion—right?—but cannot identify the invader. So far—let's be blunt—this proves nothing, one way or the other."

"I haven't begun to fight," Bruce said grimly. "Ruth, your turn."

"I told you my impressions of the séance," Ruth began.

"I don't mean that. I want to know whether you've noticed anything else out of the ordinary."

"Where? When?"

"Any time, but probably recently. Here. In this house."

"The house," Ruth exclaimed. "You think—"

"Let's not jump the gun. Anything, any impression at all."

For a few seconds Ruth could not think. Her glance wandered around the kitchen—polished brass winking, smooth scrubbed counter tops, mellow brown maple. . . . Then, from nowhere, it came back.

"I had a dream," she said slowly. "Probably just—"

"Describe it."

She did; and it lost considerably in the telling, as dreams usually do.

"The shadow loomed up," she ended, lamely. "And I thought I was awake, but I wasn't. It was an awful feeling, trying to get up, and not being able to move."

"What did awaken you?" Bruce asked. He had begun to lose interest. It was obvious he had no great hopes for the dream.

"I don't remember. . . ." Ruth wrinkled her brows. Then memory dawned, with such impact that she knocked her coffee cup over. Sara dived for it, but Ruth caught at her arm.

"Wait, wait. The voice. Sara, you heard it too; it must mean something. That was what woke me—the same voice you heard. Only there isn't any animal named Sammie!"

It took Bruce almost five minutes to extract a coherent story.

"The time," he said, almost as excited as she was. "What time was it when you woke up?"

"Almost two A.M. And Sara heard it just before dawn. That

in itself makes our first assumption ridiculous; who would be chasing a lost pet around at that hour?"

"And through a yard which is completely enclosed," Bruce agreed. "Ruth, we may have something here."

In her triumph Ruth turned toward Pat; and his expression punctured her like a pricked balloon. He looked so sorry for her.

"Now," Bruce said, "I'm going to give Pat a chance for a big ha-ha at my expense. Ruth, did you ever hear any stories about the house being haunted?"

"No. . . ."

"But then you don't know much about the place, do you?"

"I guess nobody does, nobody in the family, at any rate. Cousin Hattie was here so long. . . ."

"Still, it seems to me that we ought to start with the house," Bruce argued. "Nothing like this ever happened to Sara until she came here, and. . . ."

He broke off, his mouth hanging open; and Ruth said hopefully, "And what?"

"Nothing, I guess. I thought for a minute I had an idea, but it got away."

"Maybe you'll catch it in the morning," Ruth said. "It's been a hard day. We all could do with a good night's sleep."

But she knew that none of them would sleep well that night.

# III

"How about the Civil War?" Bruce asked.

They were sitting around the kitchen table the following afternoon. Rain slid tearily down the windowpanes, blurring the garden into a gray dismal landscape of bare trees and withered vines.

Inside, the coffeepot was perking and the kitchen was warm and bright as usual; the tiles over the stove glowed in the light of the hanging copper lamp. Ruth had worn pink that day, a bright glowing rose, and Sara's crimson sweater and royal Stewart plaid skirt made another patch of brightness. They had turned to vivid colors as a protest—and not only against the dreary weather.

Bruce leaned across the table, one hand wrapped around his coffee cup, the other shuffling through a pile of papers. He wore a checked waistcoat, which Ruth privately considered the height of affectation; yet somehow it suited the period air of his facial adornment and finely cut features.

The front door slammed and heavy footsteps announced the arrival of the missing member of the impromptu committee. Pat's red head gleamed with rain, challenging the copper-bottomed pans on the wall.

He stood across the room from the others, with one hand braced against the wall, and looked down at them.

"How did it go?"

"We just got here ourselves," Bruce said. "We were starting to compare notes."

"And what a day," Sara said gloomily. "Remember our conversation about Georgetown traditions, Pat? If I was rude to you, I've been punished. I spent the whole morning and most of the afternoon plowing through books on Georgetown history."

"Serves you right." Pat's voice was casual and his smile bland, but Ruth fancied that his eyes lingered on Sara's face with an almost clinical curiosity.

"Some of it was sort of interesting, at that," Sara admitted. "Ruth, did you ever run across the story of Baron Bodisco, who, at the age of sixty-three, fell in love with a sixteen-year-old girl?"

"No. Who was Baron Bodisco?"

"Russian ambassador, about 1850. He lived a couple of blocks from here, on O Street." Sara's eyes twinkled with amusement. "He was a sprightly old gent, obviously. The girl came to a Christmas party he gave for his nephews, and he married her six months later."

"Nasty old man," Bruce muttered.

"No," Sara said, surprisingly. "It was sort of pathetic. He said she might find someone younger and better looking, but no one who would love her more. And he absolutely showered her with jewels and money and gorgeous clothes. There was a description of one of her dresses—white watered silk embroidered with pale pink rosebuds and green leaves. With it she wore emeralds and diamonds."

"I'd be inclined to suspect the young lady's motives, myself," Ruth said, amused at Sara's unexpected streak of romanticism. Did the miniskirted young really yearn, deep down inside, for ruffles and pink rosebuds?

"There was a picture of her in one of the books," Sara said. "She was pretty, all right; but her mouth had a sort of self-satisfied smirk. . . ."

"Did you find time," Bruce inquired with commendable restraint, "to spend maybe five minutes on the Civil War?"

"Why the Civil War?" Pat dumped his coat on a chair, found a cup, and poured himself some coffee.

"The General," Bruce said.

"What?" Pat looked blank. "Oh. Sara said that, didn't she?"

"So Ruth believes. She didn't say it the first time. The words she spoke at the séance were significant, though. I forgot to mention them last night; but they are part of my evidence."

"Ghosts?" Pat asked amiably, sitting down at the table and stretching out a long arm for the sugar bowl.

"Pat," Ruth said warningly.

"Never mind, let him have his fun." Bruce shrugged. "Yes, ghosts. The phenomenon of possession is defined—"

"By those who believe in it—"

"By those who believe in it," Bruce accepted the amendment without a visible change of expression, "as being invasion by the spirit of someone who has died. Oh, sometimes you hear talk of elementals, demons and the like, but I think we can dismiss that for now. The theory is borne out by Sara's own words, which have been reiterated several times. 'Not dead.' That's what the Invader says. It sounds to me like an assertion, almost a defiance."

He lit a cigarette and waited for a comment. None came. Pat's eyes were hooded by drooping lids.

"Additional confirmation—the behavior of the medium at the séance. She said she felt an intrusion—one which frightened her so much that she was reluctant to continue. Now, since she maintains that her contacts come from the spirit world—"

"You suggest," Pat interrupted, without looking up from his contemplation of his coffee cup, "that the Invader tried Madame Nada first, found her unsatisfactory, for one reason or another, and then took over Sara."

"Not exactly. But I think the Madame did sense the Invader. Which doesn't mean that she isn't faking ninety-nine percent of the time."

"That was what scared her," Ruth said. "When she did encounter something genuine, she was petrified."

"And yet she does have a certain talent," Bruce insisted. "I'm thinking of the sensation of cold in that particular part of the living room. She felt that acutely. Ruth and Sara are aware of it—correct me if I'm not putting this accurately—but it doesn't affect them so much."

"That's right," Ruth agreed. "The others didn't seem to notice it at all. Mrs. MacDougal said she didn't."

"I don't either," Bruce said. "Not a quiver. Come on, now, Pat, be honest—you sense it quite strongly, don't you? It almost doubled you up the other night; I thought for a minute you were having a heart attack."

"I felt a chill," Pat said; and, catching Ruth's expressive gaze, he widened his eyes innocently. "I'm giving you as precise and unemotional a description as I can."

"Okay, I won't push," Bruce said wearily. "I won't even mention Ruth's dream, or the voice that calls in the night. We haven't proved yet that they are relevant. I think we have enough, without them, to formulate a theory. As Pat says— ghosts. So I spent the day at the Georgetown branch of the library reading ghost stories."

"While I was plodding through big fat history books!" Sara exclaimed. "You have your nerve."

"I used to enjoy them," Bruce said briefly. "Point is, there is usually a key motif for hauntings. Violence—that's the most common cause. A suicide seeking rest, a victim seeking revenge, a murderer doomed by his sin to linger at the scene of the crime."

"Those aren't the only reasons." Sara began foraging in the cupboards. She put a plate of cookies and another of crackers and cheese on the table, and sat down. Leaning forward, with her chin propped on her hands and her hair swinging in black satin waves across her cheek, she looked enchanting. Only Ruth saw, with an inner pang, the faintest smudge of dark shadow under her eyes.

"Buried treasure," Sara said. "That's a reason. Remember *Tom Sawyer?* Or protection—warning the living of danger to come."

"They may be motives for hauntings, but not for physical possession," Bruce said direly. He swallowed a cookie—it was a small one—whole, and looked a bit more cheerful. "There's another point I wanted to make. Last night I said that nothing had happened to Sara till she came to the house. I was too beat to see the converse—nothing seems to have happened in the house until Sara arrived. That suggests that something lingers, in the house, which finds Sara a suitable host."

He reached for another handful of cookies; and Pat took advantage of his enforced silence to say thoughtfully, "That's ingenious. Completely without solid foundations, of course. . . ."

For a few minutes there was silence except for the sound of Bruce munching. Then Ruth murmured, "It's getting dark. So early these days. . . ."

"We're going out," Pat said firmly. "Out among the bright lights. I need a couple of drinks before I listen to any more of Bruce's theories."

# IV

It had stopped raining, but the wind howled mournfully through the trees and shook sprays of leftover raindrops down on their heads. After the sedate silence and darkness of the side street, the garish lights and traffic of Wisconsin seemed like another world. The neon signs and the shifting colors of the stoplights reflected in the shiny wet blackness of the pavement made weird psychedelic patterns of crimson and green and yellow.

The picturesque brick sidewalks of Georgetown were slippery and uneven. Ruth clung to her escort's arm, and found its solidity reassuring in more ways than one. In the light and the cold, rushing air her spirits rose; ahead of her, Bruce looked down at Sara and spoke, and the girl's light laughter floated back to her.

As they passed the entrance to one of the new nightclubs they encountered a group of the new youth who frequented them. Long flowing locks and faded jeans adorned boys and girls alike, and the only distinguishing characteristic of the male was the shaggy, drooping mustache. One of the girls was barefoot. Ruth shivered in sympathy, and Pat began to chuckle softly.

"Quite a contrast," he said.

"Georgetown past and present," Ruth agreed.

"Hoopskirts and hippies? True, but that wasn't what I

meant. How the hell can conventional spooks exist in a world which produces that?"

The restaurant—soft lights, candles flickering, the murmur of relaxed conversation—made spooks, conventional or otherwise, seem even less likely. Pat got his drink or two; when the second round arrived he lifted his glass and made Bruce a small ironic bow.

"Go on with the lecture. I'm sorry to have interrupted you, but you must agree that these surroundings are more cheerful."

"Too cheerful," Bruce said dryly. "They cast a glare of absolute unreality over the whole business. Okay, okay. So I gave you the reasoning—much abbreviated—which led me to start investigating the history of the house and the family. The conventional theme of violence, and the mention of 'the General' made me think of wartime; that's why I keep harping on the Civil War. It was a time when sympathies in Maryland were bitterly divided, and when family tragedies often arose out of the tragedy of war. But I don't insist on that; I asked the girls to find out anything they could about family history."

"Well, I'm sorry to disappoint you," Ruth said. "But I found very little. Surprisingly little, in view of how much has been written about Georgetown. Wait a minute. Where did I put those notes?"

She disappeared under the table and the others heard her scrabbling and muttering as she went with both hands into the big black purse, which had to sit on the floor because it was too large to stay on her lap. When she emerged, flushed and sheepish, she met Pat's amused eye and blushed more deeply.

"I have to carry a big purse," she explained defensively. "I have all these papers. . . ."

"You can carry a suitcase if you want to," Pat said tenderly. Bruce cleared his throat and looked disapproving.

"Anyhow." Ruth leafed through the spiral notebook she had unearthed. "Here it is. The house was built about 1810 by Jedediah Campbell (good heavens, what a name!). He was a tobacco dealer."

"Everybody was," Sara remarked.

"Since tobacco warehousing and shipping were the main industries of Georgetown, that isn't surprising," Bruce said impatiently. "Go on, Ruth."

"We'd better order," Pat said, indicating a hovering waiter.

Bruce growled under his breath and ordered chicken without bothering to look at the menu. Pat deliberated over the wine list. Bruce politely intimated that perhaps wine struck the wrong note for the occasion, and Pat ordered it anyhow. Then, just in time to prevent an explosion from Bruce, they got back to business.

"All this is just genealogy," Ruth admitted. "Jedediah's oldest son Ebeneezer inherited the house, and so on, down to eternity. There is absolutely nothing interesting about any of them."

"Then I took up the tale from 1850 on," Sara said, through a mouthful of paté. "Remember the story about the Civil War Campbell that Madame Nada used at the séance? It's the only well-known story connected with the house. But he was an old man when the war broke out and nobody bothered him. Even though by then Georgetown was part of the District of Columbia, a lot of Georgetowners had Southern sympathies."

"It doesn't seem to help," Bruce admitted. "And later?"

"Goodness, I couldn't even find any names of people, not in the books. They must have been nobodies."

"I can give you the names, from family records," Ruth said. "After all, Cousin Hattie was born in the 1880's. Her father's family was large and prolific; when the family fortunes declined, the children scattered. Their children are all over the place now—California, Canada, New England. And my bunch, in the Midwest. And none of them, I assure you, has even been inclined toward violence."

"I'm not interested in the diasporic Campbells." Bruce put a hand over his glass to prevent Pat's refilling it. "Had Cousin Hattie any dark secrets?"

Ruth sputtered into her wine.

"Sorry! But that really is ludicrous. She was the most proper old lady who ever lived; she wore long black dresses from the day her father died till she passed on in 1965. And she died of old age, peacefully, in her bed."

"What a letdown," Pat said with a grin. "I hoped she would turn out to be a secret Satanist, indulging in wild sexual orgies in her parlor, and kissing—"

"Never mind," Ruth said.

"Where did you read about that charming little rite?" Bruce asked. He too was smiling; his mood had lightened considerably.

"I didn't; I don't read that sort of thing!" They all laughed at her indignation, and she added, smiling, "It was obvious from Pat's expression what he was going to say."

Pat sobered.

"Cousin Hattie is a case in point, though. I'm not seriously suggesting that she was a devil-worshiper; but she could have been, with nobody one whit the wiser. Even if you're right about the roots of this trouble lying in the past, you haven't the slightest hope of finding out the truth."

"I knew it wouldn't be easy." Eyes on his plate, Bruce was crumbling a roll into fragments.

"Easy! It's impossible by its very nature. Look here, don't you see that your theory of a violent act can be proved only if the violence was public knowledge at the time? *Which it wasn't.* If there had been any tragedy, such as murder or suicide, connected with that house, we would have known about it. It would be part of the family history and probably one of the classic legends of Georgetown. The fact that we haven't come across any such legends means that one of two alternatives must be true: Either there was no tragedy, or it was so well concealed that there is no record of it—no trial, no funeral, not even any gossip. And in the latter case—how do you propose to find out about it?"

There was a short but poignant silence.

"Oogh," Sara said, groaning. "That's a nasty one, Pat."

"Nasty, but not unexpected." Bruce sounded confident; but he drained his wineglass with more speed than good manners permitted.

"You mean you knew there wouldn't be anything in the books?" Sara demanded. "And you made me read all those dusty—"

"They had to be checked!" Bruce flung his hands out. "Can't any of you understand? We're all crazy—all but Pat—and our hypothesis is wildly insane; if we are to get anywhere with it, we must handle our research as sanely as possible."

There was no satisfaction in Pat's expression at this half-submission. Instead his face softened sympathetically.

"I see your point and I agree, absolutely. I'm just a tired old pessimist. . . . What do you plan to do next?"

"The obvious thing. Public records failed, as we expected them to. Now we try the unpublished material."

Pat shook his head.

"Damn it, Bruce, I don't like to be the perpetual wet blanket, but I've had personal experience with the family records of old Georgetown families. I did a paper once, in my distant undergraduate days, on the attitudes of Georgetowners toward the Revolution and separation from England. I went calling, with my big toothy grin, on several little old ladies, looking for letters and family papers. Talk about violence! One of the old darlings chased me out of the house with a rolled-up newspaper."

"Oh, Pat, how lovely," Sara chortled. "What did you do to annoy her?"

"I intimated that maybe her revered ancestor had not been, after all, a Patriot. You know these screwy organizations like the Colonial Dames and the Daughters of the American Revolution insist that you have an ancestor who fought in the Revolution. Turns out, oddly enough, that practically everybody in the Revolutionary Army was a lieutenant or better. . . . You can imagine the furor that would arise if some old biddy's great-great-great were found to have fought in the wrong army! I think they would cheerfully commit murder to keep it a secret."

"How ridiculous," Sara said contemptuously.

"You didn't tell me that you'd done research on Georgetown," Bruce said.

"Hardly amounted to that."

"I'd like to see that paper sometime."

"I don't even know where it is."

"Could you look for it?"

"Oh, for— If it would make you any happier."

"Oh, it would," Bruce murmured. "It sure would. . . . No thanks, no coffee for me. Nor brandy. Haven't you had enough, Pat?"

The sudden animosity in the last question brought into the open the hostility he had been concealing. Pat refused to take offense. Smiling lazily, he said, "Tact, tact, my boy."

"Sorry." Bruce flushed. "But damn it all, we've got to keep our wits about us."

"Oh, I agree." Pat raised hand sent the waiter running for the check. "You want to get back, I gather. So let's go."

As they walked back to the house, Bruce explained his plans.

"Tomorrow I'm going downtown. I'm not sure whether it's the Archives or the Library of Congress I want, but I know a guy who's majoring in American history, and I can ask him about sources. I might even try to call him tonight. What time is it?"

"Only about ten."

"I thought it was later. It feels later."

"It's a miserable night," Ruth said, shivering as a spray of icy water swept her face. "All sensible people are indoors, in front of a fire."

"I'll call Ted tonight, then. And maybe we can start on another project. One that ought to keep you girls busy all day tomorrow."

"What's that?" Sara asked in a muffled voice. The hair blowing around her face got in her mouth; she pawed at it.

"Seems to me Cousin Hattie ought to have left some papers. What about it, Ruth?"

"She left an incredible amount of junk, certainly. I've never looked through it. There might be something in the attic, I guess."

They turned up the short walk toward the house. Ruth was in the lead, since she had the key; but as her foot touched the bottom step she stopped, so suddenly that Pat bumped into her. He began to expostulate. Then he saw what she had seen, and fell silent.

The balanced Georgian facade had a door in the center, with long windows on either side—those of the dining room, now dark, on the right, the living-room windows on the left. They had left the latter room brightly lit. The light, shining through the blue satin drapes, gave them a heavenly azure glow, like the robes of a lady saint. But the shining folds were moving.

Ruth's gloved hand clutched at Pat's sleeve.

"Look—"

"Don't say anything," Bruce ordered. Instinctively they spoke in low voices, as though something could hear them. With an equally atavistic impulse they all moved close together, in a huddled, shivering group.

"I'm not going in that door," Sara said.

"Me neither," Pat agreed. "You realize, don't you, that this could be anything from a burglar to an open window elsewhere in the room?"

"Then why don't you want to go in?" Bruce made his challenge in a fierce whisper.

"I'm afraid of burglars," Pat said equably. "Is there a back door?"

"Of course, the kitchen. Come on."

This time no one laughed when Ruth groped in her purse for the back-door key. It took her a long time to locate it. Her fingers were icy cold. The shivering, quivering movement of the curtains continued.

The house was so close to its neighbor that the passageway between them looked like a black tunnel.

"Why the hell didn't I bring a flashlight?" Pat shouldered Ruth out of the way. A tiny flame sprang up and promptly went out. The wind blowing down the passageway was too strong for his lighter. He swore and plunged into the blackness. The others followed, with Bruce bringing up the rear.

The passageway was not only dark, it was cold and windy and damp. Puddles squished under Ruth's feet and splashed her ankles. She was glad to get out of the tunnel. But the backyard was not much better. They huddled again on the paved stones of the patio, now dangerously slippery with rain. Behind them the gloom of the night-dark garden, shaded by pines and unlit even by moonlight, was filled with constant uneasy movement.

The kitchen windows were dark. Ruth silently cursed her inherited Scottish thrift. From now on she would leave every light in the blasted house on, day and night! Very dimly she could make out the white painted steps that led to a little wooden annex at the back, where she kept mops and garbage cans. Through this annex entry to the kitchen was gained.

"Give me the key," Pat muttered, and Ruth gladly allowed him to precede her up the stairs. After a few seconds of muttering and scratching he said grumpily, "I can't see a damn thing. Bruce, come up and hold the lighter, will you?"

Then, for the second time that night, they were gripped simultaneously by the unexpected. Ruth had been hearing the noise for some time. She told herself it was the wind in the trees, but she didn't believe it. But not until Bruce started up the stairs did the moaning sigh form audible words. They were the words she had heard before; but now, with no walls between her and the source (what source???) they were much more distinct. The great sighing voice came at her from all sides and from no sides; from inside her head, from every point of the compass, from the cloudy turmoil of the sky . . . and died away in a long, sobbing cry.

". . . come . . . hooooome. . . ."

Pat said something; it was rather a wordless snarl of anger than articulate profanity. There was a sharp snap, and the door, caught by the wind, crashed back against the wall. The three who stood below fled up the stairs and into the entryway. By that time Pat had the inner door open, and they plunged pell-mell into the warmth of the kitchen, and into a sudden glare of light as Pat found the switch by the door.

Bruce slammed the door shut, and they all stood blinking and gasping—all except Pat, who had not even paused. Huddled in his overcoat with his head retracted like a turtle's, he was plodding toward the room at the front of the house—the uninhabited room where something had shaken the drapes.

They stopped at the door of the dining room; no one cared to go any farther than that. Looking across the hallway and the foot of the stairs, they saw the living room, as calm and bright as any room could be. It was perhaps only Ruth's imagination that made her detect the faintest wisp of gray, no thicker than the smoke from a cigarette, lifting in a lazy coil. . . . The draperies hung in sculptured folds, unmoving.

"Nothing there," Bruce said. His hand touched the light switch in the dining room, and the chandelier blazed on. They stared at one another; and Pat put one big hand on Sara's shoulder where she stood clinging to the wall like a limp strand of ivy.

"Are you all right?"

"Of course she's all right," Bruce snapped.

"Let her talk for once!"

"Stop it, both of you," Ruth ordered. "We're all wound up like clocks, and no wonder. Bruce, what about that brandy now?"

"Best idea I've heard all evening."

Ruth got the decanter from the side cabinet, and Bruce collected the glasses. Holding them by the stems, two in each hand, like big blown crystal flowers, he looked warily at Pat.

"We're going to have to go into that room sometime."

"Brandy," Ruth said hastily, and swallowed hers in one breath-snatching gulp.

Sara made a face as hers went down; brandy had never been one of her favorite drinks. But it restored some of the color to her cheeks, and Bruce promptly poured another inch of liquid all around.

"I needed that," he admitted. "The place is really turned on tonight. I wonder how much of this activity is in response to what we're doing?"

"Who knows?" Pat muttered. "Who knows anything?"

They stared at one another in bemused silence for a time. Pat's eyes were glazed, and Ruth was conscious of an insidious, what-the-hell warmth that was the product of alcohol on an overstrained nervous system.

"Look here," she said, a bit thickly, "we don't have to do this."

"Do what?" Bruce asked.

"Stand around shaking in our shoes. If the trouble is in the house—then get rid of the house."

"Ruth." Sara held out her hand; her eyes were shining suspiciously. "You can't do that. You love this place."

"My dear child, I'm not proposing a dramatic houseburning by midnight. For one thing, the neighbors might object. I can sell the place. It's worth a lot of money. You and I could go live in a nice apartment on Connecticut, or in Chevy Chase."

"One objection," Bruce said carefully. "You're ash—ashum—damn it!—assuming that my hypothesis is the right one. If Sara is schizoid she'll be schizoid wherever she is."

"I don't believe in collective hallucinations," Ruth said. "Sara didn't make that sound we heard tonight."

"Not Sammie," Pat said suddenly. "The name was not Sammie."

It was the first sentence he had spoken since Ruth made her proposition, and its very irrelevance had an oddly calming effect. Sara dropped into a chair and rested her head on her folded arms. She looked sideways at Pat with round solemn eyes, like a pensive owl's; and Bruce's breath went out in a theatrical sigh.

"I hate to admit it," he said, "but I was too shook to notice details. What was the name, then?"

"Now who's being unscientific?" Pat said irritably. He rubbed his head, making his hair stand up like a crest, and scowled thoughtfully. "I don't know that it was a name. I do know that there was no 's' sound, that strong sibilant would have been unmistakable. Sara heard the words as 'Sammie' because that is a familiar combination of sounds. Ruth heard the same thing because Sara had prepared her to hear it. To tell the truth, it sounded to me more like 'mammy.' "

After a moment Ruth burst out laughing.

"I'm . . . sorry! Oh, dear! But, Pat—mammy? Shades of Al Jolson! Some poor old nursemaid, like the one in *Gone with the Wind?* And if you knew how funny you all look, standing around this table with your coats on, like visiting burglars. . . ."

They waited respectfully until she had composed herself and dried her eyes. Then Pat remarked, "I'm glad I can supply some comic relief. As for your idea of selling the house—it has some merit, but we don't have to decide anything yet."

"We?" Bruce repeated. He leaned on the table, arms stiff, and looked at the older man. "How do you feel about your theory now, Pat?"

Pat shrugged.

"Unlike Ruth, I do believe in collective hallucinations. Wait a minute—I'm not saying that was what happened tonight. Though both you and I, Bruce, heard that voice described. . . . You said forty-eight hours. You've still got twenty-four to go."

# Chapter

## 6

LYING FLAT ON HER BACK, STARING UP AT THE CEILING, RUTH heard the clock strike four. The clock stood on the landing, probably in the same position it had occupied since it was bought from Josiah Harper, Clockmaker, in 1836. Josiah had built well. The chimes echoed in silver clarity, precise as notes struck on a harpsichord.

As she had done a dozen times since they retired, Ruth raised herself cautiously on her elbow and looked over at Sara. It hadn't taken much persuasion to convince Sara to share her room that night. The room was lit by two rose-shaded lamps on the dressing table; Ruth wondered whether she would ever be able to sleep in a darkened room again.

Sara slept on her back, with her hair cascading over the pillow like spilled ink, and the small movement of her lips, her furled brows, showed that she was dreaming. As Ruth watched, a shade of that alien look spread like a film of water over her features, and faded.

Breathless, Ruth sank back onto her pillow, turning on her side so that she could watch the girl. So this was what it was like, the emotion she had seen in other women's faces. None of the other basic instincts had come down to man from the animals quite so uncontrolled and so primitive. Even the sexual urge had been twisted and condemned and veiled until it was barely recognizable as the simple, amoral need it once had been. Humanity had tried to turn the maternal instinct into a pretty lace-trimmed valentine too, but it had not succeeded;

women who would turn sick at the sight of a dead bird could
commit any kind of violence to preserve their young.

It was raining again. The soft rustle of raindrops against the
window should have been soothing, but Ruth found it too suggestive of other sounds—dry fingers scratching on the glass, for
instance, or small bony feet crawling along the sill. The house
itself was quiet, except for one oddly soothing sound—that of
Pat's resounding masculine snores from across the hall.

Ruth's mouth relaxed as she listened. She was no expert on
snoring, but she was willing to bet that Pat's efforts ranked high
on any scale. She was getting almost the full effect, since all the
bedroom doors were wide open. There was nothing like a
haunted house to dispel artificial notions of propriety.

No sound came from Sara's room, which Bruce was now
occupying, but the comforting yellow light from his door filled
the hall. Ruth had found a box of old family papers in a drawer
in the escritoire and Bruce had declared his intention of sitting
up with them.

Ruth could remember having seen other papers in the attic.
Most of them were obviously junk, the pack-rat hoarding of a
fussy old lady; but she had not wanted to discard them as trash
until she had time to sort through them. That time, like other
hours for matters not urgently desired or needed, had never
materialized. Tomorrow—no, today—she would look for them.
Though their collective courage, bolstered by brandy, had
taken them into the chilly living room, Ruth had flatly refused
to enter the dark, gusty attic at night, and no one seemed to
blame her.

Tomorrow—today, now—there would be so much to do.
Yet they were groping in the dark, clutching a few tattered
scraps of isolated fact, with no sign of a pattern and no promise,
even, that a pattern existed. Shivering in the warm bed, Ruth
faced the dismal fact that no one had yet admitted—that if
Bruce's incredible notion was correct, the chances for Sara's
cure were even feebler than those promised by psychiatry. The
thought brought her drooping lids open and focused her eyes on
her niece, searching, and fearing to find. . . .

Sara slept peacefully now. She was young enough to look
delectable when she slept, her skin flushed and damp, her
lashes long and black on her smooth cheeks. Ruth lay stiff as a

piece of wood. Bruce had the right idea; he wasn't even trying to sleep. Sleep was impossible, when the sense of urgency was so great. If there were only something she could do. . . .

The sound almost lifted her bodily out of bed. The muffled crash was followed, after a second, by a faint rustling—innocent enough sounds, both of them, except for the fact that there was no one to make them. They had come from downstairs.

Bruce, in stocking feet and shirt sleeves, materialized in the doorway. He stared at her, and Ruth shook her head mutely.

"I'm going down," he whispered.

"Not alone. Wait, Bruce—"

The sounds of imminent strangulation across the hall stopped; and a few seconds later Pat made his appearance. He was blinking and groggy; the hair stood up on his head like fire on a boulder. He too was fully dressed except for his shoes.

"Where'd it come from?" he mumbled.

"Downstairs."

"Ummm." Pat scratched his head. It was obvious that he was not one of those hearty people who leap, fully aware and ready for burglars, out of their warm beds. He blinked, rubbed his hands over his eyes, and came one stage nearer to consciousness. "Go down," he said vaguely.

By that time Sara was stirring, and when she found out what had roused the others she decided to join the expedition. Bruce had long since left; he had scant patience with the weaknesses of the elderly.

The lights were still on in the living room. Leading the way down the stairs, Ruth could see Bruce bending over some object on the floor near the built-in bookcases. He straightened as she reached the foot of the stairs and came toward her, carrying the object; it seemed to be a book, bound in red leather.

Ruth stopped on the threshold of the living room. It was cold, much colder than it had been upstairs; she was shivering, even in her wool robe. Halfway across the room, Bruce stopped short. She saw the color drain from his face, saw him recoil as if he had run into some solid but invisible barrier; then her eyes turned in the direction of his wide-eyed stare, and she let out a cry of alarm.

"Something's on fire—Bruce—"

Bruce jerked as though he had been stung; the sound of her

voice, or her incipient movement, into the room, roused him
from his paralysis, and he came bounding toward her, his head
averted and one arm up before his face. He cannoned into her,
sending her staggering back; and then he turned to face the
thing that had sent him into flight—the rising coil of oily black
smoke which was forming in the part of the room near the window.

The cold was not the normal cold of a winter night. It rolled
out of the room in unseen waves that pulled like quicksand.
When Bruce pushed her back she had fancied she felt a sucking, reluctant release. The tentacles still fingered her body; she
retreated farther, breathing in harsh gasps that hurt her lungs,
back into the space under the stairs. She stopped only when her
back touched the wall, and gave another cry as a new wave of
cold touched her shrinking side. This was a more natural cold;
it came from the cellar door, which was, unaccountably, wide
open. Another foot to the left and she would have backed
straight down the stairs in her mindless flight.

Bruce had retreated too, step by slow step, as though he
were fighting a pull stronger than gravity. He came to a halt at
the bottom of the stairs. Pat had seen the thing by now; Ruth
heard his wordless bellow of consternation, and Sara's stifled
shriek. But most of her awareness was focused on the impossible—the moving blackness that swayed to no breeze, that
twisted in upon itself as if in a struggle for form. Smoke where
there was no fire; greasy, oily black smoke, that emitted waves
of *cold* instead of heat.

Bruce stopped at the bottom of the stairs, one hand on the
newel post. By accident or design his body barred the stairs, his
arms extended across the narrow space from wall to bannister.
He called out something, and Ruth heard the feet above stumble
back, up, a few steps. The cold was sickening; it sucked at the
warmth of the body like a leech. Ruth knew she was only on the
fringe of its malice; the full effect was directed at Bruce.

She saw the book, still clutched in the whitened fingers of
the boy's left hand, and in her bemused state she wondered, insanely, where he had found a Bible, and what good he thought
it would do. Then she remembered where the thick red volume
had come from; she also caught the accidentally blasphemous
resemblance, in Bruce's taut body and outstretched arms, which
had brought the first idea into her head. She tried to think of a

prayer and finally, as her frozen brain caught up with her instinct, she realized that she had been praying, snatches of incoherent invocation from half-forgotten rituals; and she also knew
that the symbols, verbal or physical, were meaningless in the
face of the abyss. For the Thing moved, swaying toward them,
and put out pseudopods—shapeless, wavering extensions of
darkness that pawed the air like half-formed arms.

Then, through the ringing in her ears she heard a sound, as
wildly incongruous as shepherd's pipes on a battlefield. It was a
small sound, precise and crystalline: the sleepy twitter of a bird
on a tree outside the house.

The hovering blackness began to fade.

Once the process of dissolution had begun, it proceeded
rapidly; in seconds the pale blue satin drapes showed clear, un-
fogged, on the wall of the living room.

Through the dead silence she heard again the querulous
sleepy chirp; and from Bruce came a shocking, ragged gasp of
laughter.

" 'It faded on the crowing of the cock . . .' Or was that a
sparrow? 'The bird of dawning . . .' " And, flinging out his arm
toward the door, where a streak of sickly gray sky showed
through the fanlight, he sat down with a thud on the bottom step
and hid his face in his folded arms.

Ruth put out one hand, as delicately as though she feared it
might break off, and pushed at the open cellar door. The slam
brought another alarmed bellow from Pat.

"I just closed the basement door," she called. "It was wide
open."

She detached herself from the wall, feeling as though she
must have left the imprint of her body on the plaster, and
moved out to where she could see the two faces staring down
over the bannister. Sara's was green.

"I'm going to be sick," she said.

Bruce lifted his head. He was still clutching the book; one
finger was jammed between the pages like a marker, and the
grip of his other fingers was convulsively tight. He was shaking
violently, and his face was ashen under a glistening sheen of
perspiration; but his mouth was stretched in a wide, exultant
grin, and his eyes went straight to Pat's face.

"By God," he said, "how did you like *that,* you damned
skeptic?"

## II

"I'm selling the house. I won't let Sara spend another night in this chamber of horrors."

Ruth meant every word; but she was forced to admit that Sara looked in splendid condition for a girl who had spent the night in a chamber of horrors. Slim and supple in her emerald green velvet robe, she was scrambling eggs with hungry efficiency.

"Get your hair out of the way," Ruth added irritably. "We've had trouble enough tonight without having you catch on fire."

"Sorry," said Sara amiably. "Ruth, why don't you relax? I'm fine. Bruce is the one I'm worried about."

Wrapped in a blanket and ensconced in a chair by the oven door, Bruce had almost stopped shivering. His symptoms had resembled those of shock; Pat and Ruth had had to drag him out to the warmth of the kitchen. He gave Sara a reassuring grin, but did not speak; there was a glitter in his eyes, though, that suggested he would have plenty to say when the time came.

"He needs food," Pat said, flipping toast onto a plate. "We all do. I'm starved."

Ruth lifted bacon out of the pan onto a paper towel, judged the coffee with an experienced eye, and began laying out silver with more speed than elegance.

"I am too. It must be the nervous strain. I remember once before when—when I was worried and upset, I ate constantly."

"Is that what you were tonight—nervous? Personally," said Pat, "I was terrified. Come on, Bruce, get some of these eggs into you. That cold is incredibly enervating, and you got the worst of the blast. Hero type," he added amiably.

"Hero, hell; I just had the farthest to run." Bruce took a mouthful of eggs and meditated. "I wonder how many of the great heroes of history would turn out to be slow runners, if you ever investigated the circumstances."

"Let's not be cynical," Ruth said.

They ate in silence for a while, ravenously and with concentration. Ruth finished first; as she reached for her cigarettes she looked around the table at the other three with sudden intense affection. Pat happened to glance up as her eyes reached his face; he grinned, and echoed her thoughts with unnerving accuracy.

" *'Ich hatte eine Kameraden,'* " he quoted.

"How did you know what I was thinking? Yes; I know now why soldiers under fire get so devoted to their buddies."

"There's nobody nicer than the guy who has just saved your life," Pat agreed. "Unless it's the guy who might save it tomorrow."

"Now you're being cynical. It's more than that."

"It must have something to do with trust," Sara offered shyly. "Knowing you can depend on someone, literally to the death."

"Well, you can't depend on me." Ruth pushed her chair back and stared at them defiantly. "I meant it. Sara is not spending another night here."

"Surrender, hmm?"

"Pat, we're not accomplishing anything! It's getting stronger, and we're helpless. It's dangerous—horribly dangerous—"

"How do you know?" Bruce asked.

Blank silence followed. Finally Ruth said, "You're a fine one to ask that! You looked like a dead man when we pulled you out of there."

"Another cup of coffee and he'll be his old argumentative self," Pat said. "What happened to him was damned unpleasant, but surely it's the worst that abominable Thing can do. It's non-material, after all; how much damage can It inflict?"

"Exactly." Bruce's cheeks were flushed with excitement. "Ruth, I know how you feel. But we are making progress. Don't you realize how much we learned tonight?"

"We learned one of its limitations," Ruth admitted. "Apparently it can't function in daylight."

"Which lends some credence to one of the aspects of spiritualism that has always roused my loudest jeers—the statement that spirits are disturbed by too much light."

"Right. When you stop to think about it, you may recall that the other manifestations—Sara's seizures, and the voice—have also occurred at night."

"Swell," Ruth said gloomily. "A house isn't much good, though, if you can't sleep in it."

"That's not all we learned. Remember this?"

Bruce held up the red book. He had been cradling it in his lap like a baby.

"I'd almost forgotten that. You think we were supposed to find it?"

"I don't think it just happened to fall. You aren't in the habit of leaving heavy books balanced on the edge of the shelf, are you?"

"I don't remember ever touching that one," Ruth admitted. "What is it? Myers' *History of Maryland.* No, it's one of Cousin Hattie's books. It's been there forever."

"Not only was it moved, it lay open," Bruce went on. "That might be accident; but I'm inclined to think that—whatever—could push a book off a shelf could also turn pages."

"The proof of the pudding," Pat said sententiously. "What does your prize say?"

Bruce opened the book.

"This section concerns a minor skirmish known as the Loyalist Plot." He scanned the page, muttering. "Free the prisoners of war . . . hmmph. Yes. It happened in 1780, after the Revolution had begun. Contrary to what the high school history books tell us, not everybody in the Colonies was all that keen on independence. Some fanatical Tory citizens of Maryland decided to strike a blow for the King. They were planning to free the British prisoners at Frederick, and take the armory *at Georgetown.* The Patriots got wind of the plan, caught the leaders, and finally hanged them."

The ensuing silence rang with speculation.

"I don't see it," Ruth said finally.

"Hell's bells, it's just what we've been looking for." Bruce closed the book and put it tenderly on the table. "We're looking for a General and a violent deed. Here's a war situation, divided loyalties—and a specific mention of Georgetown, for God's sake. Somebody—something—has kindly narrowed down our search through history, not only to a given period, but to a particular year!"

"But, Bruce," Ruth protested, "there wasn't even a house here at that time."

Bruce's face went blank—eyes round, mouth ajar. He looked so vacuous that Ruth, in a spasm of alarm, reached out and jogged his arm.

"Huh? No, I'm all right. I just remembered. . . . I'll be damned! I had just found that deed when the big bang came. . . . Sorry, I don't mean to be incoherent. Look here; I was poking around in that box of papers you gave me, and I found the photostat of a deed. It was a sale of land by Ninian Beall, the original proprietor of all this territory—he called it the Rock of Dumbarton—to one Douglass Campbell. And it was dated in the 1760's."

Ruth poured coffee into her cup so briskly that it splashed. She felt as if her brains needed lubricating.

"Campbell," she muttered. "One of the ancestors, obviously. . . . This house wasn't built till 1810. But there could have been an earlier house. . . ."

"If there was, what happened to it?" Pat demanded. He reached for the coffeepot and Ruth pushed it toward him.

"Torn down, maybe," she offered. "As the family prospered and needed bigger quarters. But Bruce—I thought ghosts were laid when the places they haunt are destroyed."

"Expert authorities differ on that," Bruce said oratorically, and then spoiled the effect by grinning. "You know, when I actually listen to the things we're saying, I can't believe it myself. No, but according to some of the tales I've read, the haunting is connected with a specific building; in others the very soil seems to be permeated with—whatever it is."

"Whatever it is," Sara repeated. "You all sit talking and talking, and all the time I keep remembering . . . that horrible Thing. . . ."

Bruce caught Ruth's anxious eye and nodded.

"Yes. Well, we'd better talk about It. We weren't any of us too coherent the first time we tried."

"It was so *cold*," Ruth said, with a strong shudder. "Was It—that Thing—always there, invisible, when we felt the cold?"

"What a happy thought," Bruce murmured. "Damned if I know. Pat?"

"I don't know either."

The answer was brief, the tone flat. Bruce, after one penetrating look, picked up the coffeepot and tilted it. A feeble trickle of extremely black liquid dripped into his cup.

"Somebody forgot to fill it," he said mildly, and rose to do so. Over his shoulder and over the rush of running water he said, "Still hedging, Pat, after this morning?"

"I'm trying desperately to keep an open mind," Pat said stubbornly. "Ruth, don't get mad, but—I've seen too much of this sort of thing, all over the world."

"But we all saw it!"

"What did we see? I could have kicked myself later," he added bitterly. "But I was too damned shook up at first to think straight. You know what we did. We sat here shaking and gabbling and compared notes, one after the other. You especially must know, Bruce, how witnesses unconsciously influence one another. What we should have done was write out our separate impressions, without speaking to each other, and then compare them."

"He's right," Bruce said, over Ruth's indignant sniff. He came back to the table carrying the coffeepot, and plugged it in. "Absolutely right. I should have thought of it myself, but I'm damned if I apologize. If that was just a harmless little old hallucination, God save me from the real thing!"

"Even at that," Pat went on doggedly, "we didn't actually see the same thing. Ruth saw smoke—dark, oily smoke. Bruce was babbling about the pillar of darkness by day—not a very apt analogy, if I remember my Bible—whereas, to Sara the thing had shape. It was man-high and roughly anthropomorphic."

"It had arms," said Sara, from behind a veil of hair. "Stubs, that were trying to turn into arms."

"Thanks," Pat said. "I'll dream about that one. Bruce, you can see my point, can't you?"

"Sure," Bruce said agreeably. "We've got to be as critical and logical about the evidence as we can. Hell, I said that myself. But I do think you're leaning over backwards so far you're about to fall on your can. Excuse me, Ruth."

"Don't be so darned polite," Ruth said irritably. "You make me feel like a little gray-haired old lady. I know, I am, but still. . . . Pat, I don't care what Bruce thinks, I'm sick and tired of your attitude. Are you with us or not?"

"Oh, I'm with you," Pat said unexpectedly; and smiled at their stupefied expressions. "At least I'm willing to extend the deadline you proposed. In fact, I'll prove my loyalty by pointing out something you seem to have overlooked. Ruth, did you leave the cellar door open before we went to bed?"

"Why, no; I haven't been in the cellar for ages. Pat! Do you think—"

"I think we may have a very busy ghost. Could the wind have blown the door open?"

"No, no, it catches quite firmly."

Bruce licked his finger and drew an invisible stroke on the air. "One to you, Pat. Ruth, I want to see your cellar."

He streaked out the door without waiting for an answer. They caught up with him at the top of the cellar stairs.

"Where's the light switch?"

"At the bottom of the stairs."

"Stupid place for it."

"I know." Ruth proffered a box of kitchen matches which she had picked up on the way out. "That's one of the reasons why I detest the basement. I haven't been down here since I moved in."

"You must have," Sara said, picking up her long skirts.

"Wait till he gets the light on; the stairs are steep. No, really, I haven't. The furnace runs like the proverbial charm. People come—" Ruth gestured vaguely— "you know, for meters and things. They go down, I stay up."

The light went on down below, and Bruce called them to descend.

One bare bulb, hanging limply, shed a dismal light over a small cement-lined chamber, occupied only by the big bulk of the furnace and by two ancient iron sinks. There were three windows, all at the front of the house; they were small, even for basement windows, barred and high up.

"It's smaller than I expected," Pat said, after a brief inspection. "Doesn't go under the whole house, does it?"

"No, just the dining room and kitchen half."

"I can't see anything significant down here." Bruce tugged at his beard. "No moldering, brass-bound chests filled with stolen pirate loot, no ancient portraits. . . ."

"The place is far too damp for storage," Ruth said practically. "That's why Hattie kept all her junk in the attic."

"The attic." Bruce gave his beard another tug, harder than he had intended. He let out a yelp. "Damn. There's so much to do—"

"I want to get out of this place," Sara said distinctly.

"What's wrong?" Ruth asked anxiously. "Do you feel—"

"I wish you'd stop jumping at me every time I open my mouth," Sara said. "I just don't like this place."

"I don't either," Pat said. His tone was so peculiar that Ruth transferred her anxious stare to him. He shook himself, like a dog coming out of the water, and smiled at her. "I didn't get my eight hours last night," he said.

"You do look tired, all of a sudden." Ruth took his arm. "Why don't you try to take a nap? Come on, everybody; I hate this place myself and we aren't getting anywhere just standing around."

Bruce waited until they had gone up, and then turned out the light. When he emerged he was still worrying his beard, and Pat had to address him twice before he responded.

"I said, I'm sorry the basement was a bust. Maybe the open door was an accident after all."

"Oh, I dunno," Bruce said vaguely. "Pat, are you going to the university this morning?"

"Hadn't planned to. Why?"

"I want to shower and change, I'm short on sleep myself." Bruce yawned so widely Ruth feared his jaws would split. "And I want to see Ted. His field is Colonial America."

"Georgetown?"

"No. No, he won't know anything I need to know," Bruce said stupidly. He yawned again. "Brrr. He will know what the sources are. And where they're kept—Archives, Library of Congress, the local historical association. Then I'll go there. Wherever there is."

"Take the car, I won't need it. And Bruce—"

"Mmmm?"

"Don't take too many of those damned pep pills—or whatever kind of pills Ted is peddling these days along with advice on Colonial history."

"Ted doesn't—"

"The hell he doesn't. Oh, he's generally harmless; that's why I've left him alone. And I know you don't generally indulge. Just don't start now—especially now. There's no need to push yourself; we've got time."

"I hope you're right," Bruce said.

"We'll start on the attic," Ruth said, still slightly bewildered by the exchange. "And the closets. What are we supposed to be looking for, exactly?"

"Deeds, letters, old newspapers. I've been thinking," Bruce said. "I did get the full blast from our not so friendly ghost, and I'm beginning to think it was no accident. If I had dropped that book, I'd have lost the page and we'd still be groping. So I suggest we look particularly for anything that mentions the name of Master Douglass Campbell."

## III

Bruce went upstairs to get his sweater and Ruth headed for the kitchen to clear, accompanied by Pat, who was making hopeful suggestions about more coffee. Ruth plugged the pot in and started to collect eggy plates. She was thinking that nothing is nastier than the remains of cold scrambled eggs when she realized that Sara had not followed her out. It was—she told herself—only concern that made her return, quietly, through the dining room, while Pat was looking for clean cups.

They stood in the hallway, and Ruth's approach would not have been heard if she had worn boots instead of soft slippers. Though Sara was a tall girl, she had to tilt her head back to look up into Bruce's face. Her hands lay on his breast, and his held her shoulders; the curve of her body, in the clinging softness of green velvet, was as eloquent as it was beautiful.

"I hate like hell to leave you alone," Bruce said softly.

"I won't be alone. Ruth and Pat—"

"You know what I mean."

"I know."

"Say it, then."

"I'm alone in a crowd of people, if you aren't there," she said.

His mouth closed over hers, and her head fell back so that the hair streamed in a shining cascade over the arm that had pulled her against him.

Ruth had no conscious intention of moving or speaking; but she must have made some sound, for they broke apart as suddenly as they had come together. Bruce looked at Ruth and started to speak. Then he shrugged slightly, put Sara gently away from him, and left.

Sara stood with hands clasped. She looked, as even the plainest girl can look under some circumstances, utterly beautiful. Ruth said sharply, "Go upstairs and get dressed."

Sara's eyes cleared and focused. She gave Ruth an incredulous look; but her aunt's expression told her that she had not heard wrong. She swung on her heel and fled up the stairs.

"What hit you?" Pat asked, from behind Ruth.

"Nothing," she said shortly. Pat caught her by the elbow as she tried to pass him.

"Nothing my eye. Why so nasty about a couple of kids kissing?"

"I didn't say anything."

"It wasn't what you said, it was the way you said it."

"They're too young to be thinking of—"

"Of what? If they're thinking about what I think they're thinking about, more power to them."

"Oh, Pat! This is no time for—for—"

He waited, giving her plenty of time to find the word. When she did not he said softly, "You've got a problem yourself, haven't you? What—"

Sara came clattering down the stairs. She was wearing stretch slacks and a shirt, and, Ruth suspected, very little else. Her feeling that the slacks were too tight was confirmed by Pat's appreciative stare. The rich raspberry of the slacks and the pink and lemon striped shirt set off Sara's vivid coloring, but her expression was as bleak as the colors were warm. She brushed past Ruth without meeting her eye.

"I'll do the dishes," she said, and vanished into the kitchen.

"She's angry with me," Ruth said wretchedly.

"I don't blame her. Your voice was like ice water; and coming when it did, after a transcendental minute and a half—"

"I'm going to get dressed," Ruth said. "Then I'm going to look at the closet shelves."

But she knew, as she ascended the stairs, that he was staring speculatively at her; and she knew also that the confrontation she had been expecting had only become more imminent.


## IV

By five o'clock Bruce had not returned, and Sara was vibrating nervously between the kitchen window and the tray of cocktails she had prepared.

"Come on in and sit down," Ruth said, taking the tray. "He'll be along any minute."

"You go ahead." Sara was courteous but remote; it was clear

that she had not forgotten the morning's episode. "I'm going to start dinner."

Ruth found Pat in the living room lighting the fire. He looked up as she came sidling around the door; they had all started to adopt a circuitous route through the room, avoiding its street end as much as possible.

"Maybe we ought to sit in the kitchen," Ruth said.

Pat took the tray of drinks and set it firmly on the coffee table.

"I don't think anything is likely to happen much before midnight, to judge by past events. Sit down. I'll sit on this side, just in case, and keep an eye on—things."

"No, I'd rather keep my eye on them too." Ruth sat down beside him, on the couch that faced the pertinent end of the room. "Pat, I think we ought to get out of here. At least for the night."

"It's okay by me. But I doubt if Bruce will agree. He'll want to sit and observe manifestations."

"And Sara probably won't go without him. Damn the boy; why doesn't he come home?"

"Tsk, tsk, such language," Pat said comfortably. "What have you got against the kid?"

"Nothing, really. It's just—"

"The beard and the clothes and the supercilious air? I know; they gripe me too. But these things are only a superficial facade; underneath, the little devils are a lot more like the rest of the human race than they care to admit. Bruce is a very sound specimen; Sara could do a lot worse."

"They aren't that serious about each other."

"I don't know about her feelings, but there's no question about his. He's fighting for her, Ruth—tooth and nail."

"Yes, I know . . . and I'm grateful . . . but, Pat, in a way he's enjoying this. It's a game to him—outsmarting you, and me, and the rational universe!"

"I still think you aren't giving him credit. We'll talk to him when he comes in and see if we can't convince him to leave. You and Sara can spend the night at my place, I've got plenty of room."

"That's very nice of you, but. . . ."

He met her quizzical look with one of amusement, but there was a subtle change in his expression.

"Don't worry, you'll be perfectly safe. If I had in mind what you think I have in mind, I wouldn't include Sara."

Ruth leaned back, staring into the leaping flames, and feeling Pat's arm move along the back of the couch behind her. Middle age had its disadvantages, certainly, and one of the losses was the wild singing in the blood; but if one extreme had flattened out, so had the other. The anxieties were gone; the terrors had become only mild anxieties.

"Don't be coy," Pat said softly. His fingers touched her chin. She turned her face toward him, smiling.

"I'm not coy, dear. Only tired."

"That sounds like a challenge."

He was no longer smiling; his eyes moved from her eyes to her lips, and Ruth was aware of the mixed emotions which no woman with any feminine instincts can help feeling under such circumstances—triumph, mingled with a small, exciting touch of alarm.

"Men are so conceited," she murmured. "They—"

His lips cut off the rest of the sentence. It was a cautious embrace, restrained on her side and exploratory on his; when he raised his head, neither had spilled a drop from the glasses they still held, and his hand had not moved from her shoulder.

Ruth let her smile widen just a trifle. He could control his features, but not his breathing; holding the glass was pure affectation, a little boy pretending to show off. Pat's eyes narrowed. He put his glass on the table and took hers from her hand. Without speaking, but with the same look of concentration with which, she imagined, he began a lecture, he took her into his arms.

At first she felt like laughing, there was such deliberation in his movements. She felt pleasantly relaxed, like a cat being stroked; and then, with a jarring realization, she felt her head turning, seeking the mouth which had avoided hers but was moving effectively elsewhere. Pat felt the movement too; his warm breath, then approximately under her left ear, came out in a gust of amusement. Annoyed, she tried to free herself, and found her hands ineffective.

For the first few seconds of the second kiss she was unaware of any emotion except gratification; this, then, was what men starving on a desert island experienced when confronted with their first full meal in months. Only for her it had been years. . . . The new sensation came gradually, insidiously. It was some time before she realized that pleasure had been replaced by terror, and that her body was stiff with revulsion. She tried to move and found she could not; the weight of his body forced her back onto the couch, the pressure of his hands was so painful she wanted to cry out, but could not, because his mouth was a gag, stifling sound and breath. . . . It was a nightmare, all the worse because it had happened before, and because she had not expected, from him, such ruthless contempt for her pain, physical and mental.

Then all the lights in the room went on, in a blinding flash that penetrated even her squeezed eyelids; and from some infinite distance a voice spoke loudly.

Pat was still a dead weight—almost as if he had collapsed—but his hands and body were passive now, no longer actively hurting. After a moment he sat up; and Ruth, blinking through tears of fright and pain, saw Bruce standing in the doorway, his hand on the light switch. He was wearing his coat, but no hat, as was his habit; and the expression on his face made Ruth want to shriek with hysterical amusement.

He's shocked, she thought wildly; poor child, they really are so conventional. . . . Then she realized that she was sprawled awkwardly and embarrassingly across the couch. She sat up and tried to rearrange her skirt.

Bruce gave Pat one quick, appraising look, and then vanished, without comment or apology—an omission which made Ruth think highly of his tact. She had not dared to look at Pat, but she was intensely aware of him. He was hunched over, his face hidden in his hands; but he must have been looking through his fingers, because as soon as Bruce left he turned to Ruth.

"Is there any point in asking you to forgive me?"

"My dear, there's no need—" Ruth's voice was a croak; she had to stop and clear her throat. "You didn't—"

"I hurt you; and that was unforgivable. Good God, I don't know what came over me!" His clenched hands went to his forehead, and Ruth reached over to pat his shoulder.

"Stop beating yourself. It's happened before—"

She had not meant to say that, nor had she anticipated what the impact of the words would be. They literally caught in her throat and left her staring dumbly at her glass of wine.

"I know it has," Pat said quietly. "I knew something was wrong; it was unmistakable. That's what makes my behavior so viciously stupid."

"How—how did you know?"

"I can't explain; I just—well, felt it. The first time I kissed you I felt it—a mixed-up combination of desire and fear. I knew that; I was so careful—and now I had the unforgivable effrontery to try to force you. Ruth, I'm not apologizing for my instincts, I'm proud of 'em; but I can't forgive myself for my stupidity and clumsiness."

"It's all right."

"No, it's not. But the situation is so fouled up now I might as well plunge on. It's your husband, isn't it? I know about that; he was killed in the Second World War, when you'd only been married a few months."

"Harry. . . ." She let the word linger on her tongue, wondering why, after twenty years, the taste of it should be so bitter.

"It was a tragedy, darling, I know. A terrible thing. But it's been twenty years, and more. You can't bury your emotions for the rest of your life out of some sickly romanticism, no one demands or deserves such distorted loyalty. . . ."

"Loyalty?" She turned, staring at him; and the glass she had picked up began to shake, spilling white liquid, and her whole body shook with silent, painful laughter. "The day I got the telegram from the War Department I got down on my knees and thanked God."

"Was it as bad as that?" he asked, after a moment of silence, in which the truth burst on him like a blinding light.

"It was—there are no words. I was only twenty—Sara's age—and I was so naïve, you wouldn't believe—none of these sophisticated modern children would believe—how dumb I was. At first I thought it was my fault. He called me a prig, and talked about middle-class morality. And I believed him; I was sunk in guilt at my own abhorrence. Oh, Pat, there wasn't a thing he missed!" She gave a choked laugh. The tears were pouring down her cheeks and she swiped at them with the back of her hand. "I read the books later, you know the ones I mean; there was hardly a page I hadn't known, firsthand."

"Why didn't you divorce him?" Pat asked in a deadly quiet voice.

"I told you, at first I thought it was my fault, I thought I would learn. . . . Then, later, he was going away. They were talking about the big invasion, and we knew he would be in it. I couldn't—"

"Yes, I see." Pat's fist beat a soft tattoo against his knee. "It's frustrating," he said casually, "to want to kill a man who's been dead for twenty years. I hope he's rotting."

"I can see now that he was sick," Ruth said, fumbling in her pocket. "I can be sorry for him—now. I didn't realize myself how it had affected me, I just—never thought about it."

"No wonder. All the same, it would have been better if you had proceeded to have a big noisy nervous breakdown and gotten this out of your system. You never had psychiatric help? No, you wouldn't. Excuse me just a minute while I go out on the front steps and shoot myself."

"But—don't. How could you possibly know?"

"I should have known. What the hell are you looking for? Oh, take my handkerchief. Blow your nose. Have another drink. Ruth, I should have known because I love you. Love is supposed to give people insight, isn't it?"

"I think that's one of the sadder delusions of youth." Ruth blew, loudly and satisfyingly. "Unfortunately, it seems to cloud one's vision instead."

"You may be right," Pat said, eying her nervously. "Is that any way to respond to my announcement?"

"I am sorry! I just—"

"I'm not expecting any enthusiasm, under the circumstances. Just think about it." His hands clenched till the knuckles whitened and she knew it was with the effort of not reaching out to touch her. "You feel better now, I know. It was a beautiful catharsis. But it was only temporary; Ruth, you're not through this yet. Just let me try. I'll be careful. This won't happen again. I'll be damned if I know what came over me."

# Chapter

## 7

THE PORK CHOPS WERE SIZZLING IN THE PAN; SARA COOKED them as Ruth had taught her, in bacon fat with plenty of garlic salt and pepper. She looked up at her aunt as the latter came in. Ruth had been upstairs to repair the ravages of the past half hour, but she knew her eyes were red, and she had never appreciated Sara more than now, when the girl greeted her with a smile which held no recollection of the morning's unpleasantness. It was Bruce, vigorously mashing potatoes, who avoided Ruth's eye.

"Do you mind making the gravy, Ruth?" Sara asked prosaically. "I still can't do it without lumps."

"Of course. It was nice of you two to get dinner. But, Bruce—I wondered. . . . I mean, it's after dark. . . ."

"I agree," Bruce said. "We'll leave as soon as we finish eating."

He turned to the table and began ladling potatoes out onto plates.

"Bruce, for goodness sake!" Sara exclaimed. "Put them in a bowl."

"Why get more dishes dirty?" Bruce said.

"Quite right." Pat took the frying pan from Sara and forked chops out onto plates. "Let's eat and run. You girls are spending the night at my place."

He handed the frying pan back to Ruth.

"Now you can make the gravy," he explained.

"Men," Sara said.

"Impossible," Ruth agreed. They nodded solemnly at each other.

They ate hastily, and in silence. Ruth was occupied with her own thoughts; she was aware that Bruce seemed preoccupied and unusually quiet, but in the confusion of new personal ideas that had overwhelmed her she paid less attention than she might otherwise have done. Bruce finished before the others; he scraped his plate energetically into the sink and began clearing the table with such vigor that Pat had to snatch his plate, with his third pork chop, back.

"Wait a minute. What's the hurry?"

"Ruth is right." Bruce reached for a glass. "We'd better get out of here. I was late getting back. I'd have suggested going then, only Sara had dinner ready. . . . Hurry up, will you? We can leave the dishes till morning; I'll help out then. . . ."

The stammering voice was so unlike Bruce's that Ruth could only stare.

"You must have found out something today," Pat said, studying the younger man curiously.

"Well, sort of. I mean, it doesn't. . . . Look, let's go! I'll talk about it at your place."

Sara rose obediently; and in a quick, convulsive movement Bruce dived across the table and caught her arm.

"Not you—not that way!"

"What on earth—" Ruth began.

"Ruth, will you pack some things for her and get her coat? Then we can go out the kitchen door."

"Why—of course."

As she packed Sara's robe and nightgown and toothbrush, along with her own things, Ruth wondered what Bruce had discovered that frightened him so badly. For he was afraid, and not on his own account. What could be worse than the things they had already experienced?

## II

During the drive Bruce continued to ramble, suggesting that the two women go to a hotel, offering to sleep on Pat's living-room floor, and being generally irrelevant. His conversation sounded like the noises people make to conceal the fact that they are not listening to themselves talk—that they are thinking about something else altogether.

Pat lived near Spring Valley, in a tiny house set in what seemed—and proved, by daylight—to be a neatly kept little garden.

"I like gardens," he explained. "Otherwise I'd have taken an apartment. The house is a little large for one person, but I have a lot of books."

That, Ruth decided, was an understatement. Her first impression of Pat's house was that it was built of books. Every wall in the downstairs rooms that was not otherwise occupied was lined with bookcases. There were books on tables, on chairs, on Pat's desk in his study. There were more books on beds and on night tables, and books on every flat surface in the bathroom, including the floor.

Ruth's second impression was that it was the grubbiest house she had ever seen.

Pat surveyed his living room with mild astonishment.

"It's sort of messy, isn't it? I guess what's-her-name didn't come this week."

He leaned over and blew the dust off the coffee table.

"What's-her-name being the cleaning woman, I gather," Ruth said. She picked up a sock from the back of a chair. "It wouldn't be so bad if you wouldn't leave your clothes lying around—and would pick up the newspaper instead of leaving it spread out on the floor—and take out your used coffee cups—and empty an ashtray occasionally. . . ."

She suited the action to the words, and finished by handing Pat the overflowing wastebasket into which she had forced the contents of the ashtrays.

"Amazing," Pat said. Clutching the wastebasket to his chest he looked around the room. "Looks better already."

"Where's the vacuum cleaner? Do you have a vacuum cleaner?"

"Certainly I do. But it's none of your business." Pat put the wastebasket down in the middle of the floor. "You can be housewifely tomorrow, if you insist, but tonight we're going to talk. Don't you want to hear what Bruce has to say?"

"Yes, of course," Ruth said absently.

Even in its present clutter and dust, which had been barely touched by her efforts, the room was a pleasant place, with that air of comfort which comes when a basically well-decorated room is inhabited by someone who cares more for comfort than for elegance. She suspected that Pat's mother had donated the furniture; the chintz on the chairs and couch, with its delicate pattern of lilac and delphinium, in soft blues and lavenders, had certainly not been Pat's choice, but it suited the room, with its low-beamed ceiling and brick fireplace. The rug was a soft textured blue that repeated one color of the flowered print. Coffee table and lamps looked like Pat's contributions; they were of heavy cut glass and their simple, modern lines went surprisingly well with the traditional furniture.

Pursuing her investigations Ruth rounded the corner of the couch and stopped with a nervous squeal. Lying on the floor behind the couch, unmoved by their entrance, was what appeared to be a dead dog.

Pat rushed to join her, to see what had prompted her yell. Then he relaxed, eyeing the recumbent form—which was that of a very big, brown German shepherd—with disgust.

"That's Lady," he said.

Lady opened one eye and regarded him with remote interest. She let out a short unemphatic bark and closed the eye again.

"Laziest damn' dog I've ever seen," Pat said gloomily.

Sara dropped to the floor and began to rub the dog's head.

"Pretty girl," she crooned. "Nice Lady. Poor thing; how old is she, Pat?"

"Two years old," Pat said. "It's not her age, it's her disposition. She spends half her time lying in front of her food dish where I fall over her every time I go in the kitchen and the rest of her time lying in front of the fireplace waiting for me to make a fire. I've made more fires for that stupid dog."

He was building another one as he spoke, crumpling newspapers and jamming them under the waiting logs. Lady roused, and rolled over from her front to her side. She gave Pat a look of weary approval and he paused long enough to scratch her stomach. "Stupid dog," he muttered. Lady's mouth opened in a grin of affectionate contempt.

"You understand each other," Ruth said, laughing.

"Too true. All right, you stupid dog, there's your fire. Now perhaps I may be allowed to tend to my guests. Coffee? Brandy?"

"Both, please," Ruth said, and went along to help. When they finally settled down, she gave a sigh of contentment. The atmosphere was so restful that she felt completely at home. All of them might have been old inhabitants. Sara was squatting, with black boots crossed, on the hearthrug, and Lady had condescended to shift her big head into the girl's lap, where she lay snuffling and sighing in the throes of an exciting dream. Bruce had propped himself in a somewhat self-conscious pose against the mantel and was staring off into space and displaying his handsome profile to good effect. His close-fitting dark trousers and gaudy waistcoat might have been the doublet and hose of a medieval squire; they suited Bruce's lean height and long legs.

Pat was sprawled out in what was evidently his favorite chair; its cracking leather folds had molded themselves to the shape of his body. He smiled lazily at Ruth and lifted his glass in salute.

"I hate to dispel the mood," Bruce said waspishly.

"Then don't," Pat said.

"Time's running out. In fact, it's run. Forty-eight hours, remember?"

"Oh, that." Pat shrugged.

"You're awfully goddamn' casual about it!"

"I'm sorry," Pat said patiently. "I merely meant to remind you that you don't need to worry about deadlines."

"Deadlines! I'm worried about what we're going to do. Or do you expect Ruth to live with that chunk of fog indefinitely?"

"Don't loose your cool," said Pat, and looked idiotically pleased with himself for remembering this gem of modern idiom. "Naturally we'll have to do something. Let's talk about it. Have a Socratic dialogue."

He smiled at Ruth with the same lazy charm which seemed, at the moment, to be slightly tinged with alcohol. She shared his mood, however, and knew that he was not drunk, except with reaction. One simply did not realize how unnatural the atmosphere of the Georgetown house had become until one got out of it.

Bruce flushed with anger or frustration. Then he took a grip of his beard with both hands, and nodded.

"Okay. Geez, you make me mad," he added plaintively.

"I really am sorry, Bruce. Suppose you do the talking."

"I never refuse that invitation." Bruce's cheerful grin reappeared. "Okay, we'll have that dialogue. Answer Yes or No. We all agree that Sara is not psychotic, and that the manifestations we have seen are, in fact, from the realm which is called supernatural or paranormal."

"Right," Pat said.

"Then let's summarize what we've got. Sara, there's some blank paper in that hodgepodge on the table, you'd better jot this down. If anyone disagrees, or has a point to add, feel free to interrupt."

"Okay," Pat said meekly. If there was a gleam of amusement in his eye Ruth did not see it, but Bruce gave him a sharp glance before going on.

"Point one, a personality has on three occasions taken over Sara's body. Technical term: possession, or, as the English sometimes call it, overshadowing. This entity—whom we will call, for purposes of identification, A—has been pretty damned vague. Its only contribution has been the reference to the general, and a reiteration to the effect that It is not dead."

"Added comment," Pat said. "The accent was not Sara's normal one, but I could not identify it."

"Okay, that's a good point." Bruce sounded mollified. "I couldn't identify it either, except that it sounded softer and broader."

"What we need is a speech expert," Ruth said.

"We can't bring an outsider into this," Bruce said. Then he smote himself heavily on the brow. "Damn it; that's the trouble with us, we just aren't organized. We ought to have had a tape recorder going. We could let someone listen to a tape without giving away the circumstances."

"Thinking about what we should have done is futile," Pat said. "Go on, Bruce. Apparition A is not very helpful."

"Apparition B isn't either. That's what I propose to call that—unspeakable darkness. Yet we respond a lot more strongly to it than we do the other. I do, anyhow. The entity that overshadows Sara bugs me, I'll admit, but I think mostly because it's not Sara. At the same time it is diluted, so to speak, by being contained in Sara. Whereas the darkness—appalls. The cold which accompanies it is a traditional manifestation of the supernatural, just about the only classic ghostly feature we've encountered. The cold is unnaturally violent and enervating. But the apparition is worse. It is evil."

The dog chose that moment to groan heartrendingly, and Ruth shivered.

"We all agree on that, don't we?" Pat said. "The impression of active, condensed evil—which is interesting. How do we know it's evil? That's a word and a concept which is out of fashion. Is there really such a thing as spiritual evil, and is there a human faculty, a seventh or eighth sense, that can smell it out?"

"You're getting into theology," Sara murmured. "Pretty soon you'll be asking, 'What is the good, Alcibiades?' and then I'll go to sleep."

"Yes, we're getting too philosophical," Bruce agreed. "Though I'd love to go into the problem if we didn't have more pressing matters on hand. All right. Apparition B is evil but otherwise without distinguishing characteristics. Now we come to Apparition C, if you can call a voice an apparition. The Voice. Capital V."

"You're too young to find that amusing," Ruth said, with a chuckle. "Remember, Pat?"

Bruce gave her a glance of dignified disdain.

"Apparition C, if you prefer that, seems to me the most potentially hopeful clue. It has been heard by all of us and it says definite words. 'Come home—Sammie.' "

"Query," Pat's drawl interrupted. "Name uncertain, if it is a name."

"Okay, query Sammie. The voice is indeterminate in terms of sex—"

"Or anything else," Pat muttered. "Direction, location, sense—"

"Or accent. It sounds," said Bruce, with unconscious poetry, "the way the wind would sound if it could speak. Rushing, hollow, immense."

"Good or bad?" Sara asked.

"Neutral, I'd say; wouldn't you?"

"I guess so. It's scary, but just because it is unnormal."

"Right. If Saint Peter himself appeared to me I'd scream and run, just from the unexpectedness of him. Anything else?"

"The book," suggested Ruth. "You believe something moved it."

"Apparition D?" Bruce scowled; he looked beautifully satanic with his brows coming together in a V. "Well, that plunges us into the next question. Which is—do these apparitions overlap?"

"Now you're talking," Pat said. He was so interested that he made the effort of sitting erect. "A and B might be the same entity."

"That occurred to me. The Thing—damn it, we need a name for It; It sounds like something out of a horror movie—"

"I think of It," Sara said, "as the Adversary."

"Hmm. Okay, the Adversary might try to work through Sara first. If it finds her unacceptable, or too fragile physically, it might try materializing."

"It's not a well-read ghost," Pat said. "The ones I've heard about are all tall white things. This dirty, dark mess—"

"Is the only genuine specter I've ever met," Ruth said, with a faint smile. "I've really no basis for comparison."

"Now is there anything to substantiate the impression that A and B are the same?" Bruce continued doggedly.

"No," Pat said.

"No," Bruce agreed. "Possible but not proved. Apparitions C and D—if we call the one who moved the book D—may also be identical. But, whether they are one or two, I think they are distinct from A-B and, what is more, hostile to it."

"Let's have that again," Sara said.

"I think I follow," Pat said. "The entity that moved the book is trying to tell us something. Its action is followed almost at once by the appearance of B, malignant and threatening. And the threat seems to be directed at the person who has the book."

"It's weak," Bruce muttered. "But it's the best we can do. The Voice seems to all of us neutral, if not benevolent. D is presumably benevolent, since it wants to give us some help. A and B definitely are not benevolent. So maybe C and D are the same, as are A and B. Criminey. As logic that isn't very impressive."

"No, but there's a feeling about it. . . . Hell, I can believe in one ghost, or maybe two; but four or five is surely stretching belief pretty thin." Pat tapped his fingers on the arm of the chair. "Suppose we reduce our apparitions to two. You have produced some evidence to indicate that one is helpful and the other hostile."

Sara gave a sigh and stretched out full length on the rug, hands clasped under her head.

"I warned you I'd get sleepy if the conversation got dull," she murmured.

Pat eyed her approvingly.

"You look like a parody of a tombstone," he said. "With the dog's head on your stomach instead of at your feet."

"All bosom and leg," Ruth commented unkindly. "Pull your skirt down."

"I don't think it will go down any farther," Pat said agreeably. "Anyhow, the dog's lying on it."

"You're a hell of a lot of help," Bruce said, addressing his lady love in bitter tones. "You haven't got a thing to contribute, and now you sprawl all over the room, taking people's minds off serious matters. Get up, wench."

"Let's get on to the historical research," Pat said, stifling a yawn. "Then we can get to bed."

"We didn't find much," Ruth admitted. "There's a lot of material around, but it takes ages to go through it."

"Don't I know," Bruce agreed feelingly. "I had a hell of a frustrating day myself. The records for that period are practically nonexistent."

"As the skeptic of this crowd I'd like to raise an objection," Pat said. "You seem to be basing your research on one item—the book. Are you sure you ought to limit yourself to that?"

"Oh, I'm all in favor of cross-checks. If the 1780 Campbell was named Samuel instead of Douglass, I'd be 100 percent sure we were on the right track. Matter of fact, I looked for Sammie today. And I found one. Samuel Campbell, son of George. Died in infancy around—I regret to say—1847."

"Oh, Bruce," Sara whispered. Her mouth had a pitiful droop. "That must be it. Think of it, calling your baby all those years. . . ."

"Samuel was one of twelve children," Bruce said calmly. "Both his parents seem to have been sanctimonious prigs who died in the overpowering odor of sanctity years later. And, if this means anything, there was nothing to indicate that the baby wasn't properly baptized, and all the rest. With all due deference to your sentimentality, luv, I think we can scratch Sammie."

"Your day was a bust, then." Pat yawned. "Sorry. I think maybe—"

"Okay." Bruce extended a hand to Sara and with one seemingly effortless movement pulled her to her feet. There was more muscle in his languid-looking frame than there appeared to be.

"What do we do tomorrow?" Sara asked, leaning against him.

"I go to the Columbia Historical Association. You keep on looking through the house."

"That worries me," Ruth admitted. "Are you sure it's safe for Sara?"

"I'm making two assumptions," Bruce said. "And I hope to God I'm right. One is that the manifestations occur only at night. The other—the other is that they occur only in the house."

Ruth was sodden with fatigue; it took her several seconds to comprehend the last sentence, which Pat had apparently anticipated; he was studying Sara with thoughtful eyes.

"You mean—here? Something might happen here?"

"Not if Bruce is right," Pat said. "You know, Bruce, there is a test we could make."

"What do you mean?" Ruth demanded.

"Hypnosis. Now, Ruth, don't look at me that way. It's a perfectly valid medical technique, not black magic; and I have done it before. I could do it now."

"No," Bruce said. "It's too dangerous."

"But I've had occasion—"

"It's dangerous because it's inconclusive. You guys talk about your friend the subconscious as if you had lunch with it every Tuesday, but the fact is you don't know much about the mind and the way it works. You could unwittingly suggest all kinds of things to Sara, and her subconscious might obligingly produce an imitation of Apparition A just because she thinks we want one. No. I won't allow it."

"Nor I," Ruth said flatly. "Pat, I suspect I'm going to have to make my own bed. Let's get at it, shall we?"

Pat looked stubborn; every hair on his head bristled.

"Very well," he said stiffly. "Bruce, do you want to call a cab?"

Bruce was gnawing his knuckles. He looked up.

"Would you mind if I just flopped down on the couch?"

"Afraid I'm going to pull a Svengali on Sara when your back is turned?" Pat asked nastily.

"It's late, that's all," the boy said mildly. "I won't be in the way."

As it turned out, there were three bedrooms upstairs, and Sara offered to share the big fourposter in one of them with Ruth. So it all worked out, and Pat was suddenly bland and amiable about the whole thing. Ruth was left to wonder precisely what he had had in mind when he made the original sleeping arrangements.

Not until she was almost asleep did it occur to her that there had been nothing in Bruce's discoveries to account for his strange, panicky behavior that evening.

# III

Next day was one of the days Washingtonians brag about—brilliant, mild and balmy, with only a hint of cold under the soft breeze, like the bones under a cat's fur. Pat had the car windows rolled down when he drove them to the house, and he said regretfully, "It's too nice a day for that damned museum. If I hadn't had this appointment for a month—"

"You've got to keep it. We'll be all right."

"Hey, I've got an idea. Why don't I bring some stuff— Chinese food, maybe—and we'll have lunch in the garden."

"I thought you were having lunch with the curator."

"I'll get out of that." Pat stopped the car in front of the house.

"But Pat—"

"Look, today I feel like eating lunch with you. Both of you," he added.

Sara giggled, and Pat reached over to give her a fatherly smack as she got out of the car. Or maybe, Ruth thought, it wasn't so fatherly.

"Bruce may be back for lunch," she reported, putting her head back in the car window.

"The more the merrier," Pat said resignedly. He put the car into gear. "What do you like? Sweet-and-sour pork? Egg foo yung?"

"Anything but chop suey," Ruth said, and followed the car with her eyes as it swooped down the street, avoided a woman with a perambulator, and darted around the corner into the stream of traffic on Wisconsin.

Sunlight twinkled off the windshields and chrome of passing cars and warmed the rosy red brick of the houses opposite,
bringing out the precise, geometric patterns of the whitened
mortar. Most of the shades were still drawn and the dignified
facades looked like sleepy old ladies snatching a catnap with
hands folded primly in their laps, dreaming of their long honorable lives. One of the trees was alive with starlings holding one
of their mysterious conferences; the squawking, which sounded
like the United Nations in the lively old Khrushchev era, was
unmusical but vigorously alive, and the sidewalk under the tree
was already white with droppings. Washingtonians cursed the
starlings, but Ruth had a sneaking sympathy for their vulgar,
uproarious bustle. They were ugly rusty-looking birds, but
when the sunlight glanced off their feathers they glowed with
iridescence as brilliant as that of a sequined dress. It was with
conscious reluctance that Ruth turned away from the sun and
life of the street into the quiet house.

The living room was shadowy and still with all the drapes
pulled; when Ruth opened them the sunlight streamed in, filled
with dancing dust motes.

"Goodness, the place is dirty," she muttered.

"Ruth—"

"What's wrong? Do you feel—"

"No, nothing. That's what amazes me. How can the place
look so normal?"

"Yes, I know. . . ." Ruth's eyes traveled from the window,
where the drapes hung placidly in azure blue folds, across the
patterns of the carpet. There ought to be a great charred spot,
the mark of burning. . . .

"Well," she said, giving herself a brisk shake to dispel
phantoms, "I think perhaps we ought to stay out of this room,
for all it feels so innocent. I remember that there were some papers that looked like letters in a box in the hall closet. Let's take
them into the kitchen and look them over while we have another cup of coffee. Then we can try the attic."

The letters turned out to be fascinating; they were still reading them several hours later when Pat's emphatic pounding was
heard at the front door. He was using his foot, not his fist, as
Ruth discovered when she opened the door; his arms were
loaded with parcels which he dumped on the kitchen table, demanding, "Where's Bruce?"

"Not back yet."

"Let's eat this while it's hot. We can warm his up for him."

Bruce appeared while Pat was still sorting little packages of soy sauce and mustard, and they all sat down together.

"You look particularly smug," Ruth remarked, as Bruce dug into a beautiful concoction with an unpronounceable name which contained, among other commodities, shrimp and snow peas. "You must have made a discovery."

"Something," Bruce swallowed, and the rest of his speech became considerably more intelligible. "But I don't want to discuss it while we're eating."

"We got bogged down," Sara said. "I've been reading some ancestress's love letters, and they are a panic. Do you know she called her husband 'Mr. Campbell' after they had been married thirty years?"

"That's what's wrong with our modern society." Pat shook his head and spread mustard with a lavish hand. "No respect. Old values breaking down."

Ruth laughed.

"Gosh, it's a beautiful day," she exclaimed, in a sudden burst of well-being. "Let's not talk about anything important till after lunch. I feel too good to start worrying."

"It's partly the weather and partly this damned picnic atmosphere," Bruce said. He stabbed a shrimp and looked at it fondly. "We seem to spend half our time eating and/or drinking, under the most peculiar conditions."

" 'And, my dear husband, do not forget to take food regularly and in good quantity,' " Sara quoted. "She wrote him that when he was off on a business trip. I think it's great advice."

Looking at Bruce, Ruth was inclined to agree. He was beginning to develop visible shadows under his eyes, and there was a look in them, particularly when he watched Sara, that Ruth found disturbing.

The light mood lasted through the meal, which Pat cleared by dumping everything into a paper bag and depositing it in the garbage can. When he came back in, he said,

"Are we having coffee or more tea? Whichever, let's take it outside."

The sunlight was seductively warm. Ruth produced a blanket for Sara, knowing her habit of sprawling on the lowest surface available, and Bruce sat down beside her on a pile of leaves.

"I feel like Luther," Pat announced, and they all stared at him. "I don't believe in anything," he explained.

"No ghosts," Bruce said, with a faint smile.

"No ghosts."

"I wish you were right." Bruce leaned back on his elbows and contemplated the sky.

"What did you find out today?" Sara asked. The question broke the relaxed, sunny mood; Bruce sat erect, and Ruth felt herself stiffening.

"There was a house here in 1780," he said. "Douglass Campbell's house. I ran into a piece of luck, a collection of family letters. The Page letters, they're called. The Pages lived up the street a way, but the family died out in the late nineteenth century and the last Page left the papers to the Columbia Historical Society. That's where I've been all morning."

"Okay, okay," Pat said. "You don't have to explain every goddamned source. What did the Pages have to say about the Campbells?"

"Not much, most of them were business letters about land and tobacco. But in 1805 Alexander Page's eldest daughter got married and moved to Annapolis. Mrs. Page wrote the girl several letters telling her the hometown gossip. The Campbell fire was a good juicy tidbit."

"Fire?" Sara repeated.

"The house burned down . . . and Douglass Campbell with it."

In the silence the squawk of a blue jay sounded like a scream. Ruth was remembering the impression she had felt that morning—that there should be marks of scorching where the apparition had been. As she looked at Sara she knew her niece was thinking along the same lines; her face was pale with horror.

"That black, coiling smoke," she said in a whisper. "Bruce, could it be—*him?*"

"Cut that out!" Bruce exclaimed.

Simultaneously Pat said sharply, "Don't be morbid, Sara. The suggestion of smoke is purely subjective. Bruce, what happened, that the old boy was caught in the house? He must have been old, if he had already built his house by 1780."

"The fire was thirty years later," Bruce said. "He could have been as young as fifty-five or as old as eighty. It's possible that the smoke knocked him out before anyone realized that the house was on fire. It was stone; the letter mentioned that. The walls weren't burned, of course, but the whole inside was gutted and the roof collapsed. When the heir, who was Campbell's sister's son, moved to Georgetown from Frederick, he leveled the walls and built a new house."

Ruth was silent. The sunshine and birdsongs seemed far away, and the orange beads of the bittersweet against the fence had faded. The ancient tragedy had affected her spirits unaccountably.

"I don't see any connection between this story and our apparitions," Pat said. "The smoky impression is meaningless. If the old man's name had been Samuel, now. . . ."

"It wasn't. But there was something funny. . . ."

"In the letter?"

"Yeah. The trouble with letters is that the writers have all sorts of background knowledge they don't bother to explain. Why should they? Their readers know it. But it leaves a modern researcher groping. Old Lady Page described the fire and clucked over the sad tragedy. Then she said—wait a minute. I wrote it down." Bruce pulled a notebook out of his pocket. "Here we go: 'Some have been heard to say that it is a judgment for his having withdrawn, not only from the offices of his neighbors but from the loving kindness of God following his affliction, he not having been seen at the services these thirty years. But I am sensible of his former zeal as a true Samson among the Philistines, not only in support of the Sunday laws, but in despising the heretics who are now so favored by the wretches across Rock Creek.'"

Bruce closed the notebook.

"Then she starts to complain about how dear muslin has become. She's a rip-roaring old Tory. Her handwriting was vile, too."

"Who were the wretches across Rock Creek?"

"The distinguished officials of the United States Government," Bruce said with a grin. "Many Georgetowners resented having the seat of government so close, and some were lukewarm about the whole idea of independence."

"How about the heretics?" Ruth asked. "The old lady had a fine vocabulary, didn't she?"

"She was a mean old bitch," Bruce replied briefly. "The

heretics, I'm pretty sure, were the Catholics. They weren't allowed to build churches around here until after the Revolution, you know."

"The letter is funny, all right, but not, I expect, in the sense you meant," Pat said. "What struck you as odd?"

A mockingbird swung from a branch of bittersweet and addressed them mellifluously. Bruce contemplated the bird before answering.

"Let me restate what she says. Douglass Campbell, back in the 1770's, was a good devout Protestant and a man of some substance—you got that reference to supporting the Sunday laws? Then something happened to him—some affliction—and he shut himself up in his house. He didn't even go to church. There is no mention of anyone else's dying in the fire, which suggests that he was a widower or a bachelor."

"If the heir was his nephew, maybe he was a bachelor," Sara said.

"Bachelors were rarer in those days," Pat pointed out. "He could just as well have been a widower whose children had died young. Infant mortality was high."

"Maybe that was the affliction," Sara said. "The death of a child, an only child."

"Hmm." Pat leaned back against the tree, staring up through the leafless branches at the cloudless blue sky. "Possibly. You know, Bruce, we may be interpreting the clue of the book too literally. Our invisible informant may have wanted to indicate a date, not a connection with a specific event."

"I thought of that. You realize that the Page letter gives us that cross-check we hoped for? The affliction occurred thirty years before the fire, which was in 1810. That takes us back to the crucial year, 1780. But I can't get around the fact that the Loyalist Plot involved Georgetown and Georgetowners. Can that be a coincidence?"

"Was Campbell a Tory?" Ruth asked.

"He wasn't involved in the Plot, that's for sure; the book mentions not only the names of the men who were hanged, but also the ones who were accused and acquitted."

"Maybe," Pat suggested, "he was one of the loyal—damn it, terms are confusing—loyal Patriots who helped foil the Plot. Then, thirty years later—"

"That's rather long to wait for revenge," Bruce said.

"So he died a natural death. But he could have suffered his affliction during the Plot. Some personal tragedy. Maybe he was blinded, or crippled."

"Or he could have lost his child or his wife or his money." Bruce banged his knee with his fist. "Damn it, we're just guessing. It's all so vague!"

"If you could find out whether he was married and all like that, it might help?" Sara asked anxiously, with the air of a mother looking through her purse for a lollipop. "Ruth, what about the genealogy?"

"Good gracious, I am a dolt," Ruth exclaimed. "Of course—the Bible."

"What Bible?"

"It's old; I don't know how old, but the pages are so fragile they crumble when you touch them. Cousin Hattie kept it wrapped in dozens of layers of plastic. It's one of those enormous ancient Bibles with a family tree in the front, and it was kept up for generations. Sara, there's a copy of the genealogy somewhere—in the desk, I think. See if you can find it. I hate to disturb the book, I've been meaning to take it to some museum to see about preserving it, but. . . ."

Sara was off, her hair flying. She came back with a sizable scroll, which Ruth passed on to Bruce without unrolling it.

"This must have been Hattie's copy. She was rotten with family pride."

Bruce unrolled the parchment on the grass; his black head and Sara's bent over it.

"Here's Douglass," Bruce said, his finger tracing the family tree, with its brilliantly colored coats of arms and crabbed writing. "Halfway down the tree. Wow—Cousin Hattie wasn't modest, was she? Here's Robert the Bruce back here, and Alfred, King of England. . . . This later part looks a little more authentic. She must have picked it up from family papers and tacked the royalty on to make it look more impressive."

"Her writing was nothing to brag about either," Sara said, crouched over the scroll.

"Get your hair out of the way." Bruce brushed at it; his hand lingered, but not for long. "Douglass Campbell, 1720–1810. Married Elizabeth Sanger, 1740–1756. . . ."

Sara caught her breath.

"Sixteen years old! That must be wrong."

"Not necessarily," Ruth said. "They did marry young. If he married her when she was fifteen, and she died, perhaps in childbirth. . . ."

"Yes, look here. There was a child, born the same year, 1756. . . . That's funny," Bruce said. "No name. Just a question mark."

Sara sat up, tossing her hair back over her shoulders.

"What a terrible thing. Sixteen years old, dying when she had her baby. . . . That's four years younger than I am."

"If I were a parent," Ruth remarked, "I couldn't let that one pass."

"You'd be right too, much as I hate to admit it." Sara smiled at her. "So we don't have it so bad these days. And he was . . . let's see. . . ." She crouched over the chart again. "He was thirty-five when he married her, twenty years older. . . ."

"A real aged creep," Pat said morosely. "Thirty-five, my God."

"Oh, Pat! To a girl of fifteen—"

"Maybe he was romantic as hell."

"And maybe not."

"Bruce, what's the matter?" Ruth asked, interrupting the dialogue.

"I'm trying to figure out why Douglass's only child has no name."

"Maybe it died before it was baptized," Sara suggested.

"I don't think they would even mention a stillborn child, and any other would have been baptized. The dates are odd, too—1756, and then a blank. Do you suppose Cousin Hattie got this from the family Bible?"

"I don't think the Bible could be that old," Ruth said.

"Do you mind if I look?"

"Well, I do, rather. It's very fragile."

"I'll be careful."

Ruth looked at his protruding, lower lip and grimaced. She was coming to know that expression well.

"All right," she said coolly. "Sara, it's in the lower drawer of the bookcase. . . ." She shivered. The sun had gone behind a cloud and the garden suddenly looked bleak and depressing. "Let's all go in," she said. "It's getting cold."

The book was enormous. It was wrapped in two layers of plastic and one of faded silk. As Ruth carefully unswathed it, on the piecrust table in the living room, Pat gave an exclamation.

"What criminal neglect! This should have been under glass years ago. The old lady's cheap plastic bags are no substitute."

"I meant to have it looked at, but you know how it is. . . ."

"You find the place, Ruth," Bruce ordered. "I'm afraid to touch it. Sorry; I didn't realize how delicate it was."

Ruth found the place, at the cost of some destruction. The yellowing pages were almost impossible to touch without crumbling the edges.

"Goodness," she said, forgetting her irritation with Bruce in her interest. "Here's Douglass—the first name. Looks as if he must be the original ancestor."

"He was probably the first one to emigrate," Bruce said. "Starting a new line in a new land, that sort of thing."

"I keep telling you, I don't know a thing about the family history. But he was a Scot; a lot of them left in something of a hurry after the '45."

"This must have been his Bible," Sara exclaimed. "How amazing. Two hundred years old!"

"And a bit," Pat said. "He wrote a fine, bold black hand, didn't he?"

They contemplated the page in awed silence. It is said that Americans are unduly impressed by sheer age, being so relatively young in the world scheme themselves. But there was something breathtaking about the angles and curves of the thick black ink, unfaded by time—the visible remnant of a man whose other remains were long since dust.

"Campbell and wife," Pat muttered. "Here she is—Elizabeth. . . . Yes, Hattie must have cribbed that part of the genealogy out of the Bible. The names and dates are the same."

"And here," said Bruce, in an odd voice, "is why there was a question mark for Douglass's child."

The entry was there: one name among the many blank spaces provided for possible progeny. It had been covered completely by a wide, dark blot.

"Somebody goofed," Sara said.

"Hardly." Bruce bent over the page till his delicately chiseled nose almost touched it. "This was deliberate; it's too neat to be accidental. Looks as if Douglass scratched the kid's name out. Corny, weren't they?"

"The ink used for the scratching out is paler than the original," Ruth said. "I can see marks underneath."

"You're right." Before Ruth realized what he was about, Bruce had begun picking at the page with his fingernail. A flake of blue ink chipped off.

"Bruce," she warned.

"It's okay, I'm not doing anything," Bruce said with palpable untruth, amid a shower of fine flakes. "This is cheap ink—locally made, maybe. It's coming. . . . That's an A, surely A-M—"

"Amaryllis," Sara suggested.

"Well, it obviously isn't Samuel," Pat said. "Damn. Another good theory gone west."

". . . A-N . . ."

"Amanias." Sara giggled.

"Shut up. . . . D . . . A."

"Amanda."

"A daughter," Ruth said.

"A bad daughter," Pat contributed.

Transfixed, Bruce remained in the same position, like Brer Rabbit stuck to the Tar Baby. When he straightened, his eyes had a wild glitter.

"Don't any of you see it? I guess maybe you wouldn't. I happened to run across it, as a nickname, in that book on Georgetown ghosts, and I never thought. . . ."

"What on earth are you talking about?"

"Not Sammie. Pat was right about that. But it is a name. It's not Samuel the voice is calling. It's Amanda. Ammie."

# Chapter

## 8

THE FIRST RECOGNIZABLE SOUND TO COME OUT OF THE BABBLE was Pat's unmelodious baritone crooning, "I think he's got it," to the well-known tune from "My Fair Lady."

"You're awfully frivolous for an anthropologist," Ruth told him.

"Anthropologists have a reputation for frivolity. It's the wild lives we lead. 'Exotic sex customs among the Andaman Islanders. . . .' Sorry—I'm babbling. But, by God, now I really am convinced. It's too neat to be wrong."

"Almost too neat." Bruce tried to sound calm, but he was grinning from ear to ear. "But it's got to be right, it was so damned unexpected. I felt the same way you did, Pat; I was sure the name would be Samuel, and my heart went down into my boots when it wasn't."

"Then. . . . It is Douglass Campbell who calls," Ruth said, and her tone sobered them all. "He's calling his daughter. Ammie. Who died. But she says she isn't dead. . . ."

Pat turned to look at her from the middle of the rug, where he had chasséd, a la Henry Higgins, to the tune of his song. The late afternoon sunlight slanted through the window, setting fire to his coppery hair and exposing the lines that had appeared around his mouth.

"Wait a minute, let's not jump to any more conclusions than we have to. It was not death that caused a beloved only daughter to be erased from the pages of the family Bible."

"Beloved?" Bruce repeated in a peculiar voice.

"Oh, all right, scratch the adjective. It just seemed to me. . . ."

"Yes, well . . . the point remains." Bruce scowled; his hand went up to his beard. "If she had died he'd have recorded the year in the usual way. Let's see. There's no record of any marriage for Amanda. In 1780 she was twenty-four—a hopeless old maid, in those days. She must have been the dutiful daughter who kept house for dear old dad. What could she have done to make him want to obliterate her name?"

Sara curled up on the couch, kicking her shoes off and tucking her feet under her.

"They used to disinherit boys for disobedience," she offered. "Like taking up a profession the father didn't approve of."

"There were only two disgraceful professions open to women in those days." Pat grinned. "The other one was the stage."

"But Campbell was one of the gentry," Bruce objected. "His well-bred daughter wouldn't cut loose at the sedate age of twenty-four and join a bawdy house."

"Oh, men are so obtuse," Ruth said impatiently. "She ran off, of course. With some worthless rapscallion her father didn't approve of. Or she got pregnant by same."

"Is that the famous woman's intuition I keep hearing about?" Pat was amused.

"Well, what else could the girl do?" Ruth demanded. "This wasn't London, with its organized sin and gaudy night life; it was a provincial village. And if she reached the age of twenty-four without marrying, she'd be ripe for seduction by any glib male who passed through town."

"And they say men are cynical!" Pat shook his head.

"Oh, you're being silly. Let's have some sherry. We need to talk about this."

Ruth switched on the lights as she went out. When she came back with a tray, the other three were still arguing.

"It doesn't matter," Bruce said, nailing down the essential point. "We'll probably never know what she did. The thing that matters is that she left, under a cloud."

"Okay, I'll buy that," Pat said, taking the tray from Ruth. "What does this do to our varied alphabetical apparitions?"

"The Voice is Douglass," Ruth repeated. "And if C and D— the entity that moved the book—are the same, then—then Douglass is trying to help us."

"Poor guy," Pat muttered.

"Why poor?" Bruce took a sip of his sherry, grimaced, and set the glass down. "Seems to me he was a mean old bastard. There's malevolence in that big ink blot."

"Oh, no, Bruce," Ruth exclaimed. "The voice is terribly pathetic; I've felt that all along. Of course he'd be angry at first, especially if she had left him to go to certain misery or disgrace. But afterward. . . . He still misses her and wants her back, can't you feel that?"

"I guess so." Bruce scowled at his glass.

"Is there something wrong with the sherry?" Ruth asked.

"Well, to tell you the truth—" He grinned sheepishly at her. "I can't stand sherry."

"Then for goodness sake don't drink it! You poor suffering martyr, when I think of all the times. . . . Make yourself a drink, the stuff is in the dining room."

"No, never mind. Thanks. Listen, it's getting late. Maybe—"

"Let's talk about our other apparitions," Pat interrupted. "I want to get this straight while I can. We hypothesized two ghosts, one hostile and one neutral or helpful. I think what we learned today bears this out. Douglass may or may not be the Voice, but he certainly is not the entity who speaks through Sara."

"Of course," Ruth said slowly. "We forgot to make that point because it was so obvious. Apparition B is female. Not just the voice—the gestures, the manner. . . ."

"Oh, yes," Bruce agreed. He had forgotten his preoccupation with the time in contemplating this new idea. "No doubt about it, I'd say. Apparition B is Ammie, all right."

"Yes," Sara said. "I wonder what she wants."

"Ugh," Ruth said, with an involuntary shudder. "Nothing good."

"How do you know?" Bruce asked.

"Why, I—she—maybe I'm prejudiced, but there's something wicked about walking into another person's mind."

"Not very ladylike," Bruce said. "Maybe she was desperate."

"For what?" Ruth repeated. "And why Sara?"

"That's not hard." Bruce began pacing, hands behind his back. "Sara makes a perfect vehicle for Amanda—blood kin, same sex, approximately the same age."

"But what does she *want?*" Ruth slammed her fist down on the table, and the others stared at her. "I'm sorry," she muttered. "But this is. . . . Bruce, I think we've done amazingly well, far better than we ever hoped, and most of the credit goes to you. But don't you see—practically speaking, we haven't made any progress. What, precisely, are we going to do?"

"Ruth, we are doing something." Bruce stopped his pacing and sat down beside her. "If we can find out what the girl does want—"

"And suppose she wants Sara's body?"

It was out at last, the fear that had haunted at least three of the four. Ruth knew by Sara's face that this was not a new idea for her; surely it would be the ultimate in horror to feel one's own body slipping out of control—as annihilating as death, but malignant, personalized. And Bruce's silence showed that he had no immediate answer.

"That's only one possibility," Pat said; but his voice lacked conviction. "Maybe she wants to reach her father. To be forgiven."

"I don't really care what she wants," Ruth said clearly. "I want to get rid of her."

"There is a way," Pat said. "Bruce mentioned it, that first night."

"Exorcism. Well—why not?"

"You know what it signifies," Bruce said. "The ritual casts It—the intruder—out into oblivion."

"Why not?" Ruth repeated stubbornly.

"It does seem awfully final," Sara said, with a feeble smile.

"Worse than that. It probably won't work."

"It's worth a try," Ruth insisted.

Bruce glanced helplessly at Pat, and seemed to find some support in his answering shrug.

"Ruth, how the hell do you propose to go about it? I can see myself telling this yarn to some priest."

"What's the alternative?"

"Continuing to search for the rest of the story. We may find—"

"And we may not. Bruce, don't you see how dangerous it is to wait?"

"I see something else," Bruce said, in a voice that turned her cold. "Look at the window."

The balmy weather had betrayed them. It was not spring; it was late fall, almost winter, and however brilliant the sun it had to obey the laws of nature. In winter the sun sets earlier than in summer. The days are shorter. This day was over.

Ruth got to her feet. There was no sign as yet of the ominous thickening of the air near the window, but in this she preferred to take no chances.

"Come on, Sara," she said.

Then she saw her niece's face.

"No," said the light girl's voice. "No, not . . . help!"

"Good God," Pat whispered. "Do you think she heard what we said—Ammie?"

"I don't know." Ruth took a step forward, toward the stiff body of her niece. "Amanda. You are Amanda?"

"Ammie," the voice agreed, and faded into a sigh. "Help . . . Ammie."

The light outside the window was gone; Ruth was cold with apprehension, not only for what had happened, but for what might yet occur.

"Help you?" she said sharply. Her tone was the one she might have used to a stenographer at work, but she was unaware of the incongruity. "How can we help you? Why don't you go away and leave Sara alone? Go to—to your father."

Bruce moved, his eyes wide and startled; he held up one hand as if in warning. It was too late. The stiff figure on the couch doubled up and then soared erect, hands lifted.

"Father . . . no," It cried. "No, hate, hate, hate. . . ."

Ruth had never heard a word that expressed its own meaning so vividly. Sara's body stumbled clumsily to its feet, still clawing the air. No wonder it's awkward, Ruth thought, no wonder it speaks with such difficulty. It's like trying to drive an unfamiliar type of car, when you haven't driven for—for two hundred years. . . .

She cried out and fell back as the familiar, unrecognizable

figure stumbled toward her, mouthing hate. Bruce was the first
of the two men to move and he did so with obvious reluctance.
Ruth saw the last vestige of color drain from his face when his
hand touched the girl's arm, and she remembered, only too
well, the reaction of her own body to contact with that abnormally occupied flesh. Bruce's mouth twisted as if in pain, but
he kept his hold. Swinging the shambling figure around he
brought his fist up in a careful arc. Sara folded like a doll, into
his arms; and without a glance for anyone or anything else in
the room, Bruce left—down the length of the living room,
through the arch, and straight out the front door. If it had not
been for Pat, Ruth would never have made it; his hand pro-
pelled her through the door. Huddled in his car they sat and
watched the windows, where the folds of the satin curtains had
begun to move.

## II

They stood on the doorstep of the neat new house in its well-
tended lawn. Pat's hand was on the knocker, but he was still
arguing.

"Ruth, I wish you wouldn't do this."

"I told you you didn't have to come." She reached past him
and pushed the bell.

"You'll need my help," he said significantly. "But I keep
telling you; this man is not the right man. Let me try downtown—"

"I know this man personally and he knows me. That's important, considering how crazy—" She broke off, smiling formally at the elderly woman who had opened the door. "Is
Father Bishko in, please? Mrs. Bennett to see him."

Father Bishko greeted them with the suave charm Ruth had
encountered at several Georgetown dinner parties. He was a
strikingly handsome man, with dark hair and gentle brown
eyes. He blinked once or twice during Ruth's story, but did not
interrupt. When she had finished he said mildly, "I—er—must
confess, Mrs. Bennett, that you leave me—er—speechless. If
anyone but you had told me this story—"

"I hope you consider my corroboration worth something,"
Pat interrupted.

"Naturally. If it had not been you two—"

"Then may we ask your help, Father?"

"But, my dear Mrs. Bennett!" Father Bishko waved his hands in the air. "This is not a project to be undertaken lightly."

"You can do it, can't you?"

"There is such a procedure," Father Bishko admitted.

"Then—"

"It is necessary to consult other authorities. For permission to act."

"Oh, dear." Ruth felt her smile sagging. "How long will it take?"

"Why, that is difficult to say. Several days, I expect. Assuming that the response is favorable."

"We can't wait. . . ." Ruth broke off, hearing her voice quiver.

"Is it that serious?" The priest's voice had more warmth; her distress had moved him more than her reasoned description.

"Yes, it is," Pat said. "Father, I know I haven't so much as made my confession for a good many years, but—"

"Are you by any chance trying to bribe me, Pat?" the priest asked. He sounded less vague, much younger, and wholly human; there was a faint grin on his face.

"With my immortal soul?" Pat returned the grin, and shook his head. "You know me too well, Dennie. But this lady is in serious trouble and she thinks you might be able to help her."

"You don't think so, do you?"

"Well, I—"

"Never mind. Well." Father Bishko rubbed his chin with a long ivory finger. "I'm not sure I can help either, but I'll certainly be happy to try. Suppose I drop by one day, just to look the situation over."

"Would you really?" Ruth was limp with gratitude and relief. "I don't know how to thank you."

"Don't get your hopes up," the priest warned. "If you weren't a pair of unbelievers I'd admit I have certain reservations about parts of the ritual. And, Pat—I don't believe in ghosts."

"Come on around this afternoon," Pat said, rising. "And we'll see what we can do to convince you."

When they were once more outside, Ruth turned impulsively to her companion.

"I'm sorry, Pat. Why didn't you tell me you and Father Bishko were friends?"

"Or that I, like Bruce, am a renegade?" Pat smiled down at her, not at all discomposed. "It seemed irrelevant."

"Well, he was awfully nice. It's funny; he didn't promise a thing, and yet I can't help feeling encouraged."

"That feeling is Dennie Bishko's stock in trade," Pat said, a bit grimly. "And that's why I said he wasn't the man for the job. Oh, sure, he's a howling success in a fashionable sophisticated parish; maybe he has even given genuine spiritual comfort to some people. But behind that handsome face of his there is not enough strength of faith or belief. We'd do better with a man from a slum parish—someone who has had to wrestle, if not with malignant spirits, at least with the vile things human beings do to one another."

"We'll see," Ruth said.

Pat took her elbow to help her across the street and looked down ruefully at the shining head that barely reached his shoulder.

"In your own quiet, ladylike way, you're just as bullheaded as I am," he said.

# III

It was many months before Ruth could recall that afternoon without an inward shudder. The Terror—and it rated a capital letter in her thoughts—was painful enough, but this episode violated a sense of human decency as well.

Father Bishko was looking slightly wary when she opened the door, but the charm of the house and of the formal tea service she had carefully arranged soon relaxed him.

"This is a selfish pleasure for me, in fact," he said, graciously waving away her expression of thanks. "I've longed to see this house. Now that our acquaintance has developed, I may venture to ask if we may include it on our house tour next spring. It's for a very worthy cause, you know."

"She may not be here next spring," Pat said, before Ruth

could compose a suitably vague but pleasant reply. Father Bishko, accepting a cup of tea with lemon, looked up at him with an arch smile.

"Indeed? Well, we shall just have to make sure that if Mrs. Bennett does leave it will not be because her charming house is inhabited by unwelcome guests."

They had agreed, during an impassioned consultation the previous evening, that the clerical visitor should not be informed of the details they had worked out.

"It sounds convincing to us," Bruce had insisted, "because we've seen it develop and we've experienced the disturbances personally. But to an outsider it will seem absolute balderdash. If you insist on this dam' fool stunt, just tell him it's spooks and let him cope."

"That's all he needs to know," Pat had agreed. "Furthermore, it will provide another check. If he sees anything, it will not be influenced by our descriptions."

Ruth was to recall, later, the strange expression on Bruce's face when Pat said this. Bruce had been, unaccountably, against the whole idea of exorcism. Or perhaps, Ruth thought, offering Father Bishko a plate of cookies, it was not so unaccountable. Bruce was probably as ill at ease as his coreligionist in the presence of a priest.

By now, though, Pat had gotten over his self-consciousness and was behaving charmingly. He and Father Bishko were reminiscing about their mutual school days, and both of them seemed to be enjoying themselves.

The streaks of sunlight on the floor were turning from gold to bronze before Sara came in. With her, of course, was Bruce, looking particularly bland and blank. He shook hands with the priest, bowing slightly as he did so, and joined amiably in a discussion of the avant-garde theater. After another half hour of polite chitchat, Father Bishko began making going-home signs.

"Mrs. Bennett, I assure you I'll try to bring your problem before my superiors at once. You'll forgive me if I was a bit brusque this morning—"

"Oh, you could never be that."

"Incredulous, then. But now that I've gotten to know you better, you and your charming niece. . . . Obviously, if this matter distresses you, it must be looked into. That in itself is cause enough for me to take action."

"You are very kind," Ruth said sincerely. "Especially since you must rely on our word alone for what is admittedly an extraordinary story."

"I could hardly expect you to conjure up an apparition for me," Father Bishko said with a smile.

"I was hoping we could do just that," Pat said. "It's getting on toward that time of day. . . ."

The priest put his cup on the table and looked up alertly.

"Do you mean that it consistently appears at a particular time? And, by the by, what is It? You haven't been very clear in your description."

"To the first question—no, not exactly, but It normally does not appear until after dark. As for a description—" Pat hesitated, and Father Bishko nodded.

"Yes, I quite see your point. Independent corroboration. Dear me; I must confess, this intrigues me."

"If you could stay a little longer. . . ." Sara suggested.

"Unfortunately, I'm dining out. In fact, I'm already late for an appointment." He smiled at Pat with the quick, mischievous look which undoubtedly entranced a number of his parishioners. "If you were alone in this, Pat, I'd suspect you of putting me on. As it is . . . well, my morbid curiosity is nearly at fever pitch. I would dearly love to see something of this sort with my own eyes."

Studying those bright, innocent eyes, Ruth was seized by a horrid qualm of apprehension which twisted her stomach muscles into knots. It was a common enough feeling, the sort of feeling that is hailed as a premonition if later events bear it out, and dismissed as "nerves" if they do not. Pat had been right. This nice, happy, shallow man must not encounter their dark visitant. His combination of rationalism and optimism would be the worst possible equipment for such a meeting; they might even act as a challenge to the malignant darkness.

"I'm sorry we can't oblige," she said with a forced smile, in the tone experienced hostesses adopt to indicate—to experienced guests—that the party is over. Father Bishko rose to his feet.

"Is your apparition confined in space as well as in time?" he asked, peering hopefully about as if he expected a misty white form to be lurking behind the couch.

"It comes—there," Pat said, pointing.

"Where? Here?"

Father Bishko stood motionless, his face lifted and his eyes half closed, as if he were listening to a voice inaudible to the others. Ruth's apprehension lightened momentarily. Perhaps he might sense something after all.

"No," Father Bishko said, in a matter-of-fact voice. "I sense nothing abnormal. But my gift does not lie along those lines, as I ought to have warned you."

"Nothing at all?" Pat asked. He was standing next to the slighter, shorter man and Ruth saw him give a quickly controlled shiver. The priest shook his head. Evidently he did not even feel the cold which was apparent to Pat.

Casually Bruce had wandered down the room into the entrance doorway, drawing Sara with him. From the gathering shadows of the hall his pale face, oddly distorted by the camouflaging beard, peered into the living room like a mask hanging on a wall.

"Before I go," Father Bishko said, "perhaps you would allow me to say a blessing. It can do no harm and—who knows?—it might do some good."

He bowed his head without waiting for the answer which common courtesy would have forced on Ruth. She was unable to speak. The formless apprehension had gripped her even more strongly than before, dulling all her senses but one. "Do no harm?" Or would it? She felt something now, just as, it is said, a few individuals sense an earthquake before the first tremor rips the earth apart. The signs were the same—the constricted, aching head, the breathlessness, the hushed air. And the sensation struck her dumb. She could not speak nor move, not even to call a warning.

Father Bishko, his eyes closed and his other senses apparently unresponsive, had no warning from within. Pat had fallen back a few paces at the beginning of the prayer—a rather childish attempt at dissociation, Ruth thought at the time—and when the darkening of the air became visible, he recoiled still farther.

Thus it was from Bruce, hitherto demurely silent, that the

shout came. He bellowed, "Father!" in a voice that would have roused the dead, and simultaneously the effect seemed to strike the priest. He opened his eyes then, to find himself face to face with a boiling, seething mass of blackness. It had taken shape with frantic speed—gathering strength with practice, Ruth wondered, or stimulated somehow by the presence of the priest? For Father Bishko, the effect was like waking from sleep to find a visage of dreadful, distorted hate pressed against one's own; the sudden shock of such abominable proximity would have been as bad as the horror itself. But this was infinitely worse; for few men can claim to have found themselves rubbing noses with evil incarnate.

Perhaps no human being could have withstood such a shock; and Father Bishko, despite his calling, was only human. He let out a high, shrill cry, and stumbled back; and the thing bubbled and slid after him.

Bruce's face disappeared, and then a flood of gray light poured into the hall as the front door opened. Ruth knew he was getting Sara out of the house.

Then she caught her breath as Father Bishko, in the doorway, turned at bay. She had never—as yet—seen a more magnificent exhibition of sheer courage, for the man was obviously frightened almost out of his wits. Shaking and pale, he nevertheless stood firm, and presented his crucifix to the face of the Adversary.

It stopped, swaying; again Ruth half expected to see a charred, smoking spot where it had been. For a second it seemed to shrink in, and she felt an upsurge of hope. But it was only gathering itself for the next move. With a sudden, jerking shiver it shook itself into a new shape. The column thickened and darkened, the top shrank and grew round; two projections shot out from a spot about three-fourths of the way up. Ruth cried out and threw her hands up before her eyes; in another moment the Thing would have had the form, but not the face, of a human being.

It was too much for flesh and blood to bear. Father Bishko finally broke, broke and ran, his face altering terribly, dropping the crucifix in his wild flight and sending Pat staggering back.

Not until that moment did Ruth realize that the sounds she had been hearing were coming from Pat. They were not cries of anger or fear, but they were, in a way, even more shocking. Pat was laughing.

## IV

"I'll never forgive myself," Ruth said. "Never."

They sat in Pat's dusty living room. All the feeble aids of physical comfort had been applied—a bright fire, brandy glasses and cigarettes, draperies pulled against the night. Night lights, as Bruce had said, for the frightened children. Each time the efficacy of the gestures grew less; each time it took more effort to shut out the memory of the inconceivable.

"You've no reason to reproach yourself." Pat's face was lined with chagrin. "I'm the one who should be ashamed. To laugh at a man at a time like that. . . . But, you know—if you had seen his face—"

"I did," Ruth said. "Pat, call him again."

"Honey, he must have gotten home, or to help of some kind. Bruce saw him catch a taxi."

"I was so worried about you, Ruth," Sara said. "I couldn't see how you were going to get out. But it just—went away?"

"Yes, as suddenly as it came. It came for him—Father Bishko—didn't it?"

"I'm afraid so," Bruce said tightly. The physical strain seemed to be telling on him, even more than on the others; his lean cheeks looked sunken, and the glitter in his eyes was almost feverish. Strangely enough it made him look younger instead of older.

"Why afraid?" Sara asked.

"Because the strength and rage are so violent. I swear, it looked like a deliberate attack. But that's not all. I didn't really believe any of the conventional symbols would affect it, but I guess I was still hoping. . . ."

"It means we've found that one potential weapon does not work," Pat agreed heavily.

"One? What potential weapons are there?" Ruth demanded.

"Oh, dozens, that's the trouble. The religious symbols are the most popular—crucifix, holy water, prayer—but there's garlic, iron, various herbs, beeswax, fire—you name it. You can get rid of an evil spirit by transferring it into a stone, or an animal. . . ."

"How?"

Pat glanced at her and laughed mirthlessly.

"I never imagined I'd use this book this way." He went to the bookcase by the fire and pulled out a worn green volume, one of a set that filled half the shelf. "Here's the encyclopedia of magical lore, the recipe book for witches, Frazer's *The Golden Bough.* I've acquired a few new ones, but he has most of the tricks right here."

"Are you ruling them all out because the crucifix had no effect?" Bruce asked. He joined Pat at the bookcase and took down another volume of the set.

"I'm not ruling anything out. I just don't know where to begin. But can you really bring yourself to believe that we should hang a chicken around Sara's neck and wait for Ammie to move into it?"

"Fire," Bruce muttered. "That doesn't seem very helpful in the present case, does it?" He flipped another page.

"I remember the iron bit," Sara said. "It's in that lovely Kipling book, is it *Puck of Pook's Hill,* or the sequel? 'Iron, cold iron, is the master of them all. . . .' "

"I loved that book too," Ruth said, momentarily diverted. "The fairy people can't stand iron; that's because they aren't cute little sprites in nylon petticoats, but the Old People, the little dark people who used bronze and were driven underground by the iron weapons of the new invaders."

"How cute," Bruce said crushingly, without lifting his eyes from the book.

"Something about running water, too," Sara muttered.

"Or we could acquire some masks and dance around Sara banging pots," Pat said with sudden violence. "How can one decide which of two impossibilities is more possible?"

Bruce looked up.

"I thought we had agreed that this is possible. Damned if I see why you cavil over a little thing like devil dances, if you admit devils. Or," he added gently, "do you?"

"Of course I'm still fighting it," Pat shouted. "Everything I've been taught for fifty years is fighting it. Danm it, Bruce, allow me my moments of sheer incredulity, can't you?"

"I'm not sure I can." Bruce closed the book but kept one finger inside the pages; Ruth was reminded of that other book and the circumstances of its discovery. "Pat, if you weaken. . . . We need all the belief we can get."

"I'm trying."

"Are you? Or do you begin to suspect, again, that we're hallucinating? You can't claim anything so simple as schizophrenia now. Not with that ghastly thing in the parlor every afternoon."

"I don't make any such claim, of course."

"There's another possibility," Bruce went on carefully. "One we've not mentioned, but one which I'm sure has occurred to you."

"Some natural phenomenon? Gas, or subterranean tremors, or something?"

"No, not something. I mean fraud. Deliberate, conscious fakery."

"I'd have been a fool not to have thought of it," Pat said.

Bruce put one hand casually on the back of a chair. Ruth was the only person near enough to see that he was inobtrusively supporting a good deal of his weight on that hand, and to note the tiny beads of sweat on his upper lip.

"We know you aren't a fool. All right, let's drag it out and look at it; I hate things festering in the subconscious. If it were fraud, who would be promoting it—besides Sara?"

Sara smiled; Ruth gave a gasp of protest.

"Naturally Sara would have to be in on it," Pat said calmly. "She's Ammie. The medium as well—the séance was the opening gun in the affair."

"I had the dream," Ruth said.

"That could have been induced—by the same phonograph record or tape that produces the 'Ammie-Come-Home' voice."

"You're crazy," Ruth said indignantly. "And the—the Adversary? I suppose that could be produced by a tape?"

"It could be produced," Bruce said coolly. "I don't know how, just off hand, but I'll bet any good stage magician could reproduce any of the effects we have seen. Including the cold."

"And the story of Douglass Campbell and his daughter, which we so painfully ferreted out?"

"If we found it, someone else could. Someone who used it as the basis of the plot."

"You'd make a good Devil's Advocate," Pat said, smiling

reluctantly. "Now you've got me turned around so that I have to defend the case. What about motive?"

"I can think of at least three possibilities, just off hand."

"One," Sara challenged.

"Someone wants to buy Ruth's house cheap," Bruce said promptly. "Buried treasure in the basement, maybe, or just a passion for old houses."

"Two?"

"Hatred. Of Ruth, or you, or even Pat. Get him mixed up in something like this and then expose it in a blaze of publicity. It wouldn't do his scholarly reputation much good. Three, some nut trying to prove spiritualism—and don't ask me to explain the kind of mentality that creates fakes to prove truths; I can't. I just know they exist."

"I see you've given the matter some thought," Pat said.

"I'm no fool either. Only I happen to know Sara wouldn't do such an insane thing. Of course there is that convenient item, hypnosis. Sara could be unwittingly producing her bit of the supernatural through posthypnotic suggestion."

"An outside villain?" Pat considered the suggestion.

"Not necessarily." Bruce cleared his throat. "I thought of you, naturally. In a mystery story you'd be the obvious suspect. You protest too much."

Pat choked; then his sense of humor came to the rescue, and he laughed.

"Okay, Bruce, you win again. We're committed. Let's be consistent in our folly, at least, and not waste time."

Bruce's breath came out in a louder gasp than was compatible with calm nerves. But he said coolly enough,

"Then let's look at Frazer. I balk myself at the Bantu ceremonies, but we could try some of the herbs. Vervain, Saint John's-wort, garlic—"

Sara giggled.

"What are you going to do, make a lei and hang it around my neck?"

"The big problem will be finding the stuff," Ruth said. "Garlic we can get, but vervain is not exactly in stock at the grocer's."

"You can look for it tomorrow," Bruce said. "It'll be a nice job, out in the open air for a change. Find out the scientific name of the stuff, it's in here someplace—" He was again flicking through the pages of Sir James Frazer's classic. "Funny," he muttered. "The standard remedies, in western culture, are the holy relics. We lost a big group there."

"You know," Sara said, "that reminds me of something I read—"

At the same time Pat remarked, "Maybe we need holier relics. A sliver of the True Cross or a bone of a saint."

And Ruth chimed in with, "Pat, do try to call him again!"

Faced with two people talking at once, Pat turned to Ruth. "Okay, dear. If it will make you feel better."

The telephone was on a table by the couch. They could all hear the muffled ringing at the other end, and they heard the ringing stop when the instrument was lifted.

"Dennie?" Pat's face lightened. He had not voiced his concern, for fear of encouraging Ruth's, but it had been profound. "Are you all right? Where've you been?"

The listeners could hear the tinny rattle of the other voice, but could not distinguish words. For them the conversation was one-sided but perfectly intelligible.

"I'm more relieved than I can say. . . . No, no, Dennie, you mustn't feel that way; quite the contrary. Mrs. Bennett has been beside herself with worry. . . . Yes, she's here. . . . Sure."

Ruth took the telephone with some trepidation. The priest brushed her stumbling apologies aside; he had other, more important things on his mind.

"Mrs. Bennett, I've made an appointment, the first of the necessary steps for the procedure we discussed. It will take a little time; this is a busy archdiocese. In the meantime, I want you to promise me that you won't enter that house again, or allow anyone else to do so."

"But, Father. . . ."

"I am . . . deeply shaken and ashamed. I do not say this in defense of my own behavior, but in fear for you—this visitation is strong, strong and evil. You must not risk yourself."

"I know the sensations are dreadful," Ruth said, very much moved. "But you saw it at its worst—and faced it, may I say, with a courage that few people could have shown. But it is impalpable; I'm sure it can't do any physical harm."

"Physical?" Father Bishko's voice rose. "My dear, my dear—that is not the danger. Promise me. I shan't sleep tonight unless I have your promise."

"I promise," she said; and then, on request, handed the instrument back to Pat. A few more sentences passed, and then Pat hung up.

"Poor guy," he said. "He's all shaken up."

"It might not do him any harm," Bruce said sharply. "A priest, enduring the universe, ought to be shaken up now and then. People ought to be shaken up."

"The trouble with the young," Pat remarked, "is not that they speak in platitudes, but that they are so damned intense about them."

"Don't, Pat."

"Sorry, dear. We are none of us at our best." He ran his fingers through his hair so that it stood up in the familiar cockatoo crest. "What did you promise?"

"That I wouldn't go back to the house. I had to," she said defensively. "He was genuinely distressed. And say what you will, I feel responsible. We should have warned him."

Bruce gave her a disdainful glance. He did not need to tell her that he did not feel himself bound by her promise. All he said was, "He's going to try the exorcism?"

"When he gets permission."

"I have to admit I admire his guts, then," Bruce said grumpily. "If a little bitty prayer produced that outburst today, God knows what a full-scale exorcism will bring out. I wouldn't care to face it myself."

"Maybe it will work. He seems to think so."

"He's going on the theory that if one pill doesn't do the trick, maybe six pills will," Bruce said. "I'm afraid this is a case of if one pill doesn't work, why bother with more? The technique is wrong. Sara, let's start on *The Golden Bough*."

It was like a well-rehearsed play, Ruth thought; take your places for Act One, Scene Two. They had only played these roles for a few days, but they had come to accept them. Sara found pen and paper; she made an unorthodox secretary, squatting cross-legged on the hearth rug, with the falling waves of her hair curtaining her face. Bruce, shoulder against the mantel, slim height lounging, moved his hands as he spoke; Pat slouched in his worn leather chair with the light setting the crest of his hair ablaze and leaving his face shadowed, remote. And Ruth herself was on her way to the kitchen to put the coffeepot on, so that the great minds might be stimulated to think. In the doorway she paused, appreciating the warmth and homely charm of the family scene: the vivid colors of Sara's forest green skirt and sweater, Pat's coppery bright hair, Bruce's black-and-white elegance, the glint of light off the silver bowl on the table. They might have been any comfortable family, chatting casually after dinner.

"Transference into a tree," Bruce said. "Bore a hole in the trunk, insert a lock of the sufferer's hair. Then plug up the hole. . . ."

Ruth didn't know whether to laugh or cry.

# Chapter

## 9

THEY ALL OVERSLEPT THE NEXT MORNING, AND TWO OF THEM refused breakfast.

"And it's not because I'm hung over, either," Ruth said sullenly. "I had the most ghastly dream last night—witch doctors in feathers and masks chasing Sara around a fire. It ended with somebody getting eaten, I'm not quite sure whom. Me, probably. I'll just have coffee, thanks."

Sara rose and obliged.

"I had a dream, too," she said; and something in her tone made the others stop in mid-swallow and mid-bite to look at her.

"Messages from the beyond?" Pat asked. His attempt at lightness was not a success.

"I don't know."

"Well, what did you dream?" Bruce asked.

Sara settled down with her elbows on the table. Ruth started to point out that her hair was unsanitarily involved with her plate of scrambled eggs, and then decided not to bother. There were obviously more important matters at stake.

"I dreamed I was in the house," Sara began. "Just walking through the rooms. I started out in the kitchen, and it looked funny; I mean, I couldn't make out any of the details, just the view of the garden. The room was all blurry and unshaped. Then I walked through the dining room and things got a little clearer, but the furniture was still shapeless blobs."

She paused, her eyes dark with memory, trying to choose her words.

"I couldn't see into the living room. There was like a curtain pulled over the doorway. In the hall things were still misty, but I noticed one thing. The cellar door was open."

"The cellar again," Bruce muttered. "Damn it, I just don't see. . . ."

Pat waved him to silence.

"Was that all you dreamed?"

"No, there was one bit more. I tried—I wanted—" Again she paused; she had gone a trifle pale. "This was the only bad part," she said. "I told you what happened in the dream, but I haven't described the atmosphere. The feeling of it. I was anxious all through this, but not really frightened; just—like trying to sneak something out of the house before Mother could catch me. But it kept building up, the anxiety, and when I was in the hallway I knew I was getting near the source of the trouble. I wanted to go into the living room. But I couldn't. Something held me back, something that almost gibbered with terror. Finally the struggle got to be too much. I woke up."

She took a large bite of toast, and Ruth said, in a voice that was tart with relief, "You don't seem particularly upset this morning."

"No, I told you it wasn't that bad," Sara said thickly.

"The cellar," Bruce mumbled. "It must mean something."

"What?" Pat demanded. "We looked once. There wasn't an extra cobweb that shouldn't have been there."

"Something under the cellar?" Sara said. Ruth looked at her, somewhat startled.

"Douglass Campbell's buried treasure?"

"God, I hope not," Bruce said morosely. "The floor is concrete. If we have to drill that out and then excavate the whole bloody floor area—"

"Our spirit guides are going to have to be a little more specific before I tackle that one," Pat agreed. "I suggest that if the dream does have meaning it lies in the latter part. The suggestion that there is something in the living room that we haven't found."

"Books?" Ruth guessed wildly. "There are more of Hattie's in the bookcase at the back, the same one the Maryland history book came from."

"It sounds crazy," Bruce said despondently. "But we might

as well look. I keep thinking that, with the old lady's interest in family, there ought to be more in the house that we've missed."

"I promised Father Bishko—"

"Well, I didn't," Bruce said. "I wouldn't consider such a promise binding, Ruth. I'd like you to come, if only to show me likely places to look, but you don't need to."

"Bruce is right," Pat said. "I don't consider myself bound by any such promise."

Bruce studied him thoughtfully; Ruth thought she could see the dark eyes weighing possibilities.

"There's something you could do that would be a helluva lot more useful."

"What's that?"

"Trot over to Annapolis," Bruce said.

"What the hell for?"

"State papers. I've gone through most of the material at the Library of Congress, but there are all kinds of local records at Annapolis. Two such collections—the Red and Blue Book papers—have letters relating to Georgetown people during this period. And somebody ought to look through the newspapers. *The Maryland Journal and Baltimore Advertiser* is the one covering our period, I think. They'll have it on microfilm at Annapolis."

Pat's face took on the stubborn look Ruth was coming to know so well. She could understand his reaction. Bruce was right; but his glibness and inclination to assume authority were extremely irritating.

"Why don't you go?"

"A, I don't have a car. B, I lack your academic prestige. And C," he added quickly, as Pat's mouth opened in protest, "I'm having trouble with my eyes and I'd rather not drive."

"I didn't know you had eye trouble," Sara said. "Bruce, what is it?"

"I have to use drops, and they blur my sight," Bruce said.

"But you never told me—"

"What do you expect me to do, give every girl I date a list of my physical disabilities? Forget it. Well, Pat?"

"I can hardly refuse, can I? Okay. I'd better start right away. It's getting late."

"We'll meet you back here about six," Bruce said. "The Hall of Records probably closes about four or five. We'll have left the other house by that time, so don't go there. Can you give us an extra key, in case we get here before you do?"

"All right," Pat said without enthusiasm.

He got up and promptly tripped over Lady, who was, as predicted, flat on the floor in front of her food dish.

"Stupid dog," Pat said automatically.

Lady moaned.

Bruce stared at the dog.

"Hey, Pat. Can we borrow Lady?"

"What in heaven's name for?"

"As a canary," Bruce explained.

Sara giggled, Ruth stared, and Pat explained, "He's not over the edge yet. They used to use birds in coal mines in the old days to detect the presence of lethal gases. Being so much smaller the birds passed out before the concentration got high enough to damage men. You may certainly borrow Lady, but you ought to consider three factors. First, you will probably have to carry her out to the car, and she weighs almost as much as Sara; second, we have no proof that the supposed sensitivity of animals to supernatural influences is anything more than an old wives' tale; third, even if most animals are sensitive, Lady is such a lump that she probably wouldn't stir if Satan himself came up and leered in her face."

"I'll risk it," Bruce said. "It's worth a try."

As she went in search of her purse and coat, Ruth knew that there was one implication of the dream which none of them cared to explore, or even comment upon. If Sara had been visited in sleep, then her immunity was broken. She was no safer out of the house than in it.

## II

Bruce refused Pat's offer to drive them to the house. Ruth felt almost certain that he had been lying about his eye trouble. The conclusion was inescapable: He did not want Pat to come with them. Why?

On the way over, Bruce made the taxi stop before a supermarket. He came out carrying a small bag and wearing a slightly sheepish expression. He refused to let Sara see what was in the bag. She took it as a joke, teasing and pretending to snatch; but

Ruth could not enter into the game. Doubt assailed her. Was it possible that, after all, she had been led astray, her weakness expertly played upon by an unscrupulous or deranged young man? When they reached the house it took all her willpower to force her to enter. With every visit the atmosphere got worse; the whole house now seemed to vibrate with sounds just below the range of hearing, the air to quiver with unseen forces. Her newborn doubts made the situation even more unpleasant.

Once inside, however, Bruce seemed to improve. At least his odd behavior about his purchase was explained, to Ruth's satisfaction, when she saw what it was. Bruce opened the bag in the kitchen and produced a handful of objects that looked like little gray-white oranges.

"Garlic!" Sara said, with a whoop of laughter. Then she suddenly sobered. "Oh, no, you're not," she said, backing away. "Oh, no!"

"Oh, yes." Bruce eyed his purchase doubtfully. "Ruth, have you got a drill? I don't know how else—"

"I think a big darning needle," Ruth said, smiling. "I suppose you want to release the juices? Otherwise we could just tape the bits all over her."

Sara exclaimed in outrage, and Bruce began to laugh.

"What a gaudy picture! We'll settle for the conventional necklace."

When it was done, Sara studied herself critically in the mirror and admitted, "It's not bad. I've seen worse-looking things in those psychedelic shops on Wisconsin."

"And you could always give away a free set of nose plugs with each ensemble," Ruth suggested, pinching her nostrils together.

"I don't know what you're complaining about," Sara said. "You're a lot farther away from it than I am. Luckily I like the smell of garlic."

They dragged the banter and laughter out a little too long, reluctant to leave the warm modernity of the kitchen for that other room. But when they entered, they found Lady stretched out in front of the fireplace, and Ruth's spirits rose. Up to this point they had not found the conventional trappings of the supernatural particularly reliable, so Lady's calm was meaningless until it had been tested—an eventuality which Ruth hoped would never occur. But she felt, somehow, that it would be impossible for anything to look so comfortable unless the room really was clear. Bruce obviously felt the same way; he made a detour just to scratch Lady behind the ears. She twitched one of the ears feebly but made no other acknowledgment, and Bruce said, as he straightened, "That dog manages to convey the impression that she's worn out from a hard day's work. I wish I knew how to do it."

"It makes me feel one hundred percent better just to look at her," Ruth said. "Now. Where do we start?"

"Here." Bruce advanced upon the bookcase.

They found several astounding things, including a copy of *Ruth Fielding in the Rockies,* whose cover showed an adventurous damsel in long skirts and a pompadour preparing to mount a horse. Sara appropriated this masterpiece, and sat chortling over it for some time, reading excerpts aloud.

"It's the old-time equivalent of Nancy Drew," she said. "Imagine Cousin Hattie keeping this around."

"Who's Nancy Drew?" Bruce asked, distracted.

"The girl's equivalent of the Hardy Boys," Ruth said. "Bruce, here's something called *Recollections of Old Georgetown.*"

"No soap. I looked through it at the library." Bruce got up off the floor in one effortless movement. "Nothing else. Let's try the attic."

Ruth groaned with dismay at the sight of the place; she had forgotten how many articles had been put away "till I have time to sort through them." There were boxes and cartons and old trunks and suitcases; there was a dress form, and a chair with one leg broken, and a sofa that had lost most of its stuffing. There was an untidy stack of old pictures. . . .

"I wonder," Bruce said, heading toward them, "if anybody we know is here?"

Nobody was. The pictures were daguerreotypes of desperately bearded gentlemen and grim-faced ladies, or engravings of classical subjects in funereal black frames.

"You wouldn't find anything that old in the attic," Ruth said, as Bruce tossed the last of the pile aside with a gesture of disgust. "Colonial portraits are chic; they would be downstairs."

"I can't help wondering what she looked like," Bruce murmured. Ruth nodded.

"I know. I've wondered too. But it would be too much luck to discover a portrait of her."

"I guess so. Well . . . I'll take the big trunk, you take the little one."

They worked steadily for three more hours and then stopped for a quick lunch. Lady roused at that—Sara swore she heard the can opener being removed from the drawer—and dragged herself out to the kitchen to indicate that she might consider joining them. Bruce pointed out that she was only supposed to be fed twice a day, but the argument convinced neither Lady nor Sara, who persisted in sneaking tidbits to her under the table.

The hours in the airless, dusty attic had given Ruth a headache, so after lunch they adjourned to the living room, whither Bruce had taken several promising-looking cartons. They spent an unprofitable and increasingly tedious afternoon reading yellowing newspapers and clippings of recipes, fashions and gossip columns—all fascinating under most circumstances, but none dating back to the period they were interested in. Finally Ruth's eyes gave out; she rose, stretching cramped muscles, and went to draw the drapes. The sunlight was too explicit; it showed the dust on tables and bookcases.

"Don't do that," Bruce said, looking up. "I don't want to lose track of the time. You ought to have a clock in this room."

"Don't you trust the garlic?" Sara asked lightly.

"No, and I suspect Pat may be right about Lady. She doesn't look very sensitive."

"She wants me to light the fire," Sara said.

Bruce gave the recumbent rump of Lady a disparaging glance.

"How can you tell?"

"She communicates. Telepathy."

"Go ahead and light it," Ruth said. "It seems chilly in here to me. . . ."

She stopped, with a catch of breath, but Bruce shook his head.

"No, it's not that kind of cold. I turned the thermostat down when we came in."

Sara crawled over to the fire, and soon the flames were leaping up. Lady grunted appreciatively and rolled over.

"Stupid dog," Sara said affectionately.

"Are you giving up?" Bruce asked severely. "There are two more boxes upstairs."

"We'd better have some coffee," Ruth said. "I'm falling asleep over this stuff."

When she came back with the tray she found her assistants in a state of semicollapse, Sara in her favorite prone position before the fire and Bruce stretched out vertically across the couch like an exclamation mark. They stirred when she put the tray down.

"I guess we'd better not start another box," Bruce said, with a wide yawn. "Wait a minute. There was one thing I did want to look at. The cellar."

"But we've been down there," Ruth said. The coffee had revived her a bit, but she was not fond of the gloomy basement.

"One more look." Bruce's beard jutted out in a way which was becoming too familiar.

"Shall we take Lady?" Sara asked.

"Not unless you feel like carrying her down. I don't."

At Bruce's suggestion Ruth found a flashlight and located a hammer and screwdriver in the pantry drawer when he asked for tools. He gave the screwdriver back to her but kept the hammer; and when they had descended the stairs he began banging on the walls.

"My dear boy," Ruth said, amused.

"We've tried everything else." Bruce vanished behind the furnace. The beam of the flashlight wavered like a big firefly, and steadied. "By God! Ruth, come here."

"Not on your life." Ruth advanced to the side of the furnace and peered behind it. "What's back there?"

She could see for herself. No one had made any attempt to hide it, but she had never poked her nose into the dark, spidery corner.

"A door. Where does it go to, I wonder?"

Bruce gave the encrusted wooden panel an exploratory tap with the hammer. The sound that came back was not encouraging; it had a solid thunk that denied any idea of empty space.

"The panels must be six inches thick," he said. "This isn't a door, it's a barricade. And it's going to be a helluva job breaking it down."

"Why should we want to break it down?" Ruth asked in surprise. "This part of the cellar is bad enough."

Bruce sneezed violently and wiped his face with his sleeve.

He backed out of the corner. His eyes were bright with excitement and his beard was draped with cobwebs.

"The outer part of the cellar only goes under the dining-kitchen area. This other section must lie beneath the living room. Once upon a time somebody was moved to block it off. That would be reason enough to explore it, even without the other clues."

"Oh, dear," Ruth said blankly. "I don't think I like this."

"I don't either. I'm the one who'll have to swing the ax. But it's got to be done."

"Bruce, I don't even own an ax. There's a little hatchet someplace. . . ."

"No, I'll have to pick up some tools. This is going to be a rough job. And I don't intend to start today, it's getting late. Why don't we—"

At the top of the cellar stairs the door stood open. They heard the sounds at the outer, street door—the turn and click of the knob, the slam of the door closing. Footsteps echoed in the hall.

Ruth's reaction was puzzlement rather than alarm. Those sounds were not connected in her mind with the manifestations. Bruce's response alarmed her more than the sounds. He made a convulsive movement with the flashlight in his right hand. The footsteps were on the stairs now. Before Ruth had time to be frightened Pat's familiar form came into view.

"I thought you'd still be here," he said. "Wait till you hear—"

"I told you not to come to the house," Bruce said shrilly.

"I finished early." Pat raised his eyebrows and sat down unceremoniously on the bottom step. "What are you all doing down here?"

"Bruce found another part of the cellar," Sara explained. "There's a door, all blocked up, behind the furnace."

"Really?" Pat's eyebrows shot up to his hairline. He stood up and wandered over to investigate the discovery, and Ruth felt her neck prickle, for as the older man passed him, Bruce made another of those abortive, violent gestures.

"I can't see much." Pat drew back. "It's not important anyhow."

"How do you know it's not?" Bruce asked.

"Because today I found out the missing parts of the story."
Pat beamed, waiting for the effect of his verbal bombshell to be
felt. "I know what happened to Amanda Campbell."

"Really? Pat, that's marvelous."

"How did you find out?"

The two women spoke at once. Bruce said nothing.

Pat propped himself up against the wall.

"It was in the newspaper," he said. "Amazing, eh? I found it
right away; if I were endowed with psi faculties, I'd think I had
been led to it."

He took a deep breath, prepared, it was clear, to launch into
a detailed account.

"Let's go to your place and you can tell us all about it,"
Bruce said.

Pat glared.

"You trying to spoil my effect? What's the matter—mad because the wild goose chase laid a golden egg after all?"

"Pat, of course we're pleased," Ruth said hastily. "I'm dying
to know. What did happen to Ammie?"

Pat's scowl relaxed.

"You were right, Ruth, I'll never sneer at your intuition
again. She did elope. Wait a minute, let me read this to you. It's
classic. I copied it word for word."

He searched the pockets of his overcoat and jacket before
he found the paper. Bruce moistened his lips nervously and
shifted from one foot to the other. Ruth met his eye and
shrugged slightly. Short of picking him up bodily she did not
see how they were going to move Pat. He was never very
amenable to suggestion, and this afternoon he seemed so delighted by his find that he was more stubborn than ever. Undoubtedly the boy's earlier successes had riled him; he was
prepared to rub this one in just a bit.

"Here it is," Pat said, unfolding his paper. "You know, I
didn't realize they did this sort of thing back in Colonial times.
It's like a 'Whereas' ad in a modern newspaper, only much
more detailed." He cleared his throat and began to read:

"With regret and shame the undersigned finds himself under the necessity of advertising his daughter. Painful though it
may be to a fond parent, he does by these presents make known
that Amanda, his daughter, has eloped from his house with one

Anthony Doyle, Captain in the Army of Independence, who has long attempted to seduce her from her faith and her loving duty to her parent, and has finally succeeded; for which her disconsolate father does not hold her to blame, but promises that, should she discover her error and regret her sin, she shall be received into his home without question." Pat glanced up. "The signature," he concluded, "I leave to your imaginations."

"Douglass Campbell," Ruth whispered. "Oh, Pat, you were right too—the poor man."

"You two are prejudiced," Sara said, lifting a firm chin. "You always side with the parents. I think it was frightful of him to make a public announcement of her elopement!"

"The ad was meant for her," Pat said. "Can't you read the real meaning? He wasn't trying to shame her, he wanted her to know that she could always come home."

"That's sweet, I'm sure," Sara said impudently. "But I'll bet she was glad to get away. Who wouldn't prefer a dashing Irishman, and an officer at that, to a dull dad?"

"Perhaps the young man had tried to court her properly," Ruth said, trying to be fair; she was somewhat stung by Sara's remark about prejudice. "And Douglass considered him unsuitable."

"Naturally," Pat said. "He was Catholic."

"How do you—oh, that business about seducing her from her faith. And it's an Irish name, of course. . . ."

"A Catholic and a Patriot," Pat said. "Campbell was a fiercely intolerant Protestant and a Tory. She couldn't have picked a more unpopular combination in a boyfriend."

"You're awfully damn dogmatic about your deductions," Bruce said spitefully.

"They seem quite reasonable to me," Ruth said, trying to make peace; Pat's face had darkened again.

"Okay, okay," Bruce mumbled. "Do you mind if we—"

"I wonder what Doyle was doing in Georgetown?" Sara said. "Were there any battles in these parts?"

"There must have been a detachment guarding the British prisoners," Pat said. "He may have been in command of that."

"We might look him up," Ruth suggested. "Aren't there army records? We don't even know where he came from. Maybe he took Ammie home, wherever home was."

"Camden, New Jersey," Pat said absently. He was staring at the furnace with his forehead slightly furrowed, as if some new, disturbing thought had just entered his mind.

"Was that in the newspaper too?" Bruce asked. He had become very still, the nervous gestures in abeyance; and his eyes seemed to want to follow Pat's gaze toward the blocked and hidden door.

Pat did not reply. Bruce walked toward him, stepping delicately.

"Pat, could we—look, I don't know what time it is, but it must be late. Can't we adjourn now?"

"Sure," Pat said. "It's a nasty night out, though. It started to rain when I turned off Wisconsin, and the wind is rising."

The words were simply descriptive; there was no reason why they should have created such an unpleasant picture in Ruth's mind. When she reached the top of the stairs she could not repress an exclamation of dismay. The splintered reflection of the streetlight brightened the fanlight over the door. It was not quite night, but it was too near to be comfortable—dusk, twilight, deepening into darkness. She plunged toward the hall closet where they had left their coats, calling Sara.

Bruce was the third person up the stairs, and he was as anxious as Ruth to be gone. Pat, still carrying his coat, followed them obediently along the hall. Ruth thought he seemed subdued, and attributed it to their reception of his news. She promised herself she would make it up to him as soon as they reached a safe place.

Safe. . . . The house was not. She could almost hear the humming, like an electric motor, plugged in and building up a charge. . . .

"Wait a minute," Pat said, as Bruce reached for his raincoat. "Where's that stupid dog?"

"Oh, goodness, I almost forgot her." Ruth, already wearing coat and hat, went back toward the living room. It was in darkness except for a faint glow from the fire, but she could make out Lady's silhouette, like a low lump, against the reddish glare. She switched on the lights.

"Come on, baby," Pat said.

Bruce dropped his coat.

"I'll get her. Pat, why don't you go on out and—uh—get the car started?"

"The car'll start when I want it to," Pat said, giving him a puzzled look. "Get up, Lady, come with Papa."

Ruth stood just inside the doorway, her hand still on the light switch. As she watched Bruce her suspicion and alarm came back in double strength. He was so nervous that she expected momentarily to see him start wringing his hands. He vibrated distractedly just outside the door, looking from Sara, who watched him in growing bewilderment, to Pat, who was nudging the dog's snoring form with his toe. Indecisiveness was not normally one of Bruce's problems.

"I am not going to carry you," Pat told his dog. She was not visibly moved by the statement.

Bruce hunched his shoulder, in a gesture that resembled a shudder, and made up his mind. He plunged into the room like a swimmer entering a lake in December.

"I'll carry her," he said. "Pat, you go on and—"

"Are you crazy?" Pat demanded. "She'll walk, it just takes me a while. . . ."

"She'll come for me," Sara said. She threw her coat down on a chair and entered the living room. "Lady, baby, come to Sara."

They were all there. It came to Ruth with the sharpness of a blow in the face. They were all in the living room and night crouched outside the walls. She could hear the wind moaning like a frightened child around the eaves, and through the trees, lashing the windows with raindrops.

"Sara," she said, her voice strangely hoarse. "Sara."

At the same moment Pat bent over to touch the dog.

Lady roused. She came up stiff-legged and aware, in the instantaneous response to peril which no human being can learn. Her haunches had been under the coffee table; she sent it over, spilling decanter, glasses, and ashtrays. Ruth did not even glance at the havoc. She had eyes only for the dog—for Lady, the somnolent, who stood with every hair on her neck up and bristling, with lips drawn back to display long ivory fangs. Her dark eyes were fixed on her master, and for a moment Ruth thought the hundred pounds of bone and muscle and tearing fangs were about to spring. But what happened was, in its way, infinitely worse. The snarl in Lady's throat changed to a horrible whine. She dropped to her belly and began to crawl, whimpering like a puppy. When she had cleared the couch she sprang up and fled. Ruth heard the crash of the heavy body against the front door, and the howl, the almost human howl of frustration and terror when the door refused to yield. Then there was another muffled crashing sound, and silence.

Ruth had no conscious memory of having moved. Her body had simply recoiled, with the same sort of reflex that jerks a hand back from a licking flame. There was no way out through the door, it was too perilously close to the spot where, once again, the foul blackness seethed and coiled. It was stronger tonight, worse than she had yet seen it, as if it drew strength from each successive appearance. And the cold beat at them in pulsating, paralyzing waves.

"The French doors," a voice said. "Out . . . into garden. . . ."

Ruth's retreat had carried her halfway down the length of the room. She stood pressed up against the wall, next to the round piecrust table. She could not turn her back on the blackness, nor could she bring herself to look at it directly; it contaminated the air by its very existence; it was an affront, a violation of normalcy so acute that it amounted to blasphemy.

And Pat was facing it. Ruth felt a touch of dim pride that penetrated even her terror as she saw him stop after the first automatic withdrawal. His face was hard and expressionless; his feet were planted widely apart, like those of a man thigh-deep in racing water.

By contrast, Bruce made a pitiable showing. Stumbling, making odd inarticulate sounds, dragging Sara by the hand, he retreated toward the tall French doors at the end of the room. When he reached them he dropped Sara's hand and began struggling with the catch that held the windows closed. The clumsiness of fear frustrated his intent; the catch refused to give, and when Bruce brought his fist down on it, his hand slipped, slamming into one of the glass panes. The glass broke, letting in a gust of freezing rain; and Bruce pulled back a hand that was streaming blood from half a dozen cuts. He held it up before his face, staring blindly.

"Bruce—wait—" Ruth found speech incredibly difficult. Her vocal cords, like her other muscles, seemed frozen.

The boy heard her; he whirled around, his movements still erratic and undisciplined. Then his expression changed, altering his features so terribly that if Ruth had met him on the street she would not have recognized him. He plunged forward; his hands clawed at Pat's sleeve.

"Pat . . . don't. For God's sake—"

"It can't hurt," Pat said dully. "Can't hurt me. Let go. Got to do something. . . ."

"Don't . . . no . . . stop. . . . Pat, wait, let me tell you—"

Pat's rigidly controlled expression did not change. He simply lifted his heavy shoulders and heaved. Bruce went reeling back, missing the fireplace by two feet, and hit the wall so hard that one of the pictures fell with a crash.

There had been no sound from Sara; Ruth could see her at the edge of her vision, standing near the window, staring blank-faced. Ruth's time-sense was completely distorted; the scene seemed to have been going on forever, yet she knew everything was happening very quickly. Pat was on the move even before Bruce's body struck the wall. The column of darkness did not move as he came toward it. It waited. It did not menace or threaten, rather it shrank in on itself like—

Like a coiled spring. The analogy completed itself in Ruth's muddled brain, as the spring was released.

Standing off to one side, she had a clear unobstructed view of what happened. But at the final moment something fogged her eyes—mercifully, for such things were not meant to be seen, could not be seen in safety. When her vision cleared, the coiling smoke had disappeared. But it was not gone. It looked at her from Pat's eyes.

Ruth heard the whistling exhalation of Sara's breath, and the sound of her body dropping to the floor. She wished she could faint too. Pat was a big man, tall and heavily built. He looked bigger now. His hunched shoulders seemed hulking and swollen.

The eyes—not his eyes—saw her, and were indifferent, and passed on. But that one fleeting contact with the venom of the Adversary, now concentrated and focused, wiped every emotion out of her except for a sneaking, cowardly relief: She was not in Its direct path; It did not want her. She fell to her knees, huddled like an embryo, making herself small. Anything to avoid meeting, ever again, the blackness of its regard.

From first to last her heart had not measured more than a dozen beats. It took Bruce that long to get his breath back and to move out, from the opposite wall, into Its path.

Movement seemed difficult for It. Its steps dragged. It stopped when Bruce barred Its way, and raised Its heavy head to look at him; and Ruth saw him jerk back and fling a hand up before his face. She knew the impact of that gaze; and she knew the effort it cost Bruce to stay where he was, on his feet, and to lower his shielding hand. The change in his demeanor, from the terrified panic which had driven him, woke an answering spark in Ruth's brain. Now that the thing he most feared had happened—the thing he alone of them all had seemed to foresee—he was ready to face it. Slowly and painfully Ruth began to drag herself erect. That brand of courage demanded all the support she could give it.

Even as she swayed to her feet the final transformation came, the great overshadowing of the present by the shapes of the dead past. The bodies of the two men seemed to waver and grow insubstantial. They were the same, but not quite the same; surely, she knew, these two, or two others identical in intent, had stood like this, in silent confrontation, once before. The older man, a heavy, hulking shape, head lowered like a bull ready to charge, fists clenched, arms dangling at his sides; the younger, slender and poised in breeches and ruffled shirt, the long blade in his right hand ready but not yet raised, his coat discarded in the warmth of a spring night. . . .

A gust of air from the shattered pane struck Ruth's face, and her mind went reeling; for the air was not the damp cold air of a winter night in Washington. It was balmy and fragrant with the scent of lilac: the smell of an April night which had passed out of time two centuries before.

# Chapter
## 10

"CALL HIM, RUTH."

The voice came from far away. Ruth shook her head, feeling the soft spring breeze against her closed eyelids. The fragrance of lilac filled the room, heavy and sweet.

"Call him. Call his name. Ruth, please. Help me."

The voice was nearer now, and somehow familiar. It was a man's voice. The wind touched her face. . . .

The wind was cold, carrying rain. Ruth opened her eyes.

She was looking straight at Bruce, who stood swaying on unsteady feet, his face ashen and his eyes fixed unblinkingly on that other face, as if the force of his gaze held it back. Then the looming form took a step forward, and Bruce's right arm lifted. Blood still dripped from the cuts on his hand; his stained fingers were tight around the handle of the poker from the fireplace set.

"Call him, Ruth, see if you can get through to him. . . . I don't want to have to kill him. . . ."

As the Other moved again, Bruce fell back a step, casting a frantic glance over his shoulder. He could not retreat much farther. Behind him was the closed window, and Sara, sprawled like a dead woman against the wall.

"Pat," Ruth said. "Pat, it's me, Ruth. Can you hear me?"

For an instant she thought the heavy shoulders shifted. Only for an instant.

"Pat—darling. Listen to me. Pat. . . ."

"It's no use," Bruce said. "Ruth, get out of the way. It's as strong as an ox. It doesn't know you. . . . God!"

The last word was a gasp, half-drowned by the rush of the heavy body across the carpet. It was quick, for all Its bulk, and Bruce was slowed by a fatal handicap—the body It occupied. Ruth had not even thought of it as Pat; it was so unlike him in all the significant ways. Yet the head at which Bruce aimed the poker was Pat's red head. He brought the weapon up in a whistling arc; but he could not bring it down. And in the instant of hesitation, the thing was upon him.

They went crashing backwards together. The impact of the fall, and of the heavy body on top of him, knocked Bruce out as he hit the floor. He lay still, face upturned and eyes closed, the poker fallen from his hand, while the blunt fingers settled around his bared throat, and squeezed.

Ruth was so close that she could see the separate reddish hairs on the backs of the hands, red-gold lifted threads in the lamplight—the same light which fell brilliantly on Bruce's face; and she watched while his cheeks and forehead turned from white to mottled red, and darkened.

Forever afterward she was to wonder what will guided her hand—blind luck, or unconscious knowledge, or—something else. The object her groping fingers lifted from the table at her side was heavy enough to stun, and necessity guided her aim. But there was this, and she would never forget it: As the Book left her grasp, the thing that crouched on the floor reared up, lifting clawed hands in menace or protest, Its face upraised, Its mouth stretched in a snarl. The massive volume struck It full in the face, obliterating Its features momentarily, and then dropped back onto Bruce's chest. The Thing followed the book down, falling flat across the boy's body; but not before Ruth had caught one glimpse of a face which was, once again, the face she knew, gone lax in unconsciousness.

She ran forward, avoiding the fallen figures. The window latch gave sweetly, and she shrank back, throwing her arms up before her face, as the wind shrieked in, snatching the double leaves of the window and hurling them back against the wall. The lash of the cold rain stung her forehead; the blowing drapes bellied out like live things.

She heard Sara groan and stir as the freezing damp struck her face, but she had no time for lesser casualties. Pat was lying face down on the floor, arms out above his head. She caught him under the arms and tugged. Nothing happened, his dead weight was too much for her. She transferred her grip to one wrist, straightened up, and leaned back on her heels. The heavy body moved a few inches.

Ruth gasped with terror and frustration. She had to get him out of here before he woke, and the rough handling itself might rouse him faster.

She heard a gasp and a whimper from Sara, and turned. The girl was on her feet, one hand twisted in the lashing folds of the drapes. She was staring wide-eyed at Bruce. The dusky color had faded from the boy's face, but the marks of Pat's hands, and nails, were plain on his throat. He wouldn't be of any help for a while, Ruth thought coldly. She reached out and caught Sara by a strand of black hair as the girl stumbled past her.

"He'll be all right, there's no time for that now, I need help," she said, in one breath, as Sara's head jerked back and she gave a squeal of pain. "Take his other arm. Hurry, for God's sake, before he wakes up."

Sara gave one agonized look at Bruce and obeyed.

Between them they got Pat as far as the windows, and there Sara got some of her wits back.

"He'll catch pneumonia," she said, between chattering teeth. "And it's t-t-ten feet down into the rosebushes. Ruth, you can't—"

"Oh, yes, I can." Pat was beginning to mutter and move. Fear gave the final surge of strength to Ruth's muscles. She grabbed his legs and shifted him so that he lay across the ledge; after that one good hard push was all it took.

From the sounds, she could tell that he had landed, and hard. She turned on Sara and caught her by the shoulders.

"Out you go," she said, and shoved.

She did not wait to see what happened, but whirled in the same movement and ran back to where Bruce lay. She dropped to her knees beside him; but her shaking concern was not for the unconscious boy. It was the poker in his hand that she wanted. If Pat tried to climb back through the window she would have to use it.

The sounds from outside, audible even over the sigh of the wind, were reassuring. Pat was plainly awake now, he was thrashing and bellowing in the bushes; but the tone of his fury was obviously, blessedly, Pat and no one else.

The handle of the poker was unpleasantly sticky when Ruth touched it; when she pulled her fingers back, they were smeared with red. Bruce's hand had stopped bleeding, but it was a gory mess. She had not been able to bring herself to look at his face for, despite her reassurance of Sara, she feared he was dead. But she could not leave him without so much as a glance; pity and affection and profound gratitude finally broke the shell of ice that had shielded her, and the tears began to slide down her cheeks as she shifted, still on her knees, to where she could touch his face.

# II

The car slid jerkily through a red light and went on.

"It's a good thing there isn't any traffic," Ruth said, with a shaky laugh. "I'm not at my best tonight."

Her efforts at conversation fell flat. In the back seat Sara was too preoccupied with Bruce to hear an explosion. He was awake, but his sole remark so far had been to the effect that his head felt as if it were about to fall off and roll across the floor. Ruth was not too concerned about him; since the moment when her hand had touched his cheek and his eyes had opened and stared quizzically at her, she had simply thanked heaven for the resilience of youth.

It was Pat she was worried about—Pat, who sat hunched and silent beside her, his head bent and his eyes focused on his own limp hands, where they hung between his knees. One of the reasons why she had run the red light was the certainty that a sudden halt would have flung him against the windshield.

It took them some time to get settled down after they reached Pat's house. First aid and dry clothes were the immediate needs, and Ruth had to tend to the dog, whom she had found shivering and pathetically subdued by the front door and had bundled into the car with the other wounded. Lady seemed to feel that a hearty snack would do wonders for her nerves, so Ruth took the hint, and also scrambled eggs and made coffee for the others. Finally she had them all settled down before the fire. Sara, in her green velvet, looked unbelievably normal. Seeing her clear eyes and unmarked skin, Ruth felt another deep surge of gratitude for the boy who occupied the couch.

They had bedded Bruce down though Ruth suspected, from the gleam in his eye, that he had no intention of remaining down. He was the most battered of the lot; there was a lump the size of an egg on the back of his head, and the marks on his throat had begun to darken.

Pat's injuries were superficial. His face and arms were crisscrossed with scratches from the rosebushes. All down the bridge of his nose, extending across his forehead, was a curious reddening and roughening of the skin. Ruth told herself that this must have come from the harsh nap of the carpet when she had dragged him. Oddly enough, however, there was no corresponding patch on his chin, and this area, it seemed to her, would have borne the brunt of the rubbing.

Whatever its origin, the physical manifestation was only a chafing of the skin. What frightened Ruth was the look in Pat's eye, and the frightening formality of his manner. He moved like something that had to be wound up, and was almost run down. It was not the overshadowing that she feared now. She knew what was tormenting him; and she gave Bruce a look of furious reproach when he said in his frog's croak, "You've got a grip like a wrestler, Pat. No more soapboxes for me for a few days. Talk about a fate worse than death!"

"Bruce—" Ruth began.

"It's all right," Pat said. "We might as well discuss the fact. The fact that tonight I tried to kill Bruce and almost succeeded."

"It wasn't you," Sara said.

Pat lifted his hands before his face and looked at them.

"Your hands but not your will," Ruth said intensely. "You're no more responsible than someone under hypnosis."

"A hypnotized subject," Pat quoted, "cannot be made to do anything against his will."

It was as if he had plucked the words out of a box of alphabet letters and arranged them on the table for their inspection.

After a moment Bruce said, "I've heard that theory questioned, as a matter of fact. But it's irrelevant. You weren't hypnotized. You were being used, just as a gun is used by the man who squeezes the trigger." The lecture ended in a squawk as his vocal cords protested, and he added, in a voice which was less formal and far more convincing, "Hell, Pat, don't be morbid. I know you think I'm a pain in the neck, but you wouldn't try to kill me under any circumstances, in your right mind or out of it."

There was a clicking sound from the hall, like steel knitting needles, and they all looked up as the dog padded sedately into the room. She stood next to the fireplace regarding them all in turn, with her red tongue lolling; then she walked over to Pat and collapsed at his feet with a weary sigh, putting her chin on his shoe.

Pat reached down and patted the dog's big head. When he straightened up his expression was almost normal.

"I wonder what she thinks of it all," he said. "Has she already forgotten, or does she shrug mentally and write it all off as human folly, beyond a sensible dog's comprehension?"

"No," Ruth said with conviction. "She's welcoming you back. She knows that wasn't you, back there. Pat, you have no idea—I can't explain—how alien It was."

"Trouble was," Bruce croaked, "it was your body wrapped around the damn thing. I couldn't bring myself to smash your skull."

"I appreciate your consideration, believe me. But if you didn't stop me, who did? I feel like Snoopy, I don't even know what was going on. I could feel the thing come into me, and it was just as Sara said—something pouring in, filling me up, something that didn't quite fit. That was a bad moment, the thing was so ravenously triumphant; and after that I don't remember a thing."

"I stopped you," Ruth said. She held out her hands. "So don't give us any more of your melodrama. How the hell do you think I feel about these hands of mine?"

"Language, language." Pat grinned at her and took her shaking hands into his own scratched palms. "When I came up out of that hellish rosebush you were hovering in the window with the poker. Would you really have used it?"

"Yes."

"Thanks." He lifted her hands to his face and then held them on his knee. Ruth moved closer and the dog, drowsing, made a soft grumbling noise.

"I missed the exciting part myself," Bruce remarked. "What did you do, Ruth? Not that I mind being outsmarted by a mere woman, but still. . . ."

"I threw the Book at him," Ruth said, and then gave an astonished gasp of laughter. "Sorry about that. . . . I did, literally. It was the big family Bible."

"That must have been some pitch," Pat said. "I didn't think

the Book was massive enough to knock me out. It's big, and clumsy, but. . . ."

"I don't know!" Ruth exclaimed. "I wonder. . . . But it couldn't be that. The crucifix didn't work. . . ."

"I wonder myself," Bruce said. He was sitting up, despite Sara's objections; wrapped in one of Pat's wilder robes, a silk paisley affair that must have been a Christmas present because it had so obviously never been worn, he looked like an Eastern prince instead of a Spanish grandee.

"You know what really burns me?" Pat asked. "Not my attempted murder so much as my incredible stupidity. Bruce, you knew what was going to happen; you tried to stop me; I remember that much. You expected this."

"Suspect is the word, not expect. But—my God!—I died a thousand deaths trying to get you out of that room before it happened. I was sweating bullets."

"Why the hell didn't you tell me?"

Bruce flung out his hands. His eyes were wide and dark with the memory of that terrible frustration.

"How could I? You wouldn't have believed me, any of you. I didn't have a fact to my name, just a crazy hunch. . . . And you're so bloody bull-headed, Pat, you'd have stuck around just to show me."

"Hmmmph," Pat muttered. He cocked his head, eyebrows lifted, and studied the younger man with unwilling respect. "What made you suspect?"

"Oh, don't be so stinking humble; you couldn't have seen it coming—don't you understand? You were already half-shadowed."

Ruth moved, with a soft questioning sound, and Bruce nodded gravely at her.

"Yes, the night he had you down on the couch was the first time. I gather you were all wound up in certain private emotions, so you didn't see, as I did, how nasty it looked. It was out of character for Pat, very much out of character, especially with you—it was pretty obvious that he was getting—uh—sentimental about you. I mean, there are women you seduce and women you rape, and the women you—"

"You make your point," Pat said, trying to maintain a feeble semblance of dignity, although his face was almost as red as his hair.

"Oh. Well, the second time was when Father Bishko ran. You may not be devout, but you're polite. Your behavior on that occasion, again, was alarmingly atypical. But tonight, in the cellar, you really scared hell out of me. You kept coming up with those odd flashes of intuition, bits of knowledge you couldn't possibly have known—unless you were in some sort of contact with It, getting Its thoughts."

"Yes, I see," Pat said thoughtfully. "Amanda failed with Sara. She had to try someone else."

"No!" Bruce's voice rose. "No, Pat, you still don't get it. You've got it wrong. We all have it wrong. We were on the wrong track from the beginning."

In the silence the crackling and hissing of the flames were the only sounds, except for the dog's comfortable snoring breaths. Ruth never forgot the picture they made, her friends and allies, wearing their battle scars and fatigue like medals. The firelight ran bronze fingers through Sara's tumbled hair and made dark sweet shadows at the corner of her mouth. Bruce, leaning forward in his eagerness, his bandaged hand lifted for emphasis; Pat swathed in a horrible old bathrobe furred with dog hairs, his own hair standing on end like a cockatoo's crest, and his face crisscrossed with scratches. . . . And her own hands, at rest in his.

When Bruce began to speak, he had as intent an audience as any lecturer could hope for.

"We decided, early in the game, that we might have two ghosts. As soon as we learned about Ammie, it was obvious that she was the entity who came to Sara. Where we made our big mistake was in identifying her with A, the thing that materializes in the living room. I'd begun to have my doubts about that even before tonight; because, if there was one thing we agreed on, it was that the smoke, or fog, was evil. It produced an overpowering repulsion and terror. Ammie never affected us that way."

"But, Bruce," Ruth protested. "She wasn't very—well, very nice."

"She was frightened and confused," Bruce said, with a curious gentleness. "The—well, the residue, let's call it—of Amanda Campbell that lingers in the house is not a conventional ghost, a complete sensate personality. She's more like a phonograph record, stuck at a certain point. That's why she has been so incoherent and so unhelpful when we have contacted her."

He paused, waiting for a comment. None came, not even from Pat; and Bruce continued, "But Ammie, though vital in the arousing of the house, is not the source of danger. That entity, as dark and violent as the smoke and fire it suggests, is still aware, still reacting."

"Smoke and fire," Ruth said thoughtfully.

"No." Bruce answered her thought rather than her words. "I don't think the form of the apparition is necessarily conditioned by physical fire. It conveys the emotions that drive him, even beyond death—violence, darkness, threat. That was what possessed you tonight, Pat. And it was not a woman, however malevolent. I had already come to sense this presence as that of a man, a man like you in many ways, Pat—hot-tempered, passionate, potentially violent. That's why he was able to reach you, and why you didn't sense the change yourself. Ruth didn't realize because—well, because . . ."

"That's all right," Ruth said wryly. "This is no time to spare my feelings. I didn't realize because I was operating on the assumption that all men are beasts."

"You saw the overshadowing tonight," Bruce said, passing over the admission. "Was there any doubt in your mind that what you saw was male, not female?"

"Overpoweringly male," Ruth said promptly. "Bruce, of course! It works out like those little syllogisms of Lewis Carroll's. The thing that overshadowed Pat was a man. The thing that overshadowed Pat was the blackness. Therefore the blackness is male. Ammie is female. . . ."

"Ammie is not the blackness," Bruce finished. "So who is? It can only be one person, I think."

"Samson among the Philistines," Ruth said. "Samson was a husky specimen, wasn't he? The man who died by fire. . . . I know you don't agree with that, Bruce, but I can't help feeling that it must have shaped him, somehow. Of course. It's Douglass Campbell."

Bruce nodded.

"That explains why the Bible stopped It, when the crucifix didn't."

"You're so damned smart I can't stand you," Pat said gloomily.

"Douglass was a rabid Protestant," Bruce said with a grin. "He had no respect for Papist mummeries while he was alive. Why should he pay attention to them after he was dead?"

"Whereas the Bible. . . ." Ruth began. "Good heavens—it was probably Douglass's own Bible! How pertinent can you get?"

"But that's what I tried to say once before!" Sara's voice rose, and they all stopped talking to stare at her.

"What was it you tried to say?" Bruce asked.

"Oh, I didn't think much of the idea myself," Sara said. "And then you all drowned me out the way you do. . . . It was just something I read in a book of ghost stories. The man who wrote it was a psychic investigator and he said, someplace or other, that he always suspected ghosts couldn't be exorcised by rites they didn't accept when they were alive."

Bruce sank back onto the couch. Pat hid his face in his hands.

"Sara. . . ." Ruth began.

"Well, I'm sorry," the girl said defensively.

"What are you sorry about?" Pat's hands dropped from his face; it was red with amused chagrin. "It's so damned typical of us, bellowing our loud-mouthed theories, and ignoring the small voice that had the vital clue."

"I don't suppose we'd have paid any attention if she had been able to get it out," Bruce said glumly. "Sara, I've been lectured on my sins by a lot of people, but nobody ever made me feel quite so small and wormy."

"If it's true," Ruth murmured. "If it should be true—it opens up a number of incredible possibilities. . . ."

"All sorts of possibilities," Pat agreed. "Multiple afterworlds, diverse heavens, created by the belief of the worshipers. . . ."

"And it explains why the methods of exorcising evil spirits vary so much from culture to culture," Bruce said. "Devil masks and loud noises in Africa, crosses and holy water in Europe. And—" he glanced with oblique humor at Pat—"the analyst's couch and hypnotism today."

"What a heaven that would be," said Pat, still fascinated by his idea. "The Great God Freud and his disciples. Sort of a Brave New World, without sex taboos and frustrations. . . ."

Bruce sat up with a grimace of pain.

"There are more immediate applications for us." He leaned forward, and the firelight played on his set features, deepening the shadows under his eyes and cheekbones, giving a satanic flush to the flat planes of cheek and forehead. "We're all a little giddy with relief just now, but we have to face the unpleasant truth. Which is that our situation, bad enough to begin with, is steadily getting worse. Now that this force has been aroused, it is gaining strength." He looked at Ruth. "You said once that It was impalpable, and thus incapable of doing physical harm. Maybe that was true at one time. But now Douglass has found himself a body."

Pat stirred.

"No, he hasn't. Once, maybe, because I didn't know what to expect. . . ."

"We can't count on your powers of resistance," Bruce said ruthlessly. "It took Douglass longer to find a host than it did Ammie; maybe the tie of blood relationship has meaning, I wouldn't know. But now that Douglass has succeeded once, he may find it easier a second time. Your friend Bishko has the wrong idea, Pat. It's not Ruth who's in danger in that house. It's you."

"And Sara," Ruth said. "You think Ammie is harmless, but I'm not convinced."

Sara tossed her head, throwing the hair back from her face, and smiled at her aunt.

"Ammie won't hurt me, Ruth. I guess I've always known that."

"No, not Ammie," Bruce said. He heaved himself up with a grunt of pain, and extracted a sheaf of papers from his hip pocket. "Maybe you've forgotten that dream of yours, Ruth; but I wrote it down, that first morning. The core of it was a threat to Sara, and the thing that threatened her was a shapeless darkness. Why do you think I got in the way of that hellish thing tonight? Because I could see where its eyes were looking and where its steps were heading. It wanted Sara."

"I knew that too," Ruth said dully. "And even then I couldn't—do what you did. If you hadn't. . . . I can't say it. I can't even think about it. Bruce, I've made up my mind. I'm going to sell the house."

There was no immediate reaction. Bruce sat back, lids lowered. Pat, intent on the cigarette he was lighting, said nothing.

"You could," Bruce said finally.

Pat raised his eyes from his match to encounter Ruth's waiting gaze. His mouth twisted in a grimace which was a poor imitation of the smile he intended.

"You aren't beating a dead horse, Ruth; you're beating the wrong horse. If you mean to give up, the thing to avoid is not the house. It's me."

It was an inappropriate moment for Ruth to become aware, finally and positively, of the fact she had denied so long.

"We'll be living here," she said calmly. "I won't need the house in any case."

Pat swallowed his protest the wrong way and began to cough violently.

"You're both jumping to conclusions," Bruce said; his expression was an odd blend of amusement, embarrassment, and sympathy. "Ruth, you can't sell the house; if someone else had experiences there your finicky conscience would devil you all the rest of your life. And, while I think Douglass is bound to the house, I can't be certain; and you can't spend your declining years toting a twenty-pound Bible around under one arm."

Cherry red with coughing and emotion, Pat tried to speak, but Bruce cut him off with an autocratic wave of his hand. Ruth was brooding about the phrase "declining years," and did not interrupt.

"We've got to get rid of Campbell for good," Bruce went on. "That's the only way out. The situation is not as hopeless as it looks, we've already learned a great deal. So far the only thing that has had the slightest effect on our visitant is the Bible. The logical conclusion, I suppose, would be that we should turn for help to a Protestant minister. But frankly, I'm dubious. I don't think there is such a thing as a ritual for exorcism in any of the Protestant creeds; and even if there were we'd be taking a terrible risk in exposing someone else to Douglass. A certain type of personality might be driven hopelessly insane."

"What a cheery little optimist you are," Pat said bitterly. "You've just eliminated the last possible hope."

"Man, you are obtuse," Bruce said scornfully. "We've found out a helluva lot in the last couple of days, but we're still missing the one vital clue. What does Douglass want? What is it that is keeping him from his rest?"

"He wants her—Ammie," Ruth said despairingly. "How can we satisfy that desire?"

"How do you know that's what he wants?" Bruce countered. "Even if it were—suppose he's obsessed and haunted by not knowing what became of her. Maybe we could find out. Maybe that would satisfy him. Myself, I can't believe his desires are that innocent. He's seething with rage and malevolence; the whole house is rotten with his hate. Why? I tell you, there's a part of the story we still don't know."

"You may be right, at that." Pat was looking more cheerful. "You know, Bruce, there are several factors that don't fit into your interpretation. The voice, for instance. It's not malevolent; it's kind of pathetic. How do you account for that?"

"I can't, and I'm not sure I need to. Maybe it's Douglass, at one moment of time, and the apparition is the old man at a less attractive period. Maybe the voice is Ammie, echoing the cry that calls her back. The thing that interests me is what we called Apparition D. The one that moved the book."

"It wasn't Douglass," Ruth said. "He was the one who tried to prevent us from finding it. So it must be—"

"Ammie," Pat finished. "But she isn't much help, is she? Was the book only meant to give us the year, so that we could identify the right Campbell? Or does the Loyalist Plot have a specific meaning that we haven't yet discovered?"

Sara, pensive and shy in her squatting position, raised her head, swept the hair back from her brow, and broke her long silence.

"Why," she said simply, "don't you ask Ammie?"

## III

The clock struck midnight, and they were still arguing. Bruce had worn himself out in outraged argument; he was reclining, his profile very young and sulky.

"I won't do it," Pat said. He folded his arms. "That's final."

"We'll never find out otherwise," Sara said, for the fifth or sixth time. "It's the only way."

"But the risk, Sara," Ruth exclaimed. "We opened the door once before for Ammie, and see what happened! So far this place is safe—uninvaded. We can't—"

"You said that before," Sara pointed out. "And I said you have to take risks to gain anything worth having. Even safety."

"It's more than safety that interests you," said Bruce, staring malevolently at the ceiling.

"I feel so sorry for her!" Sara burst out. "I've felt her; you haven't. Bruce is right, she's confused and lonely. . . ."

"Emotionally involved with a ghost!" Pat groaned. "Well, I won't hypnotize you, and that's flat."

"She would come tonight," Sara pleaded.

"Well, she can't come." Bruce continued to contemplate the ceiling. "Tomorrow Ruth and I are going to finish searching the attic. We haven't exhausted the conventional sources yet."

"Bruce," Ruth said reluctantly, "I hate to bring this up, but—maybe I'd better search the attic alone."

She had never seen Bruce so surprised. He swung his feet to the floor and sat up.

"Why?"

"It just occurred to me tonight, when I saw you and Pat facing one another. . . . There was a third person involved in the story. If Captain Doyle was a young man, desperately in love with Sara—I mean, Amanda—"

"A third overshadowing?" Bruce brooded. "I never thought of that. . . ."

Pat was staring.

"I don't like the way this is going," he said slowly. "Are we still on the wrong track, even now? If three of the four of us repeat a pattern of dead time, what about the fourth? Douglass Campbell was married. Are we trapped in some ghastly repetition of history?"

"Campbell's wife died in childbirth," Ruth reminded him, "and there's no hint of another woman. No, Pat; I didn't feel myself—shadowed—ever. But I did feel, tonight, as if that confrontation had happened before. If Campbell found you a suitable host, what about Anthony Doyle and Bruce?"

"No," Bruce said, with a finality that surprised them all. "I'd have felt it, Ruth. If I'm sure of anything, I'm sure that Doyle is, in his own way, at rest."

"You didn't see yourself," Ruth insisted. "You didn't feel. . . ."

She knew then that she would never, ever, be able to tell anyone about the final collapse of the fabric of time, when she had smelled lilac that had withered two hundred springs before. "It had happened, another time," she said stubbornly. "You and Pat, Campbell and young Anthony. The same positions, the same emotions—"

She was expressing herself badly, she knew that; but Bruce seemed to catch something of what she was trying to say, and his response fascinated her. His jaw dropped, with a slow, mechanical movement, and his eyes opened so widely that they seemed to fill the upper part of his face. But before he could speak the girl sitting cross-legged before the fire lifted her head.

They had all chosen to forget that Sara needed no help in doing what she wanted to do. The rapport was established; her new-found pity, and her fear for the others, did the rest. While they argued and ignored her, she made her decision. The thing was done in silence, without struggle. But they knew, even before they turned to look, that what they saw was no longer Sara.

## IV

"Sara. . . ." Bruce's voice was a groan.

"Not Sara. Gone." The dark head moved in negation, and Ruth went sick at the unfamiliarity of the gesture.

"Ammie," she said.

"Ammie . . ." the soft slurred voice agreed sweetly.

"Where is she?" Bruce demanded. He was so white that Ruth thought he was going to faint; but she could not move, not even to prevent him from falling. It was Pat who took charge; his hand on Bruce's shoulder pushed the boy back on the couch; his voice, professionally flat, took up the questioning.

"Forget that. Amanda, you come to Sara. Why do you come?"

"Help," the voice wailed, and Sara's body shook from shoulder to heels. "Help . . . Ammie. . . ."

"We will help," Pat said quickly. "Don't be afraid. You're safe here, safe with us. No one can hurt you. Whom do you fear? Is it Douglass Campbell? Is he the one who comes in the darkness?"

"Father."

"Your father, Douglass Campbell. Is he still there, in the house?"

"Still there," the soft voice whispered. "Still . . . hurting. Help . . . Ammie. . . ."

"What does he want?"

"Hurt . . . oh. . . ."

The voice was unbearably pitiful. Pat's face was as pale as Bruce's, but his voice retained the professional calm of the trained hypnotist's.

"He can't hurt you, Amanda. You are safe. Safe. I tell you that, and you know it is true. But you must help us, so that we can keep you safe. What does your father fear? Was he involved in the Plot—when they were trying to free the British soldiers in Georgetown?"

"George Town," said Ammie's voice; and Ruth heard, with a terrible thrill, that it broke the word into two parts. "Father helped. . . . Anthony knew. . . ."

"Anthony Doyle?"

"Anthony . . . knew father. . . ."

"I understand," Pat said, as the voice rose. "Anthony knew your father was a traitor. Anthony was a soldier, wasn't he? In the Continental army?"

"General's . . . aid. . . ." The voice had an echo of dead pride that struck Ruth more coldly than anything it had yet said.

"Why didn't he tell the General?" Pat asked. "About your father?"

"Told . . . father. . . ."

Ruth writhed with the ambiguity of it; she wanted to take Amanda by the shoulders and shake some sense into her. But she knew this would be dangerous, for Sara as well as for the dazed girl ghost. And Pat seemed intuitively to understand the incoherent words.

"He told your father he knew? Is that right? He wanted to warn him?"

"Told father. Fair. . . ." Sara's lips twisted in a spasm of silent laughter, and Ruth shrank back against the couch.

"Of course, that was the only fair thing to do," Pat agreed soothingly, though his forehead was shining with perspiration. "He was your father, and Doyle loved you. He came for you, didn't he? Now, Amanda, listen to me. You are safe; no one can hurt you here. Tell me what happened the day Captain Doyle came to take you away."

"Night," Amanda said strongly. Sara's eyes, and what lay behind them, grew glazed and fixed. "Came . . . night. . . ."

"At night," Pat agreed. "What happened, Amanda?"

"Night. Came . . . Father saw . . . Father. . . ."

The glazed eyes lifted, and for the first and only time Ruth saw the living face of Amanda Campbell, as it had looked on that night in April (oh, the lilacs!) of 1780. It was the same face she had seen in her dream.

"Father," the voice began again, with obvious strain; and then the last syllable lifted and soared into a scream that made Ruth's heart stop. "Not dead! Not dead!" the dead girl cried, and the body of the living girl wrung its hands and twisted as if in pain.

Pat's arm swept out just in time to heave Bruce back onto the couch. He dropped out of his chair onto one knee before Sara, and took her by the shoulders.

"Ammie, be still, stop, be quiet, everything is all right. . . ."

It was the tone rather than the words that did the job, the blend of firm confidence and cajolery. The screams died to a wild sobbing; and finally the mesmerist, now gray to the lips, was able to insinuate his final command.

"All right, Amanda, you're a good girl. . . . You helped, you helped very much, it's all over now. . . . Forget. Safe. . . . You're safe. It's time for you to go now, time for Sara to come back. Time for Amanda to go home."

The sobbing was quieter and less endurable; it had a piteous quality that wrung the heart. The fading voice said, in tones of infinite desolation,

"Can't. Ammie can't . . . go home."

# V

A single silver chime sounded. Ruth looked dazedly at the clock. Only an hour, for all that turmoil. . . . She turned back to Pat, putting the fat-bellied glass into his lax hand.

"Drink it, all of it. You need something."

"She's asleep?"

"Yes, finally. The sleeping pill worked."

"God, I hated to give it to her! I'm terrified of drugs in these abnormal states. But what could I do?"

"Nothing. You had to." Ruth sat down on the couch beside him. She was abnormally calm herself; seeing everyone break down all around her had strengthened her will. Resolutely she pushed to the back of her brain the memory of Sara after the invader had finally gone. Or had she? In the moments before the sleep of exhaustion and drugs had claimed her niece, she had not been at all sure what part was Sara and what the lingering remnant of Amanda Campbell, now firmly implanted in the channels of another girl's brain.

"I sent her away," Pat insisted, as if to convince himself. "I tried, Ruth."

"You did marvelously, I couldn't have spoken, let alone handled her as you did. Pat, it's all right! She'll be fine in the morning."

"Is Bruce still up there?" Pat gulped roughly two ounces of brandy and sat up a little straighter.

"Yes, I told him to lie down on the other bed. This is no time for the conventions."

"I don't give a damn about the conventions; the kid needs sleep himself. You'll have to sit up with her, Ruth. We can't risk it. I'd do it myself, only. . . ."

He hid his face in his hands with a painful groan, and Ruth rescued the brandy glass just before it baptized him.

"It was a crazy, touching thing for her to do," he said between his fingers.

"In a way I know how she felt—and I don't even have this fantastic empathy with Ammie. She's desperate to end it, Pat. We'll all go out of our minds from the strain, even if nothing worse happens."

"Bruce has an idea." Pat took the glass back and finished its contents. He gave a short, unpleasant laugh. "I never thought I'd see the day when I would hang breathless on the words of a young twerp like that."

"He's better able to handle this. More involved than you, brighter than I. And less hidebound than either. He was right about that, Pat; they all are, darn them. You do get petrified in your thinking as you grow older."

"Not in all your thinking." He gave her a feeble, sidelong smile, and then withdrew his hand from her touch. "Ruth, I'm afraid to touch you, and that's the truth. But you know—"

"Yes, I know. This can't last forever, Pat."

"Then the other ghosts are laid?"

"I think so. Yes."

"Then maybe some good has come out of this ghastly mess. I'd like to believe it. I'd like to believe something."

The low flames on the hearth sputtered, dying, and the stillness of late night gathered closer.

"My own beliefs are all jumbled up," Ruth said somewhat shyly. "But, Pat, I can see hints of things I never dared believe before. . . . Isn't this one of the great questions? Survival?"

"Yes, survival—but of what? We've been given no proof of Heaven, Ruth. Only of Hell."

# Chapter
## 11

SARA PICKED UP A FORK AND STARED AT IT BLANKLY; AND Ruth's heart stopped. Her panic was only slightly lessened when Sara shrugged and plunged the fork into a piece of bacon. There had been too many such incidents already this morning, and it was not even eleven o'clock.

Ruth had not meant to sleep at all, but her body was too much for her; it demanded rest. She fell into a solid, dreamless sleep at dawn. Bruce had already eaten and left the house by the time the others stumbled downstairs, and there was no sign in the kitchen that he had any breakfast beyond a cup of coffee.

The doorbell rang as they were finishing breakfast, and Pat went to answer it. The ringer was Bruce, who ambled into the kitchen with something less than his usual grace. He looked like Death—a decadent, elegant Renaissance version, bearded and long-haired.

"I borrowed your car," he told Pat, and held out a bunch of keys on one forefinger. "Hope you don't mind."

Pat took the keys and looked at them stupidly for a moment before shrugging and putting them in his pocket. They were all stupid with weariness, Ruth thought; and felt a surge of hope. Maybe Sara's frightening moments of unresponsiveness meant no more than that.

"Where'd you go?" Pat asked, pouring more coffee.

"Huh? Oh. Hardware store."

"Did you have any breakfast?" Sara seemed more alert in Bruce's presence. "I'll cook you some eggs."

"No, thanks," Bruce said. A look of profound distaste curled his lips. "Not hungry."

"Well," Ruth said, with a bright air which even she found hideously inapropos, "let's get to work, shall we? The attic for me and Bruce—"

"Not the attic," Bruce cut in. "Have you got some slacks with you? Well, you can change after we get there."

"What do you—Bruce. What did you get at the hardware store?"

"Tools. Ax, crowbar, wrenches."

"The cellar door," Pat said. "Is that it, Bruce?"

The eyes of the two men met and a flash of understanding passed between them.

"We've a problem of tactics," Pat went on, while Ruth sat speechless. "Ruth isn't exactly bulging with muscle, and it's your right hand, isn't it, that's damaged. If I remember that door, you need a bulldozer. Or two strong right arms."

"Of all the people who shouldn't—" Bruce began.

"I couldn't agree more. But I don't see how you can do it otherwise."

Bruce said nothing, but his shoulders sagged visibly. His hands lay on the table, curled around his cup of coffee. The bandages on the right hand were amateurishly clumsy, bulky enough in themselves to make any effort awkward.

"You should have a doctor look at that hand," Ruth said, still groping. "I used half a bottle of iodine, but—"

"Time for that later," Bruce said. The implication hung heavy in the air, but he did not voice it. "God. I wish I knew what to do."

"You can't call anyone else in to help," Pat continued, with hard insistence. "If what we suspect is true, this is going to be a hell of a mess. Don't forget, Bruce, we haven't seen Douglass materialize in the daytime yet."

"Yet," Bruce repeated witlessly.

"If we keep the women out. . . ."

"Sara, yes," Ruth said. "But I'm coming."

In the end it was decided that they should all go. Ruth knew that Bruce gave in to Sara's insistence only because he was equally afraid of leaving the girl alone. And as they prepared to leave the house he took Ruth aside for a moment, and she learned the other, principal reason for his surrender.

"I want you to have this," he said, and handed her a can, a fat aerosol spray container.

"What on earth. . . ."

"Sssh!" Bruce glanced over his shoulder. Pat's footsteps could be heard in the hall upstairs; Sara was finishing the breakfast dishes in the kitchen. "It's one of those chemical gas sprays they use in riots. You know how to operate it, don't you? Point it, like shaving cream—what else comes in these cans? Furniture polish? Then you've operated them before."

"But what—" Ruth was beginning to feel as if she had never been allowed to finish a sentence. Bruce interrupted, "You pick out a nice safe spot, out of the way, near the exit. Keep this thing handy, but out of sight, your finger on the nozzle. If you see the slightest sign of anything you don't like, from Pat or Sara—or me, for that matter—point the thing and let 'em have it. It's a new kind, works instantaneously. Remember to hold your breath; but since you'll be behind it—"

"I don't believe it," Ruth muttered. She eyed the harmless-looking can with repugnant incredulity.

"Ruth, I'm counting on you! I don't think we're in any danger at this time of day, otherwise I wouldn't dare risk it. But you're the reserves. I was planning to keep this can myself if Pat and I went down there together; I don't much enjoy the idea of meeting Douglass Campbell when he's armed with an ax. But this is better. You can keep it ready, and he won't know. . . . Sssh, here they come. It's important that he doesn't know you have it, stick it in your purse till we—"

He turned to give Sara a fairly convincing smile; and Ruth, her hands trembling, jammed the can into her bag.

## II

The atmosphere of the cellar had not improved since their last visit; it was still dusty, damp, and grim. After the ominous, unused stillness that overlay the rest of the house, a stillness that seemed to Ruth to hum with ominous anticipation, the cellar was even worse.

With a meaningful glance at Ruth, Bruce turned on the electric lantern he had brought and ducked into the space behind the furnace. Pat followed without a word, heaving the heavier of the two crowbars onto his shoulder. He had shed coat and overcoat, as well as his tie, upstairs, and the muscles of his back and shoulders, visible through his thin shirt, were impressive. Ruth felt a shiver slide down her spine. She had never had a higher opinion of Bruce's courage. To be trapped in that dusty, confined space, with something armed for murder, something that still raged with an insane fury that had survived two centuries. . . .

"Sit here," she said to Sara, indicating a place on the stair; and, rising, she went to stand near the wall in a spot from which she could see the two men. She still wore her coat, on the not invalid excuse that the basement was chilly, and her right hand was in the large patch pocket.

Bruce glanced at her over his shoulder and Ruth smiled at him, willing him all the strength she could give, by her presence and her knowledge. He produced a rather strained smile in response; and she thought, I've done him an injustice. If Sara can catch him, she'll have a prize. This isn't an intellectual game for him; he's risking his life for her sanity. How many men would do that for a girl?

Then the ax in Pat's hands came down with a crash that echoed through the close, dank air.

After all it took less than an hour to force the door. Pat's strength made the difference. The solid planks had hardened with age, the nails had rusted in place, and each piece of wood had to be hacked to pieces before it could be wrenched out. But finally only an inch of wood lay between them and the hidden space beyond. Nothing could be seen; there was not a trace of light from the inner cellar. But a breath of dead, noisome air penetrated the cracks and made both men back away.

"Why don't you rest for a minute?" Ruth suggested.

She was half sick herself with apprehension. It had gone too smoothly; she could not believe that they would accomplish their aim without interference. Unless, she reminded herself, it was pointless. Perhaps their effort had been for nothing, and the mysterious blocked-off space was only an empty, abandoned cellar.

But in her innermost mind she did not believe it. The tension could not be all imaginary; some of it, thickening as the moments wore on, must come from the outer air. At one point she had thought she felt a breath of the familiar, deadly cold, and she had risked leaving her post just long enough to dash up the stairs and close the door. Illogically, she felt more secure with even that frail barrier between her and the ominously quiet living room. On her way down she had almost stumbled over an object which lay on the stairs beside Sara. She recognized it—the big Bible, which the girl had evidently carried down from the living room. Ruth approved the thought, but her glance at Sara did nothing to lighten her apprehension. Silent and withdrawn, the girl sat on the step staring into nothing, like a statue.

Now as the final barrier lay before them, ready to be breached, her fingers were so wet with perspiration that they slipped on the slick surface of the can in her pocket.

"Why don't you rest for a minute?" she repeated.

"Better not wait," Pat said briefly and significantly. He inserted his crowbar into the center boards. They gave, with a creak and a screech, and Pat stepped back, his hand before his face, as the unwholesome air gushed out.

"Whew," he said. "The place is like an ancient tomb. Wait a minute, Bruce, and let the air clear."

Bruce nodded. He was leaning frankly against the wall, his chest heaving in and out, his shirt clinging damply to his body. Ruth knew that his exhaustion was not solely the product of physical exertion. After a few minutes Pat said, "It's better now."

He picked up the ax and knocked out the remaining fragments of wood. Hoisting the lantern, he vanished into the hole, which brightened with wavering light.

Bruce gave Ruth a desperate, wordless look, and followed.

Ruth glanced from the rigid form of her niece to the dusty yellow-lit hole in the wall. She did not like Sara's look or Sara's position, so near the upper doorway; but she knew her presence was more badly needed elsewhere.

It would have taken some resolution to enter the condensed atmosphere of the hidden room under ordinary circumstances. But for Ruth, personal distaste was swallowed up by her fear for the others. She was afraid to let Pat out of her sight for an instant; and, under the other emotions that drove her, she was conscious of a feeble flicker of plain, ordinary curiosity.

At first glance the old cellar was a disappointment.

It had even fewer features of interest than the outer room. It had always been windowless. The walls, of heavy stone instead of cement, were covered with slimy lichen, of a sickly yellow-green, and they gleamed wetly in the light of the lantern. The floor was beaten earth, so hard that the dampness lay on its surface in oily-looking beads. In a corner, out of the direct lantern light, something shone with pale luminosity. The basement made a splendid nursery for mushrooms, very big, very white, and oddly swollen-looking.

Despite the seeming normalcy of the room, Bruce was not at ease. He had gotten his back up against the wall—or as close against it as he could get without actually touching the slimy surface—and he still held, with an attempt at casualness that was definitely unconvincing, one of the crowbars. Pat seemed comparatively unmoved. He looked up as Ruth hesitated fastidiously on the threshold.

"Hand me that shovel, Ruth, will you?"

Ruth obeyed, concealing her reluctance at stepping onto the nasty-looking floor. The space was larger than she had anticipated. It must lie under most of the long living room area, and—she shied back, uncontrollably, as the realization struck her—it must be, in actual fact, the original stone-built foundations of the first house. Douglass Campbell's house.

After a wordless consultation with Bruce, who only shrugged helplessly, Pat went to the far, back corner and shoved the spade into the earth. The floor was not as hard as it looked; Pat's big foot, placed firmly on the head of the spade, forced it several inches into the ground.

It was as if the shovel touched a spring buried deep in the earth, and set off the reaction. Ruth had turned to watch Pat. She was still puzzled as to his intent, though it seemed clear enough to Bruce, and for a moment she had forgotten nervous fears in curiosity. Bruce was the first to see it come, perhaps because he was expecting it. His mouth opened in a shout which never emerged; and Ruth's eyes followed the direction of his pointing hand.

She had actually expected to see Sara, once more in the

grasp of her unwelcome visitant. But the other—no, she had always seen it in a certain spot, and never expected to see it elsewhere. The cloud of black was dim; it writhed as if in struggle. Douglass Campbell did not like the daylight. But his need, now, was more desperate than custom.

"Not here," Ruth said, hardly aware that she had spoken. "No . . . not here. . . ."

"This is where it comes from, this is the center," Bruce shot at her. "The spray, Ruth—get it. Pat. . . ."

Ruth obeyed, though with difficulty; her fingers were already numb with cold. Balancing the crowbar in unsteady hands, Bruce swung around to face Pat; and Ruth hesitated, because the field of her weapon included both men.

And because, this time, Douglass Campbell was not having it all his own way. Perhaps it was because he was weaker, between cockcrow and dusk; perhaps because Pat now was warned and reacting with all the strength of his will. From first to last he did not utter a sound, nor move beyond the first involuntary start of surprise that swung him back, away from the shovel. Somehow his immobility only made the struggle more apparent, and its ferocity more felt. Ruth watched the perspiration gather and stream down his face, saw the muscles tighten in the arms that still gripped the spade handle. His lips were drawn back in a spasm that bared his teeth. She stood waiting, her hand on the incongruous weapon, and as she watched the wavering column of darkness seemed to shrink.

Then the cry she had choked back rose up in her throat. In the doorway, behind the Thing, stood Sara. It was Sara, not the other girl, but a Sara who appeared to be walking in her sleep. In her arms she cradled the heavy Book as another woman might hold a baby.

Bruce lunged forward, raising the heavy steel bar. Ruth never knew what he intended to do with it, for as he moved his foot slipped and he skidded to his knees. Before he could rise, Sara spoke.

"It's no use." She spoke in a conversational tone, and Ruth's blood froze as she realized that Sara was not addressing any of the three human beings in the room. "It's over, can't you see that? You can't silence all of us."

She paused, her head tilted in an uncanny listening look.

"It was never any use," she went on, in the same reasonable voice. "Who were you trying to fool? He beholdeth all the sons of man."

Ruth wondered who "he" might be. Then she knew, and her breath caught painfully in her throat.

" 'Behold, the eye of the Lord is upon them that fear him,' " Sara said. "It was all known, and the end determined, from the beginning. Now go, and seek the hope that even such as you were promised. Go . . . in peace."

The smoky column swayed and shrank. Then, with an absurd little pop, it was gone; and Ruth, running through the space it had occupied, caught Sara in her arms as the girl collapsed.

# III

They found what they were seeking almost at once, in the very spot where Pat had begun to dig. Sara had recovered from her faint almost at once, and with only the vaguest memories of what she had said. Standing with her arm around the girl, Ruth looked down at the pitiful remnants of mortality. Some quality in the clayey soil had preserved them well.

"So he was here," she said. "Douglass Campbell."

"No." Bruce shook his head. "These bones have never been touched by fire. And Douglass's remains would have been gathered up with the debris of the upper stories of the house." He stooped, and with careful fingers pulled from the earth a twisted piece of corroded metal. "The buckle of the belt of a military uniform," he said, holding it up. "This wasn't Douglass, Ruth. It was Anthony Doyle."

The light shone steadily on the four white faces and motionless hands, but there was nothing in the foul air now beyond its own natural gases.

"He came that night for Ammie," Bruce went on, "but he never left. He's been here ever since—ever since Douglass Campbell murdered him and buried him in the cellar."

"And that was the secret Douglass Campbell tried to hide for two centuries," Ruth said; but she knew the truth, even before Bruce's head moved, again, in the slow gesture of negation.

"No. Douglass Campbell went mad that night, but not because of Doyle's murder. I can almost predict the spot where we'll find her—right under that certain area in the room above—the opposite corner from this, as far away from her lover as he could put her. Even in death he couldn't endure to have them lie together."

# IV

It was like being born again, to come up the stairs into the thin sunlight of a winter day. Ruth went to change her clothes and found herself scrubbing her hands over and over, as if the miasma of the cellar and what it contained could be washed away. When the four gathered, in the kitchen, Ruth suggested lunch, like a good hostess; but it was unanimously and immediately refused. Her offer of wine was more acceptable and as she poured the sherry, Ruth remarked,

"If this hadn't ended we'd all have become alcoholics. I've never drunk so much, at such peculiar times of day, as I lave lately."

"If this hadn't ended," Sara repeated, and stared rather blankly around the circle of pallid faces. "I can't believe it. This," she indicated, with a wave of her hand, the smug modern kitchen. "This is anticlimactic."

"But it is over," Ruth said. "He won't be back. I don't know why I'm so sure, but I am."

"Yes, he's gone. And how the hell Sara ever—" Ruth caught Pat's eye and shook her head in silent warning, but he had already stopped speaking. They all felt, somehow, that Sara's last seizure had better not be discussed, at least not then. Instead Pat turned to Bruce.

"He wasn't normal, was he? That was the terror we felt, his madness."

"He lived the last forty years of his life, and died, insane," Bruce said soberly. "That was the state in which his spirit lingered. Imagine those years, month after month, cooped up in this house, with what lay below in the cellar, rotting. . . ."

"Don't," Ruth said faintly.

"That wasn't the worst—not what was in the cellar but what still clung to the house and the old man's mad, decaying brain. He must have seen her in every room, heard her at every moment of his waking life—and in his dreams. . . ."

"He had to kill her, after he killed Doyle," Pat said more prosaically. "She'd have destroyed him if he hadn't stopped her. She must have known; maybe she saw it done."

"Oh, yes, she saw it done," Ruth said; she was shaken by a sudden fit of shivering. "She saw it done. . . . Dear heaven, don't you remember? We heard her screaming, just as she must have done that night. . . ."

" 'Not dead,' " Sara repeated. "She wasn't talking about herself when she said that. A phonograph record, cracked and caught, repeating—repeating the words she said when she saw Anthony Doyle fall, by her father's hand. 'He can't be dead—he's not dead. . . .' "

"At least she didn't have much time in which to suffer," Ruth said.

"Only an eternity." Bruce's face was pinched. "However the dead reckon time. . . . She never stopped suffering; she was caught in that one unendurable moment like a fly in a spider's web. Both of them, she and her father—murderer and victim. . . ."

"Maybe the first murder—Doyle's—was an accident," Ruth said. "Surely he wouldn't have had to kill the boy to keep Ammie from eloping."

Bruce shook his head.

"Part of it will always be conjecture; but—remember Ammie's own words. Doyle was the General's aide. I'll give you three guesses which general," he added.

"There were lots of 'em," Pat said practically. "Gates, Greene, von Steuben—"

"I know which General," Ruth said. "You be logical. I know."

"Me, too." Bruce smiled at her. "Hopeless romantics, both of us. Anyhow, the General, whoever he was, sent Doyle to this area. He fell in love with Ammie, and she with him; but he never had a chance with the old man. In the course of his duties Doyle came across the Plot. Imagine his feelings when he discovered that the old rat Campbell, who had thrown him out of the house, was up to his neck in treason! He had a perfect instrument of revenge—but he couldn't use it without destroying his fondest hopes. The other conspirators were hanged, if you recall. How could he expect to marry the girl after he had, in effect, killed her father? So he came that night to warn the old

S.O.B. to give up his dangerous activities. Remember Ammie's own words; he wanted to be fair. I would guess that he had already recorded the names of the other conspirators, but he omitted Douglass Campbell's name. He came in good faith; but he underestimated Campbell's hate. He probably never even had a chance to defend himself."

"And yet you say he is at rest," Ruth said wonderingly.

"Ruth, I don't pretend to account for this world, let alone the next. But maybe . . . Doyle died in what you might call a state of grace. His intentions were honorable, his actions harmless; hell, he probably wasn't even mad at anybody. There was no guilt on his soul, to keep it from the peace his faith had taught him to expect. But Campbell—by the terms of his own creed he was damned! He expected to go straight to Hell, and he did. I can't think of any greater hell than to endlessly relive the act that destroyed you."

"And Ammie?"

Bruce's face assumed the curiously gentle expression it wore when Ammie's name was mentioned.

"Ammie. He wouldn't let her go, in life or in death. And she—she had time, before she died, not only for terror and the last extremity of fear, but for hate. How could she help but hate him, after what she had seen him do?"

"But how did you know?" Ruth demanded. "You did know—both of you. Pat even knew where to start digging."

"You, of all people, should have seen the truth," Bruce said. "Good Lord, you were the one who told me about your feeling, when you saw me and Pat squaring off, that it had all happened before. You even suggested that it must have been Douglass and Doyle who were the original antagonists. But if they had ever met in such an encounter—one so violent that it left an imprint on the very air of the house. . . . Doyle would have been as helpless as I was. He couldn't have killed her father, any more than I could slug Pat."

"I knew after that last talk with Ammie," Pat said. "It seemed so hellishly plain to me—maybe because I was still getting flashes of Douglass's memories. She tried so hard to tell us what happened. . . ."

"We should have suspected from the first," Bruce concluded. "All the clues were there. Ammie's terror and shock in-

2049daBarbara Michaels

dicated a violent end in the house to which she was bound, not
a peaceful death in Camden, New Jersey, at the ripe old age of
eighty. And there was Douglass's behavior—shutting himself
up, not even going to church—that suggested something
stronger than grief. He was afraid to face his angry God with
that black sin on his soul."

"His own daughter," Ruth murmured. "Infanticide. The
worst possible sin. . . ."

"No." The boy's dark head moved in the now-familiar gesture. "It was bad enough, but it wasn't the worst. The thing that
drove Douglass Campbell mad was not so much his crime as
the reason for it. He didn't kill Ammie to keep her from betraying his other murder. No normal father could have done that.
He killed her because—"

His eyes met Pat's; and the older man's head bowed.

"You felt it," Bruce said.

"I felt it," Pat agreed heavily. "But I didn't know what it
was, not until we had the whole story. The ravenous desire, and
the sick hatred of that same desire. . . . It's in here, somewhere. . . ." He pulled the Bible toward him; Ruth had carried it
up from the basement. He began leafing through the pages.

"He never remarried," Bruce said. "Not in all those years,
when other men acquired three and four wives. She was all he
wanted, or needed. And then she tried to leave him. . . ."

He broke off, as something in the quality of Pat's silence
struck him. Pat had found the reference he wanted; he sat staring down at the page, where a passage was savagely underlined
in strokes of dark blue ink—the same ink which had obliterated
Ammie's name.

"But I say unto you, that whosoever looketh on a woman to
lust after her hath committed adultery with her already in his
heart."


V


The words had all been said; but the final scene was not played
until some weeks later. The famous oaks of St. Stephen's raised
bare branches into a sky sagging with iron-gray clouds, and the
somber green of the pines made a dark background for the

white marble of crosses and headstones. When the first flakes of snow began to drift down, Father Bishko excused himself and went in. The others lingered, looking down at the simple stone with its paired names and dates.

"How did you ever get Anthony's birth date?" Ruth asked.

"Oh—from the army records, of course. I'm amazed that they go back so far."

"Not only that, but they can be revised," Pat said with an air of modest triumph. "I told you about Doyle's being listed as a deserter."

"Yes. Final confirmation of the truth, if we needed confirmation. . . ."

"Hardly," Bruce said grimly. "I didn't know it was possible to tell so much, just from bones."

"Age, sex, manner of death," Pat said. "I took that course in physical anthropology twenty years ago, but a fractured skull and a broken neck aren't hard to spot. Campbell must have been a giant of a man. . . ." Ruth shivered. He put his arm around her, and went on more cheerfully, "Anyhow, Doyle has been reinstated. I don't know that he cares; but I feel better, somehow."

"How on earth did you accomplish that?" Ruth asked.

"I found a General with some imagination." Pat laughed, and gave Bruce a friendly slap on the back that almost sent the boy sprawling. "Bruce is still sulking. He hates to admit that any army officer can have a heart."

"He's an Irishman," Bruce said sourly. "As you might expect."

"And a friend of Pat's?" Sara guessed.

"Like Father Bishko," Ruth said. "Thanks to Pat's wide circle of acquaintances, we've managed to do this without publicity. I didn't think we could. Father Bishko was splendid."

"He's a master at tactful planning," Pat said. "And think how relieved he was to find out that all he needed to arrange was a memorial Mass and a cemetery plot. Not much compared with a full-scale exorcism—and the distinct probability of another encounter with evil incarnate."

"How you can find it amusing, even now. . . ."

"It's been over a month," Pat said. "And not a sign."

"Yes, I can put the house up for sale with a clear conscience."

Hands jammed in his pockets, black hair powdered with snow, Bruce glanced at Ruth.

"You really intend to sell the house? After all the years it's been in the family?"

"I offered it to you and Sara," Ruth said, and smiled, a bit wryly, at the boy's involuntary gesture of rejection. "Yes, well, you know how I feel, then. The place is purged, I'm sure. But. . . ."

"Anyhow, family pride is the emptiest of vanities," Sara said firmly. She bent over to straighten the sheaf of flowers that lay against the stone.

"Where did you find lilac, at this time of year?" Ruth asked.

"You can get anything anytime, if you pay enough for it," Bruce said. "And we paid enough."

"You're already starting to sound like a husband," Ruth warned. Bruce gave her a sheepish smile.

"I was just kidding. Sara had this thing about lilac; she kept insisting it's what Ammie would have liked."

"Oh, yes," Ruth said. She looked at Sara. So she was not the only one who had smelled the scent of lilac on a night in November. "Yes, nothing could be more suitable."

"I'm freezing," Bruce said crankily. "And I've already missed one class today. Since I've got to get that damned degree before Sara's mother will let us get married. . . ."

"It's easier than dragons," Ruth pointed out.

"One thing still bugs me," Pat remarked, as they started to turn away from the quiet earth, now blanketed by the soft white purity of the snow. "The voice. It must have been Douglass. But it sounded so pathetic. . . ."

"No," Ruth said. "Ha—beat you to it, Bruce. You know everything, so you must have an idea about this too. You never did think the voice was Douglass, did you?"

"No." Bruce drew lines in the snow with his toe, and studied them intently.

"Well?"

"It sounds so damned . . . sentimental," Bruce complained.

"What's wrong with being sentimental?" Pat asked.

"Well. . . ." Bruce added two more lines, making a rectangle. "He was safe," he said, addressing the tip of his shoe. "But how could he rest quietly, knowing that she was still lost?"

"Oh," Ruth said. "I see."

"He doesn't need to call her anymore." Bruce's eyes went to the sheaf of delicate purple flowers, sending their sharp perfume through the falling snow. "Because now, finally, Ammie has come home."

# *The Dark on the Other Side*

# Chapter
## 1

THE HOUSE TALKED.

The objects in it talked, too—chairs, tables, couches, a big, squashy hassock that squatted obscenely in a corner of the bedroom. But the voice of the house was loudest. It was a thin, high voice, like that of an old woman. Hunched on its hill, like a fat old woman crouching on her haunches, its wings spread out like the folds of a ragged skirt, its wide terrace apronlike, its tower a thin neck, wattled and scaled with lichen, the house talked. Sometimes it said, *Run away . . . leave him . . . if you can.* Sometimes it wailed, *I wish he'd die. . . .*

Sometimes its suggestion was more direct.

## II

Gordon didn't tell her that there would be a guest until just before dinner. Linda was sitting at her dressing table, elbows carelessly asprawl on the polished glass top. In the tall triple mirrors, her bedroom looked strange—not like a reflection of reality, but like another room, all the more disturbing because it contained the same furniture as her room, in the same positions, and yet looked subtly wrong. Like hers, it was decorated in shades of blue and white—cool, virginal colors, restful and remote. The drapes framing the tall windows were the deep, rich blue of the sky at late evening; their heavy velvet did not reflect

light, but drank it in and absorbed it, so that the hoarded gold
gave the blue a glowing luster. Because she had expressed a dislike for wall-to-wall carpeting, Gordon had had the floors redone; they were stained dark, unvarnished but shining like
black glass with repeated applications of wax. Glass, or black
water. . . . The scattered rugs lay like little icebergs on a dark
sea. Now, reflected, the ragged white islands seemed to move,
rocking slightly as if shifted by the dark, shimmery surface on
which they lay.

When Gordon came in, she didn't look up. Behind her mirrored image his face floated into view like something conjured
up into a crystal ball—but familiar, wearing its old look of fond
anxiety.

He was a very handsome man, Gordon. He'd be forty on his
next birthday; and he was as alarmed, and as amused at his own
alarm, as any pretty woman would be at the onset of that ominous day. The years had only added to his good looks—a brush
of white at the temples, stark and distinctive against his thick
black hair, a deepening of the lines of laughter that fanned out
from the corners of his eyes. A man with eyes like that oughtn't
to look so masculine; they were big and dark and luminous,
fringed with lashes so long and thick they looked artificial. But
there was nothing in the least effeminate about Gordon's face—
or mind, or body.

Next to his, her own face was wraithlike. Too pale, too thin,
with suggestive dark circles under the eyes and an undue
prominence of certain muscles. Those long tendons in the
throat especially—the throat he had admired, had compared
with that of the lovely statue of Nefertiti . . .

She turned her head, watching the effect, and her pale
mouth, as yet unpainted for public appearance, writhed dis-
tastefully as the lines tightened and drew. Gordon's mouth
moved. She raised her eyes to meet his mirrored eyes, and felt
herself frowning.

"What?"

"I said," he repeated patiently, "that we have a guest for dinner, and the weekend. So look your loveliest, won't you? If you
are to be immortalized, I want it to be as you really are."

He was always so patient. It was almost the most maddening thing about him.

Then the meaning of what he had said finally penetrated, and she turned her head to stare at him.

He had retreated to the hassock, the one she particularly loathed, and was sitting with a grace a twenty-year-old might have envied, one knee bent, his long brown hands curled around it.

"Immortalized?" she repeated, articulating carefully.

"But, darling, I told you last week. . . ." He stopped. That was one of the things he must never do, remind her that she kept forgetting things. He started all over again, as if she had never heard the subject mentioned; only the straight vertical line between his brows showed his perturbation.

"Our guest's name is Michael Collins. He's the young man *Manhattan* magazine has commissioned to do a series of profiles on me. I'm very flattered, you know; usually they select important people as subjects."

"You're important," she said. It was not a compliment. It was simply a statement.

"Maybe I was, once. But you know I don't give a damn about being what the idiot world calls important."

Linda shrugged and turned back to the mirror. The top of her dressing table was covered with bottles and jars, with creams and lotions and cosmetics, all the expensive playthings of a woman of wealth and fashion. They were in perfect order, their shining caps free of the slightest speck of dust. Anna, her maid, straightened them every day.

She reached out at random and took a lipstick out of a jeweled holder that held a dozen of them. Applying it to her mouth, she said, "I suppose you want me to get dressed up."

"What about that robe I got you last week? The one with the gold threads?"

"It's too big." She tipped her head, studying her mouth. "My lipstick's on crooked."

"As a mere male it's not up to me to comment," said Gordon drily. "But if you will insist on talking while you apply the stuff—"

He broke off at the sound of a knock on the door. In some big houses servants weren't supposed to knock; so Linda had read. But Gordon insisted on his privacy. She watched, in the mirror, as the door of that other room opened, and the reflected image of her maid, Anna, sidled in. The girl looked even sillier in the glass. She was a silly-looking creature at best, with her teased blond wig and adenoidal, half-witted gape; and the mirror distorted her face as it warped every other object it reflected. The sidelong glance she gave Gordon had a sly, conspiratorial gleam. Of course, she had a crush on him; all the women in the house had, from the fat Bavarian cook to the gardener's ten-year-old daughter.

Even in the foul mirror Gordon's face remained unchanged. She couldn't accuse him of leering at the maids. But he had better taste than that. Anna's figure was good, and was adequately displayed; Gordon insisted on uniforms, but he went along, good-humoredly, with the shorter skirts, and Anna's black dress verged on a musical-comedy maid's outfit. She had good legs. But that staring, vacant face . . .

Linda whirled around.

"I don't want you," she said. "Get out."

"Now, honey." Gordon rose; coming up behind her, he lifted the heavy masses of her black hair between his hands. "Let the poor girl fix your hair, at any rate. I told you, I want you to look beautiful. Anna, Mrs. Randolph will wear that gold thing—I don't know what you women call it—"

"The Persian brocade hostess gown," Anna said promptly. "If you mean the dress you bought last week, Mr. Randolph."

"That's the one. Hostess gown? You're right; that's what the salesgirl called it." He grinned at Anna, who, without moving a muscle, managed to suggest a puppy wriggling happily at a caress. "Well, I'll get out of the way and leave you to it."

Linda wiped off the crooked outline on her upper lip and sat with lipstick poised, watching Anna trot over to the long closet and take out the dress. As the girl laid it carefully across the bed her hands lingered, smoothing the heavy fabric. It was a beautiful thing; heaven only knew what treasured antique the dressmaker had cut up in order to make it. It didn't look like modern fabric; the muted blues and pinks and golds might have formed part of a sultan's regalia a century before. Linda reapplied her lipstick. It was a bright orange-red. The color would clash horribly with the dress. She ought to use another shade.

She dropped the carved gold case on the table top and reached down into the lowest drawer of the dressing table.

"Get me a glass," she ordered, taking the top off the bottle.

The contents, half gone, swam amber gold with the movement of her hands.

Anna hesitated, her eyes bulging as they focused on the bottle.

"Didn't you hear me?" Linda asked gently. "Hurry up. You lazy little fool."

Anna jumped, and then ran into the bathroom. Linda took the glass without looking at it or the girl who held it. She poured it half full. Her elbows on the table, she sipped, and watched Anna in the mirror; and Anna stared back with her big, bulging, watery-blue eyes.

Cocktails in the den before dinner. Very classy, Linda thought, for a cop's daughter from Cleveland. She came down the stairs carefully, holding up her heavy skirts with one hand. The other hand, beringed and graceful, trailed nonchalantly along the curved mahogany rail. She didn't need to hold on. A couple of drinks—or even three or four—didn't affect her at all, physically, except to dull the sharpness of her hearing. With a couple of drinks—or maybe three or four—she could hardly hear the voice of the house.

There was no one in the marble-floored foyer to appreciate her entrance, so she turned to the right and went along the hall, past the drawing room, past the morning room, past the dining room; her skirts rustling stiffly, her head high. Why not the drawing room for cocktails? she wondered. Why the study? That was Gordon's room, as the dainty-chintz morning room was supposed to be hers. Usually he didn't allow casual visitors into his sanctum. Oh, but this man was not a casual visitor. He was . . . something about a biography. That explained the study. Michael What's-'is-name was going to get the full effect—the rows on rows of learned volumes, the windows opening onto the beauty of the countryside. And in the midst of it all, Gordon himself, the sage, the scholar, who had abandoned the hollow sham of the world for a life of contemplation.

The door was open. She could hear their voices as she approached: Gordon's mellow baritone, the softer, higher voice of Jack Briggs, Gordon's secretary, and another voice . . . deeper even than Gordon's, slower, drawling. For no reason at all, a shiver ran through her and she stopped, knees waxy-soft, and put one hand out blindly for support against the satiny surface of the paneled wall.

The spasm lasted only a second. She shook herself and went on, wondering. Something was going to happen. Good or bad? Were there such categories, or were things—happenings, people—amoral, to be judged only by their effects on others? "There is nothing either good or bad, but thinking makes it so. . . ."

She came to the door and stood there, looking at them.

Amid the bustle of their rising, she caught two swift impressions. One was the barely perceptible relief in Gordon's face as he took in her appearance: exquisitely gowned, coiffed, and made up, poised and calm. The other impression was simply that of a man, a stranger, and never, afterward, could she reduce it to details. He was there; his presence was enough.

Yet he was not, on second glance, a particularly good-looking man. A few inches taller even than Gordon's respectable height, he seemed to be strung together with old elastic, so that his movements looked gawky and abrupt beside Gordon's disciplined grace. His hair was mousy brown, combed carelessly back from a side parting; his mouth was too wide and his face had a lopsided look, as if one jaw were longer than the other. The only feature that might be called handsome were his eyes, and their beauty lay in their expression rather than their color, which was a brown slightly darker than his hair.

"How do you do," she said, and gave him her hand. With the touch of his hard, square fingers, the flash of empathy faded. He was just another man, and this was just another normal social occasion.

She sat down in one of the big, soft leather chairs and watched with amusement as Collins tried to get his long arms and legs folded back into a sitting position. Gordon was hovering. He looked pathetically pleased, and it was significant, she knew, that he nodded at Briggs without making her ask for a drink.

Briggs bustled over to the bar and began fussing with ice cubes, bottles, and glasses. Linda's nerves tightened as she watched him. She detested him even more than she did the other servants—although, as Gordon's secretary, he was not to be regarded, or treated, as a servant. He was a pale, puffy man;

the texture of his skin suggested clay or bread dough, some substance that would not rebound elastically from the prod of a finger, but would retain the impression. Gordon claimed that he was a very efficient secretary. She found that hard to believe. His movements, when away from the typewriter, were fussy, slow, and inept. Finally he came back with her drink, and she tried not to touch his hand as she took it. His fingers were always damp.

"We were just discussing Michael's last book, Linda," Gordon said. "I think you read it; I know I recommended it to you."

So they were on first-name terms already.

"Oh, yes," she said, and sipped her drink. "I read it. It was very good."

She saw Michael flush a little at the coldness of the compliment, and added smoothly, "I particularly liked the chapter on the relationship between Emily and Bramwell. You caught something there which no other biographer has understood."

His wide mouth curved up, bringing out a line in one cheek, a line too long to be called a dimple.

"What was that?"

Linda looked at him in surprise. So Michael Collins wasn't quite the gauche young fool he looked. A compliment was meaningless to him unless it was genuine.

"The fact that, though he loved her desperately, he resented her talent. Oh, I know the point's been made; but you seemed to comprehend so fully the effect on the frustrated male ego, and the conflict between her feeling of feminine inferiority and the inevitable awareness of her own genius. Very few men can look at that problem dispassionately, with sympathy for both points of view."

He settled back in his chair, nursing his glass between his hands and smiling. His eyes were remarkable, Linda thought; they mirrored his feelings candidly, without evasion or concealment.

"And," she added, "you did it without resorting to the psychological jargon that's so popular today."

"It's hard to avoid," Michael said. "It has become part of our unconscious thinking."

Gordon said interestedly, "A person untrained in psychology—which includes most of us, I suppose—doesn't even use the jargon accurately. If a psychiatrist speaks of paranoia, he is trying to pinpoint a specific syndrome. Whereas a writer, and the majority of his readers, get a much more generalized, and probably wildly inaccurate, picture of behavior."

"That's true," Michael agreed. "But I was thinking more in terms of the way vocabulary reflects changing cultural patterns. Words don't convey a single specific image; they suggest a vast complex of ideas, emotions, and states of knowledge. When we speak of 'guilt,' for instance, we're using the same word that occurs in—oh, St. Augustine, let's say, and Sophocles. But for each of them the word had implications which a modern jurist no longer considers."

"A better example might be the word 'mad.' "

The voice was soft and gentle. There was no reason why it should have startled Linda so badly that the glass almost fell from her hand. She drained its contents. Briggs, rising to refill it, continued in the same mellifluous voice.

"The medieval world, assured of the reality of God and the devil, regarded madness as possession by an evil spirit. We have murdered God by reason; we try to deny the powers of evil by inventing new terms to explain the aberrant behavior that men of the Middle Ages attributed to demons."

"Yes, that's exactly what I meant," Michael said. "Vocabulary reflects the accepted world view of the period. Psychological terminology, however badly used, indicates our rejection of the cruder superstitions of the past."

There was silence when he stopped speaking. Linda sat upright in her chair, feeling, but not responding to, the intense anxiety of Gordon's regard. Belatedly, Michael seemed to sense the change in the atmosphere.

"I try to avoid jargon of all kinds in my writing," he said awkwardly. "Just as I try to avoid strained interpretations of human relationships based on the standard perversions."

"Well, I'm glad to hear that," Gordon said heartily, and Michael laughed. Linda's hand clenched around the glass Briggs handed her. The secretary went to refill the other glasses.

"Gordon's dying to know what you'll say about him," Linda said. "But of course he's too smart to ask outright."

Gordon started to speak, but Michael anticipated him, so smoothly that perhaps no one except Linda noticed how he used the words like a barrier, to shield Gordon from the malice of the speech.

"I don't know myself, yet. What I'm doing now is soaking up atmosphere, if you'll pardon the expression. And very pleasant it is—thank you."

He lifted his glass with a slight bow that was aimed, impartially, at a spot midway between his host and hostess.

"We're trying to prejudice you," Gordon said, smiling.

"I'm always prejudiced right from the first. I'm in favor of people."

"How nice of you," Linda murmured.

This time it was Gordon who came to the aid of his guest. The two of them, Linda thought irritably, worked together as smoothly as Laurel and Hardy. The flush on Michael's face subsided as Gordon talked, blandly and inconsequentially, of words and their meanings, of books and authors and libraries.

"I covet your library," Michael said, looking appreciatively around the room. "When I was an impractical college student I dreamed of having a place like this."

"It's copied from a library in an English country house," Linda said. She smiled sweetly at Gordon. "Volume for volume."

She finished her drink, and Briggs waddled over to take the empty glass.

"I don't think we have time for another, do we?"

The pause, before Gordon spoke, was just long enough to underline the fact that the mistress of the house should have made this comment. "Didn't you order dinner at eight, darling? Ah, yes—here's Haworth."

The butler's quiet "Dinner is served" brought the men to their feet. Linda rose more slowly.

"I'll take my drink with me—darling," she said.

Taking the glass Briggs handed her, she led the way to the dining room.

## III

It was a good many years before Michael could think of his first dinner with the Randolphs without a reminiscent shudder. His host was too nervous to eat, his hostess steadily drank herself, not into a coma but into sharp-tongued virulence, and the pallid secretary stealthily gobbled enormous quantities of food.

When Linda Randolph first entered the library, he realized that she had been drinking; but that fact seemed irrelevant in the presence of such unusual beauty. Her hair was the rare, true black, with a sheen like that of silk; its heavy masses framed a face modeled with a precise delicacy that he had, up till now, seen only in a few masterpieces of sculpture. It was not a conventional type of beauty; many people would think it flawed by the character which gave the features their final definition—a character too strong, too individual for a woman's face. She would never get past the semifinals in a Miss Wheat Cereal contest. But the Wheat Cereal queens didn't have the kind of face that launched ships or burned towers. Linda Randolph did. Helen and Cleopatra probably hadn't been conventional beauties either.

He knew why he had thought of Cleopatra. Linda . . . what an insipid name for that dark, exotic girl. The heavy, gold-trimmed dress emphasized the Egyptian look, but it didn't suit her; stiff with embroidery and gold thread, it stood away from her body and made her look like a well-dressed doll. Her shoulders seemed bowed under the weight of it. She was too thin.

How thin he didn't realize until she came nearer and sat down in a chair only a few feet away. The contrast between the splendid, remote figure in the doorway and the same woman at close range was a little shocking. Michael assumed she was painted and powdered, as all women were, but the best cosmetics in the world could not conceal the underlying pallor and tension of her face. Her hands, dwarfed by the wide sleeves of the robe, looked like little white claws.

He had known a lot of people who drank too much, and some who were genuine alcoholics. Linda Randolph wasn't an alcoholic yet. Not quite.

She held her liquor well, he had to admit that. She'd probably had a few before she came down, but her conversation in the library had been reasonably coherent, even bright. Those digs at her husband . . . Well, married couples did that, especially after a few drinks. *In vino veritas*—and, apparently, the closer the relationship, the nastier the truth. Parents and children, husbands and wives . . . Maybe that was why he'd chosen to remain a bachelor.

During the meal she finished her drink and then started on the wine—a superb Montrachet, too good to be swallowed down like water. The silent butler kept her glass filled. Well, Michael thought, what else can he do? She spoke to the man sharply once, when he was a little slow. Gordon, who would probably behave like a gentleman on his way to be hanged, couldn't object without risking a scene. But his conversational abilities declined noticeably. Finally, in desperation, Michael broke the rule he had made, about discussing business during social hours, and started asking questions.

"Athletic career?" Gordon smiled, and shrugged. "I quit while I was ahead. Never had the necessary motivation to become a professional. That takes concentration. I was interested in too many other things."

He broke off, to sample the wine that was being served with the next course, and Michael brooded. Motivation? Lack of interest? That was the obvious answer to the enigma of Gordon Randolph—athlete, writer, politician, teacher—who had abandoned, of his own choice, each of the professions in which he was expected to excel. The man who had everything—and who wanted nothing. But lack of ambition was too facile an answer.

"Anyhow," Randolph went on, with a nod at the butler, "I was never an all-round athletic type."

"Tennis and swimming," Michael said. "You know, I'd have thought you'd be a good quarterback. You have the build for it, and the coordination."

Gordon grinned.

"I'm a coward," he said amiably. "Didn't care for the prospect of being jumped on by all those big, booted feet."

"No contact sports," Michael said thoughtfully. "And no team sports."

"That's rather perceptive. Even if it does make me sound like a cowardly snob. Or a snobbish coward."

"Maybe just a man of sense," Michael said, smiling. "I can see why those activities might have bored you eventually. What a lot of people hold against you is your failure to write another book."

"Again, I stopped while I was ahead. They say, don't they, that everyone has one good book in him? But how many people have two?"

"Most people don't even have one. And very few have a book as good as *The Smoke of Her Burning*. It's a good title."

"Rather unsubtle, I'm afraid."

"The allusion is to Revelations?"

"Yes. The destruction of the whore of Babylon. Very theatrical."

The conversation had degenerated into a dialogue. Michael preferred it that way. Briggs never had his mouth empty long enough to frame an intelligible comment, and Linda had relapsed into a silence so profound that she might not have been there at all. Only the dress, holding its own shape, sitting empty at the foot of the table . . . It was a gruesomely vivid image, and when his hostess spoke, Michael flinched.

"You haven't read Gordon's masterpiece?"

"Not yet."

"Dear, dear. How inefficient of you." Her voice wasn't slurred; only the extra precision of her enunciation betrayed her condition.

"Well, you see, I have a theory. This is the first time I've tried a biography of a living person. I thought I'd get a personal, over-all impression first, like a quick outline sketch. Then I'll start filling in details."

"But you already knew some of the details. Like the tennis."

"Unfortunately, I can't start with a clean slate in the case of a man like Gordon. I knew most of the basic facts; a lot of people know them. He is a well-known figure."

"Was," Gordon corrected.

At the same moment, his wife said, "The famous, brilliant Gordon Randolph."

Most wives could have said that, in the right tone and with the right kind of smile, and made it sound like an affectionate little joke. Michael thought he had never heard an obscenity that sounded quite as vicious. He said quickly, "That's quite true. Of course I have a certain personal interest. You were one of my father's students in college, weren't you, Gordon?"

"Yes. And going back to that word 'brilliant,' which we use so freely these days, your father was one of the few teachers who really merited the adjective."

"Thank you. I was an uncouth high school brat at that time, but I seem to recall his speaking of you."

"Then you can't claim to have approached me without prejudice," Gordon said pleasantly.

"Yes, I can. I was only interested in two things then—one of them was basketball—and I'm afraid I didn't pay much attention to the conversation of the over-thirty crowd."

"Over thirty or under thirty, they were all the same," Linda said. Her voice had become a little thick. "Members of the fan club. The St. Gordon fan club."

Gordon gave his wife an anguished look, and Michael burst into speech.

"Speaking of my father reminds me of something I've been wondering about. Call it idle curiosity. But I know you haven't permitted an interview for many years. What I wondered was— why me? Sam Cohen, my agent, said you'd specifically mentioned my name. I'm not the most modest member of the Author's Guild, but neither am I the most famous. Was it because of Dad?"

He had meant to insinuate that question at some point, but it came out sounding a good deal more gauche than it might have under other circumstances. He could feel his face getting red as Gordon's quizzical eyes studied him, and he was painfully aware of Linda's unconcealed amusement. She wasn't too drunk to be unaware of his embarrassment.

"What are you doing, fishing for an insult?" Gordon asked with a smile. "Naturally I followed your career with more interest than I would have done, because of your father. But that career itself impressed me with your ability. I like the way you approach your subjects; Linda summed up my feelings exactly. There's warmth and sympathy in your interpretations, and you always see both sides. And, lest your vanity get too swollen, I might add that I mentioned several names. Yours was one."

Michael hadn't gotten that impression; but then, he thought, a good agent—and Sam was one of the best—automatically administered periodic doses of ego booster. Writers needed compliments. The ones who said they welcomed criticism were liars; what they wanted was praise—the more effusive, the better. But then, he thought, who didn't? Probe deeply enough, under the slickest façade of confidence, and you tapped a vein of self-doubt or a hidden fear. Irrational fears and baseless doubts, many of them, but that was precisely why constant reassurance was necessary to the human animal. Maybe, if you reduced the thing to its simplest terms, that was the secret of his success as a biographer. Find the Hidden Fear. Well, at least he didn't sneer at other people's weaknesses, even if they were not his own.

With an effort Michael brought his mind back from one of the peripheral, fascinating side tracks in which it was only too prone to get lost. He was neglecting his duties as guest. With his withdrawal from the conversation, a heavy silence had fallen. Gordon had turned to look at his wife, and the expression on his face, momentarily unguarded, was a graphic and pitiful example of what Michael had been thinking about. He knew what Gordon Randolph's hidden weakness was. Linda was as unresponsive as a Sphinx. (That Egyptian motif again!) She had withdrawn into her own thoughts (and what a hell that world must be), and again Michael had the grisly impression that the far end of the table was occupied by an empty gold-trimmed dress.

He stared blankly down at his empty plate. What the hell had he been eating? The others were finished, except for Briggs, who was methodically chasing down a last fragment of meat. What a pig the man was. Not a fat, healthy, pink pig; a dead pig, already soft with incipient corruption . . .

Michael made a voiceless movement of disgust and protest; and Briggs, having captured and subdued the last bite, looked up.

"Dear me," he said mildly. "I'm afraid I'm keeping you. Gordon's cook is marvelous. And gluttony is, I fear, my abiding sin."

He passed the tip of his tongue over his pale lips, and Michael forced a stiff smile. Taking his secretary's words as a sign that he had finished, Gordon pushed back his chair. Michael understood his need for haste. The man wanted to get his wife into the drawing room, and some coffee into his wife, while she could still walk. His eyes on his hostess's blank, perspiring face, Michael suspected that Gordon had waited too long.

Briggs was closer; he reached Linda first, moving with a scuttling speed that brought another unpleasant zoological comparison to Michael's mind. There was a sly violence in the way he jerked at her chair; and the readiness with which his pudgy hands caught at her, as she staggered, filled Michael with distaste. She turned on him like a cat, her lips drawn back in a snarl, and struck at his hands. Briggs retreated; and Gordon, reaching the foot of the table in two long strides, caught his wife just as she toppled ungracefully forward toward the plates and silverware. His face was a mask of controlled tragedy; but even in that moment of supreme humiliation he had grace enough left to throw a mechanical apology in Michael's direction:

". . . not feeling well."

He carried his wife out; and Michael closed his hanging jaw and looked at Briggs. The little man spread his hands and gave Michael a wistful smile.

"She doesn't like me. It hurts me so much. I have such enormous admiration for the dear lady. And I do try to spare Mr. Randolph all I can."

"I'm sure you do," Michael said.

"You can find your way to the drawing room, can't you? I'll just run along and see if I can be of any help."

Making his way down the interminable corridor, Michael wondered whether Randolph really meant to reappear that evening, much less sit and talk calmly about the projected story of his life. What a life! Didn't the poor devil have any friends, any associates who were comparatively decent and normal? Michael found himself, on that first evening of his visit, filled with a profound pity for the man who had everything.

# Chapter

## 2

MICHAEL CAME DOWN LATE THE NEXT MORNING TO FIND THE breakfast room unoccupied. Gordon had explained that they followed English country-house habits in the morning; he considered it a tyranny to demand that his guests appear at a specified hour for a meal as trying as breakfast.

One of the servants, a well-stacked blonde with skirts so short they took Michael's mind off coffee for several minutes, had shown him the way to the "small dining room." It was a sunny, pleasant room with a table in a circular bay window and silver chafing dishes set out along a sideboard. Michael surveyed the effect approvingly. He wished he knew more about furniture, and all that sort of thing. This stuff was what they called Provincial, he supposed—light in design and color, with flowered drapes and blue-and-white delft pots filled with blooming branches standing around. It was very different from the somber large dining room, with its heavy dark furniture and velvet hangings and family portraits. He wondered how much Linda had had to do with the decoration of the house, and which, if either, of the two styles represented her taste.

He forgot Linda as he foraged happily among the chafing dishes. The butler, bringing fresh coffee and toast, informed him that Mr. Randolph and his secretary had already breakfasted and gone to work; Randolph had said that they would meet for lunch, and suggested that in the meantime Michael explore the grounds. Mrs. Randolph? The butler's face was impassive. Mrs. Randolph always breakfasted in her room.

Along with one hell of a hangover, Michael thought. He finished his coffee and decided he might as well follow Gordon's suggestion of a walk. The view from the window was beautiful; it reminded him of Devon, where he had spent a memorable month slogging through the mud and declaiming the inevitable lines of Browning with the ardor of an eighteen-year-old. Illumined by sunshine, the spring colors of flowers and new leaves were as bright as if they had been freshly painted.

He had to ask directions again to get out of the house. Finally he found his way onto the terrace, an immense flagstoned expanse with half a dozen low steps leading down to a lawn like apple-green velvet. Tulips, one of the few flowers Michael knew by name, made swatches of crimson and yellow along a graveled path. There were other flowers: pink ones and blue ones and spotted ones. The air effervesced like champagne when he breathed it in; he felt dizzy with it. Something smelled good. Must be the pink and blue flowers. As an expert on tulips, he recalled that they didn't smell.

Breathing in and out with self-conscious virtue, he went down the steps, heading for a copse of trees that looked like a pale-pink, low-hanging cloud. Cherry trees, maybe. Or apple. There had been apple trees on his grandmother's farm . . . how many years ago? He was just old enough to revel in nostalgia, instead of finding it hurtful, and his mood was pleasantly self-reproachful as he wandered along the path. Something wrong with people who gave up this kind of life for a foul den in a smoggy hive of sterile buildings and packed humanity. Maybe he would buy himself a cottage someplace. If this book was a success . . .

Midway along the path he turned for a backward look, and stopped short. The night before, he had got only the vaguest impression of the house, which was approached by a long drive through a grove of pines. It had been twilight when he arrived; he had seen a vast, dark bulk, which in the tricky dusk had loomed larger than it was. Or so he had thought. The place *was* big. Built of gray stone, it had three stories and a roof with dormers that might conceal attics or servants' quarters. The wings stretched out on either side of the terrace and the garden. The tower . . . Something wrong with the tower. Michael studied it, frowning. The same gray stone, a handsome slate roof . . . The shape, that was what was wrong. It was too tall, too thin to harmonize with the bulk of the house. And the stairway that wound up, around the exterior, didn't harmonize either. It looked like an afterthought.

Still, the overall effect was impressive. It was a good-looking house. But the impression foremost in his mind was not so much aesthetic as financial. Money. What a hunk of dough this place must have cost, even in the laissez-faire days of Randolph's grandfather. And what it must cost, now, to maintain.

He wandered on, while another long-forgotten memory worked its way to the surface. His mother, in an enormous floppy straw hat and a shapeless skirt—women didn't wear slacks in those days, at least his mother didn't—kneeling on the ground, wielding a busy trowel. She had been an enthusiastic gardener. Maybe, if she had lived longer, she might have been able to impart knowledge about some other plants than tulips. He had been eight when she died. He had hated her for dying. But still there was that undefined feeling of pleasure and content when he saw flowers pink and blue and sweet-smelling. . . .

Rounding the end of the left wing, he saw a bank of flowering bushes and struck off at a tangent to investigate them. With the sunlight full upon them they blazed like fire—orange and purplish red and pink—a brighter shade of pink than the fat flowers in the beds. It was not until he got close that he saw the kneeling figure; and because of his odd mood of reminiscence and receptivity he was struck suddenly breathless. A familiar figure, in a big floppy straw hat, kneeling, the bright flash of a trowel twinkling in its gloved hands . . .

But the straw hat was circled by a strip of figured chiffon, and he had seen its like in shop windows along Fifth Avenue. The kneeling figure wore tight slacks, not a shapeless cotton skirt; and the face that looked up at him, shaded by the brim, had the wide tilted eyes of an Egyptian court lady.

It was reassuring to know that he was not facing a revenant, however fragrant her memory; but the girl who was digging in the dirt was almost as much unlike his hostess of the previous night as she was unlike his mother. If she had a hangover, it didn't show. The lock of hair hanging down over one cheek shone in the sunlight like a blackbird's wing; she brushed it back with a gloved hand and left a smudge of dirt along the exquisite cheekbone.

"Good morning," she said coolly. "I hope Haworth gave you something decent for breakfast."

"More than decent. How was yours?"

She dismissed the inanity with the shrug it deserved.

"Are you soaking up atmosphere or just taking a walk?"

"The latter," Michael said shortly.

"Then allow me to be the perfect hostess. I'll give you the guided tour."

"Don't let me interrupt you."

"This is therapy, not productive labor. There are four gardeners, and they regard me as a necessary nuisance."

She got to her feet, in a movement so smooth that Michael's incipient offer of a helping hand was left dangling. In her flat shoes she came up to his chin. The brim of the hat brushed his nose, and she swept it off, tilting her head back and laughing.

She wore a yellow sweater over her white blouse, with dark-brown slacks. He had thought of her as thin, the night before; now he searched for other adjectives. Slim; wiry; slender . . . No, not slender, that suggested a delicacy, a yielding grace; and the alert tension of her pose was the reverse of graceful. Michael damned his incurable writer's tendency to wallow in words, and smiled back at her.

"The place is beautiful. Are you the genius who planned all this?"

"Heavens, no. It's been like this for a hundred years. Roughly."

"But surely plants and flowers, even trees, need replacing from time to time."

"Gordon does that." There was a slight pause; he had a feeling that she was considering, not what she should say, but how to say it. "His taste is impeccable," she went on. "In everything."

Hm, Michael thought. Probably true. And spoken, if not with enthusiasm, at least with a courteous approval.

"I wish I knew more about these things," he said, indicating the bank of flowering bushes by which they stood. Descriptions of inanimate objects—which, to him, included landscape—were his weak point; he always had to labor over background. But now he found himself searching for color words: Salmon? Fuchsia? (What color was fuchsia, anyhow?) White, of course. That pink wasn't just pink, it was sort of rose-colored and sort of—

"They're azaleas," said his guide, with amusement. "Very common plants."

"Oh." Michael stared blankly at the bushes. "Azaleas. It does sound familiar. I've never seen so many colors."

"Some of the varieties are rare. That group over there is rhododendron."

"Oh."

"You don't have to pretend to be interested." She was laughing, openly; the expression changed her face, robbed it of its oriental elusiveness.

"I am, I am. Keep it up. I'll work it into some book or other and get gushing comments from lady reviewers."

"More likely they'll think you're a woman in disguise—or a bit odd. Men aren't supposed to be interested in flowers."

"Or cats," Michael agreed. "Or birds?"

"Definitely not. You know the stereotype of the male bird watcher."

"Skinny, bespectacled, lisping . . . Interior decoration?"

"Effete," she agreed gravely. "Fashions?"

"Times have changed. I've seen men's boutiques."

The tone of disgust made her laugh again, and after a moment he joined in.

"Sorry, I guess I'm more conventional than I thought. This last century is one of the few eras in history when men weren't concerned with looking like butterflies, when you come to think of it."

"That's right. And you can't think that dandies like Charles the Second and Francis the First weren't one hundred percent male."

"Not if the historical novelists are accurate. Okay. When I get back to town, I'll buy myself a flowered tie and a velvet jacket."

"And flaunt them publicly?"

"Certainly. When I take up a cause, I go all the way."

She looked up at him, with the laughter fading from her face.

"I think you would," she said slowly.

Michael found himself looking, not at her mouth or her chin or her nose, as people ordinarily do when they look at someone, but directly into her eyes. They were extraordinary eyes—so dark that they looked permanently dilated, with the pupils drowned and lost, luminous, shining. . . .

"But," she added, "you wouldn't be easy to convince."

Michael knew he ought to say something, but he couldn't think what. He couldn't even remember what they had been talking about.

Linda broke the spell by turning away.

"You get a good view of the house from here," she said.

Michael shook himself, like a dog coming out of the water, and turned. The view was impressive—and relaxing, after what he had just been looking at. The gray stone of the house was mellowed by sunlight, which sparkled off innumerable windows. Surrounded by a haze of newly leafed trees, with a backdrop of darker green firs, the lovely lines of the house had the appeal of a Constable painting. Except for that damned tower . . .

"It's beautiful," he said.

Linda consulted her watch.

"We can walk down to the grove, and then we'd better turn back. I think Gordon planned to work with you this afternoon, didn't he?"

"He said something about meeting at lunch."

"We'll make it a quick walk, then. You must see the meadow. Gordon's latest scheme, that is; he had it grass planted with daffodils and narcissi, like the meadow at Hampton Court; it's really gorgeous. And the grove is all flowering trees— cherry and apple and plum and almond."

"Oh."

"You'd better take notes," she advised. "Or the lady reviewers will scold you for your errors instead of gushing."

"I have an excellent memory. What are those stout pink and blue things?"

"Hyacinths."

She went on chatting lightly about flowers, pointing out different varieties, explaining that Gordon's rose garden was one of the sights of the neighborhood, and inviting him to come back in June, when it was at its best. The initial mood of their meeting, which had been shaken briefly by that odd exchange of words and glances, was back in full force. Making light conversation, Michael felt bewildered. It was impossible to reconcile this girl, composed and gracious, with the bitter-tongued drunk of the night before. He began to wonder whether he had misinterpreted the incident. Maybe something had happened the day before, something that set her off into behavior that was not a pattern, but an isolated outburst. Maybe he was starting to read too much into looks and expressions. Maybe . . .

"There's one thing I miss," he said casually, as they passed under the hanging boughs of white blossom.

"What's that?"

"The dogs."

He had gone several steps before he realized she was no longer beside him. Turning, in surprise, he saw her framed in apple blossoms, with a shaft of sunlight polishing the green leaves and spotlighting a face gone whiter than the petals.

"What's the matter? Are you ill?"

"Dogs," she said, in a breathy whisper. "What . . . dogs?"

Michael was so shocked by her sudden pallor that it took him a second or two to remember what she was talking about.

"Why—animals in general. Pets. I guess I mentioned dogs because they're always there in my mental pictures of country estates. Those brown-and-white hunting dogs . . . You look terrible. Sit down for a minute."

He put his arm around her rigid shoulders. For a moment they resisted, like rock; then her whole body sagged, so suddenly that he fell back a step under the weight of it, and put his other arm around her to steady her.

Over her bowed head he saw her husband come into sight, at the end of the avenue of cherry trees.

Michael was too concerned for his hostess and too confident of his host to feel any embarrassment at his farcical position. Randolph's smiling face changed and he began to run; but his first words made it clear that he had not misinterpreted the situation.

"Darling, what's wrong? She gets these dizzy spells," he explained distractedly. "Too much sun, or not enough vitamins, or something . . . Linda . . ."

He put his arms around his wife, and Michael hastily removed his. Linda straightened.

"I'm all right. Sorry, Mr. Collins."

"You scared the hell out of him," Gordon said, sharp in his relief. "Damn it, honey, this time I'm not kidding. You've got to see a doctor."

Linda started back toward the house.

"I don't need a doctor."

Her footsteps were a little unsteady, but Gordon made no move toward her. As if by mutual consent, the two men fell into step together, following Linda's slight figure.

"What did you say that set her off?" Randolph asked, under his breath.

Michael stiffened.

"I hope you don't think—"

"Oh, for God's sake. Don't talk like a fool. I meant, what were you talking about when she came over queer?"

Gordon's candid gaze was one of his most attractive features. It was not in evidence now; he scuffed his feet and stared at the ground like a delinquent caught in the act. Michael saw the truth then, and cursed himself for his stupidity. Alcoholism was a symptom, not a disease. Naturally Gordon couldn't come right out with it, not to a stranger . . .

"I don't remember exactly," he said truthfully. "But it certainly wasn't anything that might frighten or distress her. Something about the grounds—flowers, animals, damned if I can recall."

They had been muttering, like stage conspirators. Linda was about ten feet ahead of them. She stopped and turned, and Gordon's reply was never uttered.

"Wait up," he said easily. "What's the hurry?"

"I thought you wanted to get to work. Didn't you come in hot pursuit of your biographer?"

The color had come back to her face, and it was perfectly composed. Too composed; the animation that had given it life was gone, and she looked like a tinted statue.

"No, I finished the letters and thought I'd like a walk." Gordon came up beside her, but he did not touch her or take her arm. "It's a beautiful day," he added.

"Yes, isn't it."

They walked on together—a perfect picture, Michael thought sardonically, of a happy threesome spending a morning in the country. Diffused sunlight trickled through the overhanging boughs, waking highlights in Linda's satiny black hair, turning the tan on Gordon's bare forearms to a golden brown. They made a handsome couple.

"By the way," Linda said casually, "Andrea is back. I've asked her to dinner tonight."

"Oh, for God's sake!" The words were explosive, but there was more amusement than annoyance in Gordon's voice. "Not Andrea!"

"I thought I'd better warn you well in advance," Linda said, smiling up at her tall husband from under the brim of her hat. It was a charming, provocative look; no doubt, Michael thought, it was the oblique slant of those oriental eyes that made him think of something sly and malicious peering out between dark leaves.

"Oh, I don't mind," Gordon said resignedly. "I find the old witch amusing, even if she does hate my guts. But I don't think you're being fair to Mike."

"I thought he might find her amusing too," Linda murmured.

"Who is she?" Michael asked.

"Just what I said." Gordon was smiling. "The local witch."

"What?"

"She lives in a stone cottage that's over two hundred years old," Linda said dreamily. "She keeps cats. One whole wall of the kitchen is fireplace—brick, darkened by centuries of smoke. There's a black pot hanging over the flames, and oak settles on either side of the hearth. The roof is raftered; things hang from hooks in the beams. Bundles of herbs—vervain and mandragora, and Saint-John's-wort. And a stuffed cockatrice."

"And hams and strings of onions," Gordon said drily.

"You're putting me on," Michael said, looking from one smiling face to the other.

"Her mother was a witch, too," Linda murmured. "And her grandmother. It goes back for generations, like the house."

"Cut it out, honey." Gordon smiled. "The old lady is a little touched in the head, that's all. She calls herself a white witch and denies all traffic with the powers of darkness. I think she really believes it herself, which makes her an entertaining conversationalist."

"I'm looking forward to meeting her," Michael said. "One forgets that people really do believe these things, even in this day and age."

" 'There are more things in heaven and earth . . . ' "

"That, of course." Michael studied his host with new inter-

est; none of his perfunctory research had exposed a mystical
streak in Gordon Randolph. "The limitation of human knowledge, at any given point, must be admitted by any rational person. What I meant was that some people believe, literally, in
those old superstitions. I read some books once by a man
named Summers—a twentieth-century priest, Anglican or
Catholic, I forget which, but a trained scholar—who believed in
witchcraft. Not as a historical phenomenon, but as a living
force. He thought—"

"I remember old Montague," Gordon interrupted. "Amazing mind."

"But it follows logically, doesn't it," Linda said, in a high
voice. They had reached the terrace; she stopped, outside the
French doors. "Especially for a priest. If you believe in God,
you must admit the existence of His adversary."

"Certainly; but orthodoxy in these matters is a narrow
tightrope to walk. You can't deny Satan; but you can't attribute
too much power to him without risking the heresy of
Manichaeism. Good and evil—two equal, opposing powers—
that doctrine was condemned at some church synod or other
centuries ago."

He would have gone on, for the subject was one that had interested him once upon a time, if he had not realized, tardily,
that his audience wasn't listening. Linda's face was as blank as
a doll's, and her husband was watching her with that familiar
look of concern.

"I'd better go and change for lunch," Linda said.

Michael watched her disappear through the doors. He half
expected Gordon to speak to him, but Gordon went after his
wife, like a faithful dog. Dog . . . What the hell, Michael wondered, making up the end of the procession—what the *hell* is
going on in this house?


## II


That afternoon Linda searched her husband's room.

Though their bedrooms were connected through the twin-
mirrored dressing rooms, she had not been in Gordon's room
for almost a year. Not since that night . . . Her memory shook,
and went dark, as it always did when she thought about that

night. But surely, today, it would be safe. Gordon and his repulsive secretary were with Michael, and would be until dinnertime. The maids cleaned the bedrooms in the morning. No one else had any business upstairs, except possibly Haworth, the butler, who doubled as Gordon's valet, and she had set him to polishing the silver. It was a week before the silver was supposed to be polished, but . . . so what? That was what she had said to Haworth when he courteously pointed out the discrepancy. So what?

She repeated it now, taking an infantile pleasure in the cheap defiance of the phrase. She giggled softly, remembering Haworth's face when she said it. Then she stopped the giggle with a quick hand that covered her lips. None of that. She had done well, so far today—except for that one slip. If he hadn't sprung it on her unexpectedly, just when she was beginning to relax, to feel confident of her power to charm and convince . . . That had been a bad one. It was all the more necessary now that she be calm. Calm, and charming, and gracious and . . . sane.

Yet, when the heavy door moved under the pressure of her hand, she caught her breath with a sharp sound, and stepped back, jerking her hand away as if the door had been red hot. Fine courage, she jeered silently. You really hoped, deep down inside, that the door would be locked on the other side. It had been locked on her side; surely Gordon had an even stronger reason to keep his door bolted and barred. But he had not done so.

There had not been bolts on either side of the door at first. She had put hers on herself, after that night, on an afternoon when Gordon was out of the house. The whole thing had come in a neat package, enclosed in plastic—the bolt and the screws with which to affix it. She hadn't remembered the need—the so obvious need—for hammer and screwdriver until she stripped off the stiff plastic, kneeling with pounding heart by the closed door. Even now she could recall the wave of terror that had gripped her when she realized she couldn't do the job without tools. It had taken cunning as well as courage to get rid of *them* long enough to sneak into the hardware store in the village. She could never do it again. The thought of boldly entering the tool shed, where the gardener kept his tools, made her stomach turn over. What if he came in and caught her, standing there, with the hammer in her hand?

In the end, with a resource she had thought long forgotten, she had used the heel of a shoe and a nail file.

The whole performance had been ridiculous, of course. She could see that now. Gordon must have known about the bolt. If he had not wanted her to have it, he could have had it removed. But he had never said a word about it. Yet someone must have oiled it, because its surface shone as brightly as it had when she took it out of its plastic cover, and it had slid back without a sound.

Gradually her pounding heart slowed, as no noise came from the next room. She pushed the door open wider and looked in.

His room was the twin of hers in size and shape, except that the high windows on the south wall were French doors, leading out onto a stone-balustraded balcony. They had breakfasted there, on summer mornings, in the first year of their marriage. . . . The furnishings, of course, were quite different. Gordon had had her room redone. His still contained the furniture his grandfather had selected—heavy, dark mahogany, with the unique sheen produced by decades of well-trained housemaids. It was a somber room on dark days, with its dark maroon hangings and heavy carpeting of the same shade. Now the afternoon sun flooded the room, making the deep pile of the carpet glow like aged Burgundy, reflecting blindingly from the tall pier mirrors in their gilt frames. Another of Grandpa's vanities, those mirrors. Gordon looked a lot like him, according to the family pictures.

Tiptoeing, in stockinged feet, she ventured cautiously into the room, casting a frustrated glance at the door that opened into the hall. She wished there were some way of locking it, so she would have warning if anyone came. But the smooth dark surface of the door was unmarred by bolt or chain. She turned to look at the back of the door by which she had entered the room. No—no bolt there either. So, he had never had one put on.

Why had she supposed that he would? Because she had done so. That was illogical. She knew what he would say if anyone asked him—any one of those few who knew what had happened on That Night. Barring his door to her would have been a symbolic thrusting away, a rejection of need and a denial of trust.

She crossed the room. Carefully, touching only the ornate brass knob so that no smudge would mar the gleaming wood, she pulled open the top drawer of the dresser. Handkerchiefs, neat, plain, pure white, without even a monogram. She put out her hand and then drew it back, biting her lip. Damn Haworth and his neatness. It would be impossible to touch anything without leaving a sign of disturbance. The corners of the folded handkerchiefs might have been aligned with a ruler. And damn Gordon, too. He was a fanatic about neatness, he had trained Haworth, and he would be the first to notice the slightest irregularity.

More drawers. Pajamas, neatly folded. Coiled belts, looking like flat, curled snakes. Leather boxes, containing studs, cuff links, and his grandfather's ornate rings—one of the old gentleman's habits that Gordon had not emulated. More underwear. Nothing else. Nothing else visible.

She would have to risk it. Her lower lip caught between her teeth, she turned back to the top drawer and delicately lifted a pile of handkerchiefs. There was nothing underneath except the immaculate lining of the drawer. Her hands began to shake as she returned the handkerchiefs to their place and went to the next pile.

Still nothing.

It was hard to control her hands, they shook so. The silence of the room was unnatural; her ears rang with it. No—it wasn't her ears, it was a fly, trapped against one of the windows. Stupid insect. There was an open window within a few inches of its frantic lunges against the glass. For a long moment Linda stood perfectly still, staring at the small, frantic black dot. The buzzing droned in her ears. She turned back to her self-appointed chore with an abruptness that swept a pajama jacket out of alignment. What was under it?

Nothing. Nothing except the lining of the drawer.

Gradually her movements became quicker, jerkier. She shoved at the last drawer of the dresser, turned, before it had stopped moving, toward the tall bureau.

Sweaters. Folded neatly, encased in plastic bags. Nothing under the sweaters. Scarves. Nothing . . .

Slowly, like a creeping stain, the yellow path of sunlight from the window moved across the rug. As its warmth brushed her arm, Linda flinched and jerked around. It was late, dangerously late. How much longer before the conference ended, before Gordon came up to dress for dinner?

It didn't matter. She had finished the search. There was nothing here, and she ought to have known there would be nothing. Only her desperate desire for something concrete, some proof that might affect an unprejudiced mind, had driven her to what she knew would be a wasted search. It was his study she ought to investigate. His study, or . . .

The sunlight seemed brighter; it hurt her eyes. Her breathing was so uneven, it caught at her throat in sharp gasps. Nerves. She was getting upset. And that was bad, because tonight she had to be perfect. Calm, and composed, and . . . She needed something to calm her nerves.

Gordon's study, or—the other place. The most likely place, and the one room that she could not risk searching. Because the secretary had arranged with the servants to clean it himself, and there was no conceivable reason why she should need to enter Jack Briggs's private quarters. If anyone found her there—if *he* found her . . .

A long shiver ran through her body. Dropping the last scarf back into the drawer, she turned and ran across the room, on soft stockinged feet. The bottle, the comforting, reliable bottle in the bottom drawer of her dressing table . . .

She closed the door and shot the bolt into place—leaving behind the marks of her feet imprinted as clearly in velvety pile as in snow, and two drawers standing open, spilling out their contents onto the floor.

# Chapter

## 3

WHEN LINDA WOKE, IT WAS GETTING DARK OUT-SIDE. THE HIGH windows were gray oblongs; the dim light within the room reduced furniture and hangings to unfamiliar menaces.

She sat up, brushing the strands of hair back from her face. Her mouth was horribly dry. She reached for the glass of water on the bedside table and swallowed it down, so grateful for the relief to parched membranes that she hardly noticed its stale taste. Still fuzzy with sleep, she didn't think about the time until her half-closed eyes lit on the illumined dial of the clock.

She jumped up from the bed and stood swaying dizzily as the sluggish blood moved down from her head. Late. It was very late. She had meant to take extra time over her dressing, to apply makeup with extra care. She had hoped to speak privately with Andrea before the others joined them.

Where the hell was that stupid maid?

She groped for the buzzer and jabbed it impatiently. She had just found the light switch when the door burst open. Dazzled, Linda blinked at her maid.

"You're supposed to knock," she said angrily. "And why did you let me sleep so long? You know I'm late."

Anna's mouth drooped open another inch. She was silent for a moment, as if trying to decide which criticism to answer first.

"But, madam, you've told me time and again not to bother you unless you ring. And this time, the bell—it sounded sort of frantic, and I thought maybe you'd hurt yourself or something—"

"Oh, shut up," Linda said. The very reasonableness of the girl's defense infuriated her. "Straighten up this mess. Find me something to wear."

With a murmured "Yes, madam," Anna picked up the shoes Linda had left in the middle of the floor and carried them to the dressing room.

From where she stood, Linda could see the far wall of the dressing room, which was one huge mirror, polished to shining perfection. Out of its depths, another Anna advanced briskly to meet the one who was entering the room. The identical twin figures were an uncanny sight; but Linda paid no attention to that, or to the expression on the mirrored face, which had relaxed when Anna thought herself no longer under observation. Part of the bedroom was reflected in the mirror, and it was, as she had said, a mess. She had thrown herself down on the bed without turning back the spread; the satin surface was wrinkled and ugly, with a dark spot near the pillow where her mouth had rested. Her gardening clothes, which she had changed before lunch, lay in crumpled heaps on the floor. Beside the bed, as if fallen from a nerveless hand, was an empty bottle.

Linda gaped at it in vague surprise. Had she really finished the whole bottle? Surely this one had been almost full when she took it out of the drawer.

She shoved it aside with her foot, wrinkling her nose at the sour reek of spilled liquor. Her tweed skirt was twisted and her right stocking marred by a run. There were stains on the front of her blouse.

"Run my bath," she called, tugging at the zipper of the skirt.

Anna appeared in the doorway.

"But, madam, it's late—"

"Whose fault is that?" Linda asked pettishly. "Oh, for God's sake, I'll make it a shower then. Get my clothes out. The black culotte thing, stockings, the gold sandals—and hurry up, damn you."

She moved toward the bathroom, shedding clothes as she went, watching with malicious satisfaction as Anna stooped to pick up each item. Anna grunted when she bent over. She was too fat, that was her trouble. Linda gave the right hand tap a vicious twist and stepped under a spray of water that felt as if it had been refrigerated.

The treatment was drastic, but effective; she knew, from past experience, how effective. When she came out of the bathroom, she felt fairly human again, and by the time she was seated at the dressing table, with Anna's nimble fingers working at her hair, she was able to be cunning.

"I'm sorry I spoke to you as I did," she said, watching Anna's face in the mirror. "I'm always cross when I sleep in the afternoon. It was my own fault that I was late."

The sullen pink face did not change, nor the pale eyes move from their work.

"That's quite all right, madam," Anna said.

So much for that. There was no use trying to influence the girl now; she knew too much.

When Linda went down, she knew that she looked as good as skilled grooming and expensive clothes could make her look. But the black outfit had not, perhaps, been a wise choice. She liked the freedom of the wide black trousers, so full that they resembled a skirt except when the wearer was in motion; but the bodice left her arms and throat bare, and seemed to show more bone than flesh. She had had to send Anna to bore a new hole in the belt, and when it was buckled tightly it gathered the dress in unbecoming folds around the waist. *I'm too thin*, she thought, and then: *Pathos; I'm appealing to his sense of pity. Nice. And it probably won't work, either.*

The others were already assembled in the drawing room, not in the library this time. Gordon did seem to get a perverse pleasure from Andrea's company; he loved baiting her. But he would never admit her into his sanctum.

As she went down the hall, Linda knew she was walking faster than usual, almost running. Something pulled at her like a magnet acting on a lodestone. She had felt it that morning, sensing his presence even before she saw him. Tonight the tug was even stronger. That was all it was so far, nothing reasoned or desired, only a blind, mindless need. Like a fish on a line, she thought angrily, and shoved at the hangings over the doorway.

Andrea had already arrived. Sprawled with her usual lack of grace in an armchair near the fire, she raised a fat hand in greeting, and Linda saw her suddenly, not as the familiar friend, but as she must have appeared to a stranger, even one as tolerant and sophisticated as Michael Collins.

She was a very ugly old woman. Her ugliness was not the distinguished plainness some homely girls acquire in old age; it was plain, unvarnished, positive ugliness, strengthened by cultivated sloppiness. Her wrinkled face was overlaid with a thick coating of powder; her lipstick, applied in a wide slash without the aid of a mirror, always left smears on cigarettes and glasses. Her hair was another, clashing, shade of red, worn in a frizzy halo. Her dresses looked like the sort of thing that might be worn by a gypsy fortuneteller at a fair. Tonight, in honor of the occasion, she had added a few more yards of beads to the collection around her neck, and changed her long, full calico skirts for a magenta taffeta one of the same style. Long brass earrings dangled from her ears. In her left hand she held a jade cigarette holder.

*I hate her*, Linda thought. *Fat, ugly old woman . . .*

She knew a moment of despair so absolute that it felt like death. What had possessed her to ask Andrea to dinner? Some unformed idea of help, of support? But it wouldn't work that way. Andrea's weight would be on the other side of the scales, pushing them down, against her.

"Hello, Andrea," she said. "I hope the trip was successful."

"Darling girl," Andrea said effusively. She waved the cigarette holder, endangering her mop of hair. "Yes, I was just telling the boys about it. It was nasty, but I managed."

"A case of demonic possession," Gordon explained solemnly. "By—Beelzebub, was it, Andrea? Or Belial?"

"Oh, you nasty skeptic," Andrea said. She grinned at Gordon. The effect was hideous—white, unnaturally perfect teeth framed in smeary scarlet lipstick. "You know I'm never sure who it is. I just reel off a list of names and tell them all to get the hell out of the patient. It has to be one of the bunch."

Linda glanced at Michael. His expression was just what she had expected it to be—incredulity and amusement covered by a thin glaze of polite interest.

"Andrea, you are too much," she said irritably. "You sound like a charlatan."

"The fakers are the ones who bother with fancy words," said Andrea, flicking the ash off her cigarette. It landed on the Aubusson carpet, and she smeared it around with her foot. "I tell it like it is."

"Tell me," Michael said, leaning forward, "how do you go about exorcising an evil spirit? I know the Roman Church has a ritual for that purpose, but I don't imagine you—"

"No, I've got my own methods," Andrea said complacently. "Not that the other isn't effective enough. But it has to be performed by an ordained priest."

"That's right. I'd forgotten."

"You've studied the subject? Mm-hm. But you don't believe."

"No."

Reading their faces, Linda leaned back with a feeling of relief. Andrea's judgments of people were quick and violent—like or dislike, immediate and instinctive. Apparently she approved of Michael Collins. She grinned at him and he grinned back, remarking,

"At this point I'm supposed to say, 'Not that I haven't seen things, strange things, that were hard to explain by the normal laws of nature.' But I can't say that. I've never had the faintest flash of clairvoyance, nor seen a ghost."

"Never had the feeling that you'd been somewhere before, done the same thing at another time?"

"*Déjà vu?* Of course. Everyone has had that experience. It's easily explained in terms of subconscious resemblances, forgotten memories, without resorting to theories of precognition or reincarnation."

"*Touché,*" said Gordon softly, from the depths of his chair.

Andrea turned on him with a metallic jangle of jewelry.

"*Touché*, hell. Skeptics always drag that one out. They have an answer for everything—if you let them throw out half the evidence. I can quote you, offhand, a dozen cases of genuine precognition. Impressions of a scene, a house, a face—recorded and witnessed—which appeared at a later time."

It was the old familiar ground; they had been over it a dozen times, arguing in a perfectly good-humored way, which still made Linda queasy and nervous. Gordon was leading Andrea on again, not only for his own amusement but to entertain his guest. But now the conversation took an unexpected twist.

"Precognition, telepathy, clairvoyance," Michael said. "Aren't we wandering a bit from the track? ESP is one thing; demons are another. Or so it seems to me."

The room was brightly lit. One of Gordon's phobias was a dislike of darkness. There was no reason why Linda should have had the impression of something pale and shapeless stirring in a shadowy corner. There were no shadows; and the movement was only that of Jack Briggs, shifting in his chair. He was so quiet most of the time that his infrequent movements were startling.

"Your assumption is correct," he said in a precise, lisping voice, "if we accept your definitions of normal and extranormal. But there is a single consistent hypothesis which accounts both for what you call clairvoyance, and for—demons."

Andrea gave him a queer look of mingled respect and hostility.

"That's right," she said reluctantly. "Look here, Mr. Collins, do you believe in God?"

Michael was silent. Andrea chuckled. Her laugh was not the dry cackle her appearance led one to expect, but a high-pitched, childish giggle.

"Funny," she said drily. "That question really gets people these days. They'll answer impertinent questions about their sex life and their emotional hang-ups, just to prove they're modern, emancipated intellectuals. But ask 'em about God and they squirm like a spinster when you mention virginity."

"*Touché* yourself," Michael said good-humoredly. "No, I was speechless out of ignorance, not embarrassment. I just don't know. That's as honest an answer as I can give."

Andrea nodded. Her face was grave, and not without a certain dignity.

"Fair enough. Let's avoid the embarrassing word, then. Do you believe in the existence of Good?"

"Philosophically, theologically, or historically?"

"Cut that out."

"All right," Michael said resignedly. "But you'll accuse me of equivocating again. Sometimes I do believe. Sometimes I have serious doubts."

Gordon leaned forward.

"No one who has studied history can believe in a benevolent creator," he said.

Michael looked at him curiously. Andrea ignored him.

"All right, Mr. Collins," she said. "You've already answered the next question, but I'll put it anyhow. Do you believe in the existence of Evil?"

Gordon, sensing his guest's discomfort, started to protest.

"Andrea, this is a ridiculous conversation. Can't we—"

"No," Linda interrupted. She had not meant to speak. The sound of her own voice startled her; it was harsh and peremptory, unlike her usual tones. "No. Let him answer."

"Of course," Michael said easily. "I'm enjoying this, Gordon. I'm just afraid of sounding like a fool. Philosophy was never one of my subjects."

"Philosophy be damned," Andrea said rudely. "I'm not interested in quibbles about Kant's categories of whatever the hell they are. Evil is a living, conscious force, operating in this world and the next. Anyone who denies that does sound like a fool."

"Evil deeds," Michael said. "Even evil men. "But—Evil, with a capital E? An impersonal, active power?"

"There is nothing impersonal about Lucifer," said Briggs's soft voice.

The ensuing silence was broken by Gordon.

"Jack is inclined to be dogmatic about his faith."

He spoke to Michael, who smiled politely. Briggs laughed aloud.

"You needn't apologize for me, Gordon. The orthodox believer must walk softly these days, it is true. But I feel sure that Mr. Collins is not offended by any expression of honest faith."

"That depends on the faith," Michael said drily. "Some beliefs are no less pernicious for being honest. But I don't see why I should be offended at an admission of belief in the devil."

Briggs chuckled again. His pudgy hand waved his half-full glass in a mocking salute. Linda realized that no one had offered her anything to drink. For once the thought did not preoccupy her. She was too engrossed in the greater need. *Ask him,* she begged silently, focusing her demand on Andrea. *Ask him, I can't. And I've got to know.*

"Then you don't believe in Satan—the powers of evil," Andrea persisted.

Gordon groaned, half humorously.

"Andrea, you have the subtlety of a pile driver. And the mindless persistence."

"And the directness," Michael said, smiling. "After the *double-entendres* of the literary world I find it refreshing. No, Miss Baker—Andrea, then, if you insist—I do not believe in Satan."

"Then how do you explain the existence of evil?"

"Do I have to explain it? I've got problems enough."

"Don't be frivolous."

"I beg your pardon." Michael sobered. "A number of explanations have been offered, have they not?"

"None make any sense." Andrea dismissed the garnered wisdom, philosophy, and theology of the world with a shrug. "Given the omnipotence of God and His complete unshadowed benevolence, you can't account for evil."

"The finite mind of man," Michael said, with the air of someone who is quoting, "cannot comprehend the eon-long plans of the Infinite."

"Baloney," Andrea said. Michael started at the word. "If our kindness is only a weak imitation of the supreme benevolence of God, and we gag at cruelty, how can He endure it, or condone it—much less perpetrate it, as He does, by your definitions?"

"Now wait a minute," Michael protested. "They aren't my definitions. I only said—"

"Baloney," Andrea repeated. The light was merciless on her face as she leaned forward. The wrinkled, cosmetic-caked skin looked like lava that had coincidentally congealed into the simulacrum of a human face. "The only hypothesis that accounts for evil is the existence of another Power, equal to the power of good and unalterably opposed to it."

"Manichaeism," Michael muttered. He glanced at Gordon. "Odd. We were talking about it earlier today."

If he was looking for help in changing the subject, he didn't get it. Gordon simply nodded.

"You're trying to snow me with words," Andrea said. "Think I'm a dumb old woman, don't you? Well, I know what Manichaeism is, it just so happens. They were on the right track; but they were wrong, just the same. Evil is! It exists! And you've got to fight it!"

Even Linda, tense and involved, had to admit that the choice of words was unfortunate; they sounded like a parody of a football cheer, and the muffled thud of Andrea's fist, pounding the arm of the sofa, was equally anticlimactic. Linda was the only one who didn't smile. Even Andrea looked, momentarily, as if her mouth might relax. But Briggs's oily chuckle tightened it again.

"You're the worst of the bunch," she said obscurely, glaring at the secretary. "You and your damned Lucifer!"

Briggs chortled again, and Michael's laugh echoed his.
"A singularly appropriate adjective," he said, grinning.
Linda couldn't stand it any longer. It was no use. Now she
would have to try the other way. She jumped to her feet.
"Isn't it time for dinner?" she demanded; and without waiting for Gordon's answer, she went on wildly, "Of all the stupid,
idiotic conversations . . . Let's talk about heroin, or the crime
rate, or something pleasant. And someone get me a drink!"

By the time dinner was over, Linda felt better, except for the
bad taste in her mouth, which no variety of food or drink was
able to remove. They talked about heroin and the crime rate;
about massacres in Iraq and starvation in India and poverty in
Appalachia. Briggs gobbled and Andrea ate sloppily, scattering
crumbs. Gordon ate almost nothing.
    When they went back to the living room for coffee, Andrea
lingered, touching Linda's arm as if she wanted to exchange a
word in private. Linda brushed past her. There was no use talking now. Andrea was a fool, like the others, a loudmouthed,
bragging fool. She had done more harm than good. No, there
was nothing for it now but to try the only remaining means of
approach.
    It wasn't easy to arrange, though. Everyone seemed relaxed
and lethargic after a heavy meal and an abundance of wine. Andrea flung herself down in her favorite corner of the sofa.
Michael had chosen a chair by the fire; only his long legs and
the top of his head were visible. Linda sat on the edge of her
chair, nerves prickling. She didn't see how she was going to
manage it. Unless, later . . . But that was dangerous, roaming
the halls alone in the night. And it had to be tonight. He was
leaving the next morning.
    The fire crackled in the vast stone hearth, but its light was
diffused and lost in the brightness of the lamps scattered around
the room. The paneled walls and lovely stuccoed moldings of
the beamed ceiling were another successful copy of an old English original. She had been unfair, of course, to attribute this
artistic servility to Gordon. The house had been built by his
grandfather, after his first trip abroad. He had been a parvenu,
and *nouveau riche,* and all the other offensive French snob
terms; but Linda supposed she ought to give the old man credit

for realizing his own lack of taste. Rather than make a mistake, he had simply copied what he knew to be beyond criticism. It was a fault and a weakness in herself that she preferred to make her own mistakes.

Linda roused herself long enough to accept the brandy Briggs was handing around, and then slumped back into lethargy. They were at it again, Gordon and Andrea—not about demons, this time, but about gardening, which was their other major source of disagreement. If, as Gordon always said, you could call Andrea's mixture of superstition and random digging real gardening.

Characteristically, Michael was trying to keep the peace.

"I think science is now coming around to Andrea's point of view," he said. "Didn't I read somewhere that there may be a chemical present in the skin of certain people which stimulates plant growth? The old green thumb made respectable?"

Gordon made a rude noise and Michael grinned amiably at him. Linda was accustomed to her husband's ability to charm; but he had succeeded even faster than usual in winning Michael. Slouched companionably in two chairs, side by side, they gave the impression of having known one another for years. To Linda's annoyance Andrea failed to see the amused sparkle in Michael's eyes, the reflection of Gordon's sly amusement. With loud cries of pleasure, the old woman amplified Michael's comment, adding, "You don't pay enough attention to these things, Gordon. If you'd listened to me, your marjoram would be in better shape."

Gordon laughed aloud, and Andrea finally realized that she was being made fun of. Her eyes narrowed angrily.

"I didn't know you had an herb garden, Gordon," Michael said. "How did I miss it today?"

"It's on the north side. Linda was the one who wanted an herb garden, so I had it laid out according to one of the old Elizabethan manuals. But Andrea is right. My marjoram is in wretched condition."

"I thought marjoram was a girl's name," Michael admitted.

"It's a rather common plant. I've got a few of the rarer kinds that I'm quite proud of. Did you know that there are strict rules for the layout of such gardens—specific plants next to others, some which must be planted in borders, and so on? I've gotten quite fascinated by it, even though it was Linda's idea to begin with."

She felt their glances, but did not respond. Whose idea had it been? Hers, his—someone else's? Surely that was unimportant—except as another proof of her failing memory. Then, belatedly, she realized what they were talking about, and she sat up a little straighter. This might be the chance she had been waiting for.

". . . not like ordinary floodlights," Gordon was saying. "It's a new system. The effect is like very strong moonlight. No, it's no trouble; I had switches installed all over the house. And I love to show off my gadgets."

They were all at the window; Gordon was pulling back the heavy damask drapes. Linda turned in time to see Gordon touch the switch and the high oblong of black window turn silver as the outside lights went on.

Michael made appreciative noises.

"It does suggest moonlight," he said. "If I were ten years younger I'd turn it on at night and go for a moonlight stroll—tripping over things and reciting poetry."

"You can't see the herb garden, though," Gordon said, peering. "It's mostly hidden by the boxwood. Moonlight stroll? That's a good idea, Mike. It's a little chilly, but not too bad. Linda? Andrea?"

Out in the false moonlight, among the shrubbery, one person, or two, might casually wander away from the others. . . . Linda met her husband's eyes, and a cold, sobering shock ran through her. It was as if he could read her thoughts.

"No," she said. "I don't feel like it. But the rest of you go ahead."

When they had left—Andrea still arguing about marjoram, Briggs trailing his master in silent devotion—Linda got up and went to the window. The pale gray light did not suggest moonlight, not to her distorted imagination. It was a dull, unearthly light, like phosphorescence. It was bright enough; she could make out the tiny individual leaves on the boxwood hedges, twenty feet away. But instead of silvering objects as moonlight did, this light gave them a strange dead hue, between gray and green.

She shrank back into the concealment of the draperies as

the others came into view, strolling slowly across the gray-washed grass. Andrea's floppy sleeves were wrapped around the upper part of her body. It must be pretty chilly outside. Gordon, as always the perfect host, spoke to the old woman and she shook her head vehemently—denying, Linda thought, any need for a wrap. Andrea prided herself on rising above physical needs. Old fool, Linda thought angrily.

After a time her mood improved. It was fun, watching people when they thought they were unobserved, studying faces and gestures undistracted by the added element of speech. Michael was a little taller than Gordon. He had a ridiculous way of walking, like—like a—her mind fumbled for an analogy and then, suddenly, she giggled. Like a camel. The same mixture of awkward angularity and inner dignity.

Gordon's head had been turned away from her. Now he turned, stretching out his arm to indicate some point of interest. His face was alive with the inner fire of personality that gave it its charm, and his sharp-cut features had a beauty even the ghastly light could not spoil. For the first time in months Linda's body responded with an inner twist that was more painful than a physical blow. Gordon, she thought. The name was like an incantation, loosening a flood of memories.

It hadn't been so long. Five years. Was that all? It seemed longer. . . . But she could still visualize Gordon as he had looked the first time she saw him, standing by the battered desk in Room 21 of Goddard Hall—the English Department. Only a dozen of them had signed up for the course, in the Art of the Novel; the departmental chairman had restricted it to seniors. But every eligible senior had registered. They were curious. A little skeptical, some of them, of a visiting professor who was only teaching one course, a non-academician, an intruder from the world of politics and inherited wealth. The Establishment—though they didn't call it that, then. But no one was contemptuous. Whatever his background, the fact remained that Gordon Randolph had written one of the big books of the decade, which had won every literary prize of its year.

If he sensed their curiosity and skepticism, he didn't show it. The tall, well-knit figure was relaxed, leaning against the desk; the handsome face smiled slightly, a smile that warmed the dark eyes. Even his clothing was perfect—loafers, dark slacks, tweed jacket. If the jacket had been cut by a tailor whose income was higher than that of any of the professors, it did not flaunt its ancestry. A stupider man might have had unnecessary patches added to the elbows, or affected a pipe. Gordon smoked cigarettes, from a crumpled pack that lay on the desk. That might have been affectation, but Linda didn't think so. In those days he smoked incessantly, one cigarette after another. That was before the doctors had started warning about cancer. Gordon quit then. . . .

It came back to her so vividly—the shabby old room, scarred and scuffed by generations of students; the dusty sunlight pouring in through streaked panes, brightening the colors of the girls' pastel sweaters and blouses, showing the unformed contours of the boys' faces. . . . Beside Gordon's sure maturity they had seemed so young. Of course all the girls had fallen in love with him, even the ones who sneered at crushes on teachers. And the boys, after the initial antagonism, had succumbed in a different way. Linda could still feel the shock of incredulity when she realized that this god, this *man*, was looking at her with more than the smiling courtesy he displayed toward the others. That when he talked to her, his voice was different. That he really felt—

The vision was so real that the interruption made it waver and shake, like a film on a cracking screen. Linda turned with the bright shards of memory still close around her and blinked through dazzled eyes at the man whose arrival had disturbed her.

He was alone.

"Where—where are the others?" she stammered.

"Andrea's muttering incantations over some plants," Michael said with a smile. "Gordon was called to the telephone, and Briggs went with him."

"Oh."

Slowly Linda relaxed her cramped fingers, which had been clutching the edge of the drapes. Her mind began to function again. If Briggs had gone with Gordon, the telephone call must have been a business call, and it might take some time. Andrea in the garden, lost in her crazy spells . . .

*You see,* one of those disembodied voices murmured gently, *if you want something badly enough, it arranges itself.* . . .

She smiled, slowly, and saw the subtle response in Michael's face; she turned, slowly, slowly, and looked out into the palely lighted night. He would have to join her at the window; it would only be courteous. And from here she could see Andrea returning. She could hear, if she listened carefully, any footsteps approaching the room.

He came. She had known he would.

"Very effective," he said, after a moment.

Startled, Linda looked up at him. Just what had he meant by that ambiguous adjective? Whether he meant to refer to the lights or not, she would have to assume that he had.

"I don't really like it," she said. "The lighting."

"Why not?"

"Oh, I don't know. It bothers me, somehow."

"Because it's not real? You are bothered by pretense?"

This time she could not be mistaken. There was a slight but definite mocking tone in his voice.

"No," she said sharply. "I don't object to good imitations. But there's a tint in this light that is like a travesty of moonlight. Greenish. Don't you see it?"

Michael looked, frowning in concentration. That was one of the qualities that made him so attractive. He seriously considered new ideas. He might be prejudiced against her—that was inevitable—but he would not dismiss any reasonable question without thinking about it.

"You're right," he said finally. "You don't see it right away."

"No. It—grows on you."

Linda moved a little, shifting position. Her bare arm brushed his sleeve. She felt the slight recoil of his arm with satisfaction. He was not impervious. But then which of them was? Old and young, stupid and brilliant, sensitive and brutal—they were all alike in this one thing. If she couldn't reach the mind of the individual man, she would reach the male animal. But she would have to force it upon him. He was civilized enough, and cautious enough, to reject subtle advances. Some men would have responded before this.

She swayed, raising one hand to her face. Crude, this method, but time was short. Once she was in his arms, the rest would follow.

He had to put his arm around her; he couldn't let her crash to the floor at his feet.

"Feeling dizzy again?" he asked coolly. "You'd better sit down."

"No. I'll be all right in a minute."

Damn him, she thought. He was as rigid as a stick of wood. It was hard to resist his effort to move her toward a chair or couch, and still seem limp and helpless. She let go completely, clinging to him with both hands, her body against his.

There was a moment of resistance. He knew quite well what she was doing. Then it happened, as she had known it would. That the response was purely mechanical, a reflex that his mind rejected and resented, she did not care.

But as his arms tightened and his head bent, seeking her mouth, a strange thing happened. It was the first time for many months that a man had touched her in this way, and she had expected her body to respond with starved alacrity, all the more so because he was a man to whom she might have been attracted, normally, under normal circumstances. How abnormal these circumstances were she did not realize until she felt her head twist, avoiding the kiss she had invited, and sensed the pressure of her hands against his chest. His arms loosened; he could hardly escape feeling the mindless revulsion that filled her. And then, over the curve of his arm, she saw the eerily lighted window and the thing that stood outside, on the lawn, staring in at her.

Only once before had she seen it so distinctly. It stood quite still. Still as a statue, still as a figure painted by a child or a primitive artist—an outline sketched by a sharp pen and filled in, solidly, with black ink. Yet the individual hairs, bristling along the curve of the back, were distinct; so was the heavy, predatory muzzle and the thrust of the head. The only lights in the whole mass were the eyes—red, luminous, glowing like coals.

From a great distance Linda heard Michael's voice repeating her name. She wasn't pretending now, and he knew it. But his voice was lost in the shrieking cacophony of the other voices, the voices that had haunted her for months, risen now to a whirl of mocking laughter: *We told you, we told you. Now it's too late. Too late, too late, too late . . .*

Then all the voices faded into blackness and silence.

# Chapter
## 4

A SHARP, STINGING SCENT PIERCED LINDA'S LUNGS. SHE STRUG-gled, choking. Her face was all wet; cheeks and hands stung as if they had been slapped. Opening reluctant eyes, she saw a face near hers. It was not one of the faces she expected to see, and for a moment it was as unfamiliar as a total stranger's. A round, florid man's face, with horn-rimmed glasses and thick, iron-gray hair . . . Gold. Doctor Gold. Linda's eyes closed again.

"I'm all right," she muttered, as the doctor waved the horri-ble-smelling thing under her nose again. "Don't . . ."

"Sure you're all right," he agreed smoothly. "Just fainted. Take it easy for a minute."

He patted her shoulder mechanically and stood up. Gordon must have dragged him away from a quiet evening at home; he was tieless, and pepper-and-salt stubble darkened his heavy jowls. As he moved away from her, Linda saw Andrea at the foot of the couch on which she was lying. The old woman was bent like a priest bowing before the Host; her hands wove pat-terns in the air and she crooned under her breath. A wave of fee-ble dislike swept Linda. How could she have had such faith in the old witch? Not that Andrea didn't—know things. But she hadn't been much help so far. Her behavior tonight had been maddeningly wrong, evoking hostility instead of sympathy. What on earth did she think she was doing now—summoning her friend's wandering spirit back into her body?

Her ritual completed, Andrea caught Linda's eye. She leaned forward over the foot of the couch.

"What was it?" she hissed.

Linda shook her head. Stupid, stupid . . . she couldn't talk about it here, Andrea knew that. But sooner or later she would have to tell Andrea about the latest appearance. Whom else could she talk to? No one else would believe her. Andrea only believed because she was half crazy herself.

Her eyes pulled away from the avid demand in the older woman's gaze. Michael was nowhere in sight; probably he had effaced himself, as any proper visitor would when the hostess was taken ill. Linda wondered where he was. She wondered why she cared—why this one man's absence from a room could make it feel empty. Especially now, after that unexpected fiasco at the window . . .

She forced herself to concentrate on the important presences. Gordon and Hank Gold made a significant little group, standing with their backs turned, talking in voices so low she could not make out the words. She didn't need to hear, she knew what they were saying. Once Gordon had made her visit Gold professionally. The doctor had poked every muscle in her body and taken samples of everything that was detachable. Then he had sat and talked. She had not been in good shape that day; the trend of the conversation had got away from her. Finally she had had to invent an excuse for leaving. It was a flight, rather than departure, and Gold had been well aware of it. After that, she had refused to consult him again; had he not admitted that all her physical tests were normal? But she couldn't prevent Gordon from inviting his friend and neighbor to dinner occasionally. She couldn't always excuse herself on the grounds of a headache. She couldn't keep Gordon from telling him things.

And now—now she would have to fight. If there was the slightest hint, the least admission of what she thought she had seen . . . Panic twisted her stomach. Michael. Had she spoken to him in the last seconds, gasped out any damning description of the thing that stood glaring outside the window? There was no need to wonder whether he had seen it. No one saw it except she herself. Once, when she was showing Hank Gold the gardens, it had passed through the darkening twilight like a flash of black fog. Turning, at her startled exclamation, he had denied seeing anything except a shadow. That made it all the more important that she should not mention the word now—that deadly, ominous common noun.

The conference ended. They turned and came to her, Gordon first, the doctor following, scratching at his chin.

"Bed for you, baby," Gordon said, with a forced smile. "Hank says you'll be fine after a good night's sleep."

Linda gathered her wits together.

"Hank probably hates both of us," she said. "Dragging him out in the middle of the night just because I fainted."

Gordon's smile faded.

"I couldn't get you out of it," he said. "This can't go on, Linda. You must agree—"

A hand on his arm stopped him. Gold was smiling, but his eyes gave him away.

"This girl needs rest, Gordon, not a lecture. We'll discuss it in the morning."

"Sorry," Gordon muttered.

"Nothing to be sorry about." It was farcical, the contrast between Gold's smile, his casual voice, and his intent, betraying stare. "Here, Linda, pop one of these down. Then off you go. I'll see you in the morning."

It appeared as if by legerdemain, a small white capsule lost in the vast pink reaches of his hand.

"What is it?" Linda asked.

"Just a mild sedative. So you can sleep."

Trapped, Linda looked from the little pill to Gold's face—pink, smiling and inexorable.

Silently she took the capsule. What was the use?

When she had swallowed it, both men seemed to heave a simultaneous sigh of relief. They expected more of a fight, Linda thought, and derived a faint, grim satisfaction from fooling them even that much. This was right; this was how she had to behave from now on. She had been wrong, before, to struggle openly.

"I'll carry you," Gordon said.

She waved him off.

"Up all those stairs? I can walk perfectly well."

The room wavered as she sat up and Gold came to her assistance. She was glad to lean on the arm he offered. It was better than some of the other possibilities. Now that she was standing, she could see Michael, near the door. She walked slowly toward him, leaning on the doctor's arm.

It was impossible for her to tell, from his carefully controlled face, what he might have heard—or repeated. But she had to know.

"What made me faint, Hank?" she asked, in a sweet, worried voice.

"I can't be sure, my dear, until we run a few tests."

Linda stopped, pulling on his arm.

"But you gave me every test you could think of. You said I was fine." Her voice rose; with an effort, she got control of herself. "I hate being jabbed with needles," she said meekly.

"Many people do." Gold's chuckle would have deceived most listeners. "My own nurse—would you believe it, I've got to give her a tranquilizer before I can take a blood sample. I think you're very good about it, Linda."

"But if the other tests were normal—"

"My dear, that was just a routine physical. There are rare diseases and deficiencies that require specific analysis. I may have missed something."

"Such as what?"

She didn't look at the doctor; she looked at Michael, now only a few feet away. And she knew.

"My dear child, I can't possibly speculate. It could be anything from an allergy to a chemical deficiency. Perhaps you can give me the clue—something you ate or drank, something you did today. . . . Come along, now, you ought to be in bed; we'll talk about it tomorrow."

The pressure of his arm increased and Linda went with it, no longer resisting. She had found out what she needed to know. During Gold's final speech, Michael's eyes had met hers. There must be some truth to this business of ESP, she thought. She had asked, silently; and he had answered, in equal silence.

As she went through the doorway, Michael seemed far away from her. She was tired; so tired she could hardly move her feet. The doctor's strong arm half lifted her up the stairs. As she went, through the thickening mists of sleep, she heard Gordon speak his guest's name, and knew that they would be settling down for a long talk as soon as Andrea left. The pill, the damned sleeping pill; she wouldn't be able to creep downstairs to listen, as she had listened to other conversations. But it didn't matter. She knew what they would say as well as if she were in the room, invisible and percipient.

## II

"Thanks, yes," Michael said. "I could use a drink."

Gordon nodded and went to the bar, which was concealed in what had been a Hepplewhite sideboard. Glancing around the room, in the mental equivalent of a man brushing himself off after a crawl through the woods, Michael reorganized his shaken faculties. The secretary, Briggs, wasn't in the room; that was why Gordon was doing his own bartending. Come to think of it, Briggs had not reappeared after fetching the doctor. The man must have some idea of tact after all.

Andrea was still very much with them, though, and Michael wondered how Gordon planned to get rid of the old woman. The man's need to talk crackled in the air like electricity, but Michael thought he would not bare his soul in front of the witch. Witch . . . It wasn't so hard to believe, seeing Andrea as she looked now. Excitement and the damp night air had loosened her frizzled hair so that it hung in limp locks across her cheeks. Witch locks . . . another appropriate word whose meaning he had never considered.

"One for the road, Andrea?" Gordon spoke without turning from the bar.

"Subtle as a brick wall," the old woman cackled. "Forget it, Gordon, I can take a hint without being primed like a pump. I'm going."

She heaved herself up from the couch in a mammoth flutter of skirts and jangle of beads. She was too good an actress, Michael thought, to leave without a good exit line. Gordon seemed to feel the same way; he turned with a glass in each hand and stood watching Andrea. Andrea did not disappoint them. Drawing herself up to her full height, she thrust out an arm and pointed a fat finger at Gordon.

"You jeered at me tonight, Gordon Randolph, for fighting the powers of darkness. Take care—for They are not mocked. The time may come when you will beg on your knees for the help you despise now. Be sure that I will not deny you."

She spun on her heel, her skirts belling out like a monstrous purple flower, and stalked toward the door. Michael arranged his facial muscles into a conciliatory smile, but Andrea was not disarmed. She had a parting word for him, too.

"As for you—you are a mocker and a doubter. . . ."

An uncanny transformation came over voice and face, as the first trailed off into silence and the other lost its rigid anger. The old woman's throat worked hideously as she struggled to speak. When the words finally came, they were shocking because of their softness—faint and whispering, like a child's voice calling out in the terror of a nightmare.

"Help," Andrea said. "Please . . . help . . ."

Too amazed to move, Michael stood rooted, staring at her, and in another second the act was over. The wrinkled face snapped back into its malevolent expression and Andrea stamped out of the room, leaving a silence that vibrated.

"Whew," Michael said feebly. "She's really something, isn't she?"

Gordon removed himself from the sideboard, against which he had been leaning, and sauntered toward Michael, holding out one of the glasses. The incident, which had shaken Michael, seemed to have removed some of Gordon's tension. He was clearly amused.

"Sit down and have a drink, in that order. That's what I love about Andrea. She always provides me with an excuse to have another drink."

Michael laughed and followed his host's suggestions.

"How does she get home?" he asked.

He was about to add the obvious witticism, but there was no need; his eyes met Gordon's and they both grinned.

"Not by broomstick," Gordon said. "Believe it or not. No, she walks everywhere she goes; the old bitch is as tough as they come. I'd have ordered the car out for her if I hadn't known, from past experience, that she'd refuse it. With commentary."

"That I can believe. Why does she dislike you so much?"

"I can think of about ten good reasons," Gordon said promptly. "Six pathological, three socioeconomic, and one— well, maybe it's psychotic too." He tilted his head back and finished his drink in one long swallow, rising as soon as it was gone. "Another?"

"No, thanks."

Michael contemplated his barely touched glass with some

constraint. It was coming now; and he couldn't refuse to listen. Just as one human being to another, he owed Gordon that much. And as a potential biographer . . . Maybe the best thing he could do for Gordon was get him started talking.

"She hates you because of Mrs. Randolph."

"Why not call her Linda?" Gordon came back to the couch and sat down. "You're a perceptive young man, aren't you?"

"It doesn't require much perception to see that."

"No, you're right. It sticks out like a sore thumb." Gordon's shoulders relaxed as if an invisible burden had been lifted from them. The glance he gave Michael was a compound of apology and relief. "Sorry I said that."

"I'm not looking for juicy tidbits for a best seller."

"I know. Thanks."

They sat in silence for a few minutes, and then Gordon sat up straighter.

"Okay. Professionally or otherwise it's damned good of you to listen to this. Frankly, I'm at my wits' end. I don't know what to do—and this is one thing I must do right."

"I understand."

"I think you do. You see," Gordon said, staring down at his glass, "I love her." He gave a queer, smothered laugh. "The oldest, tritest cliché in the language. From a writer, at that, a man who's supposed to know something about words. But that's it. That's what it comes down to, when you strip away all the verbiage. I love her and I won't let her go."

"Go?"

"Not physically. Although she has tried . . . I mean retreat, withdraw into some dark world of her own. That's what she's trying to do."

"Neurotic? Or psychotic?"

"Words, words, words," Gordon snapped; his suave courtesy had left him, and Michael liked him all the better for it. "A psychiatrist can think up labels. I can't. But I know, better than anyone else can. She's pulling away, moving back; and now the world she's invented is becoming real, for her. She—sees things."

"Interesting," Michael said carefully. "How that phrase, which has a perfectly matter-of-fact meaning, can suggest so much that isn't at all matter-of-fact. I gather you mean she has hallucinations?"

Gordon's swift glance at his guest was not friendly; but Michael returned it equably, and after a moment the queer empathy between the two men had reestablished itself. Gordon laughed suddenly and leaned back, putting his glass down on the table.

"Thanks again. That's my greatest danger, I guess—becoming mystical myself. We all do, when catastrophe strikes. What has brought this curse upon me?—that kind of thinking. And it is, to say the least, nonconstructive. Yes, she has hallucinations."

Michael nodded silently. He was afflicted with an unusual constriction of the brain. Three words. That was all she had said—groaned, rather—just before she slid through his fumbling hands in a genuine faint. But those words, coupled with the similar incident in the grove earlier that day, had told him enough. He was on the verge of repeating his knowledge to Gordon when something made him hesitate. After a moment, Gordon went on,

"The hallucinations are only part of the problem, but to me—and to Hank Gold, whom I've consulted—they seem a particularly alarming symptom. It seems to be an animal of some kind that she fancies she sees—a dog, perhaps. Why it should throw her into such a frantic state . . ."

The black dog.

The words formed themselves in Michael's mind so clearly that for a moment he thought he had spoken them aloud. He did not; nor did he stop to analyze the reasons for his continued silence on this point. Instead, he said, "It seems to be an animal? Don't you know?"

Gordon laughed again; this time the sound made Michael wince.

"No, I don't know. Don't you understand? Whatever her fear is, I'm part of it. I'm the one she hates, Mike."

It all came out, then, like a flood from behind a broken dam. Michael sensed that this had been building up for a long time, with no outlet. Now he was the outlet. He listened in silence. Comment would have been unnecessary.

"Linda was barely twenty-one when I met her," Gordon said. "She was a student, taking the course I taught that one year—you know about that, I suppose. It was an experiment; I thought perhaps teaching might give me something I had failed to find in other pursuits. It didn't. But it gave me something that meant more.

"She was beautiful. She never knew, nor did any of the clods around her, how beautiful she really was. You can see it still, though it's contaminated now, faded. What you may not realize is that she was also one of the most brilliant human beings . . . Oh, hell, that's the wrong word; why can't I find the right words when I talk about Linda? Intelligent—yes, surely. Original, creative, one of those rare minds that sees through a problem to its essentials, whether the problem is social, arithmetical, or moral. But there's an additional quality. . . . Wisdom? Maybe that gives you a clue, even if it's not quite right. The quality of love. You know how I mean the word—'And the greatest of these . . . ' I know, I'm making her sound like a saint. She wasn't. She was still young, crude in some ways, impatient in others, but that quality was there, ready to be developed, drawing . . .

"It drew me. God, how it drew me! I couldn't sleep nights. I sat around waiting for that damned class to meet, three days a week, so that I could see her. I had every adolescent symptom you've ever heard of, including humility. It took me four months to realize that I didn't have to wait for class, or skulk around the library and the coffee shop, hoping for a glimpse of her. . . . You aren't laughing. I wouldn't blame you if you did. I mean, I wasn't precisely the greatest lover that ever lived, but I'd had some experience; there's not another woman alive or dead that I'd have dithered over for four months before I got up nerve enough to ask her to have dinner with me.

"After that," Gordon said softly, "it went quickly. We were married six weeks later."

He relapsed into silence, staring dreamily at the fire. Michael said nothing. He knew there was more to come.

"Linda's background," Gordon said suddenly. "I suppose, if you follow the current theories, that it accounts for what is happening to her now. I can't see it myself. Maybe I'm too close.

"Her father was a policeman, just an ordinary run-of-the-mill cop on the beat. He was killed in a gunfight when she was thirteen, shot dead on the spot by a nervous burglar he was trying to arrest. Posthumous medal, citation—and a collection taken up by the appreciative citizens which kept the widow and three orphans eating for about six months.

"It seems fairly clear that her father was the only member of the family with whom Linda had any emotional ties, so his death hit even harder than it would ordinarily hit a girl of that age. Her mother I've never met; she remarried and moved to some damned hole like Saskatchewan when Linda was sixteen. Linda refused to invite her to the wedding; she showed me the letter her mother wrote when she read of our engagement in the newspapers. It was fairly sickening, full of effusions about how well her baby had done for her little self, and suggestions as to how she could share the wealth with the rest of the family. Linda threw it in the fire. She must have written her mother; an absence of response wouldn't be enough to choke off that sort of greedy stupidity. Whatever she said, it was effective. We haven't heard from the mother-in-law since, nor from the two brothers. One is a merchant seaman, the other is in one of the trades out west—carpenter, plumber, I don't know what.

"That's what makes the phenomenon of Linda so hard to believe—that she could have emerged from that mess of normal, grubby people. Her father must have been an unusual person. Or else she's a throwback to something in the remote family past . . . you never know. She's always refused to let me look up her genealogy. Not that it matters, of course, but I was curious, strictly from a scientific point of view.

"So, she loved her father and hated her mother; nice, straightforward Oedipus complex. And she married me because I was a good father figure, older, successful, supportive. Christ, Mike, you don't need to nod at me; I know all this, I've been over it, to myself and with professionals, a dozen times. But the reason why psychiatry fails to satisfy me is because it invents its own data. You act in a particular way because you hate your father. You admit you hate him—fine and dandy. You say you don't hate him, you really love him? You're kidding yourself, buddy, because I know better; you wouldn't be acting this way if you loved him. You hate him. But, in a way, you love him, too, because of that thing called ambivalence. What good is that sort of thing to me, Mike? It gives too many answers."

He waited. This time he wanted a response.

Michael didn't know what to say. He never did know, when

people talked this way. What do you say to a man who has cut his heart out and put it on the table in front of you? "Nice, well-shaped specimen. There seems to be a hole in it, right here. . . ."

"It doesn't give simple answers," he said carefully.

"The question is simple."

"Is it really?"

"Why does my wife hate me?"

Michael made an impatient movement.

"Any question can be stated in simple terms. 'Why do men fight wars?' 'If we can send a man to the moon, why can't we solve the problem of poverty?' 'God is good; how can He permit evil?' That sort of simplicity is a semantic trick. You don't alter the complex structure of the problem by reducing it to basic English."

Gordon did not reply, and for some minutes the two men sat in silence, listening to the hiss of the dying fire. That sound, and Gordon's soft breathing, were the only sounds in the room. Michael realized that it must be very late. He was conscious of a deep fatigue—the sodden, futile exhaustion that resulted from wallowing in other people's emotional troubles. Too much goddamned empathy, he thought sourly. He thought also of the comfortable guest room upstairs, with its nice, soft mattress and its well-placed reading light. But he couldn't leave, not while Gordon wanted an audience. And there was something else that had to be said.

"Gordon."

"Hmmm?" Gordon stirred; he looked as if he had come back from a great distance.

"I'm wondering. Whether I should go ahead with this project."

"What do you mean?" The confessional was closed; Gordon's dark eyes were searching.

"Probing the emotional problems of a man who's been dead for a century is one thing. Obviously I can't lacerate your private emotions in that way. And I'm not sure that I can do anything worthwhile with your life without considering them, not any longer."

"I wondered too. Whether you'd say that."

Gordon stood up, stretching like a big cat. Michael noted the smooth play of muscle and the lean lines of his body, and a fleeting thought ran through his mind: *I'd hate to tangle with him, even if he is forty.*

"Another drink?" Gordon asked.

"No, thanks."

"I'll bet you're beat. You can go to bed in a minute, Mike. I appreciate all this. . . . But first I want to make a confession, and a request."

"You want me to go ahead with the biography."

"Yes."

"And the confession?"

"I hate to admit it, it's so childish." Gordon didn't look embarrassed; hands in his pockets, he stood gazing down at Michael with a faint smile. "But you are a perceptive devil, Mike. I wasn't aware of this, consciously; but I guess one of the reasons why I allowed this project to get underway was that I hoped you might come up with some burst of insight into my problem. Something I can't see because I'm too close to it."

"Something the best professionals can't see either?"

"I told you my misgivings about psychiatry. And even if the head shrinkers could help, Linda won't let them. She's refused even to see a neurologist."

"You overwhelm me," Michael said helplessly. He meant it literally; he felt as if Randolph had just dumped a load of bricks on him. He was flattened and breathless under the heap of responsibility. He was also annoyed. It was too much to ask of any man, much less a poor feeble writer.

"No, no, don't feel that way. I don't expect a thing. I just . . . hope. Look, Mike, I understand your scruples and your doubts, completely. Try it. Just try it. Work on the book for a couple of weeks, a month, see how it goes. Then we'll talk again."

"Okay."

Michael stood up. He felt stiff and queasy and in no mood to argue.

"We'll leave it that way," he said. "Damn it, Gordon, I can't help but feel that you're exaggerating. Your wife doesn't hate you."

"No?" They faced one another across the hearthrug. Gordon, hands still in his pockets, rocked gently back and forth as if limbering up for a fight. His eyes were brilliant. "Six months ago she tried to kill me."

## III

Rain fell, heavily enough to keep the windshield wipers busy and make the oily surface of the highway dangerously slick. The weekend drivers were pouring back into the city. Michael had to pay close attention to his driving. A long night's sleep had left him oddly unrefreshed; he had started out tired, and two hours on one of the nation's most expensive death traps didn't exactly help. By the time he reached his apartment he could barely drag himself upstairs. There were four flights of stairs. The old building had no elevator.

After the Randolph mansion, his two rooms and kitchenette should have looked grubby and plebeian, but Michael heaved an involuntary sigh of pleasure at the sight of his worn rugs and tattered upholstery. His desk was overflowing with unfinished work. He had left the dishes in the sink. Even so, the place felt warm and cozy compared to the atmosphere of the big handsome house in the country.

He selected two cans, more or less at random, from the collection on the kitchen shelves, and started to heat up the contents. Napoleon had been and gone; his dish on the floor was empty, but he was nowhere in sight. The kitchen window was open its usual three inches. It still amazed Michael that a cat the size of Napoleon, the scarred, muscled terror of the alleys, could get through an opening that narrow, but he had seen him do it often enough, sometimes with the speed and accuracy of a rocket.

Once he had tried shutting Napoleon in the apartment while he was away for the weekend. Napoleon had expressed his opinion of that with his usual economy of effort; he had left neat piles of the said opinions every few feet down the hall, through the living room, culminating, in the most impressive pile of all, in the center of Michael's unmade bed. Michael hadn't even bothered to speak to him about it. He was only grateful to Napoleon for skipping his desk. After that he left the window slightly open and took his chances with burglars. A closed window wouldn't deter anyone who really wanted to get in. There wasn't anything in the place worth stealing anyhow.

When the soup was hot, he carried the pan into the living room and sat down, putting his feet up on the coffee table, which bore the marks of other such moments of relaxation. He ate out of the pan, remembering, with a wry smile, the smooth, unobtrusive service of the breakfast he had eaten that morning, complete with butler and antique silver chafing dishes. Then his smile faded into an even wrier frown, as the thoughts he had successfully avoided all day forced their way into his consciousness.

Gordon Randolph had excelled at half a dozen different careers. Michael wondered why he had never gone on the stage. He had an actor's instinct for a good, punchy line of dialogue.

Then Michael shook his head, as his habitual sense of fairness reproached him. Gordon didn't have to dramatize the situation. It was theatrical enough. And he, Michael, had provoked that simple, shocking punch line. He had more or less set it up. Nobody could resist a line like that one.

"Six months ago she tried to kill me."

The man has guts, Michael thought. He's still there—not only in the same house, but right in the next room.

Gordon's description of that incredible event hadn't been theatrical at all; if anything, it had been understated. But Michael's writer's imagination had not required any details. He could picture it only too vividly: to wake from a sound sleep to see, standing over you, a figure out of a nightmare—or out of a Greek tragedy, a figure with the terrifying beauty and malignancy of Medea, arm upraised, knife poised to strike—and to know that the would-be killer was your own adored wife. . . . No wonder primitive people had believed in demoniacal possession.

Because he had the muscles of an athlete and the quickness of a cat, Randolph had survived the encounter, but he still bore the mark of it, a long, puckered scar along his forearm. Michael's insistent imagination presented him with another picture that was even worse than the first. To wrestle for your very life with some Thing that had the cunning and strength of the insane, and yet the familiar soft body of the woman you loved; held back by fear of hurting the beloved, but knowing that if you failed to hold her, the Other would have your life. Demoniac possession? God, yes, surely that was how you would think of it, despite the centuries of rational skepticism that had supposedly killed that superstition.

The soup on the bottom of the pan was scorched. Michael's food always was; he cooked everything at top heat. He ate absently, without noticing the taste. There was a bad taste in his mouth anyhow. That house—that sick, evil house . . .

He paused, the spoon dripping unnoticed onto his knee, as his mind grappled with this new and absorbing notion. Evil. Now why had he thought of that word? It was a concept he avoided because it was at once too simple and too complex— meaningless, he would have said once. And yet, during that whole weekend, the word had come up again and again. They had all used it, talked about it.

A thud and then a clatter came from the dark kitchen, and Michael jumped and swore as he noticed the puddle of soup on his trouser leg. He put the spoon back into the pan and swabbed ineffectually at the spot with his hand. That only made it worse. Then he looked up, glaring, as the pad of heavy paws announced the arrival of Napoleon.

The cat stood in the doorway, returning Michael's glare with interest. He was an enormous animal, as big as a small dog, and uglier than any dog Michael had ever met. His ancestry must have included cats of every color, for his fur was a hideous blend of every hue permitted to felines—orange, black, brown, white, gray, yellow, in incoherent patches. Now he looked leprous, having lost a good deal of fur in his encounters with other tomcats. One ear was pretty well gone, and a scar on one side of his whiskered countenance had fixed his jaws into a permanent maniacal grin. From the glow in his yellow eyes, Michael deduced that he had just returned from another victory. After a moment, Napoleon nodded to himself, sat down, lifted his back leg into an impossible position, and began licking his flank.

"Don't bleed on the rug," Michael said automatically.

Napoleon looked up from his first aid, gave Michael a contemptuous stare, and returned to his labors. Michael returned to his thoughts, which were considerably less pleasant than Napoleon's.

Homicidal mania. They didn't call it that nowadays, did they? Paranoia? Schizophrenia? He shook his head disgustedly. Gordon was right: words, words, words. They meant nothing to a man whose wife had tried to kill him.

Evil. Another word, but it was a word rooted deep in human experience; it satisfied the demand for understanding more than did the artificial composites of a new discipline. It had the solid backing of centuries of emotional connotations. It brought back

references from every literary source from Holy Writ to Fu
Manchu. Out of this accumulation of literary and racial memory, one quotation came to Michael's mind:

> *By the pricking of my thumbs,*
> *Something evil this way comes.*

Nobody ever expressed an idea quite as aptly as Shakespeare. But in this case the evil was not approaching. It was already there—in that house.

Napoleon finished his ablutions and stalked over to lean
heavily on Michael's leg. It was his only means of expressing
an emotion, which Michael, in his softer moments, liked to in-
terpret as affection. Someone had once said of that hard-bitten
monarch, Henry VII, that he was not, to put it mildly, uxorious.
In the same vein of irony one might say of Napoleon that he
was not a lap cat. He did lean, occasionally, and his weight being what it was, the effect was noticeable. Michael got up with
a weary sigh and extracted a can of cat food from the supply on
the shelf. Affection? Gluttony, rather. Napoleon applied himself
to supper with uncouth gulps, and Michael wandered back to
the couch.

Not even the cat, for whom he felt a sneaking fondness
compounded with envy, could distract him from the black current of his thoughts. How the hell could he write a biography of
a man who was as hag-ridden as Gordon Randolph without
tearing the man's soul to bloody shreds? Especially if he went
on in this vein of half-baked mysticism. Evil deeds, evil men,
he had said—but Evil, in the abstract? If there was evil in the
beautiful house, it had to emanate from some living individual.

There weren't that many candidates. The revolting old
woman, Andrea, was one of them; she was a constant visitor,
and she was crazy as a loon. Michael wondered how genuine
her belief in witchcraft was. Ninety-nine percent, he thought.
What other hang-ups did she have? Certainly the old woman's
blend of malice and superstition was not a healthy influence;
but how profoundly had it really affected Linda Randolph? Had
Andrea implanted her own insane ideas, or merely strengthened
neuroses that had already begun to form? Even insanity has its
own brand of logic. The paranoid schizophrenic may kill a
complete stranger, suddenly and seemingly without cause; but

in terms of the murderer's delusion, his action makes perfectly good sense. As the object of a widespread conspiracy aimed at his life and reason, he is only acting in self-defense when he kills one of the conspirators. Was that why Linda had attacked her husband? Could such a delusion have been planted by a third party—such as Andrea?

Then there was Briggs, the fat little man who looked like a moribund pig. Physiognomy was not a science. Under his pale, pudgy façade, Briggs might have the soul of a saint. But Michael doubted it. Briggs's feelings toward the Randolphs were obvious. He idolized his employer and resented—because he desired— his employer's wife. Which was natural. Randolph had been modestly vague about the circumstances that had brought Briggs to his present post, but Michael had got the impression of perse- cution, a miscarriage of justice, the loss of a profession for which the man had prepared all his life. Briggs wasn't the type to square his shoulders and march back out into the arena after someone had kicked him where it hurt. Randolph's offer of a job might, literally, have saved his life. No wonder the little man admired his boss. His attitude toward Linda was equally comprehensible, if less attractive. Malice—plenty of it. Michael wondered whether Gordon was too damned high-minded to see how his secretary felt about his beautiful wife. But Briggs's brand of fee- ble frustration was not evil, not in the sense Michael meant.

Randolph? Michael dismissed that hypothesis not because of Randolph's charm and talent but because of a fact that stood as solidly as Mount Everest. Randolph was genuinely, desper- ately, in love with his wife. Although Michael had interviewed a lot of people, he couldn't always tell the truth from the as- sumed; but in this case he would have staked his reputation on the genuineness of Randolph's feelings.

All of which led straight back to the most obvious source of evil. Linda herself.

Now, there, surely, he was out of his depth and could can- didly admit the fact. God damn it, he wasn't a psychiatrist. No- body but a professional had the right to speculate about a mental condition as severe as Linda's. He couldn't even consult a pro- fessional. It would be an unforgivable violation of friendship.

But the idea remained, dangling like a shiny toy in the fore- front of his mind, and for a few minutes he played with it. Often in his biographical research he had talked to Galen Rosenberg about the personalities of his subjects. Rosenberg had been one of his father's best friends, and Michael would have appreciated his pithy comments even if he had not been one of the top psychiatrists in the east. His humility and his sardonic sense of humor were as great as his all-embracing tolerance. It was a pity Gordon couldn't convince his wife to see Galen. If anyone could help her . . .

Michael shook his head. He was busy-bodying again, and if he had learned anything in the course of his thirty-three years, it was the futility of trying to force help on people who didn't want it. No, he couldn't discuss the case with Galen, not even under pseudonyms. His problem was not Linda's neuroses, it was a question of his own professional competence. Could he do a decent job with Randolph's life without mentioning the fact that Randolph's wife had tried to kill him? Another of those simple questions that weren't simple at all.

The answer, like the question, could be phrased with paradoxical simplicity. Michael realized, with a slight shock, that the answer was not the one he had hoped to get. He was a professional, and a good one; on that theme he had no false modesty whatever. Already sentences were framing themselves in his mind, possible lines of investigation were taking shape; the subject fascinated him as a problem, all personal ties aside. Oh, sure, there would be sticky moments, places were he would have to walk carefully, but they were only part of the challenge of the job. He could do it, all right. And he wanted to do it. And he didn't want to do it.

Michael bounded to his feet with a snarl, knocking two issues of *Mad,* an *American Historical Review,* and approximately two weeks of the *New York Times* off the coffee table, and evoking an answering growl from Napoleon, who was crouched on the rug by the front door. It was his favorite place. What he was waiting for, Michael never knew, though he wasted a lot of time speculating. Other cats? Not people. Napoleon hated people, all people, and departed via the window whenever a visitor approached.

"Why the hell I don't get a nice friendly dog, I don't know," Michael said aloud. "I could talk to it and get an answer now and then. I can't even kick you to relieve my spleen. You'd wait till I was asleep and then come in and tear my throat out. Who do you think you are, squatting there by the door? A watchdog?

A lion? A vulture? God damn it, I hope that old saw about animals reflecting the personalities of their owners isn't true. You make me look like some kind of nut."

Having thus relieved his spleen, he stalked toward the bedroom, shedding coat, tie, and shirt as he went. Napoleon settled back on his haunches muttering to himself. The eerie sound followed Michael all the way into the bedroom, and he kicked the dresser in passing. Why couldn't the cat purr like an ordinary feline? This sound wasn't quite a growl, but it certainly wasn't a purr; Napoleon never expressed approval in that traditional fashion. He never expressed approval at all. He just sat around muttering to himself. A helluva pet for a poor miserable bachelor . . .

No pets. No animals at all, on the whole expansive twenty acres of Randolph's estate. Surely that was not coincidental. You'd expect a man like Randolph to ride and hunt, to keep dogs.

Michael turned out the light and pulled the crumpled sheet up to his chin. He liked to consider himself above such considerations as physical comfort, but his uncooperative body remembered the smoothness of the sheets at the Randolph house, and the yielding yet firm surface of the mattress. Surely this mattress had grown another lump since the last time he slept on it. He wriggled, trying to find a smooth spot. No use. The damned mattress grew tumors, like protoplasm. . . .

There was no clue to Randolph's personality in the absence of animals; that was a pretty corny old cliché. A lot of nice people didn't like dogs. There were such things as allergies, too. And . . . of course. Linda Randolph's neurosis had to do with animals. Randolph couldn't have a dog on the place when the sight of an imaginary one sent his wife into fits. So much for the subtle analytical biographer's insight.

Michael gave up his search for comfort and lay staring up at the ceiling, hands clasped under his head. The dirty yellow light from the street filtered in through panes grimy with city dirt, past the cracks in the wooden slats of the ancient blind. Sounds filtered in, too—the soft drizzle of the rain and the hooting, honking blare of traffic. Even at this late hour there were cars on the city streets. Soon the trucks would begin their nightly deliveries, but he wouldn't hear them; his ears had become inured to the grind of brakes and the vibration that was gradually eroding the fabric of buildings and pavements. He was used to the sounds and the grime and the press of human beings. They were part of his habits; without them he probably couldn't work. Yearning for apple blossoms and fresh country air and crocuses (crocuses?) pushing their tender green tips through the damp brown earth—sentimental nonsense, that was what it was. A nice place to visit, but I wouldn't want to live there.

Soothed and comforted by the familiar cacophony and the friendly dirt, he was drifting off to sleep when he remembered something else. He hadn't paid much attention at the time to Randolph's remark; he had been tired and confused, and the remark hadn't made any sense anyhow. Now he remembered it, and the utter illogic of it brought him out of his doze, wide awake and staring.

"If she should come to you," Randolph had said, "try to get her to see a doctor. Maybe you can do it."

Had Gordon Randolph really said that? Of all the weird, crazy things to say . . . And he had simply nodded and muttered, "Sure, of course; be glad to."

Michael groaned aloud. What had he got himself into this time? What kind of tacit admission could be read into that acquiescing mumble of his? He was always doing things like that, agreeing to propositions without listening to them, letting his mind wander off into byways and returning to a conversation to find that he had committed himself to ideas he violently opposed or plans that he had no intention of carrying out. But this was his worst fiasco yet. Did Randolph really think . . . ?

Of course there had been those two episodes. When a man walks into a room and finds his wife in another man's arms, he may be excused for thinking there is something between them. Was Linda Randolph a nymphomaniac as well as an alcoholic?

Michael groaned again, so heartily that it provoked a loud response from Napoleon, out by the front door; but at the same moment he denied the thought. He had spotted Linda as a heavy drinker the first time he saw her. The symptoms of the other were just as obvious, and she wasn't . . . No, indeed, she wasn't. His face burned, in the darkness, as he remembered the strength with which she had held him off.

So, all right, he told his wounded male ego—so you made a mistake. You got carried away. Perfectly natural. But the girl really was sick, she had passed out cold.

"If she should come to you . . ."

Damn it, why didn't he listen to what people said? He should have rejected the preposterous suggestion. He shouldn't have seemed to accept any such possibility.

Then the most disturbing thought of all forced its way into his reluctant mind. Had he failed to deny the proposition because, in reality, it had not seemed so incredible? Did he, unconsciously, want Randolph's wife to seek him out—for help, for anything? He pushed the idea away, outraged; but it came back. If a desire was really unconscious, he wouldn't know it himself. If he really wanted . . .

"Oh, damn it," Michael said helplessly. There was only one thing to do with an idea like that one. He turned over and went to sleep.

# *Chapter*

## 5

THE FANTASIES AND SELF-DOUBTS OF THE NIGHT WERE EASY TO dismiss in the cold light of dawn—which was not only cold, but gray, rainy, and sooty. But it was several days before Michael could make himself stop listening for footsteps coming toward his door.

He threw himself into work as a cure for mental degeneration, and found that after a while he didn't have to force himself; the hunt was up, and as usual it gradually gripped him. Even the inevitable frustrations were minor challenges, to be overcome.

One such challenge was Randolph's book. Michael could have sworn he owned a copy of *The Smoke of Her Burning*; it took two hours of disorganized search before she would admit that he no longer owned it. He kept meaning to get his books arranged in some kind of order, but they wouldn't let themselves be arranged; every time he started the project, he ended up with piles all over the floor and himself sitting cross-legged in the middle of the debris, deep in some fascinating volume he had forgotten he owned. The bookshelves were as motley as the volumes they housed; he had always meant to have some bookcases built in. . . .

What had he done with Randolph's book? Damn it, he had to read Randolph's book, that was the least a biographer could do. Standing in the middle of the floor, like a pillar in the midst of a forum paved with literature, Michael scratched his chin. He must have given it to someone. Why hadn't he read it himself?

That was not unusual, though; he was a compulsive book buyer, and his collection included a deplorably large group that he had never had time to read. He would just have to buy another copy of *The Smoke of Her Burning*.

But it wasn't that easy. The book was out of print. After all, as the third bookdealer pointed out waspishly, the printing presses of America poured out thousands of new books every year. You couldn't expect them to keep every old title in stock. Oh, sure, *The Smoke of Her Burning* had been an important book. But you couldn't expect . . .

So Michael tried the secondhand bookstores and encountered another snare; he could waste days in such places. He finally found the book, but not until he had loaded himself with old masterpieces he hadn't been looking for and probably wouldn't read—including, for reasons he refused to consider, a worn copy of somebody's *History of Witchcraft*. By the time he got home, he had transferred his annoyance to Gordon's book, and no longer wanted to read it.

There were plenty of other things to be done. He spent two afternoons in the newspaper morgues reading about the public exploits of Gordon Randolph. It was an unexpectedly depressing activity. Some of the yellowed, crumbling clippings were over twenty years old; the face of a young Gordon Randolph mummified by antique newsprint made any attempt at immortality seem futile.

The clippings came from sports pages, literary columns, and the general-news sections, but there was one significant omission. Randolph's name did not appear in the gossip columns. Rarely, there might be a mention of his presence at some charity affair or concert, but he never escorted a lady who was not impeccable in reputation and social status. Either Randolph's private life was arranged with a circumspection that verged on Top Secret, or he was abnormally well behaved. Not a wild oat in the whole field.

His marriage had rated a long column, and the lady reporter gave it the Cinderella approach—Professor Weds Student, Millionaire Marries Policeman's Daughter. They had been married at the college chapel. There was a picture of Linda Randolph in her wedding dress, and Michael found it more depressing, for different reasons, than Gordon's photographs. Poor as the print was, it conveyed something of that quality Randolph had vainly tried to describe. It conveyed something else—happiness. She glowed with it, even through cheap paper and smeary ink. From that, Michael thought, to what I saw three days ago. He turned the page quickly.

All of it, sports achievements, literary kudos, political successes, were dry bones. This was just the beginning. The next step was to talk to people who knew Randolph. So, on Wednesday, Michael got his car out and drove up to the campus of the well-known Ivy League school where Randolph had matriculated.

He had taken the precaution of providing himself with a general letter of introduction, and it finally got him into the sanctum of a Vice-President in charge of something. Public Relations, to judge from the gray-haired gentleman's suave manner. The President of the university was unavailable. Probably away on a fund-raising campaign, Michael thought—or building barricades in preparation for the spring campaign of the SDS. Not that it mattered. Anything the President would say about one of his most illustrious alumni wouldn't be worth peanuts. The same thing was true of the Vice-President. Michael only needed him as a source of references.

"I'm afraid there are very few of Mr. Randolph's former professors available," the Vice-President explained winsomely. "Now although I was not myself in residence at the time, I have followed Mr. Randolph's career with interest, and I might say . . ."

He recapitulated Randolph's public career, which Michael could have recited from memory, for ten minutes before Michael could stop him.

"I want to talk to people who actually knew him," Michael explained.

The Vice-President hesitated, torn between irritation and caution. How these pompous asses did love to see their names in print, Michael thought. The man was smart enough to know that if he vexed the biographer, his name might appear amid adjectives that would make him writhe. The pungent style of the periodical that had commissioned the biography was well known.

"Well, of course, this was twenty years ago," the V.P. said, with a slight sniff. "Most of our professors are mature men when they are at the height of their careers; by now the majority are retired or—hem—deceased. And, while people tend to think of the academic profession as static, there is in actual fact—"

"A lot of job shifting," Michael interrupted. "I know that. I'll do the tracking down myself. All I really need are the names of Randolph's professors and their current addresses, if they are available."

"Well, if you insist, Mr.—"

Michael insisted. When the file was produced, the Vice-President brooded over it.

"Physics; Professor Kraus. Emeritus, now, of course; I believe he returned to Germany or Austria. If he's still alive . . . Sociology; that would be Professor Smith, he is now at Elm College, in the—er—Midwest somewhere."

"Chicago," Michael said.

"Somewhere of that sort, yes. I don't know that he would be of much help to you; Mr. Randolph only took one of his courses. Now his major, naturally, was English; the chairman at that time was Professor—"

He looked up, his eyes widening, and Michael nodded.

"Collins. He was my father. He's dead. Ten years ago."

"I'm sorry. . . . Well, then, let me see, there was Doctor Wilkes. . . ."

Not a single one of Randolph's former professors was still in residence. Michael finally escaped with a very short list. Four of the men were still living, two in Europe and one at Harvard, plus the unfortunate exile in the Midwest. Michael went home and wrote letters. He couldn't go traipsing off to Munich to interview a man who had taught Randolph algebra twenty years ago. The man at Harvard was on sabbatical leave.

He had begun his investigations with the academic world not only because it was more in line with his own interests but because he believed in the importance of that period in character formation. Sooner or later, he would have to interview Randolph's business associates. Talk about a subject being outside your field; he wasn't even sure what Randolph's business was. One of those massive conglomerates that included manufacturing, investments, oil wells, and God knows what else. But there were offices someplace in the city; if there wasn't a Randolph Building, it was presumably only because Randolph hadn't got around to constructing one. Yes, eventually he'd have to talk to the inhabitants of the business world, but he had no illusions about that; no one who worked for Randolph was going to tell him anything interesting.

So the next step was the college where Randolph had taught. It was in Pennsylvania; not a long drive, but he decided to plan to stay overnight, since that particular episode was fairly recent, and there ought to be a number of witnesses still available—possibly even a few students working for advanced degrees.

A sullen sun sulked above the skyscrapers when he left the city, but it wasn't until he had bypassed Philadelphia that he felt any awareness of spring. The Main Line suburbs reminded him of the countryside around Randolph's home—manicured lawns and smug, neat houses, flowers and kids playing in the front yard. Things were blooming.

This time he had taken the precaution of setting up an interview in advance, by phone, and he saw, not a Vice-President, but the Vice-Chancellor. Michael had read too much history to have much faith in revolution as a means of social progress; but every time he met a college administrator, he was aware of a sneaking sympathy for the militant students. The Vice-Chancellor might have been a brother of the Vice-President— the same graying hair and discreet tie, the same canny brown eyes. Michael sniffed. Yes; they even used the same scent. Christ, he thought; and placed a look of intelligent interest on his face as the Vice-Chancellor lectured.

"I was a mere Assistant Professor at the time," he explained with a deprecating smile. "Nor was Gordon in my department. Economics is my field."

"Then you didn't know him well?"

"We had several interesting chats at the Faculty Club."

In a pig's eyes, Michael thought crudely.

"What did you talk about? Economics?"

"Among other things. He was very well informed for a lay-man, very much so. A brilliant mind, of course. And capable in a wide range of subjects. That is of course the outstanding factor in his personality. And that's what you're interested in, isn't it, my dear fellow? His personality. I'm sure everyone who knew Gordon was struck by that—the breadth of his interests."

It went on in this vein for some time. Michael had suspected from the first that this pompous ass could not have won Gordon's friendship, and after half an hour of name dropping and burbling generalities, he was sure of it. It took him another half hour to extract the information he wanted. When he left, the Vice-Chancellor sent his regards to dear old Gordon.

On the steps of the Administration Building, Michael saw a bearded youth attired in a red plaid poncho selling copies of the school paper. He bought a copy. The picture on the front was a scurrilous caricature, badly drawn but recognizable, of the Vice-Chancellor. Michael turned back.

"Contribution to the cause," he said, and went on his way leaving the hairy young man looking in bewilderment at the five-dollar bill in his hand.

It took Michael the rest of the day to find one of the teachers who had been Randolph's colleagues. Though they all had offices and office hours, nobody seemed to be in his office at the specified time—or, if he was, he refused to answer the door. (Michael could have sworn he heard harried breathing inside one locked and unresponsive room.) What were they afraid of? he wondered. Students? Which wasn't so funny, nowadays . . . He finally caught one man as he was making a surreptitious exit, and when Martin Buchsbaum found he was not a student, he invited him in.

Buchsbaum was a youngish man, chubby and pink, with a nose that looked as if it had once been broken, and a cherubic smile.

"Randolph? Sure, I met him. But I never knew the guy, not to talk to. I had just made my Assistant Professorship, didn't even have tenure. He was one of the sheep, and I was the lowest of the goats. You know, the sheep and the—"

"I know. My father was a teacher."

"Then you do know. The gulf between the tenured and the non-tenured is wider than the one between the Elect and the Damned. I'm sorry, friend, but I can't tell you anything about the Great Man. He was lionized, idolized—"

"Even canonized?"

"Man can't even plagiarize a quotation these days," said Buchsbaum amiably. "What did your old man teach, English Lit?"

"Right."

"It doesn't follow, though. I threw a chunk of Andrew Marvell at a cop once. He not only capped the quote, he went ahead and gave me a ticket."

"A mere traffic ticket? Weren't you out there hurling obscenities and bricks at the police last fall?"

"I was." Buchsbaum's face was glum. "I slipped and fell and sprained my sacroiliac while I was running away. Cost me seventy-eight bucks for doctor bills. After that I decided I was too old and too underpaid to be a liberal."

Michael laughed. He got up to go a little reluctantly; Buchsbaum was a pleasant change from the Vice-Chancellor.

"Stick around," Buchsbaum suggested. "A man who knows his Fry is a man worth knowing. Or, better still, come home, meet the wife, have a beer. I'll try you on the more obscure metaphysical poets."

"If I didn't have eight more people to track down today, I'd accept with pleasure. I used to enjoy this sort of thing, in my younger days. You ivory-tower boys have a nice life."

"You are viewing it with the rosy glow of old age remembering lost youth. Don't kid yourself. Why do you think I skulk around the halls with my collar turned up like James Bond? Students, committees, secretaries wanting lists of things, parents, students . . ."

"Without the students you wouldn't have a job."

"Don't give me that; I've quit being a liberal." Buchsbaum put his feet up on the desk and adjusted them so that he could look between them at Michael. "We all hate students. Most of my peers aren't that blunt about it; they blather on about the book they haven't been able to finish and the vital research they can't carry out because of their onerous teaching load. The majority of them couldn't write a book if you dictated it to them. What they mean is, they hate students. Like me."

"What about Linda Randolph? Did you know her?"

Later, Michael was to wonder what made him ask the question. He had meant to throw out some feelers about Linda; this was where Randolph had met her. But she was not his main interest.

"I knew her," Buchsbaum said.

"That romance must have caused a lot of comment."

"You could say that."

"I've met her. She's charming, isn't she?"

"Is she?" The feet were still on the desk, the stout body as relaxed; but the pink face wasn't friendly any longer. Feeling idiotically rebuffed, Michael turned toward the door. Buchsbaum said suddenly,

"Sit down, Collins. Don't go away mad. I'm sorry if I sounded . . . Hell, I was in love with the girl, of course."

"Of course?"

"Most of her teachers were."

"Not the students?"

"Oddly enough, no. Caviar to the general, you know."

"Cut that out."

"Sorry, it's a bad habit. No; I think she put the kids off a bit—the callow youth. She was bright as they come, and the juvenile male doesn't care for that kind of challenge. But . . ."

He was silent for a time, staring reflectively at the tip of his left shoe; and Michael was reminded of Gordon, groping in the same way for words to describe his wife. When Buchsbaum began to speak, his voice was soft and abstracted, as if he were talking to himself.

"We make cynical remarks about the lousy students. Most of them are, you know. They don't give a damn—they lack motivation, in the current jargon—and even if they have motivation, they don't have the intelligence of a medium-bright porpoise. Day after day you stand up there on your podium and you strip your brain and throw it out, into a sea of dead faces, and it falls flat on the floor and dies there. But now and then— once a year, once out of a thousand students, if you're lucky— you look around and see a face that isn't a flat doughy mass with the right number of holes in it for eyes and nose and mouth. It's a face, a real face. The eyes are alive, the mouth responds to the things you say. When you make a joke, the eyes shine. When you throw out an idea that takes a little cogitation, the forehead actually wrinkles—something is going on behind it, some gears are really meshing. When you say something that—that moves her, the mouth curves at the corners, not much, just a little, up or down depending on whether she's moved to laughter or to tenderness. . . ."

The pronoun had slipped out, but Buchsbaum didn't try to retract it. His eyes moved from his shoe to Michael's face, and he smiled.

"The Reminiscences of a Middle-Aged Loser," he said

wryly. "It's true, though; every teacher knows about it. The quality of the response differs. Hers was unique. I won't say that I wasn't affected by the fact that she was also a gorgeous dish."

"I'm sorry," Michael said, realizing that the revelations were finished. "I didn't mean to probe into your private affairs."

"Sure you did." Buchsbaum took his feet off the desk and stood up. It was dismissal. He was friendly, but guarded, now. "Only you wanted me to talk about Gordon, not his wife. Sorry I can't help you."

"Have you read his book?"

"Naturally. It's brilliant. Like everything else the man has done." Buchsbaum beamed at his visitor. "I hate his bloody guts. You noticed that."

## II

"I hate his bloody guts."

"If it hadn't been for him, I'd have killed myself that night."

"A desperately unhappy man."

Three interviews, three different comments.

Pacing the dark streets of the town in search of a restaurant that promised something more suited to an over-thirty stomach than pizza or oliveburgers, Michael pondered the results of his day. He had located one other teacher, and one student. The latter, Tommy Scarinski, was on the last leg of his doctorate, having taken off several years because of illness. Michael was fairly sure that the illness had been what is referred to as a nervous breakdown. The boy still twitched. He was a pale, very fair youth, slender as a girl, looking much younger than his twenty-four years. He had idolized Randolph—canonized him, in fact. Michael didn't doubt that he had contemplated suicide. The impulse was far more common in this age group than most people realized. With the majority of the kids it was only an impulse. Some of them liked to believe that the influence of a friend or lover had been the catalytic agent that deterred them from that most final of all gestures of protest. In this case, though, Michael rather thought that Tommy—it was a mark of his immaturity that he still called himself by the diminutive—did owe his life to Randolph. He had been at the age, and at the stage of

mental deterioration, when the influence of an idol could make
or break his mind. But—my God, what a responsibility. What a
delicate, damnable job. Chalk one up for Randolph.

There was a sign, down the block, that said "Restaurant."
Michael opened the door and saw a dim interior, not too
crowded. A waiter appeared promptly. He ordered a drink and a
steak and let himself relax against the imitation leather of the
booth.

Buchsbaum's comment wasn't really a mark against Gordon. It was another example of the man's sophomoric attempt
at wry humor, with strong touches of masochism. Buchsbaum
had never been Gordon's rival, in the ordinary sense of the
word; he was the sort of man who would always prefer a romantic illusion to a possible rejection. Most probably he didn't
even dislike Gordon.

And why, Michael wondered irritably, should he be thinking in terms of pluses and minuses? He wasn't trying to defend
Gordon or play the part of Devil's Advocate; that wasn't the
way he worked. He wanted the truth—and he knew it was never
a single isolated fact, but a patchwork of differing, sometimes
contradictory, views.

The waiter arrived with the drink, and Michael took a
hearty swig of it. He made a wry face. Should have specified
the brand; this tasted like something out of a still. But it was
better than nothing.

The third interview had been the least productive, for all its
verbiage. Professor Seldon was almost at the compulsory retirement age of sixty-five: a diminutive, dapper old man with a
mop of white hair and a goatee and beard of the same silky hue.
He talked fluently; God, Michael thought with an inner grin,
how he did talk! He had been dependent on clichés for so long
that he couldn't have said "Good morning" if Shakespeare or
Milton hadn't happened to say it first. And he was Chairman of
the English Department.

Seldon's comments on Gordon were about as useful as the
newspaper accounts had been. Reflex reactions. The remark
about Gordon's tragic unhappiness had some normal human
spite behind it, though Professor Seldon would have been genuinely indignant if you pointed that out. He was a third-rate
scholar and a second-rate human being; envy of a better man
could not be openly expressed, so it masked itself under the

guise of benevolent pity. Translated, his remark simply meant: *This man has everything I would like to have. Nobody ought to be that happy—except me. So he must be miserable, down deep underneath, where it doesn't show.*

And, ironically, the old man was right. Randolph was an unhappy man. There was a serpent in his Eden, though that was a cliché worthy of Seldon himself. But Seldon had no knowledge of Gordon's private life. His assessment of Gordon might have come straight out of the high school Class Prophecy: "Bright, intelligent, friendly; bound to succeed."

Michael caught the waiter's eyes and nodded. The mellowing effect of the whiskey wasn't quite complete, he could stand another one. Frustration of this sort was normal, he knew that. Most people weren't perceptive about other people. Wrapped up in their own miseries, they had no energy to spare for the problems of others; anyhow, they tended to pigeonhole people as they did ideas, and reacted to deviations from a wholly imaginary picture with astonishment and annoyance. "Good old Sam wouldn't do a thing like that." "Mary, of all the people in the world; she must have changed a lot since I knew her." Whereas, of course, Mary hadn't changed at all. Mary, like everyone else, was not one Mary but a dozen. Her astonished friend had just not happened to see the Mary who finally broke out.

Then why, Michael wondered, was he so irritated by his failure to get an instant, comprehensible picture of a man as complex as Gordon Randolph? Was it because he wasn't getting any picture at all, not even a misleading one? Hadn't Randolph had any friends, only associates and disciples?

No. He had not. That was the only useful point Michael had obtained from Seldon.

"Oh, no, Randolph didn't associate with . . . us," he said. Mentally supplying the three missing words, Michael suppressed a smile. "I presume he passed his leisure hours with friends in the city. Except—yes. I recall being surprised, at the time . . . He spent a good deal of time with the students."

The emotion that colored his voice—one of the few times that genuine feeling was allowed to show—was simple astonishment. Remembering Buchsbaum's conversation, and some of the student complaints he had seen published in recent months, Michael understood. His internal amusement, this time, was rather sour. By God, things had changed. He remembered the big, echoing old house where he had grown up; the front door always open and the carpet in the hall worn threadbare with the tread of students' feet, in and out, at all hours of the day and night. His father had had a funny notion of a teacher's role. . . . Professor Seldon would probably never know why Michael left so abruptly.

But it was that very lead that had led to his present frustration. The student-teacher relationship, if it was a good one, could be one of the most important in life. He had expected some interesting material from Randolph's students. Having gone, posthaste, to look up the enrollment for Randolph's class, he was delighted to find that one of the top students was still around. Tommy Scarinski.

Maybe his reasoning had been fallacious. But he didn't think so, he was inclined to cross Tommy off as an isolated aberration. The best students in the class, the ones who got the highest grades—they still gave letter grades in those bad old days—might not necessarily be the people who had most attracted Gordon, but it was far more likely that his favorites would be found among that group than among the kids whose work had been too poor to rate Gordon's approval. Besides, the class file included Randolph's comments—terse, sympathetic, and intelligent. The four "A" students had received the most favorable comments—with one exception. Miss Alison Dupuis had been dismissed with a curt: "Idiot savant; but how can you flunk a calculating machine?" With the other three, Randolph had obviously enjoyed a personal friendship.

One of the three had been Linda.

The second, Joseph Something or Other, had dropped out of sight. The vinegary spinster at the Registrar's office could tell him only that Joseph was no longer registered. Well, that was something he could do tomorrow; he had been too pleased at the availability of Tommy Scarinski to check the other records, to see whether Joseph X had matriculated, or transferred to another institution. Graduate school somewhere was a likely possibility, in view of his scholastic record and his teacher's praise. What had Gordon said? "Genuine creativity and drive— a rare combination." Yes, Joseph was worth tracking down. The evaluation of a brain like that, sharpened by several years of maturity and by absence from his former mentor, would be valuable. That was why Tommy had been so disappointing: The years hadn't sharpened his brain, it was still mushy. . . . Poor devil.

The waiter brought his steak, and Michael finished his drink and his deliberations. As he ate he glanced around the room in search of distraction from thoughts that were becoming stale and futile. It was a pleasant, undistinguished little place, like a thousand other restaurants in a hundred other towns. The only thing that made it different was the fact that it was in a college town. There were a lot of students present, mostly couples, and they definitely brightened the scene. The voices were shrill, but they were alive; they got loud with excitement, they vibrated with laughter. Collegiate styles were undoubtedly picturesque. Floppy pants, beads and pendants, clothes that dangled, and jingled, and blazed with color. Michael approved of beards; at least you could tell the boys from the girls that way, and the Renaissance look appealed to him. A couple at a table next to the booth he occupied might have posed as models for the New Look—the boy had long brown hair, and hair over most of the rest of his face; a red kerchief was knotted around his throat. Michael's eyes lingered longer on his date. The long, straight blond hair obscured her face most of the time, but her legs were in full view. They were booted up to the knee, and what she wore above them, if anything, was hidden by the tablecloth.

Michael signaled the waiter for his coffee. The man lingered, swabbing unnecessarily at the table, and Michael resigned himself.

"Stranger in town?"

"Yes. I'm just here overnight."

"You busy tonight?"

"No," Michael admitted, wondering what form the conventional offer would take this time.

"You like music?"

"Well—some kinds," Michael said, surprised and curious.

"Stick around then, have another cup of coffee. Kwame is due in a few minutes. He's not bad, if you like that kind of music."

"Kwame?"

The waiter, a tired-looking man with receding hair, grinned.

"That's what he calls himself. Real name's Joe Schwartz."

"What does he play? The sitar? The viola d'amore?"

"Just the guitar. But, like I said, he's not bad. If you like that kind of music."

He moved on to the next table, leaving Michael feeling ashamed of his cynicism. Maybe he ought to get out of the big city more often. It was a hell of a note when you were surprised by ordinary human amiability. The conversation was a lesson for him in another way; it emphasized his point about personality stereotypes. The weary middle-aged waiter was not the sort of person you'd expect to enjoy the music produced by somebody named Kwame, even if he didn't play the sitar.

His newfound friend was on the alert, and signaled him with a jerk of the head when the performer appeared, but Michael didn't need the signal. Even in this crowd he would have spotted Kwame.

Such is the power of suggestion that Michael had unconsciously expected the performer to be black—with a name like Joe Schwartz, yet, he told himself. But the sparse expanses of skin visible were of the sickly tan that people choose, for some obscure reason, to call white. The hair was extensive; it made the efforts of the other boys look epicene. Now that, Michael thought admiringly, is a beard!

It swept down in undulating, shining ripples to the boy's diaphragm, where it mingled with the waves of long brown hair. Although the night was chill and damp, Kwame wore only jeans and a sleeveless embroidered vest, which flopped open with each step, displaying a cadaverous chest. He was barefoot. But his guitar had been carefully swathed against the damp. It was a twelve-string guitar, with a shining surface that might have been produced by Stradivarius or Amati. Expensive, loved, used, and tended like a baby.

There was a tiny podium or stage, about the size of a dining-room table, at the far end of the room, and at another gesture from the waiter, Michael took his cup and moved down to an unoccupied booth near the stage. The other habitués were doing the same thing. Kwame, who had seated himself crosslegged on the floor, placed the guitar across his lap and sat waiting. His eyes moved incuriously around the room, and as they met Michael's, the latter was conscious of an odd shock. Drugs. The eyes were unmistakable. . . . And why, he wondered cynically, was he shocked? He read the newspapers.

There was no announcement, no introduction. When everyone had seated himself, and silence had become profound, Kwame began to play.

Michael's first reaction was negative. Kwame's harsh voice had little appeal for a post-adolescent square who concealed a secret weakness for old Perry Como records, and Kwame's playing, though competent, was not remarkable. The songs were a mixture of legitimate folk music and modern rock imitations of folk music; a few of them sounded vaguely familiar, but Michael was not sufficiently knowledgeable about the popular repertoire to identify them. All had one theme in common: peace, love, innocence, and the annihilation of all these by man's cruelty. The mushroom cloud billowing up around the kids playing in the daisy field, the blast of an explosion annihilating the kids in the Sunday School . . . Kevin Barry lost his young life again, and the lambs were all a-crying. But it was effective. The images were sure fire, they couldn't miss.

Two of the songs were different. Kwame ended his recital with them, and by that time Michael had succumbed to the same spell that held the rest of the audience. He couldn't have explained why he was spellbound, none of the elements of the performance were that good. But in combination . . .

Then Kwame swept his fingers across all twelve strings in a crashing dissonant chord, and broke into a vicious, and extremely funny, satire on the Congress of the United States. Like the others, Michael ached with containing his laughter; he didn't want to miss the next line. At the same time the cruelty of the satire made him wince, even when he shared Kwame's opinion of that particular victim. The laughter burst out explosively at the end of the song.

Kwame didn't give it time to die, but went right into the next number. It was a very quiet song. It was about love, too, and about peace and innocence; but these verses allowed beauty to survive and triumph. The words were very simple, but they were selected with such skill that they struck straight home, into the heart of every compassionate hope. They were articulated with meticulous precision; and as he listened, Michael felt sure that Kwame had written the song himself—and the one that had preceded it. The boy was a magician with words. He made strong magic, did Joe Schwartz. . . . And then, with the suddenness of a blow, Michael realized who Kwame was.

The performance ended as it had begun. Kwame simply stopped playing. Some fans came over to talk to him; and Michael looked up, blinking, to see the waiter standing by him.

"Thanks for telling me," he said. "I enjoyed that."

"He's a good kid," the waiter said.

"Do you suppose I could buy him a drink, or—"

"He don't drink."

". . . a cup of coffee? Or maybe a steak?" Michael eyed the protruding ribs of Kwame.

The waiter grinned.

"This isn't Manhattan," he said obscurely. "He'll talk to anybody. Hey, Kwame—friend of mine wants to meet you."

Kwame looked up. He saw Michael, and his beard divided in a sweet smile.

"Sure," he said. His speaking voice was as harsh as the one he used for singing, but several tones higher. Two of his fans trailed him as he approached the booth and he gestured toward them, still smiling.

"Okay?"

"Sure," Michael said. "Join me."

They settled themselves, Kwame placing his guitar tenderly on a serving table against the wall, where it would not be jostled by passers-by. The waiter lingered.

"You haven't had dessert," he said, giving Michael a significant glance.

"Oh. Oh! That's right, I haven't. Will you all join me?"

They would, and their orders left Michael feeling old and decrepit. Banana split, chocolate cake *à la* mode with hot fudge sauce, and a double strawberry frappé sundae for Kwame. Michael ordered apple pie and gave the waiter a nod of thanks as he departed. He ought to have realized that Kwame would be a vegetarian, and he was glad to have been saved from the gaffe of asking the boy if he'd like a steak. It would have been tantamount to offering someone else a nice thick slice off his Uncle Harry.

The food was a useful icebreaker; conversation, at first, was difficult. Kwame spoke hardly at all. Smiling dreamily, he was far out, someplace else. His friends, a blond girl (were they all blondes these days?) and her escort, who had a long cavalry-style moustache, treated Michael with such wary deference that he felt he ought to have a long white beard—and a whip. Yes, that was what they reminded him of—two captured spies in the enemies' clutches, refusing to speak for fear of giving away vital information. Name, rank, and serial number only . . .

They loosened up after a while, as Michael plied them with coffee and sympathy, and he began to enjoy himself. They weren't any more articulate, or sincere, than his generation had been; but they sure as hell were better informed. The much-maligned boob tube, perhaps? More sophisticated; superficially, yes, the little blonde was discussing contraceptives with a wealth of detail his contemporaries had never used in mixed company. Which was okay with him; his hang-ups on that subject weren't deep seated. He wondered, though, if basically these youngsters were any wiser than he had been at their age. They knew the facts; but they didn't know what to do with them, any more than he did. Maybe he was just old and cynical. He felt old. When he looked at Kwame, he felt even older.

Time, and the double frappé, had had their effect; whatever drug it was that Kwame had taken, it was beginning to wear off. He sat up straighter and began to join in the conversation. His comments had no particular profundity. But the young pair responded like disciples to the utterances of the prophet. When Kwame cleared his throat, they stopped talking, sometimes in the middle of a word, and listened with wide, respectful eyes.

Michael, whose mental age was rapidly approaching the century mark, found himself strangely reluctant to introduce the subject he wanted to discuss. He was relieved when Kwame gave him an opening.

"You're twenty-five now? You must have been a student, six years ago."

"Bright," Kwame said. The blonde giggled appreciatively.

"You were here when Gordon Randolph was teaching here."

"Right . . ."

The response wasn't quite so prompt.

"I'm doing a biography of him."

"Groovy," Kwame said.

Michael persisted.

"I've been interviewing people who knew him because I have a weird notion that personality, or character, or whatever, isn't an objective, coherent whole. It's a composite, a patchwork of reflections of the man as he appeared to others."

That interested them. The blond girl nodded, smoothing her hair, and Kwame's dreamy eyes narrowed.

"Personality, maybe," he said. "But not character. Two different things."

"How do you mean?"

"Character, you call it—soul, inner essence—not a patchwork. One integrated essence."

"All part of the Infinite Consciousness?"

Kwame shook his head. The beard swayed.

"I don't dig that Zen stuff. All part of an infinite something. Names don't name, words don't define. You've gotta feel it, not talk about it."

"Hmmm." The collegiate atmosphere must be getting him, Michael thought; he had to resist the temptation to plunge down that fascinating side track. "But that inner core, the integrated essence—that's beyond the grasp of a finite worm like myself. All I'm trying to get is the personality. I'm hung up on words."

"All hung up on words," Kwame murmured.

"So you can't tell me anything about Randolph?"

"Man, I can't tell you anything about anything."

This was evidently one of the proverbs of the Master. The blonde looked beatific, and her escort exhaled deeply through his nostrils, fixing his eyes on Kwame. Michael turned to them with the feeling that he was fighting his way through a web of gauze.

"Neither of you knew him, I suppose?"

"My sister was here then," the blonde said. She sighed. "She said he was the sexiest man she ever saw."

"Great," Michael muttered. "Haven't any of you read his book? It's a study of one of the problems that concern you—decadence, decay, the collapse of a society's moral fiber."

Even as he spoke, he knew he was dropping words into a vacuum. They professed concern about certain issues, but the only opinions they allowed were the opinions of their contemporaries and those of a few selected "in" writers. Many of them rejected the very idea that any generation but their own had searched for universal truths. Unaccountably irritated, Michael turned to Kwame, who was nodding dreamily in rhythm to a tune only he could hear.

"If you're not hung up on words, why do you use them? You use them well. A couple of those songs were—remarkable. You wrote them, didn't you? Words as well as music?"

Kwame stopped swaying, but he didn't answer for several seconds. When he turned dark, dilated eyes on Michael, the latter felt an uneasy shock run through him. He had reached

Kwame, all right; he felt, illogically, as if he had said something deeply insulting or obscene.

"Only two," Kwame said. "I only wrote two of them."

"They were the best," Michael said. "You ought to perform more of your compositions."

A spasm contorted Kwame's face.

"I don't write songs now. Not for a long time."

"Why not?"

"I can't anymore."

Kwame put his head down on the table and began to cry.

The other two were staring at Michael with naked hostility, but he hardly noticed. The fact that he did not understand Kwame's distress did not lessen his feeling of guilt at having somehow provoked it. He felt as if he had struck out blindly with a club and maimed something small and helpless, something that responded with a shriek of pain.

"I'm sorry," he said quickly. "I didn't mean—"

Kwame raised his head. The top fringes of his beard were damp, and tears still filled his eyes; but he made no move to wipe them away.

"You don't know what you mean," he whispered. "You see the shadows on the wall of the cave and you think they're real. Man, you don't know what's out there, in the dark, on the other side of the fire."

So they still read the old-fashioned philosophers. Michael recognized the allusion, it was one of the few images that remained from his enforced study of Plato. Humanity squatting in the cave, compelled to view the shadows cast on the wall by a flickering fire as the real world, never seeing the Reality that cast the shadows. . . . But his original reading had not evoked the chill horror that gripped him at Kwame's words. What Beings, indeed, might stalk the darkness outside the world, and cast distorted shadows? Whatever They were, Kwame knew about them. Michael had the irrational feeling that if he looked long enough into the boy's wide, liquid eyes, he would begin to see what Kwame had seen. . . .

Drugs, he told himself. Drug-induced hallucinations . . . His incantation of the conventional dispelled the shadows, and he said gently, "It's all right. I'm sorry. Forget the whole thing."

Kwame shook his head.

"Can't forget . . . anything. I need something. Need . . ."

His eyes turned toward the others, silent, defensive, watching. "You got anything? Grass? Acid?"

The blonde gulped, glancing at Michael. The boy, who seemed to have better control of himself, said calmly, "Nobody carries the stuff, Kwame, you know that. Not in here, anyhow."

"Then let's go someplace." Kwame shoved futilely at the table and tried to stand. "Let's go—"

The flutter of agitation had spread out beyond their table; other patrons were staring.

Michael sat perfectly still. Kwame's agitation was beyond reassurance; all he could do was refrain from any move or comment that might seem to threaten or condemn. In fact he felt no sense of condemnation, only a profound pity. After a moment, Kwame relaxed. There was perspiration on his forehead.

"Sorry," he said, giving Michael another of those sweet smiles. "We've gotta go now."

"I've enjoyed talking to you," Michael said. "And I enjoyed your performance. You're really good."

"Sorry I couldn't help you."

"That's all right."

"And thanks for the food."

"It was a pleasure."

The other two were standing, looking nervous as singed cats. But Kwame seemed to be bogged down in a mass of conventionalities.

"Sorry I couldn't—"

"It doesn't matter."

Kwame brooded.

"I knew her," he said suddenly.

"Who? Oh . . ." Michael knew how a policeman must feel when confronting, single-handed, a hopped-up addict with a gun. He didn't know what was safe to say. Kwame spared him the trouble.

"Linda. She's his wife now."

"I know."

"Beautiful," Kwame said; Michael knew he was not referring to Linda's face or figure. "A beautiful human being. We tripped together."

Balanced between caution and curiosity, Michael still hesitated to speak. Why hadn't he thought of that? Drugs might help to explain . . . Kwame seemed to sense what he was thinking.

"Not pot, nothing like that. She didn't need it. She was on a perpetual trip." He sighed. "Beautiful human being."

"Yes," Michael ventured. "Did Randolph take—"

Kwame shook his head.

"Oh, no," he said gravely. "Not him. He didn't need it either."

He started to walk away, his companions falling in behind him like a guard of honor. Then he turned back to Michael.

"He always knew about it."

"About what?"

"The dark," Kwame said impatiently. "The dark on the other side."

# Chapter
## 6

MICHAEL SHOVED AT THE TYPEWRITER. GLUED TO THE TABLE top by a two-year accumulation of dirt, spilled coffee, and other debris, it did not move; but the movement jarred the table, which proceeded to tip half a dozen books, an empty coffee cup, and a box of paper clips onto the floor.

Michael spoke aloud, warmly. The only response was a growl from Napoleon, couchant before the door. He pushed his chair back, slumped down in it, and moodily contemplated the single sheet of paper before him.

It was raining in the city again. He could hear rain pounding on the windowpane and see the dirty trickles that slid down the glass inside, where the caulking had dried and flaked and never been replaced.

Rain. Like all words, this one had its accumulated hoard of images. Sweet spring rain, freshening the earth and washing the grubby face of the world . . . The trickles on his window were jet-black. There was enough dirt on the window, but God only knew what color the rain had been to begin with.

The desk lamp flickered ominously, and Michael cursed again. He had forgotten to buy light bulbs. There wasn't one in the apartment. He had already taken the bulb out of the kitchen.

It might not be the bulb, of course. It might be the damned fuses in the damned antiquated building, or some other failure of the outmoded and overloaded electrical system.

From the dark kitchen came a pervasive stench of scorched food. In his mental anguish over the typewriter he had forgotten about the pan of stew till it turned to a charred mass. One more pan in the trash can. . . . He stubbed his toe groping through the dark kitchen. The broken coffee cup was not one of the ones from the dime store, it was a tender memento of something or other Sandra had given him. Sandra? Joan? Hell.

The paper, the sole product of an afternoon of creative effort, brought no comfort. It was filled from top to bottom with a series of disconnected phrases that weren't even passable prose.

> *I hate his bloody guts.*
> *He saved my life.*
> *A desperately unhappy man.*
> *A brilliant scholar.*
> *Sexiest man she ever met.*
> *All-around competence.*
> *Wonderful guy, a real chip off the old block.*
> *Keen, incisive business brain.*
> *Almost too sensitive.*
> *After Budge, one of the greatest backhands I've ever seen.*
> *Brilliant . . . brilliant . . . brilliant . . .*

And, at the very bottom of the page, dug deep into the paper by the pressure of his fingers on the keys:

> *He always knew about it. The dark on the other side.*

Damn the words, and damn the doped-up infantile little hippie who had produced them, Michael thought. But this verbal incantation didn't bring relief. He saw his words too clearly for the empty things they were. They didn't describe Kwame, and they didn't cancel the impact of the words Kwame had used. He makes bigger magic than I do, Michael thought sourly. Heap strong magic . . . The words haunted him; last night he had dreamed of shadows and waked in a cold sweat, tangled in bedclothes as if he had spent eight hours battling an invisible attacker.

Still. Dismiss Kwame as a talented junkie, and what did you have left? A series of epigrams, and damned dull ones at that. He was heartily sick of that word "brilliant."

Yet as the inconclusive interviews had proceeded, one concept began to take shape. One thing about Randolph that was significant, and hard to explain. Incompleteness.

Yet you couldn't say he didn't finish what he began. He finished his book. As a writer, Michael knew the importance of that; for every completed book there are a thousand beginnings. He had finished teaching his course and he had apparently taught it well, even brilliantly—damn that word! He had not abandoned tennis or swimming until he had mastered both skills, and his retirement from politics had followed a series of almost uncontested victories.

He mastered a skill, and then he stopped. Was it because he found all of them too easy? No challenge? Or was it because, under the façade of competence, he was somehow unsure of his ability? That wasn't as ridiculous as it sounded. The severest critic was internal. If a man couldn't satisfy that, paeans of praise from the outer world couldn't convince him of his worth. He had to keep on trying, fighting, accomplishing, and never succeeding, because the inner critic was insatiable. So—eventually, suicide, alcoholism, drugs. It had happened before.

But not, Michael thought, to Gordon Randolph. His life had not followed that pattern. If he had quit competing, it was not in the spirit of defeat. He had not retreated into any of the standard forms of suicide. He seemed—yes, damn it, he was—a happy man, except for one thing, the one thing in which he had not succeeded. The one thing for which he cared most desperately. And none of the pat phrases on that sheet of paper gave any clue to his successes, or to his one great failure.

Michael reached for another sheet of paper and inserted it into the typewriter. At the top of the page he wrote:

*His wife tried to kill him.*

Was that why he couldn't make any sense out of the man who was Gordon Randolph? Because, like so many of the others who had known her, he was becoming obsessed by Randolph's wife?

In her way, Linda was an even greater enigma than Gordon. Not because the coalescing picture was incoherent. A beautiful human being—they all agreed on the content of that, if not in the exact words, including Randolph himself. He had groped for words and so had Buchsbaum, but poor old Kwame had caught it. Then what had turned her from a saint into a devil, from a beautiful human being into an alcoholic, a haunted psychotic?

If I were writing a novel, Michael thought, they would have a common cause—Gordon's incompleteness, his wife's madness. But life is rarely so tidy or so simple. Or, if it is, the connections are too complex for us to see.

The light bulb flickered again. Napoleon muttered. The rain poured down harder. Michael got up and went into the kitchen. He stubbed his toe—the same toe.

A moving streak shot past him, into the sink and out through the slit in the window, its passage marked by a crash of breaking crockery, which was Michael's last saucer. Nursing his throbbing toe, Michael restrained his curses and listened. He knew what Napoleon's abrupt departure heralded. After a moment it came. A knock on the door; simple and ordinary. There was no reason why the sound should have made an anticipatory shiver run down his spine.

## II

Linda watched the rain ripple against the window of the bus. The downpour was so heavy, it didn't look like rain, but rather like a solid wall of water against the window of a submarine. The warm, stuffy bus was a self-contained, miniature universe; and the dark on the other side of the window might have been the vacuum of outer space. A few scattered lights, blurred by the rain, were as remote as distant suns.

The bus was not crowded. Not many people would come into the city in such weather and at such an hour, too late for the theaters or for dinner. The seat next to hers was occupied by a young sailor. He had come straight to it, like an arrow into a target. When he tried to strike up a conversation, she looked at him—just once. He hadn't tried again. He hadn't changed seats, though; maybe he didn't want to seem rude.

Linda didn't care whether he moved or not. She was aware of his presence only as a physical bulk; nothing else about him could penetrate the shell of her basic need. Even her physical discomfort was barely felt. Her shoes were still soaking wet and muddy. She had squelched through the ooze of Andrea's unpaved lane, hoping against hope, even though she knew she would have seen lights from the road if anyone had been at home. She had even pounded on the door, hearing nothing except the yowl of Andrea's pride of cats. Linda knew she could get into the house without any trouble; but with Andrea gone, there was no safety there. It was the first place they would look. Only a senseless desperation had taken her to Andrea in the first place. She wasn't running *to* anything or anybody; she was running away.

The impulse which had got her onto the bus was equally senseless. She had a little money, not much, and no luggage. If she paid in advance, she could get a room in a hotel; but how long would it be before Gordon found her? If he didn't want to call the police in, there were other, more discreet, ways of tracking her down. Anna would know what clothes she was wearing. There were hundreds of hotels; but Gordon could afford to hire hundreds of searchers. She wished the bus would go on and on forever, without stopping. Then she wouldn't have to decide what to do next.

When the bus reached the terminal, she sat unmoving until all the other passengers had got off, until the driver turned and yelled. She squeezed her feet back into the sodden leather of her shoes. Another stupid move; the driver would remember her, now that she had lingered and made herself conspicuous. He wanted to clear the bus and go home; he stood by the door, tapping his fingers irritably on the back of the seat.

Linda walked through the terminal and out onto the street. It was still raining. She walked. She walked a long way. In her mind was the vague idea of confusing the trail by not taking a taxi directly from the bus station. Not that it mattered; he would find her sooner or later. But she had to keep trying.

Finally she came to a brightly lighted street where there were many people. Cars, too, on the pavement. Taxis . . . Yes, this might be a good place from which to take a cab. She stood by the curb and lifted her hand. Cars rushed by, splashing water. Some had little lights on top. None of them stopped. Linda blinked vacantly as the water ran down off her hair into her eyes. Rain. That meant taxis would be hard to find. She remembered that fact from some obliterated past.

A taxi skidded to a stop a few feet beyond her and she walked toward it, but before she could reach it a man darted out, opened the door, and jumped in. The taxi started up, splashing her feet and calves with water. She stood staring after it. Another car stopped, almost at her elbow. The driver leaned out and flung the door open.

"Okay, okay, lady; if you want it, grab it. Hop in."

She got in, sat down.

"Where to?"

The address was written down on a slip of paper inside her purse, but she didn't need to look at it. She had known, all along, that she meant to go there.

"Must be from out of town," the driver said, pulling out into the street. "Figured you were, that's why I stopped right by you so nobody could beat you to it. Chivalry's been dead for a long time, lady. You gotta move fast if you wanta survive."

"It was nice of you," Linda said politely. "Thank you."

She didn't have to talk, he talked all the rest of the way. She remembered to tip him; it was an obvious thing, but tonight nothing was obvious, every movement and every idea was a long, arduous effort. What she did not remember until it was too late was that she had meant to leave the taxi at some indeterminate corner and walk the rest of the way. Too late now . . .

The street was dimly lighted, lined with buildings. In the rain and the dark, everything looked black—sky, buildings, windows. She dragged herself up the flight of steps, her shoes squelching.

There was no list of tenants' names outside the door, and no lobby—only a small square of hallway, with the stairs rising up out of it, and two doors, one on either side. Cards were affixed to the doors. She squinted at them through the rain on her lashes. Neither bore the name she sought. She went up the stairs.

Not the second floor, not the third. Another floor, surely it must be the last. There was no elevator; it had not occurred to her to look for one. She went on climbing. The wood of the stair rail felt rough and splintery under her fingers. The whole structure, stairs and rail, felt alive; it yielded, protesting with faint sighs, to the pressure of hands and feet.

The light was dim, a single naked bulb on each landing. Luckily for her, she reached the topmost landing before they failed, every light in the building simultaneously, plunging the place into abysmal darkness.

Linda threw herself to one side, feeling for the wall, for any solid substance in the darkness; heard a door flung open and felt the rush of something past her. Something plunged down the stairs, sliding from stair to stair but never quite losing its footing, never quite falling. It sobbed as it went.

## III

So much for premonitions, Michael thought.

It was Gordon Randolph who had knocked at his door. Not Gordon's wife.

Randolph's dark hair was plastered flat to his head; the ends dripped water. The shoulders of his tan trench coat were black with wet. Wordlessly Michael stepped back, inviting Randolph in with a gesture of his hand. Closing the door, he wondered what he ought to offer first. Coffee, a drink, dry clothes . . . But one look at his guest told him that any offer would be ignored, probably unheard. Randolph stood stock-still in the middle of the rug. Only his eyes moved, darting from one side of the room to the other, questioning the darkened doorways.

"She's gone," he said.

Michael nodded. He had realized that nothing less than catastrophe would have brought Randolph here in this condition. He felt profound pity for the tragic figure that stood dripping on his rug; but a less noble emotion prompted his comment.

"Why here?" he demanded.

"I went to Andrea's place first. Nobody was there. I searched the house."

"You searched—"

"Briggs is checking the hotels. Private detectives. But I thought maybe—"

Michael took a deep breath.

"Give me your coat," he said. "You're soaking wet. I'll get you a drink."

"Thanks. I don't want a drink."

"Well, I do."

Ordinarily the relief of movement would have given him time to collect his thoughts, but fumbling around in the dark kitchen was only another irritant. When he came back into the living room, carrying two glasses, Randolph was standing in the same position, staring fixedly at the bedroom door. Michael thrust a glass into his hand.

"Now," he said, "you can tell me why you think your wife might have come here. And make it good."

For a second he thought Randolph was going to swing at him. Then the taut arm relaxed, and Randolph's pale face twitched into a smile.

"All right," he said. "I had that coming to me. Get this straight, Mike. There is not in my mind the slightest shred of doubt about you and your intentions toward Linda. This is a pattern."

"You mean—this has happened before?"

Even from the little he knew, Michael should not have been surprised. He was. He was also, though he could not have said why, repelled.

"Twice before. Both friends of mine. It isn't you, you know." Randolph glanced at Michael and added hastily, "Damn it, I seem to be saying all the wrong things. You, and the others, are symbols of something, God only knows what; if I knew, I'd be a lot closer understanding what is wrong with her. I'm grateful that you're the kind of man you are. You wouldn't take advantage of her sickness."

"Not in the sense you mean, no. I have several old-fashioned prejudices," Michael said wryly. "Well, you can see for yourself that she isn't here. What precisely do you want me to do?"

The lamp chose that moment to give a longer, more ominous flicker. It was symptomatic of the state of Randolph's nerves that he jumped like a nervous rabbit.

"The bulb's about to go," Michael said.

"Not the bulb, that reading lamp flickered too. I hope we're not in for another of those city-wide power failures."

Randolph's face was white. Michael thought he understood the reason for the man's terror. The thought of Linda, lost and confused, wandering the blacked-out streets, disturbed him too.

"If she should show up, I'll call you at once. Where?"

Randolph shook his head.

"I'll be on the move. And she's wary and suspicious. If she overheard you speaking to me, she'd run. You couldn't detain her unless you—"

"Uh-huh." He didn't have to be specific; Michael could see the picture—the struggle, the screams, the neighbors, the cops . . . "A nice mess that would be," he muttered. "Then what the hell do you want me to do?"

"The ideal thing, of course, would be to get her to see a doctor."

The prompt reply dispelled any lingering doubts Michael may have had. Though why he should have had any, he didn't know.

"Ideal but difficult, if she's as suspicious as you say."

"She's suspicious of me," Gordon said. "That's why she rejects every doctor I suggest. From you she might accept it."

"Well, I could try," Michael said dubiously. "Be sure to let me know, will you, when you find her."

"Of course."

He seemed to have nothing more to say; yet, despite his concern, he was in no hurry to leave. He stood, holding the glass he had not even sipped, his head cocked as if he were listening for something. My God, Michael thought incredulously; he does expect her. At any second. Does he walk through life that way, listening for her footsteps?

"Well," he said again, "I'll do as you suggest—if she does show up, which I don't believe she will. And if I do get a chance to telephone, you'll be . . . ?"

"I've an apartment in town," Randolph said vaguely. "Maybe you could leave a message."

He put his glass down on the desk; and then, with the suddenness of a thunderclap, without even the usual preliminary flicker of warning, every light in the apartment went out.

The effect was frightening, disorienting. There was a faint glow from the window—so the blackout was not city-wide—but in the first moment of shock Michael didn't see that, and neither, obviously, did Randolph. Michael heard his voice, but he recognized it only because it was not his own. The sound was something between a scream and a sob, and it raised the hairs on the back of Michael's neck. Before he could move or speak, Randolph had blundered toward the door. Michael heard the sound of the door being flung open, and the rush of a body out onto the landing and down the stairs. He moved then, trying to shout a warning; the old, worn steps were treacherous enough in the light, he could visualize Gordon sprawled at the bottom with a broken neck. The anticipated slither and crash never came. The sounds of frantic movement diminished, and ended in the slam of the front door.

Then, in the ringing silence that followed, Michael saw the glow of the street lights through the window. He let out his breath with an explosive sigh. Once Randolph got outside, he would realize that his worst fear was unfounded. The man's nerves were in a shocking state. Not surprising; it was bad enough to worry about what might be happening to your wife, adrift in every sense in a blacked-out city; worse to worry about what she might be doing to others.

The lights chose that moment to restore themselves, and Michael blinked and cursed them absentmindedly. He had just had another thought, no more reassuring than the others he had been thinking. Linda had tried once to commit murder. Gordon spoke of a pattern. She had run away before; and what, Michael wondered, had she done on those other occasions? Michael had no illusions about one thing. Gordon might be the most altruistic of men, but on one subject he was beyond ethics. He would protect his wife at any cost—even if the cost were another life.

It was not a cheerful thought, especially if he accepted Gordon's assumption that he himself was Linda's next quarry. Michael shivered. There was a chill draft from the door, which Gordon had left open. He turned; and saw Linda staring at him from the doorway.

Her face was alarmingly like the one he had pictured in his latest fantasy—white and drawn, with eyes dilated to blackness. The only thing missing was the knife he had placed in the imaginary woman's hand.

For a moment they stood frozen, staring at one another. Then Michael got a grip on himself.

"You sure are wet," he said conversationally. "You'd better come in and dry off before you catch pneumonia."

One small, soaked shoe slid slyly back a few inches, as if bracing itself for a sudden movement. Michael didn't stir.

"He was here," she said. "Looking for me."

"Yes."

How long had she been standing out there in the hall? She must have come up after Gordon arrived, but before he left; that blind rush of his would have knocked her flat if she had been on the stairs, and there hadn't been time for her to climb them afterward. So she had been outside the door when Gordon fled, concealed by his agitation and the coincidental darkness.

"You didn't tell him I was here?" she persisted.

"How could I? You weren't here."

She nodded.

"Are you going to call him now?"

"Not if you don't want me to."

"I don't want you to."

"Then I won't."

The conversation was unreal. Michael couldn't remember what it reminded him of—Lewis Carroll, something existentialist? No. It was of a conversation he had had with the four-year-old son of a friend, some weeks earlier. The directness, the repetition of the obvious . . . Carefully he took a step, not toward the pitiable, shivering figure in the doorway, but back, away from her.

"You might as well come in and dry off," he said. "I'll make some coffee. Something hot."

"If I ran you could chase me," she said.

"Through all this rain?" He smiled. "I'm too lazy."

Her foot moved uncertainly. It took a step; then another and another. Michael let his breath out slowly. She was in. Safe. Now why did that word come into his mind?

## IV

Linda knew she wasn't safe, not even there, where she had wanted to come. But there was nowhere else to go.

She stood and sat and moved like an obedient child, while Michael helped her off with her coat and took off her wet shoes and dried her feet on something that looked suspiciously like a shirt. He made coffee; his movements in the dark kitchen were interspersed with bumps and crashes and repressed exclamations. She could hear every move he made. In a place this small, he wouldn't have a telephone extension in the kitchen, surely. The phone in the living room was on the table that served as his desk. She could see it from where she was sitting, and she watched it as if it were alive, a black, coiled shape that might spring into sudden, serpentine threat.

When he came back, carrying two cups, he was limping slightly.

"I keep stubbing my toe," he said with an apologetic grin, as she looked at his stockinged feet.

"Why don't you turn on the light? Or wear shoes?"

Michael looked surprised. It was an endearing expression; Linda wished she could simply enjoy it, instead of wondering what lay behind it. Probably he was surprised that she could frame a sensible question.

"I'm sort of a slob," Michael admitted, handing her one of the cups. "See, no saucers. No shoes. They're around here somewhere. . . . The place is a mess. I should be ashamed, entertaining guests in a hole like this."

"You weren't expecting company," she said drily. The heat of the cup, between her hands, began to seep through her whole body. Even her mind felt clearer.

"No," he said; and then, as if anxious to change the subject, "How long has it been since you've eaten? What about a sandwich? Or some soup? That's about the extent of my talents as a cook."

"It sounds good."

"I'll see what I've got on hand."

Another period of bumping and crashing in the kitchen followed. Linda sat back, closing her eyes, and then straightened up again. The warmth and the illusion of refuge were dangerous. She mustn't give in to them. From now on she had to be on the alert every second. There was still a chance, slim but worth trying, because it was the only chance. But if he failed her, she must be ready to act, instantly. In self-defense.

There was a louder crash from the kitchen. Michael's comment had a different tone, as if he were addressing another person instead of swearing to himself. Linda started, the empty cup wavering in her hands. Then Michael reappeared, carrying a plate. At his heels was another figure. Linda stared at it in comprehension and relief.

"Hope we didn't startle you," Michael said guilelessly. "He always comes in through the window, and through anything else that may be in his way. He just broke my last decent glass."

The cat, a monstrous, ugly animal, sat down, so abruptly that Michael tripped over it and nearly dropped the plate.

"Here," he said. "Take it quick, before he gets it. I was out of bread. I'm afraid the eggs got a little burned. . . ."

There were two fried eggs on the plate. The yolks wobbed weakly, but there was a half-inch rim of brown around the whites. For the first time in weeks Linda felt like laughing.

"They look lovely," she said, and glanced nervously at the cat, who was eyeing the plate with avid interest.

"His name is Napoleon," Michael said. "He hates people. But I've never known him to actually attack anyone."

"You don't sound as if you like him very much."

"We loathe each other."

"Then why do you keep him as a pet?"

"Pet? Keep? *Me* keep *him?*"

"I see what you mean."

She finished the eggs. They tasted terrible, but she needed the energy, in case . . . Lunch. Had she eaten any? Napoleon began to make a noise like a rusty buzz saw, and she looked at him apprehensively.

"I don't know what it means," Michael said gloomily. "He isn't purring, that's for sure. But he does it to me, so don't take it personally."

"I won't. Michael—"

"Wait," he said quickly. "We'll talk. We'll talk all you like. But not just yet, not until you're comfortable and dry. I won't call Gordon, not unless you tell me to. That's a promise."

"I believe you."

"Thank you." His eyes shifted. "Oh, hell, I forgot. I'm expecting someone to drop in this evening—an old friend of mine. Shall I call and try to put him off?"

"Maybe that would be better," Linda said slowly.

"All right. It may be too late, but I'll see what I can do. In the meantime, your clothes are wet and you look like a drowned rabbit. The bathroom is through there. See if you can find my bathrobe someplace. It's in the bedroom—on the floor, probably."

He was smiling at her, his eyes as candid as a child's. Linda wished desperately that she could trust him. But she didn't dare trust anyone. The risks were too great.

"Thank you," she said. She stood up. She reached for her purse. "I won't be long," she said.

Michael followed her into the bedroom, switching on the light. Like the living room, it was big and high-ceilinged. Automatically Linda's eyes assessed the exits. One big window. No window in the bathroom, which looked as if it might have started life as a closet when the building had stood in its newly constructed elegance. An enormous carved wardrobe now served the functions of a closet. There were two doors, one into the living room and one into the bathroom. All the furniture, including the wardrobe, was battered and nondescript. Interior decoration was clearly not one of Michael's interests. Every inch of wall space, except that which was occupied by the wardrobe and the doors and windows, was covered with bookcases; even the bed had been moved out into the middle of the floor to allow more space for books. The bed was not made.

Michael ambled around muttering apologies, picking up socks and underwear and books and old letters, and heaping them unceremoniously on the single chair. His face brightened as he lifted a drab garment from the floor.

"Here's my bathrobe," he said, shaking it out. "Gosh. I'm afraid it's pretty wrinkled."

"Thank you; it looks fine to me."

"Wait a minute." He darted into the bathroom, gathered up shaving equipment, towels, and more books. "There should be a clean towel someplace. . . ."

They found one, finally, on top of one of the bookcases. Linda closed the bathroom door and turned the shower on full force. She put her ear to the door and listened. The bedroom door closed with a bang, which probably represented one of Michael's attempts at tact, or reassurance.

Linda opened the bathroom door just wide enough to slip out, and eased it shut behind her. There was a telephone extension on the bookcase by the bed. She eased the instrument out of its cradle, her fingers on the button underneath. There was a slight click; but with luck he wouldn't notice it.

The click was lost in the ringing. She had moved so quickly that he had barely had time to dial the number. She waited, her hand over the mouthpiece, so that he could not hear the sound of her ragged breathing.

Finally the receiver at the other end was picked up. She knew, from the first syllable, that the voice was not the one she feared; and the relief was so great she almost lost the words.

"Let me speak to him," Michael said; and then, after a pause, "Galen? It's me, Michael."

He had been telling the truth. Her astonishment and joy were so great that she did not concentrate on Michael's next statement: something about "said you'd drop in tonight."

"But, Michael, I'm just leaving for—" the other man said.

Michael cut him off.

"Yes, I know. Hold on a second, Galen."

That was all the warning she had, and it was barely enough. She eased the receiver back down into its slot with a care and speed she had not expected her unsteady hands to know, and then dropped down, flat on the floor beside the bed, as the bedroom door opened.

The bathroom door was closed and the rush of water was unchanged. The thud of her heart sounded like thunder in her ears, but she knew Michael could not hear it. He stood motionless for a few seconds. Then the door closed.

Linda got to her knees. She didn't dare pick up the telephone again. She didn't have to. There was something wrong, or he wouldn't have bothered to check on her before proceeding with the conversation. And now she remembered what the person on the other end of the wire had said, at first, "This is Dr. Rosenberg's residence."

The mammoth volumes of the city telephone directory were where she might have expected them to be—on the floor. She scooped up the classified directory and ran into the bathroom. On her knees on the floor, she began turning pages. "Department Stores . . . Hardware . . . Machinery . . . Physicians." And there he was. Rosenberg, Galen. A conscientious member of the medical profession; four separate numbers were listed, including his home phone. Most doctors avoided giving that one out. But her eyes were riveted to the one word that mattered, the word that told which medical specialty Dr. Galen Rosenberg practiced.

It might be a coincidence. Presumably even psychiatrists had friends, like other people. But if Rosenberg had intended to visit his friend Michael, why did Michael care whether she overheard the conversation? And why had he interrupted the other man at that particular moment? On his way to—where? Not, she thought, to Michael's apartment. Not then. He was clever, Michael Collins, but not quite clever enough.

Her mind worked with the mechanical precision it developed in moments of emergency. Coat, bag—she had those. Shoes—they were still in the living room. That was bad. Well, she would just have to leave them.

Stripping off her dress, she opened the bathroom door and walked boldly across the bedroom. The door was still closed. She opened it a crack, and called, "Would it be all right if I washed my hair? It feels horrible."

"Sure." Michael's footsteps approached the door. It started to open, but she was ready; she pushed it back, making sure he saw her bare arm and shoulder.

"Hey," she said, putting a faint amusement into her voice.

"Oh, sorry. There should be some shampoo, someplace. . . ."

"I found it. Just wanted to let you know I wasn't drowned."

"Oh. Thanks."

He sounded embarrassed. She pictured him standing outside the door, his long, thin face alert and compassionate. Linda's mouth tightened.

"Your friend," she said, through the crack. "Did you reach him?"

"Friend? Oh, I'm afraid I wasn't able to put him off. He won't stay long. Don't worry, I'll tell him something."

*I'm sure you will*, she thought.

"Okay," she said, and closed the door.

So that was that. Naïve of her to expect anything else.

Letting the water run, Linda closed the bathroom door and slipped into her dress. The skirt was still damp; it felt clammy and cold against her skin. Gathering up coat and bag, she went to the window of the bedroom.

For several terrifying minutes, she was afraid she couldn't open it. The latch was a flimsy, old-fashioned thing, but the frame refused to yield to her frantic shoves. Outside, dim through the filthy glass, the angular black shape of a fire escape mocked her efforts. When the window finally gave, it went up with such a rush that she almost fell out.

Sprawled across the sill, she lay still for a moment, with the rain beating down on her head and the cold air in her face. Then she pulled herself back. Folding her coat, she went across the room to the wardrobe and opened its wide double doors.

\* \* \*

The bedroom door opened, and Michael's voice called, with hideous cheerfulness, "Linda? Hey, are you decent? Friend of mine wants to meet you."

Huddled in the back of the wardrobe, behind a heap of old newspapers and dirty laundry, Linda held her breath. Not that she needed to; when the truth dawned on him, Michael made enough noise to drown out a squad of heavy snorers—bellowing for his friend, splashing around in the bathroom as if he expected to find her submerged in the tub, and then rushing to the open window.

"She's gone," he kept repeating. "Damn it, Galen, she's gone."

Linda heard the other man's deep voice for the first time. They had talked in the other room for some minutes, but they had kept their voices so low, they were only murmurs.

"Out through the window? That's a hell of a route, Michael. I wouldn't have thought that old rattletrap of a fire escape would hold any weight."

"It obviously did. The dust on the windowsill is smeared where she crawled out. And—yes, her coat's gone. Her purse too. But—wait a minute—" Linda heard him run out and return. "Her shoes are still here! She went out in the rain, barefoot. . . . She's out there now, somewhere. Oh, God. I muffed it, Galen. If she gets hurt, it's my fault."

"Calm yourself. You sound like a bad performer trying out for Hamlet."

"Sorry," Michael muttered. "Damn it, Galen, I don't see how she knew. I was so careful—"

"There's a telephone extension in here. If she's as intelligent as you say, she could have managed."

"You mean it isn't that hard to outsmart me. And you're right."

"Cunning and intelligence are two different things. But before you go flying off in all directions again, let's stop and figure this out. Are you sure that fire escape is still functional? She may be out there still, halfway down. Or lying below, with something broken."

Michael rejected the last suggestion with a wordless sound; but Linda scarcely heard it. Her eyes were fixed, in horror, on the doors of the wardrobe. They were old and warped and did not close completely; a narrow line of yellow had announced

the switching on of the light when Michael entered the bedroom. Now the crack altered its shape, widening and narrowing
in turn. Someone was trying to open the door.

Her attention flickering wildly from the attempt on the door
to the conversation, she realized what the older man, the one
named Galen, was saying. My God, she thought; he knows I'm
here. He's smarter than Michael, smarter and tougher; he knows
I'd be afraid to step out on that fire escape. He must be leaning
against the doors, making them move, just to frighten me.

Then the door opened and she saw the source of her terror.
Not the doctor. Something worse. The cat, the damned cat. She
was afraid of the cat. It looked like a diabolical animal, and it
hated people; Michael had said so. It would take one look at
her and yowl or spit, and back out, and then they would know
where—

Linda saw its eyes shine with that eerie fire, which is, scien-
tifically, due to a perfectly normal phenomenon of light refrac-
tion. Then the eyes disappeared. Deliberately the animal sat
down, its back to her, and began washing its tail.

"There's nothing in the alley," Michael said, with a loud
sigh of relief.

"And no signs of her having gone that way, either."

"A flashlight doesn't show that much detail from up here.
What did you expect, a glove draped daintily over a garbage
can? Damn it, Galen, she had to go that way. There's no place
to hide in here. I was in the kitchen the whole time, she couldn't
have gotten past me."

A small contorted shape in the corner of the wardrobe,
Linda could almost feel the other man's gaze, moving thoughtfully around the room. Oh, yes, he was much smarter than
Michael. It never occurred to that innocent idiot that she hadn't
left. But he knew, the doctor—he had had considerable experience with people like her.

Whether he actually bent over to look under the bed, she
did not know; a snort of amused disgust from Michael might
have been his response to such a gesture. But she knew when
the doctor's searching eyes lit on the wardrobe—the only other
place in the room where a person might be concealed.

"There's Napoleon. Still as unsociable as ever?"

"He hates everybody," Michael said absently. "Likes it in
there, though. . . . Galen, what am I going to do?"

Napoleon finished washing his tail, turned around, and prepared to go to sleep. After the first knowing look, he had not glanced in Linda's direction.

"Well," the doctor said finally, "let's sit down and talk about it. Your original account was somewhat abbreviated."

"Have you got time?"

"Sixteen minutes. Then I'll have to drive like hell. I must catch that plane."

They went out, talking about the medical conference the doctor was going to attend. Linda let her head fall back against one of Michael's coats. Against the light from the half-open door of the wardrobe she saw the solid, unmoving black lump that was Napoleon. An odd smile curved her mouth. How very appropriate, she thought.

For the moment, at least, she was safe; reprieved by the hallowed familiar of legend, by the animal sacred to the powers of evil. What would happen next she neither knew nor cared; she still had to get out of the apartment, but she would worry about that later. Now she could relax, for a little time, enjoying the omen, and listening intently to the conversation, which was clearly audible through the open door.


"I wonder," the doctor said, "why she should come to you. Is she in love with you? Or you with her?"

"I don't know what the word means," Michael said quietly.

"No more do I."

"Then why the hell did you bring it up? No, I don't think she's running to anyone, or anything—unless it's safety. She's running away from something. Not her husband—"

"How do you know?"

"Well, for God's sake! Modern women don't run away from husbands, they divorce them. Besides, he—he's devoted to her. Desperately worried about her. He's out in this filthy rain now, looking for her. He was here, not five minutes before she came."

"He was?"

"I wish to God you people could carry on a normal conversation instead of trying to make it into a Socratic dialogue," Michael said irritably. "Yes, he was. And before you can ask, I'll tell you. I don't know why he should expect to find her here—that's the truth, Galen. But he did. He says she's run away before—to other men."

"What other men?"

"How the hell should I know? I didn't ask."

"I think I might have asked," the doctor said thoughtfully. "If a nervous husband told me I was number three on any list, I'd be curious about my predecessors. All right, never mind that. She runs away. He pursues."

"You make it sound . . . Galen, I tell you the girl is off her head."

"How do you know?"

"Oh, for—"

"All I'm trying to indicate is the stupidity of jumping to conclusions. As a writer you ought to know that a single set of observed facts may be capable of varying interpretations. And you know the human tendency to misinterpret evidence in terms of a preconceived theory. So far, all you've conveyed to me is that the woman is running away from something she fears. Either her husband is the source of her fear, or he is closely connected with it. Certainly it's possible that her fears are unjustified or imaginary; that she is, as you so elegantly put it, off her head. But it is also possible that she fears a real danger, one which even you would admit to be a legitimate cause of fear if you knew what it was. Just because you can't see it doesn't mean it isn't there."

"I know what she's afraid of," Michael said reluctantly. "And it—isn't there."

"What is it?"

"A dog. A black dog. She saw it one night and it terrified her so badly she went into a fainting fit."

"You didn't see it?"

"It happens that I didn't see it. But if I had, if it was real and not a figment of her imagination—so what? The cause is inadequate to explain her response. I tell you, the girl was frantic with fear."

The doctor did not respond at once. Linda, who had followed the discussion with growing hope, sagged back. For a while he had sounded like a possibility, a potential convert. But Michael's last statement was unarguable.

"I could argue that," the doctor said after a while. "But I'll accept your hypothesis, if only to keep you from bellowing at me."

"My hypothesis? I haven't got one."

"You sure as hell have. And it's time you dragged it out into the open and had a look at it. Your voice, when you said, 'A black dog,' was significant. What does that phrase suggest to you? No fair thinking about it—give me some images."

"The Hound of the Baskervilles," Michael said promptly. "Luminous eyes, jaws dripping with phosphorescence . . . The black dog of the Celts, that presages doom . . . A grisly story I read when I was a kid, about a werewolf. . . ."

"Now I," said Galen, "had a black dog once. A big black mutt who followed me everywhere I went and chewed up my shoes and hid under the bed when my mother scolded him."

"All right," Michael muttered. "I see your point, damn your eyes. None of my dogs was black. But it's not just a personal bias, Galen. It's partly the emotional atmosphere in that damned house. There are so many sick feelings—between Linda and that foul secretary, between Linda and the old hag who calls herself a white witch. When I looked back on the weekend, it seems to me that we talked of nothing but evil, and demonology, and Satan. The house is big and brightly lit, it has every modern luxury; but it stinks of ugly emotions. It's a sick house. Now laugh."

"Why should I? That's the most important thing you've said yet. You are neither stupid nor insensitive—"

"Thanks a lot."

"—and emotional atmospheres can be felt, I'd never deny that. The origins of the feeling are another matter."

"I know. And since I don't believe in mental telepathy, I've been trying to remember what small, unnoticed clues I must have seen. There must have been something; I don't ordinarily come over psychic."

The springs of the armchair creaked.

"I must go," the doctor said. "I'll barely make it as it is. I'll call you when I get back, Michael."

"But what am I going to do?"

"What are you looking for, free advice? It's your problem."

"Consoling as always."

"You've already made up your mind what to do. You just want me to agree with you. You're planning to telephone the bereaved husband and tell him his wife was here?"

"I have no choice about that."

"Perhaps not. Good-bye, Michael."

"Here's your briefcase. . . . Your Olympian detachment is all very well, but this isn't a remote, academic problem. She's on the loose right this minute, contracting pneumonia by walking around in the rain without any shoes on, if nothing worse. I don't like the role of informer; but for her own safety I must tell Randolph that she was here. Maybe he can—"

"Randolph?"

Linda heard the sound of the front door opening. The voices had gotten fainter; but the change in the doctor's tone came from some other cause than distance.

"This is Gordon Randolph's wife you've been talking about?"

"I thought I shouldn't mention names."

"No . . . Damn it, I'm late now. I'll break my usual rule, Michael, and give you one word of advice, if you'll walk downstairs with me. If you should hear anything . . ."

Linda was on her knees, oblivious of the danger of discovery; but strain as she might, she could make out no further words, only a mutter of voices as the two men descended the stairs. She crawled out of her hiding place, over the prostrate form of Napoleon, who snarled affably at her as she passed. Her cramped muscles complained as she stood upright. Overriding physical discomfort was the agony of indecision that racked her mind.

She went to the door and looked warily out into the empty living room. The lights still burned and the front door stood open. Michael was a trusting soul. . . . From below, amplified by the funnel of the stairwell, the rumble of voices floated up.

Briefly she fought the wild, dangerous urge to rush down the stairs and catch him before he left. But she knew she couldn't take the chance. They all talked that way, the ones who considered themselves liberal and sophisticated; but when it came to action, they balked at the final conclusion. If she could only talk to him at her leisure, with some means of escape at hand in case he turned out to be the broken reed all the others had been. . . . Too late for that now. Too late for anything but escape.

In her arms she still clutched the coat and purse, which she had been holding for so long. Darting across the room, she scooped up her shoes and went out the door. She reached the floor below just before Michael's head came into view, and cowered in the shadow of the stairs as he went past. If he had turned his head he would have seen her; but he went quickly, intent on his next move. The telephone; Gordon. And Gordon would see through her trick. He knew her habits and he wouldn't accept the obvious without checking. She would have to hurry. Gordon would come. Hurry . . .

The door above slammed shut and Linda fled down the stairs, her stockinged feet making no sound. The front door of the building opened and closed, and a slight dark form blended with the darkness of the night, and disappeared.

# Chapter

## 7

WHEN MICHAEL DISCOVERED THE TRICK SHE HAD PLAYED ON him, his first reaction was anger—not at his own stupidity, but at Linda. Gordon, who had just come back after an inspection of the alley under the fire escape, smile wryly at his expression.

"I know just how you feel, but don't let it get you."

"You told me she was intelligent," Michael said, recovering. "I should have believed you."

Gordon's smile faded.

"The operative word is not intelligence. There's a special kind of cunning developed by people in her condition. . . . Oh, hell, Mike, I'm still trying to mince words. I'm sorrier than I can say that you got dragged into this mess; but now that you are involved, it would be stupid of me to hold anything back."

Michael couldn't help remembering that it was Gordon who had dragged him into the mess. Then his annoyed vanity faded at the sight of Gordon's tormented face, and he shrugged.

"I feel very bad about letting her get away. If I had realized how sick she was—"

"Precisely why you shouldn't feel guilty. It was my fault for understating the problem. Let's forget that and go on to something constructive."

"Shouldn't we be trying to trace her? There's a subway station in the next block; cabs aren't too frequent around here. . . ."

"Briggs is already on that," Gordon said.

"Oh. Sure."

Another unwelcome memory recurred to Michael—the look of unconcealed repugnance on Linda's face whenever she saw Briggs. Surely he wasn't the best person to send after a frightened woman. . . . He shrugged the doubt away. It was none of his business.

"How about a drink?"

"No, thanks; I'd better get moving."

But Gordon appeared to be in no hurry; drawing on his gloves with deliberate care, he managed to look poised and aristocratic in spite of his obvious worry. By just standing there he made the shabby little room look shabbier. His keen black eyes moved around, lingering on the paperstrewn desk.

"How do you feel about the biography now?" he asked.

"I don't know. I've put quite a bit of work into it. . . ."

"Have you really?" Gordon's dark gaze swung back to Michael. "Whom have you talked to? Or should I ask that?"

"Oh, sure, why not? I started with the colleges. You made quite an impression at both of them."

"They all mouth the conventional academic baloney," Gordon said cynically. "Wait till you talk to my former political cohorts. They won't be so complimentary."

"They were somewhat annoyed at your retirement, I suppose."

"A euphemism." Gordon smiled. "But by all means talk with them; you'll get an interesting view of my personality. Well. I'll be in touch, Mike."

"Please do. I'm concerned too."

When Gordon finally went, Michael dropped into the big overstuffed chair and put all ten fingers in his hair.

She had looked so young.

The glamorous hostess in her expensive gowns had seemed mature; the shrewish wife had a woman's cruelty. But she wasn't that many years out of college; she must be ten, even fifteen, years younger than Gordon. And when she sat huddled in his big chair, with the rain dripping down onto her pale cheeks, she had looked about sixteen. Her hands and feet were as fragile as a child's; the sodden shoes had been no longer than his hands.

Yes, he reminded himself, and she had presence of mind enough to take those pathetic little slippers with her when she outfoxed him. Poor little Cinderella? Rich little Lucrezia Borgia was more like it. But still he sat motionless, head in his hands, his fingers contracting as if their pressure could force from his mind the picture that persisted through every conscious doubt—the picture of a slight, dark figure running down a dusky corridor, growing smaller and more tenuous as it fled, until it finally vanished into air.

## II

Next morning Michael went around and heckled his agent. Sam Cohen was not noted for his equable disposition; after half an hour of querulous dithering, he exploded.

"What the hell do you mean, you don't know whether you want to write it or not? You've got to write it. We've got a contract!"

"I didn't sign it in my own blood," Michael snarled.

Sam recognized the signs; he was used to them, but he got writer's temperament so seldom from Michael that it took him by surprise. After a blink of his scanty eyelashes, he went into the routine.

"Mike, you know this is the best deal I've ever gotten for you. It's too good to pass up, even if you don't care about the damage you could do your professional reputation if you renege on a formal contract. Hell, we may have a best seller on our hands if this rumor about Randolph's going back into politics is true."

Michael sat up in his chair.

"Where did you hear that?"

"The essential criterion of a rumor is that nobody knows how it started. But I've heard it mentioned more than once."

"Hmph. I didn't know you could do that. Get back into the game, I mean."

"Why not? He never lost an election, you know. With his money and charm, the party bosses would jump at him. Sure, it will take a little time to get his name before the public again, but—didn't you ever wonder why he agreed to this biography when he's refused even an interview for years?"

"I guess I am naïve," Michael said slowly. "He's a nice guy, you know. The idea of his using me—"

"Naïve is right," Sam snorted. "So how is he using you?

Making you rich is all. Does that make him any less of a nice guy? Oh, get out of here, and let me work. And do some work yourself."

Michael grinned and wandered out. On the street he stood blinking at the feeble sunshine and wondering what he wanted to do. He had called Gordon that morning, when the latter had failed to call him. Linda was still missing. The sunshine was anemic. The smog was heavier than usual. It was a lousy day. He was in a lousy mood.

So he spent the day doing nothing. He made a feeble attempt to clean up the apartment, a chore which was weeks overdue, but he knew his real motive was to be at home in case Gordon called. He did manage to get the dirty laundry collected; there were socks under the cushion of the chair and a sock on the kitchen table. Rooting around in the bottom of the wardrobe, he found a pile of dirty shirts. On top of them lay a small, crumpled black glove.

Straightening up, with the glove in his hand, Michael abandoned the shirts. So that was where she had been; obviously, there wasn't any other place. Then he remembered something, and, turning, he bellowed loudly for the cat. Napoleon was gone. Deprived of an audience, Michael muttered to himself. The animal was obviously getting senile. Or else there was something about Linda Randolph that appealed to him. A nasty thought, that one . . .

By evening, when the phone still refused to ring, Michael was desperate. He straightened his desk. He managed to cram half the books that had been on it into one bookshelf or another, but there was no place for the rest. He needed another bookcase. Only, where was he going to put it? Every inch of wall space in living room and bedroom was already taken up. Maybe the bathroom . . . Then, on the bottom of a pile, he found the book that he had bought and then ignored. Randolph's masterpiece. With a snort, Michael threw himself into a chair and began to read.

He came to three hours later when Napoleon bit him on the ankle, milder attempts to gain attention having failed. Still carrying the book, he stumbled out into the kitchen. He gave Napoleon the hamburger he had intended for his own dinner, an error he didn't even notice till the next day. He went on reading.

At four in the morning he finished the book, and fell groggily into bed in a state of mingled exaltation and rage. The pathetic little mental image of Gordon's wife had developed a set of fangs. Anyone who could write a book like that when he was still in his twenties . . . The man needed encouragement, admiration, an atmosphere of peace and quiet—not a crazy wife who probably resented his superior talent. Lying awake in the darkness, Michael could see the ghosts of Gordon's unwritten books, laid out in a row like murdered babies. Murdered *in utero* by Gordon's wife.

This partisan mood carried Michael through the next few days. He didn't call Gordon, but Gordon called him and reported that Linda had not yet been found. He sounded less edgy. Of course, if she had been hurt or killed, she would have been heard of by this time, Michael thought. Personally, he no longer gave a damn.

He spent two infuriating days trying to track down some of Gordon's political associates, knowing full well that he would never reach the hidden men who made the real decisions, and discovering that politicians were even more peripatetic than academicians and just as impressed with their own importance. Yet through the platitudes and glittering generalities, an impression gradually formed. He believed the rumors of Gordon's return to politics. It was ridiculous, of course, to resent Gordon's failure to take him into his confidence. Maybe he hadn't made up his mind yet.

Michael found himself curious to read some of Gordon's political speeches. They were not easy to locate; the big-city newspapers had not followed out-of-state local campaigns in detail. Finally he managed to find back issues of the leading newspaper of Gordon's state.

Even in cold print the speeches were impressive. Michael could imagine their effectiveness when they were delivered with the full force of Gordon's dynamic personality. He had wondered what kind of political speech might be composed by the man who wrote that fantastic book. Now he knew. Of course the media were completely different; a political speech was not a novel. But the similarity was there, not in phrasing or in content so much as in an underlying integrity, the product of a particular kind of mind.

Gordon's candidacy had been supported by the newspaper. It got a lot of coverage, and the not-so-subtle slant in the reporting, compared with the tone taken toward Gordon's unfortunate opponent, made Michael's mouth twist in wry amusement. Politics, he thought, with the comfortable contempt of a man who has never run for office. Well, you couldn't blame Gordon for the traditional dirtiness of the game. . . . He kicked himself mentally. Blame, hell, you don't condemn or approve, he reminded himself. You just read. And write, if possible.

It was pure accident that he saw the item at all. It was on the front page, but it was hidden down in the lowest left-hand corner, and Gordon's name was mentioned only once, in small print.

There was a photograph, and he studied the inexpressive features of the young man with interest. Copied from a formal studio portrait, the face was not distinctive. High forehead, hair and eyes of some indeterminate dark color, horn-rimmed glasses so big that they reduced the features to unimportance. Gordon's campaign manager, William S. Wilson.

The name was familiar. Michael groped through his mental card file on Randolph for several seconds before he realized that the familiarity had nothing to do with contemporary events. The name was that of Edgar Allan Poe's character. A nice, cheerful story that one, about a man haunted by his own ghost.

The analogy was nonexistent. Accidental death, the police believed—the strain of an exciting campaign, and too many sleeping pills. There was no reason why the young, successful assistant of a rising politician should take his own life.

Michael was curious enough to pursue the story. The next installment had retreated from page one to page fourteen, reasonably enough, since there were no dramatic developments. The assumption of accidental death was confirmed by all the evidence the police had been able to turn up. So much for William Wilson.

Michael didn't know, then, that the seed had been planted. It had not yet taken root; it just sat there in the darkness of his subconscious mind, rubbing a little, but beginning to be encased, like a grain of sand in an oyster, by layers of protective preconceptions. But the intrusion was a seed, not a sterile piece of grit. The telephone call he got the next day started it growing.

Typically, Galen didn't waste any words.

"Have you resolved your latest problem?" he asked, as soon as he had identified himself to his surprised listener.

"No, she's still missing. Where are you?"

"Paris, of course. I told you I'd be here till the end of this week. Michael, I want you to go over to my office and—"

"You're calling me from Paris? Why?"

"If you'll be quiet for a minute, I'll tell you. I'm due at a symposium in about four and a half minutes. Go over to my office and pick up an envelope my secretary has for you. I've already spoken to her."

"You want me to mail it to you?" Michael asked, groping.

"If I wanted something mailed to me, I'd have my secretary mail it," Gordon said impatiently. "The envelope is for you. Go and get it now. Don't make any decisions until you've read the contents."

"What the hell are you talking about?"

"I don't believe I've used any words of over three syllables, have I? I must go now. I'll be in touch with you as soon as I get back. And remember, don't do anything drastic until you've seen that envelope."

The receiver went down with a decisive click. Galen never bothered with hellos and good-byes.

Michael hung up. There was no use trying to call back. He didn't know what hotel Galen was staying at, and it was more than likely that Galen would refuse to add anything to his enigmatic message even if he could be located. He was never obscure except by choice.

Michael got up and wandered over to the window. It was raining again. The sky, what little he could see of it, was a dirty gray, and the puddles in the alley reflected the sallow light with a sheen of oily iridescence. Even on the fourth floor, with the window closed, he could hear the snarl of bumper-to-bumper traffic on the street. Absently, Michael drew his initials in the smeary film on the inside of the pane. The hell with it. He wasn't going all the way across town on a day like this just to pick up an envelope.

The foul evening darkened, the rain beat a peremptory tattoo against the window. Michael wandered the apartment like a caged lion, unable to settle down or even to understand the strange sense of uneasiness that grew, slowly but steadily. Unable to concentrate and unwilling to go out, he puttered with small jobs he had been putting off; he put a new light bulb in the kitchen and started to cook himself something to eat. It was then that he discovered he had given Napoleon the hamburger. There was nothing else fit to eat except various things in cans, and he realized he wasn't hungry anyhow. He was too nervous to eat.

Nervous. Slowly Michael let himself down into a chair and considered the word. He reviewed the symptoms: taut muscles, mildly queasy stomach, restlessness, general malaise of mind. Yes, that was his trouble; he was as nervous as a cat. . . . He gave the somnolent Napoleon a look of hate, and revised the figure of speech. He hadn't had the symptoms for years, that was why he had been so slow to recognize them—not since college exams, or the early days of his working career, when a particular interview, or letter, or telephone call might make or break his new-hatched confidence in himself. So why now, when there was nothing hanging over him that really mattered?

The thing hit him with the violence of an earthquake, but it was nothing physical, nothing that any of the conventional senses would have recognized. Yet it was as peremptory as the sudden shrilling of a telephone in a silent room. It summoned, like a shout; it tugged at the mind like a grasping hand. It lasted for only a second or two, in measurable time; but while it lasted, the room faded out and gray fog closed in around him. He was conscious of nothing except the calling. Even the hard seat of the chair under him and the solidity of the floor beneath his feet seemed to dissolve. It stopped as abruptly as it had begun. There was no fading out, merely a cessation.

Michael found himself on his feet. His face was wet with perspiration, and his knees were weak. Blinking like a man who has emerged from a cave into bright sunshine, he looked around the familiar kitchen, and found its very normalcy an affront. The table was still a table; it rocked slightly under the pressure of his hand as it always did. It ought to have changed into an elephant or a tortoise. The view from the kitchen win-

dow should not be the normal view of night darkness; it ought
to show an alien sun over some weird landscape. The thing that
had invaded his mind was as shattering and as inexplicable as
any such transformation.

But the most incredible thing about the experience was that
he accepted it. He knew, not only what the calling was, but who
had sent it. Knew? The verb was too weak; there was no word in
the language for the absolute, suprarational conviction that
filled his mind.

He was still a little unsteady on his feet as he crossed the
room. He noticed that Napoleon was no longer in his favorite
place by the door. Evidently the cat had left, and he hadn't even
heard him go.

His desk was covered with papers, notes, books. Michael
didn't touch any of them. Slumped in his chair, his eyes fixed
on vacancy, he thought. It was one of the hardest jobs he
had ever done in his life; methodically, he examined and demolished all the guideposts he had established in the past
ten days—as well as a few mental monuments that had been
standing a lot longer. It left his conscious mind pretty bare.
He didn't try to construct any new theories to fill it up. He
couldn't yet.

The urgent impulse that still gripped him, even though its
stimulus had vanished, did not interfere with his thinking; it occupied a level much more basic than reason or conscious
thought. It was rather like an overpowering hunger or thirst. But
he couldn't yield to it yet; a man who walks along a contaminated stream knows, even though his throat is a dusty agony,
that he cannot relieve the pain until he finds clear water.

Why hadn't he gone out, that afternoon, to get the envelope
Galen wanted him to have? The office was closed now, and he
didn't know the secretary's last name, or address.

The contents of that envelope must concern Randolph, and
they must be important. That conclusion wasn't intuitive; it was
the result of logic. Galen's reaction that night, when he learned
the identity of the fugitive, had been markedly peculiar. He
hadn't been merely surprised; he had been worried. That last,
hasty spate of advice had also been uncharacteristic: *Don't do
anything, don't take any action whatsoever. I'll discuss it with
you when I get back.*

But Galen had decided the matter couldn't wait. That oblique reference at the beginning of the telephone conversation indicated that he had been thinking about the Randolphs, and strongly suggested that the rest of the conversation concerned them. Galen thought nothing of trans-Atlantic telephone calls, or any other obstacle that stood in the way of what he wanted done, but he did not extend himself over a mere whim. The material must be important. And if it were favorable, noncontroversial, Galen wouldn't be so cautious about it.

Unless one of the Randolphs had been Galen's patient. Michael dismissed that theory at once. Under no circumstances would Galen discuss a patient's case with him. No, the connection had to be something else; and Michael had a pretty good idea as to what it must be.

He tried to remember his first impressions of Galen, but he couldn't pin them down; Galen had just been one of the Old Man's friends, too antique to be interesting. Galen must be over sixty—he had to be, if he and the Old Man had been at school together in Europe, before the last big war. He didn't look it. Physical fitness was something of a fetish with him. Not surprising, perhaps, after the two-year hell of a concentration camp and the desperate years of underground fighting that had preceded the camp. More surprising was Galen's mental stability. There was a certain ruthlessness under that passionless exterior of his, but he was as free of bitterness as he was free of optimism. It was revealing, perhaps, that he never spoke of the war years, or of the wife and small son who had been devoured by the holocaust. His reference to his boyhood pet was one of the few times Michael had ever heard him mention his childhood. His parents, too . . .

It was Michael's father who had been primarily responsible for getting Galen out of the chaos of postwar Germany; the kind of help the old man had given during those years had never been made explicit to Michael, by either man; but after his father's death, Galen was—there. Silent, withdrawn, unsentimental—but there.

Michael shook himself mentally. This was a sidetrack, a waste of time. There was no point in speculating when, in a few hours, he would have the answer in his hands. In the meantime . . .

He thought for another hour. At the end of that time he finally moved, but not much; when he finished, there was on the table a single sheet of paper. It contained only four names, in Michael's cramped writing, but he contemplated the meager results of his labors with grim satisfaction.

Then he picked up the pen and added a phrase after three of the names.

*William Wilson. Dead. Suicide?*

*Tommy Scarinski. Nervous breakdown; attempted suicide.*

*Joseph Schwartz. Breakdown; drugs.*

He paused, pen poised, studying the list. Incredulity was hard to conquer. It seemed so unlikely. . . . Yet there they were, four of the people who had been closest to Gordon Randolph in his adult life. His campaign manager and friend, and his three prize students during that single year as a teacher—a position, surely, that gives a man or woman enormous influence over younger minds. And of those three, one was still a nervous wreck, and another had retreated from a promising career into a world of drug-induced terrors. And the third . . .

The third was Randolph's wife.

## III

Threading a tempestuous path through a mammoth traffic jam, Michael blasphemed the beautiful weather and the long weekend. The balmy sunshine had infected half the inhabitants of the city with the urge to flee to Nature. Galen's secretary was one of them. It was after ten that morning when the answering service told him the office wouldn't be open, and he had wasted more time in a futile attempt to track down Galen's secretary. Finally he drove to Galen's house and harassed his manservant until the poor devil consented to open up the office and help him search. That had taken several more hours— the harassment, not the search. Whatever her other failings, Galen's secretary did what she was told. The envelope, with Michael's name typed neatly on it, was in the top drawer of her desk.

Badly as he wanted to examine the contents, another need was stronger. He had wakened that morning with a renewed uneasiness, not so demolishing as the call that had summoned him the night before, but constant and peremptory. He was on his way now to answer it.

He braked, swearing, as a blue Volkswagen roared blithely past on the left and ducked into the nice legal margin between Michael's car and the rear of the one ahead of him. He couldn't even think in this chaos; driving took too much concentration, with so many morons on the road.

He resisted the childish desire to drive right up onto the back fender of the Volkswagen. Today, of all days, he couldn't take any chances. The afternoon was far gone; but he would reach his destination in two or three hours, and by that time he had to have a clearer idea of what he meant to do when he got there. So far the demand had been strong and basic, blotting out all thoughts but one: Get there. Sooner or later, though, he would have to make a plan. He couldn't stand on Andrea's doorstep waiting for another message from Beyond.

Linda must be at Andrea's. It was the only place she knew, the only potential ally who had not failed her. Michael had reached that conclusion logically; direction was one of the elements the mental call had lacked. Gordon had already searched the witch's cottage, which did not lessen the probability of Linda's being there now; the safest hiding place is one that has already been investigated. But she would be wary of visitors in general and hostile toward Michael in particular. Remembering the telephone book, open to the page with Galen's name, Michael felt the same mixture of shame and chagrin that had moved him originally. He wasn't proud of his performance that night. To say the least, it had been stupid. She probably thought of it as betrayal. No, she wouldn't let him into the house, not unless the days of loneliness and fear had reduced her courage to the breaking point. He might have to break into the house— a prospect he faced with surprising equanimity. For such a purpose, darkness would be useful.

But when he stopped at a restaurant in the next town, it was not only because of the need to kill a little more time. He couldn't wait any longer to see what was in Galen's envelope.

It was a big Manila envelope and it was sealed not only by tape but by a heavy wad of sealing wax. The wax was fresh and the envelope clean, which meant that the material it contained must have been gathered together only recently. It was not one of those envelopes so dear to writers of sensational fiction, which has been moldering for years in a secret hiding place until the *deus ex machina* of the book produces it just in time to foil the villain. The envelope was not bulky. It could not contain more than a dozen sheets of paper.

When he had the papers in his hand, Michael sat staring blindly at them for a while before he started to read. He had been expecting what he found; it was, after all, the most logical connecting link between Galen and Randolph. But it was still something of a shock to see again the sprawling, angular handwriting that had once been as familiar as his own.

A letter a week for almost seven years, arriving every Tuesday morning. Careless and unmethodical as his father was about other things, he wrote every Sunday. Michael never kept personal letters after he answered them; there certainly had been no particular point in saving his father's. They were good letters, informative and amusing because of their acidulous comments on people, books, and events. So far as he could remember, the old man had never mentioned Randolph. Which was not surprising; by the time he had left home, Randolph was no longer a student.

His father had written less frequently to Galen, but he had kept up a regular correspondence with his old friend. Galen never threw anything away. These letters were only a small part of the mass of materials that were docketed, labeled, and filed—both in the neat cabinets filling several rooms of Galen's house, and in the latter's capacious memory. Galen had not kept these letters because of a premonition. But he would not have produced them now unless they had significance.

After these optimistic deductions, the first letter was a disappointment. It didn't even mention Randolph's name.

Professor Collins rambled on for two pages about the petty gossip and activities of the university. Michael knew that some of the ivory towers were rat infested, but he had forgotten how largely small malices can loom, even to a mind that is supposed to wander in the airy realms of ideas. Cheating on examinations, unexpected pregnancies, a rumor of students dabbling in black magic . . . Nothing was new on the campuses. There was only one name mentioned in the letter, that of a student for whom his father had high hopes. His name was not Randolph.

Puzzled and deflated, Michael put the letter aside. Maybe Galen's secretary had made a mistake, or else Galen had told her to include all the letters dated to a particular year. He could hardly quote specific identifying details over the telephone, especially when he hadn't read the letters for over ten years.

Michael felt sure of this hypothesis when he started the next letter and found Randolph's name in the opening paragraph. The context was not precisely what he had come to expect of Gordon Randolph.

"These sporadic flashes of brilliance baffle me," his father had written of the school's star athlete and president of the student body. "I expected great things of the boy, he's already a school legend, but he never happened to take any of my courses until this year—which is his last. I'd say that literature simply wasn't his field, if it weren't for that rare outstanding essay."

The rest was inconsequential, for Michael's purposes. There was another reference to the devil worshipers, whose existence was now a well-established rumor. His father found them exasperating, whoever they were: "They've been reading about the Hellfire Club and decided to imitate that bunch of nasty-minded little——"

The next word was indecipherable; which, Michael thought, with a reminiscent grin, was probably just as well. His father's collection of epithets and expletives were drawn from the riper Restoration dramatists; some of them had curled his hair even in his supercilious high school days.

As he read on, his sentimental nostalgia increased; but so did his bewilderment. There were eight letters in all. One of them didn't even mention Randolph, the others contained more references to his father's pet student—what was the kid's name?—Al Something—than to Gordon. Poor old Dad must have been losing his grip, Michael thought. Gordon was only a few years away from his great book; according to the publisher's blurb, parts of it had actually been written while he was in college. If his father hadn't spotted a talent of that magnitude . . .

The last letter was no more informative, but it was something of a shocker. His father's handwriting was shakier than usual, and his sentences were so garbled by emotion as to be relatively incoherent in parts. The feeble idiocy of the campus Hellfire Club had exploded into scandal and disaster; one student was dead as a result of an occult experiment, which his father's Victorian inhibitions had kept him from describing in detail. And that student was the boy for whom he had had such hopes—Alfred Green.

Large as the affair had been in the minuscule world of the university, it hadn't made much of a splash in the press. Michael remembered hearing something about it, but the influential board of trustees had succeeded in suppressing the details. Still, reading between the lines, it must have been a nasty business. The word was his father's. It kept recurring, through the scribbled agitation of the lines: nasty, foul, disgusting. It would seem that way to him, Michael thought. Then, at the end of the letter, came a hasty postscript.

"Young Randolph came by this evening, to express his regrets. Alfred was one of his closest friends. It was kind of the boy, and perceptive, to know that this has hurt me worse than an ordinary scandal would have done. Perhaps I haven't been fair to him. Antipathy is an odd thing."

Michael sat staring at the last page for a long time, while the cigarette burned down between his lax fingers and his second cup of coffee grew cold. He felt completely deflated. He had expected a complete, startling answer to the enigma that had begun as a simple problem of character, and which had now taken on such ominous outlines. But there was no answer in these letters, only new questions. In the back of his mind the mental call still pulled, confusing what wits he had left.

It was not until he was trudging through a blue twilight on his way to the place where he had left the car that he realized what the letters had told him. Another death. Randolph's triumphant career seemed to be unnecessarily littered with corpses.

He forgot this new piece of the puzzle, which was merely an addition to his list rather than a clue as to why the list existed, as he drove through the streets of the village near Randolph's estate. The street lights had come on and the houses looked peaceful and homey, with lights twinkling through the gathering darkness. The temperature had dropped, though; the wind that tossed the boughs was sharp. He rolled up the car window.

He hit a snag when he turned into the curving streets of the

suburb. He had already observed that the inhabitants of Brent-
wood liked their privacy. There were no quaint mailboxes with
names on them along the curving drives and walled estates.
There weren't many street lights, either. Maybe the rich didn't
need them. They had their own methods of guarding against
crime—burglar alarms, dogs, even private guards.

Nor did Andrea court publicity. Michael found the house at
last only because it was at the end of the sole road that was unpaved and unlandscaped. A survival from a simpler past, he
thought, jouncing down the rutty lane. If there was a house
down here, it was well hidden. Mud squelched under the tires,
and he had visions of being thoroughly stuck, at the end of a
road that petered out into forest.

As the thought formed, the road ended. The dark shapes of
trees loomed up, and Michael jammed on the brakes, skidding.
He saw the gate, and knew that he had arrived.

It was the sort of gate Andrea might have had constructed to
her specifications if she had set up shop as a newly certified
witch—wooden, rickety, sagging on rusted hinges. Thick,
untrimmed shrubs concealed the path beyond and leaned out
over the fence like watchful sentries. The house beyond was
visible only as a crazy shape of roofs and chimneys that cut off
a section of starry sky. There was no light, and no sign of human life.

Shapes other than man-made cut off the starlight. Half the
sky was curtained by clouds. The wind lifted Michael's hair
from his forehead and turned the boughs of the tall shrubs into
armed appendages, which thrust out in abrupt challenge. The
clouds hung heaviest toward the east. As Michael watched, distracted from his search by the eerie movement of the night, a
glow of light flickered above the tops of the pines, like the
ghost of a sick sunset. It was followed by a slow, far-off roll of
thunder.

Practical considerations intruded on the fascination of the
approaching storm. This trek might turn out to be more disas-
trous than a plain old wild-goose chase. The road was already
gluey with mud; another heavy rain could maroon him in this
abandoned lane. He had better check the house and get out.

The mental call that had brought him a hundred miles was
gone.

When it had left—if it had ever existed, save in his imagination—he could not remember. But its absence left him feeling blind or deaf, bereft of a sense that had, even in so short a time, become something he depended on as uncritically as he accepted the use of his eyes. For the first time in nearly twenty-four hours he examined his activities in the cold light of reason, and found them folly. Only his inborn stubbornness brought his hand to the latch of the gate.

It screeched rustily. He had half expected that it would, but the sound, shattering the quiet night, made him jump. As he took a tentative step forward, something streaked across the path in front of him. He grabbed instinctively at the branch of the shrub, stabbed his thumb on something sharp, and let out a yell. The shrub had thorns.

The darting streak that crossed his path hadn't triggered any fantasies, though; he knew what it was—a cat, one of the dozen that Andrea was reputed to keep. He wondered where the others were, and what arrangements Andrea made for their comfort while she was off on her frequent trips. Then he realized that all the shrubbery was alive with movement. The action of the wind made the foliage mutter; but there were other sounds. Small, ground-level movements rustled branches and made leaves whisper. He saw something glow into life at the base of a bush near the house—two small round dots of red fire. The cats prowled.

He went down the path, feeling with feet and extended hands. The clouds had grown heavier; there was no moon, and even the faint starlight became increasingly obscured. He found the house by running into it, literally. By daylight it was probably attractive; there was a low porch, flanked by pillars and draped with vines. He had banged his head on one of the pillars. The roof hung low, almost brushing his head. He made his way to the door and fumbled for a bell or a knocker.

This was the moment of low ebb. The expedition seemed utterly futile, his mood of the last few hours a wild delusion. The door did not seem to have a bell, and even if he found some means of making his presence known, he did not expect an answer. Then lightning split the sky—nearer now, a thin sword of light instead of a far-off glow. For a split second he saw the details of the door starkly outlined—brass knocker shaped like a frog's head, small leaded window, even the splinters in the wooden panels where impatient cats had demanded entry. Then the light vanished, leaving his eyes blinded. But his muscles remembered, and his hand found the knocker.

The damn thing made a sound like a bass drum. Echoes rolled into the windy night; he heard them mutter and die inside, beyond the door. Then the panels moved.

The inside of the house was darker than the night. He saw only the pale oval of her face, suspended in blackness. He never doubted her identity, even though she seemed smaller than he remembered, as small as a child, as small as a bent old woman.

"I knew it was you," she said, in a breathy whisper.

Michael nodded, then realized that she could see no more of him than he could see of her.

"I figured you'd be here."

"Why didn't you come before?"

"It wasn't until last night that I got your—" Michael stopped; it was hard enough to mention his fantastic experience, but the phrase he had been about to use reduced it to inanity, as if the thing he had received had been a telegram or phone call.

Then he realized she was not listening. She was looking past him, out into the dark garden.

He was slower to perceive. He realized first that the wind had died; leaf and bough hung motionless, as if in apprehension of what was coming. He thought, *This is going to be one hell of a storm*. And he knew the thought for what it was—the desperate defense of the commonplace against a phenomenon it was afraid to admit. For the stillness was abnormal. Linda's hand gripped his arm, her fingers digging in like claws. At the same instant the silence burst. He recognized the sounds, but they sounded different, here, than they had coming from the back alleys of the city. Cats. The howls and snarls seemed to come from more than a dozen feline throats. The shrubbery was animate with glowing eyes and flying bodies.

The fury of the cats might have warned him, if he had had time to think. The next flash of lightning came too quickly; it caught him unprepared. The storm was moving in. All the horizon was dark with boiling masses of cloud, and the thunderclap came close on the heels of the light, booming like a cannon's roar. In the ghastly gray-blue light he saw it. Standing stiff-legged and huge, it might have been only a monstrous image, cut out of basalt or obsidian. But the pricked, listening ears were alive, and so were the eyes, glowing with an inner fire. When the darkness returned, he felt as if every light in the world had failed, and the darkness was worse than the vision itself, because he knew it was still out there, waiting—the black dog.

# *Chapter*
## 8

LINDA KNEW IT WOULD BE THERE. SINCE THE THING FIRST AP-
peared to her, she had developed a special sensitivity; she
didn't have to see it now, to know it was coming. It was a tension in her very bones, like fear, a stench like the foulness of
decay. But familiarity did not breed contempt, or acceptance.
Every time she saw it, the feeling was worse. She would have
stood there, frozen, if Michael had not pushed her into the
house and slammed the door.

Two inches of wood were a frail barrier against the thing in
the garden. But it seemed to cut off some of the aura of terror
that enveloped it. Only then did she realize the enormous importance of what had happened.

"You saw it," she gasped. "Oh, God, oh, God—*you* saw it!"

"I saw it." His voice was queer; she thought that the emotion that made it shake was fear, until he went on, "God forgive
me. I thought you were imagining it."

He caught her to him, holding her so tightly that breathing
was an effort. For a long moment she stood quiescent in his
arms, recognizing the impulse for what it was, a desire untouched by ordinary physical passion. She felt it too—the reassurance of contact with another living human body.

"You're not afraid," she murmured.

"Like hell I'm not," Michael said promptly. "Linda—what
is it?"

"You saw it."

"Yes, and I know too well that eyesight is a damned unreliable witness. We can't stand here all night. Are you sure it can't get into the house?"

"I'm not sure what it can do."

"That's comforting. Aren't there any lights in this hole? I'd be happier if I could see what was coming at me. I think."

"Of course there are lights. I was afraid to use them, before."

"We'll risk it now."

As she switched the lights on, Michael turned from the door. He had been peering out through the small window, and he answered her question before she could voice it aloud.

"Nothing there now. I could see clearly during that last big flash."

"It's gone," she said. "Not—vanished. Withdrawn."

"You can feel it? Sense it? Damn the language, it's inadequate."

"I can tell when it's coming, sometimes. But not long in advance."

Michael laughed, a short, explosive sound that held no amusement. The antique wall sconce, which was the sole source of light in the hall, held pink bulbs shaped like candle flames—one of Andrea's cuter affectations. The rosy light gave Michael's cheeks a healthy flush, but she knew, by the shape of the lines around his mouth, that he was badly shaken.

"We're talking about it as if it were susceptible to natural laws," he muttered. "Damn it, I'm still not ready to admit that it isn't. It was the shock of seeing it like that, when I hadn't . . . And you've been living with that for—how long?"

"I don't know. . . . Months."

"And you've held on to your sanity."

"By the width of a fingernail," she said. "By the breadth of a hair."

Separated from her by the width of the hall, Michael did not move; but the steady dark eyes held hers with a look that was as palpable as a touch, and as expressive as a page of print. Linda knew the look; no woman with a single normal instinct could have failed to read it. Her eyes fell before his, and after a moment he spoke in a casual tone.

"As a companion in a haunted house you're not very cheering. You look like a little ghost yourself. How long has it been since you've had any sleep, or a decent meal? And speaking of food, I'm starved. Is there anything in the house except toad-stools and henbane?"

"Yes, of course. Come out to the kitchen."

While she made coffee and scraped together a scanty meal, Michael wandered around the kitchen making casual remarks. This was an interlude of comparative sanity in the midst of madness; both of them recognized its artificiality, just as they recognized the need for a breathing space. But she knew that he looked out the window each time he passed it, and she did not miss the fleeting glance he gave the door. It was bolted and chained; Andrea had left it that way, and she had checked those bolts daily, knowing their inadequacy but knowing, as well, that no precaution could be neglected. Only once did he refer to the thing that loomed large in both their minds.

"The cats," he exclaimed, as a tabby-striped tom appeared, demanding sustenance. "How do they get in and out?"

"One of those pet doors, in the cellar. No," she said, as he made an involuntary movement of alarm. "It's too small for anything but a cat. You know how they can compress them-selves—like rubber—"

"Yes, I know," he said.

The meal was a poor one—she had already depleted Andrea's stock of food—but Linda ate ravenously. She hadn't had much appetite the last few days. Michael watched her with satisfaction, eating little himself. She didn't blame him; canned lima beans and tuna fish were unappealing unless you were half starved. When she pushed her empty plate away and looked up, she found him braced and ready.

"Talk to me," he said. "I don't know how much time we have."

"About—it?" She made a helpless gesture with her hands. "How can I? How do you talk about something that is either supernatural or else a—"

"Delusion? You still believe that?"

"At first, when you saw it too, I thought . . . But Michael, you've heard of collective hallucinations."

"The fact that you can still admit that possibility is a good indication of your sanity," Michael said. "I'm willing to admit it myself, but only as one theory among others. Linda, are you sure that damned thing isn't real? That it isn't an actual, living dog?"

"There is no such animal in the neighborhood. Believe me, I made sure."

"A wild dog? Even a wolf? It sounds unlikely, I know, but—"

"Even a wolf can't live without food. Sooner or later it would rob a poultry yard, or attack a pet animal. It might not be seen, but its presence would certainly be known."

"And no one else has seen it?"

"No . . ." She found it hard to meet his eyes after that admission, but he seemed undismayed.

"Not Andrea?"

"She knows about it," Linda admitted. "She believes in it. But she's never seen it."

"Odd," Michael muttered. "That she hasn't seen it. She believes it's supernatural, of course."

"Of course. But don't make the obvious mistake about Andrea. For all her superstitions, she has a hard core of common sense. She can believe in various fantastic phenomena, but she doesn't imagine things. There's a difference."

"I know what you mean. I could believe in flying saucers without too much effort; there has been a certain amount of evidence. But I can't believe that I saw one land, and a bunch of little green guys get out of it, unless I have a screw loose somewhere."

"None of Andrea's screws are loose. She has some screws in unusual places, though."

Michael laughed.

"Then you and I are the only ones who have seen the dog," he said. "When did you see it first?"

"It's hard to remember exactly. . . . About a year ago, I guess. I remember the occasion very clearly, though."

"I can see why you might."

"I went for a walk, at twilight. I like that time of day—at least I used to. I wasn't in a very happy mood. There had been . . . words, with Gordon. I walked out under the trees, just wandering around. The ground was wet and soggy, but everything smelled so fresh and sweet. The sky was a pale greenish blue, there was a new moon. I went down that avenue of cherry trees. It ends, if you remember, at a fence; there's a pretty view from that point, out across the pastures.

"I was leaning on the fence, thinking, when—there it was. I

saw it quite distinctly; the light was fading, but it seemed to stand out, as if something shone behind it. I was frightened, but only because it appeared so suddenly, out of nowhere, and because it was a fierce-looking dog and a stranger. Honestly, Michael, I couldn't be mistaken about that, I really like dogs, I was friends with all the neighbors' pets. . . . Well, I knew better than to run, but I retreated as quickly as I could. It didn't follow me. Not until later did I realize that it hadn't moved, or made a sound, the whole time. It just stood there, looking at me. . . ."

"When did you start to think that it might not be a real dog?"

"Not that time. Not even when a search failed to turn up any sign of such an animal. Gordon was alarmed when I told him," she said expressionlessly. "He insisted on looking for it, right then, even though it was almost dark. He and the yard servants searched again next morning, and he called all the neighbors, and the police, to see if anyone else had reported seeing it. No one had. But the worst was . . . I told you the ground was soft and wet. When they searched the field where I had seen it, they found no prints."

From Michael's expression, she realized that, despite his comments, he had been clinging to the hope that the creature was material. This piece of news hit him hard.

"How could prints show on grass?"

"There were large bare patches," she said inexorably. "Something would have shown, somewhere."

"I see. But that wouldn't be enough, in itself, to convince you that you were having hallucinations."

"No. I didn't start thinking that until Jack Briggs failed to see it, the next time it came."

"If he wasn't looking . . ."

"It ran straight across the terrace while we were looking out the drawing-room window. It went fast, but it was in sight for several seconds. That's a long time, Michael."

"Long enough. Any other non-witnesses?"

"Several. My maid, for one. That was from an upstairs window, of course, and it was pretty dark."

"Not easy to see in that kind of light, especially if she had already been told you were suffering from hallucinations. Most people see only what they expect to see."

"Gordon told her something," Linda said doubtfully. "I

think he must have warned all the servants about me. They started treating me peculiarly about that time. But God knows I was acting pretty peculiarly anyhow."

"I imagine he pays excellent salaries, doesn't he? Yes; money, and his famous charm, could convince them of anything he wanted them to believe."

The room was full of cats by this time—fat cats, thin cats, striped, spotted, and Siamese. One of them jumped onto the table, with that uncanny suggestion of teleportation that surrounds a cat's suave quickness, and Linda stood up, overturning her chair.

"What are you trying to prove?" she demanded wildly. "You still don't believe in it, do you? You think it's real."

Michael stroked the cat, a round orange creature, which was investigating his half-empty plate.

"That shouldn't be the main point, for you," he said mildly.

"I'm grateful, don't think I'm not. Whether it's real or just a plain apparition, it isn't a figment of my imagination, or you wouldn't have seen it too. You aren't the suggestible type. You've come a long way to bolster me up, to support me. But you'd stop—you couldn't go on—if you knew what I really believe. . . ."

The lights flickered and faded, leaving the room in brown obscurity; and a violent clap of thunder seemed to rock the foundations of the house. Linda covered her face with her hands. On the roof, a thousand minuscule feet began dancing. The rain had started.

Michael stood up. He had scooped up the cat, to keep it out of his food; and the animal, already full, hung complacently from his hands with a full-moon smirk on its fat face. The contrast between its furry blandness and Michael's drawn features turned Linda's cry of alarm into a semihysterical gasp of laughter.

"Stop it," Michael said sharply. "You're losing your grip— no wonder, in this place. . . ."

He turned, looking helplessly around the room, which still swam in an evil dimness. The stuffed monster dangling from the ceiling seemed to grin more broadly, and the heavy beams seemed to sag. Outside the window, the night was livid with the fury of the storm. But Linda noticed how gentle his hands were, holding the unwanted bundle of cat. Finally he put it back on the table, with the air of a man who is abandoning lesser niceties, and sat down firmly on his chair. The cat started licking his plate. Michael regarded it curiously.

"The cats are calm enough now," he said. "They blew their stacks when it was outside."

Linda dropped back into her chair.

"Cats are traditionally sensitive to influences from the other side," she said dully.

Michael's head turned sharply; on the verge of speaking, he caught himself, and she knew that his comment, when he did speak, was not the one he had meant to make.

"It only appears at dusk, or in a dim light?"

"Yes. Michael, I know what you're trying to do. But it won't work. The fact that the thing only comes at night is just as much confirmation of my theory as of yours."

"You think it's supernatural, then," he said calmly. "Something from—the dark on the other side."

"Don't! Why did you say that?"

"Never mind, I'll get to that later. All right, so it's supernatural. The supernatural has many forms. What precisely is this thing? A hound of hell, *à la* Conan Doyle? A manifestation of hate and ill will? The old Nick in one of his standard transformations? A werewolf, or a . . ."

His voice trailed off and his eyes widened. Linda nodded. She felt quite numb now that the moment of truth was upon her, but she felt no impulse to conceal that truth. Even if he stood up and walked out of the house, leaving her more alone than she had ever been, she had to be honest with him.

"The word is too simple," she said. "But—yes. That's what it is. It's Gordon."

## II

The lights had returned to normal. The storm muttered more softly, held in abeyance. Linda sat with her hands folded in her lap, watching Michael as he paced up and down. He was followed by an entourage of interested cats; but the sight of Michael as a feline Pied Piper did not seem amusing. His distress was too great.

"I can't buy it," he said, swinging around to face her. "I've believed in enough mad things in the last few hours so that you'd think a little detail like that wouldn't stick in my craw. But it does."

"I didn't expect you to believe it," she said.

His face twisted, as if a sudden pain had struck him. She watched the spasm with dull disinterest, wondering why he felt such distress. The lethargy that gripped her was pleasant, compared to what she had endured; she knew how a patient must feel after a critical session with his analyst, or a penitent after a bad session in the confessional—drained, empty, oddly at peace.

"How about settling for an abstract manifestation of evil?" Michael suggested hopefully, and won a wan smile in response. "I'm serious," he insisted. "Half serious, anyhow . . . Linda, you've been through a terrible strain, it would be a miracle if your nerves were normal. I'm not suggesting that you're insane, I wouldn't be talking to you like this if I thought so. But isn't it possible that you've concocted this—this fantastic theory out of a very real, legitimate fear of Gordon?"

She looked up, a faint spark of interest in her face.

"You're willing to admit that I might have a legitimate fear of a paragon like Gordon?"

"He's no paragon," Michael said slowly. "Not of virtue, anyhow. I don't know what he is. But I'm ready to concede that there's something seriously amiss with him. I'm all the more willing to admit it because it cost me such a struggle to admit it. Linda, do you remember a boy named Joe Schwartz? He was a student of Gordon's when you were in that class."

"Joe? Of course I remember him. He wrote some of the funniest, most scurrilous verses I've ever heard."

"Scurrilous?"

"About the professors, and the other students, and human foibles in general. Some topical, some more basic. He had a gift for hitting people's weaknesses, but he was never cruel; he could sting, delicately, without really hurting. None of the parties that year were a success unless Joe performed. He'd sit there on the floor whanging out chords on his guitar and bellowing out his infamous comments in a raucous voice, grinning from ear to ear. . . . Why are you looking like that?"

"It doesn't sound like the Joe Schwartz I know," Michael said grimly.

"He did get a little peculiar toward the end of the year. People said he'd changed. I'm afraid I wasn't much aware of others just then. Love's young dream, you know."

Michael looked uncomfortable, but he went on doggedly.

"What about Tommy Scarinski?"

"You've been busy, haven't you? Yes, he was one of Gordon's acolytes. Always unstable, of course . . . At the time, I thought he was preying on Gordon, instead of . . ."

"The reverse?"

"You don't understand a process, sometimes, until it happens to you personally."

"We're getting there," Michael said. He spoke slowly, without looking at her. "We try to talk around it, but we'll have to discuss it sooner or later. Why, Linda? Why is he doing this?"

"I don't think I could explain it to you—or to any other man."

She hadn't meant it to hurt, but it did; she could tell from the change in his face. She went on quickly,

"You see? I can't even talk about it without sounding like one of the militant feminists you men despise—like an embittered woman whose marriage has gone sour and who rants about the whole male sex instead of facing facts. But it wasn't like that. I'm not a romantic adolescent, I know that few relationships, marital or otherwise, are based on true equality and respect. As a rule, one partner dominates the other; and in human society there's a long tradition of masculine superiority. So—all right. I could have accepted that, I'm conditioned to it. Maybe I even wanted it. But Gordon doesn't want to dominate people; he wants to absorb them, body and soul and spirit. Living with him was—indescribable. I felt as if he were fastened to me, like a gigantic leech, pulling out every ounce of will, every thought. . . . I can see myself making that speech in a divorce court, can't you? It might come straight out of some ghastly day-time serial."

"Why didn't you leave him?"

"I did leave him. He brought me back." She laughed bitterly. "That sounds ridiculous, doesn't it? In this day and age . . . But it was so easy, really. I had to get a job, I didn't have much money. I never did. Credit cards, charge accounts, but no cash. I couldn't very well go to one of the big hotels and charge my escapade to Gordon's account. Even if I'd had the gall, I knew it would make it easier for him to find me. So I had to get a job—and quickly; I couldn't pick and choose. I have a B.A. degree, no special training; you'd be surprised how few jobs there are for women with no special skills and no experience. Even my typing was rusty, after all those years. I turned down a couple of offers because there were special conditions of employment involved, and I was in no mood for another man who wanted to own even that small part of me. I don't know . . . I've never known . . . how many jobs I lost because of Gordon's quiet influence—he must have located me immediately—and how many because of the ordinary handicaps of my situation. There were a few things I didn't try: washing dishes, ushering at movie theaters. . . . It wasn't false pride; I was afraid of places like that."

The look in Michael's eyes hurt her, and yet she found a perverse pleasure in seeing how deeply she could move him.

"I finally got a job as live-in maid and baby-sitter for a family in the suburbs," she went on. "I held it for three days before the woman told me she didn't need me. I'm pretty sure that was Gordon's pressure; household help is darned hard to get these days. Maybe he told the woman I was mentally disturbed.

"I was pretty desperate by then. When Gordon popped into my slummy little hotel room, with his tame psychiatrist in tow, I was in no condition to put up a fight. It probably wouldn't have mattered, even if I could have kept my cool; the doctor was under Gordon's famous spell. But of course I didn't stay calm, I started yelling and screaming, and got an injection for my pains. When I woke up, I was back—home. And all the servants walked around shaking their heads and sighing. I thought at first that I'd try again, plan more carefully—scrape together enough money to get away, a long way away. But it is not easy to fool Gordon. And—I just didn't have the strength. It took all the energy I had to keep myself from giving in, from admitting that I was losing my mind."

Michael stooped and picked up a tiger kitten, which had gone to sleep on his foot. The motion of bending brought a little color back to his face.

"I still don't understand why," he said.

"Why Gordon wants to have me declared insane? I wouldn't be sent to a sanatorium, you know; he'd keep me at home, in a nice quiet padded cell, with nice quiet attendants watching me every second. Gordon doesn't give things away, or let go of the things he owns. He discards them; they don't leave him. Does that degree of vanity seem monstrous to you? It does to me, too; but that's Gordon, he's always been that way, he cannot endure rejection. Especially from me. I gave him love, devotion, admiration—but they weren't enough. When he demanded more, I started to fight back. But that's the insidious thing about a plan like his. How do you prove you're sane? It's a vicious circle; the more desperate and frightened you become, the more erratically you behave; before long you begin to wonder yourself, and then the progression downhill is rapid. I started drinking. But not until after I tried—"

"I know about that," Michael said quickly.

"You do? Oh, of course, he'd tell you that. And you—you came here?"

Michael shook his head, dismissing irrelevancies.

"I don't know what made you do it," he said. "But the end result is clear."

"Oh, yes, it was the final bar on the prison door. If I tried to escape again, he had the ultimate weapon. I was dangerous—homicidal—and he had witnesses to prove it."

"Good Lord," Michael muttered. His fingers continued their automatic caress of the kitten, which was curled in the crook of his arm, purring loudly. Linda watched the animal, using it, illogically perhaps, as a kind of live barometer. So long as the cats were quiet . . .

"But I did it," Linda went on. "I don't remember anything that preceded it, but I remember lying there on the floor, with the knife beside me, where it had fallen from my hand. There was blood on the knife. . . . He'd knocked me down; you can't blame him for that. He wasn't even particularly rough about it. The lights were blazing and the room seemed to be filled with people, and Gordon stood there with blood running down the sleeve of his shirt. . . ."

"Shirt? Wasn't he in pajamas?"

"I don't think so. . . . No. Does it matter?"

"Not really. But it stimulates my nasty suspicious mind. You don't remember actually striking the blow?"

Suddenly it was difficult for her to speak, or to look at him.

"You do go all the way, when you take up a cause," she whispered. "Michael, it's no use. I wouldn't remember that, it's the one thing my mind would utterly reject, would blot out. But

I . . . had thought about it. Sometimes it seemed to me that I could hear the words, they were so loud in my mind: *Kill him. It's the only way you can ever get away.* You can twist and evade all you like, but you can't free me of that act—or excuse it. There's no excuse for killing, unless it's the only means of self-defense left to you. And he was not threatening my life."

"What about your soul?"

"Don't," she said breathlessly. "Don't talk about that. It's the excuse I've used . . . but I'm not sure I believe in the soul."

"Maybe that's not the right name. But it exists—some entity other than the body. It brought me here—your call."

"My call?"

"That's not a good word either, but I can't describe it because I've never felt anything I can compare it with. It hit me last night—a sudden, peremptory mental calling. You wanted me, you needed me, and I had to find you."

"But I didn't call you," she said slowly. "Not that way or any other way."

Michael stared.

"You must have. I couldn't have been so sure without . . . Last night, near midnight—didn't you ask for help? Not necessarily of me—a prayer, a mental plea . . ."

"No. Nothing."

"Then who . . ."

In his surprise, Michael almost dropped the kitten. It eluded his fumbling hands, jumped down, and streaked for the door. In the silence they both heard the sounds. There was someone, or something, at the front door.

They moved closer together, like children afraid of the dark; their hands groped and clasped. Linda's first impulse, to hide, was canceled by Michael's behavior. He stood rock-still, facing the darkened doorway; and Linda accepted his decision. Whatever it was, running away wouldn't help.

But when the opening door was followed by the sound of footsteps coming slowly down the hall, she went limp with relief. She recognized those footsteps.

Andrea stood in the doorway like a figure straight out of Grimm. The black, hooded cloak she wore, even while grocery shopping in the village, blended with the darkness of the hallway behind her, so that her wrinkled face stood out with uncanny distinctness. Over her arm was the basket she carried in lieu of a purse. She paid no attention to the cats, who were weaving patterns around her feet, but surveyed her unexpected visitors without surprise.

"I thought you'd be here," she said.

Linda would have accepted that statement as an example of the old woman's boasted ESP, but when Andrea raised a hand to push back her hood, she realized that there might be another explanation. Andrea was trembling. Terror and a strange exultation blended in her face.

"It's out there," she said. "Waiting for you. I saw it. Heavenly saints—I saw it!"

"It can't be," Linda gasped. "The cats didn't notice."

"There is a circle of protection woven about this house," Andrea chanted. The effect was only slightly marred by her stagger as she crossed the room to put down her basket and lay her cloak aside.

"Where was it?" Michael asked.

"Under the white lilac bush at the side of the house." Fumbling in a cupboard, Andrea accepted his presence without question. She straightened up with a bottle in her hand, jerked out the cork, and put the bottle to her lips. She drank deeply, her prominent Adam's apple bobbing up and down. When she lowered the bottle she shuddered, and wiped her mouth with the back of her hand.

"I needed that," she said. "Have some?"

"No, thanks," Michael said.

"Suit yourself."

Andrea put the bottle down on the table. Michael's eyes moved from it to Andrea, to Linda, and then off into space; and Linda knew that he had deduced the source of her private liquor supply. He must have wondered about that. . . .

Andrea got a glass from the cupboard and poured herself a stiff drink. Michael moved, as if in protest; and Andrea gave him a hostile glance.

"Need this," she muttered. "Had a bad shock."

"Why a shock?" Michael asked coldly. "You're the one who believes in demons."

Andrea collapsed onto the nearest chair. A cat left it, in the nick of time.

"Poor Tommy," Andrea crooned, reaching out an unsteady hand. "Did Mama hurt the baby?"

Michael's mouth curled expressively, and Linda turned on him.

"Leave her alone! She's not young, and her heart isn't too good."

"Nothing wrong with my heart," Andrea said decisively. She shoved the bottle away and set her empty glass down with a thud. "I said I needed that, and I did. As for you, Mr. Collins, if you're such a pretty little skeptic, what the hell are you doing here? Stooging for the great Gordon Randolph? The delectable decoy, to lead her out into his waiting—claws?"

Michael took a step toward her and stopped himself with an effort that left him shaking.

"Sit down," Andrea said gruffly. "I take it back. If you are a decoy, you're an unwitting one. I know what you're thinking— this crazy old bat has corrupted the innocent girl with her weird ideas of witchcraft. Baby, I didn't give Linda the idea. She gave it to me. And, God help me, I didn't believe her until tonight. I saw him. I knew him. He's waiting out there, waiting for her. He can't get in. Not yet. But he's summoning his powers. Can't you feel them, growing, feeding on evil? Soon he'll be strong enough. Soon he'll come."

The high, crooning voice was semihypnotic. Crouched in her chair, monotonously stroking the black cat that had sprung to her lap, Andrea cast a spell of conviction. Michael shook himself.

"I thought you said you had a protective spell around the house," he said.

"Ordinary white magic, against ordinary intruders. This isn't ordinary. He's strong. Very strong. But it takes time to build up the power. It's building now. Can't you feel it? I can feel it. Like electricity in the air. When it's strong enough—then he'll come for her."

The cat's fur crackled under her moving hand.

"What does he want?" Michael demanded. "Damn it, there has to be a reason, even if it's a crazy reason. What is he after?"

Linda felt like a spectator, or a piece of meat over which two merchants were haggling. She hated the feeling, but she could not fight it; the force of the other personalities was too strong. They faced one another like duelists. Michael's fists were clenched. Andrea's weapons were more subtle—the crooning voice, the air of conviction.

"He's after her soul," she said softly. "Her immortal soul. His own is already in pawn to the powers of darkness. He wants hers, not to redeem his own, but to suffer with him, in flames, through eternity."

Michael turned away.

"That's insane."

"Why should you stop at that, when you've accepted so much?" Andrea asked, in the same insidious whine. "You came here to save her, didn't you? Oh, you don't need to answer; I know, I know it all. I've seen the thread, the silver thread that binds the two of you. It's knotted and tarnished now, but there's no break in it. It will bind you forever, into death and beyond. It drew you here, to her side, when she needed you."

Andrea stood up. The cat slid down like a pool of viscous ink. There was a power in the old woman, if only the power of her belief. It forced Michael to face her.

"But you can't save her," she said. "Love is a strong force, the purity of the soul is stronger; but nothing can avail against the powers of darkness except the concentrated power of good. And only I can control that power. I can save her. And I will! All my life, all my studies, have led me toward this moment."

Michael spoke to Linda. He had himself under control now; there was even a certain compassion in his face as he glanced at the old woman.

"Will you stay here, with her?" he asked. "Or will you come with me, now? The choice is yours, Linda. It has to be yours."

Linda hesitated. The tone of his appeal reached her, drawing on some core of sanity and strength. The appeal of being allowed—no, forced—to decide her own fate was something only she could fully appreciate, after years of life with Gordon. Michael waited patiently for her to answer, but Andrea did not.

"No, no," she shrieked. Rushing toward Linda, she caught at the girl's shoulders with both hands. They felt like bird's claws, fragile and fleshless.

"You can't go out there," she whimpered. "Don't think it, don't dream it. He doesn't understand. He wants you, he wants you for himself, to save you for himself and keep you. Make him stay. He can help. He can help if he will, he's strong and young. . . . But if he will go, don't go with him. Stay, I'll save you. Andrea will save you, she knows. . . ."

"All right," Linda said. "All right, Andrea."

She turned to Michael.

"I can't go," she said. "It isn't only because of Andrea. I'm afraid, Michael. I'm afraid to go out into the dark—even with you."

She knew that Andrea's hysteria had convinced Michael, but not in the way she had hoped. The very wildness of Andrea's appeal had swayed his mind back toward rational rejection. If there ever was an obvious picture, this is it, Linda thought dully—a crazy old woman and a weak-minded young one. She wondered how much of her decision to stay was due to her pity for Andrea rather than fear—and how much to her instinctive recoil from one of Andrea's statements: "He wants you for himself."

"We'll stay, then," Michael said. "If that's what you want. I guess it can't do any harm."

Her purpose achieved, Andrea turned brisk and businesslike. The volte-face was so sudden that Linda was left wondering, futilely, how much of Andrea was real and how much was calculated theatricalism.

"We must begin," Andrea said, rubbing her hands together. "At once. The time is short. Purification. It must be symbolic, I daren't let you out of my sight. Come along, both of you."

Andrea's workroom, as she called it, was a small separate building, once a shed or outdoor kitchen, now connected to the house by a low-ceilinged passageway. Linda heard Michael's gasp, and sympathized; if the kitchen had been picturesque, this room came straight out of the ages of alchemy.

Its single window was heavily draped. There were no electric lights. Andrea moved about lighting candles—candles in bottles, candles in tall brass candlesticks, candles stuck onto saucers in puddles of grease, candles in glass-covered brackets on the wall. In their eerie, moving light, the room looked even more uncanny than it did by daylight.

A long, rough table was completely covered with a fantastic collection of miscellany, from papers of all sizes, shapes, and colors, to samples of dried vegetation. Small baskets, boxes, and ordinary brown paper bags were strewn about. One pile of papers, whose vivid colors and angular shapes suggested Japanese origami creations, was held down by a human skull. Another, narrower, table had oddly shaped glass bottles and beakers, filled with colored liquids, like those in an old-fashioned pharmacist's window. The contents of the flasks glowed, lambent in the mellow candlelight—sea blue, crimson, gold, and green. Rough wooden shelves along one wall held a collection of crumbling leather books. The walls, of whitewashed, unfinished planks, were hung with drawings and diagrams. Dominating the room, on the wall opposite the door, was a huge medieval crucifix with its tormented Image, flanked by glass-covered candle sconces. The center of the floor was empty and uncarpeted and almost without varnish after centuries of traffic. The air in the room was close and stale, permeated by a cloyingly sweet smell.

As soon as the candles were lighted, Andrea fumbled in the basket she had brought with her. Another scent, pungently different but equally unpleasant, wafted forth to war with the stench of stale incense. Linda recognized it; her guess was confirmed when Andrea scooped up a double handful of small whitish-gray bulbs. She opened her hands and the bulbs separated, like the Dutch chocolate apples which are made up of pre-formed slices; but instead of dropping to the floor, the segments of garlic hung from her hands, suspended on long pieces of twine.

Michael sneezed.

"God bless you," Andrea said, with the force of an incantation.

She draped the threaded cloves of garlic over the window and the threshold of the closed door. Michael watched silently. Linda watched Michael. She saw, with growing despair, that the pendulum of his thinking had swung back, toward the rational world and away from her. Andrea's mumbo jumbo had destroyed his sensitivities; his hostility and distaste for her were so strong that he couldn't feel that dreadful reality behind the ritual. Linda felt it even more strongly here, in this frail wooden box that was exposed to the night on all four sides. No. Not four sides—five. On the roof, the rain drummed with importunate demand; but above the normal pressure of the storm, Linda was conscious of other forces gathering, closing in.

When the garlic was in place, Andrea went to a cupboard and took out a flask, crossing herself as she did so.

"Sit over there," she ordered brusquely, indicating the spot with a jerk of her head. "In the middle of the floor. Take some cushions from that corner. We'll be here for a good long time."

Michael muttered something under his breath, but obeyed. As he and Linda seated themselves, Andrea anointed the doors and windows with liquid from the flask and then, walking backward, dribbled the contents of the flask in a wide circle around the seated pair. She was careful to stay within the circle. When it was closed, a dark, unbroken wetness on the worn boards of the floor, she came to Linda.

"Hold out your hands," she ordered, and poured a few drops of the remaining liquid into Linda's cupped palms. As she directed, Linda touched the water to her forehead. Michael followed the same procedure, reluctance slowing his movements.

Andrea scrambled to her feet. She seemed to have regressed, both mentally and in time; hobbling, mumbling, she might have stepped out of a sixteenth-century village street—the wise woman, the white witch, Old Mother Demdike. She took a piece of chalk from one of the pockets concealed in her ample skirts and crawled around the interior circumference of the circle of holy water, scribbling designs and symbols onto the floorboards, taking care not to touch the dark dribble of wetness. When she had finished, she crouched down on the floor facing the other two, and poured the last few drops of water into her right hand, crossing herself repeatedly. Her scarlet skirts made a puddle of bright color in the candlelight; her back was curved. The drone of her voice was unbroken except for quick, shallow breaths that came faster and faster and reminded Linda unpleasantly of an animal panting.

Gradually, as Linda watched the old woman's intent face and glazing eyes, the drone of her voice and the monotonous drumming of the rain blended into a single soft whine, like the buzz of a giant insect. Linda's cramped legs grew numb. She tried to move her hand and found it would not respond to her will. The man beside her, the other objects in the room, drew back and lost reality. There was nothing else in the universe except the mingled drone of voice and rain, and the steadily mounting pressure of an invisible force.

The room seemed darker—or were her eyes failing? The low sound was inside her head now, reverberating against the bony dome of her skull. She could hardly feel the wooden floor under her bent legs, but every inch of her skin tingled with the force. It was as if the encompassing air had grown heavier, or as if she were newly sensitized to its constant, unfelt pressure. A picture began to form behind her eyes. She saw the room in miniature, like a small cube of light in the midst of towering, indistinct shapes of darkness, which surrounded it like storm clouds. Featureless and black, yet living, they leaned in over the frail walls; but within, another force moved and grew, holding back the dark. She saw it all, in that moment, as a cosmic manifestation—the struggle of light against darkness. Across the world and the ages the battle raged, unseen, with the balance swaying now to one side and now to the other. In their small microcosm of the universe, the scales were balanced; but the struggle was not static. The pans dipped and swayed as the opposing strengths changed to counter each other's weight. She could not see beyond the darkness; but within the light, the power emanated from one hunched figure. She herself was not part of that cosmic struggle; she was only a pawn, a fly trapped by two great winds, an animal caught between two armies massed for battle. . . .

Deep down inside her dazed consciousness, a small spark of outrage flared. True or false, a cosmic vision or a fancy of hysteria, that view of the universe was not to her liking. She would not surrender her will, even to good, without a voice in the decision. Linda made the greatest effort of her life—an effort all the harder because it was without a physical counterpart. It was like pushing, with her mind, against a barred and bolted door. Then something gave way, with an almost audible snap, and the room flashed back into focus.

Michael's hand clasped hers; she felt the pain of his grasp now. He was not looking at her, but at Andrea; his face was as white as paper. As Linda turned dazed eyes on the old woman, Andrea's voice faltered, caught, and stopped. The rain pounded on the roof in a roar of water. Linda saw the candle flames swaying like live things trying to escape from an attacker. The gritty boards of the floor were harsh against her bare legs. Only one residue of her vanished vision remained: the consciousness of pressures mounting, building up to a tension that could not hold. Like an overload on an electrical system . . . Sooner or later something would blow.

Andrea raised clawed hands to her throat. Her mouth gaped open. She made hoarse sounds, her eyes bulged. Then her hands fell, and for a dreadful moment she balanced on hands and knees, head dangling, like a sick animal. Knees and elbows gave way; she rolled over onto her side and lay still.

The storm rose up, howling with wild winds around the eaves, battering at the walls. As Linda sat frozen, staring at the old woman's empty eyes and still face, Michael got to his feet. He staggered as his numbed legs took his weight, and then leaned forward over Andrea's body. When he turned, Linda knew what he was going to say.

"She's dead. We must—good God Almighty!"

The impact of the mighty wind was strong enough to break the window; but it was not wet air that came through the shattered pane in one great leap. Michael's left arm swept out, catching Linda as she stood up, and throwing her back against the wall. Most of the candles died in the gust of rain and wind. The pair that flanked the crucifix wavered and held. Pressed against the same wall, her body aching with the violence of the impact, Linda saw him go down, buried under the solid black mass of the thing that had come through the window. It made no sound, none that she could hear over the agonized wail of the storm, which was whistling through some crevice in the broken glass with a noise like that of a pipe or whistle. And there was another sound—the sound of Michael's gasps, as he fought for his life.

# Chapter

## 9

LINDA'S OUTFLUNG HAND TOUCHED AN OBJECT, AND SHE SEIZED it without looking to see what it was. She felt only its weight and convenience of shape, fit for grasping; she wanted a weapon, and that was how she used it, swinging it high and bringing it down with all her strength. If it struck home, she never felt the impact; at the same moment the air erupted like a volcano, deafening her with sound, blinding her eyes, shaking the floor under her feet. Swaying, her hands over her dazzled eyes, she heard the echoes roll and die. Echoes of thunder . . . The lightning bolt must have struck the roof, or something just outside.

Linda opened her eyes. Through the chaos of wind and rain, the two small lights on the wall burned steadily.

Andrea's body lay huddled on the floor, grotesquely tumbled by the struggle that had gone on over it. Michael was on the floor too, flat on his back, his arm thrown up across his face. The curtains billowed at the broken window; a branch protruded like a bony arm through the gap between the torn curtains. The big oak tree outside the window had been the lightning's target. There was nothing else. Whatever else had been in the room, it was gone.

On the floor beside Michael lay the crucifix, which she had used as a club. It was cracked, straight across the stem.

She went to Michael and bent over him. His eyes were closed. His sleeve, and the arm under it, were shredded. Blood dripped down and formed in a dreadful pool beside his head.

But the gesture had saved his life. The dog had gone for his throat.

He opened his eyes when she touched him.

"It's gone," she said quickly, feeling him stiffen under her hands as memory returned.

"Gone? How?"

"I don't know. I hit it—with that." She touched the crucifix. "But the last lightning flash was so violent that it stunned me for a few seconds. It hit the tree outside the window, and—" She broke off, her eyes widening with a new fear. "Michael, there's fire out there. I can see the light. The rain is stopping, too."

The light was only a flickering redness, but as she spoke the curtains at the window caught in a flare of flame.

"That does it," Michael muttered, struggling to stand. "The outside of the house is soaked, but inside it's as dry as sawdust. It will go up in a second. We've got to get out of here."

"Get out!" She caught at his injured arm, heard him groan, and transferred her weight to support him as he swayed. "We can't just walk out and leave the house to burn!"

"How can we stop it? The wood is dry with rot, and there are all these papers and books. Someone will see the flames and call the fire department. We must be away from here before anyone comes."

"I can't leave."

"You aren't afraid of—what's out there, are you? It, or its master, will be too canny to stick around. The place will be swarming with people in five minutes. There couldn't be a safer time for us."

"It's not that. I can't leave . . . her."

She was surprised to feel wetness on her face. Michael's own face, bloodless with pain and shock, softened. They looked at the huddled body, roused to a terrible imitation of movement by the flickering light of the fire, which had seized avidly on the wooden walls.

"She's dead," Michael said. "There's no doubt of that, Linda—I know. What else can you do for her? It's purifying— fire." He added, with a glance around the strange little room, "I know, she thought she was doing good. All the same, it seems fitting, somehow, that this should burn. . . . Linda, please."

His weight was heavy against her; the fact that he made no mention of his own need was the strongest appeal of all. With one last look at the still body, she turned, bracing him; as they passed through the door, the flames leaped from walls to floor. Half the room was ablaze. As they went down the passageway, Linda wondered why Andrea's body had looked so small. Shrunken, almost, as if part of its substance had been sucked out.

One good look at Michael's arm made Linda forget her other concerns, but he wouldn't let her do much, except apply a bandage to stop the bleeding, and arrange a rough sling. A swig of brandy from the bottle on the table brought some of the color back to his face. It also brought him to his feet.

"Take the bottle," he said, thrusting it at her. "Hurry. God, I can hear the fire now, it's not raining hard enough to stop it. Let's go, Linda."

She lingered, looking affectionately at the old kitchen.

"I hate to see it go without making a fight to save it. The house is two hundred years old."

"Yes, you're a fighter, aren't you. But pick your causes, for God's sake. Do you want to be found here, with the house ablaze, a dead body, and signs of what the newspapers will be delighted to refer to as unholy practices? The least that can happen is that I'll go to jail and Gordon will lock you up for the rest of your life. I can just see what his tame psychiatrists could do with this mess."

It was brutal but effective. She turned, without another word, and started toward the door.

"Wait a minute," Michael said. "The cats. We can't leave them inside."

"They can get out, through the cellar."

"Just in case . . ."

Michael drew the bolts on the back door and threw it open. The rain was falling gently now, as if spent by its effort.

"Come on," he said, and led the way to the front of the house.

## II

They made it, but with only seconds to spare. As the car skidded onto the paved road and turned, they heard sirens and saw the flashing red lights of fire engines coming the other way.

Linda was driving. Michael had tried to, but the effort of

turning the car in the narrow lane, which was now a bog of mud, was too much for him; he blacked out, over the wheel, with the first movement.

"Stupid," he said hazily, as she took his place. "Too dangerous, on the highway . . . I hope you can drive. I forgot to ask."

"I hope so too. It's funny, though," she added, nursing the wheel and the brake as the car curtsied coyly into a rut, "how it comes back to you. I drove one of my boyfriends' jalopies through an entire Cleveland winter. Ice and snow and mud and . . . woops."

He didn't answer, either to commend her skill or to make suggestions; she knew he was fighting to stay conscious, and she did her best to avoid jolting him. When she swung onto the highway, she was conscious of an absurdly warming glow of pride. It was a long time since she had done anything for herself. Some of the dependence was inevitable when you were married to a man as wealthy as Gordon; you didn't mend your own socks or scrub scorched pans. Even so—hadn't Gordon overdone the servant bit? He didn't do anything himself, except for the exercise necessary to preserve his splendid physical condition. He didn't even drive a car; he hired the best chauffeurs that were to be had. He didn't build a fire in the fireplace, or plant a bulb, or groom a horse. The moral value of work was a myth, of course; or was it? Surely there was a healthy feeling of satisfaction in doing some small, needed job and doing it well: cleaning a dirty kitchen, mending a piece of broken furniture—getting a car out of a muddy back lane.

She thought Michael had lost consciousness, he was so still; but once they were on the paved road, he spoke.

"You've got a good, efficient fire department. There they come now. Maybe they can save the house after all."

"I hope so. Don't think I'm sentimental—"

"What's wrong with being sentimental?"

"Well, this is no time for it," she admitted. "I don't know what you want to do now; I didn't think about anything except getting away from there. But you've got to see a doctor, Michael, right away."

"Sounds good," Michael said.

"Doctor Gold lives down the next street," she said, her eyes on the road.

"Isn't he your little pal? The one I met?"

"Yes."

"I think we'll pass him up."

"But, Michael, he's the closest."

"Too close. He'd be on the phone to Gordon before he did anything else."

"I could stay in the car."

"Alone? No."

"I can't stand knowing how much it hurts you," she said unsteadily. The car swerved.

"Keep your eyes on the road. . . . Don't waste your sympathy. I am just about to pass out. . . . Thank God."

"There must be a doctor in the next town," Linda said, putting her foot down.

"No, wait. . . ." Michael roused himself; his voice sounded miles away. "Whatever you do, don't panic. Keep at the speed limit, we can't risk . . . a wreck, or a cop. One thing to do . . . obvious . . ."

"Michael . . . Michael!"

"Don't wreck the car," he said; weak as it was, his voice was amused, and Linda was conscious of a strange constriction somewhere in the region of her diaphragm. "Don't stop . . . Put a couple of dozen miles between us and the house. . . ."

She heard his sigh of exhaled breath as his head fell back against the seat.

The drive was almost too much of a challenge; it was one of the worst jobs she had ever undertaken. Terror is strong and breath-stopping, but it is usually brief; it passes quickly. Fear, the kind that had haunted her for months, has its own built-in anesthesia. And when despair is deepest there is no need to struggle, only to endure. What made the drive so bad was the need to keep constantly on the alert, to anticipate, not only the normal hazards of the road, but any unexpected, almost unimagined supranormal danger. She realized that the worst kind of fear is fear for someone else. She damned herself for involving Michael in her danger, and speculated wildly as to how she could extricate him—if it wasn't already too late.

Through it all she drove steadily, surely, never taking her eyes from the road. The torrential rains had flooded out many sections, and she drove through shallow sheets of water at a crawl, her throat tight with fear of flooding the engine. But the worst moment was the roadblock.

A tree was down on the road ahead; but she didn't know that, not at first, she saw only the barriers and the flashing lights of the police car.

Her foot hit the brake and her hand fumbled for the gear lever. There was a side road, a block or two back. . . . She realized the stupidity of that move, just in time, and brought the car to a sedate stop. She had barely time to reach over and pull Michael's jacket across his slung arm as the police officer came up to the side of the car.

She rolled down the window.

"What's the trouble?" she demanded, with the ordinary annoyance of an innocent motorist who is delayed.

"Tree across the road. The crew is working on it, but you'll be better off going around; it'll take some time." The man's eyes moved past her, to the silent figure sprawled across the other seat. "Something wrong, miss? Need any help?"

He was very young, the policeman; his voice was kind. Momentarily Linda fought the urge to break down and tell him the truth. A doctor, a nice safe hospital for Michael . . . Then she saw the boy's nostrils quiver, and she realized that the brandy bottle must be leaking. Either that, or Michael had taken more than she thought.

"That must have been quite a party," the policeman said. "Your husband, ma'am?"

"What makes you so sure we're married?" Linda asked, with an attempt at a smile.

He was young, but he wasn't stupid. Pushing his cap back, he smiled back at her.

"I didn't see your ring at first," he explained, indicating her left hand, which was taut on the wheel. "But, you know, it's a funny thing; we see a lot of drunks, you can imagine. Sometimes a girl's date passes out, but usually it's a married guy."

"That must give you rather a jaundiced view of marriage."

"No, not really. Oh—oh, I get it. You mean the husbands are driven to drink?" The young man laughed. He had pink cheeks and even, white teeth, and he was obviously bored with his dull post. "Well, maybe. But what I always figured was, I figured the boyfriends were more anxious to look good. It's not a very nice thing to do, pass out on a date and make her drive you home."

"I'm sure you'd never do a thing like that, whether you were married to the girl or not," Linda said. Every nerve in her body was screaming for haste, but she couldn't show it. If she gave him any cause to ask for her driver's license, they were finished.

"Well, I'll tell you, ma'am, you pull a few bodies out of the wrecks and you get to realize it isn't worth it. Well, I guess you don't need a lecture; you look like you'd never had a drink in your life."

"Thank you," Linda said sweetly. She batted her lashes at him. "I certainly haven't had one tonight."

"No, I could tell that. If you had—well, I'd have wanted to stop you from driving. It's even more dangerous on a bad night like this. You sure you don't need any help with your husband?"

"Thank you, but I can manage." Michael stirred and muttered; and Linda said quickly, "I'd better get him home to bed. You say there's a detour?"

"Yes, ma'am. Two blocks back, you turn right, then left at the next corner, and you're on Main Street. . . ."

She didn't need the directions, but she nodded her thanks and pretended to listen intently. She turned the car carefully under his benevolent but critical eyes, and started back; wondering, as she did so, why she had the urge to hide their tracks. She was acting as if they might be objects of an ordinary search, instead of a quest by something not limited by human senses. Was that her intelligence, struggling against superstition, or simply overcaution? She gave it up, with a shrug that was a little desperate. Rational or not, the purpose was achieved; that nice boy would not think of her and her drunken bum of a husband if anyone came looking for a crazy girl fleeing with her lover.

Her lover. She drove on, automatically, through the night. Once, at her worst, she had prayed that she would never love anyone again. Love had betrayed her too often. With her father, who had died and left her, and her mother, who had never given a damn about her because she was a girl, and had "all these funny ideas." And, after she had gone to him for the security her childhood had lacked, with Gordon. He had not only failed, he had used love as a weapon against her, a blindfold to hide his true nature, a spy that betrayed her own weaknesses. Love? It was a chameleon word with a thousand meanings. There were as many kinds of love as there were human beings—a hundred times more, because every human being had that many different feelings which he called by the same name.

Beside her, Michael moaned and shifted. His head dropped

onto her shoulder. She adjusted her weight and kept on driving, eyes steady on the road.

When she first saw him, she regarded him not as a man but as a ladder by means of which she might climb out of the pit where Gordon held her prisoner. She had meant to ensnare his senses so that his reasoning faculties would be blinded, and he would obey her demands with the uncritical partisanship which that kind of "love" induced in the victim. It was a blindness with which she was only too familiar.

Not that she had meant to tell him the truth. Some tale of conventional "mental cruelty" would have done the trick—or so she thought. She knew now that she would never have caught this man with anything so crude. She might more safely have appealed to his sense of compassion. But that was a double-edged weapon, too easily turned against her—"poor girl, she needs help but doesn't know it; we must hurt her for her own good." Gordon had already used that, and it had almost worked. But that was Michael's strength; no appeal that was purely emotional could convince him completely. He had a critical brain, critical even of himself, and it functioned. Even now, though he "loved" her—whatever he might mean by that word—he was still asking questions. He had come to her defense not because of "love" but because the tireless critical brain had produced facts that cracked his first predilection in favor of Gordon and Gordon's explanations.

With that kind of intelligence she had no quarrel; in fact, it might be the only solid thing in a shifting universe, and the one quality above all others that had made her turn to him. But love, whatever else it was, was not a sterile agreement of similar minds. And, after the last agonizing months, she was no longer sure of her capacity to give anything beyond that.

The inert mass beside her stirred again, and she started.

"Are you awake?"

"I'm not sure. . . . Where are we?"

"About halfway to the city. I haven't been planning; I've just been driving."

"Pull over as soon as you can find a place."

They were approaching a town, and she found the parking lot of an all-night diner. She left the engine idling, pushed down the parking brake, and turned to Michael.

He was upright and aware, but the dull look in his eyes alarmed her.

"You've got to have a doctor. I'll ask, at the diner."

"Wait a minute. I've got to think. . . . What sort of story are we going to tell a doctor?"

"But it's nothing the police need to . . . Oh, I see. He'll know it was an animal, won't he? He'll start fussing about rabies. He'll want us to report it, describe where it happened, so the police can check. If we said the dog belonged to a friend of ours—"

"He may wonder what kind of friends we have, that they didn't call in their family doctor. Lying is complicated, isn't it?"

"Sometimes telling the truth is more complicated. Michael, we'll have to risk it. Maybe he'll be sleepy and bored and won't care."

"Yes, we'll have to risk it."

"Does it hurt terribly?"

"Yes, damn it, it hurts. But that's not what's bothering me. I can't risk being incapacitated. Don't you understand? What happened tonight was the first round. And we lost. You don't think he'll give up now, do you?"

"No. But I wouldn't say we lost. We got away."

"Leaving one dead on the field of battle. She lost. She's dead because she lost. Whatever she was doing, or thought she was doing, it failed."

"That couldn't have been part of his plan. He didn't know she'd be there."

"I don't know what his plan is, that's why I feel so helpless. But I'm beginning to suspect that my involvement isn't coincidental. Why he's got it in for me I don't know, but he asked for me; he did everything he could to throw us together. He has something in mind. And until we figure out what, we're fighting blind. Let's locate that doctor. You go and ask while I try to think of some disarming lie."

The doctor was suspicious and hard to soothe. Groggy and querulous at first, he woke up completely after a look at Michael's injuries, and only the latter's quick imagination kept him from calling the police. Michael managed to suggest a drunken party and considerable provocation; the smell of brandy on his breath went a long way toward convincing the doctor that the affair had been an ordinarily middle-class brawl, with possibilities of scandal, in which he was better not involved. They left as soon as they could get away.

"Well," Linda said, when they were back in the car, "if the police make any inquiries, we won't be hard to trace this far."

Michael shook his head. The pills the doctor had given him were working. He looked much better.

"I don't think we need to worry about the police. Not that we can go to them for help; our story is too wild. And if we'd been found there, with Andrea dead and the house blazing, we'd have had some embarrassing questions to answer. But a common garden-variety scandal can't be Gordon's aim. He won't turn us in, and nobody else knows we were at Andrea's."

"I'll bet the police would love to have some witnesses as to what happened there."

"Not even that. Even if they find the—evidence intact, the logical conclusion will be that Andrea was carried away by her histrionics and had a heart attack. There wasn't a mark on her. In fact—that may have been just what did happen."

"You don't believe—"

"I don't know what to believe."

"The dog. It was real enough."

"Too real. I felt it, all hundred pounds of it. It felt like a dog; it even smelled like a dog."

"But the others—the supernatural animals—"

"Werewolves," Michael said roughly. "Say it. My God, are we going to cringe away from words?"

"Werewolves are real; they take material form."

"I know, I've read all the horror stories. Everything works two ways, doesn't it? Do you realize that nothing that has happened couldn't be explained in rational terms?"

"But Andrea . . . I see. Self-induced?"

"She had a bad heart. And a firm belief. Linda, the phenomenon is known, documented—not only in the jungles of Haiti and Africa but in American hospitals."

Linda's eyes were straight ahead, watching the dark ribbon of road unwind.

"You know what your rationalist interpretation means, don't you? You're sitting next to an attempted murderess."

"Forget that!"

"I can't forget it. I'll try not to think about it, but . . . Where are we going, Michael? We'll be in the city soon. I'd suggest some place brightly lit, with lots of people around you. . . ."

"All right, then." Michael turned, his arm over the back of the seat. "We may as well drag all the dirt out into the open. Those other times, when you ran away to other men—what happened? What did you do?"

Linda didn't answer at first. She had to fight to keep her voice steady.

"I ran away once. I told you about that. There was no other man, then or ever."

"Then Gordon lied?"

"He's a very convincing liar. It's his word against mine, of course, and I'd have a hard time proving I was telling the truth. What difference does it make? How many times do I have to try to kill someone before you'll admit—"

"Stop it! Under any circumstances, by any possible interpretation, that kind of thinking is dangerous. Don't . . . open your mind to it."

"I'm afraid!"

"I'm not. Not of you. Remember that. We do have to decide where we're going, though. I know where I'd like to go."

"To your friend—Galen. I've forgotten his last name. The doctor."

"Reading my mind? How much of that conversation with Galen did you overhear?"

"All of it. Except when you went downstairs with him."

"I hate women who are smarter than I am," Michael said, amusement coloring his voice.

"Do you know, I almost ran out and tried to catch him. He sounded . . . wise. Wise and stable."

"He's the wisest man I know, and the sanest. That's why I want to consult him. Not because—"

"You don't have to reassure me. Not any longer."

"Furthermore," Michael muttered, "he knows something. Something about Gordon."

"I wondered, when I heard the way his voice changed when you mentioned Gordon's name. Do you think Gordon was ever a patient of his?"

"No, it was something else." Michael told her about the letters. "I don't know what they mean, though," he ended. "There's some hint there. . . . But it slipped past me."

"I'd like to see them."

"Yes, I think you'd better. But they date to a period some years back, before you met him. When I get my hands on that cautious psychiatrist, I'll interrogate him. The son of a gun must know more than what is in the letters. My dad may have talked to him."

"Then let's go to his place."

"Can't. He's not back yet."

"When will he be back?"

"The weekend, he said. Not before tomorrow."

"Then where do we go? There's the bridge, up ahead."

"My place, I guess."

"He'll know. . . ."

"What can he do there that he couldn't do anywhere else?" Michael asked reasonably. "I thought of a hotel, but I don't like the idea, I'd feel more insecure in an unfamiliar place. It isn't physical attack we're worried about, is it?"

"No, but . . ."

"Any other ideas?"

His voice was calm and patient, but Linda sensed his utter exhaustion. They were both exhausted, not only by long hours of wakefulness, but by mental strain. She couldn't think clearly. Certainly she couldn't think of any rational objection to his idea.

"I guess you're right," she said slowly. "Give me directions, then. I wasn't paying attention the last time I came to your apartment."

The streets were not crowded; it was well after midnight. Linda drove slowly, nursing her growing fatigue. The rain had stopped, but the streets were shiny with water, and clouds bumped the tops of the tallest buildings. They left the car in the garage, for which Michael paid, he informed her, a rent equal to that of his apartment, and walked the short distance in exhausted silence. There were no pedestrians on the street. The city might have been struck by some silent science-fictional weapon, and all life destroyed except their own.

The presence of Napoleon, squatting like a leopard by the door, should have been reassuring, for he was obviously glad to see them. But as she bent to fondle the scarred head that was banging against her ankles, Linda was conscious of an increase in her dark forebodings.

"He must have eaten up all the food," Michael said, watching Napoleon's activities cynically.

"I'll get him something. You sit down."

"There's some of the canned cat tuna on one of the shelves," Michael said as she went into the kitchen.

The sight of the littered sink and empty refrigerator made Linda wrinkle her nose in disgust.

"It's a wonder you don't both have rickets and scurvy," she said, searching the drawers for a can opener. "There isn't a drop of milk. I should think you could at least feed that poor cat milk."

"He hates milk," Michael said. "Whiskey, gin, beer, Coke— he loves Coke, but he'll drink anything. Anything but milk."

Linda found the can opener in the sink, and went to call Napoleon. The cat was sitting on Michael's stomach, glowering.

"He knows I've been in a fight," Michael said. "And he has a pretty good idea as to who lost."

The cat sneezed and walked back down the length of Michael's semirecumbent form, planting his feet heavily. He went into the kitchen, contempt radiating from every hair.

"I've lost face," Michael said.

Linda was unable to be amused. Michael didn't seem to feel anything wrong. What was the matter with her, that she couldn't give way to the fatigue that dragged at every muscle? Unable to relax, she began to walk up and down the room. Her eyes felt hot and her skin had begun to prickle. Not for the first time, she speculated about drugs. Gordon had every opportunity to administer anything he chose. Coffee, wine, even the aspirin in her bathroom . . . What a nice, neat, satisfying solution that would be. It explained so much. . . . But not, unfortunately, quite enough. She turned.

"Where are those letters you mentioned?"

"What?" Michael started; he had fallen into a doze, slumped in the big chair. Linda's heart—or whatever internal organ it is that behaves so peculiarly in moments of emotion— twisted as she watched him blink and brush at his ruffled hair. "They're in that envelope I brought up from the car," he said, yawning. "Why don't we wait till morning? We can think better after we get some sleep."

"I'm too keyed up to sleep yet," she said. "What about a nice soothing cup of tea?"

"Okay."

Linda went into the kitchen. She couldn't tell him of her feelings; he was too tired to cope with anything else tonight. But her panic was real, and it was steadily growing. She had to see the letters now, without delay, as a hunted man, feeling the approach of the hunters, might desperately try to fashion the smallest scrap of wood or metal into a weapon.

The letters were too small a scrap. They told her nothing she didn't already know. But the warm drink and the forced concentration helped her nerves. Lethargy replaced her earlier anxiety. Even the sudden movement of the cat did not startle her; but Michael started and swore as the long, lean body streaked for the kitchen.

"That's funny," he said.

"What?"

"There goes a plate. . . . Oh, nothing. But he usually doesn't move that fast unless he hears someone coming."

He was sitting upright, frowning. Funny, Linda thought. Now he's getting nervy, and I'm falling asleep. She put the last letter down.

"Your father didn't like Gordon," she said.

"No. I wonder why."

"Antipathy, he says."

"That's just a word people use to explain reasoning they aren't consciously aware of. What I don't understand is that letter about the Hellfire Club."

"Oh, that was Gordon," she said vaguely. She yawned.

"What do you mean?"

"He's been dabbling with demonology for years. Good God," she said, roused by anger, "you still think I invented all this, don't you? Where do you think I got my ideas? Why did you think Gordon and Andrea were at swords' points? Why do you think she hated him?"

"I never imagined . . ." Michael looked dazed. "He's such a fastidious person. . . ."

"You're thinking of Satanism in terms of Aleister Crowley, and the Great Beast, and sexual orgies. That's only a perversion added by some psychotics. It was never like that with Gordon. If anything, he's too puritanical, too cold. It's power he wants, power and control. Isn't that the ultimate control—over the minds and the will of others? He tried teaching and he tried politics, but they weren't enough. Through them he could partially dominate certain types, but there were always a few who were immune, and they were the ones he wanted most to dominate."

Another wide yawn interrupted her. It was a pity, she thought sleepily, that she should be so tired. This was an important point, something Michael hadn't realized, something he had to know.

"The clue to Gordon Randolph," Michael muttered. "Is this what I've been groping for? Hey—you're going to fall apart, you're yawning so. We'll talk more in the morning. Bed for you."

Linda let him lead her toward the bedroom, knowing that she ought to be tending to him, but too sleepy to care, too sleepy to pay attention to his explanations and his arrangements. He said something about sleeping on the couch. Linda looked up at him, blinking; her eyelids were so heavy.

"All right," she said obediently.

She might have been able to prevent it if she had seen it coming; but she was too sleepy, and he was too strong. His arms went around her; even the arm that was bandaged from wrist to elbow held her close. His mouth was warm and hard and insistent on hers. For a few sleep-dazed moments she was lax in his embrace, not responding, but not resisting. Then a frenzy of revulsion filled her, and she struggled.

He let her go at once.

"I'm sorry," he said. "I didn't mean to do that. But you looked so . . ."

He was pale; whether with pain or anger, she could not tell. Linda swayed, gasping for breath; and the words that came out of her mouth were not the words she had meant to say.

"Michael. Lock me in!"

His eyes widened, and then narrowed to slits as the meaning of her words struck him.

"No," he said violently.

"Please."

"No." His voice was gentler but inexorable. "I won't, even if I could. Hell, I don't know where the key is, if there is a key. There is no need for me to lock you in. Now go to sleep. Sleep well."

With a whimper she turned away, stumbling, and threw herself down on the bed. The movement took the last of her strength; a great weight seemed to be pressing down on her, on mind as well as body. But her mind fought off the pressure for several seconds after her body had succumbed; she knew what was coming. And knew also that those few seconds of awareness were part of Gordon's plan—the realization of danger coupled with the inability to avoid it is the highest refinement of cruelty. Then, finally, the weight closed in, and her last spark of will flickered out.

# III

Michael watched until her breathing slowedand she lay quiet. His hand went to the light switch, and then withdrew. If she woke, in the dark . . .

Was it only an irrational symbol, this concept of darkness versus light? Darkness concealed; but why need the objects it hid be objects of fear? They might be friendly things, things of beauty. Perhaps they only feared the dark who had seen some frightful thing come at them out of the veils of darkness. From the dark, the dark on the other side . . .

Turning away from the door, Michael wished fervently that he had never met Kwame nor heard that enigmatically threatening phrase. What did it really mean? It meant something to Kwame, something he felt so strongly that he could transfer the impression to other people. Michael remembered the horrifying vision he had had when Kwame first spoke the words. That had to have been some kind of ESP; he couldn't have thought of it by himself.

And it was a hell of a picture to have in the back of his mind, especially after a night like this one. Michael found himself reluctant to turn out the lights in the living room, though the glow from the open bedroom door was brighter than his sleeping room usually was.

He threw himself down on the couch, too tired to look for blanket or pillow. His feet were propped on one arm of the couch. It was too short for comfort, but tonight he didn't care; he could have slept on a stone. He was too tired to think—and that was just as well, because the thoughts foremost in his mind were ugly thoughts. Satanism, possession, werewolves, the dark on the other side . . . His arm was throbbing. The pain killer was wearing off. He thought about getting up and taking another pill. But the bottle was in his coat pocket and his coat was in the closet and the closet was ten feet away, and that was just too damned far for a man who had been up all night, battling werewolves and witches and . . . Heavily, Michael slept.

And woke, with one of the wrenching starts that sometimes rouse a sleeper from a dream of falling. He had only been asleep for a few minutes; his muscles still ached with fatigue. Something had wakened him.

Mind and body drugged by the short, annihilating nap, Michael lay quiescent and listened. There were sounds, out in the kitchen. That was what had roused him. Someone was in the kitchen, moving around.

The most logical source of noise was Napoleon. But his sleeping mind was accustomed to the cat's comings and goings, it would have noted the sounds, classified them, and let him sleep. These were not the noises the cat made when it thudded down into the sink or lapped water or chewed the hard, crunchy bits of cat food. These were small, metallic sounds, like coins chinking in someone's pocket . . . a loose metal strip blown by the wind against another piece of metal . . . knives and forks in a drawer, being shifted. . . .

When he recognized the sounds and identified the key word, his brain refused to accept the conclusion. Maybe Linda had been unable to sleep. Looking for the wherewithal to make coffee or food, she would naturally move quietly, so as not to disturb him.

Then he saw her. The kitchen, out of the direct beam of light from the bedroom door, was very dark. As she moved out into the diffused dimness of the living room, her slim body seemed to be forming out of shadows like a dark ectoplasmic ghost. She stood still for several seconds, as if listening; and Michael remained quiet, not from design, but because his paralyzed body was incapable of movement. There was just enough light to reflect, with a pale glitter, from the long shiny object in her right hand.

# Chapter
## 10

SHE MOVED VERY SLOWLY. WHEN SHE REACHED THE COUCH, she stood motionless for several long moments. He could see the knife distinctly now, it was only inches from his face. It hung from fingers so lax that they seemed about to lose their grip altogether. He could hear her breathing. It was quick and deep, long gasps of effort.

Her fingers tightened and her arm began to move. Up—slowly, in abrupt jerks and starts, as if struggling against a force that tried to hold it. Michael watched in an unholy fascination; the whole bizarre episode might have been happening to someone else, with himself an unwilling and helpless spectator. Now her arm was high above her head. A strained, impractical position for a downward blow . . . The arm started down.

Michael moved. To his outraged nerves it seemed as if the whole thing were taking place in slow motion: that he had an infinite amount of time in which to act before the knife struck. In an almost leisurely movement his right arm lifted and his fingers clamped around the wrist of the hand that held the knife.

His touch affected her like a jolt of electric current; every muscle in her body stiffened, her wrist twisted frantically in his grasp. She screamed, a thin, high sound that was more like the voice of an animal in agony than anything human. It was the scream as much as anything else that made Michael take more than defensive action. A few more moments of that, and someone would call a cop.

He tried not to hurt her. Rolling sideways off the couch, he pulled her down with him, pinning her kicking legs with his body, his right hand still tight around her wrist, his left fumbling for her mouth. They struggled in darkness; the back of the couch cut off the feeble light from the bedroom. He could feel her struggling, feel the writhing of her lips against his palm. He had half expected the maniacal strength he had read about, but he encountered very little difficulty; she was a small woman, and it took only seconds to immobilize and quiet her. Flaccid and cold under his hands, she lay still. He couldn't even feel her breathing.

It never occurred to him that her collapse might have been a ruse. He scrambled up. His need for light was more than a need to see, it was a craving for the power that opposed the dark.

She looked like a sick child in a sleep troubled by pain— tumbled hair, pale face, mouth drawn down in a pathetic grimace. She was wearing his old bathrobe, which had helped to hamper her movements; the struggle had torn it open, but she was still wearing her slip and underclothing. Michael revised his comparison. Not a child, no. But she looked pitifully young. The wrist he had twisted seemed too fragile to resist the lightest touch. By her right hand lay his big carving knife.

Michael kicked it out of the way. He knelt down and put his ear to her breast. Faint and abnormally slow, but it was there— the pounding of her heart. He straightened, studying the pale face with a mixture of different terrors. The closed lids veiled the eyes; he wondered what he would see in those eyes when the lids lifted.

After a moment he stood up and went into the bedroom. When he came back, she hadn't moved. Carefully he wrapped the bathrobe around her; the coldness of her skin and the sluggish pulse suggested shock. Then he set about the rest of the job. His mouth was set in a tight, twisted line as, using the neckties he had brought from the bedroom, he tied her wrists and ankles together.

A pale, ugly dawn was breaking before she came to. Michael had tried everything he could think of to bring her out of her faint—wondering, all the while, whether he really wanted her to wake up. Faces in sleep or unconsciousness were like blank pages; waking intelligence, the expression of eyes and mouth, are what give individuality and character. What would he see when her eyes opened? The face, now familiar and beloved, of the girl he wanted; or the Medea figure who had stood over him with a knife?

He had carried her back into the bedroom and piled every blanket he owned over the waxen body. He had bathed her face and rubbed her wrists. The slow, mechanical breathing did not change; the muscles of face and body remained flaccid. And the night wore on. It seemed to Michael at times as if the sun would never rise, as if some astronomical miscalculation had stopped the earth on its axis. Then the first sullen streaks stained the clouds; and her eyes opened.

Michael saw what he had hoped, but not really expected, to see. His relief was so great that he dropped with a thud onto the edge of the bed. But the realization that dawned in her face, as memory returned, was almost worse than the madness he had feared. Her horror and consternation were genuine; if he had had any lingering doubts of her honesty, they vanished then. Her eyes moved from his face, downward, toward her bound wrists and ankles. They were hidden under the piles of blankets, but he knew she could feel the bonds.

"I'll take them off," he said quickly. "I just wasn't sure . . . It's all right now, I'll get them off. . . ."

He turned the covers back, and she twisted frantically away from his hands.

"No—no! Leave them on, don't let me—"

"It's gone," Michael said, hardly knowing what he was saying. "It's all right."

"How do you know?" Her voice was quieter, under a fierce control, but she still held herself away from him. Michael's hands dropped back onto the blankets.

"Don't you see," she went on, "that we can't take the chance? I can't take it, even if you will. Call your friend. Call Bellevue, some hospital. And leave me tied until they come for me."

Michael shook his head dumbly. He was incapable of speech, but she read his face, and her own expression changed. Her eyes flickered and then dropped away from his.

"All right," she said. "I'm sorry. I was upset. Untie me."

She held her bound wrists toward him. The cloth was soft, and he had not tied the knots tightly; but he saw the red marks on her wrists, and his first impulse was to do as she asked. Yet he hesitated—noting her reluctance to meet his eyes, remembering the quick, cunning expression that had flickered across her face.

"What will you do if I untie you?" he asked.

Her silence was all the answer he needed. The minute his back was turned, she would run, and not stop running until she had found a safe padded cell in which to hide. She might even go back to Gordon, she was desperate enough for that. . . . And through the black despair that enveloped him he felt an incongruous flash of something like triumph. She hadn't reacted this way after her attempt on Gordon. Rather than risk hurting him, she would run to meet the fate she had been fleeing.

"No," he said decisively. "Not that way, Linda."

Her eyes blazed up at him, and she started to speak. The words caught in her throat as they heard the sound of a knock at the front door.

The same idea came to both their minds simultaneously: Gordon. Michael moved just in time to stop the scream that had gathered in her throat. He knew what she meant to do, and he knew what his course of action must be. The struggle was short but ugly, because now he was not fighting some sick manifestation of hate, but Linda herself. When he stood up, he was wet with perspiration. His stomach contracted in a spasm of sickness as he looked down at the writhing figure on the bed—gagged with a towel, its wrists and ankles tied firmly to the bedposts. The knock was repeated. It had come again twice while he was . . . Whoever it was must know he was there.

Michael turned on his heel and went out, closing the bedroom door tightly behind him. As he reached the front door the knock was repeated. He wrenched the door open with a violence that did little to relieve his fury and frustration. He was almost hoping that his surmise was correct. It would have been a pleasure to get his hands on Randolph.

But it was not Randolph. It was his secretary.

"Good morning," Briggs said politely.

Michael stared back at him, deflated and uncertain. He was not sure of Briggs's role. Involved he must be, but perhaps only as one of Gordon's blinded disciples. If that was the case . . . Michael's stomach contracted as he remembered what lay on the bed in the next room. Linda wouldn't be the only one to be locked up if Briggs happened to see that pretty picture.

"Good morning," he answered, wondering how his voice could sound so normal. "Looking for something?"

Briggs blinked; a sly, appreciative smile moved his mouth. The expression was so ugly that Michael fell back a step. Briggs took advantage of his movement to enter.

The man was dressed in an imitation of Gordon's impeccable taste. The suit had been well fitted; but not even Savile Row could have done much with Briggs's figure. The expensive leather belt had slid down below the equator of his round belly, and the Italian silk tie curved out to follow the hump. In his hand Briggs held a hat. He put it down on a table and glanced around the room.

"Nice place you have here," he said.

There was no sound from the bedroom. Michael wondered whether Linda had recognized Briggs's voice and found him too much even for her new resolution. He couldn't risk it, though. He had to get the man out of here.

"I don't like to seem inhospitable," he said, "but I'm just about to go out."

It was such a glaring lie, considering the hour and the state of Michael's apparel, that Briggs didn't bother to comment. But another of those faint, unpleasant smiles touched his pale mouth.

"Oh, I shan't stay. I just came by at Mr. Randolph's request. You haven't seen anything of Mrs. Randolph, I suppose?"

A series of soft thuds came from behind the closed door. Michael glanced at it.

"That damned cat," he said.

"Your cat? How nice that you have a pet."

"If you don't mind . . ." Michael felt he couldn't control himself much longer. In about thirty seconds he was going to grab Briggs by the collar of his pretty suit and heave him out the door.

"Yes . . . You see, there was a sad occurrence last night. You remember our local witch, I'm sure. Apparently she got carried away by one of her experiments and set her house on fire."

"Really?" His tone didn't even convince Michael himself, but suddenly he no longer cared. Briggs knew. He knew all about everything.

"Yes," Briggs cooed. "Very sad. Burned to a crisp, the poor old lady was. Well, naturally Mr. Randolph thought Linda might have been involved."

"Linda," Michael repeated.

"I think of her that way," Briggs said, with an indescribable smirk. "I wish we could find her, help her. . . . She's a beautiful young lady. A shame to have all that go to waste in some asylum."

Two things kept Michael from planting his fist right in the center of Briggs's leer. One was the thought that it would be like hitting a fat woman. The other was the knowledge that Briggs was trying to anger him into an indiscreet act.

"How is Mr. Randolph?" he asked.

"Not well." Briggs shook his head sadly. "He's very upset, naturally. Knowing Linda's sad history as he does, he wondered about what happened to Andrea. Luckily the evidence was destroyed. The body, I mean."

"I'm late now," Michael said.

"How thoughtless of me to keep you, then." Briggs turned toward the door. Then he made a sudden dart to the side, his pudgy hand shooting out.

"Here it is," he exclaimed guilelessly, holding up a small black notebook. "Mr. Randolph thought he might have misplaced it here."

Michael looked at it.

"Randolph's? But it must have been here for days. I never saw it."

"Somehow it seems to have worked its way under a heap of magazines," Briggs said blandly. "You busy writers aren't the neatest housekeepers in the world, are you? He'll be glad to have this back. And to think this was the reason why he asked me to stop by. I declare I'd have forgotten to ask if I hadn't seen it, peeping out. Well, then . . ."

"Wait a minute," Michael said. An insane suspicion had entered his mind. "Let me see that."

Briggs surrendered the notebook without comment. Only his raised eyebrows indicated courteous surprise.

Michael flipped through the pages of the notebook. It was an ordinary little loose-leaf pad, except that its cover was of tooled leather instead of plastic. It was certainly not Michael's property, and the handwriting on the pages resembled what he remembered of Gordon's script. The entries were cryptic and abbreviated; they might have been written in the sort of personal shorthand a busy man had developed in order to jot down appointments and reminders. A few of the signs reminded Michael of chemical or mathematical symbols.

With some reluctance he returned the notebook to Briggs. He had an odd feeling that if he could study those entries at leisure, he might learn something important. But he couldn't refuse to let the man have it, and the need to get Briggs out was stronger than any possible gain from the book.

"Well, I must be running along," Briggs said affably. "I hope you'll excuse the intrusion, at this hour. I have a busy day ahead of me. Oh, and by the way . . ."

Already in the doorway, he turned.

"If Linda should turn up, do be kind to the poor girl."

"Naturally."

"But don't forget . . ."

"Forget what?" Michael snapped.

"She might be dangerous," Briggs said softly. "Be careful."

He went out, and just in time; the itching in Michael's fingers was almost intolerable. He slammed the door and leaned against it, twisting his hands together. When he was able to speak without stammering, he went back to the bedroom.

She lay quiet, staring at him over the gag, her eyes liquid and enormous. Michael took the gag off and untied the cords that held her down. Neither spoke. He sat down on the edge of the bed, knowing he dared not touch her, and watched the tears slide down her cheeks and soak into the pillow on either side of her face.

## II

Michael put down the telephone.

"They expect him tonight or early tomorrow," he said. Sun streamed in the window. It was midmorning, and a beautiful spring day. Outside. The room had another atmosphere. They had both fought their way back to some kind of calm, but the air was cold with tension.

"Tonight," Linda repeated thoughtfully.

"Or tomorrow. He never knows till the last minute what

plane he'll be catching. Usually he wires to let them know, but not always; he drives himself, so he doesn't have to be met."

Michael knew he must sound like a host trying to entertain an unwanted guest. He couldn't help it; something had happened to his brain. Up to this point he had been able to consider and discuss everything that had happened; he had even been able to apply logic to a concept that was considered to be beyond logic. But last night . . . His mind balked at that, he couldn't even think about it, much less discuss it. He was behaving as if it hadn't happened. Which was not only stupid; it was potentially dangerous.

He looked at Linda. Sitting upright on the bed, she sipped her coffee. Her hands were free, but her ankles were still bound; at her insistence, he had again fastened them to the footboard of the bed. He had felt sick while doing it, and he felt sick every time he looked. But it was a small price to pay for the composure of her face. She had fought this latest catastrophe, and come through it, as she had come through all the others; but he thought that she must be like someone clinging to a single strand of rope, over an abyss, slipping inexorably down each time her grasp on reality failed. The frantic hands might tighten, temporarily stopping the descent, or even claw their way back up the rope, a few precious inches toward safety. But inevitably the grasp would weaken again, and each time the fall would be arrested a little farther down, toward the end of the rope and the final plunge.

"I left a message," he said. "Asking him to call the minute he gets in."

"We're acting like children," Linda said. "Waiting for this man as if he were God, or . . . Why do you think he can help us?"

"I don't. I just don't know what else to do."

"How is your arm?"

"Hurts. It's not that, nor the fact that I'm bushed. Something's happened to what passes for my brain. I can't . . . I can't think."

"Physical exhaustion doesn't help," she said, with a briskness that was contradicted by the tenderness of her mouth. They both knew that they could not afford an exchange of sympathies. In a battle, minor wounds must go untended.

"My own brain isn't working very well either," she went on.

"But one thing is clear, Michael. I can't spend another night with you."

"It's a good thing nobody is listening to this conversation," Michael said wryly.

She gave him a strained smile.

"I mean it, though."

"Why is it night you're afraid of? Isn't that childish too?"

"Fear of the dark . . . Maybe. But everything that has happened so far happened at night."

"When the powers of evil walk abroad . . ."

"You see? It means something to you. What was it you said, last night—about the dark on the other side?"

Michael twitched uncomfortably.

"Kwame—Joe Schwartz—said that. About Gordon. He was talking about the old Platonic image of the shadows on the wall of the cave, but it turned me cold to hear him, I can tell you. Not the shadows, but the Things that cast the shadows, the Things that prowl the dark, on the other side of the fire. Gordon knows about them, he said. It was pretty obvious that he did, too."

"Poor Joe."

"He takes dope," Michael said. "Some kind of hallucinogenic."

"But you don't. Why does the phrase make you so uncomfortable?"

"Racial memory?" Michael offered wildly. "Some hairy, beetle-browed ancestor of mine, squatting in his cave, with his puny fire and his club the only defense against the things that prowled outside in the dark. Saber-toothed tigers and mastodons . . ."

There was no answering spark of amusement in her face.

"Go on," she said.

"Well . . . Too many horror stories when I was a kid. The other side of what? Eternity? The threshold of this world? The doorway that separates the living from the dead? Spiritualists talk about 'the other world,' don't they, to describe the region from which they get their communications?" He was getting interested; he went on, catching the impressions as they floated up into consciousness. "When Kwame talked of the dark on the other side of the fire, he was thinking of *The Republic*, but also of that other image. This world, narrow and circumscribed as opposed to the spiritual reality of the other side. The dark . . . That idea is not in Plato, damn it, if I remember my classics, which I probably don't. For him, the non-material, ideal world was one of light, of true consciousness. A spiritualist would see it that way, too. What do the discarnate entities keep mumbling when they are asked about their world?"

"Sunshine, light, flowers, love," Linda said promptly.

"Right. So why does this world of light and flowers seem to Kwame to be transmuted into darkness—not empty night, but a place where shadows live? Darkness and light, the primeval symbols of evil and good; the notion of a balance of forces, eternally warring, never ending. There are times, for everyone, when he feels himself the plaything of forces from somewhere outside, forces beyond his control, which strike him when he least expects it. 'Out of the night that covers me . . . ' "

"Imagery, poetic," Linda said, as his voice trailed away. "It's frightening, though, isn't it? 'Black as the pit from pole to pole . . . ' "

"Poetic imagery is part of the picture I get. Black as the pit . . . black as Hell . . . There's a nice conventional image of fire and darkness for you."

"The familiar Calvinist Hell."

"It's funny," Michael went on thoughtfully, "how many of the pre-Christian afterworlds were dark. That terrible twilight place the classical poets describe, where the dead speak with faint voices like the piping of birds. . . . Didn't the Egyptians go down under the earth into darkness where the sun-god never came?"

"You're out of my field," Linda said.

"Darkness and light, black and white; even the colors have symbolism. White is the color of purity, the garments of the Virgin and the priest. . . . What's the matter?"

"Sorry. It reminded me of Briggs, and every time I think of him I get a chill."

"Why Briggs?" Michael grinned. "Not the color of purity, surely."

"Didn't you know? No, I suppose you wouldn't. Gordon must have told you about Briggs's being unfairly dismissed from his job, and all that? He never told you what the job was, though. . . . Briggs is an unfrocked priest."

"What?"

"I guess that sounds melodramatic. Actually, he was a student for the priesthood. They threw him out. Very politely, I imagine. I can also imagine why."

"My God . . . Linda, what is Briggs? I mean, what role does he play in relation to Gordon?"

"I've wondered so often myself. Sometimes I think he's just another victim, but a willing one. Sometimes I see him as the *éminence grise* behind Gordon's latest activities. They're hand in glove, anyway, never doubt that."

Her face was averted, her voice rapid. She could hardly speak of the man, her loathing was so great. Michael realized that the basis for her aversion was more than a spiritual rejection. Perhaps it had not been Briggs's dabbling in questionable theology that had caused his expulsion, but rather his inability to conform to the basic tenets of the priestly orders. He wondered whether Gordon was aware of his colleague's attitude toward his wife; and knew that, if Gordon was what they had conjectured him to be, this would only be another weapon in his hands.

In the middle of the afternoon, Napoleon returned.

Michael hadn't noticed his long absence; he had too many other things to worry about. He was in the kitchen making another pot of coffee when the heavy body thudded down onto the counter; and then he remembered that Napoleon never missed coming home for breakfast.

He reached out for the animal, expecting the usual snarl and rebuff. But Napoleon's lackluster stare remained fixed on thin air and he did not move. Michael passed his hands over the cat's body. He found no new wounds. Whatever else he had been doing, Napoleon had not been fighting. Which was in itself a sign of something wrong.

Lifting the unresponsive bulk, he carried it into the bedroom.

"He's sick," he said, sounding like a nervous parent.

Linda looked up from the book she was not reading.

"Let me see."

Michael dumped the cat onto her lap and Linda investigated.

"I don't know," she said doubtfully. "He's a mess—why don't you chaperon him better?—but what's left of his fur feels sleek enough. And his eyes look okay. . . ."

Returning her look owlishly, Napoleon made the rusty grinding noise that passed for a purr. When Michael reached out for him, he eluded his master's hand with the old agility, and leaped down off the bed. Michael trailed along after him while Napoleon made a thorough inspection of the apartment, from bathroom to kitchen. Having arrived at his food dish, he squatted down in front of it and began to gulp with a ravenous intensity that relieved much of Michael's worry.

He wandered back into the bedroom.

"He's eating."

"I expect he's all right, then. Michael . . . Would you think me ridiculous if I found his return reassuring?"

"I never thought of that. Hell, honey, it's illogical. Cats are supposed to fawn on demons."

She didn't answer. Michael sat down wearily on the edge of the bed and put his hand on her ankles. He ran his finger under the thick silk, making sure it was not too tight.

"Don't," she said.

"It's stupid," Michael burst out. "You can untie it yourself any time you want to."

"But it would take time. You'd have some warning."

"For God's sake—"

"What time is it?' "

"About two."

"Don't lie."

"All right! Three. Well, maybe three thirty . . ."

"Another hour," she said. "We must leave a wide margin."

"I'll call Galen again."

"You've called twice in the last hour. They'll give him your message."

"And if he doesn't come by the time your deadline is up?"

"I won't stay here tonight."

"A hotel room won't be any safer," Michael said, deliberately misunderstanding her.

"It's not a hotel room I'm contemplating."

"Linda, you can't do that! If you get yourself committed to some hospital, the only one who could possibly get you out is Gordon himself. I don't even have the legal right to ask questions. You can't lock yourself into a room and throw away the key."

"I will not stay here tonight."

"You'll have to," Michael said. "I won't let you go."

She looked up at him, a pale ghost of humor in her face.

"Funny. You're driven to the same extremity I tried to force you to earlier. Yes, you can keep me here. Bound and gagged . . . Have you thought about how it would look, if someone forced his way in and found me like that?"

"Constantly," Michael said with a groan.

"And you'd risk that?"

Michael reached out for her, compulsively, but she fended him off with a strength that had panic behind it.

"Don't, don't ever do that! You kissed me last night, before—"

"You don't mean . . ." Michael hesitated. He was surprised, and disgusted, to realize that his predominant emotion was jealousy.

"There may be a connection," she said. Her eyes refused to meet his. "I won't . . . go into details. But there may be."

"I see."

"That would have to be one of the conditions we must agree to, if I do stay."

"I'm not that big a fool," Michael said roughly. "Even if I do act like it most of the time. What other conditions?"

"Have you got any sleeping pills?"

"Never use the things. What makes you think they would help? I'd be inclined to suspect the reverse. The less control you have over your conscious mind . . ."

"Since you don't have any, there's not much point in debating that."

"How true. Anything else?"

"Find a key for that door. And barricade it."

"Honey, for the love of Mike—what if there's a fire, or a burglar, or—something else? We can't anticipate his moves; he might do anything. If I couldn't get to you—"

"It's a risk we must take." Her eyes were hard as stone; the eyes of a fanatic. "Another thing. I want you to search this place from top to bottom. Make sure Gordon hasn't left any other little souvenirs, like the notebook."

"You think . . . ?" Michael cogitated. "I wonder."

"I'm not thinking, I'm just grasping at straws. But according to some occult theories, there must be a physical connection between the spell and the person whom it is meant to affect—

like the doll, which uses the victim's own hair or nail clippings. Why not a physical connection, a focus, for the warlock's spells? Gordon isn't careless about his belongings. That notebook was left here deliberately."

"I agree. I'm sloppy, but not unconscious; the book was planted under a pile of material I wouldn't ordinarily refer to. Wait a minute. If your theory is right, he must have planted something at Andrea's house."

"He's been there any number of times."

"He went there looking for you, before you came here the first time," Michael said. "He admitted entering the house."

"So it's possible. I'm not sure of this, Michael. I think it's worth checking, though."

"I'm trying to figure out when he could have hidden the notebook."

"Hiding it wouldn't take more than a few seconds. It must have been here for several days, Michael. Because the summoning that brought you to Andrea's didn't come from me. There's only one person who could have sent it."

"The idea had occurred to me. But I can't think of any reason why he should do such a thing."

"His reasons aren't comprehensible to normal people. I can think of an analogy, though: the pathologically jealous husband who keeps accusing his wife of infidelity until finally, in sheer desperation, she goes out and acquires a lover."

"Yeah, I knew a guy like that. His wife finally left him, and he took it as proof that he'd been right about her all along. All right." Michael stood up. "I'll search the place. The fact that Briggs was so ostentatious about removing the notebook might have been a bluff, to conceal the existence of something else."

He was not willing to admit, even to himself, the flaw in his reasoning: that if Briggs had removed the notebook, it might be because Gordon no longer needed it. Once the link was established . . .


When he had finished his search, the apartment was neater than it had been for months. He found nothing, but he was aware that the negative results were not conclusive. Unless he tore furniture and walls to pieces, he could not be sure that some small object was not still concealed.

He searched the bedroom last, at Linda's request; he knew that, as twilight closed in, she wanted him near by, where he could watch her. She seemed convinced of her theory of a physical link; Michael found it weaker and less convincing the longer he thought about it.

Napoleon, fully restored to health and malevolence, was still with them. Curled up on the foot of the bed, he watched Michael suspiciously.

Michael backed out of the interior of the wardrobe, carrying the pile of dirty shirts he had inspected several times before. He shook each one out, feeling in the pockets, and dropping them one by one to the floor as he finished. He viewed the untidy pile indecisively, and then shrugged and left it there.

"Can you think of any place I missed?" he asked.

"No." Linda's voice was strained. "Michael, it's almost dark."

"Not yet."

"Yes. Now." She held out her hands.

When he had done it, Michael was shaking. It got worse every time he did it. Napoleon's disapproval didn't help matters. The cat protested so violently that Michael finally had to shut him in the bathroom.

"All right," he said, straightening up after he had tied the final knot. "That's it. I'm not going to gag you, I don't see the need for it; and anyhow, it is simply too goddamn much for me to stomach."

"Okay," she said submissively.

Michael had turned on the lights; the darkness outside was complete. The lamp by the bed cast a warm glow on Linda's face, and he was outraged to see that she was smiling. Maybe she felt better this way. He sure as hell didn't.

He couldn't look at her any longer. He couldn't stand the thoughts that kept worming into his mind. Abruptly, he turned and blundered out of the room; when he was out of her sight he leaned up against the wall, his head resting on his arm. It was barely seven o'clock. How in the name of God was he going to get through the rest of the night?

It was the hour of midnight he dreaded most. Superstition . . . but no more mad than any of the other things that had happened. He forced himself back to Linda and found, as people usually do, that he could stand it, and would stand it, because he had to.

They talked, but no longer of theories and interpretations. They spoke of defense, like the decimated garrison of a beleaguered fortress. But the weapons they discussed were not in any modern arsenal.

"I don't happen to have any holy water on hand," Michael said, driven to a fruitless sarcasm. "Ran out last week. . . . It didn't help Andrea, remember?"

"Could you—could you pray?" she asked diffidently.

"No." Michael looked at her. "Yes. I could pray. If I knew What to pray to."

The idea came into both their minds at the same moment, or else she read his face with uncanny quickness.

"You can't do that," she said.

"Why not? If we're right—or even if we're wrong. Any kind of mental assurance, confidence—"

"Not that kind, no—there's a limit, Michael. It would be spiritual prostitution, unimaginably worse than any physical contamination. You couldn't do it—not if you really believed. And if you didn't, it would just be a dirty game."

Again Michael was reminded of the gulf between their minds. His idea of trying to fight Gordon on his own ground had been partly a counsel of desperation, partly an academic theory. There was nothing academic about Linda's attitude; she looked sick with disgust.

"Besides," she went on; her voice was shaking. "Besides, you'd be a novice, a probationer. He's studied these things for years. All you would do is weaken yourself, don't you see? He could walk right into your mind and destroy it."

"Okay, okay. It was just an idea. Then what can we do?"

Linda relaxed.

"Do you love me?" she asked.

The question was so unexpected that it caught Michael off guard.

"Someone asked me that, once," he said slowly.

"Well?"

"I said I didn't know what the word meant. I still don't. But I love you."

"Then love me. No—" His hand came toward her and she shook her head. "Don't touch me, don't think of touching me. Think of love. Not of desire; they aren't the same. I don't know what love means either. But most people confuse loving with being loved. Love isn't reciprocal. It doesn't ask, or expect, or demand. It isn't an emotion, it's a state of being. Love me, Michael."

"It sounds rather one-sided to me," Michael said; for the life of him, he could not have kept the bitterness out of his voice. "And also rather esoteric. You aren't talking to Saint Francis, you know."

"I noticed that. . . . Oh, Michael, I'm sorry! I'm sorry you're involved in this, I'm sorry for talking to you like a third-rate mystic, I'm sorriest of all for asking, demanding, and not offering you anything in return. I haven't anything to give, not any longer. I did once; I think I did. . . . But I lost it, somewhere along the way, when Gordon taught me his way of loving. He does love me, you know. He calls it that. And I'm almost as bad as he is now; the only difference is that I know that that insatiable demand is not love, but a perversion of it. That's why I can't fight him. But you can."

Without answering, Michael stood up and walked across the room. From Linda's earnest confusion of half-digested philosophy he derived only despair. Even if they fought their way out of the present crisis, there was no future for him with a woman who was literally frightened to death of loving. She was sick, incurably sick, if she could believe what she said she believed. Like most theories, hers sounded fine on the surface; but if love was not reciprocal, only the saints could derive much satisfaction from it. A normal human being had only so much to give without getting something in return. Depletion was inevitable.

And this present situation, which she had talked him into, was impossible. Linda was immobilized, defenseless. If she was wrong—and she had to be wrong!—about her idea of vulnerability through the lack of love, then he was as susceptible to mental invasion as she was. The logic of Gordon's next move came to him so strongly that it was as if he had read the other's mind. Even if Linda had not been bound, she would be no match for him; he was stronger and heavier. She could scream; and she would, as long as she had breath left with which to scream, long enough for the neighbors to call the police, who would not arrive in time. . . . They would find him standing there, over the bloody thing on the bed. Gordon would keep control over him that long. Just that long. He would release the mental bonds in time for Michael to see, and comprehend, what he had done. . . .

Just in time, Michael realized what was happening. He flung himself around, grasping blindly at the first solid object that came within reach. Something rocked under the thrust of his body, something fell and crashed; and he found himself leaning against the big dresser, his arms grasping it as a drowning man would clutch an oar. A broken ashtray lay on the floor. His face was streaming with perspiration, and his heart pounded as if he had been running a race. Something else was pounding—an irate neighbor, from the floor below. The howls of Napoleon, imprisoned in the bathroom, were loud enough to wake the dead.

"Michael! Michael—is something wrong?"

How long had she been calling him? With an enormous effort, Michael removed his hands from the dresser and turned around.

"It's all right," he said thickly; and then said it again, because his voice had been almost inaudible.

He saw Linda staring at him. There was concern in her face, but no fear; apparently the meaning of his sudden movement had escaped her.

"What is it?" she repeated.

"Liver, or something," Michael said promptly. His voice and body were once again under his control. The mental grasp had left his mind, but he derived no comfort from his victory. This might have been only a preliminary, testing thrust. He knew that he did not dare tell Linda what had happened.

"Hadn't you better let Napoleon out?" she asked. "He's beside himself."

"Huh? Oh, yeah."

Michael opened the door warily, putting himself into a posture of defense. Napoleon's shrieks stopped abruptly, but he did not appear; looking around the corner of the door, Michael saw him crouched in the farthest corner, behind the hamper.

"It's all right," he said. "You can come out now."

The cat refused to move until Linda called him. He curled up on the foot of the bed.

"I'll make some coffee," Michael mumbled, and fled without waiting for an answer.

He got to the kitchen before his legs gave way, and collapsed into a chair, letting his head drop down onto the table. For a long time he sat and shook, while his mind raced desperately from one blank wall to another. He had thought, when he fought Linda for his life, that that was the worst thing that could happen. He knew now that he had yet to experience the worst. If he hurt Linda, Gordon wouldn't have to take any further steps; he would sit screaming in a cell for the rest of his life, until he found some means of ending it. And even this might not be the ultimate disaster. Gordon had a fertility of imagination that was far beyond his own feeble concepts of evil. . . .

And the end of it all was that there was nothing he could do. He was boxed into a corner. Whatever he did now would be dangerous. He could lock himself in one room and Linda in another; but his controlled mind would find some means of breaking through any barricade he could construct. He could go out, and smash a window, or insult a cop, and maybe get thrown in jail—if he could find a cop willing to arrest him. That would leave Linda alone, at the mercy of whatever attack Gordon planned next. He could let the police take Linda—which would be just what Gordon wanted. If he untied her, and begged her to immobilize him, she would know what had happened, and with her susceptibility to suggestion—or mental control, call it what you liked—she would then become his Nemesis, instead of the reverse. There was no way out.

The sound of knocking roused him, after a timeless interval of sheer despair; and he was, somehow, not surprised to realize that his lips were moving soundlessly in words he hadn't used since childhood. He moved like a machine to answer the door. Neither hope nor fear drove him; he was simply geared to accept, and deal with, whatever was there.

For a few seconds after he had opened the door he stood with his mouth slightly ajar, assessing the man on the threshold as he might have studied a perfect stranger. The tall, spare figure and unlined face; the odd, silvery-gray eyes and the close-cropped hair that was a matching silver . . . Galen had been gray ever since Michael had known him. He carried a light suitcase and a topcoat. No hat. Galen never wore a hat.

Michael stepped back, throwing the door wide.

"How did you know I wanted you?" he asked.

"I called from the airport," Galen said prosaically. He threw his coat onto a chair and put his case down on the floor beside it. "Henry said you'd been phoning all day."

His gaze swept the room and returned to Michael; and the

latter was conscious of his appearance, which was both haggard and unkempt. He ran his hand self-conciously over the stubble of beard on his jaw and glanced down at his unspeakable shirt—rumpled, sweat-stained, dirty—before meeting Galen's eyes.

"I'm glad you're back," he said inadequately.

"Why?"

Michael opened his mouth, and closed it again. Coherent explanation was beyond him.

"You might as well see the worst," he said. "Come into the bedroom."

He had always admired Galen's phlegm, and wondered what degree of shock it would take to startle him out of it. He found out. Galen paled visibly at the sight that met his eyes.

Flat on the bed, arms outstretched and bound, ankles tied to the footboard, Linda looked like a character out of one of the books Michael never read, much less wrote. Apparently she had recognized Galen's voice; she was not surprised to see him, but she blushed slightly as the incredulous gray eyes swept over her.

"It isn't what you think," she said.

"I'm not sure what I think." Galen sat down in the nearest chair. "Give me a minute to catch my breath. Michael . . ."

Michael talked. It was an unspeakable relief; he knew how Linda had felt all those months, bottling up her fears. He talked without critical intent or editing, mixing theory and fact, interpretation and actuality. And Galen listened. He blinked, a little more often than was normal, but his face had smoothed out into its professional mask. Michael finished with an account of the mental attack he had just experienced. Linda, who was hearing this for the first time, gasped audibly, but Galen went on nodding.

"Well, well," he said, after Michael's voice had stopped. "No wonder you look like hell."

"Is that all you can say?"

"What do you want me to say?" He glanced from one of them to the other, and smiled faintly. "If it comes to that—what do you want me to do? Put on my wizard's robes and exorcise the devil?"

Michael sat down on the bed. He grinned.

"I rather expected you to put in a call for the men in the white coats, and order rooms for two."

"I may yet," Galen said coolly. "You realize—neither of you is unintelligent—that everything you've told me can be explained in terms of pathological mental conditions?"

Michael glanced apprehensively at Linda and was reassured by what he saw. The strain, the underlying fear were still there, but Galen's comment had not shaken her. She had anticipated it. Perversely, he was moved to marshal the very arguments he had once demolished himself.

"Andrea's death?"

Galen shrugged.

"The phenomenon is sometimes called thanatomania. With the heart condition you mentioned, the result was virtually a foregone conclusion. I've seen several cases myself where there was no diagnosable organic weakness. You must have read the newspaper accounts, a few years ago, of an excellent example of thanatomania. The woman had been told, by a soothsayer, that she would die on a certain date. She died. In a modern hospital, under professional care."

"I read about it," Michael admitted unwillingly. "What about the dog, then? I saw it too."

"Then the dog is a collective hallucination, or a real dog."

"Hallucinations don't bite," Michael said.

Galen glanced at the dirty bandage on his arm.

"I'll have a look at that later," he said calmly. "Aside from my concern, personal and professional, for your physical health, I'd like to examine the marks."

Bemused by fatigue and relief, Michael grappled with that one for several seconds before he understood enough to get angry.

"Another example of thanatomania?" he said sarcastically.

Galen's tone of annoyance was indicative; he usually had better control of himself.

"Good God Almighty, Michael, do I have to synopsize the professional journals? You've read enough of the popular literature to know that patients have inflicted everything from fake stigmata to signs of rape on themselves, in order to prove whatever point feel they must make. And don't try to tell me you aren't deeply enough involved, emotionally, with Mrs. Randolph, to be suggestible."

Linda spoke for the first time.

"So involved that he would be forced to concoct a crazy

theory in order to excuse my attempt to kill him." It was a statement, not a question. Galen nodded, watching her. She went on
calmly, "Yes, I can understand that kind of reasoning. But I do
have one question, Doctor. Why did you give Michael his father's letters?"

Galen's slow, close-lipped smile spread across his face.

"The first sensible question anyone has asked yet," he said.
"The answer is complex, however. I suggest we adjourn."

"Where?" Michael asked.

"My house, naturally. I want to have a look at that arm.
And I agree that, for whatever reason, this atmosphere is un-
healthy for both of you. Pack a bag, Michael, while I untie Mrs.
Randolph."

Michael turned to obey, but he was diverted by the specta-
cle of Galen, every professional hair in place, calmly untying
the knots that bound Linda to the bed. Glancing up, Galen met
his eyes and smiled affably.

"This is not, by any means, my most unusual experience,"
he said, and turned his attention back to his work.

# Chapter
## 11

"NOT SELF-INFLICTED," GALEN SAID.

"Thanks a lot."

Michael rolled down his sleeve. Linda knew he had been trying not to wince; Galen's poking and probing, which appeared to be prompted more by a spirit of scientific inquiry than concern for his patient's pains, must have hurt more than the original dressing of the wound.

Galen leaned back in his chair.

"Unless you found a cooperative dog," he qualified.

Linda bit back the comment that was on the tip of her tongue. She did not have Michael's lifelong experience with the older man, which had apparently given him a childlike faith in the great father figure. She had welcomed Galen's appearance for two reasons: first as an ally, who would help guard Michael from herself, and, second, as the key to the final door through which she meant to pass when all other means were exhausted. But although she herself had anticipated and considered every one of Galen's rational objections, she found them irritating coming from him.

Glancing around the doctor's study, she thought she would like the man if she weren't prejudiced against his profession. The furnishings of the room were so luxurious that they were inobtrusive; every object was so exactly right, in function and design, that it blended into a perfect whole. The exquisite marble head on the bookshelf looked like one she had seen in an

Athens museum, but it was not a copy. The rugs were modern Scandinavian designs; their abstract whirls of color went equally well with the classical sculpture, the Monet over the fireplace, and the geometric lines of the rosewood tables and desk. Heavy hangings, deep chairs, beautiful ornaments—they made up a room of soft lights and warm, bright coloring, as soothing to the nerves as it was stimulating to the senses. Only one object—Linda's eyes went to the soft couch, piled with cushions; and Galen, who saw everything, smiled at her.

"I use it more than my patients do," he said. "Most of them prefer to confront me, face to face."

"I didn't think you ever slept," Michael said.

"Catnaps. Like all the other great men of history. Hence the couch, in here."

He had a beautiful speaking voice, as modulated and controlled as an actor's. And used for the same purpose, Linda thought. Fighting the influence of the voice and the room, she returned to the attack.

"You don't honestly believe we went looking for a dog and provoked him into attacking Michael?"

"It does seem unlikely," Galen admitted.

"But not impossible?"

"Trite as it may sound . . ."

"Nothing is impossible. Damn you," Linda said.

Galen's fixed smile widened, very slightly, and Linda flung herself out of her chair and began to pace. That was one of the reasons why she hated psychiatrists; she had the feeling that her every action was not only anticipated, but provoked.

"However," Galen went on calmly, "unless the evidence to the contrary is strong, I generally prefer the simplest hypothesis."

"A real dog," Michael said.

"A real dog," Galen agreed.

Linda turned, to find both of them watching her. For a moment, the open amusement in Galen's face almost provoked an outburst; then she saw the strained pallor of Michael's face, and she dropped into her chair.

"I'm sorry," she said.

"You asked me a question," Galen said. "About the letters. What did you make of them, Michael?"

"Not much. I was hoping you'd have more to say on the subject."

"I do. But I want your interpretation first."

"The thing that struck me was the Jonah effect," Michael said slowly. "The doom and destruction that hit the people closest to Randolph. That, and my father's inexplicable dislike of him. It was Linda who told me he must have been the head of the witchcraft cult, and thus directly responsible for the death of that boy—"

"Green. The author of *The Smoke of Her Burning.*" As they both sat speechless, Galen turned to Linda. "Didn't you suspect, Mrs. Randolph, that your husband never wrote that book?"

"I—I don't know. I never—" Linda rallied. "I guess I did. But not for a long time, and it was never more than a suspicion. I loved the author of that book before I ever met Gordon; I think it was one of the reasons why I loved him. The external brilliance, the polish—Gordon could have done that. What he lacked, what he never could have produced, was the soul of the book—the compassion, the tenderness."

Galen nodded. He turned back to Michael.

"That was what your father suspected, knowing both students as he did. That was what he told me, privately. Of course he could prove nothing. Green had told him he was working on a book, but had never showed him any of the manuscript. He said he wanted to have it complete before he submitted it for criticism."

"I should have known," Michael said, flushed with self-contempt. "I call myself a writer. . . . But there were other things. The campaign speeches, even Kwame's songs . . . For a while I played with the idea that he had stolen them from Gordon."

"They were not written by the same man; but they were written by the same kind of man," Galen said. "Despite my reluctance to accept your theories of diabolic possession, I do believe in what you might call mental vampirism—a spiritual blood sucking, a leechlike drain of the intelligence and emotions of others. You've met people, I'm sure, who left you feeling drained and depressed after a few hours' conversation. Usually this is an unconscious demand, but Randolph is quite conscious of what he's doing. Make no mistake, he was never guilty of ordinary plagiarism. His victims gave him what he wanted, half convinced themselves that it was his work.

"Eventually, however, the vampire goes too far, and destroys the source from which it draws its vitality. It is symptomatic, not only of Randolph's effect on others, but of their personality weaknesses, that they should resort to suicide, or some other form of escape, rather than attacking Randolph. For it was not only intellectual brilliance he sought, it was brilliance coupled with a sense of insecurity. You might say, if you were mystically inclined—which I am not—that Randolph was drawn, by a kind of spiritual chemistry, to people of this sort, just as they were attracted to him. The stronger souls—pardon the expression—resisted him. As you did, Mrs. Randolph. He miscalculated with you, possibly because his instincts were confused by a more basic desire. But there lay the danger to you. Randolph literally could not let you go. What he fails to fascinate he must destroy. And eventually he destroys even that which he fascinates."

"Then everything he's done," Michael muttered, "all his success—a fraud. A gigantic fraud."

"Not at all. He has one undeniable talent: Charisma, we call it—the ability to charm and command affection, loyalty. All leaders have it, to some extent, and all of them depend on advisers, speech writers, hired experts, to supply any qualities they may lack. If Randolph had accepted that kind of help, he might have been a successful politician and a good teacher; he is not a stupid man. But he isn't content with mere competence. A healthy, strong body, and the finest of training, let him excel in the sports he selected—and don't underestimate the power of that confident personality on his opponents. But he knew that eventually he would lose, when he got into the big leagues, against opponents who were simply better than he was. So he quit."

"Well, I'll be damned," Michael said. "You're on our side after all, you old—"

"I am merely presenting what seems to me, at the moment, the most logical hypothesis. I've followed Randolph's career with some interest, since your father told me his suspicions. I respected his judgment, and I was intrigued by Randolph's behavior. If your father was correct, there were certain alarming tendencies. . . . Well. Candidly, I was relieved when he decided to give up his political career."

Michael opened his mouth to speak, but Linda forestalled him.

"So you believe in a perfectly materialist, rational explanation."

"Yes. Given your husband's personality, and motives, the rest is clear. The dog is a real dog, manipulated and concealed by Randolph in an attempt to play on your nerves. Your erratic behavior is a result of secretly administered drugs and a form of hypnotic control, intensified by your increasing suggestibility as doubts of your own sanity increased."

"But I thought no one could be hypnotized to do something he wouldn't consciously do."

"An error," Galen said succinctly. "Or, shall we say a great oversimplification."

"My attack on Michael—"

"Posthypnotic suggestion, conditioning . . ." Galen paused. The Gray eyes appraised her coldly. "I am not saying that your mental and emotional state is normal, at the present time."

"I know that," Linda said. "What I don't know is how abnormal it is."

"You mean, are you still a potential threat to Michael?" Galen pondered the problem without visible emotion. "I would guess that you may well be."

"God damn it!" Michael was on his feet, ignoring Linda's outstretched hand, and Galen's unperturbed smile. "Your theory stinks, Galen. Oh, I know, it all makes sense. It even explains why the dog attacked me, and yet left before it did any serious damage. The storm excited it, so that it broke away from its handlers, and they called it back before it could be killed or captured because they didn't want their supernatural effect ruined. I'll even admit to hearing a funny whistling sound that might have been Gordon, calling the dog. But your version doesn't explain Gordon's motive. Why the elaborate plot? Why all the hocus-pocus? And why me, for God's sake?"

"Your theory isn't strong on motive either," Galen pointed out. "The mechanism isn't that complicated, or obscure; Randolph's original reason for inviting you to his home had nothing to do with plots, supernatural or otherwise. He may have selected you, in preference to others, because of some amorphous idea of getting back at your father, who was one of the few people who never succumbed to the myth; after that, the development of the relationship between you and Mrs. Randolph would give even a balanced mind cause for dislike. What do you consider a motive, anyway? Four million dollars? You're talking about human behavior, which is difficult enough to comprehend even in so-called normal individuals. People have committed murder over a dirty plate, or a sum as small as three dollars."

"All right, all right," Michael said irritably. "Stop talking down to me. I'll accept any hypothesis you shove at me, if you'll just tell me what to do about it."

"You know better than to ask me for advice."

"Professional reticence?" Linda asked, too politely.

"Professionally I'm full of advice. As a human being I'll be damned if I will take on the combined role of leaning post and punching bag. Make your own decisions and kick yourself if they turn out badly."

"There's something you may not know," Michael said. His voice was quiet, but he was furious; Linda knew him well enough now to recognize the signs. "If Randolph were just our personal Nemesis, you'd be justified in staying out of this. But he is planning to go back into politics. That's a fact; I've checked it out. By your own description he's a paranoidal maniac with enormous charm. Does that remind you of any other political figure in recent history? Gordon isn't a runty paperhanger with a funny moustache; he's got a lot more on the ball."

Galen's lips tightened. He showed no other reaction; but after a moment Michael flushed and turned away.

"I have not refused to concern myself," Galen said quietly. "What I'm trying to do is make this a joint project."

"I'm sorry," Michael muttered. "You're right; the long-range effects aren't important now. The main thing is to get Linda free of him. At the risk of sounding simpleminded, I suggest one of the quick divorce mills."

"What's happened to your brain?" Galen asked nastily. "You can't treat this as an ordinary case of mental cruelty. Randolph is not an ordinary man."

"He doesn't own the whole goddamned world."

"He owns her." Galen's head jerked in Linda's direction. Illogically, it was at that moment, with the impact of his brutal statement still aching, that Linda decided to trust him.

"He's right," she said to Michael. "Call it what you like— obsession, neurosis, whatever. He does own me." She turned to the psychiatrist. "You've been very persuasive, Doctor. But I don't believe any of it. Gordon isn't an ordinary man, you're right. He's not a man at all, not any longer."

Galen leaned back in his chair.

"At last," he said, with a sigh. "I thought I spotted something. . . . What do you think he is? Demon, disciple of Satan, werewolf . . . Ah. The dog."

In Michael's hurried, incoherent account, this theory had somehow escaped mention—probably because he rejected it himself. Linda knew there was no use trying to avoid it. Squaring her shoulders, she looked Galen straight in the eye.

"Yes," she said. "That's what I think he is."

"Hmph." Galen rocked back and forth. "Why?"

"If you don't stop saying that—" Michael began.

"Shut up. I'm investigating Linda's crazy ideas, not yours. Lycanthropy . . . You are not referring, I'm sure, to the mental aberration which involves cannibalism, necrophilia, sadism, and a craving for raw meat, among other symptoms?"

"Is there such a thing?" Linda asked incredulously.

"As a form of psychotic paranoia, sometimes called zoanthropy, there certainly is such a thing. It is comparatively rare, but well documented; some of the famous mass murderers of history probably suffered from a form of this complaint—Gilles de Rais, Jack the Ripper. . . .

"But that's not what you mean. You are referring to the belief that some human beings can transform themselves into animal form, through the application of various magical techniques. The werewolf is the most familiar to us, because it is a product of European mythology and is described by the classical authors. In the East, however, one encounters weretigers, and in Africa the supernatural beast may be a hyena or a leopard. The leopard societies of West Africa, which terrorized whole villages, are well known; there was a strong element of such a cult in the Mau Mau atrocities, in Kenya. The mutilations inflicted on the victims of these societies resemble those made by the claws of a predatory animal, and were done with artificial instruments designed to resemble claws.

"Of course it's impossible to separate the supernatural and pathological elements. A culture with an implicit faith in lycanthropy produces men who are susceptible to the mania, and an individual who found it impossible to attain prestige by normal

methods might well turn to lycanthropy as a means of intimi-
dating those he cannot otherwise control."

"Good God," Michael muttered.

"There is, as well, a connection between lycanthropy and
witchcraft," Galen went on calmly. "The tradition of supernatural animals is widespread and very ancient. The ability of a
witch or warlock to assume animal form was one of the powers
granted by Satan to his disciples. Often witches made their way
to the Sabbath meeting in animal form. The great black goat
was a manifestation of Lucifer. Black is, of course, the color of
evil. And the black dog is not unknown as a supernatural animal, sometimes representing the warlock and sometimes Satan
himself. The wild dog or wolflike beast is a symbol of the bestial qualities of the human mind, freed from the bonds of reason
and conscience."

"A vile slander on animals," Michael said.

Galen went on, without appearing to hear him.

"You see, I am sure, how the various traditions mingle—
pre-Christian superstitions, perversions of Christian theology,
and a variety of mental aberrations, ranging from paranoia to
autohypnosis and hallucination. But the elements of the classic
Western werewolf legend are explicit. Some werewolves, as in
the popular films, are helpless victims of a curse, involuntary
skin-turners. Most are not innocent; they seek the change by diabolical means and use their animal form to satisfy bestial desires. According to these accounts, it is the soul, or astral body,
of the man that takes the animal form. The real body lies in a
cataleptic coma, barely breathing; but the astral form is actual,
physical, in that it can inflict pain and death, and feel pain and
death. Any wound inflicted on the animal is reproduced on the
sleeping human body, and drawing the animal's blood forces it
to resume human shape. In some traditions, the beast can only
be killed by a silver bullet, or by a sword which has been
blessed by a priest. When death occurs, the body of the beast
disappears and the body of the lycanthrope is found with the
same wounds that killed the animal. Intelligent observers have
already suspected the werewolf's human identity because of
such signs as hairy palms and eyebrows that meet in the middle.
He is often strangely affected by the full moon. Has Gordon
any of these traits, Mrs. Randolph?"

"Don't be ridiculous," Linda said disgustedly. "Those are old wives' tales."

Meeting Galen's gently ironic eye, she began to laugh, helplessly.

"Oh, dear . . . that's probably the craziest thing I've said yet. Maybe I'm not as far gone as I thought I was. No, I think Gordon belongs to your second category. How was it you phrased it? 'The ability of a warlock to assume animal form was one of the powers granted by Satan to his disciples.' "

"It makes sense," Galen said. "Given his past history, his dabbling in demonology as a young man, and his desire for control over others."

Linda's insane desire to laugh broke out again at the sight of Michael's stupefied expression.

"Wait a minute," he gasped. "First you said . . . And now you're saying . . ."

"You seem to be degenerating," Galen snapped. "I'm not telling you what I believe. I am endeavoring to ascertain what Randolph himself believes."

"I think he believes it," Linda said stubbornly. "What I just said."

"I don't know," Michael said.

Galen rose. He seemed taller; from where Linda sat, on a low chair by the desk, he seemed to tower over her.

"Maybe we'd better ask him," he said.

For the last few minutes, Linda had been partially aware of background noises, but in the immediacy of the conversation she had paid little attention. Now the meaning of the muffled sounds came home to her—a doorbell ringing, footsteps down the stairs and along the hall, the rattle of locks, and the opening and closing of the door. She sprang to her feet. The footsteps were coming down the hall, toward the study. Footsteps she knew. Gordon's steps.

## II

She was on her feet, halfway to the window in a mindless flight, when Galen's hand caught her arm. His grip was as hard as steel.

"I'm sorry, I meant to warn you," he said; the even voice contrasted alarmingly with the intensity of the hard hand on her wrist. "He came more promptly than I expected. Trust me, Linda. This has to be done."

Without waiting for an answer, he turned to Michael.

"Just keep quiet," he said rapidly. "Don't look surprised, at whatever I say, and don't contradict me or volunteer anything. If you weren't half-witted tonight, I wouldn't have to tell you—"

There was no time for further speech. The door of the study opened. Linda had a glimpse of the impassive manservant who had admitted them to the house; behind him was Gordon.

Without meaning to move, Linda managed to get behind Galen. He had released his grip on her arm. There was no need for further constraint, and he must have known it. She was as incapable of movement as she was of speech.

Gordon's fine dark eyes moved slowly over the three faces confronting him.

"My poor little errant wife," he said, "and—friend. I've never had the pleasure of meeting you, Dr. Rosenberg, but of course your reputation is well known. It was good of you to call me."

"Sit down, Mr. Randolph," Galen said equably. He did not, Linda noticed, offer the other man his hand.

Gordon took the chair indicated. He seemed perfectly at ease, except for the weariness in his face—normal in a man who has been trying to track down an insane wife.

Carefully, he did not look at Linda. He was acting again, and doing it well, simulating wary concern, pretending he didn't want to frighten her. . . . He looked at Michael instead, and a pathetic shadow of his old charming smile touched his mouth.

"Sorry, Mike. I've been a little off my head the last few days, or I wouldn't have thought—what I've been thinking. And all the time you were planning this. I'm eternally in your debt."

It was a little obvious, even for Gordon. Linda knew quite well what he was doing, but being able to analyze his methods did not make her immune. Huddled on the low hassock where Galen's ruthless arm had deposited her, she fought a doubt she had thought long conquered—doubt of Michael, and of the doctor to whom he had brought her.

Michael said nothing. He was standing, as if he felt more secure on his feet. His wooden-faced silence did nothing to relieve Linda's doubts.

The silence deepened. Galen, who had seated himself behind his desk, picked up a pen and began scribbling with it. His eyes intent on the meaningless doodles with which he disfigured the pristine surface of the desk blotter, he was humming under his breath, and—Linda realized—flatting badly.

It was a crude trick, but Gordon succumbed. Linda didn't see the crack in the barrier at first, it was so small. Only later, when she recalled the interview, did she appreciate Galen's over-all strategy.

"I'm grateful to you, too, Doctor," Gordon said. "But I don't quite understand . . . May I speak to you alone?"

"Why?"

Galen did not look up from his doodling. Critically he studied a scribble which looked like an arrow, and carefully added three oblique lines to represent the feather at the end of the shaft.

"To discuss what's to be done."

"That concerns all of us," Galen pointed out. "Your wife has told me a very disturbing story, Mr. Randolph."

He looked up; and Linda, who had felt the full effect of that passionless stare, was not surprised to see Gordon recoil slightly.

"Disturbing?" he repeated.

Galen, who had returned to his drawing, nodded vaguely.

"In what way?"

Galen shook his head and went on doodling. By now the precise movements of his pen had caught everyone's attention. Gordon was almost craning his neck to watch, and the distraction had shaken his concentration.

"I must insist, Doctor," he said; his voice was no longer pleasant.

"On what grounds?"

"Why—because she is my wife. I have the right—"

"You have no right." Galen's voice was remote. "Your wife has placed herself under my care. I called you in to ask you about certain statements she has made, not to report to you."

Gordon rose to his feet in a single powerful surge, his face distorted by the expression few people other than Linda had seen. Disregarding his instructions, Michael took a step forward, but it was Galen who stopped Randolph, with a single small gesture of his right hand, so quickly done that Linda could not have described it.

The effect on Gordon was astounding. He fell back, his face losing its color. Then, as if compelled, he leaned forward and looked at the drawing Galen had made.

"The College," he said, in a choked voice. "You are one—"

"Oh, yes," Galen said cheerfully.

Because she was sitting by the desk, next to his right hand, Linda was the only one who saw that hand move. A long index finger flicked a switch; and all the lights went out.

With the curtains drawn and the door closed, the room was plunged into primeval blackness. Linda heard the long, shaken intake of breath that came from Gordon; it went on so long it seemed impossible that human lungs could hold so much air. Then it burst out, in a sound that shocked the brain and senses as it affronted the ears. She heard a heavy chair fall, and the rush of something through the dark, and she dropped to the floor, crouching, for fear his blind rush would bring him to her. He found the door, after an interval that seemed interminable; the light from the hall was yellow and comforting, silhouetting his tall body. Then he was gone. The front door slammed, waking echoes from the lovely crystal chandelier in the hall.

The lights came on again.

"Hmph," Galen said.

Crouching on the floor behind his chair, Linda was busy shaking. A pair of hands caught her by the shoulders and hauled her to her feet. She stared into Michael's face.

"You all right?"

He didn't wait for an answer, but dumped her unceremoniously on the hassock, and wheeled on the figure pensively posed behind the desk.

"What College, you congenital liar?"

"I haven't the faintest idea," Galen said placidly.

"Another lie . . . The drawing. What is it?"

Galen stirred and stretched.

"The drawing, like the gesture I made, is an invention. A meaningless hodgepodge of symbols and Hebrew letters. I regret to say that my years of Hebrew school are far behind me, and my knowledge of the Cabala is even vaguer. The effect on Mr. Randolph was interesting, though, wasn't it?"

Michael regarded him with no admiration whatever.

"Of the two of you, I almost think I prefer Randolph. The College, I suppose, is an equally imaginary group of—what? Adepts in magic, squatting on top of Mount Everest thinking about the universe? You deliberately let him think . . ."

"I let him think what he wanted to think. And I found out what I wanted to know." He turned a contemplative stare on Linda, huddled on the hassock. "You were right. I felt sure that you were, but I had to check. And implant a certain useful suggestion."

Michael picked up the chair Gordon had overturned in his flight, and sat down. Under its drawn pallor, his face held the first gleam of hope Linda had seen for hours.

"He thinks you're a powerful warlock yourself. That isn't all you learned, is it?"

"I wondered if you'd notice."

"I was blind not to see it before."

"When you described his reaction to the power failure in your apartment, I wondered. Knowing that his concern for Mrs. Randolph was only problematical, I suspected another, more immediate cause for his panic."

"He's afraid of the dark," Michael said. Linda saw him shiver, and felt the same chill. She would never hear that word again without remembering.

"Yes. Significant, in view of the poetic words of your young friend at the college." Galen's voice changed. "Damn you for mentioning it, Michael; I should be immune to that kind of verbal magic, but when I think of what that poor devil sees, when the lights go out . . ."

"It isn't only the dark Gordon fears." For once Linda was immune to that kind of magic. "He's afraid of flying. He doesn't drive a car. He quit smoking."

"No contact sports," Michael muttered. "Even then . . . Swimming? Lots of other people around, spectators, competitors, just in case . . ."

"I believe that Elliott Jacques is correct when he states that this particular anxiety comes to its peak during the crisis of middle life. Randolph is about forty, isn't he? I've seen a num-

ber of such cases, since the realization often produces symptoms which require psychotherapeutic treatment—psychosomatic illness, insomnia, claustrophobia, to mention only a few.
Randolph's reactive symptoms are new to me; but they have a
dreadful logic of their own. He fears, not only the dark, but the
ultimate darkness. He is afraid of dying."

"And that's why he turned to Satanism," Michael muttered.
"Those conversations we had about good and evil . . . He
doesn't believe in God, but he can't accept the inevitability of
death. There's only one other dispenser of immortality. 'Better
to reign in Hell than serve in Heaven.' "

"Especially if you don't believe in Heaven," Galen said. "I
hope you're enjoying your abstract intellectualizing, Michael.
You may drown in it."

"What do you mean?"

"I took a calculated risk with Randolph. We've learned
some interesting and useful things about him, but we've also
stirred him up. He left here in a frenzy of rage and fear."

"You mean—he'll try something else?"

"Almost immediately, I should say."

Slowly, the two pairs of eyes turned to focus on Linda.

## III

"No," she said. "No, he wouldn't dare. He was frightened. "I've
never seen him so upset."

"That's precisely the danger. A man of his temperament
doesn't back down under a challenge. He'll be all the more eager to strike before, as he thinks, I have time to conjure up all
my powers."

"God damn your arrogant soul," Michael said softly. "You
deliberately, cold-bloodedly, stirred up that rattlesnake, knowing he can—"

"It had to be done." Galen's seldom-aroused temper showed
in his flushed cheeks. "Oh, hell . . . I ought to know better. One
of the basic rules of this trade is not to meddle with your
friends' problems. . . . Tell him, Linda."

"Michael, he's right. How long could we go on, with this
hanging over us? Watching each other out of the corners of our
eyes, afraid to sleep. . . . Twice I've tried to kill someone," she

said, feeling Galen's silent commendation like a rock at her back. "If I have to go on dreading that, I'd rather be dead. Gordon is off balance, for the first time since I've known him. We've got to keep him on the defensive."

"How?" Michael demanded.

"Don't look at me," Galen snapped.

"He's afraid of dying," Michael said. "Why?"

"Give me five years of analysis and maybe I can tell you," Galen said. "What the hell do you think I am, a mind reader?"

Linda wrapped both arms around her body, but their limited animal warmth did not touch the chill that froze her mind.

"You both know," she said, shaping the words with difficulty because her lips were stiff with that inner cold. "You know what we have to do. Force the issue, keep him off balance. We'll have to follow him."

"Where?" Michael's voice sounded as stiff and difficult as hers.

"Back home, of course. Back to the house. Galen's absolutely right, he'll be wild with an-ger, he won't be able to wait; he'll try something tonight. And all his—his materials are back there."

"Doesn't he have a place here in town?" It was Galen who spoke; Michael was visibly struggling with conflicting emotions.

"A small apartment. He couldn't keep anything concealed there."

"Especially a large black dog," Galen murmured.

Michael, who had arranged a truce in his internal civil war, nodded thoughtfully. Having scaled one barrier, Linda faced the next.

"Doctor. I don't—I don't want to say this, but I must, I can't keep anything back now. Your theory appeals to me a great deal. If Gordon is a conscious villain, that makes me innocent, not only of intent to harm, but of serious mental instability. I'd like—oh, how I'd like!—to believe it. *But I don't.*"

Galen nodded. She knew that she had told him nothing he hadn't suspected, but that he was relieved by her candor. He turned to the other man.

"How about you, Michael?"

"I don't know. I just don't know."

"It doesn't matter." Galen got to his feet, rather heavily; for the first time Linda was conscious of his real age. "We'll go after Randolph. I have a few business matters to arrange before we leave, though. You two had better have some food. I ate on the plane."

Michael shook his head.

"I have some matters to arrange too. Can I borrow your car?"

"What for?"

"Never mind, then. I'll take a taxi."

"I'm incurably nosy," Galen said mildly. "Here, take the keys."

Michael caught the bright jingle out of the air with one hand. He looked at Linda with an expression that she was to remember, often, in the next hours. Then he turned on his heel and was gone.

# Chapter

## 12

BY THE TIME MICHAEL RETURNED WITH THE CAR, THE OTHER two were ready and waiting. The night had turned clear and chilly; Linda was wrapped in a huge cloak, which the doctor had mysteriously produced from some vast storehouse of improbable needs. Galen wore no coat, and his silvery head was bare. He carried a small flat case, like a briefcase.

As soon as the car stopped, Galen led Linda down the steps. He opened the back door of the car.

"You drive," he said to Michael, who was brooding over the wheel. "We'll sit in back where—For God's sake!"

Linda flexed her muscles just in time. From under her skirts came a wail of protest, and she reached down and lifted a dangling, muttering bundle of fur.

"Why the hell?" Galen demanded, slamming the car door.

His haste was unnecessary; Napoleon had no intention of going anywhere. He subsided onto Linda's lap and looked abused.

"He likes to ride in cars. Besides," Michael said, in a voice that ended Galen's objections, "I have a feeling he might be useful."

Fondling the scarred ears, Linda did not look up.

"The canary in the coal mine," she said. "Michael, I wish you hadn't."

"If he goes berserk, he can wreck the damned car," Galen said. "Haven't you got a carrying case for him?"

"On the floor," Michael said briefly, and put the car into gear.

They made good time; the streets were emptying. Staring out through the closed windows, Linda remembered that other, recent night drive. Night and darkness, the recurring motifs; there had been sunshine, once, but she could hardly remember that such a phenomenon existed. She was tired, so tired; not only in body but in every cell of brain and nerve. Desire for the endless sleep of death was comprehensible to her now; perhaps, she thought, it was not grief or despair that prompted suicide, but only sheer exhaustion.

Her eyes fixed unseeingly on the flashing, multicolored lights of the city, Linda knew that that was the solution none of them would admit. Sick or sane, right or wrong, she was not normal, and perhaps she never would be. While she lived, Michael would not abandon her—and neither would Gordon. Even if Gordon were defeated, Michael would be stuck with her and her inability to love; he was a stubborn man, he would keep on trying even though it was hopeless. But without her, Gordon would have no reason to attack Michael. He would be safe; and she could rest.

Dreamily and without interest, she wondered whether this black mood was Gordon's latest move. She didn't think so. It was far too pleasant a feeling to have emanated from Gordon's mind. And so reasonable . . .

In the warm, smothering shadow of the idea of death, two small, dissenting sparks burned. One was Michael—not desire, not even hope, just the thought of him. The other, absurdly, came from the scrubby patch of fur in which her fingers were entwined.

Napoleon stirred restlessly under her tightening hands, but she didn't let go. A mangy lifeline, that was what he was. A fighter. Battered and scarred and bloody, he had never thought pensively of the sweet sleep of death. Swaggering like Cyrano, his tail a scrawny panache, he took on all comers for the sheer glory of the fray: "Give me giants!"

The lights had disappeared now, except for isolated lighted windows. Linda recognized the terrain. Another hour . . . Even that thought could not rouse her from the drowsiness which numbed her limbs. Normal weariness—or the dangerous false sleep of Gordon's inducing? She could not tell, nor could she fight it. The solid, silent bulk of the man beside her gave her failing courage a slight lift, but even that faded out as the darkness closed in around her.

## II

Absorbed in his driving and in the hagridden thoughts that made every effort doubly difficult, Michael had no warning. He didn't realize what was happening until he heard the sudden flurry of movement from the back seat, and the animal screams, and Galen's voice, sharp in command:

"Pull over! Quick!"

Michael jerked the car to a stop, half on and half off the road. He turned.

On the back seat, Galen's briefcase gaped open. Galen, kneeling on a heaving dark cylinder that sprawled half on the seat and half on the floor, held a hypodermic high, checking it. He must have had it ready and waiting, in that convenient case. . . .

Before Michael could move, Galen plunged the needle home in a reckless disregard of antisepsis. Hampered by the muffling folds of the cloak, Linda went limp as the drug took hold. Then Michael heard the sound that was coming from the floor of the front seat. Napoleon, inflated to twice his normal size, had removed himself as far as possible from what was happening in the back. Once before, Michael had heard him make a noise like that.

Galen looked up, his face a white oval in the shadows.

"Get that cat," he said briefly, and reached down to tug at something on the floor, pinned by Linda's legs.

Napoleon erupted into hysteria when Michael tried to hand him into the back; and Galen, cursing in four languages, heaved the cat's carrying case into the front seat. Between them they got the frantic animal into the case and his cries stopped.

Nursing a bleeding hand, Galen spoke again.

"If a patrol car spots us, we're in trouble. Find a parking lot or a side street."

Michael obeyed. His own hands were scratched and painful. It seemed like hours before he found a place to park— a driveway leading to a private house, whose dark shape was hidden by trees. The muffled sounds from the back were driving him frantic. Almost as bad was the deadly silence from Napoleon's box.

He switched off lights and engine and made sure the doors were locked before he turned. Galen had propped Linda up in a corner of the seat. He was checking her pulse and respiration.

"How is—"

"She's okay. Physically. I was careful with the dosage."

"You expected this."

"For God's sake—didn't you? It was as predictable as sunrise."

"I'm sorry. I'm not thinking very clearly."

*"You* aren't?" Galen's voice was bitter. "For the last hours everything I've done has been in direct opposition to every medical ethic I've ever held. If I'm not caught in the act, and drummed out of the profession, I'll probably shoot myself in sheer self-loathing. . . . That reminds me. Hand it over."

"What?"

Galen snapped his fingers impatiently.

"You know what. The 'business matter' you had to arrange before we left. Give it to me, Michael. . . . Thanks. Do you have a permit for this?"

"I do. If it matters."

"Probably not. What's a permit more or less?"

"Give it back to me, Galen. You've risked enough already."

"No, thank you. If any shooting needs to be done, I'll do it."

There was a moment of silence. Then Michael said, "I brought it for the dog."

"And that's not a bad idea," Galen admitted. "If the animal has been trained as an attack dog, it may take a bullet to stop it. No, Michael, I will keep the gun. I commend your intentions, but I cannot trust your judgment. Not in this case."

"Why?" Michael asked suddenly. "Why are you doing this? Risking your reputation, perhaps your freedom—"

"Arrogance. I think so highly of my own judgment, I even follow my hunches."

"You came," Michael said, "because you knew I'd do this anyhow, with you or without you. And because I—hit below the belt with a reference to your personal tragedies. What makes my remark so inexcusable is that I didn't give a damn about that aspect of Randolph; I just wanted to get you mad enough so you'd help us."

"Forget it," Galen said brusquely. "I don't know why I'm here myself; at the moment I couldn't analyze an arithmetic problem. Get on, Michael. Randolph must be home by now; we're over an hour behind him."

"What are we going to do when we get there?"

"I'll be looking up my horoscope for today while you drive."

"What about Linda?"

"She should be waking up by the time we arrive."

"I meant as a source of information."

Galen stared at him; Michael saw the faint glimmer of his eyes in the starlight.

"You have got a few brain cells working after all. It wasn't scopalamine I gave her, you know. However, she is in an extremely suggestible state, if Randolph has been working on her. . . . Oh, hell. Drive, will you? I'll see what I can do."

After twenty interminable minutes, while Michael drove like an automaton, Galen leaned forward to report.

"No dice. I'll try again when she starts to come out of it."

The night had sunk into its deadest hours by the time they arrived. Passing the now familiar landmarks, Michael recognized the entrance to the unpaved lane that led to Andrea's house. Darkness and silence, now, along its length . . . He wondered where, and how, the old woman had been buried, and who had come to mourn her. Poor old witch—another victim of Gordon's insane urge for human souls, or the victim of her own—what had Galen called it?—thanatomania. The ability to induce death by suggestion alone. Mental aberration, or genuine curse, it didn't matter. Linda had it too.

The ornate gates that marked the entrance to the Randolph estate stood open. Michael brought the car to a stop just inside, switching off the lights. The house was invisible from this spot, and he doubted that anyone could have heard the car. Unless someone had been watching for it . . .

Linda was awake. For several minutes now he had heard the mumble of voices from the back seat. With the engine no longer running, he was able to make out the words.

"What the hell are you doing?" he demanded.

"Shut up," Galen said. "All right, Linda, you believe me, don't you? Say you do."

"I believe you."

Her voice was slurred and drowsy.

"Tell me again."

"I can't hurt you," Linda said obediently. "I can't hurt Michael. I don't want to hurt anyone. No one is going to hurt me. . . ."

"And you aren't afraid."

"I'm not afraid," said the soft doll's voice. The hairs on Michael's neck lifted.

"You," said Galen, turning on him with a cold savagery that made him flinch, "are going to keep quiet. You will not speak unless I tell you to, or move unless I tell you to. Understand?"

"Yes, master. . . . What did you do, hypnotize her?"

"No," Galen said, in a peculiar voice. "I didn't. Just keep your mouth shut and come along. We must get into the house. Linda, you have a key?"

"Yes."

"Where is it?"

"In my pocket."

"Get it out."

The way she moved made Michael feel cold. Her gestures were competent, without fumbling or hesitation, but they lacked all her normal grace. He followed the stiff, mechanical figure up the driveway, and he let Galen take her arm; he had the feeling that it would have had the solidity and coldness of wood under his fingers.

After some probing—she only answered direct questions, and those absolutely literally—Galen had got her to produce a back-door key, and lead them to that entrance.

The servants' rooms were on the upper floors, so there was no danger from them; but the kitchen entrance was the length of the house from their ultimate destination. That couldn't be helped; Linda had no key to the other doors, and to climb the twisting stairs around the tower would give those within warning of their approach.

Michael could see the light in the tower window; it shone like a sleepless eye on the topmost floor, the window of Briggs's study. His sleeping quarters were on the floor below; the secretary was the only inhabitant of this part of the house, which was out of bounds to the servants. Briggs did his own cleaning. Linda herself had not been in the tower since the man moved in.

Galen elicited this information while they stood shivering in the shadows outside the house. He had already made it plain that he wanted no conversation after they entered. A slim sliver of moon had risen, and its rays were enough to show Michael the tension of Galen's body and the waxlike calm of Linda's face. Her face, and her soft, docile voice, gripped him with a pain as sharp as an actual wound. How much more could she stand? He had read some of the literature of witchcraft, and he had seen Gordon's livid face; he had an excellent idea of what they might discover in the tower room. The sacrifice, the shrouded altar, drugs and incense . . . A sight like that might break her mind completely.

"It's not too late to turn back," he said, turning to Galen.

"It is too late."

"We're guilty of breaking and entering. . . ."

"Don't be melodramatic. Mrs. Randolph is the mistress of the house. She has every legal right to go where she chooses, and to invite her friends to accompany her."

The shrubbery rustled as they crossed the wide lawn, silver-washed by moonlight. On such a pale expanse an object would be clearly visible; but the absence of any seen threat did not calm Michael's nerves. He was half hoping that the dog would come. It was better to know where it was than to imagine it, lurking unseen.

Somewhere, back on a tree near the gate, a petrified cat squatted on a branch. It had been Galen's suggestion that they free Napoleon; he had not needed to give his reasons. Gordon's malice might extend to any creature Michael was fond of, and the cat had a better chance, free, against danger. As Michael extracted the limp, unprotesting body from the carrying case, he recognized the symptoms. Only one thing roused Napoleon to his former fury, and that was when Michael inadvertently brought him near Linda—one of the few people for whom he had displayed a tolerance verging on affection. Michael had to lift him up into the lower branches of the tree, and as he turned away he saw Napoleon squatting there, motionless, looking like the Cheshire cat, even to the twisted snarl of his teeth. There was a certain element of the gruesome in *Alice,* come to think of it. . . .

They made their way through the darkened kitchen, with its vagrant gleams of chrome, and down the hallways. Wide double doors admitted them to a part of the house Michael had never seen. At the end of a long corridor, flanked by closed doors on either side, the tower steps led up. One window gave a scant light—a narrow, mullioned window half obscured by tendrils of ivy through which the moonlight slid in surreptitious trickles, casting more shadows than it relieved.

Linda stopped. It was so dark Michael could not see her face. Not until he put a steadying hand on her shoulder did he realize that she was shaking from head to foot.

His hand was struck down.

"Don't touch her," Galen hissed in his ear. "Linda. Go on. Up the stairs."

Michael didn't need to touch her to feel her resistance. It was a painful thing to witness, for the struggle was mute and confined. Galen's command broke her will instead of calming it. She shivered violently, and went on.

They were almost at the top of the stairs before Michael heard the sound. Its faintness made it worse, for it seemed to come from the inner chambers of his brain instead of an outside source.

Michael half recognized it, and wondered why his mind should reject the attempt at identification so violently. A picture formed in his mind, to match the sound: a high-vaulted place, great expanses of marbled flooring, adorned with columns . . . the walls a blend of colors and shapes . . . and the high, pure, sexless voices filling the echoing heights of the . . .

"God!" he said, involuntarily, and heard Galen's hand thrust heavily against the panels of the door.

The entire picture came at him in a single vast blasphemy; it was much later before he could isolate the details, and by that time he was already trying to forget them. Lights all around the room, burning with the clear softness of wax. Lights on the black-draped, tablelike object at the far side of the circular chamber. Black candles. Black hangings, draping walls and ceiling. Briggs stood before the altar; and as Michael's mind had denied the parody of the ritual music, it rejected the obscene caricature of priestly vestments that adorned Briggs's fat body and set off the pallor of the pale, epicene face. The reek of incense he had expected was present; some of it came from the golden censer in Briggs's hand. It was mixed with another smell. Michael averted his eyes from the thing that lay, mercifully motionless now, on the table.

Even Galen was struck dumb and motionless; and while the two men stood frozen, Linda moved past them, out into the room. Michael made a futile grab at her. Before he could move again, Briggs spoke.

"Gentlemen," he said, "pray don't be hasty."

He had a gun. Michael repeated the words incredulously to himself. Proud Satan's aide, allied with the powers of Hell— Briggs had a gun. A pretty little pearl-handled job, which he held as demurely as a woman might fondle a flower. It seemed innocuous after the things Michael had imagined.

It was enough to stop him, though, even without the restraint of Galen's outflung arm.

"Linda," he said helplessly, knowing he could not reach her.

She had advanced into the center of the room. The hood of the cloak had fallen back over her shoulders, and her hair streamed down around her face. It had the pure pallor of a saint's image as she stopped, facing the man who stood in the middle of an elaborately figured, colored carpet. Behind him the black draperies billowed, and Michael realized there must be a window there, or a door, leading to the outside stairs.

Unlike his coactor, Gordon was not in costume. He had discarded coat and tie; his shirt was open at the throat and his sleeves were rolled up. Hands and bare forearms were splashed with drying stains. His handsome, tanned face was calm. Michael was struck with a realization of the man's power— physical strength and beauty, combined with enormous will, and with another quality that Michael had not recognized until he saw the slender, submissive figure of Gordon's wife facing him with bowed head. A surge of hate rose up and nearly choked him. He would have moved then, forgetting the gun, if Galen's arm had not barred his way.

"You'd better come in and close the door," Gordon said calmly. "There. That's far enough."

He lifted both hands in a convoluted, ritual gesture.

He believes it, Michael thought. He really believes he can stop us, like that. . . . Glancing at Briggs, he felt sure that the secretary had no such faith. His narrowed eyes were as cynical as his gun. He was leaning back against the table; the plump pink feet and calves were bare.

"Briggs," Galen said. "Don't be a fool. So far you're guilty of nothing the law can touch you for. You can't possibly expect to get away with murder. Put down the gun."

"Gun?" Gordon seemed to see the weapon for the first time. His face twisted with annoyance. "Come, now, Briggs, you know we don't need that. I can hold them."

Galen ignored him. ·

"I'm a doctor, Briggs. This man is psychotic, and very dangerous. If you cooperate with us, I'll see that you get away scot-free."

For a second Michael thought it was going to work. The fat man's eyes narrowed until they almost disappeared. Briggs was perfectly sane, in the usual sense of the word; his faith in his dark master was almost all sham. Michael could see him weighing the advantages: Gordon's money and influence, the satisfaction of the various lusts of the flesh to which Gordon's patronage gave him access, against—what? Freedom and immunity? Freedom to return to the cold, hostile outer world and abandon his nice soft nest.

"Briggs," Gordon said impatiently. "Put away that silly toy and go on with the ceremony. Our audience has arrived. I want them to see everything."

"Yes, master," Briggs said quickly. "But—can you keep your control of them, and give your mind and heart to the offering?"

"I have bound them in the web of darkness. There they will stand until they rot, unless my will releases them."

Michael was dangerously close to jumping the main actor. Briggs's ridiculous gun had destroyed the aura of superstitious terror that had hitherto shielded Gordon; he saw the man for what he was, half mad, wholly evil. He felt light-headed with relief at the removal of that greatest fear, and was inclined to dismiss the menace of the weapon. A little thing like that, in Briggs's pudgy, womanish hand—hell, he probably couldn't hit a barn door at ten paces. Two things kept him in his place. One was his promise to Galen, silent at his side. The other was the sight of Gordon's big-muscled hands, so close to Linda. He could snap her neck with one twist of those brown hands. And he was capable of doing it, if his fantasy world was destroyed.

Michael heard a controlled, barely audible intake of breath from the man beside him. Galen's first attempt had failed. Briggs's weapon enforced, and reinforced, Gordon's madness, and Briggs was now committed. In seeming obedience he had stepped back behind the makeshift altar, his hands outstretched over it; but the wide sleeves of his robe, and the spacing of the candles, left those hands in shadow, and Michael had no doubt of what they still held.

Galen knew the danger as well as he did, or better. But his friend's next move took Michael completely by surprise.

"I am bound in the web of darkness," Galen said suddenly. "But not forever. I call upon the Masters of the Great College to come to me."

Hands lifted, he spat out a string of strange syllables, rich in gutturals. Michael wondered what half-forgotten adolescent lesson he was using; but he forgot that when he saw the impact of the words on the other listeners. Linda's body jerked violently, as if something had struck her. Gordon went pale. He fell back a step, and after a moment his voice rose up, clashing with the other voice in an equally unintelligible chant.

Galen, rock-still in his place, waved his hands and switched to Latin.

His attention fixed on the combatants, Michael did not see what, if anything, Briggs was doing; later, he had to admit that Briggs might have thrown some new chemical into the smoldering bowls on the altar. But he felt the change in the air; it smelled like the acrid stench of burning flesh, and it made his head spin.

Backing away, step by dragging step, Gordon resembled a fighter reeling under the blows of invisible fists. His face was no longer pale; it was dark with fury, and swollen out of recognizable shape. The words still poured from his distorted mouth; and Michael imagined, insanely, that he could see them take shape in the air and strike back, against the shapes of Galen's incantation.

Galen had gone back to Hebrew, having exhausted his stock of appropriate Latin and Greek. Alone in the center of the room, Linda swayed back and forth, eyes glassy. Michael had forgotten his desire to go to her; he was only half aware of a pudgy, dark form, creeping at them from the direction of the altar.

Gordon was back now within a few feet of the shrouded

window, his hands writhing, his face unrecognizable. Then Galen's breath failed; and in the split-second lull, Gordon's voice rose to a howl. The curtains behind him bellied out as if in a sudden gust of wind; the nearby candles flickered and went out. The black draperies wrapped Gordon around like enormous sable wings. Within their shelter he swayed, staggered, and dropped to his hands and knees.

Galen's voice faltered and went on; Gordon's answered. The droning beat of the two voices, the evil stench in the air—untouched by the chill blast of wind—the effect of shadows and the movement of the shaken draperies . . . All these, and other, equally explicable factors, might have explained what Michael saw. The shape of Gordon Randolph—on hands and knees, four-footed like a beast, dark head lowered—blurred and shifted. When the outlines coalesced, they were no longer those of a man.

He was not the only one to see it. Linda screamed and covered her face with both hands. Michael moved, without plan, his only motive the need to get between Linda and the thing that paced slowly down the length of the floor toward her.

What Briggs saw, or thought he saw, they would never know for certain. Michael heard the gun go off, at close range; the entire magazine let loose in one undirected, hysterical burst. The bullets had no visible effect on the dog. It came on, with the unnatural slowness of nightmare, its padded feet making no sound on the carpet. Michael saw something fat and black in his way; he removed it with one sweep of his hand and then caught Linda in his arms, turning, holding her head against his chest so that she could not see.

Another shot and another . . . or was it the blood pounding in his ears? The room had gone dark—or was it because his eyes were closed? There was only one sense left to him, but it was enough—the feel of the warm, living body in his arms, and its response.

Galen had to shake him, hard, before he opened his eyes. The older man's pallor was so pronounced that he looked bleached—hair, face, eyes.

"It's all right," Galen said. He laughed, shortly and humorlessly. "What a description . . ."

"You got it?" Michael asked.

"Got it? What?"

"The dog . . . Don't, I don't want her to see." He stiffened, trying to shield Linda as Galen's impersonal hand caught her chin and forced her face up.

"She's all right, too," Galen said. "I'm sorry, Linda; you're entitled to a nice long bout of hysterics, but not just yet and certainly not here. The servants must have been wakened by that cannonade. We must leave before someone comes."

"I don't want her to see . . ." Michael repeated, with idiot persistence.

"She had better see it." Galen turned them both, and Michael saw the sprawled body of Gordon Randolph. The white shirt was no longer white. The face was as blank as a wax dummy's.

"Dead," Galen said. "Like any other mortal creature."

Michael felt Linda shiver, and lifted her into his arms as he heard the first tentative rap on the door.

"It's locked," Galen said softly. "But we'd better get going. Down the outside staircase."

When they got to the car, Michael was somehow not surprised to see a familiar shape sitting on the roof. Galen grabbed Napoleon, who came without protest. They were back on the main highway before anyone spoke.

"Put about ten miles behind us and then find a place to stop," Galen ordered. "I'm going to put Linda to sleep. And you aren't fit to drive far."

Michael nodded. He knew, better than Galen possibly could, how unfit he was. When Galen told him to pull over, he was glad to change places with the other man. Linda was already half asleep. She looked so fragile that Michael was almost afraid to touch her. She opened her eyes and gave him a wavering smile.

". . . Love you. . . ." she whispered, and drifted off.

"I wonder," Galen said, after a time.

"Wonder what? Whether she loves me?"

"Oh, that. No, I think you'll make out all right there. You're her hero, aren't you? Fighting the powers of darkness for her soul . . . What are lions compared to that?"

The familiar sardonic tones woke Michael completely. He leaned forward, arms folded on the back of the seat.

"What did you see, Galen?"

"At the end?" Galen slowed for a blinking stop light, and

then picked up speed. "The original delusion of lycanthropy was Randolph's, as I suspected. He reverted completely."

"I saw him change," Michael said quietly. "I saw the dog. How do you define a hallucination, Galen? If three people out of four see one thing, and the fourth sees something else—which of them is hallucinating?"

Galen's silence was eloquent—of what, Michael wasn't sure.

"How do you know Briggs saw a dog?" he asked finally.

"What was he shooting at, his beloved employer?"

"He flipped," Galen said shortly.

"I admire your technical vocabulary. Where did he go, by the way?"

"Out and down. I didn't think the little swine could move that fast. . . . It's possible that he was aiming at you. When the gun was empty, he made a dash for it, and I can tell you I didn't try to stop him."

"And then you walked out on a murder. In view of your haste to leave, I gather you don't intend to inform the police that we were there."

"No."

"Why not, Galen?"

"There is no purpose to be served by such an act. Briggs killed his employer during one of their insane rites. If the police wish to question Mrs. Randolph, she has been with me. No problems."

"What a nice bloody liar you are," Michael said admiringly. "It all spells Merry Christmas, doesn't it? Satisfies you completely?"

"I've explained everything."

"Yes, you have. Galen—what did you see? Honestly?"

There was a pause. Finally Galen said,

"Drop it, Michael."

"But if you—"

"Drop it, I said." Eyes steady on the road, Galen drove on. "I saw what I wanted to see. Collective hallucination is a catchword, but it satisfies me. I don't want any glimpses of the dark on the other side."

"Only one problem," Michael said.

"What's that?"

"They'll do an autopsy, of course. On Randolph's body."

"Naturally."

"Which gun fired the shot that killed him, Galen?"

Galen didn't answer immediately. When he did, it was not in words. Michael took the object that was passed to him. To his overheated imagination, the barrel still felt warm.

"Are you sure?"

"Not of which shot killed him, no. I fired at Briggs. He was spraying bullets around like a machine gun, and I thought he was aiming at you. But people were moving pretty fast."

"They'll be able to tell, if it was a bullet from this gun."

"They won't find either gun. Briggs took his with him, and if he has a grain of sense he'll destroy it."

"And this one?"

"I've got to go back to Europe next week."

"Some convenient lake in France, or a ditch in Holland . . . Nice."

"What do you suggest I do, hand it over to the police?"

"Don't lose your temper. I'll never be able to thank you for what you've done tonight. . . . Maybe I shouldn't tell you."

"Tell me what?"

"It was a bullet from this gun that killed Randolph."

"That wouldn't keep me awake nights," Galen said icily. "But how do you know?"

"There was only one bullet in it."

"So?"

Michael put his head down on his arms. His bad arm ached and he was sick with exhaustion. But tonight he would sleep without fear, or remorse.

"It was a silver bullet."

# Prince of Darkness

# PROLOGUE
## *Meet*

THE TEASHOP WAS LOCATED ON ONE OF THE DINGY DISCOUR-aged streets on the wrong side of the Thames, not far from Waterloo. Its interior appearance matched the neighborhood. Torn plastic mats failed to conceal the streaked grease on the table-tops, and the floor was strewn with the crumbs of a thousand vanished biscuits. The afternoon sun of September fought its way in through windows begrimed with dust.

It was early in the day for the peculiar meal which only the British could have invented; the hour, and the unprepossessing atmosphere of the shop, perhaps explained why there were only three people in the place: two customers, at a back table, and a drowsy-looking waitress, whose teased blond hairdo was pressed up against the transistor radio which filled the room with the jerky rhythms of modern dance.

The two men who sat hunched over untouched cups of a suspicious-looking dark-brown liquid were in complete har-mony with their surroundings. The elder of the two was a tiny man, wizened and bent like a gnome. His sharp nose would one day meet his pointed chin, if the teeth in between abandoned their posts. His eyes were small and close set, and heavily shut-tered, not only by drooping lids, but by a kind of opacity; the thoughts that burgeoned inside the domed head, sparsely cov-ered by graying hair, would never be read through those win-dows. He wore a chartreuse-and-burgundy tweed jacket and a cap of the sort that is associated with gentlemen who frequent the race tracks. His hands were small and delicately shaped.

The younger man's most conspicuous feature was a head of thick flaxen hair which hung in ragged locks over his ears and brushed the back of his collar. The collar was frayed; the suit jacket was shiny with age and seemed not to have been constructed for its present owner. Though slightly built, the man was too thin even for his normal bone structure. His skin had the distinctive grayish pallor which innocent observers might have interpreted as the result of long illness, or—more accurately—long confinement away from the sun. There were good bones under the tight-drawn skin of his face, but his features were marred by their expression. The blue eyes were set too deeply in their sockets, the mouth was too tight, the jaw heavy and arrogant. Like his face, his hands bore the signs of his recent activities; long-fingered and slender, they were heavily calloused, with broken nails and ragged cuticles.

He picked up his teacup clumsily, as if he were not accustomed to handling anything so comparatively fragile as the thick white china, took a sip, and grimaced.

"No wonder so many people are emigrating."

"Sure, and it wasn't for the beverage that a good Irishman like meself would suggest meeting here."

"Irishman, hell. You haven't seen Dublin for fifty years. And do drop the phony accent, can't you?"

"Limerick," said the older man equably. "And be damned to you. Seems to me you've picked up a bit of an American twang yourself."

"My late—er—roommate was an American."

"And what would he be doin' so far from home, I wonder?" cooed the older man. He met his companion's cold stare and bared his teeth in a grin. "Allow me me little eccentricities, lad. So long as I do the job you've no ground for complaint."

"I'll give you that much," the younger man said grudgingly. "You're the best in the business. That's why I got in touch with you."

"That and old friendship, eh?" The older man grinned more broadly, and his companion responded with a slightly upward curve of the corners of his mouth. It could hardly have been called a smile, but it was evidently the closest approximation he could manage to that expression, and the slight relaxation of his taut shoulders indicated that his mood was improving.

"Hardly friendship," he said. "You seem to have flourished

since those days, Sam. You're looking older and more wicked than ever."

"I can't say the same for you. How long is it you've been . . ."

"Back?" The younger man supplied gently. "Six days."

"Six, is it? You wired me four days ago."

"Yes."

"In a hurry, weren't you?"

"Yes."

Sam sucked his lower lip. He gave his companion a sidelong glance.

"And what have you been doin' with yerself since then?"

"This and that."

"You've not spent your time in Savile Row, that's for certain," Sam said, with a glance at his companion's shabby suit. He gave his own lapel a complacent tug. "Nor at your barber."

"What's that supposed to mean?"

"Why should it mean anything, then?"

His companion gave him another grudging smile.

"Everything you say means something, you old devil. Are you suggesting I get my hair cut, or the reverse?"

"Ah, it's a sad world when a man can't make a casual remark without starting nasty suspicions." Absently Sam took a sip of tea, choked theatrically, and settled back. "The reverse. You're right up with the current fashions. Why don't you grow a beard?"

"No beard. All right, Sam, let's have it."

Sam sighed profoundly.

"You didn't give me much time, you know."

"You never need much time."

"In this case I didn't. Most of it's public knowledge." Sam sat up straighter. When he spoke, his accents were unaffected, average American.

"Name of Katharine More. Dr. More. It used to be Moretszki, in case you didn't know."

"She changed it?"

"Not she. She's got a towering pride, but not of that variety. The grandfather changed the name when he came from Russia in the eighteen eighties. He proceeded to do two impressive deeds: make a fortune in real estate and engender twelve children. The lady you've inquired about is the daughter of the second son, Carl. By one of those odd quirks of fate which occur in the best of families, she is the only surviving descendant of that prolific old gent."

"Which makes her the surviving heir to the prolific old gent's money."

"Precisely." Sam shot a keen glance through scanty lashes at the other man's face; it was impassive as stone. He continued.

"The money went, in actual fact, to the eldest son, Stephan. He had a stepdaughter, child of his wife's first marriage, but no offspring of his own. So the money went to Kate."

"Kate? Not Shakespearean, I hope."

"I think of her that way," Sam said, with hideous sentimentality. His companion winced perceptibly. Sam smirked. "Indeed, but there are suggestions of the shrew. The lady is fairly young—late twenties—very rich, very intelligent—"

"Please." The younger man raised a peremptory hand. "Don't say very beautiful."

"Well." Sam masticated his lower lip thoughtfully. "That she isn't. Not that her face would stop a clock, mind, but she's the image of the lady professor, which is what she was. Everything but the horn-rimmed glasses. She has twenty-twenty vision."

"You would know that." The younger man sounded resigned. "Well, I've never believed in those films anyhow."

"Which films? Oh, I get you; the ones where the frigid old bag takes off the horn-rimmed specs in the last reel and turns out to be Sophia Loren. No such luck, my boy. But three or four million bucks should gild even a withered lily."

"You're a dirty-minded old man entirely," said his companion, in a vile imitation of a brogue. "Professor of what?"

"Assistant prof, to be precise. Of Sociology. Her field is folk-lore and superstition, ethnic survivals in isolated communities, et cetera. She's written one book, on superstition and witchcraft in America. It's been compared with Margaret Murray's work on the witchcraft problem, but is more highly regarded by the scholarly reviewers; traces the cult of—"

"Is there anything you don't know?" The younger man ran a hand through his shaggy hair.

"That's my business, me boy. Information."

"Well, you needn't give me a synopsis. I've read Murray's books, as it happens. She claims, I believe, that the witchcraft of the Middle Ages was the remnant of a prehistoric European religion which survived into late times. The horned god, fertility rites, and so on."

"That's right. Your girl friend has carried the idea one step further. She thinks the Old Religion still survives."

"Oh, it does, it does," the younger man murmured. "The powers of darkness are considerably stronger than the powers of good. What student of world affairs could doubt that? All right, Sam, let us not philosophize. Is the lady still professing? Or professoring?"

"No, she quit after she inherited her petty millions. Retired to the old family homestead."

"Which is where?"

"It's all in my report." Sam indicated the sheaf of papers which lay on the table between them. "Middleburg, Maryland, U.S.A. No, I'm not kidding. It's a misnomer, though; the town is an unusual place."

"Go on."

Sam settled back in his chair, comtemplated his tea balefully, and settled for a cigar. When it was lit he blew out a cloud of dark smoke that made his companion wrinkle a fastidious nose, and began his lecture.

"Middleburg is one of the oldest settlements in the States, goes back to the early seventeenth century and Lord Baltimore—you've heard of him? Religious freedom, Catholic English fleeing persecution, all that stuff. Well, so the town sat there, peacefully rotting, for three hundred years. About thirty years ago it was discovered by the overflow gentry from Baltimore and Washington. They thought it was quaint, and I guess it was; if you like quaintness. Now the place is transformed, but selectively. The idle rich bought up the old houses and restored them, and built big estates outside town. They've got a committee which supervises new construction; I hear you can't build a house in the area for under a hundred thousand, but that may be exaggerated. Slightly exaggerated.

"The citizens are an ungodly mixture. Along with the inbred descendants of the original boys and girls you'll find some of the bluest blood money can buy. The country club is so exclusive that the President—of the U.S., that is—was recently blackballed. It's huntin' country and drinkin' country. I don't know about merrie olde England, but in the States those two often coincide. How are you at riding? Horses, I mean."

"Fair."

"Oh, that English modesty," Sam said, beaming. "What about hunting? Riding to hounds, I believe it's called."

"I'm not awfully keen these days on hunting things," the younger man said. His tone was calm, even pleasant; but a shiver went up Sam's well-insulated backbone.

"Well, then," he said, studiously contemplating his stone-cold cup of tea, "we'll have to find some other way for you to ingratiate yourself. The lady doesn't hunt, in any case."

"Doesn't she?"

Sam looked up quickly, but his companion's face was as affable as it ever permitted itself to be.

"Want more tea?" he asked, more disturbed than he cared to admit.

"God forbid."

"All right, five more minutes and you can be on your way to wherever you're going, and I'll be on my way to—wherever I'm going. Where was I? Oh, yes, the town. If you want to know more about it, there've been articles in some of the glossier magazines. They like their privacy, in Middleburg—for a variety of reasons, probably—but they can't keep all the curious out, and it is a strange place, with the mixture of old and new. The old boy, Kate's Uncle Stephan, was one of the people who bridged the gap. He had the dough, and his mother was a daughter of one of the old families. A Device, no less. All right, shrug, but in Middleburg that means something. Uncle Stephan was a weirdo himself. Didn't marry till late in life, a widow with a child. He brought the kid up after his wife died, but never officially adopted her; that's why the dough went to Kate when he kicked the bucket. She's got the girl living with her now. They tell me she's quite a dish."

"Your slang is at least twenty years out of date. All right, you've given me a picture of the lady, and a damned unattractive one it is. What about her weaknesses?"

"Rumor says she hasn't any."

"Rumor. What about you?"

"A compliment, is it?" Sam grinned. "Praise from Caesar . . . I'll admit I've found a few weaknesses. For one, the doctor has gone off the deep end."

"Which one?"

"Well, you might call it lunatic-fringe scholarship, or just plain stupidity. She's come to believe in her own subject, or at the least she's doing some curious research."

"Sticking pins in waxen images?"

"She may be, for all I know. Spiritualism, at least; and not the usual psychic bit, holding hands around a table in the dark. 'Tis a cult of some kind, with false priests and rituals. She has meetings in her house."

"Charming. I used to dabble in magic myself, in my ill-spent youth."

"Well, that's a possible lead. If, indeed, it's winning the lady's confidence that you've got in mind. . . ." He paused, his odd opaque eyes wide in pretended innocence. His companion's face became, if possible, even blanker. Sam seemed to find in this the answer he expected; his voice had a hint of satisfaction as he continued.

"To the most popular and attractive weakness of the flesh the doctor seems to be impervious. Like all these brainy women, she despises men. However"—Sam lifted one dainty forefinger and wagged it in front of his companion's amused face—"there was one weak moment, about two years back. When she fell, she fell hard. The whole town knew about it; and, my God, how the old ladies' tongues wagged. Not that Middleburg isn't as susceptible as any town to the good old human habit of casual adultery. But middle-class Americans are a hypocritical lot; they like to have the game, but not the name. Hypocrisy is not one of the doc's weaknesses; in fact she seems to enjoy rubbing people's noses in unpopular facts. Naturally, they responded by hating her guts."

"Naturally."

"Well, that's irrelevant. What may help you is the fact— mark this—that the lucky fellow somewhat resembled you."

The younger man made a rude noise.

"Not the old double routine, Sam. That isn't done nowadays."

"No, no, nothing so unlikely. 'Tis said that every man has an exact duplicate of himself walking the world; but how many people d'you know who've actually met theirs? I was speaking of a general type. Slight build, fair hair and—this is important—an Englishman."

"Why important?"

Sam leaned back in the chair and assumed the position he favored for lecturing. The sunlight had deepened to bronze; in the back of the teashop shadows gathered.

"I suppose you're too young to know these things," he said tolerantly, ignoring his companion's raised eyebrow. "You see, me boy, women aren't logical. Vessels of pure emotion they are, poor darlings; and their emotions tend to get fixed on particular types. No doubt the Freudians could explain it all in terms of father images. Unlike ourselves, the ladies—bless 'em—are not so much impressed by the important physical features as by minor characteristics like hands, voice, hair color, and so on. And you needn't be lookin' at me with your eyebrows like that. A lady friend of mine explained it all to me, once upon a time."

"A lady friend of yours?" the younger man said incredulously.

"Yes, indeed." Unoffended, Sam smiled complacently. "Didn't I say that they were illogical little creatures? It was me hands that won her heart; me hands and the lovely shape of the back of me neck."

He rubbed the last-named feature fondly.

"How very poetic."

"Yes; I've me sentimental side, though few ever see it." Sam sighed deeply and then got back to business. "You'll see the implications. Mind, I'm not claiming the resemblance will bring the lady rushing to your arms; but you've a better chance of being well receved than if you were tall and dark and heavy-set."

"Puts me right in there with about half the men in the world," the younger man agreed sarcastically.

"A quarter," Sam said pedantically. "Tall and fair, tall and dark—"

"The redheads further confuse your categories. How many million fortunate males share my admirable characteristics, I wonder?"

"Don't forget the voice," Sam reminded him. "That's one of the things that gets them."

"Don't be vulgar. Two million instead of two billion, then."

"Well, if you want to pick flaws—"

"No, I think you've done splendidly. I shall sally forth to—what's its ghastly name?—Middleburg, and imitate a blond Englishman. I take it he wore his hair long?"

"You are the bright lad." Sam smiled sunnily.

"Too bright for my own good." His companion shoved back his chair and stood up, in a quick, abrupt movement that jarred the comatose waitress out of her dreams. "All right, Sam. I appreciate this," he added awkwardly. "Especially your seeing me personally."

"It was on me way." Sam pushed the sheaf of papers across the table. "Don't forget these. Are you just going to vanish into the Limbo, now, or will I be hearing from you?"

"Why should you be hearing from me?"

"Oh . . . sometimes these matters can't be handled by one person. If you should need any assistance . . ."

The younger man stood quite still, his hand resting lightly on the back of his chair; but his pose suggested that the slightest sound or movement might send him into flight.

"And what makes you think I'm up to anything that will require handling? Or assistance?"

Sam made a vulgar noise in the back of his throat.

"Come off it, me lad. I'll be back in about a week. You know how to reach me. The usual rates, of course," he added, with one of his unpleasant smiles.

"Of course."

There was a moment of silence, during which the two contemplated one another with expressions which were as different as they were mutually unreadable. Then the younger man said,

"Good luck, then. I expect you'll need it."

"I always do," Sam agreed calmly; and, as his companion turned, he added, "One more thing."

"What's that?"

"I neglected to mention it. The fellow you're . . . impersonating. The great lover."

"Well?"

"Well," Sam said pensively, "he's dead, you see."

# PART ONE
## *Huntsman*

# Chapter

## 1

MIDDLEBURG, MARYLAND, POSSESSED A POPULATION OF 9300 and one of the finest small airports one descending passenger had ever seen. For a place of its size it had a surprising amount of traffic. There were several daily shuttle flights to Washington and New York, and this plane, the Friday afternoon flight from Washington, had been nearly full.

The passenger in question, a slight, fair-haired man, was the last one off the plane. He stopped at the foot of the ramp and stared across the field, noting the number of private planes and hangars. The field was miniature, but equipped with all the latest gadgetry; it looked like a rich man's toy. The setting was equally perfect. Beyond the strips of concrete and the fences a gently rolling countryside had taken on the rich colors of autumn. The grain fields were stubble now, but much of the land was wooded; the gold of maples and the crimson of oak and sumac made vivid splashes of brightness against the somber green background of firs. A faint haze lay over the land, but the day was fine, almost too warm for October. The visitor reflected that this must be what the natives called Indian summer. He shrugged out of his coat, draped it over his arm, and started off across the field toward the terminal.

It was small, like the airport, and equally perfect; built of fieldstone and timber, it looked more like a private hunting lodge than a public building. The young man joined the group waiting at the luggage counter. Only a handful of the passengers had waited; most of them, carrying briefcases, had gone directly to waiting cars. Weekenders, evidently; and week-enders who could afford two separate wardrobes and homes.

The people waiting for luggage were of the same type, and the young man categorized them with the quick impatience which was one of his many failings. The Rich. Bureaucrats or businessmen or idlers, they were all alike: people with too much money and too much leisure, so that they spent large quantities of the former trying to occupy the latter.

He himself did not fit in with the crowd, though he had a chameleonlike instinct for protective coloring. The business he was presently engaged in required another type of costume. His suit—one of his own, recently retailored to fit his reduced mea-surements—was old but good. His tie was modest in design, but he wore it with a slightly stifled look, as if he were unused to even that moderate formality. By the standards of the over-forty generation he still needed a haircut. He had considered horn-rimmed glasses, and had abandoned them as being a bit too much, and also as too obviously fraudulent; his vision, like Katherine More's, was twenty-twenty. But the most important part of the disguise was attitude. He had thought himself into his role so thoroughly that when the man standing next to him spoke he came out of an artistic fog with a slight jerk.

"Stupid bastards get slower every week." The man, a stocky individual, had shoulders like a bull's and a belligerent, feet-wide-apart stance. His close-cropped gray hair failed to conceal a skull as hard and round as a cannonball, or soften features which looked like something an inexperienced sculptor had roughed out and then given up as a hopeless job.

"Hmmm? Oh. I haven't been waiting very long."

"Stranger here?" The older man sized him up with a long, appraising stare, and extended a brown hand. "Volz is my name. U.S. Army, retired."

"Peter Stewart. I'm a writer." He let the U.S. Army, retired, wring his hand, and produced a pained smile. "General, were you, sir?"

"How did you know?"

"The . . . general air," Peter murmured, and grinned mod-estly when the general gave a short brusque laugh that sounded like a dog barking.

"Very good. The writer's touch, eh? Have I read any of your books?"

"I very much doubt it."

Suitcases began rolling onto the rack and Volz, with an unexpurgated comment, darted forward. Peter followed more slowly. When he had retrieved his battered case he found the general still at his side.

"Going into town?"

"Yes. There are taxis, I suppose?"

"Probably taken by now. I'll give you a lift, if you like."

"That's very good of you." Peter spoke stiffly; then he reminded himself that he was being too suspicious. He knew the automatic if superficial friendliness of Americans. This loudmouthed idiot couldn't possibly know anything about him or his past—or his present intentions. He added more warmly, "I've booked a room at the Inn, but if that's out of your way—"

"No, no, got to go through town anyway. My place is on the other side. This way."

His car was just what Peter had expected: a black, shiny Lincoln with a uniformed chauffeur, who leaped out as his employer came stamping up. The chauffeur was black, six and a half feet tall, with a profile like that of the Apollo on the temple of Olympia. Even the flat crisp curls looked Greek.

Belatedly Peter tried to conceal his fascinated stare with an inane smile and a murmured greeting. The black statue responded with a stiff inclination of his head and no change of expression whatever. Chastened, Peter climbed into the back seat, and the door slammed smartly, just missing his heel.

On the way into town the general told four dirty jokes and a long tedious story about some minor skirmish during the Battle of the Bulge. Peter laughed immoderately at the jokes and made admiring noises during the anecdote. By the time they neared the outskirts of Middleburg, Volz had also extracted a major portion of Peter's biography. It was a good biography, and Peter was proud of it. He had spent two days composing it and another week gathering the documents which backed it up.

"Folklore," Volz repeated. "Thought you said you wrote fiction."

"Actually, I do write novels under another name."

"What name?"

"Ah." Peter shook his head, smiling. "That's a secret, I'm afraid."

"What?" Volz stared at him suspiciously, and Peter had to

remind himself that impertinent curiosity was a normal American trait. Then the general's face broadened in a smile which was more than impertinent; it was downright offensive. "Oh, that sort of novel. I'll bet I've read some of them at that."

Peter returned the smile, reflecting with some complacency on the advantages of the writer's trade as cover for even less wholesome activities. Anonymity was not only understandable, it was the norm; within twenty-four hours the whole town would be speculating on his pseudonyms and identifying him with everybody from Norman Mailer to Agatha Christie. He could deny all the rumors with perfect sincerity, and never be believed.

Volz abandoned the question of identity as they approached the town. He was now exhibiting another notorious American characteristic—pointing out uninteresting local sights to a visitor. The Foundling Home, the hospital, the Catholic Church— all new, handsome buildings, which suggested sizable private support. Peter made appropriate noises.

"The Club's down there," Volz said, indicating a drive flanked by impressive stone pillars. Peter just had time to catch the sign, which added an emphatic "Private Drive—Members Only" to the name of the country club.

"I don't suppose you ride," Volz said, with unconsicous contempt.

"I used to."

"You said you'd been sick, so I figured—"

"Exercise is what I need. Healthy outdoor life, and all that. So the doctor says."

"I suppose you'll be wanting a local doctor? We've got a good man. Paul Martin."

"So I've heard. Matter of fact, I've got a letter of introduction to him. From Sir George Macpherson."

He watched, out of the corner of his eye, and saw that the name had registered.

"The British Ambassador? You know him?"

"Not personally. Just the family." He dropped it there, knowing the error of elaborating a good lie.

Volz's stare was perceptibly more friendly.

"Great guy, Sir George. When he was out with the hunt last year, he was quite impressed with my stable. Are you a hunting man?"

"I have hunted."

"Give me a call if you'd like to join us one day."

"I'd like that. But I haven't been near a horse for several years; I might disgrace myself."

"Oh, well, come out to my place someday and try my horses. I've got a new hunter, name of Sultan; cost me a pretty penny, I can tell you. Like to see you on him."

Volz grinned wickedly, and Peter made a mental note to watch out for Sultan's tricks.

"When does your season begin?" he asked.

"October; we start earlier than you people, I'm told. We meet three times a week."

"I just might join you one day. If you're sure I won't be intruding."

"Any friend of Sir George's," Volz assured him. "You'll like the other members. Important people."

"Mmm." Peter wondered how he could ascertain the one point he was most interested in. To mention Katharine More by name would be too crude even for Volz. "I understand that Middleburg has an inordinate number of nationally prominent citizens."

"Sure does. An ex-governor, several Congressmen, some of the big banking families. All friends of mine. Not that I pick my friends for that. They're all . . . interesting people. Very interesting . . ."

Before Peter could pursue the subject, Volz changed it. He leaned forward, pointing.

"Here we are. Middleburg. Not much of it, but what there is, we like."

The outskirts of the town were unusual in that the common highway deformities—neon signs, gas stations, factories—were absent. The main street was narrow, and lined with old trees whose carefully tended branches met above in a multicolored arch. The houses were set in wide lawns, with shrubbery and ornamental trees. Massed beds of chrysanthemum and aster made patches of color, from white and gold to deeper bronze and a glowing crimson. Many of the homes were white-painted wood, their size and wide verandas dating them to an era when household help was cheap, and available. Judging from the superb condition of lawns and paint, Peter concluded that help was available, if not cheap.

"Main Street," Volz said. Peter suppressed a smile. "That's Jefferson Avenue over there, where Martin lives."

"It's an attractive town. Is it all as—prosperous as this section?"

"Yep. We're pretty proud of the place. Of course we have a few slums, like everybody else. Down by the creek is Shantytown, where the niggers live."

There was no glass partition between front seat and back. Peter glanced at the rigid back of the chauffeur and said blandly, "I'm surprised you folks haven't cleaned it up."

"You can't get trash like that to take any pride in their homes. Only way to clean the place up would be to run 'em out. And we need 'em. Servants."

"Of course."

The chauffeur's dark hand reached for the turn signal, and the car slowed. They turned left, past a white, steepled church, onto a street lined with shops. Peter frowned thoughtfully at the uniform facades, with their bow windows set in aged brick and their discreet little signs; then he remembered what the place reminded him of. Reconstructed . . . Williamsburg, was it? . . . a travel brochure, glanced at some years back, which advertised one of the restored Colonial towns of which Americans were so proud. Such places always had an air of selfconsciousness; they were not the result of slow natural growth, but of a planned effect, like a set for a film.

He caught a few of the signs, noting thankfully that there were no atrocities such as "Ye Olde Curiosity Shoppe," and then the car slid smoothly to a stop in front of a larger, more distinctive, building.

The sign read simply "Middleburg Inn," and the place looked as if it had been built as a tavern or hotel several centuries ago. A long wooden building, painted yellow, with black shutters and shingles, it had three floors, and a flat-roofed veranda, supported by black columns stretching along the length of the facade. The windows of the topmost floor were gabled. A pair of tall brick chimneys reared up from the far end; and on the left was a five-floored annex, built of the same yellow clapboard, but clearly of later date.

"Here we are," Volz said unnecessarily. "Give me a call, Stewart, about the hunt. Always happy to have a friend of Sir George's."

"Thanks for the ride." Peter accepted his suitcase from the stiffly correct chauffeur and stood watching as the car glided away. The two figures in front and back were as isolated from one another as if they had been on two different planets.

"Curious people," he said aloud, and headed for the registration desk.

His room was small and extremely Early American, with yards of flowered chintz draped here and there, and a quantity of maple furniture. The mattress was comfortable, though, and the small bathroom gleamed with gadgetry, including heated towel racks and glasses done up in paper, a custom which Peter had always considered evidence of a basically nasty mind. His eyebrows rose slightly at the rates quoted on the discreet card placed beside the telephone.

The air conditioner was going full blast. As soon as the bellboy had left, Peter turned it off and wrestled successfully with the window.

His room was in the annex, at the back; front rooms, of course, would be reserved for more important visitors. Peter had expected this, but had been prepared to find some fault with the room if necessary in order to get the location he wanted. This was quite satisfactory. Nothing faced onto the alley behind the hotel except the back doors of other business establishments; they would be closed and deserted after dark. By American standards it was a very clean alley. The trash cans were tightly lidded and placed off to one side to keep the center of the pavement free for traffic. High board fences lined both sides. And off to the right, not far from his window, was a fire escape. It was almost too perfect.

He took off his jacket, loosened his tie, and started to unpack. The domestic staff of the hotel was clearly well trained; everything was painfully neat. Even the drawers of bureau and desk had been relined with fresh white paper. That was how he knew that the singular object in the top left bureau drawer could not have been left by mistake.

It was a gold crucifix, about an inch and a half long, and distinctive in its design. The anguished figure on the cross had a simplicity of structure which marked it as modern work, but the artist had managed to suggest, in the droop of the head and the twist of the limbs, a degree of agony which reminded Peter of some of the more sadistic medieval depictions of the Crucifixion. He picked it up, conscious of an odd aversion; and as he examined it more closely his curiosity and repugnance grew. It was damned skillful work; there was no explicit detail in the beautifully modeled figure which would account for his distaste.

With an abrupt movement he put the ornament into his pocket, straightened his tie, and reached for his jacket. He needed a drink. Several drinks, in fact, if his imagination was getting that far out of hand.

He had the drinks, in a lounge which was free of the Early American touch, but which reeked equally effusively of Ye Olde English Pub, and then had dinner. The Inn, as he might have anticipated, had an excellent dining room. After dinner he went to the desk.

"I'd like to speak to the manager."

The clerk was a type: supercilious, thin, middle-aged, with a consciously well-modulated voice. It took Peter several minutes of argument, in an accent which he deliberately exaggerated, to win his point. There was more than the normal officiousness in the clerk's reluctance; Peter got the impression that the manager and owner—who was not male, but female, a Mrs. Adams—was something of a tartar. But when the clerk returned from his expedition into the inner sanctum, he was looking almost human in his surprise.

"Mrs. Adams will see you," he said in hushed tones.

Peter knew, at first glance, that he and Mrs. Adams were not going to be friends. From the clerk's attitude he had expected to find one of those frail, white-haired aristocrats whose cooing voice conceals a will as dictatorial as Hitler's. He had nothing against old ladies, even vicious aristocratic old ladies, and he had always been successful with them. He assumed the charm automatically, bending so low over Mrs. Adams' extended hand that his lips almost touched it, but he had no illusions as to the effectiveness of the performance.

Mrs. Adams was neither frail nor white-haired. Her hand showed the painfully twisted joints of arthritis, but it was still big and powerful. She had been a big-boned, tall woman, and she had not lost much of her bulk with age. Her hair was tinted an improbable shade of red, and the eyes that met his in a long, appraising stare had once been beautiful, before they sank into folds of mottled skin. They were an unusual clear green, with flecks of amber.

"I don't see people," said Mrs. Adams. Her voice reminded him of the general's; it was almost as deep and it had the same peremptory, barking tone. The habit of command, Peter thought wryly; he could picture the old lady with a whip, bullying a shivering huddle of field hands. She added, "What the hell's the idea of barging in here?"

Peter had not been invited to sit down. He folded his hands, shifted his feet, and looked guileless.

"You could have said no," he reminded her gently.

She cocked her head and peered up at him. Bad vision? Perhaps, partly, but there was a ghostly air of coquetry about the pose that reminded Peter of the fact that once, God knows how many eons before, she must have been a handsome woman. The green eyes began to sparkle and she said, less gruffly, "Sit down, I hate being loomed over. So, all right, I was curious. Hell, I'm not that old! Bennie said you were a good-looking devil, and he's usually right, if for the wrong reasons."

She burst into laughter at the sight of Peter's face.

"Relax, sonny; he won't bother you. I make damn good and sure my employees know the score. Besides, he has his own arrangements. Private ones. Now then. What's your excuse for shoving in here?"

"If I had known the charms that awaited, I'd have shoved sooner," Peter said. "And planned to stay longer. But since you force me to get to the point—"

"Don't be impertinent."

"Sorry. I found something in one of the drawers in my room. Must have been overlooked by the previous occupant. Since it appears to be gold, and may have a sentimental value, I thought I ought to give it to you personally."

Mrs. Adams took the crucifix and examined it with mild interest.

"Sentimental value?" The mass of wrinkles which was her face writhed. "That's an odd way of putting it. All right, Stewart. You've been a good little Boy Scout. Of course you could just as well have given it to Bennie. My people are honest. They know better than to try anything on me."

"I'm sure they do."

"Sentimental value." She chuckled. "A writer, are you, Stewart?"

"Yes." Peter gave the word a rising inflexion, and Mrs. Adams grinned at him.

"Hell's bells, boy, this is a small town, in spite of all the pretentiousness. And I hear everything that goes on, not only because I'm the boss here, but because I'm one of the local gentry."

"I guessed it at once, from the charming formality of your manner," Peter said.

Her grin faded, but he sensed that she was not displeased with him. Some other thought drew her face into deeper lines that made her look centuries old.

"These new people," she muttered. "What do they know? My family goes back three hundred years in this town. Upstarts . . . carpetbaggers . . ." Then her eyes came alive; for a few seconds they had been as vacant as glass marbles. "Some of 'em aren't so bad, though. The general's a pompous ass, but he's not stupid. By tomorrow everything you told him will be all over town. Yes," she said softly, and now her grin was overtly unpleasant, "we'll know all about you, Mr. Stewart."

Peter had planned to take a walk after dinner. The night was fine, starlit and cool, with a snap of frost in the air, and he wanted to orient himself. But the conversation with Mrs. Adams had disturbed him more than he liked to admit. Certain old phobias, which he had thought to be conquered, reasserted themselves. He felt a need to get inside four walls, with a locked door between himself and the rest of the world. It might seem an unreasonable desire for a man who had spent two years staring with sick frustration and hate at another locked door; but a cell is protection as well as confinement, and freedom is not necessarily comfortable.

The window had been closed and the air conditioner turned on. Peter turned it off and opened the window. He switched off the overhead light and leaned out across the sill.

A breeze stirred the drying leaves on branch and ground, making a barely audible background rustle under the normal night sounds—the swish of cars passing on the street beyond the alley, a woman's clear voice laughing, the unmusical howl of an optimistic tomcat. Beyond the shuttered walled-in shapes of the stores in the foreground Peter could see the waving branches of trees outlined against the lighter dark of the sky, and a few cheerfully lighted windows in some of the taller houses. A nice peaceful town, Middleburg; full of nice, average people.

Under those sheltering roofs, to be sure, lay hidden all the miseries and thwarted passions which humanity brings upon itself: drugs, alcoholism, adultery, hate, frustration. . . .

The corners of Peter's mouth turned up in a smile which his friend Sam would have recognized. That was just the sort of smug superficial remark a second-rate writer might be expected to produce. Which didn't mean it wasn't accurate; the same thing could be said, without saying anything meaningful, about any nice average town anywhere in the world. In the igloos and grass huts the problems were different, but they were no less painful.

Then why did he feel that there was something particularly malevolent about Middleburg—that the peaceful-looking town was really as alert as a sleeping cat, and that the yellow windows were like slitted eyes, through which he was being studied with a concentrated inimical intelligence?

Because I'm neurotic as hell, Peter told himself. It'll take a while to get over those years, more time than I've had. Got to remember that, take it into account. Forget it. Go to bed and get some sleep.

Still he stayed at the window, arms crossed on the sill, enjoying the feel of the clean country air. It must be admitted that the inhabitants of Middleburg whom he had met so far were not attractive human beings. Mrs. Adams was not unique; he had encountered the type before, in other settings: the foul-mouthed bellowing country squiress, more at home in a paddock than a parlor, displaying an aristocrat's deliberate contempt for conventional social behavior. In her way, she was just as much a caricature as Volz was a caricature of the military man. Caricatures . . . Peter's tired brain fumbled with the idea and then gave it up. He couldn't distinguish his own neuroses from valid judgments, that was the trouble. No wonder everyone he met seemed masked.

It was while he was preparing for bed, with all the lights sanely burning, that he realized what specific point had set him off. The crucifix. There had been one inconspicuous detail wrong, besides the indefinable sense of corruption in the modeling. Such ornaments were often worn on a chain around the neck. This cross had welded to it a small gold ring through which such a chain might have been passed. But the ring was in the wrong place—at the end of the long part of the cross. If that crucifix had been worn around someone's neck, it would have hung upside down.

# Chapter

## 2

IMMEDIATELY AFTER BREAKFAST NEXT MORNING PETER PUT through a call to Dr. Paul Martin, introducing himself and mentioning the magic name of the Ambassador. As he accepted Martin's invitation to drop over later for a cup of coffee, he wondered whether he ought to inquire into Martin's training in psychiatry. The fantasies of the previous night had induced some singularly disquieting dreams; even in broad daylight he could not completely shake off the impression of intent yellow eyes, staring and aware.

Once he got out onto the street he forgot his mental quirks in the normalcy of the scene. The weather was so good as to be almost a legitimate topic of conversation. Dry leaves crackled pleasantly under his feet as he strolled down Adams Avenue, past a row of shops. The stores included the usual—grocery, shoe store, cleaner's, and the like—but the effect was quite unlike that of the other small towns Peter had seen in the States. None of the buildings were garish or run down; they conformed to the imposed code, almost all being of rosy aged brick with white trim around doors and windows, and a superfluity of black wrought-iron hinges. The grocer's window displayed jars of caviar and snails and at least two vintages of wine which Peter had never seen west or south of Manhattan. There were other establishments which few villages of Middleburg's size could have supported: a saddlery, a jeweler's whose other branches were in Amsterdam and Cape Town, and a well-stocked bookstore.

On a sudden impulse Peter went into the bookstore. As he had expected, they had the book in stock; frugally he bought the soft-cover edition and tucked it into his pocket.

Martin's house wasn't far from the hotel. It was in a neighborhood of smaller but very comfortable homes, which looked newer than the old mansions of Main Street. Again Peter was struck by the well-tended lawns and shrubbery, and the fine old trees.

The doctor's office was in his home. A swinging sign by the front gate announced the office hours, and Peter saw that he had arrived at the end of the morning session. In the semi-seclusion of the entryway, which was shielded by trellises and flowers, he dealt with the book he had just purchased. He dog-eared several pages, bent the spine back ruthlessly, and rubbed the edges and the front and back covers along a concrete planter which held geraniums. A handful of dirt from the planter, applied lightly to the edges, completed the aging process. Peter put the book back in his pocket and applied his finger to the bell.

The door was opened by a plain, elderly woman in a white uniform, who showed him to the waiting room and explained that the doctor had not quite finished with his last patient. If Mr. Stewart wouldn't mind . . .

Peter said he didn't mind, and took a chair as the nurse went on into the inner office. The room was a pleasant enough place, furnished like any private sitting room except for the usual out-of-date magazines on a table; but he had a feeling he was going to get awfully sick of Early American before he left Middleburg.

Pessimistically he looked through the pile of magazines and found, as he had expected, that there was nothing he wanted to read. A more promising periodical lay on the maple-and-chintz sofa—a copy of the local paper, abandoned by an earlier patient.

The *Middleburg Herald* wasn't as pretentious as the town it served. Presumably the inhabitants got the two *Times* and the Washington papers for their main source of news; this twelve-page weekly gave only token attention to the international and national scenes and devoted the rest of the issue to burning local questions. Two pages of want ads were concerned chiefly with maids and antiques. There was a column of high-school news, written by some budding journalist of sixteen; Peter found, to his amused dismay, that he only understood about half the slang.

The Social Column was more impressive. Accustomed as he was to the unique status of Middleburg, Peter's lips pursed in a silent whistle more than once as he read through the lists of events and names. Dances, dinners, committee meetings; trips to Bermuda and Cannes—blue blood was right, dark blue. The Hunt Club was one of the more publicized groups, and its members seemed to include the most indigo of the blue blood, plus a number of names Peter didn't recognize. Local aristocracy, presumably. He was interested to note that his hostess, Mrs. Adams, figured prominently in the social news.

But the Middleburg scene was not all sweetness and light. He was just beginning the lead editorial, an indignant tirade about vandalism in the churchyard and desecration of graves, when the door of the inner office opened. A young, very pregnant woman emerged and followed the nurse to the desk. Peter got to his feet. The doctor was ready for him.

Paul Martin was not a young man, but his hair was still thick and brown, and his tall frame was in excellent physical condition. There were a few wrinkles in his cheeks and forehead, but they were lines of laughter, which deepened attractively as he shook hands with Peter. His was a generally attractive face, with candid brown eyes and a broad, easy smile; a slight Bostonian twang did not distort his soft baritone voice.

He read Peter's letter of introduction while the nurse brought in rolls and coffee. When she had left, he looked Peter up and down, without prejudice, but intently enough to make the younger man squirm internally. He had never before felt so unmistakably that he was being inspected, inside and out.

"Kind of Sir George to remember me," Martin said. "I've only met him once."

His modesty was in refreshing contrast to Volz's immediate assumption of intimacy. Peter found himself warming to the doctor.

"I gather he knows your reputation."

"Hmmm." Martin's eyes continued their inspection. "I'm not a specialist, you know; just a country GP. He doesn't mention the nature of your recent illness . . ."

Peter dropped his eyes and toyed with the coffee spoon. A mild embarrassment was, he thought, the proper reaction; and it was a relief to release his eyes from that searching scrutiny.

"Well," Martin said after a moment, "it doesn't matter. You're not in need of regular medical care now, what you want is a backstop in case of trouble. Right? It might be a good idea for me to give you a physical checkup—"

"That won't be necessary. It wasn't . . . that is . . ."

"Of course," Martin said quickly. "You look fit enough. Any complaints at the moment? Sleeping well? Good. You're a few pounds under your proper weight, I'd say, but that's nothing to worry about."

Still intent on the pattern of the silverware, Peter nodded mutely. The point had been made. Had it been made a little too easily? He was beginning to see why Sam had mentioned Paul Martin as a leading citizen, a man whose friendship might be important. Though the doctor lacked both money and family connections, he had an air of quiet competence and authority which inspired respect. When Martin changed the subject, Peter knew it was not because of consideration for his pretended embarrassment, but because the doctor had learned all he needed to know.

"More coffee? So you're a writer, Mr. Stewart. Interesting occupation. I gather you use a pseudonym. What sort of thing do you write about, if that question doesn't threaten your anonymity?"

"Not at all. I've done a lot of things, actually, from fiction to popular science. Popular nonfiction, pseudotechnical stuff, is what I prefer. My agent thinks just now that a book on folklore might do well. That's why Sir George suggested I spend a few weeks here. Combine rest with business, so to speak."

"Folklore." Martin leaned back in his chair and selected a pipe from the assortment on his desk. "And why, I wonder, would Sir George think of Middleburg in that connection? Why not Transylvania? Or some of the more remote areas of your own country?"

"Vampires and little old ladies pretending to be white witches? That sort of thing has been done to death, Doctor. I'm looking for something more sensational; got to think of the money, you know. Black Masses, pacts with the devil—that's the thing nowadays."

He didn't know precisely what had moved him to make that statement, unless it was the faint nagging memory connected with the reversed crucifix. Martin's reaction was somewhat unexpected. He threw back his head and laughed heartily.

"You won't find any Black Masses in Middleburg," he said. "In a somewhat more prosaic sense, though, Sir George was quite right. I just wondered how he happened to know about it; when he was here, his sole interest seemed to be pursuing a series of miserable foxes. Middleburg is a very old community, Mr. Stewart, and there are some interesting survivals. Not black magic, of course, but superstitions, traditions, old songs—even some very quaint bits of folk medicine among the old farming families. Have you visited our museum?"

"I only arrived yesterday."

"Oh, of course. Well, you may find it worth your while. It's small, but rather fine, we think. It's run by our own Folklore Society. We've a very active group. Perhaps you'd like to attend a meeting?"

"Very much."

"Then you're in luck." Martin smiled. "There's a meeting tomorrow night."

"Splendid. How many members do you have?"

"Only about a dozen. When we started out we admitted everyone, but those of us who were hard-core enthusiasts found that we were wasting a lot of time on purely social activities, so we began weeding out the dilettantes. It works much better this way. We're amateurs, but serious amateurs."

"Amateurs?" Peter repeated. "But you have at least one professional here in Middleburg. I confess I've been looking forward to meeting her."

He pulled the book from his pocket and placed it on the desk. His eyes were on the book, so he didn't see Martin's face, but he did see the sudden uncontrolled twitch of the doctor's hand. When he looked up, Martin's expression was unremarkable.

"Dr. More. Yes, she's certainly a professional. Unfortunately, she's not a member of our little group."

"Intellectual snob?"

"No, no, not at all. Well, perhaps just a bit. . . . She's a friend as well as a patient, you see, and I don't like—"

"I'm sorry, I shouldn't have said that. I don't even know the woman. Only it seemed natural . . ."

"Natural," Martin repeated. "Yes, yes, of course. And it's natural that you should want to meet her, with your interest in the field. . . . And *The Old Religion in the New World* is a splendid book, really first-rate. I see you've studied it thoroughly. But I'm afraid Kate doesn't—meet people."

"Something of a recluse, is she?"

"Not at all," Martin said stiffly. Peter wondered at his defensiveness. Was he in love with the woman? If not, why was he so desirous of making her appear less offensive than she almost certainly was? Why didn't he simply drop the subject, as he had every right to do with an inquisitive stranger?

"You'll probably see her around town," Martin went on more easily. "She comes and goes, she's not a hermit; and if we should encounter her, naturally I'll introduce you. Be glad to. What I meant was that she isn't the sort of person who joins societies. Not a joiner," he repeated, clearly relieved to have found a nonpejorative adjective.

Peter was silent, weighing the value of what he might learn from further questioning against the disadvantage of risking Martin's friendship by boorish inquisitiveness. He was still weighing when the telephone on Martin's desk gave a discreet buzz, and the doctor reached out for it. "What? Oh, I suppose so. Tell him to come in."

He hung up the phone.

"Will you excuse me just a moment?"

Peter nodded. The door opened, and the nurse ushered in the chauffeur who had driven Peter from the airport.

"Come in, Hilary," said Martin. Peter blinked at the name. "The general wants an immediate answer? Why the devil doesn't the man use the telephone? Splendid invention, the telephone. Sit down, man, sit down; it'll take me a while to write an answer. Oh—this is Mr. Stewart. Hilary Jackson, Peter."

"I've met Mr. Stewart, sir," said Hilary Jackson.

"But not formally." Peter put out his hand. "How do you do."

Jackson gave him the cut direct, staring straight ahead and ignoring his hand.

"Very well, sir, thank you."

The man's voice was a rich bass, with no particular accent. He remained standing, hat in hand, until Martin looked up from the note, which he was perusing with a scowl, and indicated a chair.

"Sit down, Hilary, you make me nervous."

"Thank you, sir, but I'm quite comfortable."

Martin opened his mouth to expostulate, and changed his mind after a quick glance.

"All right," he muttered. "Just a minute."

Snatching a pen he scribbled a few lines on the back of the note and handed it back to the chauffeur, who took it with a slight bow which narrowly missed being a burlesque.

"Thank you, Doctor."

When the door had closed behind him, Peter turned a quizzical gaze on the doctor. Martin did not notice him. He was staring at the door, and his homely, pleasant face looked gloomy.

"Sad case, that," he muttered. "He's a bright boy—"

"Boy?" Peter said involuntarily.

"He's only eighteen."

"Oh. I wonder how big he'll be when he grows up."

Martin smiled.

"Splendid physical specimen, isn't he? And mentally just about as fine."

"What's he doing chauffeuring a . . . man like the general?"

Martin caught the slight pause; the lines at the corners of his mouth deepened briefly and then faded.

"Don't knock one of the bulwarks of our local society," he said drily. "Volz inherited money, from his wife. His ex-rank gives him even more prestige. But he's not a stupid man; don't be fooled by his manner. Why does Hilary choose to work for him? Money, my boy, filthy lucre. Volz is so objectionable that he has to pay through the nose to get any help at all. Hilary is saving for college. He'll make it, one day; but at the cost, I'm afraid, of considerable bitterness."

"But for God's sake, don't you have what-d'you-call-'ems—scholarships, grants?"

"It's not that simple," Martin explained patiently. "Hilary is bright, but he's a product of the local high school and of a home which isn't exactly an intellectual haven. Scholarships exist, but few pay all expenses. And I wonder whether Hilary doesn't . . . Well. My theories about my patients' neuroses aren't worth repeating."

"Where did he get a name like that?" Peter asked curiously.

"His mother liked it."

"Oh."

"I worry about too many things," Martin said, with a wry smile.

"And I'm taking up too much of your time." Peter rose. "You've been very kind, Doctor."

"I've enjoyed it." Martin stood up, towering over the younger man by several inches. "Come over tomorrow night for supper, why don't you? About six. We'll go on to the meeting together."

Peter went off down the street at a leisurely pace, hands in his pockets, face turned up toward the gentle breeze with a look of bland innocence. He was thinking:

Patient. A friend and patient. In what sense? Even learned sociologists get stomachaches and colds. . . . They get other things, too. If Katharine More had diabetes or tuberculosis, her doctor might not care to discuss her malady with strangers; but Martin had been more than reticent, he had been ill at ease. Odd, how the old stigma attached to mental illness still lingered, even in educated minds. . . .

It would be quite a coincidence if Katherine More really suffered from the complaint he was pretending to have had. "The doctor's gone off the deep end"; according to Sam's report she was dabbling in peculiar hobbies. But why should a woman who was successful, rich, and still young suffer from nervous complaints?

When he got back to the center of town, Peter looked for a restaurant. The Inn had lost its charm since he had met the proprietress; besides, the prices were too high. He had some money saved, the bonus for the last job; it had paid well, even if it had ended disastrously. But his resources were not unlimited, and it was beginning to look as if his present project might take longer than he had expected.

Middleburg was singularly lacking in public eating places. The fact wasn't surprising; the country club and the hotel dining room probably provided enough facilities for people who did most of their entertaining in well-staffed homes. The cheaper restaurants and lunch counters were full, with waiting lines. Seeing the number of young people and children, Peter realized that it was Saturday. No school.

They were handsome kids, taller and healthier-looking than the ones he had seen recently; in their bright, mod clothes they looked like a flock of exotic shrill-voiced birds. Peter wondered which of the ingenuous scrubbed young faces had been out digging up graves the previous week. He had passed the modest white church on the way to town and had noticed workmen replanting turf and replacing stones. All at once he felt depressed, and not only by the obvious irony of the contrast between the bright shining faces of the young and their equivocal minds. The shining faces alone were enough to make a man who had passed the fatal age of thirty feel seventy years older. Peter decided he'd have lunch at the hotel after all.

It was a near thing. If he had been ten minutes later he would have missed her.

She stood in the doorway which led into the proprietress's lair, and as Peter entered the lobby he could hear Mrs. Adams' stentorian tones, though he could not see her. The woman in the doorway answered, in a lower voice; Peter heard a reference to "tonight."

He would have known her at once, he told himself, by the pricking of his thumbs. More practically, he had seen the photograph on the back of her book—one of those carefully casual poses, like a snapshot: Dr. More in the yard of her lovely home in Maryland.

She hadn't changed much since the picture was taken. The close-cropped dark hair, hardly longer than his, fitted her head like a black velvet cap. Her spare figure was as slim as a boy's and as sexless as a statue's; its thinness was emphasized by the clothes she wore, tight faded blue jeans and a checked shirt with rolled-up sleeves.

Finally she closed the door, ending the conversation; and the familiar, narrow face turned toward Peter. He knew every feature—the high forehead, with a lock of black hair falling carelessly aslant, the full mouth which was unmarked by lipstick. The eyes were hidden. She was wearing enormous, very dark glasses, which rendered even more expressionless a face which would not under any circumstances have been called mobile.

For a moment the round black eyepieces seemed to stare directly at Peter. Then something caught the woman's attention, and she turned her head toward the girl who was approaching her from across the lobby.

Absorbed as he was by this first sight of his quarry, Peter was human enough to be distracted by the newcomer. On her, the female uniform of the town—jeans and a tailored shirt—looked incongruous, like La Belle Dame sans Merci in a bikini, or the Queen of Elfland in boots and a mini skirt. The long fair hair was so fine it floated out around her shoulders like a luminous cloud; she moved with steps so light and quick that they looked like dancing. The fair-skinned face was luminous too, as if a light shone within, and blazed out through the wide-set blue eyes. She moved with joy, and shone with delight. . . .

And her figure wasn't half bad, either. Peter shook himself mentally. Ordinarily he didn't go around rhapsodizing like an adolescent. What the hell was coming over him?

More important than face or figure was the fact that this girl was undoubtedly Tiphaine Blake, the little cousin whom Sam had mentioned. ("Screwy name!!" his notes had added.) She joined Katharine More and they stood talking. Peter noticed that for all her fragile air Tiphaine was the taller of the two. The More woman was small, not many inches over five feet; her arrogance and that black, blank stare made her look taller.

After a discussion which seemed to produce disagreement, with Tiphaine indicating the dining room and Katharine jerking her head in peremptory negation, the two women moved toward the door. Always a believer in directness, Peter had considered forcing an encounter; but the plan which was beginning to shape itself in his mind made him decide against it. He moved casually out of their path. Still, he was unable to avoid the younger girl's alert eyes; she gave him a friendly smile, the smile a woman gives a man whose appearance attracts her, but warmed by something else. General *joie de vivre*, probably, Peter thought morosely; and went into the dining room in search of Chicken Maryland and beer. According to Sam's inclusive report, the local beer was terrible, but the hotel had every imported variety.

He spent the afternoon reclining on his bed, hands under his head, staring at the ceiling. By four o'clock his plan was in fairly good shape. He put on coat and tie and sallied forth in search of a car rental agency.

As he drove the nondescript blue Falcon out of town, he had some second thoughts. Was he rushing things? Possibly. But inactivity was bad for him; the longer he waited the more impatient he became, and with impatience came recklessness. Better to move soon and avoid that danger. Anyhow, he wasn't committed to anything yet. Reconnoitering wouldn't do any harm. He had to play the hand as it was dealt to him.

He returned to the hotel at seven, exchanged comments with Bennie about the beauty of the town, and after dinner went straight up to his room.

At 11 P.M. he went out again, but not through the door.

Access to the fire escape from the inside of the hotel was gained not through a private room but from the corridor—a sensible practice of which Peter approved, particularly since it meant that he wouldn't have to pass any lighted open windows. He had to play human fly for a few feet, from his own windowsill across to the fire escape, but the handholds were numerous. The fire escape was admirably solid; it hardly creaked as Peter crept down it, stepping lightly in rubber-soled sneakers.

He hung by his hands and dropped from the landing on the first-floor level; the raised bottom flight of stairs was probably wired into some sort of alarm system. His progress down the dark alley would have been unseen, if anyone had been watching; his black sweater and slacks blended with the shadows, and he moved like a cat. Once out on the open street, though, he straightened up and walked slowly, hands in his pockets. His precautions were probably needless. But, just in case, it might be useful to have the hotel staff willing to swear he hadn't left his room. On the street, though, skulking was dangerous. A stroller out for a late walk wouldn't be noticed, but a lurker in the shadows would only arouse suspicion.

He had left the car on a side street. Five minutes after leaving the hotel he was on his way out of town. A leisurely fifteen-minute drive, with meticulous observation of the traffic laws, brought him to the estate. He had located it that afternoon, without having to ask questions. The name on the stone gateposts identified it without equivocation. "Malking Tower" was an odd name for a house, particularly when there wasn't a tower anywhere in sight, but at least it was unmistakable.

The iron gates, which had stood ajar that afternoon, were now closed. Peter left the car under a tree half a mile down the narrow country road, and climbed the wall, avoiding the gates. It was a substantial wall for these parts, where fences were intended more as a request for privacy than as physical defense; but it had no complications such as ground glass or barbed wire, and the stone of which it was built provided plenty of convenient hand- and footholds. He had checked that point during the afternoon visit.

There was a half-moon hanging in a cloudless sky; it gave just enough light to let him pick his way. As soon as he had penetrated the trees, which formed a second barrier, he saw the house before him. It was an unimpressive place, except for its size; it sprawled out over a considerable amount of territory, with wings jutting out in unexpected places. Part stone, part wood, with brick chimneys at frequent intervals, it had grown over the years from a central core which probably dated back to the early eighteenth century. Peter had been pleased to see that the landscaping was extensive; shrubs and bushes masked the foundations, affording admirable hiding places for snoopers, and some splendid old trees practically invited visitors to second-story windows.

There were gardens and outbuildings behind the house, but he was not interested in them at the moment. The front of the house faced him and he moved directly toward it, slipping like a shadow from tree to tree. The faint sound of leaves crackling underfoot didn't worry him; it blended with other nocturnal noises. The air was cold, now that the sun had fallen; it carried the faint acrid tang of wood smoke.

He stopped, paralyzed, as the air above him solidified and dropped down toward him. A faint hollow cry echoed and faded as the shape which had uttered it winged off toward the trees. Peter straightened from his instinctive crouch. An owl. Uncanny creatures. Probably the woods were full of them. Bats, too.

He reached the house without further interruption. At first he thought everyone had gone to bed. Then he caught a faint glow of light from somewhere on the first floor, and headed toward it. It was a puzzling sort of light, as ambiguous and elusive as fox fire, from behind curtained windows, possibly, but faint and oddly colored for all that.

The lighted window was in a wing north of the central portion of the house. Standing below, Peter frowned up at the source of the light. He was not puzzled as to how to reach it; the windows were on the order of French doors, opening onto one of those useless little iron balconies—useless to anyone except burglars. What was so strange was the quality of the light. The window was heavily curtained, all right, but—he noted approvingly—one of the windows had been left ajar, and the movement of the draperies let gleams and glows of illumination seep through. The light was not that of electricity, neither the yellow glow of a normal bulb nor the bluish pallor of fluorescence. It was an ugly gray light that was almost worse than darkness.

The rim of the balcony was just beyond the tips of his extended fingers. Flexing his knees, Peter jumped, and caught the edge of the platform. As he pulled himself up, he remembered his "roommate," and the "keeping fit" routine the idiot had insisted upon, and the corners of his mouth curled up in a sardonic smile. You never knew what was going to be useful. That was one of the things that made life so interesting.

The door was open just far enough for him to get his head through; the movement of the drapes, in the night breeze, was sufficiently erratic that the additional movement caused by his careful hands would not be noticeable. In less than a minute he was crouched by the door, with a peephole at eye level.

No wonder there were no lights anywhere else in the house. The entire household was gathered in this one room, and a singular room it was. Peter realized that it must have been a small ballroom or main salon at one time, for it was of considerable size, with a high, carved ceiling and a fireplace on each of the long walls. He saw shapes only dimly in the gloom, but the room seemed to have been almost entirely cleared of furniture except for low tables set at intervals around the walls, and a peculiar structure at the far end of the room under a raised semicircular alcove that might have been a musicians' platform. A low, rectangular shape draped in dark cloth, it bore a pair of candelabra, a wide shallow bowl, and a pitcher. Bowl and pitcher were made of metal, which shone with a faint silvery luster in the dim light.

The only light in the room came from the candles, nine in all, which were neither wax nor tallow nor any other substance the unseen watcher knew. He had never seen such a light. The figures standing in a semicircle before the altar—the word was unavoidable—were barely visible, but Peter could identify them, even though their backs were turned toward him. He recognized the floating, shining hair of the girl called Tiphaine, and the rigid thinness of Katharine More. An elderly man and woman, on her left, must be the house servants. The fifth member of the group was also familiar. Dr. Paul Martin.

The sixth person in the room stood with her back to the others, facing the altar. Her robes were white, with some sort of symbol embroidered on the back in gold thread. Peter caught the glitter of it as she swayed, in rhythm to the words she muttered, in a half chant, half recitation. The candlelight focused on her lifted hands and on her frizz of hennaed hair.

Mrs. Adams turned, slowly and ungracefully, and the others dropped to their knees. Martin was the last to kneel; he turned his head to look at Katharine, and Peter caught a glimpse of his face. Lined and frowning, it betrayed his abhorrence of the bizarre rite, and also his deep concern for the woman in the center of the half-circle.

Then the priestess's voice rose, and Peter made out the words.

"Magna Mater, mother of all, give us that boon we seek! Restore what you have taken, as your right, as part of all that which is born of woman, your heir, and comes back at last to your universal womb! Restore it, not to break the eternal barrier of your law, but to comfort your daughter, who sits in darkness seeking a sign!"

She broke into bastard Latin, and then into another language which Peter did not recognize. Hebrew?

He sat back on his heels, a slow, unpleasant smile tugging at the corners of his mouth. Was the woman really such a fool as to fall for an obvious hodgepodge of fakery like this? It wasn't even one of the well-known nut cults, but a conglomeration of half-baked scraps from a dozen different magical idioms.

The Magna Mater. Kate More, of all people, ought to know what that ambiguous cult had involved. If she was desperate enough to resort to this, she needed comfort very badly. For the intent of the service was as clear as the identity of the person for whom it was being performed. It was the same pitiful demand made of many spiritualists, whether they called themselves mediums, witches, or high priests. Communication with the spirits of the dead.

There was no pity in Peter's face, or mind, as he slowly straightened up and stood waiting.

# Chapter

## 3

HE HAD TO WAIT FOR ALMOST A QUARTER OF AN HOUR. IT seemed longer. The cold wind numbed his motionless body and hissed drearily in the branches above, but he didn't dare retire to a less vulnerable position for fear of missing the strategic moment. The ceremony wasn't especially enthralling. Mrs. Adams wouldn't dare use any of the more exotic props with this audience and, even at their dramatic best, these affairs tended to be dull. The smell of incense made him want to sneeze. The old lady must be using the stuff lavishly if its odor wafted all the way down the room to him.

The effect of incense and ritual on the participants, who were getting the full treatment, was different. Peter's eyes narrowed thoughtfully as he saw the elderly servant woman begin to sway, slowly at first, then with a jerky, spasmodic rhythm. The older man—her husband?—was uttering low gutteral growls that sounded like a bass accompaniment to the priestess's chant. Tiphaine and the doctor stood still as statues; Tiphaine's profile, oddly shadowed by the flickering light, had a look of frozen fascination. And in the center of the half-circle Katharine More leaned slightly forward, as if in anticipation.

Peter, who had speculated cynically about drugs and too much predinner gin, realized that only the chilly air and the distance kept him from succumbing too. The old hag at the altar had power; the chanting voice, mouthing rotund syllables that had no clear meaning, began to drum hollowly inside his head. He shook the affected member vigorously, and flattened his windblown hair with a hard palm. He had to keep alert. The climax of the ceremony was due at any minute. These mass-hypnotism jobs had to be calculated carefully, so that the high point of the ceremony caught the participants at the peak of their receptivity, before they progressed to coma or fits, or the effect of the drug and ritual wore off.

Peter eased the door open a little farther. They wouldn't notice a breeze; they probably wouldn't notice anything less than a tornado. All eyes were fixed on Mrs. Adams, who was facing the altar, half-crouched, hands extended. Yes—here it came. The priestess's voice rose to an eldritch screech as she whirled, the folds of her robe flying out.

"Come! By Asmodeus and Hecate and Diana of the Three Faces, I summon you from the shades! Appear!"

All the candles went out.

Peter never learned what the next item on the program was meant to be. The cue was too good to miss, and he felt sure that the original effect wouldn't have been half so impressive. As the flames died, he grasped the heavy drapes with both hands and flung them open.

The silence in the pitch-black room was so complete that he could hear them breathing. The change in that breathing, to a harsh, collective gasp, told him that they had seen him. In actual fact they could not have seen much. His features were in shadow and his body, if visible at all against the dark background of trees and grass, was only a darker silhouette. But there was enough moonlight to give an unearthly shimmer to ruffled hair so flaxen that it must have looked silver.

Peter knew the power of imagination when heightened by anticipation. By morning, most of them would be willing to swear that they had seen a face, and recognized it. One, at least, would think so. He had never heard Katharine More speak, but he knew that it was her voice which broke the rapt silence with a short, ugly sound that was half scream and half sob.

He didn't wait for further reactions; the spell was broken, they would move now. His arms, invisible in their black sleeves, were already raised, the fingers curled over the top of the doorframe. When he pulled himself up, it must have appeared to some of the watchers as if he had floated up into the dark sky.

For an instant Peter balanced precariously, one foot on the opened leaf of the door, and then caught the rim of the matching balcony of the upper story. He reached the roof as a rush of footsteps thudded across the bare floor of the room below.

Lying flat and motionless along the edge of the sloping roof, foot and hand braced against the gutter, he heard the doctor's voice. It would be Martin who had had the fortitude to investigate.

"There's no one here," the familiar baritone, now somewhat shaken, reported. "Get some light, for God's sake."

He was answered by a glare of light—yellow, electric light—which poured out onto the balcony. Peter could see its glow from up above, but he didn't raise his head. He doubted that Martin could see him from below, the angle was too acute; but the slightest movement would attract attention.

Someone spoke from inside the room, and Martin said, "No one. How could there be? It was a hallucination, I told you. . . . Katharine. Is Katharine all right?"

"Out on her feet. Stop making like Sherlock Holmes and give me a hand with her." The voice was that of Mrs. Adams, and it sounded just as perturbed as Martin's. Peter didn't bother suppressing a grin. The old bitch wasn't even an honest nut. She hadn't expected her solemn prayers to be answered so literally.

Then a babble of sound broke out as they all started to talk at once. One woman, presumably the cook, was shrieking. Martin's voice rose over the uproar in a tone which made Peter comprehend some of his charisma.

"Stop that, all of you! Upstairs to bed, Kate, and take two of those capsules. None of your phobias about pills, that's an order. Tiphaine, go with her. Will, get a ladder and a couple of flashlights. You and I are going to have a look around."

The voices retreated, and Peter pushed himself upright.

"For a hallucination?" he jeered inaudibly. Then he shinnied up the slope of the roof, slanting toward the side of the house where he had spotted a gnarled ivy winding around the brick chimney. If he couldn't get down that before Martin found his ladder, he had really lost his touch.

Martin had a wife. Peter didn't know why this fact should have surprised him, but it did. She was such a drab, brown, self-effacing little woman that he had a hard time remembering that she existed even when she was in the same room. As he chatted with the doctor over cocktails, he wondered idly why such a popular, successful citizen had married a woman with no visible good points.

At dinner he found out. Mrs. Martin was a superlative cook. He told her so, with such enthusiasm that a faint shade of color came into the woman's pale cheeks. She glanced shyly at her husband, and Martin smiled fondly.

"I keep telling her she's wasted on me," he said. "But she thinks I'm prejudiced."

Mrs. Martin responded with a look of such intense animal devotion that Peter felt a poignant twinge. I'm getting old, he thought resignedly; must be, to consider good cooking and dog-like devotion attractive qualities in a wife. He accepted a second piece of apple pie.

"Keep that up and you won't need to worry about being underweight," Martin said with a grin.

"Oh, I never gain weight," Peter said, surreptitiously flexing sore leg muscles. "I keep busy."

"I ought to be a good host, then, and urge you to keep eating. But I'm afraid that we'll be late if we don't leave now. We can get coffee at the meeting."

They walked the two blocks to the hotel through a night hazy with leaf fires and crisp enough to make ears and fingers tingle. Martin took a deep breath.

"This is my favorite time of year," he said. "Is it like this in England?"

"Much the same. But it doesn't seem quite so spectacular. Everything's on such a large scale here."

"Not Middleburg. I've always imagined that it was very much like an English village."

Peter glanced up and down the street, with its stretches of wide lawn and its huge houses.

"Something like it," he said.

Since the Folklore Society of Middleburg met at the Inn, Peter was not surprised to see the proprietress among the members who were already gathered there. She was dressed in a shapeless tweed suit and "sensible" shoes—a far cry from the fantastic robes of the previous night. Peter was amused to note a touch of coolness in Martin's greeting. He wondered if there had been words between the two that same night.

The second familiar face he saw did surprise him. Somehow he hadn't expected General Volz to be interested in ethnology. Volz, who was wearing riding attire whose flared trousers made him look almost square, greeted Peter and reminded him of his invitation. Martin nodded approval.

"Good idea, for everyone concerned. Those animals of yours don't get enough exercise, General."

"Gonna report me to the SPCA?" Volz inquired, grinning.

Martin gave him a perfunctory social smile and excused himself.

"I would be willing to wager that Dr. Martin is not a member of the hunt," Peter said.

"You'd win that bet. Like he keeps saying, he worries too much; gets into a sweat about every stray dog and dirty kid in town. He's a great guy, though, in his own funny way. Come on and meet the other members."

They were an oddly assorted crowd, Peter thought. A white-maned Senator rubbed shoulders with a local merchant, and a faded maiden lady named Device, who looked like the popular conception of a librarian, chatted amiably with two fashionably dressed young housewives.

Instead of the usual rows of folding chairs facing a speaker's podium, this room had sofas and upholstered chairs arranged before a white-framed colonial fireplace, in which flames leaped comfortably. A large round table, of the sort used for conferences, had been pushed back against the wall. A coffee urn stood on another table, and the members helped themselves when they felt the need for refreshment.

It appeared to be an informal sort of organization and, despite Martin's claims, Peter suspected that it was an organization of dilettantes. A motley crowd like this one, whose only commonality was its membership in the gentry, blooded or moneyed, of the town, could hardly produce many serious students of any subject. Yet they seemed to know one another well, and to be at ease together. One of the young matrons was telling Miss Device a funny story; the older woman began to titter, and laughed so hard she had to cover her mouth with a bony hand.

Peter eyed the hilarious group enviously. It was hard to imagine the sort of joke two such disparate women would both find amusing, but at least they were having a good time. He wasn't. Volz's only topic of conversation, except for his own wealth and social position, seemed to be those useless bums in the slums who wanted the government to support them. Peter glanced surreptitiously at his watch and swallowed a yawn. This was not only going to be a dull evening, but a wasted one. He had hoped to meet Katharine More, but—

The door opened, and all conversation stopped. Even Volz broke off in the middle of his polemic. Peter turned, and saw in the doorway the girl who had been with Katharine More in the lobby of the hotel.

She was wearing a full, very short red skirt which showed off her long slim legs, and a low-cut white blouse which did equally pleasant things for other parts of her admirable anatomy. She carried a guitar case, and her hair brushed her shoulders.

It was remarkable hair—not blond, now that he saw it again, but pure gold, with a touch of copper. She turned her head, with a grace that characterized all her movements, and the heavy mane swung out, ripples of light running down its waves. Martin had come over to speak to her. Tall as she was, she had to look up to him, and the posture showed the beautiful line of her throat and chin.

So the evening wasn't going to be a total waste after all. One of Peter's alternate plans had included Katharine's little cousin; after seeing her that afternoon, he had considered it more enthusiastically. Now it was up to him to use the opening Fate and the Folklore Society had so unexpectedly presented. He didn't have to strain his dramatic talents when Martin led her over to him; nine tenths of his fascinated stare was genuine.

"Tiphaine Blake, this is Peter Stewart." Martin gave the name only two syllables, with the accent on the last; the *i* was short, and the diphthong like a nasalized French *a*.

"When I said you were in luck, I meant it." Martin's eyes were twinkling as he glanced from Peter to the girl, and Peter damned him silently. "Tiphaine is going to sing for us. She's wonderful; we're looking forward to it ourselves."

They joined the rest of the group, who had already taken seats. Tiphaine selected a low stool before the fire. She took her guitar from its case and sat with it across her knees, head bent, striking soft chords and tuning the instrument.

Martin's voice stilled the murmur of conversation. Slouched in his chair, filling his pipe, he spoke in a casual voice but with his usual air of authority.

"We'll skip the business meeting tonight," he began, and

grinned amiably as a murmur of laughter rippled through the room. "I'm sure it wouldn't amuse our visitor."

The smiling faces turned toward Peter. A private joke, clearly; maybe Martin's distaste for formal meetings amused the other members. Jolly for them.

"Anyhow," Martin continued, "it would be a shame to waste time on other matters when we could be listening to Tiphaine. My dear, will you tell Peter what you've been doing?"

She raised her head and smiled directly at Peter.

"Everything I've been doing?" she asked. Another communal chuckle passed through the room. They are a cheery little bunch, Peter thought disagreeably.

Discounting the feeble joke, her voice was as charming as he had expected it to be, a soft contralto, rich and low, but with a clarity usually found only in higher voices. She was sensitive to people's feelings; she sensed Peter's impatience, though he felt sure it had not been visible, and immediately sobered.

"As you may have guessed, Mr. Stewart, I sing folk songs. I'm not really a serious student, like these people. I just like to sing. But folk music, though a legitimate part of folklore, is a pretty big field. Paul suggested I specialize—collect particular types of songs. And since many of the members are interested in magic and superstition, I've learned some songs which deal with the supernatural. It's amazing how many there are. I'm going to sing a few of them now."

She ran her fingers over the strings and began to sing.

The soft, unemphatic speaking voice was transformed. She had not been formally trained, but she had a natural sense of pitch and rhythm, and superb control. She had something else which some trained singers lack—a fantastic range, with no awkward break between the contralto and soprano registers. Over and above the technical beauty of her voice, there was the special magic which the best folk singers have—an empathy with the song which made it come alive.

The song was of the Child ballads. "The Wife of Usher's Well." The story conformed to the theme of the supernatural which Tiphaine had chosen, telling of the return to the mourning mother of her three dead sons. Peter didn't pay much attention to the words; he was more interested in the performer. He wondered how she would come over on a recording. Her face and figure certainly didn't detract from the total effect.

The applause was enthusiastic. But when it had died away, the members of the Folklore Society plunged into a discussion which left Peter amazed. He had underestimated them; they really did know a lot about the subject. The housewife on his left pointed out that there was a variant of the song in which the boys left home for the purpose of studying "grammarie"—not grammar, but an old term for magic. The Senator asked Tiphaine to repeat the fourth verse, the mother's incantation, and she did so:

> *"I wish the wind may never cease,*
> *Nor storms in the flood,*
> *Till my three sons come home to me,*
> *In earthly flesh and blood."*

"You comprehend the reference to wind and storm," the Senator chirped, when she had finished. "Obviously the lady was no common grieving mother, but a trained witch."

"How's that?" Peter asked involuntarily.

"But these were talents attributed to witches," the Senator explained mildly. "The ability to command the wind and to raise storms at sea. You will remember, of course, the famous case of the Earl of Bothwell, who was accused of trying to kill the queen by raising a storm while her ship was at sea?"

"Oh, of course," Peter murmured. "It's just that I had never thought of it in connection with this song."

"That's what makes Tiphaine's research so interesting," Martin said, around the stem of his pipe. "Any more discussion? Next, my dear, if you please."

And so it went, through several more songs—"The Demon Lover," "Clerk Colville," "The Elfin Knight." Peter found himself getting interested. His scanty knowledge of Black Magic was a hangover from an adolescent hobby; he had never realized it was so pervasive. He was roused from his pedantic musings by Tiphaine's next song. It was "Scarborough Fair," and with a perfectly straight face she gave them the Simon and Garfunkel adaptation instead of the original. Most of the members missed the joke; it was Miss Device, of all the unlikely pop music fans, who pointed it out.

"Trying to catch us, were you, dear?" she said sweetly.

"Not you, Miss Device," Tiphaine said with a smile. "You do know the most amazing things!"

"Well, I know why this one fits your typology," the spinster said complacently. "The herbs. They didn't use them to flavor the soup!"

"A love charm," Peter added, entering into the spirit of the thing. "I wonder whether it works."

He looked at Tiphaine; she responded with a sweet smile and a flick of her hand across the guitar strings in a strikingly dissonant chord.

"It doesn't," she said.

"All right." Martin indicated his watch. "You know the agreement, ladies and gentlemen; Mrs. Adams is kind enough to let us meet here, but we must wind up early so the guests can get some sleep. Anything else, Tiphaine?"

The girl brushed her hair back from her face.

"One more. And I bet I can baffle you this time."

She struck a slow, broken chord. Then her voice began, muted as a whisper, but so distinct that every syllable was clear.

*"Cold blows the wind to my true love,*
*And gently falls the rain.*
*I've never had but one true love,*
*And in greenwood he lies slain."*

It was the old ballad of "The Unquiet Grave," and the dead lover who cannot rest because of the excessive grieving of his sweetheart. By the time she had finished, the hairs were standing up on the back of Peter's neck. Empathy was too weak a word. She sang like someone who has herself kissed the cold lips of the dead.

He sat in silence while the babble of discussion went on. The listeners had a lot of theories, but finally Miss Device said decisively, "What's the problem about this one, Tiphaine? Of course it's a familiar superstition, that the dead are kept from their rest by the tears of the living, but—"

"It's not my idea," Tiphaine interrupted. "Katharine suggested it. She doesn't take it seriously, but she said it might be fun to throw the suggestion out and see what you made of it."

There was a long, echoing pause. Peter looked up alertly as he realized that the name which had caught his wandering attention was the cause of the general uneasiness. This was an amiable gesture, showing that Katharine More took an interest in their activities and in those of her companion and cousin. Why the chilly silence at the mention of her name?

Martin, whose smile had solidified into a grimace, was the first to recover. "You've got us all intrigued, Tiphaine. What is the suggestion?"

Tiphaine seemed unaware of the consternation she had caused. Leaning forward eagerly, she said, "The lover is lying dead in the greenwood, right? Not just dead, murdered. But the song doesn't say why, or how."

"It may be a fragment of a longer song," Mrs. Adams began, and was interrupted by the general.

"Maybe she murdered him. The girlfriend. Guilt, not grief, makes her disturb his rest."

Peter stared at Volz. It was an ingenious idea, and quite in tune with Volz's philosophy of life. He would think of murder.

"No, no." Tiphaine chuckled; it was a charming sound, like bubbling water. "Well, maybe you're right. But look at the list of things he gives her—impossible things, like water from the desert and blood from a stone. Sounds like a formula for a spell, doesn't it? Why does he want these things, if his desire is to be left in peace? Then in the last verse he says he'll see her again when the leaves are green. In the spring."

There was a blank silence when she had finished. She chuckled again and shrugged. One sleeve slid down from her tanned shoulder, and Peter momentarily lost track of what she was saying.

". . . of course it's been changed over the centuries. In some versions the true love is a woman instead of a man. But Kate says it reminds her of William Rufus, and Murray's theory of the sacrifice of the god."

Again that odd, frozen silence. It was broken by Volz.

"Murray who?" he inquired.

Laughter ended the discomfort, and Martin shook his head in mock reproach.

"Harry, you've got to read a few books or we'll drum you out of the club. Margaret Murray, an authority on the witch cult. You know her theory, that the witchcraft of the Middle Ages was simply a survival of an old pagan religion?"

"Nope," Volz said blandly.

"Well, now you know."

"Interesting," Volz muttered thoughtfully; and Peter thought he knew why such an apparent ignoramus was accepted by a group like this one. Volz was barely literate, but his intelligence could not be denied. Like other famous military men, he was simply unable to absorb the printed word. Once he heard an idea he dealt with it efficiently.

"Yes, it is interesting," Martin said drily. "But the particular theory Tiphaine mentioned goes even further. The head of the witch cult, or Old Religion, was a god to his followers—and, *ipso facto*, a Devil to the outraged Christians. Miss Murray believed that the Incarnate God had to be sacrificed periodically to ensure the well-being of his worshipers. The notion of the dying god, who is reborn in the spring, is very ancient; you find it in Egypt and Babylonia and, later, in Greece. Death and resurrection; not only a symbol of the new life which comes forth from the earth each spring, from the quickened seed, but an assurance, through sympathetic magic, that that rebirth would surely come. A symbol and a promise."

Martin's voice was soft and slow; the rest of the group sat in respectful silence. Then the doctor shook himself and went on more briskly.

"You're aware of the significance of the one Resurrection, of course, but as students you must remember that the concept has historical precedents. It is found in many fertility cults, and if you remember the descriptions of the Witches' Sabbath you'll see why Miss Murray believes that the Old Religion was a kind of fertility cult. She suggests that Joan of Arc, for instance, was a head of the cult, and that she accepted her own execution as the inevitable sacrifice. William Rufus—for your information, Harry—was a very early king of England who was murdered while hunting. Murray indentifies him as another witch "god," whose death was the cult sacrifice. Most authorities disagree, but—"

"But it does fit the song," Miss Device said. "Slain in the greenwood. And the rest of it is a corrupt reference to the resurrection of the god."

"Very ingenious," Martin agreed. "And very hazardous."

"I don't know," one of the housewives said. "What about . . ."

Peter looked at Tiphaine. It was becoming his favorite occupation. Having thrown her little bombshell she had withdrawn again, but she was clearly enjoying the effect, smiling as

her eyes moved from one animated face to the next. They met
Peter's waiting eyes, and were held.

He put his cup down on the table, rose, and held out his
hand.

"May I?" he asked.

She came slowly to her feet and put the guitar into his
hands. She was almost as tall as he; the wide blue eyes met his
with satisfaction and—he had almost thought—recognition.

He motioned her back to her seat and stood with one knee
raised to support the guitar. The others had stopped talking as
they watched. Peter turned to them with a deprecating smile.

"I have some evidence to support Miss Blake's idea," he
said. "If you don't mind."

"Of course not," Martin said quickly. "Have we by any
chance touched upon your specialty. Peter? I wish you'd warned
me."

"Not a specialty, no. Just an odd coincidence. I happened to
be in northern Scotland a few years ago, and heard an elderly
lady sing a version of this song which I'd never encountered before. It has two additional verses which may interest you."

He felt for a C major chord and missed by a quarter of an
inch. Martin gave him an encouraging nod, and Peter winced
theatrically.

"I am out of practice. There, that's got it.

*'Go fetch me persil and cinquefoil,*
*Poplar leaves and rue,*
*And we will rise through the windy night,*
*As we were wont to do,*

*'When the oaken leaves that fall are green,*
*And the dying year's reborn,*
*When the seed of the withered flower swells,*
*You'll have no need to mourn.'"*

Peter ended with a flourish, and glanced up.

"She put them in at the end," he said.

Either his singing was even worse than he had imagined, or
his verses were better; the whole group sat still, with faces set
in expressions of deep concentration. Or was the word consternation?

Martin was the first to speak.

"Splendid," he said, patting the tips of his fingers together. "I might even say, brilliant."

Peter tried to look modest, but he was inclined to agree—in view of the fact that he had invented the new verses himself, within the last ten minutes. He looked at Tiphaine.

"Cheater," she whispered.

"I wasn't trying to upstage you, honestly."

"Bad enough that you're an expert in sheep's clothing. If I'd known you could sing like that—"

"You would never have let me begin."

The discussion went on around them; Peter paid no attention until Volz banged him on the back demanding further details, which he cheerfully supplied. His powers of invention were flourishing after that auspicious beginning. It was a good thing he had glanced at Katharine's book that afternoon. The discussion of the "flying ointment" used by the witches had interested him, and he had remembered some of the ingredients. The well-informed folklorists caught every one of them. Martin had to exert all his authority to break up the meeting. As the others straggled out, still arguing, Martin joined the performers.

"We've entertained a savant unawares," he said with a smile. "Is making people underestimate you part of your professional technique, Peter?"

"And he sings almost as well as Glen Campbell," Tiphaine murmured, with a sidelong glance at Peter's outraged face. "I'd love to sing duets with you, Mr. Stewart. How are you on the Beatles?"

Martin laughed and put an avuncular arm around the girl's shoulders.

"Stop that," he said affectionately. "I think you've hit upon a splendid idea. Why don't you two work up a program for us? And I wasn't thinking of the compositions of the—er—Beatles."

"Some of their compositions are pretty folksy," Peter said. "Or do I mean folkish?"

"I apologize," Tiphaine said, smiling at him. "I think it's a marvelous idea. Are you going to be in town long, Mr. Stewart?"

"I plan to be," Peter said, looking steadily at her.

"Good, I'll call you."

"I'll call you. Better still, I'll see you home."

She looked up from fastening the guitar case; her eyes were twinkling.

"How very conventional, Mr. Stewart! Thanks, but that's quite unnecessary. Also impractical, unless you can make like young Lochinvar."

Peter looked blank, but Martin understood. His brows came together.

"Are you riding that brute again, Tiphaine? I told you—"

"I love riding at night," she said dreamily. "With Sultan it's like riding the wind, with the stars shooting by overhead. . . . Don't be square, Paul."

"I'm going to speak to Volz. If he wants to lend you one of his horses, he ought to pick one that's more manageable. And how does Sultan get home from your place?"

"Timmy brought him over. He'll take him back."

The doctor's face reddened.

"That makes it worse," he growled.

"Who is Timmy?" Peter asked curiously. "Your local ax murderer?"

Tiphaine laughed and did a little dance step.

"You'd think so, to hear Martin. He's just a poor, half-witted boy, the general's stablehand. I think it's sweet of General Volz to keep him. Nobody else would hire Timmy."

"I suspect he gets Timmy's services cheap," Peter said, before he could stop himself. Martin gave a sharp laugh.

"That's the correct explanation of the general's charity. Timmy is mentally retarded, but physically he's a full-grown man. I keep telling you, Tiphaine—"

"Oh, Martin!" She spun around in sheer exuberance. "I'm not afraid of Timmy. He adores me."

"I know," Martin said. His tone was so grim that Peter glanced at him in sudden comprehension.

"Maybe the doctor's right," he said. "Let me take you home. I've always wanted to try that Lochinvar stunt."

"Now you're both being square." Tiphaine bounced up on tiptoe, deposited a kiss on the doctor's cheek, and darted away. "I'll telephone you tomorrow, Mr. Stewart," she called back over her shoulder. "Just to assure you that I'm still alive and un-raped!" Her laughter was cut off by the closing door.

Peter turned, brows raised, to meet Martin's thunderous

glare. After a moment the doctor laughed ruefully and reached for his pipe, his usual solace in times of stress.

"I told you, I worry too much."

"You've got me worried too."

"Why?" the doctor asked bluntly.

"She's so sweet," Peter said fatuously. "So innocent. . . . I mean, without meaning to, she's probably driving the poor devil out of his mind. What there is of it."

The doctor laughed, and clapped Peter on the shoulder.

"You sound quite incoherent," he said. "Love at first sight?"

"Second. I've seen her once before, with an older, dark-haired woman. I thought she looked familiar—the dark woman. Was it, by any chance . . . ?"

"Yes, it probably was." Martin's friendly hand fell away. "Tiphaine lives with Dr. More. They're distantly related."

The doctor's farewells were uncharacteristically abrupt, and as Peter headed for his room, he was more than ever eager to meet his elusive quarry. What was there about Katharine More that caused the townspeople to react so oddly to the very mention of her name? His own phrase lingered in his mind: the dark woman. From the way people acted, you'd think she was a witch, or something.

## Chapter

### 4

"I WANT TO SEE YOU," PETER SAID.

"How about tomorrow morning?" Tiphaine's voice had a musical lilt which was unmarred even by the distortion of the telephone.

"Today. This minute."

"What a pity. Because I'm going riding today."

"By a strange coincidence," Peter said smoothly, "General Volz has offered me the use of his stable. I'll meet you there—when?"

The faint laughter sounded like bells.

"Three o'clock."

"That's too far away."

"Have a good hearty lunch," she advised. "That'll take your mind off."

"Off what?" Peter asked, and heard the laughter again, just before she hung up.

She was there before him when he arrived at the general's estate. That was what Volz called it, and for once he wasn't bragging. The house was almost too new for Peter's taste, which had become accustomed to the gracious lines of the older homes of the area. Volz's house was an enormous block of concrete and glass; one wall, jutting out over the ridge of a low hill, was all windows, which caught the sunlight in a blinding glitter. Peter wondered how this anomaly had passed the Architectural Committee. Was it too far out of town to be included in the regulations; or was the answer just plain bribery?

The stables, behind the house, were more conventional; it would take a wilder mind than Volz's to come up with anything *outré* in the way of a stable. The general didn't stint himself on horses any more than he did on the other comforts of life. Half a dozen of the stalls were occupied, and the tack room, into which Peter glanced, was filled with expensive leather.

As he crossed the stone-paved stableyard, Tiphaine came out of the second stall, leading a horse which was already bridled and saddled. She greeted Peter with a dazzling smile and a casual "Hi." He returned the smile, but the horse held his attention.

He had no doubt that this was Sultan, to whom the doctor had objected, and he was inclined to agree with Martin. Sultan was big, well over the sixteen hands that was considered a good height for a hunter; a chestnut, he was one of the handsomest animals Peter had ever seen. His conformation was faultless, from the small, well-set ears to the clean, big-boned hocks. But there was something about him. . . .

Peter eyed the horse with disfavor, and Sultan's wicked rolling eyes returned the look, with interest. He strolled over and put a casual hand on the arched neck. Sultan's head whipped around. Peter didn't move; and after a moment Sultan snorted and decided to pretend he had only been yawning. He looked out over the stableyard with an air of supreme disdain.

"Terrible actor, isn't he?" Peter said, still stroking the animal's neck.

"Oh, yes, you always know exactly what he's thinking."

"I don't think I like what he's thinking. Look here, why don't you let me take this monster?"

"I'm tempted to agree. Just out of natural wickedness."

"All right. I promise to fall off a few times if that will amuse you."

"It's a deal. I'll take Starlight. Timmy!"

The name, as much as the sudden rising of her voice, made Peter start. Since his professed concern for Tiphaine had been part of the act which would, he hoped, get him into the confidence of Tiphaine's cousin, he had forgotten about the feeble-witted stableboy. But at the sight of the figure which came shambling out of one of the stalls he felt a stir of real revulsion.

Timmy was short and slender. From that point of view he

didn't look very dangerous. He was also incredibly dirty, far filthier than his occupation gave him any excuse for being. His tattered shirt and shapeless trousers exuded a powerful atmosphere that made Peter wrinkle his nose, even at a distance. Or was the atmosphere pure Timmy? A shock of dusty-looking brown hair obviously hadn't been washed in weeks; it had straw, and other less wholesome fragments, stuck in it.

Timmy's features would long remain a blur to Peter. After the first casual glance he found himself unable to look at the man's face. The birthmark was incredible; Peter had seen similar marks, but never one so extensive. It turned almost half of Timmy's face into a liver-red horror. Peter was moved by an unwilling surge of pity. Talk about Job. When the benevolent Creator afflicted His creatures, He did a good, thorough job of it. To take another viewpoint, and get God off the hook, you could assume that Timmy had been something nasty in his previous incarnation. Something very, very nasty.

Apparently Timmy didn't talk. He could hear all right, responding to the girl's request with a sickening, shambling alacrity, so Peter gathered he wasn't deaf and dumb. Perhaps he didn't have anything to say. Peter watched, studying the man's bare arms—which were tanned and fairly well muscled—and his back rather than his face. But when the little silver-gray mare was saddled, and Timmy turned, hands out, to assist the girl to mount, Peter moved, out of an instinct which for the moment was stronger than any rational reason.

"Let me, Tiphaine," he said.

Timmy fell back as he approached, for which Peter was grateful; the smell of Timmy would have been overpowering at close quarters. He didn't see Timmy's expression, since he didn't look at Timmy's face. He didn't need to. The wave of hate was almost palpable. This time Peter didn't care about making unnecessary enemies, though he usually avoided doing so as a principle of good business. He was inclined to agree with the doctor that Timmy, unlike most of his afflicted fellows, was potentially dangerous; but so long as he was on guard, the miserable creature couldn't do him any harm.

Tiphaine turned to wave at Timmy as they walked the horses out of the stableyard, and then gave Peter a taunting smile.

"Welcome to the club," she said.

"The 'Hate Timmy' club?"

"The 'Timmy-ugh' club would be more like it."

"That one I'll join. Martin is right, Tiphaine; there's something wrong with that lad. And I don't mean his intelligence quotient. Most mental deficients are gentle as lambs. But Timmy—"

"There are two paths," she said blandly. "Through the fields and through the woods. Which do you prefer?"

"Stop trying to change the subject. Haven't you ever heard about the birds and the bees?"

For answer Tiphaine leaned forward and brought her crop down on the mare's flank. The little animal leaped forward. Automatically Peter's legs closed in on Sultan's sides and his hands relaxed; two years of inactivity had not dulled the reflexes acquired from earlier years of practice. But he was accustomed to riding horses, not thunderbolts; Sultan's jet-propelled takeoff nearly unseated him. His grip on the reins tightened. It was close enough to have slowed a more sensitive animal, but sensitivity, he had observed, was not one of Sultan's character traits. How the hell, he wondered, did Tiphaine ride this brute with a simple snaffle bit? What Sultan needed was a chunk of barbed wire in his mouth. Good thing he wasn't wearing a hat; he'd have lost it in that first rush.

Ahead of him Tiphaine leaned forward over the horse's neck, her blowing hair like a stream of molten copper. She glanced back over her shoulder, saw the hurricane bearing down on her, and straightened, slowing Starlight to a trot. Peter gathered his own reins in as they came abreast. Sultan hesitated perceptibly; then, gauging his rider's temper correctly, he changed to a slower gait, so abruptly that Peter's teeth clashed together. Torn between reluctant admiration for Sultan's speed, and irritation at his deliberately uncomfortable trot, he used the powerful pulley rein to bring the big animal to a sudden stop. Now he knew why Volz had bought the horse, who was probably anathema to every other hunting man in the neighborhood. With the general, flashy performance would win out over disposition any day.

Tiphaine came cantering sedately up to join him. Her hair had coiled itself around her neck and shoulders, and her face was flushed.

"You *are* a cheater," she said, grinning broadly. "You promised you'd fall off."

"Or are you under the mistaken impression," Peter said, as if the conversation had never been interrupted, "that that moldy specimen's hormones have been inhibited along with his brains?"

Tiphaine doubled up with laughter, falling forward over the horse's neck till her bright locks mingled with the silver-gray mane.

"You win," she said, raising a flushed face. "Aren't you ever distracted by anything?"

Peter let his gaze move from the V of her blouse, where a pulse throbbed in the little hollow at the base of her throat, to the slim thighs, encased in skin-tight jeans.

"Try me," he suggested.

Instead of blushing or giggling, she returned the look, inspecting him from head to foot.

"You're too thin," she said coolly. "But that's all right, I like thin men. Good shoulders. And a nice mouth—when you let it relax. Ah, there it goes, all tightened up!"

Peter grinned unwillingly; he had just remembered Sam's lecture on the foibles of the female sex. Was the old devil ever wrong?

"That's better," Tiphaine said, her own mouth relaxing. "I like your hands, too. Nice thin hands. No hair."

"No hair?" Peter repeated, fascinated.

"On your hands. Some men have big thick tufts on the backs of their fingers." She shivered delicately. "And mats of it on their chests, like bears. Or dogs. You're all right."

She extended one finger and poked him on the skin exposed by the open neck of his shirt. Peter flinched.

"You make me feel like a horse," he said lightly, trying to conceal an unexpected surge of annoyance.

Tiphaine laughed.

"Come on, I'll show you the sights. No more lectures, promise?"

"I'm speechless," Peter said.

They talked about horses, and songs, and things in general. Not about Timmy, or Katharine More, though Peter was aching to work his way into that subject. An instinctive sense kept him from doing so. This was his afternoon for Tiphaine, and a hint of any other interest might queer the pitch. It was a successful afternoon—from that point of view, and from others. Peter was beginning to sympathize with Martin's sentiments, if not about the town, at least about the surrounding countryside. Placid, inhabited, well cultivated, it still had an air of extravagance; the rolling land, the vast blue of the arching sky, the crisp purity of the air, and over all the landscape the brilliant sweep of fall foliage—it was far from the smoggy industrial America which is all many visitors ever see. He hadn't been out like this, with a good horse under him and a pretty girl beside him, for a long time. He wondered what it would be like to have these things without any reservations or hidden purpose clouding the brightness of the day, and then dismissed the thought with a brusque mental expletive. He had ridden with dark thoughts too long. It was impossible to go back now.

The sun slid westward, reddening. Tiphaine glanced at it, and then at her watch. A shadow dimmed the brightness of her face.

"Time to go back," she said. "I promised to be home by five."

"Promised your parents?" Peter said casually, as they turned the horses.

"My parents are dead."

"I'm sorry."

"Oh, years ago. I live with my cousin. Katharine More." She gave him a quick sidelong glance which was half veiled by her falling hair. "Martin said you knew her."

"I know her name, that's all." Peter guided Sultan, unnecessarily, around a heap of rocks. "I've read her book."

"She's a marvelous person," Tiphaine said, her blue eyes fixed on the horizon. "She isn't really my cousin; she's the niece of my stepfather."

"Sounds like one of those genealogical French exercises."

"What I mean is, she has no obligation toward me at all. But she took me in after Stephan died; he left her all the money, you see. I mean, he didn't make a will. So it all went to her."

It would have been fairly incoherent if Peter hadn't already known the story. Tiphaine's voice had become higher, with a slight stammer. He said casually,

"Stephan being your stepfather? It seems to me that there was an obligation. Moral, if not legal; his, if not hers."

"But that's just it," Tiphaine said eagerly. "She didn't owe me a thing."

"So she took you in. What do you do to earn your keep? Wash her socks?" The look in her eyes hit Peter hard. He added, in a smooth even voice, "Or scrub the floors, perhaps? While she paces the hall muttering, 'Mirror, mirror, on the wall'?"

He half expected her to fly to Katharine's defense; she surprised him with a splutter of laughter and a shining glance.

"How did you know? And you," she said mockingly, "only need a plumed velvet cap on those golden locks. Come around tomorrow and sing under my balcony."

"Not me," Peter said, recovering himself. "If I remember the original, the prince got thrown into the dungeon."

"You wouldn't be put off by a little dungeon, would you?"

"Too damp. Bad for my cough."

"Chicken. Oh, gosh, it's late. We'll have to hurry."

When they reached the stableyard, Timmy was nowhere in sight. Volz had returned from wherever he had been; his big black car stood in the stableyard, and his chauffeur was washing it. In shirt sleeves Jackson looked even bigger and more muscular than Peter remembered him. He greeted the man with a smile and a wave as Jackson looked up, and got a cool inclination of the head in return.

"Where's Timmy, Hilary?" Tiphaine asked, sliding off the mare's back.

"He's . . . busy," the chauffeur answered. "I'll take care of your horse, Miss Tiphaine."

She nodded casually. Peter dismounted.

"I'll drive you home. Just a second."

He started unbuckling the girth. Jackson put down his cloth and came over.

"I'll do that. Sir."

Peter straightened to his full height and stared up—way up—into the other man's face. It had the splendid blankness, and the chiseled regularity, of a granite statue's. He wondered how anyone could kid himself into feeling superior to a specimen like Jackson. He was not usually sensitive to his own lack of inches, but the chauffeur made him feel like a worm.

"Thanks," he said wanly.

There was a flicker of movement in one of the stalls. Peter caught a glimpse of rusty-brown hair and an intensely malevolent stare before Timmy ducked back out of sight. Jackson saw it too. With one hand he made a quick, twisting gesture. Then he looked guiltily at Peter, and the latter saw the first crack in the granite of his face. He grinned.

"If that means what I think it means . . ." he said. "Maybe you could show me how to do it?"

He turned away without waiting for an answer which he probably wouldn't have gotten anyway. Tiphaine was waiting in the car, and he slid behind the wheel with an apology for the delay. Tiphaine gave him directions which he solemnly followed. The drive took about ten minutes. It was the long way around, Tiphaine explained; there was a path through the woods which she took when she came on foot.

"You're back in plenty of time," Peter said, as he stopped the car in front of the house. "And please give my regards to the Wicked Queen."

Sooner or later, if their acquaintance developed—and he intended that it should—she would have to invite him into the house. Apparently Tiphaine had come to the same conclusion. She said, without any perceptible hesitation.

"Come in and give them yourself. No, really, I know she'd like to meet you. I told her about your new verses and she was intrigued. Unfortunately I couldn't remember all the words."

Peter hoped devoutly that he could.

He was a little keyed up, and therefore looking particularly casual, as he followed Tiphaine into the hall and through a door on the left.

The afternoon sunlight, pouring through wide French windows along the far wall, gave a luminous glow to the mellow brown leather of the chairs and brought out the rich reds of the huge Bokhara which covered most of the floor. Katharine More sat on the couch, stockinged feet tucked under her; the pale blue of her slacks and the white of her shirt stood out against the crimson upholstery. Curled up in her lap was an enormous black cat. The sunlight gave his plushy fur a kind of iridescence. Kate's hair was exactly the same shade of black.

Tiphaine performed the introductions with less than her usual charm, and, at her cousin's suggestion, went off to make cocktails. Peter, impaled by his hostess's considering eye, sought desperately for a topic of conversation other than folk music. He was afraid she was going to mention that damned song, and he hadn't got the words quite straight.

"I admire your house. This room, especially."

"It's very definitely a man's room." Her lips parted in a smile which did suggest the Wicked Stepmother, strong white teeth and all. "My uncle furnished it. With his usual taste, and lots and lots of money."

He understood, now, why she wore dark glasses in public. Her face was young and unlined, but the eyes betrayed her—not her age, which wasn't that great, but something worse. Whatever it was, it was eating her away inside; the result showed in the darkly shadowed eye sockets and the fixity of her look. He had seen eyes like those on men just before they started screaming and clawing at the bars.

There were other betraying signs—the jerkiness of the movement with which she turned to take a tall frosted glass from Tiphaine, the unnecessary tension of her hand around its curved surface. Peter accepted a Scotch and water, and Tiphaine sat down with her own drink. The cat had lifted its head and was regarding the visitor with a fixed feline stare which strongly resembled that of its mistress.

"I see you keep a familiar," Peter said at random. He was not prepared for the reaction. Tiphaine gasped, and Katharine More almost dropped her glass.

"He was my uncle's cat," she said harshly.

"He seems to approve of you." Peter snapped his fingers at the animal. Its eyes narrowed contemptuously.

"He approves of everyone; he's a big, fat sentimentalist in spite of his appearance." Kate had recovered herself; there was amusement in her voice as she watched Peter's attempts to ingratiate himself. "But he has his dignity. Don't address him as 'kitty, kitty.' "

"What's his name?"

"What would you expect—for a familiar?" Her smile was strained. "Pyewacket."

At the sound of his name the cat stood up and stretched, looking fantastically like a miniature black leopard. He jumped down off Kate's lap and stalked toward the closed door, where he stood on his hind legs, wrapped both black paws around the doorknob, and twisted. There was a click. The cat dropped down, inserted one paw into the crack, and pulled the door open. He left without once looking at Peter, who was frankly gaping.

"I'd like to have known your uncle," he said.

"That's a simple trick," Kate said scornfully. "Many cats can do it."

"First time I've ever seen it."

"You're probably a dog lover. Cats are just as bright. They just don't give a damn about pleasing people. But they can learn anything they choose to learn, if it's to their advantage."

"They're uncanny beasts, though. That combination of grace and ferocity . . ."

"Which is why so many of the poor things were burned as witches' familiars. You, as an expert on folklore, know all about that, of course."

"Of course." Peter cast about for another change of subject. "Uh . . . your uncle preferred cats to dogs?"

"Pyewacket was the only exception. He didn't like other animals. Or people."

Well, well, Peter thought. Before he could inquire further into Katharine's obvious dislike of the uncle who had endowed her with a tidy fortune, Tiphaine broke her long silence.

"That's not very polite, Kate."

"To you or Stephan? It's true; he approved of you."

Her hostility was poorly concealed. Tiphaine's cheeks flushed with embarrassment, but her mouth was set stubbornly.

"He'd have to approve of you," Peter said. "Didn't he bring you up?"

"And gave me my name."

"I wondered how you came by it. I've never heard the name before."

"My real name is Melanie." Tiphaine shook her head. "Isn't it insipid? When I got to be about twelve I insisted it had to be changed. Stephan named me Tiphaine. He said it was the proper name for an elf."

"How very imaginative."

"Oh, he was certainly imaginative," Kate said drily. "You seem to be interested in my uncle, Mr. Stewart. That's his portrait."

Peter had noticed the painting, but the stiff, archaic style and the old-fashioned garb of the subject had given him an impression of greater age. As he studied it, he realized that the effect was intentional. The black suit, and the column, topped with a marble urn, on which the man's hand rested, were done with sketchy disinterest, but the face and hands came out of the canvas with a near three-dimensional effect—long cadaverous white hands, and a face set in a wide, sneering smile which showed a set of splendid teeth.

Privately, Peter thought it would make a nice decoration for the office of a dentist with morbid tastes. He leaned back in his chair.

"He looks like someone who might haunt a house, doesn't he?"

"They say he does." Tiphaine came over to sit on the arm of Peter's chair.

"Who says he does?"

"The Negroes. Of course they're a superstitious lot."

"So far as Stephan was concerned, they have reason. He was a real bastard." Katharine's voice was calm, but the word dropped like a stone.

"Simon Legree?" Peter raised an eyebrow. "I thought you people had done away with that sort of thing."

Katharine's mouth twisted, but she said nothing.

"Oh, it wasn't anything like that," Tiphaine exclaimed. "They thought he was a magician—a warlock. They were scared to death of him. Imagine!"

"Oh, I can," Katharine said sarcastically. "After all, when a man insists on stalking around the village in a long black cape, baring his teeth at everyone . . ."

"It was a game," Tiphaine said defensively. "He happened to have two fingers which were precisely the same length. When he found out about the old werewolf stories it amused him to pretend. He even let his eyebrows grow together."

"What did he do about reflections in a mirror?" Peter asked, with genuine interest.

"He ostentatiously avoided mirrors." Tiphaine giggled. "It really was funny, Peter, watching him stalk around town swishing that cape. He'd come home and laugh and laugh."

"Sounds like a fun-loving old gentleman," Peter agreed politely.

Katharine gave him a quick look.

"I'm sure our family eccentricities don't interest Mr. Stewart."

"Oh, but they do. I hadn't realized that the interest in magic and folklore ran in the family."

"I suppose it does," Katharine said. "I remember visiting Stephan when I was a little girl. He had a fantastic library, and I was a compulsive reader. Maybe that started me on my—peculiar career."

"Library?" Peter saw the opening and dived in, head first. "I say, that must be fascinating. I know it's presumptuous of me to ask . . ."

"To use the library? Certainly. Martin said you were going to do a book." Katharine gave him another of those wide, white smiles. "And you'll sing me those fabulous new verses to "The Unquiet Grave," won't you?"

"Certainly." Peter put his glass down and rose, without haste. "Next time. I've kept you too long as it is. The charm of your hospitality made me forget the time."

Katharine uncoiled herself and stood up. Once again it struck Peter with a slight shock to see how small she was; in stocking feet she barely reached to his nose.

"It has been fun, hasn't it?" she said clearly.

When she tipped her head back to look up at him, there was not the slightest hint of coquetry in her manner. Quite the contrary; war had been declared. But in her direct gaze there was something else, considerably more basic. The feeling was mutual. And Peter knew she disliked it as much as he did.


According to the radio, a storm was on its way. After sundown the temperature dropped sharply, and when Peter slid out of his window into the night, the sky was spotted with sly little clouds. He dropped his chin into the high neck of his sweater and walked faster. What a climate! Well, he wouldn't suffer from the cold tonight. He'd be moving too fast.

His next supernatural appearance was going to be even more dramatic than the first. He had acquired the necessary paraphernalia at a pharmacist's in the next town, twenty miles away. It fit nicely into the briecase he carried.

He had taken careful mental notes on the arrangement of Volz's place that afternoon. It ought to be an easy job. The biggest potential fly in the ointment was the problem of the dogs. There hadn't been any.

Since Volz was Master of the Hunt, it was reasonable to suppose that he had some foxhounds around somewhere. In Peter's experience, dogs did bark in the night, at friend or foe; he had to know where the general's hounds were kenneled, if he wanted his nocturnal presence to be unannounced. But he had neither heard nor seen any sign of canine life that afternoon.

Guiding the car with one casual hand, Peter decided that maybe Volz just didn't like dogs. An infallible sign of character, liking or not liking dogs. From what he knew of the general he wouldn't expect Volz to like them.

Timmy was another potential problem, but a minor one. Peter assumed that the repulsive young man sometimes slept in the stables; he certainly smelled as if he did. But surely, on a cold night even a half-witted stableboy would be entitled to four walls and a fire. Peter was prepared to deal with Timmy, though, if he had to. He wasn't expecting any trouble from that quarter.

Volz was remarkably careless about protecting his property. The wall around the stableyard was a flimsy wooden affair, and the gate didn't even have a padlock. In a spirit of fair-mindedness Peter had to admit that horse thieves were pretty much out of style. He suspected that the house was loaded with bolts and chains and burglar alarms, but that was fine with him. He had no designs on the house.

The wind whistled through the trees and tugged irritably at his hair as he approched the back of the house, moving silently but with no attempt at concealment. One set of windows in an upper floor was alight. Presumably Volz was about to retire to his bachelor bed. Peter wondered idly how he spent his evenings. The man couldn't read. Watching television, probably.

He checked the tack room and the stalls and found them, if not empty, at least empty of Timmy. So the man did sleep indoors. That made life somewhat simpler. He found Sultan's stall and stopped the incipient snort with a handful of sugar. While Sultan was munching, he got to work. He was crouched on the floor, tying the second of the cloths around Sultan's near fore, when the roof fell in on him.

It was instinct that saved him, the reflexive spasm of a hunted creature who has learned he must fight for the privilege of breathing. He twisted himself out from under the falling bulk just before it mashed him flat, and swung his clasped hands down on the back of the other man's neck. The next movement brought him to his feet, headed out. Timmy was one thing, and dogs were another thing. This lad was something else.

But Sultan's massive posterior blocked the exit, and Sultan's sudden cupboard love was his undoing. The big head butted him in the chest and snuffled down the front of his sweater looking for more sugar. It caught Peter off balance for a moment, and while he was trying to wriggle past Sultan's tail a hand wrapped around his ankle. His feet went out from under him and he landed flat on his back with a thud that knocked the breath out of his lungs. Before he could get it back, the other man was on top of him.

Jackson was no judo expert; he didn't need to be. His wrists pinned by two big hands, wheezing for breath, Peter looked up at the handsome black face staring down at him, and sighed. He blew up out of the corner of his mouth, trying to get the hair out of his eyes, and said mildly, "Would you mind shifting weight just a bit? You're sitting on my diaphragm."

To his surprise Jackson obeyed, leaning forward so that most of his weight rested on his knees. It was a naive move; he was now in an extremely vulnerable position, and Peter rapidly reviewed three different dirty tricks by which he could free himself. But the very innocence of the gesture disarmed him— that, and the fact that Jackson had a head like cast iron and a reach like a python's. He produced his most disarming smile.

"What happens now?" he asked. "Do you march me up to the house and deliver me to the boss man?"

Jackson's lower lip went out and his brow furrowed. He wasn't stupid; he was just confused. Peter could see his difficulty. When you hate everybody, it's hard to decide whom to fight.

Peter waited patiently, practicing breathing. His wrists hurt. He had a feeling that the circulation was being cut off. But he didn't mention it. Jackson was capable of seeing the subtler points. Most kids his age wouldn't be; he was not only smarter than most kids his age, he had had more experience—all bad, probably.

"Okay," Jackson said finally. He released Peter's wrists and leaned back.

Peter tried to keep his face straight; he wasn't entirely successful. Jackson caught the flicker of expression in the dim light from the door, and a grudging half-smile touched his mouth.

"You think I'm pretty stupid, don't you?" he said.

"Just trusting," Peter said. He pantomimed the move, in

slow motion, so Jackson wouldn't take offense. "Not that you'll ever need tricks like that," he added, as he rolled himself out from under Jackson's body. "You scare the hell out of most people just standing there. If I'd known you were the watchman, I'd never have tried this."

"I need all the tricks I can get," Jackson said.

"Maybe you do," Peter agreed. He sat down, with his back up against the wall, and reached in his pocket. "Cigarette?"

"Not in here."

"Where?" Peter shoved at the equine head which was bruising his chest. Sultan had misinterpreted his gesture toward his pocket. "Damn this animal. I'd like to talk to you."

"And I want to talk to you," Jackson said grimly.

They found a sheltered spot in the pasture, behind a rock that gave some protection against the chilly wind. Jackson was in shirt sleeves, but he didn't seem to notice the cold. He squatted, his back against the rock, and fixed his eyes intently on Peter.

"Whatchu up to in there, man?"

"Spare me the dialect," Peter said, cupping his hands around a match, and extending it toward Jackson's cigarette.

"And you spare me the stalling." Jackson took a drag and blew out smoke. The vapor was torn to tatters by the wind. "What were you doing in the stables? I've got a good imagination, but I can't think of any legal reason."

"How about illegal?"

"Quite a few. But none of them seem to apply."

"I felt like a midnight ride," Peter said.

Jackson's fist shot out toward Peter's throat, and then dropped as if it had been amputated. Still sprawled comfortably on the grass, Peter lowered his hand and said mildly, "Don't shove, Jackson. I don't like it any more than you do."

The boy rubbed his forearm.

"Where did you learn that one?"

"I watch a lot of television."

"No, come on. Show me."

Peter started to remonstrate, and then reminded himself of several not so extraneous factors. He glanced at his watch. The luminous dial showed eleven forty. He had time.

"All right," he said, rising to his feet with a groan. "Do that again, slowly, and I'll show you."

The next ten minutes were strenuous. Peter ended the demonstration by letting Jackson hook his feet out from under him, and gave a realistic grunt as he fell. From a prone and slightly theatrical position he smiled affably up at the boy's grinning face.

"Now do I get that horse?"

"Nope."

"Why not?"

Jackson sat down beside him and pulled out a crumpled pack of cigarettes. After a slight hesitation he extended it to Peter.

"You're crazy," he muttered, his head bent over the match. "I never spent such a crazy night. I catch you trying to steal a horse, and ten minutes later you're teaching me judo, or whatever the hell it is. Crazy."

"I impress some people that way," Peter agreed, still prone. The ground was cold, but not quite as cold as the upper air.

Jackson scowled at the glowing end of his cigarette. He didn't find conversation easy, probably because there were so many ideas burgeoning in that well-endowed head of his, and too few people to whom he could express them. Peter wriggled into a more comfortable position, hands clasped under his head, and pensively contemplated the firmament. He had plenty of time. It was beginning to look as if the evening's performance would be called off.

Finally Jackson mashed his cigarette out.

"Who are you, anyhow?"

"Just a peaceful tourist."

"Peaceful like a bomb. But you know what you remind me of? You remind me of old Daniel in the lions' den. The lions stand 'round, smiling and showing all those pretty white teeth. But those teeth bite, friend. And Daniel knew they were lions."

Peter turned his head. This wasn't what he had expected.

"You speak in parables, my son. Was that a warning?"

"Forget it. I said more than I should have. Don't expect any help from me. I don't stick my neck out for anybody."

"Especially for Whitey?"

The boy glanced at him. Peter thought he had never seen a look so devoid of emotion. It was not hostile, merely set in an intensity of purpose which negated feeling.

"Some of the boys get their kicks out of name calling. Me, I'm not that stupid."

"That must make you unpopular in certain quarters," Peter said.

"It makes me unpopular in all quarters." Jackson gave him a sudden ferocious grin. "That's why I collect all the dirty tricks I can find."

"Thanks for the warning." Peter stood up. "Well. No more tricks, dirty or otherwise, from me. I've got to have something in reserve for the next time you jump me."

"Don't try it."

"Another warning?" Peter braced himself; Jackson had risen, and was looming.

"What you're up to is none of my business, Stewart. If you can pull something on that bastard up at the house, I'll cheer you on. But from the sidelines, mister—from way out on the sidelines. And if I can make a buck by acting like a big faithful watchdog, I'll make it. At your expense."

Peter shrugged.

"Fair enough. Can I collect my belongings? I left them in the stall."

They walked back in silence through the windy night. Still in silence Jackson watched Peter stuff his possessions into his bag. After the third item he couldn't stand it any longer.

"I would sort of like to know what you were going to do."

"I'll bet you would."

"Luminous paint; that stuff around Sultan's feet—black cloth—"

"It'll give you something to think about during the long nights." Peter straightened, bag in hand. "No dice, Jackson. I'm going home in a huff. You won't let me steal your horse, I won't let you play. You're better off not being involved, really."

"Sure, sure," Jackson muttered.

Peter left without a formal good-night. As he turned the corner of the stable, he heard something rustle, and he whirled, dropping his bag and raising his hands. There was nothing to be seen. Not at first. His back flat up against the rough wooden planks, he saw a slim dark shadow scuttle across a patch of moonlight and disappear as the moon hid behind a cloud.

# Chapter

## 5

THE PERFORMANCE PETER HAD PLANNED WAS USELESS WITHOUT Sultan. He went back to the car, wondering about alternatives; so long as he was out, it seemed a pity to waste the evening. The night was perfect; scudding clouds, flickering moonlight, a wind keening high in the trees. Still cogitating, he drove the few miles to the other house, parked in his former spot, and climbed the wall as before.

As soon as he got through the belt of trees he realized that something was going on. The house was a blaze of light.

By now it was well past midnight. Knowing Katharine's habits, he would not have expected her to be entertaining. The absence of cars in the driveway confirmed the assumption. He wondered what had happened.

He investigated the downstairs rooms first, and found lights shining in rooms which were uninhabited, except for the kitchen. The two elderly servants were there; both had on night attire, with robes over pajamas. The cook's graying hair was done up in pink curlers. Something was boiling on the stove, and the cook was preparing a tray. She looked sleepy and disgruntled. Her husband sat at the table, elbows propped, blinking groggily into a cup of coffee. Peter watched them for a few minutes, and then decided there was nothing to be gained by waiting. With the windows shut he wouldn't be able to hear anything even if they spoke.

The upstairs window he selected had two things to recommend it. Its frontal location, above the room in which the séance had been held, suggested that it might be the master bedroom, and an old oak tree provided a convenient ladder to the small balcony. He swarmed up the tree with only one broken branch to mark his progress; the snap was lost in the general uproar of the wind. At least he hoped it was. When he stood on the balcony, outside the French doors which were the counterparts of the doors below, he saw that he had struck pay dirt.

It was Katharine's room. He would have recognized it from its air of austerity, plain furniture, and walls lined with bookcases, even if the woman herself had not been sprawled face down across the bed. Tiphaine was bending over her, one hand on her cousin's shoulder. Every light in the room was on—the overhead chandelier, the desk and dressing-table lamps, two bed lamps. Tiphaine's molten hair threw the light back like a polished bronze mirror, and swung down, half hiding her face. She wore plain white silk tailored pajamas and looked good enough to eat.

As Peter moved in closer for a better look, some slight sound must have reached the older woman's ears, for she sat bolt upright, both hands going out in a spasmodic gesture.

"What was that?"

"The wind. Only the wind. Kate, it's all right; try to relax."

Katharine nodded. She looked like hell, Peter thought clinically. Her eyes were sunken and a muscle at the corner of her mouth beat frantically, like a tiny pulse. He was sardonically amused to note that the woman who dressed in tailored slacks and shirt during the day had a less Spartan taste in nightwear. Her gown was pale green; the full skirt spread out across the bed in agitated ripples the color and opacity of seawater. One slender strap had slipped down off her shoulder. She was definitely too thin. Still, the general effect would have been arresting, if it had not been for the face—a study in sheer terror, unmasked . . .

"There's someone out there," she insisted.

Peter took one noiseless step backward and stood poised at the rim of the balcony. But Tiphaine shook her head and did not stir.

"Kate, I looked. When I first came up. There never was anyone there. It must have been a dream."

"It was his voice. Saying . . . saying . . ."

"Saying what?" Tiphaine sat down on the edge of the bed.

"Saying he wanted . . . that I should . . ." Kate shivered.

Tiphaine put her arms around her cousin, and Kate caught at her with frantic hands.

"Don't go away," she muttered. "Don't leave me alone . . ."

A soft knock sounded at the door, and she started violently.

"It's only Mrs. Schmidt," Tiphaine said soothingly. She called, "Come in."

The cook entered, carrying a tray. The pink curlers looked like some barbaric hair adornment.

"This is too hot," Tiphaine said, taking the cup. "I'll put some cold water in."

She vanished into the bathroom. Katharine was quiet now, her hands and face controlled; putting on a good front before the servants. It was hard to believe that she was the same woman who had been cowering and moaning a few moments earlier.

"Did Will search the house?" she asked.

"Yes, miss."

"Was there—anything?"

"Not a sign of anything, miss."

Having seen Will dozing over his coffee in the kitchen not five minutes before, Peter knew the woman was lying. It was fortunate for him that the household had grown accustomed to Kate's hallucinations; he could come and go without too much fear of being seen by the Schmidts. Old Will was not the man to prowl the grounds on a cold autumn night unless he had to. And it was becoming clear that he would have to pay Kate More several more visits. The damned woman had nerves, not of steel, but of rubber; they bounced back after every shock. But not all the way. A few more surprises . . .

Tiphaine came back with the cup of tea. Over Kate's bowed head a significant glance passed between the two other women, and Peter deduced that Tiphaine had added some sort of sedative to the tea. Kate certainly needed something. Despite her control, her hands shook so badly when she took the cup that tea slopped over onto the bedspread.

The cook left, taking the tray, and Tiphaine switched off the overhead light.

"Leave it on," Kate gasped. "Don't leave me. . . ."

"You can't sleep with all the lights blazing. I'll be here, Kate. All night, if you want me."

"Kind . . ." Kate slumped back against the pillows; in her exhausted state the drug had taken quick effect.

The room was now dim except for the circles of light shed by the lamps on the desk and bedside tables. Now, before she sank into drugged sleep, was the time for the next move.

Peter climbed onto the roof. It was within arms' reach of the top of the balcony rail. Hanging head down, held by his knees and one hand, he twisted around so that he could see into the room. It was an uncomfortable position, but he didn't have to hold it long. Just long enough to give the knife the proper flip, that would make it curve down from a high point that was above normal eye level. To a mind already attuned to the supernatural it would seem to have materialized in midair. That was the explanation of the poltergeist legend; careful misdirection by the person responsible for the flying objects, so that no one noticed where they originated.

One quick movement of his wrist and it was done; he saw it thud, the carved hilt quivering, into the wooden footboard of the bed.

He twisted himself up and caught the gutter with his other hand. Much as he would have liked to see the results with his own eyes, he couldn't spare the time. There must be no sign of a material agent, or the game was spoiled; this time old Will might actually be moved to look around.

He was half way across the roof when the scream began, and it went on for some time, even after he had descended to the ground and was running toward the wall.

Peter slept the dreamless sleep which is erroneously attributed to the just. There is, after all, nothing like exercise in the fresh air before retiring. When he awoke, he lay still, blinking in the daylight, and planning his next move.

The first part of his project was easier than he had expected. Thanks to Katharine's own overactive conscience, she was already in a state of extreme nervous tension. The next step wasn't going to be so easy. He had never had any hard-and-fast scheme for getting invited to the house, though he had considered possible openings. One potential means of entree was definitely out. Katharine was not only unimpressed, she was hostile and suspicious. Tiphaine was a more hopeful prospect, but Peter's personal vanity was not so exaggerated as to make him believe he could sweep the girl off her feet within the next few days. The very success of the initial phase made haste essential. If Kate went on the way she was going, she might crack up fairly soon. He had to be on hand when the moment arrived, and that meant residence in the house, not casual lurking.

Maybe, after all, the hoary old tricks were the best.

Without rising, he stretched out one arm for the telephone and ordered breakfast. Then he asked for a local number.

Volz sounded as if he had been up, swinging from the trees, since dawn. Peter moved the telephone three inches away from his ear. He was in luck. The hunt was meeting next day.

His second outside call was less productive. Mrs. Martin's feeble voice informed him that the doctor had gone out on a call late last night and wasn't back yet. Peter said he would stop by later that afternoon, and hung up, smiling nastily. He didn't have to ask where Martin had gone.

He amused himself for the rest of the morning by a visit to Greer's Saddlery. He had been tempted to appear next day in old slacks and sweater, but that would have been indulging his sense of humor too far. At Greer's he contemplated himself in the mirror with a grimace of amusement. The uniform was as archaistic as tights and a doublet, and much more uncomfortable. The white stock tickled his chin, and the black derby hat gave him a headache. He tapped the shining boots with the crop, fingered the chaste gold bar that adorned his stock, and bought the lot, over the moans of Mr. Greer, who insisted that everything needed taking in at the waist.

"I'll tighten my belt," Peter said shortly, and left, after paying out a sum which made him grimace again, but not with amusement.

He went to Martin's house just after three, and had to wait. Martin had a backlog of patients from that morning. When Peter was finally shown into the sanctum, he found Martin pouring himself a shot from a bottle which normally lived in the bottom drawer of his desk.

"Join me?"

"No, thanks." Peter sat down, looking concerned, and Martin shrugged.

"I don't ordinarily do this. But today has been one of those days."

"Not much sleep?"

"None." Martin swallowed his dosage, made a wry face, and then glanced keenly at Peter. "How did you know?"

"The word gets around," Peter said vaguely.

"God yes." Martin sighed. "What are people saying?"

"Rather peculiar things. It depends on whom you're talking to, of course."

"Of course," Martin said mechanically. "It's good of you to be so discreet, Stewart, but there's not much point in discretion when the whole damned town is whispering. You've met Dr. More?"

"Yesterday. And professional reticence is unnecessary with anyone who's seen her. What's wrong with the woman? Drugs? Guilty conscience?"

"What makes you say that?"

"You mean, what business is it of mine? Because Tiphaine is out there, two miles from the nearest neighbor, with only a pair of doddering old servants. Drug addicts aren't precisely the safest companions."

"It isn't drugs."

"I don't give a damn what it is. The woman is unstable. She might—hurt Tiphaine."

"Take it easy," Martin said. "You're interested in Tiphaine?"

"I'm in love with her," Peter said, and met the doctor's eyes with one of his best candid stares.

"Does she reciprocate your feelings?" Despite his furrowed brows there was a hint of amusement in the doctor's voice.

"I know it sounds ridiculous," Peter said shyly. "But sometimes it happens that way. . . . No, of course she doesn't. Not yet. If I had time . . . but in the meanwhile, what's happening out there? The situation is unhealthy, whatever the cause."

"The situation is even worse than you think," Martin said, and then fell silent. Peter waited, while Martin filled his pipe; the doctor's own concern was warring with his professional caution, and as Peter watched he could almost see the other factors being weighed—his own respectable introduction and exemplary behavior, plus the fact that this wasn't really . . .

"It isn't really a question of professional ethics," Martin said. "Of course the problem may be one of hallucinations—visual and auditory—but she isn't the sort of woman who is ordinarily affected in that way. I'm afraid, Stewart, that someone has been playing some malicious and dangerous tricks."

Peter widened his eyes and looked baffled.

"Why would anyone do a thing like that?"

"I can't imagine." Martin made a sweeping, frustrated gesture. "It can't be personal enmity, so I can only conclude that someone here in town has it in for the family. You may have heard some of the stories about Stephan . . ."

"Tiphaine told me about his werewolf game."

"It wasn't exactly a game," Martin said. "He was always good to Tiphaine, so naturally she takes his part. But Stephan had a mean streak. He enjoyed frightening people, and he dabbled in some of the nastier magical practices. Katharine herself isn't popular; she's never done the town any harm—quite the contrary, but her charities are, at her own insistence, anonymous, and there are wild tales among the more superstitious older residents that she's inherited Stephan's talent for magic. Black magic."

"It's unbelievable," Peter murmured.

"You know better. You've traveled in backward country areas, must have, to collect your songs. How many witches have you met?"

"A few. But that was England and Scotland, little country villages. This is a modern, sophisticated town."

"Science and sophistication don't kill superstition," Martin said heavily. "Look at the newspapers—ads for palmists and astrologers, fortune-telling columns. You can find a section "Spiritualists" in the Yellow Pages. Add to that a long tradition of superstition, and you're in trouble. You've met Mrs. Adams, at the hotel? Fine horsewoman, canny businesswoman; but she's a member of some wild cult that calls on Mother Earth. Not," he added quickly, "that I think Mrs. Adams is behind these tricks that are being played on Kate. I visualize someone simpler and more easily frightened. Someone who is suffering from illness or financial trouble, and blames it on Kate."

"But, look here!" Peter sat up, gripping the arms of his chair. "If some madman thinks she's put a spell on him—the most effective ways of canceling such a spell is to kill the witch!"

"That's what I'm afraid of." Martin knocked out his dead pipe. "At first it was simply malice, no physical threats. But last night someone threw a knife. It just missed Tiphaine."

Peter's look of dismay was genuine this time. Unless Tiphaine had moved at the last moment, he didn't see how the knife could have come anywhere near her. What was Martin trying to prove? Or had he gotten a hysterical version of the story from two frightened women?

"You have a nice, neat theory, Doctor," he said. "But isn't it also possible that Dr. More herself is playing the tricks?"

He expected a bellow of protest. Instead, Martin's shoulders sagged.

"I don't know why I'm discussing this with you," he murmured.

"Because you're worn out and worried sick. Look here, Martin, it's Tiphaine I care about. Doesn't my interest in her give me a right to be concerned?" Martin nodded heavily, without looking up, and Peter went on earnestly, "I'm not trying to build a case against Dr. More. I don't know what to think—except that Tiphaine may be in danger, either from her cousin or as one of those innocent bystanders who are always getting clobbered by careless assassins. I'm as anxious to find out the truth as you are."

"Calm down, Peter. I agree completely." Martin looked at him with a faint, haggard smile. "I must admit, it's a relief to share this with someone I can trust."

"We'll think of something," Peter said confidently. "What about a hired guard?"

"I suggested that. There isn't a man in the house except old Will, and he's as timid as a rabbit. Superstitious, too; his family has lived here for three hundred years. But Kate refused."

"She did, eh?"

"Yes, but I may yet convince her." Martin's tone was less assured than his words. "I'm going out there tonight myself."

"I wish I were. Well, if you're going to be up all night again, I'd better leave so you can nap this afternoon." Peter rose. At the door he turned, as if some sudden idea had come to him.

"Martin, I wonder . . ."

"What?" The doctor looked at him hopefully.

"I haven't quite got it worked out yet. But I may need your cooperation."

"Anything. Anything that will help."

"This might help," Peter assured him.

He left the office with the smug feeling that for once he had told the simple truth. He simply hadn't specified who would be helped by his plan.


"One of the reasons why I always hated hunting," Peter muttered, "is that you have to get up so early in the morning."

His companion, one of the plump matrons whom he had met at the Folklore Society meeting, giggled nervously. She had an improbable name—Marlene, or something like that—and teeth that looked as if they had been meant to protrude slightly before an orthodontist got his hands on her.

"It's a nice day for it, anyhow," she said. "For hunting, I mean. It's not a nice day really . . ."

Peter wiped beads of moisture from his boot. The weather was foul. In Scotland it might have been called a mist; fog shrouded the lower patches of ground, and moisture collected on every possible surface. Marlene assured him earnestly that the fog would lift by ten, and that it would be a marvelous day. Peter gave her a glance of hatred. Her riding habit was too tight; the buttons at her middle were strained. At least he wouldn't have her beside him once the hunt got underway; she sat her horse, a timid-looking filly, like a blob of jelly, and her hands were nervous on the reins.

"The unspeakable chasing the uneatable," he muttered, and gave Marlene a bland smile as she glanced at him uncertainly.

"What did you say?"

"I was admiring your horse."

"She was very expensive," Marlene said complacently. "My husband *raved* when he saw the bill."

"He doesn't hunt?"

"He doesn't do *anything*," said Marlene. "Except make money."

"Well, that's not such a bad occupation. It allows you to buy very expensive horses."

"Not all that expensive," Marlene said perversely. "Sultan cost four times as much. I sure do admire your nerve, riding that mean animal. He always tries to bite me."

As if he had understood the words, Sultan stamped and glared. His feeble wits had completely forgotten Peter's sugar the night before, and twice he had absentmindedly started to nibble his rider's boot. Peter dealt with that problem the second time. Now Sultan sulked and bided his time. Peter felt fairly sure that the noble steed would head for the first tree he saw, and try to scrape his rider off.

"He tries to bite me, too," Peter said truthfully. "Oops." He jerked in the saddle and gathered the reins closer. "He seems edgy today. Hope I haven't taken on more than I can handle."

A cacaphony of excited barking announced the arrival of the MFH and his canine entourage. Peter studied the square, squat figure, which looked like a toad in a top hat, with disapproval.

"Volz isn't his own Huntsman, I see. How did he get to be Master?"

"It's a lot of work. He has the time and the money. He doesn't like dogs, but there's no rule that says he has to be Huntsman."

She trotted off, bouncing emphatically, toward the other riders. Peter pushed his hat back off his aching brow and glanced around. Most of the other members had arrived by now. Mrs. Adams was one of them; she was at her best in the masculine garb, and the hunt colors she wore testified to her skill. Peter recognized some of the others, from the Folklore meeting. Martin was conspicuously absent, but everyone else who was anybody seemed to be present. All the white folks, that is. Middleburg had its town Negro, a distinguished State Department official, who lived in a particularly isolated house outside the town limits, but the only black face visible here was that of Hilary Jackson, and Hilary was busy trying to hold the pack of yelling hounds.

Peter had seen Timmy's fleeting form, but the half-wit kept out of sight except when actually called upon to perform some service. At the moment, he was invisible, which suited Peter fine; the shambling, secretive form looked absolutely eerie sliding along through patches of mist. He touched Sultan's side and walked the horse over to where Hilary stood, feet braced, magnificent muscles taut against the pull of the leads. He hadn't planned to start a conversation, under the eyes of the town gentry; but he was unprepared for the hostile look Jackson gave him. The boy deliberately looked away, leaving Peter feeling rebuffed.

Two hours later he was still feeling rebuffed. He was also bored. They had killed once. As a guest, Peter kept behind, and he made a show of Sultan's wildness as they stood around the miserable remains of the fox. Sultan reared, in response to a surreptitious jab, and Volz turned from his contemplation of the bloody mess on the ground.

"Having trouble, Stewart?"

"No," Peter said. "He's just a little—oops!—nervous."

"Better go back and change mounts."

"Oh, no, that's not necessary."

"All right. Just don't get in the way."

Hounds and riders were off again. The next chase went as Peter had hoped, into the woods. It was a messy sort of forest, overgrown and thick with fallen trees; he lost himself without any trouble. He got rid of his hat along the way and loosened his stock; a few swipes with a handy bramble branch gave his face that extra touch of verisimilitude. Then he set off at a leisurely pace toward the edge of Katharine's property.

The wooded area ended about a hundred yards from the stone wall which marked the back boundaries. The wall was lower here in back, easily within a horse's jumping ability.

He reined the stallion in at the edge of the wood. Even from that point he could hear sounds of activity on the other side of the wall. They were odd sounds—a regular, monotonous thunk, thunk, like someone beating a rug. From his early investigations Peter was able to identify the sounds. There was an archery target back here, a good safe distance from the house. He was in luck. Now he wouldn't have to play his little drama right up under the kitchen windows.

He sent Sultan plunging out of the woods at a gallop and put him at the wall. He learned then another reason for Sultan's high price. The big animal jumped like Pegasus, soaring so lightly that it almost hurt Peter to spoil the picture. He came back into the saddle too hard and too soon; Sultan came down practically flat-footed, and Peter didn't have to pretend when he lost one stirrup and slipped sideways, like Tom Mix ducking Indian arrows. When he straightened up, he saw that the analogy was only too apt. He was being covered by a pair of steely eyes and an even harder steel point.

Katharine wore her usual costume, with a sweater instead of a shirt, and very dirty sneakers. Her sleeves were pushed up to the elbow to leave room for the leather archer's guard. The pose showed her slight figure to its best advantage, erect, balanced, and straight as the arrow she was aiming at the center of Peter's chest.

Peter sat very still. The black-and-red-feathered arrow had a field point, not one of the deadly broad-bladed hunting points; but it was steel, for all that, and the arms that held it had an unmistakable look of competence. Her stance was that of a professional, wrist and arm perfectly straight but not rigid. The bow was equipped with a sight, which confirmed his suspicion that she had done a lot of target shooting. The point of the arrow dropped as he watched her warily, but he was not reassured; from the point of aim, it was clear that she was pulling an unusually heavy bow for a woman of her size—thirty or thirty-five pounds, maybe.

"Out," she said succinctly. "Turn around and go back where you came from."

"Over that?" Peter nodded at the wall. "I barely made it the first time."

"You shouldn't have tried."

"I couldn't help it."

She squinted, studying his scratched face and general dishevelment.

"I'm afraid Tiphaine is too impressionable. She raved about your riding."

"Sultan seems a little nervous," Peter said defensively. He raised one hand to brush his hair back, and Sultan danced.

"So he does. How unfortunate. Out."

"But, look here! I'm sorry about intruding, but it was an accident."

"I don't allow hunting, or any other sort of intrusion. If you want to see me, come to the front door."

"But, Dr. More—"

"Out."

Peter started to expostulate, then closed his mouth and shrugged. He wasn't at all sure she wouldn't shoot him. He turned Sultan. They were not far enough from the wall for a good approach, and both he and the horse knew it, but by that time Sultan was so annoyed he didn't care. He flung himself up and barely made it, his heels scraping the stone; and Peter, releasing reins and stirrups at the same moment, slid ungracefully out of the saddle.

He landed on the outer side of the wall, with a crash and rattle of shrubbery which was as spectacular as he had hoped, and lay as he had fallen, with one eye cocked toward the wall.

Katharine's startled face appeared above it, and Peter closed the eye. He heard her scramble down and approach. He was sprawled on his back, one leg twisted under him. A cold hand touched his forehead, brushing the hair back and lingering on a rising lump. He heard a soft intake of breath and got ready to respond, with pathetic weakness, to cries of feminine distress and pity.

"Damn it to hell," Katharine said to herself. "The stupid fool's killed himself."

An hour later Peter was reclining in bed upstairs, with a splitting headache whose discomfort was mitigated by the knowledge that Phase Two of the plan had been successful. Martin had come and gone; he had given Peter a reproachful look, but one which was tempered by amusement and relief, and he had spoken gravely of possible concussion. In view of the fact that the poor chap was living at the hotel, where service, though splendid, was not designed for the sick . . .

"What about the hospital?" Katharine interrupted.

Peter looked up at her from under his lashes as she stood by the bed, fingers tapping impatiently on the footboard. Her mouth was a tight slit and her eyes were narrowed with a fury which the doctor's diagnosis had only slightly calmed.

"You know how crowded we are, Kate. Besides, moving him would be ill advised. If you need help, I might be able to send a nurse. . . ."

"From your overworked hospital? Oh, all right, Martin. I can't very well throw him out bodily, can I? But I wish you weren't so damned *nice!*"

She flung out of the room, closing the door with exaggerated care. Peter grinned at Martin, who answered with a wink and a slight nod toward Tiphaine, who stood by the door.

"Just stay in bed and take it easy," Martin said casually. "Tiphaine will keep an eye on you, you don't really need a nurse. Child, you know what to watch out for—bleeding from ears or nostrils, drowsiness, nausea. . . ."

"I know." Tiphaine glided forward, giving Peter a smile that made his abused head swim. "Don't worry, Paul, I'll take care of him."

When the doctor had left, she sat down on the edge of the

bed and took Peter's hand in both hers. She was very lovely, with her vibrant features and that unbelievable hair, between gold and copper. Peter was wondering how soon he could reasonably recover from a slight concussion when she spoke.

"What happened, Peter?"

"I fell off," Peter said literally.

"You forget, darling, I've seen you ride. Did someone—do something to Sultan?"

"Now what," Peter said, "would make you think a thing like that?"

"Stop it." Color flamed in her cheeks; she looked beautiful and rather alarming. "The whole town is gossiping about what's happening here. Paul knows. You've been talking to him, haven't you?"

"Well, yes. But . . ."

"So you decided you were going to rush in and rescue us." The blue eyes were blazing; the fine hairs lifted about her face as if electrified. "The big hero. Prying and prowling and . . . Why don't you leave us alone? Everything was fine until you came. . . ."

Peter, who had been trying ineffectually to get a word in, decided that there was only one way to shut her up. He caught her clenched fists and pulled her down, so hard that several hitherto unnoticed bruises complained; but after the first twinge Peter was in no state to notice. For the first second or two she twisted like an eel in his grasp. This stage was succeeded by one of enthusiastic cooperation. But as soon as his grip relaxed she was up, and out of his arms, in one lithe movement. Peter was left with his mouth open and his arms out. He closed the former, dropped the latter, and looked reproachfully at Tiphaine.

She was still flushed, but not with anger; after a moment her wide mouth curved up and she sat down again.

"Bad to worse," she said, a little breathlessly. "Is that any way to calm a girl's suspicions?"

"I'm sorry." They contemplated one another solemnly for a moment. Then Peter said, "I'm also a liar."

"I guess I should apologize." There were lines in her face that shouldn't have been there, and Peter felt an emotion so unfamiliar that it took him some time to identify it. He felt like a heel.

"I was answering your suspicions," he said, drowning out the small voice of his conscience. "And explaining—in pantomime, that is—why I'm here."

"That's sweet of you. But unnecessary. There's no reason why you should worry about me."

"Yes, there is. What's wrong with Kate?"

Tiphaine was silent, scrutinizing him with an intensity which was almost as uncomfortable as the doctor's had been. But her questioning eyes were harder to face than Martin's. Finally she gave a long sigh.

"It's Mark. That's what is wrong with Kate."

"Who," Peter said carefully, "is Mark?"

"Someone we—Kate used to know. Her . . . well, he was . . ."

"Mmmhmm," Peter said.

"She was in love with him, and he died."

"How?"

"He was out with a gun. Alone. The gun went off, somehow, and killed him."

"I see. And he's the one she wants—" Peter caught himself just in time. He wasn't supposed to know about the cult of Mother Earth. "To forget," he ended lamely.

Tiphaine didn't seem to have noticed the tiny pause.

"That's the trouble, she can't forget him. It's been almost a year, but she's still—haunted."

Peter leaned back against his pillow.

"He must have been quite a guy."

"He was," Tiphaine said softly, "quite a guy."

"You liked him too?"

"Liked him? Mark?" She considered the question, smiling faintly, eyes remote. "You didn't like Mark. You hated him or you were crazy about him." She smiled suddenly, mockingly. "Most men hated him."

"Oh, that type."

"No, not that type! Well, I guess he was . . . sort of. Women adored him. That was enough to make other men dislike him," she added with a worldly air. "And he could be pretty sarcastic. One look, and one comment in that drawly voice of his, and people just shriveled."

"I don't think I'd have liked him," Peter said.

"Probably not. Though you reminded me of him, at first,"

she said thoughtfully; and Peter thought, hell, not again. "Until you kissed me," she added.

"I gather you have a basis for comparison," Peter said coolly. He had been wondering why he was so ridiculously jealous of a dead man.

"Mark kissed all the girls. No offense, no hard feelings." Smiling, she put out a delicate finger and ran it down his face from temple to cheek to mouth. "You're dying to know what the difference is, aren't you?"

Peter took her hand and put it firmly down on the spread.

"What are you up to now. Distraction?"

"But there's nothing else to say," she exclaimed. "I don't know any more."

"I think you do."

"Then—if I do—I can't tell you." She stood up and started for the door. With her hand on the knob, she turned to look at him. "But I'm glad you're here, Peter," she said softly.

# Chapter

## 6

AS SOON AS THE HOUSEHOLD HAD GONE TO BED, PETER prowled. No incidents were scheduled for that night—it would be too suspicious, on his first night in the house—but he wanted to get the interior geography of the placc clear in his mind. After an hour of sitting in the dark, his night vision was complete. He couldn't risk even the smallest light, not with the household in its present state of nerves.

Like the downstairs, with its wings and additions, the upstairs was a rabbit warren. Luckily only one wing was in full use, the one over the huge séance room he had seen the first night. It had one corridor with rooms on either side. Katharine's rooms, the master suite, occupied the entire end of the wing. His room was as far away from hers as possible, next to the staircase. Tiphaine's smaller chamber adjoined her cousin's, and there were two other rooms, empty guest chambers.

Peter approved the thick carpeting of the corridor, which muffled footsteps, and was happy to find that door hinges and knobs were well oiled. He discovered this by looking into the two unoccupied rooms; he would like to have ascertained whether Katharine locked her door, but was afraid to try it. Ten to one she was lying awake, staring into the darkness; the slightest sound, at door or window, would set her screeching.

If he were in her shoes, he wouldn't know what to do about locks. Do you lock the door against intruders, or leave it unlocked so that help can reach you quickly? After all, ghosts aren't hindered by locks and bolts.

The room across the hall from Tiphaine's was as dark as the proverbial cow's interior, once he had closed the door. Shades and curtains were drawn, and he had to inch his way across the floor, feeling with hands and feet. He didn't pull the drapes back; they were on rings, which might rattle. Instead he slid between them, raised the blind, and pushed back the bolt that kept the window locked.

The first gust of wind set the drapes swinging and produced a slight rattle from the rings. Peter pulled his head back in and got the window shut in a hurry, though he doubted that the sound had been loud enough to rouse anyone. He had seen enough. The window ledges were wide and the wall was covered with vines and trellises. A careful climber could get around from this room to Kate's balcony. He was on his way out of the room when another idea came to him, and he investigated. As he had hoped, the bathroom adjoining his room was meant to serve this room too. The connecting door was closed, but the bolt on this side was not drawn.

Peter studied it for a moment, and a slow smile spread over his face. Yes, it was definitely an idea; and a nice effect it would make, too, if he could work it properly.

He spent the next half hour practicing, with a shoelace and a drawing pin—they called them thumbtacks here—which had held back the curtains in his room. The shoelace was too thick, naturally; he would have to get another kind of twine, white, or transparent plastic, that wouldn't show againt the white paint of the door. Plastic fishline, that was the stuff; strong enough to do the job, and thin enough to slide easily through the crack between door and doorframe. He could pick that up in town tomorrow, along with some white-head thumbtacks. At least he had the positions of the latter figured out, along the minute cracks in the inner molding of the door, so there wouldn't be any betraying holes after the pins were removed.

He returned to his room through the bathroom, and went on through into the hall. The servants didn't sleep in this wing, and it would be a good idea to locate their bedrooms, so he would know how to avoid them.

The Schmidts slept at the other end of the house, over the kitchen; Peter identified the room some distance away by the resounding duet of snores. A good safe distance from the gentry, near the cook's domain; still, if he had been Kate he would have gathered them in closer. He doubted whether they would hear a machine gun, let alone a scream, over the sounds of their own snores. He wanted to explore the downstairs, particularly the library. He fancied he would find Katharine's working desk there, and he was curious to see whether papers, such as her bank receipts, would contain any interesting material. But he decided not to risk the trip. Give her one quiet night, to calm her nerves. Then the next performance would hit her even harder.

Peter spent the morning in bed, catching up on his sleep. It was a very comfortable bed. The cook brought him his lunch, but refused to be inveigled into conversation. Philosophically Peter turned his attention to food. It was excellent. All the homely women he had met so far in this peculiar town were splendid cooks. He wondered if the converse was true.

After lunch he decided that he had loafed long enough, and got dressed. The sound of guitar music led him to the living room. Tiphaine was wearing stretch pants and a striped jersey in an electric shade of green that made her hair blaze like a fire. She looked up from the guitar in her lap with some surprise.

"Should you be up?" she asked.

"No bleeding from the ears, no excessive drowsiness, no—"

"I haven't been a very good nurse, have I?" Her smile was just a little sarcastic. It did not become her, Peter decided.

"I haven't been a very good patient," he admitted, dropping into a chair. "I got bored, I'm afraid. Sing something."

She did some of the familiar ones, "Venezuela" and "Barbara Allen"; then she began "The False Lover Regained," and Peter obligingly joined in. They did several other songs together, but Tiphaine's voice had lost some of its sparkle; before long she put the guitar down and leaned forward, chin on her hands.

"Peter. How much longer are you going to stay?"

"I'll leave today, if you want me to."

"You will?"

"I'll leave the house. But I'll be sitting out there tonight, watching your window. Probably in a patch of poison ivy," he added more lightly. "That's the sort of thing that generally happens to my grand gestures."

She gave him a slow, bewitching smile.

"Then you really meant it, about being worried about me?"

Peter decided, against his will, that his lady love was a bit laborious.

"Yes, I really meant it."

"And I meant it when I said I was glad you were here. I wanted to tell you—look out, someone's coming. . . ."

She struck a chord at random. Peter leaned back, hands clasped around his raised knee.

"If you sing 'Greensleeves,' " he said in a loud voice, "I'm leaving."

"How did you know?" Tiphaine played up beautifully, raising her own voice just a little.

"That old familiar E minor chord. Not that you don't have the voice for it. It's just that I've rendered that cursed song, and heard it rendered, at every school and village concert since I was three years old. It palls. It's beautiful, but it palls."

He turned his head casually, and then started to get up.

"Don't stand," said Kate, framed in the doorway. "I'd feel bad if gallantry made you swoon at my feet."

After that, of course, he had no choice but to rise.

"If that really worries you, you'd better sit down yourself."

Kate dropped onto the sofa and reached for a cigarette.

"Don't let me interrupt you. Maybe now I'll hear those famous verses."

"Glad to oblige," Peter said. He had spent some of his spare time that morning polishing the said verses. Silently Tiphaine handed him the guitar.

"Interesting," Kate said when he had finished. She blew out a cloud of smoke which hid her expression, but her voice held a note Peter didn't like at all. It was amused, and a little respectful. Still, it was the most pleasant tone he had heard from the lady so far.

"I've been thinking, Tiphaine," she went on casually, "that perhaps Mr. Stewart ought to attend the meeting tonight."

The silence was so thick it could have been cut with a knife. Tiphaine sat motionless, hands clasped on her knee.

"It's up to you," she said finally. "But do you think . . . ?"

Kate's hand moved to her mouth; she took a deep drag on her cigarette.

"Oh, I definitely do think."

Tiphaine turned her head so that the waves of hair veiled her face, and Peter said easily, "What's the meeting about? More folklore?"

"A little experiment," Kate said. "I shan't tell you about it in order not to prejudice you. Unbiased observers are so important, don't you think?"

"Definitely," Peter murmured. Their glances locked, and once again he was aware of that strong, physical pull which had nothing to do with likes and dislikes. To cover his confusion he ran his fingers over the guitar strings, and Kate said sweetly.

"You have such a pleasant voice, Mr. Stewart. Sing something for me, won't you? Some other gem from your own private researches."


Dinner that night was as good as the meals Peter had been getting on trays, if not better. They ate this one in the formal dining room downstairs, *en famille*. His hostess had said nothing about dressing for dinner, so Peter was surprised to see her sweep into the room in what was almost formal evening attire—a long red skirt, which rustled and flared as she walked, and one of her favorite tailored blouses, silk this time, with wide sleeves caught at the wrists by jeweled links, and a barbaric tangle of gold and colored stones around her neck. Tiphaine wore something blue, pale and flowing. In her case, one noticed the girl rather than the clothes.

Conversation was spasmodic. Toward the end of the meal Kate fell into a frowning silence and didn't even pretend to follow the talk of the other two. Her hands were restless, toying with the silverware, and with her wineglass. They waited on themselves, and Kate kept her glass filled.

They were still at the table, and Kate was pouring coffee when Peter heard the doorbell chime. A few minutes later Martin entered, pulling off his driving gloves. His face was ruddy and his hair windblown.

"Colder tonight," he announced, putting his hand on Kate's shoulder. "Thanks, I would like some coffee. My heater seems to be on the blink."

"You ought to trade that old wreck in," Tiphaine said.

"Can't afford it." Martin sat down at Kate's left and accepted a steaming cup of coffee. "No self-respecting dealer would offer me more than a couple of hundred on a trade-in, so I might as well wear it out."

A casual conversation, over coffee, with old friends—but it wasn't even a good performance, Peter thought. The women were both tense as horses before a storm, and Martin's eyes kept coming back to Kate's face. All pretense ended when Kate broke into a discussion of American cars versus foreign cars.

"Mr. Stewart is sitting in tonight, Paul."

Martin couldn't be much of a poker player, his face was too mobile. It registered first surprise, then pleasure.

"Good," he said emphatically. "We need a skeptic."

"But I'm not," Peter said blandly. "I believe in everything. Ghosts, and werewolves, and succubi—"

"We'd better go," Kate said, starting to her feet. She was white to the lips.

Mrs. Adams was already in the séance room when they got there, and Peter wondered uneasily whether the woman had the run of the house, and her own key. She was squatting, in an ungainly fashion, tracing some design on the polished floor with a piece of chalk. In her trailing robes she ought to have looked absurd; but when she straightened up and turned her hard green eyes to him, Peter had no desire to laugh.

"Evening, everybody. Mr. Stewart."

"You don't seem surprised to see Peter," Tiphaine said.

"I knew he'd be here."

"How?"

"They told me." Her voice was brusque, almost impatient, quite unlike the mystical whine in which Peter had heard similar announcements made. Somehow this effect was more chilling.

Peter inspected the room with the sort of interest he might be expected to display on seeing it for the first time. It looked much the same as it had that other night, except that now it was brilliantly lit by two crystal chandeliers. The altar was in place, with fresh candles in the holders. The only difference was the odd diagram which Mrs. Adams had just finished inscribing in the middle of the floor.

It consisted of four concentric circles, of considerable size; the innermost was about four feet in diameter, with each additional circle adding another foot or so. In the center was the familiar six-pointed star, each point ending in a cross, with cabalistic signs occupying each outer angle. The three outer circles had crosses alternating with mystic names; from where he stood Peter could make out a few of them: Jehova, Adonai, Agia.

"Agrippa's circle," he said. "So it's a good spirit you're summoning, is it?"

The listeners were visibly impressed, and Peter thanked his encyclopedic memory and his childhood interest in the macabre.

"Is that what it is?" Martin said. "I'm afraid this particular aspect of folklore has never interested me."

"Since you are an adept," Mrs. Adams said, "perhaps you would like to perform the ceremony?"

"I'm no adept, not even a humble practitioner of the Art. Nor is it my specialty. I'll leave the witchcraft to you, Mrs. Adams."

Tiphaine chuckled softly, but Mrs. Adams was unmoved.

"The Art is not witchcraft—as you know quite well, Mr. Stewart. All right, we've got to start pretty soon. The hour is propitious after eight and before nine. Where are the Schmidts?"

As if on cue, the Schmidts made their appearance, and Mrs. Adams moved to the altar.

"Lights," she said—for all the world like a bloody film director, Peter thought disgustedly. Will Schmidt found the switch, and the room plunged into darkness.

Darkness complete and without alleviation. The drapes covering the windows were drawn tight. Then a faint glow of light appeared. Mrs. Adams had lit the first candle—by second sight, Peter presumed. The other candles followed, and in the sickly half-light the priestess turned and genuflected toward the altar. She turned the wrong way, though, and a genuine chill ruffled the hair on Peter's neck.

Agrippa and the good spirits be damned; if this old hag wasn't a witch, and a black one at that, he would eat his shoes.

He didn't believe that she was going to summon up any spirits, good or evil. But in a sense she was just as much a witch as the poor bedlamites who were burned for that crime during the ghastly witch hunts of the Middle Ages. She thought she was. The atmosphere was already curdling; his first instant distaste for Mrs. Adams was intensifying into full-blown repulsion.

Mrs. Adams poured some of the liquid from the pitcher into

the basin. The liquid was hot; the effect of the steam rising around the old woman's wrinkled features and barbaric hair was enough to set a nervous person screaming. From somewhere in her ample robes Mrs. Adams pulled out a little bag and threw a pinch of its contents into the steaming bowl. A sharp acrid smell of something nasty rose up. Peter coughed.

With peremptory gestures Mrs. Adams beckoned them into the circle, cautioning them in sharp whispers not to scuff out any of the lines. Peter doubted that, in the darkness, the precaution could have been observed. He wasn't particularly worried about it. The magic circle was for the protection of the magician and his friends, in case the spirits summoned got out of hand. Either Adams was a true believer in which case no spirits were going to materialize, or she was cynic enough to provide a material "ghost"—in which case chalk lines wouldn't be much protection. Peter didn't know what to expect, but he wanted to be prepared for anything; he spent the next few minutes of the ceremony removing his shoes.

The witch was now holding a short stick or baton—her magic wand—which she had produced from among the folds of her robe. Raising the wand she intoned the words, "Raphael, Rael, Miraton, Tarmiel, Rex."

The circle was crowded, with all of them in it, but no one moved. It was also far enough from the dull candlelight so that Peter found it hard to tell who was who; he was surrounded by dark, heavily breathing shapes, and for a mad moment it seemed to him that there were more such shapes than there had been at first. Then he caught a faint gleam from Tiphaine's hair, and felt a warm hand fumble and slip into his hand. He gave it a reassuring squeeze and let it go.

The priestess spoke again, this time in English.

"Infernal powers, you who carry disturbance into the universe, leave your somber habitation and render yourselves to the place beyond the Styx. If you hold in your power him whom I call, I conjure you, in the name of the King of Kings, to let this person appear at the hour which I will indicate."

The voice stopped, and Peter raised his drooping head. Damn the woman; the words were prosaic, almost pedantic, but the tone was hypnotic as hell. Again he speculated about drugs. Something in the coffee at dinner? Something in that vile-smelling liquid in the bowl?

Adams stepped back out of the circle and Peter took advantage of her movement to shuffle out of Tiphaine's reach. He could see why she wanted to hold hands, and he would have enjoyed it himself, for other reasons. But if he decided to take a walk, he didn't want any clinging fingers holding him back.

Crouching, Mrs. Adams sprinkled something over the floor, something that pattered faintly, like sand or fine birdseed. Peter knew it wasn't either one. Then she rose to her full height, stretched out her wand, and shouted, "May he who is dust wake from his sleep. May he step out of his dust and answer to my demands, which I will make in the name of the Father of all men."

Nice, ambiguous invocation, Peter thought, trying to keep his critical sense awake under the bombardment of gibberish. Sounded like an appeal to the Christian God; but the witches used the same terms for their dark Master. What a voice the woman had! She bellowed like a bull. But her shrieks were spookier than the usual medium's shivery whisper. And, in a dreadful fashion, they made better sense. The voice that summons the strengthless dead must carry a long, long way.

Mrs. Adams squatted again and flung two small objects down among the scattered dirt on the floor—white, hard objects, that contacted the wood with a brittle click.

*"Exurgent mortui et ad me veniunt! Ego sum, te peto et videre queo!"*

She made a series of rapid gestures with her hands. All the candles went out.

Momentarily impressed, Peter realized that it had been expert legerdemain. He had seen good stage magicians do that with candles. The smell of hot wax did not overcome the pungent smell of the liquid, which now seemed overpowering. Peter felt his head spin. The room was closed in, and dead; yet he had a sense that somewhere, someone was waiting. After the first startled gasp the others had fallen silent, but Katharine's breath rattled in her throat.

If anything was going to appear, it would appear now. The ceremony was complete, the adjuration had been made. More practically, the total darkness was very useful to the appearance of nonspiritual spirits. Pete left his shoes and slid away. It was so dark he couldn't see his hand in front of his face, so he felt sure his absence wouldn't be noticed immediately. Only his sense of location told him where he was; he knew where he was going. The door or the window, both at the far ends of the room. He suspected the latter. It was a convenient spot for material-ization, as he knew from personal experience.

Something was happening, down there by the windows. The curtains were moving, back from the center. He heard the rattle of the wooden rings and saw a pale rectangle appear, and widen. The light seemed bright after the intense blackness. Only one problem. There was no one in sight who could have pulled those draperies.

The figure did not appear in the window, as he had. They—whoever they were—had had more time to plan their effect. It was a good one, too. The figure that rose slowly up from the floor was featureless, only a black silhouette—a man's silhou-ette, that of a young man, erect and slender.

Peter, halfway between the stunned, huddled group in the circle and the "materialization," stopped short as a sudden sus-picion fired his brain. That silhouette was oddly familiar. It looked . . . it looked like . . .

"God Almighty," he said in a whisper which echoed through the hushed room. Then he launched himself in the longest tackle he had ever made in his life.

He was so relieved when his outflund arms met solid, hu-man flesh that he almost lost his grip.

"Lights," he yelled and added an expletive as a pair of very material teeth found his hand. The creature he was holding had turned into an animal; wriggling, writhing, kicking, biting, it kept him fully occupied till the lights finally went on. Blinded, Peter fought off one final spasm; then his opponent subsided into a sobbing heap, and Peter, slightly nauseated, rose to his feet.

It was Timmy, of course; he was unique, though the marred face was now hidden in his bent arms. Martin was the one who had responded to Peter's demand for light. He came trotting down the length of the room, reaching the spot just as Timmy flung himself over in a violent spasm. His body stiffened, his eyes rolled back into his head, and a trace of foam appeared at the corner of his distorted mouth. Peter stepped back, and Mar-tin dropped to his knees by the writhing body, mercifully hid-ing the ghastly face.

"Epilepsy?" Peter asked.

"Yes. Poor devil, that on top of everything else." Martin shifted slightly to one side and Peter saw, before he hastily averted his eyes, that the doctor had jammed a folded handkerchief into Timmy's mouth. "That's all I can do now; the attack should pass off in a few minutes. No, Kate, don't look at him, he's not—a very attractive sight."

Kate stopped where she was, a good ten feet away. Her face looked like a death mask, skin stretched whitely over the bones; but under her pallor there was a look of pitiful relief.

"Timmy?" she said. "Only . . . Timmy?"

"Only," Peter said bitterly. He had unconsciously been scrubbing at his hands with his own handkerchief; looking down at it, he was surprised to see that it was stained with red. Katharine's eyes followed his.

"You're hurt," she said; and Peter, fascinated, watched a new trickle slither down from under his cuff.

"He's got a knife," he said urgently, turning to the doctor. "Find it before he wakes up, for God's sake."

"Here it is." Martin pulled it out from under the body, whose spasms seemed to be subsiding. "Lucky he didn't fall on the blade."

"Lucky for whom?" Peter asked nobody in particular. He pushed back his sleeve and found a slit in shirt and skin which ran for several inches along his forearm.

Martin took his hand and pulled it down to eye level.

"Had a tetanus shot lately? That's good; the knife is an ordinary switchblade, looks new, but anything that's been in contact with Timmy is bound to be filthy. It's just a cut, Kate can handle the first aid. I've got to get this boy to the hospital right away."

Peter nodded, distracted by this description of Timmy. He couldn't be very old, at that; but it was hard to think of him in terms of anything so normal as years old. Now that he had had it brought to his attention, the cut was beginning to sting. In the excitement he hadn't even noticed when it was inflicted.

"Shall I call an ambulance for you?" Katharine asked calmly. Martin shook his head.

"No, no, he'll be all right when he comes out of it, just a little shaky. I'll drive him myself. There—it's passing now."

Timmy's legs were flat, except for an occasional twitch. As the doctor lifted his patient's filthy head, Peter turned away.

"Come upstairs, Mr. Stewart, and I'll find a Band-Aid for you," Kate said. "I'd leave the TLC to Tiphaine, but she'll be busy soothing Bertha for some time yet."

Peter glanced at the group that was still huddled in the circle. Tiphaine, white-faced and tight-lipped, had her arms around the cook's heaving shoulders. Will Schmidt wasn't being much help; he looked as if he wanted to run.

Peter followed Katharine's rustling skirts to the door and then stopped.

"I don't want to bleed all over that Persian rug."

Turning, she took him by the wrist and raised his arm.

"Your shirt's ruined anyway," she said unconcernedly. "Drip down into your sleeve."

Her fingers were firm and cold as ice. The contact, the first physical one that had occurred between them, startled both, and for a second Katharine stood motionless, staring at their joined hands. There was blood on her fingers now, and when she turned away and started up the stairs, she kept her right hand out away from her body, holding her skirts with the other. At the top of the stairs she stopped with a sudden startled intake of breath and whirled, so abruptly that she almost bumped into him.

"Peter. I just realized—"

"What?"

"It was Timmy. Only Timmy."

"Yes. Just a crude, cheap trick," Peter said soothingly.

He had underestimated the lady; this time she was not seeking reassurance. She shook her head impatiently.

"No, no, that's just it. How could he have done anything so stupid? We'd have recognized him."

"It was pretty dark. . . ."

"It wouldn't have been." From a pocket hidden in the sweeping folds of her skirt she produced a small flashlight.

Peter's lips pursed in a silent whistle, and he studied her resolute face with reluctant admiration.

"Timmy didn't plan this," he said thoughtfully. "He hasn't the wits. And if someone else put him up to it, that someone would have taken precautions. Timmy's face is unique. He would have been supplied with—is that what you're thinking?"

"A mask, yes. You didn't search him?"

"I didn't even know he had a knife," Peter said ruefully; and her face softened, minutely.

"I'm sorry, I forgot. Come along."

Ten minutes later she surveyed her handiwork critically, and nodded.

"I'll ask Martin to have a look at it in the morning, but that should do. You're looking a little green. Have you any other injuries?"

"No," Peter said, trying to ignore the various areas which Timmy's feet and fists had contacted.

"Do you need any help getting to bed?"

Peter looked at her. After a moment the corners of her mouth turned up, stiffly, as if not used to such exercise, and she said, "I'll send Will up."

"Never mind," Peter said sadly. He wondered what she would look like if she really smiled. The sardonic grimace that passed for that expression wasn't really a smile; it never reached her eyes.

"While I'm thinking about it . . ." Katharine reached for the telephone by the bed and dialed a number.

"Is Dr. Martin there yet? . . . Yes, please. I'll wait. . . . Paul, it's Kate. Everything all right? . . . Good. I want to ask you something. It occurred to me that Timmy might have been prepared for a masquerade. Could you check to see whether he had any sort of disguise, a wig or a mask, tucked away? One of those thin plastic masks would fit into a pocket. . . ."

She listened, and her face changed. "Oh. I see . . . No, that's all right. Good night, Paul."

She hung up.

"They looked through his clothing when they undressed him. Paul says he plans to burn the foul stuff."

"No mask?"

"No nothing. Good night, Mr. Stewart. Thank you."

"You called me Peter before."

"A momentary aberration."

She went out, closing the door emphatically.

Richard is himself again, Peter thought. At least she had the grace to say thanks. Damn the woman, she had a brain like a razor. She wasn't thanking him for the damage he had incurred on her behalf; that had been pure bad luck, and she gave it precisely the value it deserved. She was thanking him for helping to restore her slipping grasp on reality.

He slid between the sheets with a muffled groan. He was

going to have a few sore spots tomorrow. Damn Timmy, too. . . .

That same keen brain of Kate's wouldn't miss the other implications of this evening's fascinating performance. It had worked out fine, just as well as anything he could have engineered. Give her another day or two, to relax—and to think. To realize that, by no stretch of the imagination, could the figure she had seen on the balcony have been that of Timmy. To wonder why anything so unconvincing as Timmy had been presented at all. To begin to imagine horrors all the worse for being unknown. One more day, then a quick, hard blow straight to the core of the problem. That ought to do it.

# Chapter
## 7

"YOU LET HIM GO?" PETER REPEATED INCREDULOUSLY. THE news took his mind momentarily off his aches and pains; Martin was rebandaging his arm, and was being unexpectedly heavy-handed about it.

"What else could I do with him?"

"I can think of several things."

"He isn't aggressive," Martin said. "He fought back when you attacked him, as any animal would."

"Attacked him!"

"Oh, you had to, I'm not blaming you. But that's all he is— an animal, barely functioning beyond instinctive behavior. What else could I do, Peter? The state institutions are over-crowded, and pretty horrible. Volz knows how to handle Timmy. I've told him about the knife, and he's promised to keep a closer eye on the poor devil. Of course, if you insist on preferring charges . . ."

They were in Martin's office. Peter had driven himself to town instead of waiting for the doctor to make a house call, so that he could pick up his belongings from the Inn. Kate had indeed been thinking. She had come in with Peter's breakfast tray and asked him to stay on for a few days. She mentioned his desire to do some reading in Stephan's library, but neither of them was fooled by that excuse. Timmy's downfall had convinced her, if not of Peter's *bona fides*, at least of his usefulness.

"Oh, the hell with it," Peter said. "Why should I prefer charges?"

"That's decent of you," Martin said gratefully. "Wait a minute, you'd better have a sling for that arm, for a day or two anyway."

Peter started to protest and then thought better of it. He had no objection to publicity, nor to appearing more helpless than he was. Beneath his satisfaction at the way things were working out, a small ugly doubt festered. Since he hadn't engineered the Timmy episode—who had?

"I suppose Mrs. A. is keeping quiet this morning," he said casually.

"I had a few words to say to her," Martin admitted, with a faint smile. "Of course she denies putting Timmy up to it."

"Who else could have done it?"

"The evidence certainly seems to point to her. Still . . ." The doctor stepped back to inspect his work, and nodded. "Still, I was frankly surprised. She's a genuine fanatic; really believes in all that nonsense. I wouldn't have thought she'd descend to trickery."

"Isn't that one of the odd vagaries these people have? I've heard of séance mediums caught in the most flagrant deceit, who stoutly maintained that the rest of the phenomena were genuine."

"I know. As you say, it's a psychological quirk and we just have to accept it. But I think I put the fear of God into Mrs. Adams. She won't be trying anything else."

Peter didn't voice his skepticism. Mrs. Adams was a tough customer—too tough, he suspected, for the mild doctor. Still, Martin had a way with him and perhaps he could be forceful when he got angry enough.

As he went along the hall, trying to keep his coat from falling off the shoulder whose sleeve wasn't occupied, a dim little figure darted out from under the stairs.

"Oh . . . Mrs. Martin." Peter relaxed. "You startled me."

"You ought to button that coat," she said faintly, and did so. Then she looked up at him, her hands still on his coat front.

"Mr. Stewart," she whispered, "how much longer are you staying in Middleburg?"

"I don't know. I thought—"

"Sssh." Her hands covered his mouth. "Please, not so loudly. You must go away. Go away now. And take her with you."

"Who?" Peter obediently lowered his voice. "Tiphaine?"

"No, no. No. The other one. Today, go today. Next week will be—"

The office door opened and Mrs. Martin froze.

"Oh . . . my dear. I see you had the same thought I did," Martin said affectionately. "Have you persuaded Mr. Stewart to stay for a cup of coffee?"

She shook her head mutely.

"Mrs. Martin was kind enough to come to my rescue," Peter said. "I must have looked like a contortionist coming down the hall."

"Oh, I see. Should have thought of it myself. How about that coffee, though?"

"I'd better not. Got a few errands to do. Will I see you later?"

"Tomorrow, if not this afternoon. I'll be out."

"Good. Thank you, Mrs. Martin."

At the door he hesitated for a moment, looking back into the semidusk of the hall; but Mrs. Martin had already disappeared. Timmy wasn't the only one who was a little off. But the cause of Mrs. Martin's distress was only too obvious, and too normal. Martin had been spending a lot of time with a younger, richer, more attractive, woman. Even without the millions, Kate's physical attraction was enough to—

Peter stopped himself right there, none too pleased at the direction his thoughts were taking.

It was almost the end of October, and if he stayed around much longer, he was going to start liking this part of the world. The sunlight was warm and seductive, with just enough snap in the air to be invigorating. A carpet of colored leaves covered streets and sidewalks and lawns, but many of the trees were still spectacular in gold and red.

As he strolled down the street, he passed children rolling in leaf piles, shrieking with pleasure. The busy rakers were almost all black, and as Peter walked on he noticed something. As soon as they saw him coming, they retreated. It wasn't just his imagination. One man, who had worked his heap of fallen leaves almost up to the sidewalk, literally dropped his rake and fled.

On impulse he turned right, onto a side street, instead of continuing toward the shopping area. This was a block of smaller houses, and there were fewer hired workers. Peter went on at a deliberately leisurely pace, like a visitor admiring the well-tended gardens and neat lawns. Then it happened again. The yardman, a young fellow of about Jackson's age, took his rake with him when he retreated, but the intent was the same.

Peter proceeded, frowning. Small incidents, both of them, but they were disturbing, because they recalled other incidents and impressions which he hadn't wanted to contemplate. That first night in Middleburg, when he had thought of it as a cattown, pretending to sleep, but watching through slitted eyes . . . maybe it hadn't been just a neurotic fancy. Maybe his busy subconscious mind had been formulating data which he hadn't consciously noticed.

When he roused himself from his musings, he realized that he was in a part of town which he hadn't explored. He couldn't be far from the center of town; it was ridiculous to get lost in a hick town the size of Middleburg. He turned right, went on a few steps—and found himself facing a big white house, built in the gingerbread style of the 1880's. It looked like many of its neighbors, except for one thing—a sign which read "Middleburg Historical Association and City Museum."

There must be someone in the museum who could give him directions. He turned up the walk.

On the front door another sign gave the hours: 9 to 5 weekdays, 1 to 5 Saturdays and Sundays. The door was unlocked. There was no one in sight when Peter stepped into the hall, which was furnished like that of an ordinary dwelling house except that the antique furniture bore neat labels, and the walls were covered with old prints and paintings.

A door on the right opened, just a crack, and a face peered out, a thin spectacled face crowned with an untidy coil of gray hair. Peter recognized the woman who had been introduced to him at the Folklore Society meeting. Miss . . . Device—that was it; he remembered the name because it had struck a familiar note, though he couldn't remember offhand where he had heard it.

Either Miss Device needed a new pair of glasses, or she was preoccupied; it was several seconds before her thin lips cracked in a smile of welcome. She came out of the other room in sections, first an arm, then a leg modestly covered by heavy stockings and a skirt which reached three inches below her knee, then the rest of her body.

"Mr. Stewart, is it not? We've been hoping you'd pay us a visit."

She looked as if she meant it; the greedy gleam in her gray eyes reminded Peter of other faces, those of guards and curators in various unpopular tourist attractions which he had had occasion to visit. The poor devils got bored, sitting around all day with no one to talk to, and when an unwary visitor did appear, they leaped on him like ghouls.

Peter sighed, but not audibly. It would be gauche and unkind to tell the woman that he had only been looking for directions. It would also be useless. He wasn't going to get out of here without the full tour.

First he heard the interminable, dull life history of every town worthy whose portrait adorned the walls of the entrance hall. The contents of the next room were no more enthralling. The objects lovingly preserved in glass cases were just as boring as the ones he had viewed in little local museums abroad: old letters, receipts for tallow and wool and tobacco, corroded tools, patched coarse pottery.

Without Miss Device, he would have passed straight through the next room. But this exhibit, which filled half a dozen case, was clearly her pride and joy, and a blush colored her thin cheeks as she admitted that she had done the work with her own hands.

"It took me over ten years," she said.

Peter murmured something appreciative, and gave the contents of the nearest case a closer look.

They were clever, if you cared for that sort of thing: dolls, dozens of dolls, dressed with meticulous attention to detail in the costumes of the various historical eras since the founding of the town. Bearded courtiers of the time of James I, in cloaks and ruffs; little-girl dolls in homespun gowns and caps; a court lady dressed in satin, with a diminutive lace collar and curled ringlets. Intrigued, Peter bent over the case. The lady's curls looked like real hair, and the face, modeled out of clay or—no, something finer—wax, perhaps, was so individualistic as to suggest an attempt at portraiture.

He turned to the next case, which contained costumes of the eighteenth century—workmen in leather aprons, ladies in towering powdered wigs, gentlemen in embroidered waistcoats. These were no ready-made dolls, dressed by a clever seamstress; the figures themselves had been individually modeled and painted.

The exhibit was an impressive piece of work, and Peter said so; this time, for a change, his good manners paid an unexpected dividend. Miss Device became so flustered that she excused herself and left him alone.

Peter glanced again at the dolls. His unexpressed opinion would not have pleased Miss Device; he was brooding on the sterility of ten years spent on such a hobby. The ancient and no doubt honorable line of the Device family was ending with the conventional whimper. Once again the name struck that odd note of familiarity, but try as he might he couldn't place it.

He had had enough of dolls and shy spinsters, and just about enough of the prim little museum. He might as well go on through the other rooms—at a fast walk—and try to sneak out without Miss Device's seeing him.

But the next room was something of a surprise. The contents were familiar enough, but they seemed out of place in this tidy Victorian house. Not so incongruous to the room was the figure which stood, hands clasped behind its back, staring at a particularly elegant example of a pillory.

"Hello, General," Peter said. "I didn't know you liked museums."

Volz turned.

"So you're up and about, are you? What's the idea of damaging a perfectly good stablehand?"

He snorted. Evidently this was supposed to be a joke.

"You people amaze me," Peter said. "Back in the old country we have our share of village idiots, but we don't accept their iniquities quite so casually."

"Like hell you don't. Old Sam, who beats his wife to a pulp whenever he gets drunk; little Mamie, who sets fire to things . . . You just don't expect to find the same tolerance here. Damned British arrogance," he added, and went off into a paroxysm of grating laughter.

Feeling himself at a slight disadvantage—the old so-and-so definitely had a point—Peter joined him as he turned his fascinated gaze back toward the infernal device before him. The wood had weathered over the years, but was still intact. Rusty chains dangled from the cross bars, and the holes were suggestive, even now.

Flanking the pillory were the stocks, with holes for hands and feet instead of for the head, and an object which Peter was slower to recognize. Somehow—damned British arrogance?— he hadn't expected to find one here. Pillory and stocks were common punishment in the Colonial period, but a ducking stool? Then he remembered that it had been used to rehabilitate shrews and nags as well as to test witches; for some reason the recollection made him feel better.

"Where's the Iron Maiden?" he asked facetiously; and was decidedly taken aback when Volz bobbed his head at the other corner.

Peter turned. They were all there, the objects he had seen in the musty dungeons of Nuremberg and the Tower of London— the rack, the boot, thumbscrews. They looked even worse set against the clean-painted walls of this sunny room than they had in the stone-walled grimness of the fortresses.

Volz watched his face with ugly amusement.

"Why so surprised? This stuff goes back to the seventeenth century. That's when the colony was founded. The boys brought along some little bits of home, that's all."

"But I thought the colony was founded on the basis of religious freedom."

"Too much freedom," said Volz, not so cryptically. "I can see you don't know much history, Stewart. Thinking in terms of the Inquisition? All this stuff was part of the normal interrogation process, for criminals of various kinds. Heresy and witchcraft were crimes, sure; but we had our share of that here too, you know. Remember Salem?"

"Certainly. But I thought it was an isolated instance. The last flowering of a vicious belief."

"No, no. Just the most publicized. Look here."

He indicated a glass case in the center of the room. At first glance its contents were a refreshing change from the rusty horrors which filled the rest of the room. They were, for the most part, old books and documents. Peter's attention was caught by the central exhibit, a badly executed but evocative drawing of a woman's face. The features were uncannily familiar, from the pale thin mouth to the untidy gray hair; but the style of the drawing dated its subject to a far earlier century than the one Miss Device now graced. Yet the contrast jogged that one hitherto elusive memory. Peter didn't need the identifying label to recall the affair, with all its ugly details.

"Elizabeth Device," he muttered. "Good God, of course!

The Lancashire Witches. Sixteen . . . thirty-something? Old Demdike, the head witch of the coven, her real name was Device. The whole damned family were witches. Oh, no. Don't tell me—"

"Oh, yes." Volz gave a hoarse shout of laughter, and one of the vile gadgets caught the vibration and whispered rustily. "Our little lady is the last descendant of one of the most notorious families in the history of witchcraft. Funniest thing I ever heard of. Especially when . . ." He added a description of Miss Device which, while probably accurate, was unquestionably defamatory. Peter grinned unwillingly. Volz had a mind like a sewer, but he also had a gift for pungent description.

"I didn't know any of the family emigrated," he said, turning back to the glass case.

"It wasn't publicized," Volz said dryly. "The boys—two brothers they were—denied the family. But they made the mistake of bringing along a gossipy aunt—that one—and it wasn't long before the town found out. Those"—his nod indicated the moldering documents in the case—"those are the records of the trial."

Peter studied the long wrinkled face and squinted eyes. Not a pretty face, no; but still . . .

"What did they do to her?"

"She died during the ducking procedure. Third time down."

"Drowned?"

"Probably a heart attack, from terror," Volz said indifferently. "The men who handled the stool were experts; they didn't want the suspects to drown. It must have frustrated the hell out of them when the old lady died on their hands." He chuckled.

Peter looked at him in distaste, and had a sudden, horrific vision of Volz's stocky form clad in the doublet and ruff of the period he was talking about. Black doublet, of course, and cropped hair; he'd be a Puritan, and a great little prosecutor. Studying Volz's pouting mouth and beady eyes, Peter amended the description. A witch pricker, that's what he'd have been, enjoying the shame of the exposed witches as much as the money he received for sticking pins in strategic parts of their bodies.

Volz was not completely insensitive; his eyes narrowed at Peter's unconcealed disgust, and he said, "Let me show you the Iron Maiden. It's a particularly good one."

"No thanks. I'm weak already, and I don't want to spoil my appetite."

"Yes. Too bad about last night." Volz's eyes lingered pleasurably on Peter's sling.

You little bastard, Peter thought. Aloud he said, "Someone put Timmy up to that performance. Aren't you even slightly curious about who is corrupting your servants?"

"He might of thought of it himself. Who knows how these crazy people think?"

Peter gave him a sweet smile; his accompanying thoughts were better not revealed. Whatever the mess going on in this town, Volz had to be part of it. He wasn't even bothering any longer to conceal his hostility.

"I didn't see your car in front," he said. "Or I'd ask for a lift."

"Having a little trouble with the carburetor, left it at the garage." Volz puffed out his chest. "Great exercise, walking. Be good for you."

"Mmm." Peter said. He left Volz in rapt contemplation of the rack.

At the corner of the next street he caught sight of the church steeple, and knew where he was. He also knew where he was going. To the gentry of Middleburg, only one of the town's three garages was The Garage. Tom and Mack's, not far from the hotel.

Volz's shiny Lincoln was parked in the lot, but there was no sign of Jackson. Peter found him in the alley behind the garage, having a cigarette with two young men about his own age. At the sight of Peter, the two boys simply melted away. Jackson stood his ground, tossing his cigarette butt to the ground, but his expression was sullen.

"Got time for a cup of coffee?" Peter asked.

"Where? In the Colonial Room?"

"Anywhere you say."

"Ain't you scared you'll get in bad with my boss?"

Peter, who was already exasperated by his most recent encounter with Volz, made a grimace. Jackson's face did not relax.

"Leave me alone," he said. "I told you before, I'm not sticking my neck out."

"Jackson, why don't you get the hell out of this town? This isn't all the world, not even all the country. This place—"

"Stinks. So how do I get out? You gonna adopt me? Listen, Stewart, you're trouble. It was bad enough before, now you've had the sign put on you." Jackson's voice dropped to a whisper. He glanced uneasily over his shoulder; and Peter's nerves tightened. The signs of fear, which would have been disturbing enough in an ordinary man, were unnerving coming from Jackson.

"What sign?" Peter asked; unconsciously, his voice had also become lower.

"I've already said more than I should. For God's sake. Stewart, I told you, you're poison. Do you really want to drag me down too? Then stick around; that's all you have to do to finish me, just—stick around."

There was only one possible answer to that agonized plea, Peter turned on his heel and walked away.

On his way back to the hotel he stopped in several shops, to pick up odds and ends such as toothpaste, and a gift for his un-enthusiastic hostess. The drugstore still retained its small town apothecary atmosphere; as Peter stood brooding darkly over the brightly colored rows of toothpaste, the proprietor spoke from behind the counter.

"Looking for something in particular, mister?"

"Just trying to make up my mind." Peter selected a package at random. "Is there any difference, really?"

"Not much. It's kind of confusing, I guess, for a furriner." Peter glanced up, eyebrows raised, and the man said, "You must be the writer fella who's staying at the Inn. English, ain't you?"

Peter admitted the fact, and the man extended his hand.

"Olivetti's my name."

"Stewart."

"Oh. Then you ain't related to that other young fella who used to come in here. English, too, he was."

Peter pocketed his change.

"Was?"

"Yep, he's dead. Shot hisself."

"Shot . . ." Peter turned back. "Suicide?"

"Well, the coroner *said* it was a accident." Olivetti leaned both elbows on the counter and prepared to enjoy himself. "But everybody knew he wasn't the careless sort. Got mixed up with that female, old Stephan's niece. She's poison, she is."

"Killed himself for love?" Peter leaned his elbows on the counter too. When in Rome . . .

"Well, now, he didn't seem like that kind neither."

"What kind was he?" Peter asked.

Olivetti turned and spat neatly into some invisible container behind the counter. A melodious echo sounded, but Peter was too absorbed in the conversation to appreciate this survival from America's past.

"Owed me fifty bucks," Olivetti said briefly. "I wasn't the only one, neither. You figure it."

A fussy old lady hobbled up, demanding advice, and Olivetti turned away, with an invitation to drop in any time. Peter left.

There were, actually, several ways of "figuring it." Peter considered them as he did his other errands. His conversations with the shop attendants were not so casual as they seemed, and the comments he heard interested him very much. The languishing lady who ran the flower shop remembered Kate's dead lover as a "sweet boy, with the most sensitive eyes"; the grocer referred darkly to ruined village maidens and irate fathers; the high school girl behind the counter in Woolworth's had never met him, but she remembered him, "you bet your sweet life, mister, you couldn't forget a guy like that." Loaded with parcels, an inappropriate bunch of red roses, and a mass of vital but indigested information, Peter headed hotelward.

His room was neat and airless; it was odd how even a few days of nonoccupancy could remove the lived-in look of a room. Peter collected his clothes and tossed them into his suitcase. Habit, born of years of transient lodgings, made him recheck all the drawers.

He found it in the bureau, in the upper drawer, the same one in which he had found the crucifix. The meaning of this object was not so ambiguous.

It was a doll. No, Peter thought; the old word came, unsought and unwelcome, into his mind. A poppet. The old word, which sounded so cute and innocuous, and which had such a deadly significance.

This was no crude clay image bristling with pins. It was a work of art, a miniature model, barely eight inches high, dressed in tiny slacks and doll-sized sweater; there were even little leather shoes on the feet. The features were modeled with loving—no, scratch that word—with care. And—this was the detail that really got him—the shaggy cap of blond hair was not only a good imitation of his, it *was* his. Real hair.

Peter picked the doll up. As he studied the features more carefully, a wry smile touched his face. Clever; yes, clever as hell, but there was a hint of caricature which was reassuringly malicious and, therefore, human. Was his nose really that long?

The eyes—he couldn't judge them. They were covered with a narrow wisp of black cloth tied around the head like a blindfold. The miniature hands were bound together at the wrists.

Peter weighed the image in his hand. It wasn't very heavy. Just cloth, from the look of it, stuffed with cotton or some similar material. Except for the head. The intent was clear enough, but puzzling in its very lack of violence. No pins. If his memory served him correctly, they usually used pins.

"They" being the witches and warlocks who fashioned little images of their enemies, using the principle of sympathetic magic to give them the identity of the would-be victim, so that any indignity or harm perpetrated on the image would be suffered by the living man or woman.

So, no pins. It was a warning—perhaps a threat—and a hindrance. The bound hands and blinded eyes—ignorance and impotence, that was what they had wished upon him.

They, again. The doll certainly suggested one specific person. But if he hadn't happened to pass the museum, by pure accident, he wouldn't have known about Miss Device's pretty little hobby.

Mrs. Adams, and the cult of Magna Mater; Miss Device and her dolls; Volz's filthy mind and overt antagonism; Timmy . . . How many of them were there? Or had one person employed a variety of devices to incriminate the innocent and blur the picture?

It certainly seemed that some other person in Middleburg besides himself had it, as they said, "in for" Kate More. Now he had got the sign, as Jackson put it. Why? Did the unknown view him as an ally of Kate's? Possibly. The doll had not turned up until after the Timmy episode, in which he had openly supported Kate. On the other hand, he didn't know when the doll had been put in the drawer; he hadn't been in his room for several days. A complicated image like that one would take some little time to make.

Another possibility was that he was interfering, somehow, with the unknown plotter's purpose; that his subversive activities against Kate had been observed, and disapproved of. But that didn't make sense, because the end result of the series of supernatural happenings, his own and the others, must be the same: the annihilation of Katharine More. Unless . . . unless the other person (or persons) wanted the same result, for a different reason. A hypothesis slid sneakily into his unreceptive mind, and he considered it sourly. No use thinking about it; he would have to do some more investigating before he had enough data to work with. It was only one of a number of possibilities, after all.

Peter shelved that idea for future consideration, and went on to his third possibility: that Kate Ross herself was the perpetrator of the other tricks, including the ones which had been aimed against him. So far as he knew, nothing had happened which she couldn't have engineered herself, from the phony nightmares to the involvement of Timmy. Why she should want to make herself look like a budding psychotic he didn't know. Again, there were a few possible explanations, but no proof. But that was the trouble with all his ideas: nobody, except himself, had any obvious motives.

One thing was clear—and it was just about the only thing that was. He had to know more. Unknown quantities were always potentially dangerous; in this case the danger was no longer merely potential.

He looked down at the doll and moved by a wild impulse, began to pluck at the string that bound the small hands. He felt a crazy reluctance to damage the image; it took him some time to unwind the string without hurting the inanimate wrists. As he did so, something sharp pricked the ball of his finger. Maybe he'd been wrong about the pins. . . . But when he located the almost invisible end of the sharp object, and pulled it out of the stuffed palm, it was not a pin. It was a fingernail clipping, curved and thin and pointed.

His fingernail clipping, just as it was his hair—parts of himself, added to the image, which gave the sympathetic identification greater force. The last time he had performed that particular hygienic ceremony had been—here, at the hotel? Or at Kate's house? He couldn't remember. The hair must have come from the barbershop. Or had someone sneaked in while he was asleep, and raped a lock? Either notion was impossible. He had a mental image of Miss Device scuttling into the masculine confines of Alfie's Barber Shop and snatching a lock of hair from under Alfie's broom. His mind reeled.

It would be difficult to imitate one of Miss Device's dolls, but not impossible. The blind, helpless eyes bothered him. He plucked at the blindfold, but it didn't move. Sewn into place, perhaps. He turned the doll over to look, and his lips pursed in a silent whistle.

Not just a hindrance; a definite warning. On the back of the image was a tiny white patch; the color made its shape quite distinct against the black fabric. It was in the shape of a heart, and it was sewn, or glued, slightly to the left of center, just under the shoulder blade.

Symbolic, not anatomically accurate. But clear. The heart is just as easily reached from the back as from the front. Peter had the distinct impression that the symbolism was not that of a love charm.

When he left the hotel, the doll was in his suitcase. He told himself, ironically, that he was getting quite attached to the thing—even if its nose was too long. He wasn't quite willing to admit that he wanted to keep it safe—away from any sharp objects which just might be inserted into that target on its back.

# Chapter

## 8

PETER HAD LUNCH IN TOWN AND GOT BACK TO THE HOUSE AT a time when he knew half the inhabitants would be taking naps. Kate usually slept after lunch; no wonder, with the disturbed nights she had been having. The Schmidts would be in the kitchen or in their room, and Tiphaine was probably out somewhere. At any rate, she wouldn't be looking for him in the library.

Like the living room, it was definitely a man's room, but not that of a man whose acquaintance Peter would have been keen on having. The deep leather armchairs and dark, heavy furniture were all right; so were the fine oak paneling and the walls lined with books. But there was a suggestion of feminine luxuriousness about the embroidered cushions and soft hassocks scattered about; and who in his right mind would want to live with those pictures? Hans Baldung's "Witches at the Sabbath"; the Durer engraving of the four beefy females—who might simply have been having a girlish chat, *au naturel*, if Peter hadn't known the title of the picture; a set of medieval woodcuts, crude in style and even cruder in subject, showing executions of various kinds—hanging, burning, the headsman's block . . .

Dear old Uncle Stephan, Peter thought, and turned his attention to the books.

Magic and witchcraft, sorcery and alchemy; volumes in German and French and Arabic, scholarly works such as Murray and Frazer; the classics, Reginald Scot and James I; the screwballs, such as Montague Summers. It was the most complete collection of books on the occult Peter had ever seen; fifteen years ago he would have rubbed his hands together and sailed in. Now he felt bored and slightly disgusted. It was a hell of a hobby for a grown man.

But everything he might need was here. He found a number of references to the poppets, or dolls; the idea of waxen images was old, very old, and distributed through many cultures. Sympathetic magic, according to Sir James Frazer. Used for love charms, ritual murder, even curing illness. And probably quite effective too, in a culture where people believed in its efficacy. But the books only confirmed his vague memories; they told him nothing new.

He put the *History of Magic* back on the shelf and went to the ornate mahogany desk that stood in front of the windows. A cursory investigation told him that he was wasting his time. Kate didn't work in this room; none of her papers, scholarly or financial, were here. He could see her point.

For want of anything better to do, he selected a book at random and sat down in a chair. It was a comfortable chair—almost too comfortable. It didn't feel like leather, but like some softer, more yielding, substance, and Peter was unpleasantly reminded of a horror story he had once read about furniture which embraced its owner. He grimaced, and settled himself firmly. Jolly old Uncle Stephan . . .

Two hours later there were books all over the floor around the chair, and Peter was still reading. A watcher, if there had been one, might have deduced that he was not at all happy about what he was reading.


Katharine remained invisible the rest of the day. She didn't appear for dinner, and Peter asked about her.

"No, she's all right," Tiphaine said. "Just resting. She often has a tray in her room when she's working, or just feeling antisocial."

They served themselves, as was the household custom; Mrs. Schmidt put a savory-smelling casserole and a salad in front of Tiphaine, and left the room.

"Smells good," Peter said, accepting a full plate.

"Mrs. Schmidt is a marvelous cook, even if she isn't the

most cheerful companion in the world. She grows her own herbs. Fresh seasoning makes a tremendous difference in cooking."

"Parsley, sage, rosemary and thyme," Peter murmured, poking at the heap on his plate.

"And savory, dill, basil and tarragon," Tiphaine said mockingly. "They are used for just plain ordinary cooking, you know. Have some salad. Basil and dill in that."

Peter sampled the salad.

"You're right; the woman's a witch at cooking."

Tiphaine put her fork down and looked exasperated.

"Peter, just for once, can't you—"

"The subject seems to be on my mind."

"The trouble is you're fighting it," Tiphaine said shrewdly. "You don't want to believe that things like that can happen."

"That's probably true. Which is not very rational of me; I know perfectly well that people do believe in the occult. What I can't understand is how a woman like Kate could fall for such rot. I could see the first time I met her that she was under an abnormal strain. Ordinarily I'd have thought of blackmail, anonymous letters, the usual things."

"Anonymous letters?" Tiphaine shrugged. "You don't know Kate. Her reaction to a poison-pen letter would be a shout of laughter and a clinical analysis of the mental state of the writer. You've heard people say that they don't care what the rest of the world thinks. Mostly they're lying. But Kate really doesn't care."

Peter nodded. He was remembering Sam's comment: "She takes a kind of pleasure in rubbing people's noses in facts they don't want to face."

"You mean she does whatever she pleases, and to hell with gossip."

"Not exactly," Tiphaine said. "She doesn't do things for the hell of it. But if she felt she had a good reason for behaving in a certain way, she wouldn't let gossip bother her."

"And that," Peter pointed out, "is why her present state of nerves is so surprising. I agree; she isn't susceptible to blackmail or threats for the ordinary peccadilloes that terrify most people. But there's a difference between fear of losing one's reputation and fear of—death, shall we say?"

Tiphaine's head jerked up. For a moment her face was unguarded, and Peter saw that the idea was not new to her.

"Not necessarily death," he went on. "But every human being has some weakness. Every one. Remember *Nineteen Eight-Four* and Room One-oh-one. That was where they took the stubborn ones, the rebels whom nothing else could break. And the thing that waited for them in Room One-oh-one was simply the worst thing in the world. The one thing that they couldn't endure. Different for every person; but for every person there was something. What is it for Kate? What one thing is it that she can't endure?"

"Loss?" Tiphaine said softly; chin propped on her hands, she had listened intently. "Mark?"

"You've been singing too many folks songs," Peter said rudely.

" 'Cold blows the wind to my true love, And gently falls the rain . . . ' " She sang it, unselfconsciously, in an eerie little voice that was hardly more than a whisper. "It would be . . . funny . . . wouldn't it, if it were true . . ."

"Funny is not precisely the word." Peter didn't care for the look in her eyes. "Snap out of it, Tiphaine. Kate is no simpleminded romantic. How do you know she isn't inventing her apparitions?"

"Pretending, you mean?"

"She may not be doing it deliberately," Peter conceded.

"Deliberate or not, that's not possible. I've seen things myself, Peter."

"That doesn't mean Kate couldn't have engineered them."

"Oh, that's absurd. Why on earth should she?"

"How the hell should I know? None of it makes any sense. It's you I'm worried about. If I could be sure you were in no danger . . ."

His hand slid up her bare arm. She was wearing something sleeveless and low-cut, of a pale ivory that set off her tan. After a moment Peter removed his hand.

"Sorry again."

"Mrs. Schmidt will be bringing in the coffee at any moment," she murmured. "Peter, I can tell; you have something in mind. What is it?"

"Just a tentative scheme for catching the person who's behind these tricks. If it turns out to be someone other than Kate, at least I'll know that the malice is directed against her. I don't mean to sound callous, but you're my chief concern."

"That's very sweet."

"Not so sweet, no. Look here. Sooner or later, some night, if not tonight, another incident will occur. Whoever it was who prompted Timmy, he'll have to act again, to destroy the confidence Timmy's capture gave Kate. And I think he'll act soon."

"Soon? Then you think—"

Peter drew his chair closer to hers.

"Tonight . . ."

When Tiphaine came out of her cousin's room Peter was waiting in the hall. She put her finger to her lips.

"I slipped one of the pills Paul left into her tea. She'll be asleep in minutes."

"Martin prescribed them?"

"Do you wonder? She has a thing about drugs, that's why I have to sneak." Tiphaine grimaced. "I hate doing it, but—"

"You have to. I know. Then you're sure she won't be walking around anymore tonight?"

"Yes."

"Any luck with locking the doors onto the balcony?"

"No. I tried, but she told me to leave them open. She likes fresh air."

Peter had been fairly sure of that, but he was relieved to hear it.

"Never mind. I strung thread all over those bushes under the window. If anything goes up that way, we'll know about it. Now for the inside of the house. Got the stuff?"

"I'll get it." Tiphaine went into her room and came back with a box of talcum. Peter sprinkled it lightly but thoroughly over the hall carpet, beginning at Kate's door. When the whiteness reached down to the door of the adjoining room, he stopped as if struck by a sudden thought.

"My bathroom. Doesn't it communicate with this room?"

"Yes. But what—"

While she stood in the doorway watching, Peter crossed the spare room and slid the bolt in place. The white-headed pins and the plastic twine were completely invisible from where she stood, but she saw his ostentatious manipulation of the bolt.

"Door's bolted," he said, coming back. "On this side."

"Right. What does that prove?"

"I hope it will prove something, if anything untoward occurs. She's suspicious of me, and if you're not, you ought to be."

"What do you mean by that?"

"I mean you shouldn't trust anyone."

He finished sprinkling the hallway, leaving Tiphaine marooned in her own doorway. She watched while he finished the job, backing into his own room like a painter who has painted himself into a corner. He waved the near-empty can of talcum cheerfully at Tiphaine, who responded with a faint smile. She closed her door, and Peter followed suit. Now no one could enter the hall without leaving traces in the even coating of powder.

Peter read for an hour. Then he turned out his light and sat in the dark for another hour. By this time it was nearly 1 A.M., and he decided it was safe to proceed.

Most of his precautions were already made: the rumpled bed, the mechanism on the bathroom door, the chair under the doorknob of the bedroom door. Changing clothes was unnecessary; his gray slacks and shirt would be better camouflage against the pale facade of the house than dark clothing. He had already removed his shoes.

He went to the door on the other side of the bathroom and took hold of the left-hand pair of threads. The plastic fishline was made for the job; invisible against any surface, it was stronger than twine. He pulled slowly and steadily, and felt the bolt slide back.

The adjoining room was dark, and he didn't dare turn on the light. A small pocket flashlight, gripped uncomfortably in his teeth, let him rearrange the device which controlled the bolt. He removed the pair of thumbtacks to the right of the bolt, and the length of fishline which had passed over them, from the head of the bolt, back through the crack between door and doorframe. He tested the tacks on the other side, and the piece of fishline which would shoot the bolt again after he got back into his room. Perfect.

So far so good. He opened the window, and got out as quickly as he could. The wind was stronger than he realized. It tore at him as he moved crabwise along the window ledge and groped for a handhold among the tough vines to the left of the window. It was a cold wind. "Cold blows the wind . . ." The plaintive little melody Tiphaine had sung began running through his head. "And gently falls the rain . . ." No rain. Thank

God for that, he couldn't have tried this stunt in wet weather. He must appear at the strategic moment looking as if he had just been summoned from a warm, dry bed.

"I've never had but one true love . . ." He couldn't get the tune out of his head. His toes jammed painfully into a crack in the stone. Peter fumbled for his next handhold. "Funny if it were true," Tiphaine had said. The Unquiet Grave. No . . . not funny at all.

His reverie ended when he reached the corner of the wing and the only really sticky part of the trip. The ivy was old and solidly entrenched; it was climbing a cargo net. But there was no ivy on the end of the house, near Kate's balcony.

Clinging like a chimpanzee to the drainpipe on the corner, Peter eyed the six-foot gap between his perch and the edge of the balcony. It was an easy jump, if there had been any solid ground from which to launch himself. He had seen the problem before, but there wasn't really any sure solution to it. Getting to the balcony wasn't so hard; it was getting back that bothered him. Shinnying up the pipe a few feet, he hooked his heels into the space between wall and pipe and fell forward, arms extended and body straight. His hands caught the edge of the balcony with inches to spare, and in a moment he was climbing over the rail.

What he saw brought him to a dead stop. There was a light inside the room.

Peter stood on the balcony, stockinged toes curled up against the chill of the flooring, and swore under his breath. All his work was for nothing if she was still awake. Hell of a doctor Martin was; he couldn't even prescribe sleeping pills that worked. But when he peered through the curtains he framed a mental apology. She was asleep all right, and breathing heavily. But she had left a night light burning. He ought to have expected that.

Holding the curtains slightly apart, he studied the situation before he ventured in. She was sleeping soundly now, but she hadn't dropped off easily; the bedclothes were twisted into knots and pushed down toward the bottom of the bed. She slept on her side, curled up protectively; her arms were wrapped around the pillow which she held close to her, like a baby—or a shield. The nightgown was black lace this time. Clearly she was no sunbather. The tan on her legs faded above the knees. . . .

Peter's cold feet reminded him that he had no time for that. She wouldn't hear anything short of a yell, that was the important thing. He slid into the room and got his second surprise when an object popped up from among the tumbled bedclothes. It was small, round, black, and had pointed ears, now pricked inquiringly.

Peter and Pyewacket contemplated one another. The cat was curious but not perturbed. Peter glowered at it. He knew how unpredictably a sleeper's sense of hearing functions; people can snore through a parade of fire engines, and waken at a child's whimper. The movement of the cat's heavy body might be enough to rouse Kate. He went about his business as quickly as he could.

By the time he had the arrangement set up, Pyewacket hadn't moved. His ears were still pricked, though, and his head was cocked at an inquiring angle. Peter decided to risk one more delay. He had set up his display on top of the small desk which was conveniently close to the window. He wanted very much to see what was in the drawers.

He found Kate's checkbook in the top center drawer, and a quick glance at the register of checks told him what he wanted to know. So she was impervious to blackmail, was she? A series of sizable withdrawals, made out to cash, over the past nine or ten months, might be for some innocent purpose; at the moment he couldn't think of one. Ten thousand was the highest amount, five thousand the least. They added up to a formidable sum.

Peter put the checkbook back precisely as he had found it, and closed the drawer. Everything was set. But for the best effect, that light ought to be out.

It was on the bedside table, within arm's reach of the sleeper. A risky business, especially with that damned cat staring at him, ready to jump. But it had to be risked. If the sudden darkness, or a shriek from the cat, woke her—well, she had to wake up pretty soon anyhow.

Peter started the tape recorder. One of the new, small casette types, it made only a whisper of noise. He crossed the room on tiptoe. Hand poised, he looked at Kate. She hadn't moved. Sleep wasn't knitting up any ravels for her; the long dark lashes veiled the circles under her eyes, but there were two vertical lines between her brows, and the full mouth was drawn down at the corners. The lines in her forehead deepened and she stirred, murmuring. Peter's hand slammed down on the light switch, and the room went dark. He heard a rustle of bedclothes and an inquiring meow; but by that time he was sliding through the window.

He had to make sure she was awake before he went any farther. The taped voice had begun, and grown louder; the candles were due to burst into flames at any second. It would be better if she saw them light up. Crouching, peering through the slit in the curtains, he heard, over the muttering voice on the tape, the solid thud as Pyewacket hit the floor and wandered over to see what was making all the noise. Still no movement from the sleeper.

A paw, sheathed, but ready to erupt into claws at the slightest encouragement, patted hopefully at Peter's fingers. He slid his other hand down the seductive, trusting slope of Pyewacket's back, located the waving tail, and gave it a sharp tug. An anguished cry of trust betrayed rent the night, and Peter jerked his hand back just in time to avoid an incriminating set of scratches.

He heard Kate sit up, so suddenly that the bed squealed. The candles chose that auspicious moment to light; and he had one glimpse of an ashen face and staring black eyes before he went over the edge of the balcony. The recorded voice was loud enough now to drown the sounds of his movements, including, he hoped, the only loud noise he must make.

The recording sounded good. The voices couldn't be much alike, but the tormented whispering tone concealed differences in timbre, and the accent was convincing. Good old Sam— always right about the important things. When Peter had made the recording that afternoon, in the seclusion of his bathroom, with the shower streaming, he had thought of Sam. Even the background rush of running water came through nicely. If you didn't know what it was, you'd think it might be a wind howling eerily—or the crackle of flames, maybe.

Poised on the outer edge of the balcony, Peter began his return trip. This was the only bad part. If that drainpipe wasn't sturdy enough to bear the impact of his body, or if his hands missed its narrow circumference . . . He compensated for the second difficulty by letting himself fall parallel to the wall with his shoulder actually brushing it. The pipe sagged, but held; grasping it with one hand, Peter pulled the string wound around his waist and heard the series of tiny bumps as the recorder bounded onto the balcony, hit the rim, and came up over the rail. He reeled the string in as fast as he could, but the recorder swung against the wall as it fell. It didn't matter; he probably wouldn't need it again.

With the tape recorder dangling from his belt like a scalp, Peter slithered across the side wall and in the window. He was moving fast, unbuttoning his shirt and unwinding string as he dashed across the spare bedroom. Recorder, socks, and shirt went into the bathroom hamper. Time was getting on; he could hear interesting sounds from the hall. His hand tugged gently on the remaining length of fishline; an extra sharp tug, after the bolt was drawn, dislodged the thumbtack, and the twine's full length came through the crack into his hand. Tugging at his belt, Peter ran across the room, threw the chair aside, and opened the door.

The hall was brightly lit; Kate had turned on the switch outside her door. She was standing in the doorway, arms out and braced; only their pressure on the doorframe held her erect, he could see the sag of her knees under the sheer black skirt. Her face was as white as paper, but a queer relief came over it as her eyes fell on Peter. Tiphaine, in her own doorway, had stopped to slip her arms into a robe. Following Peter's instructions, she had not stepped onto the floor of the hall, where the white powder lay virgin and unmarked.

"What happened?" Peter asked, blinking. The light hurt his eyes; it gave a fine air of verisimilitude to the picture he presented, that of a man abruptly awakened from peaceful slumbers, who has delayed answering the cries of the maiden in distress only long enough to assume his trousers. He finished rebuckling his belt and stepped carefully out into the hall.

Kate's lips parted, but no sound came out. Tiphaine was studying the unmarked surface of the talcum. She looked up, caught Peter's eyes, and nodded; and Peter made a dash forward just in time to catch Kate as she fell.

She couldn't weigh much more than a hundred pounds. The taut limbs, which looked so hard and competent when she was awake, felt thin to the point of fragility now. Tiphaine was at his shoulder when he laid Kate down on her bed. He turned her and repeated the question.

"What happened?"

"I don't know. I heard her call—look!"

She pointed.

On the desk the twelve black candles burned, the flames flickering in the breeze from the window. There was an additional effect which Peter hadn't planned: Pyewacket, fascinated by the dancing lights, sat like a black Egyptian statue between the candelabra, tail wound around his sleek flanks. But Tiphaine's eyes were focused on the small object that lay before the cat, between the candlesticks.

"Where did that come from?" she asked breathlessly.

"What is it?"

She walked to the desk, picked the object up, and held it out to Peter.

"A rabbit's foot." She added, in a flat, even voice, "Mark carried one, as a lucky piece. Some uncle from America gave it to him when he was a little boy."

"What happened to it?" Peter took Kate's hand and felt for a pulse. It was faint but steady; she'd be coming to in a minute.

"It was—buried with him, I suppose."

"There are thousands of the things around. How do you know this was his?"

"I don't. But—what point would there be to this unless it was—is—Mark's?"

"Who knew about it?"

"Most everyone. He showed it to people." She dropped the talisman back on the desk and rubbed her fingers together, shivering.

"Get it out of sight," Peter ordered. "And the candles. She's coming around. You don't want her to see that macabre arrangement again, do you?"

Tiphaine obeyed, but she moved so slowly that Kate's eyes flickered open before she had finished clearing away. From her prone position Kate could look straight across the room at the desk. Her mouth twisted, and Peter felt the hand he held tighten around his fingers.

"The voice," she muttered. "It was yours. Had to be . . . yours."

Peter was silent, partly because it was a reasonable reaction, partly because he was struck momentarily speechless. Damn the woman; what did it take to break her down, gibbering phosphorescent wraiths and skeletal fingers on her throat?

She had been frightened into a fainting fit, but that subborn core of strength had led her straight to the only rational answer. Now he was glad he had taken those seemingly unnecessary precautions.

"You heard a voice?" he said calmly.

"In the darkness . . . the candles flared up . . . A voice like . . . yours."

"It wasn't Peter." Tiphaine had swept the candles and rabbit's foot into the pocket of her robe. She came swiftly back to the bed, leaving a disappointed cat behind. "We sprinkled powder on the floor, Kate; there wasn't a mark on it when I came to the door.

"Connecting bath," Kate muttered. Incongruously, through all her accusations, she retained her desperate grip on Peter's hand.

"It's bolted. On this side."

"Go look."

Tiphaine gave Peter an expressive look and a shrug. She was back almost at once.

"Still bolted. Kate, even if he got into the next room, how could he have reached yours? Footprints would have shown in the hall; he can't walk on the ceiling, you know."

Kate's teeth began to chatter. The room wasn't particularly cold.

"That's enough for now," Peter said. "Tiphaine, you'd better call—no, I'll do it; you stay with her."

He went out, flexing ostentatiously empty hands. Kate's next thought would be for some sort of mechanical recording device; she'd insist that Tiphaine search the room. Just to be on the safe side, he'd better get rid of the tape recorder. The trip downstairs, to admit the doctor, would give him an opportunity, and it was logical that he would stop off in his own room to put on more clothes. With Katharine More you couldn't take too many precautions. But as he closed the door gently behind him, he knew he had struck a damaging blow. The last thing he heard was her admission of defeat.

"Then it was Mark. Mark's voice . . ."


"Is she still pacing up there?"

"Yes." Tiphaine was doing some pacing of her own; she

swung around on her heel, bright hair flying. "Martin says he can't give her anything more. Old maid, that's what he is! I think I'll go out of my mind if she doesn't stop!"

"She ought to get out of the house," Peter said.

"She won't go with me." The strain was telling on the girl; irritability sharpened her voice and flushed her cheeks.

"Let me see what I can do."

"I wish you luck."

Peter expected he would need it. He wanted to get Kate off by herself, preferably out of the house, where she couldn't yell for help, but he didn't expect her to acquiesce. But Kate agreed without a struggle when he suggested a walk. Apparently Tiphaine's report last night had cleared him.

They went across the yard and through the gate into the woods, Kate leading, Peter trailing like a watchdog—or keeper, he thought. He didn't try to talk. She couldn't keep up her present pace very long. After a while her steps slowed and stumbled; but when Peter took her arm she shook his hand off.

"I don't nccd any help."

"Like hell you don't," Peter said unemphatically.

She glanced up at him and then looked away. Her eyes were unfocused and dilated to blacker blackness than usual.

"Let's get off the path," she said. "Someone might come, and I don't want—"

"Lead the way."

"There's a place I go to sometimes." She pointed up the trail, to a spot where a coil of wickedly beautiful scarlet leaves twined around a tree, and a broken branch stuck out from a tall oak.

Between the oak and the poison ivy a faint path went off into the underbrush, but Peter would not have seen it without guidance. Clearly it had not been used for some time; honeysuckle and poison ivy made a thick treacherous matting underfoot, and climbed to strangle trees and bushes. Kate wiggled her way through and Peter ungallantly let her lead. He was scratched and perspiring by the time they broke through into a final tangle of thorned bushes into a small glade.

A brook ran rippling across the cleared space and vanished between trees to the right. Tall trees ringed the clearing, shading it. Some pines; the ground was covered with a thick soft carpet of browning needles, which had triumphed even over the omnipresent honeysuckle. At the far end of the clearing, to the left of the path by which they had come, stood an unusual object—a massive block of stone about ten feet high and almost as broad. Its color was dark, almost black; granite, possibly. The top was flat, like a platform, but it bore no trace of man's hand.

"A meteorite?" Peter hazarded.

"No, just a chunk of rock. The local people call it the Devil's Pulpit." Kate crossed over to the rock and dropped down beside it. She fumbled in her pocket for her cigarettes. "They avoid this place, particularly around Halloween. That's why I like to come here."

"Halloween?" Peter sat down beside her and declined a cigarette with a shake of his head. "Oh, yes, your local Allhallows. Jack-o'-lanterns and—what is it? Trick or treat."

"Haven't you ever seen it?"

"No. Sounds like a combination of Guy Fawkes and Carnival."

"When I was small, there used to be farms around here." Kate propped herself on one elbow and stared absently at a shaft of sunlight jabbing down through the trees. "The children came trick or treating to our place. Once."

"Once?"

"Uncle Stephan met them at the door," Kate said dreamingly. "I was there on a visit. He'd worked awfully hard on his costume. When they rang the bell he answered it. They were dressed . . . oh, rabbits, and little witches, and Superman. He'd painted his face dead white, except for his mouth. It was red. His canine teeth were particularly long and they shone in the dark. He made . . . noises."

Peter was silent. Comment was unnecessary.

"Two of the fathers came next day," she went on, in the same voice. "They didn't stay long."

She put her cigarette out very carefully, pinching the ends to make sure no spark remained. Then in one convulsive movement she slid down flat onto the ground and hid her face in her arms.

"Go ahead and cry," Peter said gently. "It'll do you good."

"I'm not crying." She rolled over onto her back and lay still, staring fixedly up at the blue circle of sky. "I'm trying to think. Whether I should see a psychiatrist. Or move away from here. Or do what he wants. Or just kill myself and get it over with."

"That's no solution," Peter said. The moment he had been

waiting for had arrived, and he didn't quite know what to do with it.

"That's what I'm afraid of." She gave a sudden dry laugh, like a stick snapping. " 'For in that sleep of death, what dreams may come . . . ' My dreams are bad enough now. That leaves three choices, doesn't it?"

"Who," Peter said, "is 'he'?"

"Someone I used to know." She rolled onto her side, looking at him through half-closed eyes.

It took Peter several seconds to recognize the look, not because it was new to him, but because he had never expected it from her. Yet the pull was there, he had been aware of it for some time. She looked so much smaller when she wasn't standing. He put out his hand and traced with his fingers the curve of her cheek and throat. Then her arms were around him, pulling him down.


She lay on her back, eyes closed and face lifted, her arms lax and white against the brown pine needles. Peter propped himself up on one elbow and studied her face. It hadn't changed. The tension was still there, tightening the corners of her mouth and hollowing her cheeks. Her sudden, unpremeditated try for temporary amnesia hadn't worked. She hadn't made any pretense about it; no soft murmurings about love, only wordless sounds of pure physical pleasure. Still . . . even from that point of view, it had been quite an experience.

"Want a cigarette?" he asked.

She shook her head without opening her eyes.

"Help yourself."

Peter reached across for her shirt and felt in the pocket. His hand lingered on the return trip, and a faint smile curled her mouth, but she kept her eyes closed. . . .

She must have felt the change in the pressure of his fingers, for her eyes flew open and she tried to sit up. Peter straightened his elbow, and she fell back.

"You're hurting me . . . What is it? What are you staring at?"

The signs were faint, but they couldn't be missed. On a fair-skinned blonde like Tiphaine, maybe; but Kate was dark.

From a tree high above, a mocking bird sang a long trill. It sounded miles away. Peter shook his head dazedly. Of all the unexpected . . . How the hell had Sam ever missed this? He felt her shrink under the painful pressure of his hand, and looked up to meet eyes wide with terror, and as easy to read as a page of print.

"So it's true," he said stonily. "What happened to it?"

Her answer was barely audible, even in the dead silence. The bird had stopped singing.

"She lived for eight months. It was pneumonia."

He knew what need had driven her to the cult of Mother Earth, and the resurrection of the dead.

# PART TWO
## *Quarry*

# Chapter
## 9

KATE KNEW SHE HAD BETRAYED HERSELF WITH THAT ONE SIM-
ple change of pronoun. Not only the fact, but what it had meant
to her. . . . A chink in the armor, a break in the wall; a weakness
through which she could be attacked. She closed her eyes, wondering idly whether the hard hand would move up to her throat
and tighten, and knowing that she didn't really care any longer.

He had betrayed himself as well; but she had always known,
in some remote corner of her mind, who he really was. They
weren't much alike, actually, only in superficial features like
the shape of their heads, and the unruly fair hair. Mark's delicate nose and mouth and boyishly rounded face were nothing
like Peter's features. But when Peter's eyes narrowed and his
mouth went tight, she could see him—Mark—in one of his
rages. Mark . . . one long year in his grave, and still haunting
her, in no figurative sense. Against the blackness of her closed
eyes the picture formed again, the same scene that had fought
its way past her will on countless other days and nights.

He always carried himself so arrogantly, walking on the
balls of his feet with his head thrust forward. In the moonlight,
that last night, he looked like one of Milton's fallen angels—
poised as if about to lift in flight, a thin diabolic smile on his
youthful face. It was October, and cold—October, almost exactly one year ago—but Mark was coatless, and that, too, was
typical of Mark. He expected even the elements to conform to
his requirements. When they didn't conform, he behaved as if
they had.

First she had tried to reason with him. It didn't work; it never had. Then she had tried to hurt him. The stinging words hadn't bothered Mark; they bounced back off the barrier of his fantastic ego like tennis balls off a brick wall. He couldn't believe any woman could resist him. But he had cause to think himself irresistible; once she had responded to the boyish charm and the words which seemed so much wittier and less trite than conventional wooing. Witch woman he had called her, enchantress, weaving spells. . . . Succubus, that was one of his favorite endearments—the supernaturally beautiful seductive spirit, preying on human lovers who cannot resist her deadly charms.

The epithets had palled even before Mark did; that night, in the cold passionless light of the moon, they made her angry. Mark had tried every trick in his considerable repertoire: threats, charm, even tears. Everything except reason, because that was a quality beyond Mark's comprehension. When all his devices failed, there was only one thing left. And somehow the gun was in her hand, and he was coming toward her. . . .

Katharine forced her eyes open. Peter was standing with his back to her, buttoning his shirt. The discarded sling lay on the ground at his feet.

"Your arm," she said dully. "I forgot about it."

"So did I." Peter turned, with a smile that reminded her of an archaic statue's—curved, remote, and terrible. "You're very skillful. Practice, or natural talent?"

His eyes moved over her body with an inhuman contempt, and Kate snatched at her clothing.

"Don't," she whispered.

"Mark was something of a connoisseur. I'm sure he appreciated you even more than I could. Until you tired of him."

Her head bent, Kate began to dress. But she could not close her ears to the remorseless voice.

"It must have been the final blow to him when he found out why you really wanted him. Not as a husband, not even as a lover. Just for breeding stock, like a healthly thoroughbred dog. Because it wasn't carelessness, was it? Not with a woman of your intelligence, not these days, when every gum-chewing adolescent knows how to take precautions. That's the only thing I find hard to believe: that a cold-blooded bitch like you could have one normal instinct. But then it is an instinct, isn't it—a matter of uncontrollable hormones. A sick, sentimental substitute for—"

"Stop it!" Kate clutched at her ears.

He caught her by the elbows and forced her to face him.

"What did you do to him? What happened? I've always known it wasn't an accident, Mark knew too much about guns. He killed himself, didn't he? Didn't he? And you drove him to it."

Shaken in his grasp like a doll, Kate stared up at him from under her loosened hair.

"Killed himself?" she gasped. "Himself? Mark?"

She began to laugh. It surprised her. She hadn't meant to laugh, and once she started she couldn't stop. Through a haze of dreadful, shaking mirth she saw Peter's face alter, saw his hand swing back; and then the red haze faded into a lovely blackness, a cold blackness that swallowed up the laughter and the sting of the blow across her face, and all other sensation. She fell into a deep dark hole, embracing the blackness. Maybe, if she was clever and careful, she would never have to come out of it again.

Martin's voice brought her out of it, and she hated Martin. She hated the pressure of the bedclothes on her body and the familiar smell of fresh linen and the smooth feel of it on her cheek. All her reluctant senses fought at being awakened; she curled herself up tighter inside and tried to go back into the dark.

Almost . . . She hovered on the rim of the blackness. But the hateful voice wouldn't be still.

"What the hell happened? Goddamn it, don't shake your head and look blank at me; something must have happened, something cataclysmic; she's in a catatonic state, I can't even reach her."

"Let me try." That voice. That one was worse. Kate hated it, it meant disaster; but it jabbed and prodded like a needle, sliding in past defenses that kindlier voices could not pierce.

"Kate, wake up. You can't hide, it doesn't work. Kate . . . Answer me, Kate. . . ."

Oh, now—now she was feeling more—the hand on her shoulder, the bedsprings sagging as he sat down. Tears of fury welled up and slid down from under her stubbornly closed lids; and Peter said, with a queer relief, "She's crying."

* * *

Then it was nighttime, and that seemed strange, because it was as if no time had passed at all and the same voices had been talking without interruption.

"Hasn't she been asleep a long time?"

"The injection should be wearing off soon. But if she does withdraw again—well, you brought her out of it once."

"She didn't need me. She'd have come out of it herself."

"She's tough, yes, but everyone has his breaking point."

"Wise remark number forty-two."

"I haven't had an easy day myself, Stewart."

"Sorry. You're quite fond of her, aren't you?"

"I wanted to marry her," Martin said.

Kate lay very still, her eyes closed; with that vital sense cut off, it seemed as if the others were strengthened. She could almost feel Peter's reaction, and Martin's response to it.

"I know," Martin said, after a moment or two. "I already have a wife. But that doesn't prevent a man from dreaming."

"What did prevent you?" Peter asked pleasantly.

"She was in love with someone else."

"So I've heard. What was the fellow like?"

"Rather like you. Nothing specific; but that first day, when you came into my office, there was a look. . . . I think," Martin added, "that Kate's seen it too."

Kate opened her eyes a slit. They stood at the foot of the bed, facing one another. Peter leaned wearily on the footboard; his hair looked as if he had been running both hands through it, and his face was haggard. Paul looked tired too. Poor Paul; he had probably been working over her all day.

"I don't care what he looked like," Peter said sharply. "What was he like?"

Martin took his time about answering. When he did, his comment was concise and his tone savage.

"Treacherous, arrogant, selfish."

"Mmm." Peter rubbed his chin thoughtfully. "Well, but he's dead. Has been, for almost a year. Since conventional considerations don't prevent you from—er—dreaming, why haven't you tried again?"

The smooth, sneering voice was so like Mark's that Kate made a little movement of withdrawal. Neither man noticed.

Martin stiffened and Peter straightened up. The air was electric with antagonism.

Kate pulled herself to a sitting position.

"Stop it," she said. "Paul, stop it, stop it, stop—"

"It's all right, Kate." He was beside her at once, pushing her back onto the pillows. "Be quiet now, calm down. You don't want another injection, do you?"

His hands were hard against her shoulders, and she was weaker than she had thought.

"No," she muttered; all at once she felt as limp as a rag doll, as limp as a little wax figure held over a fire, softening, melting. . . .

"Don't want . . . that," she said, with an enormous effort. "Want . . . I want . . ."

"What? What is it you want?"

"My lawyer," Kate said. "I want . . . make my will."

That was right, that was the right thing to say. She knew at once, from the heavenly feeling of lassitude that was beginning to fog her senses.

Martin sat back, lifting his hands. He looked up to exchange glances with Peter, who had come around to the side of the bed.

"I thought you'd made your will," Martin said in a puzzled voice.

Kate felt a sharp pang of anxiety. He was going to argue, he wasn't going to do what she asked.

"My lawyer," she insisted. "Tomorrow. Promise, Paul . . . promise. . . ."

"All right, all right," Martin said. "I promise, Kate. I'll call him this evening. It can't do any harm," he added, as if to himself; but Kate knew he was speaking to Peter, who stood staring down at her with his brows drawn together in a frown. It didn't matter what he thought. She let out a long sigh. Paul would keep his promise. He always kept his promise.


She was still a little weak next morning, but she insisted on getting up to meet the lawyer. Somehow that was important, that he shouldn't find her helpless in bed. Martin didn't argue. He wasn't arguing about anything. Kate knew why he responded to her slightest suggestion with such suspicious alacrity, why he watched her when he thought she wasn't looking. Deep down inside she laughed, and hugged herself with a secret joy. He didn't fool her. No, she was the one who was tricking them, all of them.

The lawyer didn't seem to notice anything unusual when she rose to greet him, slim and poised in a black suit she seldom wore except for business meetings like this one. Her instructions were simple and concise; he nodded with grave approval when she explained them. The only time he looked taken aback was when she asked him to have the will ready next day. Lawyers were like that, she told herself, and smiled tolerantly at him. They liked lots of time to quibble about nonessentials.

"You said yourself it was quite straightforward," she reminded him, and smiled her best smile. "I know it's an imposition, but—as a favor to me?"

And because I'm your richest client, she added silently. She knew he would agree; everything was going the way she wanted it to now.

"Very well, Miss More. I'll bring it out in the morning, since it's so important to you. Is tomorrow an anniversary of some sort? October—let me see, it will be the thirty-first." He laughed. "Of course, the thirty-first, Halloween."

"Yes," Kate said softly. "It's an anniversary—of some sort."


For the rest of that day her feeling of dreamy contentment persisted. In some far-off corner of her mind Kate knew the mood wouldn't last; people couldn't live their whole lives feeling as if they were wrapped in invisible cotton which insulated them against the touch of the outside world. But the feeling was so pleasant, after the long months of tension, that she wanted to enjoy it as long as she could.

Her new mood affected everyone in the house. Even Mrs. Schmidt was seen to smile as she carried in the tea tray. Tiphaine was brilliant, flushed, dancing. Martin relaxed so far as to go home in the early afternoon, announcing with a wry smile that he did, after all, have other patients. He took Kate aside to assure her that he would be back that night.

The only person unaffected by the new regime was Peter Stewart. He kept out of sight, as if he expected a dismissal once his presence was noted; but Kate caught glimpses of him, prowling the halls and peering in at windows. His expression was glum.

In the afternoon it began to rain, and when the two women sat down to dinner, the patter of water against the windows sounded like thousands of little running feet. Martin had not yet returned, and Peter was also missing. Kate didn't ask about him.

They made trivial conversation during dinner; afterward they went into the living room. Kate picked up a book and Pyewacket came purring in and settled himself on her lap. His considerable bulk made reading difficult, since the owner of the favored lap had to keep elbows out at an odd angle to avoid jabbing the black back; and tonight the cat seemed restless, never settling in one position but turning and rearranging himself like a grumpy arthritic old man. Finally he sank his claws deliberately into Kate's thigh, responded to her exclamation with a growl, and jumped down. He stood in the center of the floor, his long black tail waving like a whip, and then stalked off, pried the door open, and vanished.

Kate watched him go with mingled amusement and irritation. His restlessness had affected her; she couldn't concentrate on her book. She turned her head to look at Tiphaine, who was draped over an armchair, feet dangling across the arm. Her pretty face was set in a frown of concentration and her hands moved in quick motions, manipulating a long piece of string.

"More cats' cradles?" Kate asked. "That looks like a new one."

"Damn." The string knotted and caught, and Tiphaine began to untangle it. "It's new, and awfully complicated. I keep forgetting— There."

She put her hands inside the loop, stretching it wide, and began again.

"Funny colored string," Kate said lazily.

"Just ordinary red twine. I found it in the kitchen drawer. It must have been on a package. You know how Mrs. Schmidt is about saving things."

Again the string caught. Tiphaine shook her head and tried a third time.

Kate watched for a while. She was really too sleepy to do anything useful; even the patterned movement of the string, and the flash of Tiphaine's white fingers, made her drowsy.

"I think I'll go to bed," she said finally. "Listen to the rain. Sounds as if we're in for a spell of bad weather."

"Ah." Tiphaine made a soft sound of satisfaction and jerked her hands apart. The string slid and held, forming a pattern too complex for Kate's blinking eyes to see clearly; there seemed to be a double set of seven strands raying out from the center.

"No more rain," Tiphaine announced with a grin. "I've conjured up a wind. It should clear before morning."

"You mean you listened to the weather report," Kate said, but the words lacked her usual snap, and Tiphaine looked at her intently.

"You do look tired. Want me to come up and tuck you in?"

"Certainly not. Are you going to sit up much longer?"

"Not much longer."

"Good night, then."

Once upstairs, Kate found that she was no longer sleepy. Her bones ached with weariness, but after she was in bed, with the bed lamp turned down low, sleep would not come. That silly string game of Tiphaine's obsessed her; whenever she closed her eyes she seemed to see the pattern outlined in bright streaks of reddish light against blackness. After a period of restless tossing and turning—just like Pyewacket—she gave up, turned the lamp to a brighter setting, and reached for a book.

She had read only a few pages when she heard footsteps in the hall. They were very soft, as if tiptoeing; they sounded like a man's step.

Before she had time to become frightened, she remembered Martin. He had promised to come back and he always kept his promises. Probably he thought she was asleep and was tiptoeing in to look at her. The doorknob turned, and she looked up with a welcoming smile—a smile which froze as she recognized Peter Stewart.

He had been outside; rain flattened his hair and darkened the shoulders of his coat. While Kate stared, he raised one finger to his lips in a gesture for silence.

"I want to talk to you," he said in a low voice.

"I don't want to talk to you," Kate said childishly. "Go away."

His hand moved, so quickly that she had no chance to avoid it. The stiffened fingers struck her twice across the cheeks, sharp blows that stung the skin without rocking her head.

She gasped and clawed at him with both hands. He caught her wrists and held them. The corners of his mouth lifted in a parody of a smile which was all the more unpleasant because the cold watchful eyes did not change.

"That's better," he said. "You've been in a fog all day. What are you taking, some sort of tranquilizer?"

"I don't know. Martin gave me an injection—"

"Don't let him give you any more. You've had enough happy medicine." He released her hands and sat down on the edge of the bed. "We never finished our conversation, did we?"

"We aren't going to finish it. Get out of here. Pack your things and get out of the house."

"Not until I've found out what I came here for." He leaned forward. "What happened to Mark?"

The name was a blow, a sharp jab with a heavy implement that jarred even through the thick cotton insulation, an insulation already weakened by Peter's presence. She shook her head. "No. It's all over. I don't have to talk about—him."

"It's not over. Quite the contrary." His hands reached out for her again, gripping her shoulders and pulling her up till their faces were only inches apart. Her treacherous body betrayed her; she went limp, held erect only by the painful grip of his hands, her head fallen back. But she could not avoid his eyes. They held hers hypnotically.

"But I did it," she whispered. "I did what he told me to do."

"Who?" The intent blue eyes widened. "Mark?"

She moved her head feebly.

"Did . . . what he told me. Now he'll leave me alone."

"Leave you . . ." His grip relaxed, and Kate fell back bonelessly against the pillows. "Not an accident," he said, as if to himself. "Not suicide. You killed him, didn't you?"

The words had been there so long, buried deep in her consciousness, but always beating against the barriers that held them in.

"Yes," she said, and her voice was suddenly strong and steady. "I killed him."

His eyelids flickered, but he showed no other reaction, except for the slow draining of color from his cheeks. There was no time for anything else; the door burst open, and Martin came into the room.

"I was afraid of this," he said grimly. "Kate. What has he done to you?"

"Nothing," Kate said vaguely. "I told him. About Mark."

"Good God," Martin groaned. He turned on Peter, who hadn't moved. His lids had drooped, hiding his eyes. His lashes were darker than his hair, and very thick; Kate had noticed them on another occasion, and the memory of it must have shown in her face as she looked at him; for Martin's mouth tightened as he glanced from Peter to Kate.

"Get out, Stewart. If you try to approach Kate again, I'll call the police."

Peter stood up, stiffly. He did not speak, but when he raised his head and looked at Martin, the doctor stepped back.

"Will!"

The handyman materialized in the open doorway. Peter looked from him to Martin, and shrugged.

"You've made your point," he said, and sauntered toward the door. Will stepped back to let him pass; he left without another word or backward glance.

"Make sure he leaves the house," Martin ordered. He closed the door and came over to the bed, taking both Kate's limp hands in his.

"My poor darling. What have you done?"


Witchcraft or weather report, Tiphaine was right. Kate didn't hear the wind rise and howl around the house; she was deep in drugged sleep. She woke next morning to a bright, cold world, as brilliantly polished as a jewel. She lay unmoving for a few moments, trying to grasp the vague memory that made her uneasy; then she recalled what had happened the night before. But the recollection wasn't as painful as it might have been. Fatigue and the aftermath of shock had dulled her memories of the later part of the night, but she remembered Martin's soft voice, repeating reassurances. There was no proof; it was Peter's word against hers. She could deny ever saying it. Confessions under duress weren't evidence. It was all right. Everything was all right. . . .

Evidently Tiphaine had heard of Peter's visit, for her expression when she greeted Kate at the breakfast table was anxious.

"Mr. Watts called," she said tentatively. "He said he'd be out at ten, if that wasn't too early. I'm to call him back if you—"

"That's fine," Kate said. "Ten o'clock is fine."

She patted the younger girl's cheek and saw her face brighten at this unusual demonstration of affection.

At ten Mr. Watts duly appeared, and she signed the will. He had brought two of his clerks with him as witnesses. Common courtesy demanded that she offer him coffee, and she managed to conceal her annoyance when he accepted. Luckily he was too busy to linger long. By eleven he had left, and Kate went out of doors. The day looked so bright and fair that she was caught unawares by the strength of the wind; it swooped at her and sent her staggering. At the sound of the door being opened, Pyewacket came darting toward her like a black streak of lightning. His morning nap in the sun had proved too uncomfortable with the wind plucking at every hair. Naturally he blamed Kate for the weather; he spat at her when she held the door for him.

Kate walked around the side of the south wing, bending over to pick up fallen branches which had been blown down by the wind. That must have been a real gale last night. She found the cold air refreshing; it seemed to blow a few of the cobwebs from her brain.

When she reached the kitchen door it opened and Tiphaine came out. She was wearing a bulky cable-knit sweater of off-white over her black slacks, and she carried Kate's jacket.

"Here you are. Out in this wind without a coat?"

"I was just about to go in."

"It's too nice a day." Tiphaine held the jacket for her. "Want to beat me at archery?"

"I thought you hated it."

"I feel like doing something violent." Tiphaine grinned and clutched at her hair. It was lifting straight up off her head, like a bright flame. "Come on, it'll do you good."

"All right. But you won't even hit the target in this wind."

Her prediction proved to be correct. Tiphaine hadn't had enough experience to allow for the wind, and her arrows sailed blithely in every direction. The girl was in one of her giddily cheerful moods this morning; she laughed at each blunder. Kate shot with her usual methodical care, finding the challenge of the wild gusts interesting, and managed to get a reasonable number of black-and-red-feathered shafts into the inner circles of the target. On Tiphaine's next turn the wind, which had been playing with her hair like a lover, wrapped the whole length of its ruddy gold around her face, and her shot went so wide that Kate jumped back, even though she was standing, as prescribed, behind the archer.

"That's enough of that," Tiphaine said, muffled. She unwound herself and unstrung her bow. "I'll shoot myself if I go on this way. Coming in, Kate?"

She had to repeat the question. Kate was staring off, across the lichened gray stones of the wall, toward the woods. The brilliant colors were beginning to fade now; last night's gale had stripped many of the remaining leaves from the trees. But the effect was still glorious, and it seemed to draw her.

"What?" she said. "No, I think maybe I'll go for a walk."

"It's almost lunchtime," Tiphaine said. Kate turned to answer, and was just in time to see the look of calculation, quickly veiled, which had narrowed the girl's eyes. "Maybe there is time for a walk," she went on, too quickly. "I'll come with you. I can't after lunch; I promised Miss Device I'd help her with some sewing."

"Let's skip the walk, then," Kate said casually. "I'm getting hungry."

She waited until Tiphaine left for town before she got up from the chaise longue on which she had promised to nap. Looking out the window, she saw the car slow at the gate and then spin sharply to the right. She collected shoes, jacket, and a scarf for her hair, and went out.

She found herself tiptoeing on the stairs and listening for sounds. There should be none; Mrs. Schmidt would be busy in the kitchen, and Will always disappeared after lunch—for a nap, she suspected, though she had never caught him at it. And what difference did it make if anyone saw her? She was the mistress of the house; she was going out for a little walk. Nevertheless, she was very careful in closing the heavy front door, and she didn't put her shoes on until she was outside. As she set out across the lawn she was almost running.

She had to cross the stubble of Mr. Goldberg's cornfield to reach the wood from this direction. Walking was hard among the stiff short stalks, and she took care not to fall on any of them. Goldberg had planted a few vines of pumpkin along the edge; the big orange globes looked like fallen moons, but not pretty golden moons—more like the swollen red monsters that hang above a smoky horizon like goblin faces. Speaking of faces, the children had been busy among the pumpkins. Presumably they had carried the successful carvings off with them, but a few botched jack-o'-lanterns lay among litters of seed and pulp. One had been almost finished when the knife slipped, making a long, twisted gash of a mouth. Its big round eyes stared up at her, hollowed and empty with blackness.

Kate shivered. The jolliness gone wrong, the sinister merriment, reminded her that Halloween had originally been Allhallows' Eve, the night when the dead walk and the powers of evil have strength to work their will. That's the sort of thing we do here, she thought; we try to hide horror with a painted clown's mask. Our funerals, and embalming, and . . . She shook herself mentally and went on at a faster pace. Of all the morbid trains of thought . . .

Once inside the woods she felt better, but even the familiar, friendly terrain seemed changed. It was a wild wood, which had never been cleared; she liked its tangled freedom, even when her ankles were scratched by shoots of wild holly and fir, and trapped by the ubiquitous honeysuckle. It was a bright, vivid place even in winter; the orange berries of bittersweet stood out against the green of the pines, and blue jays and cardinals swung from graceful bare branches. There were always animals about, and she knew many of them personally; hours spent sitting, in perfect stillness, on a fallen log or rock had accustomed many of the shy wood dwellers to her presence. There was an old striped badger, who lived in a bank farther back in the woods, and a family of woodchucks, who trundled out to sun themselves on warm days. But today nothing seemed to be stirring. The woods were uncannily quiet. Once a jay shrieked, and the harsh note broke off in midcall, as if the sound of its own voice had frightened the bird.

She was on the bridle path when she heard hoofbeats coming toward her. The rider was still out of sight, and Kate looked about for a side path she could duck into. She didn't feel in the mood for people. Then the horse came into view. She recognized both horse and rider, and dashed toward the trees.

In her haste she picked a spot where honeysuckle made an almost impenetrable curtain between two pines. Tearing at the resistant stems, Kate watched his handling of the horse and knew for certain what she had only suspected before. That fall of his had been a fake.

He slid down off the horse and came toward her, and Kate abandoned her attempt at flight. Better to meet him here, in a semipublic place.

He was dressed even more carelessly than usual, in a dark sweater and slacks which needed pressing; above the black fabric his face looked bleached and spectral, the skin drawn tightly over the high cheekbones, the eyes faintly shadowed.

"I tried to see you this morning," he said. "They've got the place too well guarded."

"Naturally. You realize that what I said last night—"

"Forget about that. I'm interested in this morning. Have you signed that will?"

Kate gaped, not knowing whether to be more surprised at his casual dismissal of her admission, or at his knowledge.

"How did you know about the will? I mean, that I was signing it this morning?"

"Snooping," Peter said briefly. "Have you signed it?"

"Yes."

"Damn." He ran his fingers through his hair so that it stood up on end like a rooster's crest.

"It's none of your business, anyhow," Kate said, and tried to pass him. He caught her by the arms.

"I'm not going to struggle with you," she said distantly. "Nor argue, nor even talk. So you may as well let me go."

His fingers tightened and then relaxed, though he did not release her.

"I've been up most of the night, thinking," he muttered. "But I suppose there's nothing I could say to you, now, that would make you believe . . . Tell me something. You've been paying blackmail. For Mark's death, I suppose. To whom?"

In her numbed state, his shock tactics were very effective.

"Timmy," she said; and her hand flew to her mouth as her eyes widened in horror.

"Timmy again. Damn it all—you've no idea who's behind him, I suppose. . . . No. The Schmidts. Did you inherit them from Uncle Stephan too?"

"Yes. Damn you, damn you!" She forgot her dignity, and her decision not to struggle, and began twisting frantically. "What are you trying to do? Can't you leave me alone?"

"I wish to God I could. You'd better not do that," he added, his tight mouth relaxing a trifle, as she began pounding him on the chest with her clenched fists. "It's not only undignified, but it has a bad effect on me."

He pulled her roughly into his arms, pinning her hands between his body and hers, and kissing her with an intensity that forced her head back into the curve of his shoulder. After the first second Kate forgot the discomfort of her twisted neck and laboring lungs; she was not even aware of the moment when her body relaxed and her mouth answered the demand of his.

He let her go so suddenly that she staggered, catching blindly at the tangled vines for support, not feeling the bite of them against her palms. Something rustled in the underbrush and Peter whirled, breathing hard. Silence fell; and Peter's clenched hands relaxed.

"I'm tempted," he said, in a voice whose tone belied the mocking words, "to drag you up onto that horse and carry you off. But I wouldn't get far, would I?"

Kate tried to say something, and found that her voice had deserted her. She shook her head violently.

"No," he agreed. "Not with you screaming bloody murder every step of the way."

Kate cleared her throat.

"Anyhow," she pointed out, "you haven't got a horse."

Peter swung around with a vehement remark. Sultan was still in sight, but retreating fast, one eye cocked warily. Peter started out after him.

"I'll be back," he called out. "Try not to do anything stupid between now and six o'clock, will you?"

Kate ran.

She ran faster than she had ever run in her life, ran till her legs ached and the pain in her side finally forced her to slow to a limping walk. The thing she was trying to run away from couldn't be escaped so easily. It rode with her, step for step and yard for yard. She sank to the ground at the edge of the wood, in a tangle of arms and legs and disheveled hair. The wild wind hummed angrily in the trees above.

Her brain felt as if it were boiling like a caldron. A hodgepodge of mixed ideas, emotions, and fancies bubbled and seethed. One thought popped to the surface, and she was just beginning to see it clearly when it broke and sank, and another took its place. She sprawled in a heap of leaves, face hidden in her folded arms. As her frantic breathing slowed, so did the seething thoughts; but the mental terrain that now lay open to her was as unfamiliar as a landscape after an earthquake has tumbled mountains.

For a long time she lay still. How long she did not know, but when she finally sat up and opened her eyes, the sun was sinking westward and the shadows had grown longer. Out of the jumble of wild emotion one predominant feeling stood isolated and unshakable. She marveled that she had not recognized it long before.

Only then did she hear the voice. It must have been calling for some time; it sounded hoarse and frantic. She looked up, and saw Tiphaine standing by the wall.

She must answer; they would be worried about her. Unsteadily she got to her feet and waved. Tiphaine turned, saw her, and ran toward her.

"Kate! I've been so worried. . . . What happened?"

"Nothing happened. I just—went for a walk."

"You look so . . . You saw him, didn't you?"

"Peter? How did you know?"

Her voice was harsh; the younger girl stepped back a pace.

"Why—General Volz called. He said Peter had borrowed Sultan, and wondered if I planned to ride today."

"Oh." Kate started walking toward the house.

"What did he say?"

"Who?"

"Peter, of course. Kate, what's wrong with you? You look sort of drunk."

"It's that stuff Paul gave me, I guess." Kate stopped, turning toward her cousin. She had to look up into Tiphaine's face. "Tiphaine, I've been thinking. We haven't had a vacation for a long time. I think perhaps we ought to get away from here for a few weeks, maybe longer."

"A vacation?" Tiphaine's smooth face was expressionless.

"Yes. Tomorrow we might go to one of the travel agencies, and collect some folders. Maybe even Europe."

"Tomorrow." Tiphaine's face cleared, and Kate felt sick with relief. It was going to be easier than she had thought. "That's a wonderful idea, Kate."

The sound was faint at first, but it rapidly got louder—a wild, rhythmic pounding, like drumbeats. Tiphaine understood its meaning before Kate did; she gasped, turning toward the trees, in time to see Sultan come thundering out into the open. The reins dangled loose on his neck, and the saddle was empty.

Sultan shied violently at the sight of them, and swerved. Tiphaine ran toward him, calling; he came to a crashing stop and stood with his head drooping. Kate followed more slowly. She was a poor horsewoman at best, and Sultan had always terrified her. Nor was she as quick as Tiphaine to catch the implications. Not until she was standing beside her cousin, and caught a glimpse of Tiphaine's face, did she realize what the empty saddle might mean.

"He must have been thrown," she exclaimed.

"I guess so," Tiphaine said slowly.

"Or else he never did catch Sultan." That idea was reassuring; Kate snatched at it. "The brute was running away from him when I left him. That was—oh, a long time ago—"

"How long ago?"

"I don't know. I don't remember very well."

"Kate, you don't know much about horses, do you? Look at Sultan."

She knew that much; she had been trying not to see it. Sultan the vicious was in a state of pitiable terror. Shivering, sweating, nosing at Tiphaine's hand, he did not look like a mount which has triumphantly tossed its rider and run for home. He hadn't gone home. He had bolted, blindly and madly, and by the look of him he had been running for some time.

Kate's knees went weak. She put one hand on the saddle for support, and jerked it away as something warm and sticky smeared her fingers. In silence she held her hand out for inspection. Across the palm there was a wet reddish streak.

Tiphaine said something. Kate didn't hear the words, only a buzzing, like a fly trapped against a window. Inside her head, echoing hollowly, words had begun to form: an insane litany that beat in time with the cold, rushing wind's moan.

"Cold blows the wind . . . cold blows the wind. . . ."

Somehow she got into the saddle. The stirrups were too long, and she couldn't seem to get her feet into them. She slammed her heels into the horse's sides. Tiphaine's hands pulled at her. She shook them off and snatched at the rough mane as Sultan bolted.

Under any other circumstances she could never have controlled Sultan. He was too big and too strong-mouthed. Now he was no longer an animal; he was simply a means of locomotion, and the will that drove her mastered him.

Sultan took the main trail at a dead run. They met no one. The woods were as still as death, shadowy under the tall pines. When they neared the turnoff to the glade, the horse stopped so suddenly that only Kate's taut grip on his mane kept her from flying out over his head. She did not need the animal's signs of panic to tell her the way. A horse had been through the cutoff, though it had not been intended as a bridle trail. The hoof marks were clear on the bare patches of ground off the hard surface of the main trail.

She forced Sultan onto the cutoff, but it took all her will to do it, and that will was fading, with the fear of what she knew she would find. At the edge of the glade he balked, planting all four feet like rocks. He would go no farther. Katharine, perched precariously on his back, felt the shivering muscles under her thighs like an extension of her own shaking body.

The clearing was carpeted with gypsy-colored leaves, but enough foliage still remained on the trees to cut out the sunlight and cast a blue haze over the scene before her. In the shadows the man's body lay face down and utterly still, looking two-dimensional, like a figure cut out of black paper. One shaft of sunlight cut down like a spotlight, gilding the tumbled fair hair. Its oblique path caught the tip of the arrow that stood up from his back like a little banner. The feathers were black and red. In Kate's ears the old song rang with a sick, hollow whine, like a bad recording:

"And he in greenwood now lies slain."

## Chapter

## 10

THE TREES TURNED UPSIDE DOWN, TRUNKS UP AND BRANCHES toward her feet. Kate slid off the horse's back, landing on hands and knees.

Standing erect was out of the question. She crawled across the few feet that separated her from Peter. For a long minute she knelt there, hands on her knees, watching gravely as the tip of the arrow bobbed up and down and the trees swayed in a slow, sickening dance. It took her that long—sixty interminable seconds—to realize that the two movements were not the same. The feathers were moving, minutely but perceptibly, with the rhythm of his breathing.

She put out a shaking hand to touch his head, and saw the bizarre barometer of breath jerk more vigorously.

"Don't move," she said, in a voice which sounded too steady to be her own. "You've got an arrow sticking in you."

There was a long moment of silence, while she sat listening to Peter's breathing. It was emphatic and irregular now, punctuated with more peremptory sounds of life. Finally a muffled voice said, "What was that you said?"

"An arrow. In your back."

"Oh." He turned his head carefully, without lifting it, and Kate found herself staring into one half-closed blue eye. The eye narrowed still more as recognition dawned.

"Arrow," he repeated, as if the word were too incredible to believe. "One of yours, by any chance?"

"Yes, it's one of mine." She lifted both hands and let them

fall, in a gesture of denial. "But I didn't do it. Probably you won't believe me."

Peter's eye closed.

"How did you find me?"

"Sultan came back alone. There was blood on the saddle."

"Isn't that the title of a song?" The silence went on so long that she bent over him in a new upsurge of terror, and his eye opened again. This time it looked more alert.

"Pull it out."

"Peter, I daren't. I'll go for Paul. He'll know—"

Peter levered himself up on one elbow.

"If you didn't fire the bloody thing, someone else did. I'd rather not wait around until he comes back to dispose of the remains." His eyes narrowed as he studied her pale face and silently working mouth; then the corners of his mouth curled up in the familiar, detestable smile. "Chicken?" he inquired gently.

Kate took a deep breath.

"Brace yourself," she said, and grasped the shaft, as close to the point as she could.

It had not penetrated as deeply as she feared, but clearly it was deeper than he had thought; he was flat on his face and squirming by the time she had finished. She took advantage of his position to apply a wadded-up handkerchief to the wound, and then held the evidence in front of the face he had turned toward her.

"Hunting arrow," he muttered.

"I never use them."

"I know. Drop it, we shan't learn anything from it. Everyone in town must know your colors. Let's make ourselves scarce."

"Can you walk?"

"I'll crawl if I must," he said grimly, and pushed himself to his knees.

"I have Sultan. If you can mount . . ."

They managed it somehow, though it wasn't easy; by the time Peter was in the saddle, clutching the pommel with both hands and swaying ominously, there was a sizable wet patch on the back of his sweater.

Katharine took the reins and they started off. Sultan was unhappy, and his gait had never been noted for smoothness; she heard Peter's breath catch every time a hoof came down.

"Hold on," she said, without looking at him. "If you fall off, I'll never get you back up there."

"I'll hold on."

"Peter. What were you doing out there?"

He muttered something that sounded like "later," and swore feebly as a branch struck his bowed head. When they turned onto the bridle path the going was easier, and again Kate found time to wonder at the unnatural stillness of the woods. The shady, sun-streaked leaves seemed frozen, as if waiting. Only the creak of the saddle and the slow rhythmic plop of the horse's hooves broke the stillness. She turned to look at Peter, and saw that he had slumped forward till his head touched Sultan's neck. Her hand loosened its hold, and Sultan stopped. Peter straightened, blinking.

"What's up?"

"I'd better walk beside you, it's safer." She slapped the horse's flank. "Come on, you nasty brute, walk."

"No, wait. Where're we going?"

"To the house, I guess. Then I'd better—"

"Got to talk first," he interrupted. "Can't wait. You know . . . what . . ."

She interrupted in turn, trying to spare him the effort of talking.

"I know someone just tried to kill you. From the questions you asked me earlier, I gather you've been snooping, as you put it, into the various unpleasant things that have been happening to me. I'm assuming, as a working hypothesis, that the would-be murderer is the person who's been blackmailing me. You think the Schmidts may be involved. It's certainly a possibility. There are a lot of other things I don't understand; I don't know why a blackmailer would want to—try to drive me out of my mind. People who've been judged insane can't sign checks. And I don't know why you . . . why you . . ."

Peter was sitting up straighter and looking more alert. He did not comment on her last, unvoiced question, nor on the faltering of her voice.

"What a pleasure it is to meet someone with a logical mind," he murmured. "That's fine, as far as it goes. But you don't understand the really vital part yet. And I doubt if I could explain it. I'm not even sure I believe it myself. Do you know what today is?"

"Why—October thirty-first. What about it?"

Peter's eyes rolled expressively heavenward.

"Think, Kate, think. It's all there, if you'll just face it. Common garden-variety murderers don't use bow and arrow. In a forest glade, Kate, with a black stone and a babbling brook—in the greenwood, as the poet says. And the date—ah, I see you have thought of it."

The blue eyes met the black in a long, demanding stare; Kate's eyes were the first to fall.

"No," she said. "It isn't possible."

Sultan, sensing her agitation, stamped and snorted; and Peter exclaimed aloud and caught at his shoulder.

"Hurry," he said through clenched teeth. "We mustn't be here after the sun sets."

The sun had set before they reached the house. Behind the skeletal trees to the west the sunset flamed in angry hues of red and orange, scarred by slashes of purple and black clouds. The house swam in the dimness of twilight. There was no light, no sound, and no sign of a living occupant.

Kate, supporting most of Peter's sagging weight, let her held breath out in a sigh of relief. She hadn't wanted to come back here, but there was literally nowhere else to go. Volz's was the only nearby house, and Volz, of all people . . . But the Schmidts seemed to be gone; at least they hadn't heard her come in.

But they might come looking for her at any moment, finding her alone, burdened with an injured man. Peter was conscious, but just barely; she couldn't drag him much farther, certainly not up the stairs. She stood undecided in the dim hall, biting her lip nervously. Would it be better to get him into her car and head straight for town? The car was out in back, and if the Schmidts were in the kitchen, they would hear the engine start up. No, there was a quicker way to get help. She maneuvered her burden into the living room and let him drop onto the sofa. He moved feebly, and fell back; and Kate, rubbing aching shoulders, tiptoed out into the hall to the telephone.

Martin responded instantly, as she had known he would; no surprise, no questions, no delay. Only a few terse instructions and a promise to come at once. Luckily the capsules were in the

medicine chest in the downstairs bathroom. Martin had prescribed them for her headaches, but she had never used them—
that silly phobia of hers about drugs.

She collected the other supplies she was going to need and
fled for the living room, closing the door behind her with an absurd sense that she had reached sanctuary. There was no reason
to be afraid now; even if her wildest fears were true, even if
they found her, help was on the way.

Peter was trying to sit up when she came in, and he resisted
her attempts to get him down again.

"Too dangerous," he muttered. "Kate . . . got to talk. I'm so
damned dizzy. . . ."

"Take these." She offered him the pills, three of them, and a
glass of water.

"What . . . ?"

"They're for pain. Like aspirin, only stronger."

He was too confused to argue. The pills went down, but Peter refused the water.

"Got any brandy?"

"Maybe you shouldn't."

"I'll risk it. Need something . . . quick."

He swallowed it in one gulp, buried his face in his hands,
and then sat up, shaking his head.

"Wow. That's better. I'll need more patching up, I'm afraid,
but make it quick. We'll talk while you work."

"Try not to yell," Kate warned as he lay flat, chin supported
on his folded arms. "I don't want anyone to know we're here."

"I'm too tired to yell. You think the Schmidts are involved,
then?"

"I don't know. That's just the trouble. I feel I can't trust
anyone."

"Best possible assumption. That's what we have to talk
about. I have an idea that—ouch! What are you putting on that,
carbolic acid?"

"Peroxide. Are you all right?"

There was a lengthy pause before Peter replied.

"I'm so sleepy. What was I talking about?"

"I told you not to take that brandy. Hold still."

She applied strips of tape with a hand which was none too
steady. It was hard to see, the twilight was so far advanced. But
she didn't dare turn on a light. Her ears strained to hear the

sound she hoped for, the familiar rattle and clank of the old car. But the windows were closed; maybe she wouldn't hear the car. He could get in. The front door was unlocked.

Peter was so still she feared he had fainted under her awkward hands. The room seemed very dark. And cold. Peter had begun to shiver. She remembered the danger of shock, and squinted into the gloom, trying to find something to put over him. But she knew there was nothing of that sort in the room, not even an afghan.

"Peter. Peter, can you hear me?"

A vague murmur was the only response.

"Peter! I've got to go upstairs and get something, a blanket, or—"

He sat bolt upright, in one convulsive movement.

"You're not going upstairs. We're leaving, both of us. This was crazy, coming here. . . . I've just realized . . . they'll be looking for us, it's dark now, and this is the logical place. After dark . . . before midnight. . . ."

His voice dropped to a mumble, and Kate peered anxiously at the pale oval of his face.

"Peter, lie down. You're sick. You don't know what you're saying."

"Got to get out of here," Peter insisted querulously. "May not know we're here . . . yet . . . but they'll wait. Out there. Go out the window. Around the side to the car . . ."

"It's all right, Peter. Paul will be here any minute. I called him as soon as we arrived, and he said—"

His hands caught her by the shoulders, sinking painfully into the old bruises.

"You did what?"

"Called the doctor, of course. What—"

He let her go, so suddenly that she fell to one side; then he slumped forward, hands buried in his hair.

"God Almighty. I've got to think. . . . What the hell is wrong with me? Maybe it's not too late. The window."

"Oh, no, Peter. Not—"

"You are hard to convince, aren't you? Too damned trusting, that's your trouble. . . . Said it yourself, don't trust anybody." Peter pushed himself upright and stood swaying drunkenly. "Don't wait for me. Run. Maybe . . . not too late. . . ."

"I'm afraid it is," Martin said regretfully.

\* \* \*

The overhead chandelier went on, in a blinding burst of light, and somehow Kate found herself in Peter's arms, not quite sure who was supporting whom, but illogically reassured by the feel of him. From under blinking eyelids she saw Martin in the doorway, smiling pleasantly.

"Very touching," he said. "You make such an attractive couple. It really is a pity."

"You don't have to kill her," Peter mumbled. "She'll agree—"

"Too late for that, too. If she'd agreed to marry me . . . But I knew the other day, when I heard her disgusting babbling about you, that I hadn't a chance."

"Then it wasn't you who suggested . . ." Peter shook his head. "I can't think," he said plaintively.

"I see you've taken your medicine," Martin said with a smile. "But you suspected me, earlier; I overheard what you were saying before I came in. Where did I go wrong? I thought I was doing a magnificent job of being the stalwart, loyal family doctor."

"The will."

"Not until then? Well, that is a relief. But I don't think anyone else will find it peculiar. Even the lawyer seemed to think it was reasonable for Kate to leave her money to her sole surviving relative."

"Won't be so reasonable . . . if she dies," Peter muttered.

"Oh, it will seem quite reasonable. You don't know the rest of the plan yet. But you soon will. Come along, both of you."

Now that the first shock of his appearance had worn off, Kate was trying desperately to think. The Schmidts were involved, then; they must be, or Martin wouldn't be so confident of his control of the situation. But he hadn't called them. He didn't even have a weapon. He thought he could easily handle a woman and a man weakened by—drugs, of course. Those pills! Kate's knees buckled under Peter's weight, and as his head dropped onto her shoulder she gasped,

"You've killed him! What was in those capsules?"

"He's not dead, he's just sleeping peacefully. So much kinder that way."

Martin sauntered toward them and Kate sank to her knees, still stubbornly clutching at Peter. He was a dead weight; but as they went down she felt his elbow dig into her ribs, and she threw herself into her part with abandon, wringing her hands as she bent over him.

"He's dead, he's dead; you've killed him!"

She slid back out of the way as Martin knelt to inspect his victim; and Peter's legs came up, knees bent. But his reflexes were dulled by the drug; Martin saw the blow coming, and ducked. Instead of hitting his head, Peter's knees struck his shoulder and sent him sprawling. Peter got to his feet, teeth set in his lower lip; and as Kate sprang toward him he spun her around, put his hands in the middle of her back, and shoved.

She went staggering toward the window, knowing she couldn't stop herself. . . . Then her outflung hands struck the panel and the door leaves burst open. Kate went reeling out onto the balcony.

It was not like the sham balconies in the other rooms, being wider, longer, and railed with stone. Kate hit the balustrade with a force that knocked the breath out of her. Clinging to the cold stone with both hands, she looked back over her shoulder. Framed by the window, under the glaring lights, the interior of the room looked unreal, like a set in a play. Peter was down, and decidedly out; there was no pretense this time about his twisted limbs and head. He had used the last of his strength to give her a chance of escape. And not only her—his only hope of survival lay in her being able to get help. If she was caught, they were both lost.

The logic was inescapable. The only trouble was, Kate couldn't move.

She couldn't run away and leave him. It was stupid, it was illogical; but for the moment primitive instinct was stronger than reason, and it froze her in her place.

Then Martin rose from beside Peter's body; and, with a queer choking noise, Kate flexed her knees and jumped over the edge of the balcony.

She landed with a thud in a big yew, scratching her arms and face and doing considerable damage to one ankle; but now that the decision had been made, she no longer hesitated. Martin ran out onto the balcony, and she crawled, under the shelter of the yew, toward the corner of the house. Before he could get over the balustrade she broke free, running as fast as she could toward the front of the house.

He reacted as she had hoped. By going through the house and out the front door, he could intercept her on the route she appeared to be taking—from the house to the front gate. As soon as he disappeared into the room, Kate turned.

She was heading for the car, and she was prepared to take some risks in order to acquire a speedy means of transportation; but some rudiments of caution remained, enough to make her stop before venturing into the open lawn behind the house.

It was as well she did so. The car was there, all right; she could see its outlines through the branches of the shrub behind which she cowered. She could also see Will Schmidt. The hood of the car was up, and he was bending over the engine.

Kate gritted her teeth. Damn Martin; he would think of that. When Schmidt straightened and turned, in response to a hail from the front of the house, she knew the car was useless to her. It would take too long to find out what part Will had gimmicked. Perhaps it wasn't even repairable.

Schmidt carefully lowered the hood before setting off at an ungainly lope to join his confederate. Kate grinned savagely. If she hadn't seen him at work, she might have wasted vital moments trying to start the engine.

Instead of backtracking, she slid around the corner of the house in the same direction Schmidt had taken, but at an angle, avoiding the car. As she ran, she fought back a wild desire to go back. They must have left Peter alone. If she could rouse him . . . But the idea was absurd. He was deep in drugged sleep, and too weak to go fast and quietly even if she could waken him. She turned her mind instead to alternate means of transportation. It was miles to town, it would take too long to walk, and they would be searching for her. They . . . She had never realized the terror that could be implicit in a simple pronoun. She didn't know who they were, or how many they were. All she knew was their purpose. But that was enough.

So it would have to be the woods, and Volz's stables. Sultan had gone home a long time ago, she had been too much preoccupied with more important matters to tie him, and he was not the horse to linger when bed and breakfast beckoned. Volz might be one of *them*; he was a horrible man anyhow, and she didn't dare ask him for help. Timmy, as everyone knew, went to his own room at sunset. . . .

Timmy.

Kate set her teeth and ran faster. Timmy had always made her skin crawl, even before the recent events in which he had been so oddly involved. But in her present mood she was prepared to deal with Timmy, or anyone else near her own size. It might be just as well, though, to take some precautions. She slowed to a walk, forced to do so by the pain in her straining lungs, and put the delay to good use by scanning the shadowy sides of the path. A stout stick and—yes, there was a stone just the right size, small enough to fit comfortably into her fist, big enough to hurt. She would just have to hit Timmy if he tried to get between her and one of Volz's horses.

Or Volz's car? No. The keys wouldn't be in the ignition, they would be in Hilary's pocket, and Hilary would be shut in his own room and disinclined, in any case, to give aid and comfort to anyone. Besides, the car made too much noise.

She stumbled as her weakened ankle gave way, and fell head first against a tree trunk, hitting her forehead so hard that for an instant she saw bright lights whirling inside her eyeballs. With a whimper of pain she ran on. The lights weren't as bad as the other things she kept seeing inside her eyes, the visions of what they might be doing to Peter.

When she reached the edge of the woods she stopped, rubbing her aching head. Her vision was blurred, and she had to blink before it cleared.

What she saw made her stomach sink, sickeningly. The moonlight shone off the polished surfaces of a number of cars parked outside the stable gates, and most of the downstairs lights were blazing. Tonight, of all nights, Volz was entertaining.

Kate slumped against a tree trunk, sick with despair. She couldn't go out there when the house was full of people and the chauffeurs were standing around, smoking and talking. Surely there was someone in the town, someone among the owners of those cars, to whom she could appeal for aid?

She looked again, and gradually she realized that there was something strange about the cars. The weird outlines of Miss Device's old electric runabout were unmistakable. She was one of the sights of the town in that car, sitting bolt upright on the high seat. Miss Device would not be much of an ally. She would twitter and wring her hands.

Miss Device always drove herself. But the others . . . Joan

Solomon did too, her white Cadillac was in the lot, parked at Joan's usual, acute angle next to the Senator's Rolls. The Senator had a chauffeur. Where was he?

A cold wind put chilly fingers down her spine, and she knew the answer. In nice weather the chauffeurs hung around outside. On a night like this, with a long party in prospect, they would be in the kitchen, or with Hilary in his room. No, Hilary would probably be helping with the serving. He would be inside.

Kate straightened, her hopes rising. Maybe the situation wasn't so hopeless. She would just have to be careful. But no cars. Joan had probably left her keys. She had lost two cars that way, but she still forgot the keys. But Joan's Cadillac was too hard to get at, through the tangle of surrounding fenders.

The stableyard gates were closed, as they always were at night. Kate sighed. Another wall to climb. At least this was wooden, and slatted, instead of crumbling stone. When she was inside the yard she unbarred the gate to facilitate her retreat. Then she crept toward the stalls.

She had already decided which horse to take. Not Sultan. She would have to ride bareback; saddling up would take too much time. The little mare Starlight was the gentlest of Volz's horses. But with Starlight Kate knew she had to get out of the yard unseen and unsuspected. Sultan could outrun the mare any day of the week, and so could most of the others, especially with skilled horsemen on their backs.

Her skin crawling in spite of her resolve, she inspected all the stalls to make sure Timmy wasn't napping in one of them. Sometimes he did. But he had a catlike regard for his own comfort—or what he considered comfort, which did not include cleanliness. She was relieved, but not surprised, to find no trace of him.

In the silent stableyard, the only sounds came from the horses. Kate jumped as something touched her ankle and then relaxed when she recognized Grimalkin, the stable cat, twining himself around her ankles. He was normally an unsociable animal, but he liked her. Kate stooped to touch his fur, thinking wryly that in this town a cat's approval was not necessarily a compliment.

Her presence acknowledged, the cat stalked off, tail high, and Kate reached in to unlatch Starlight's stall door. The mare turned her head with a little inquiring sound, and Kate grabbed for her mouth. Starlight's melting brown eyes looked calmly at the intruder; she was not alarmed, because nothing alarmed her. Her placid disposition was the reason why Kate had chosen her.

Then the shadows moved.

Kate spun around. Timmy stood in the doorway. His face was a featureless darkness, but she recognized the slight figure outlined against the pale moonlight. She took in a breath which was almost a gasp. The first sight of him had had the effect of a blow in the pit of the stomach. But the stone was in her left-hand pocket. The stick was clenched in her right hand.

"Get out of the way, Timmy," she said softly. "Go back to your own room."

Timmy's shadowy head moved from side to side. His slim body didn't really block the doorway; she could see the cobbles of the courtyard on either side of him. She raised her stick.

"Go back. Or I'll tell Mr. Volz on you."

Timmy's head jerked back, and for a moment she thought her threat had frightened him. Then she heard the soft sounds he was making, and recognized them for what they were; and for a second another fear, the fear of the normal for the stain of madness, gripped her throat. It was then that she saw the others moving slowly in from behind and from both sides. Bizarre, nightmare shapes: a wolf, man-tall, walking on its hind legs; a woman in long black skirts and a stiff white cap that concealed her features as completely as the wolf-snout hid the other face; a crouching dark shape with a ghoul's face that had run like melted lava and shone with a sick green luminescence; a wrinkled harridan with long gray locks streaming under a pointed hat, carrying a broom. . . . A witch, like the witch costume the little girl had worn that night, so long ago . . .

Halloween night. Costume . . .

Kate's reeling brain swayed back from the edge of hysteria. It was Halloween, and Volz was giving a costume party.

She knew the others now, knew the faces—the familiar faces, many of which she had known all her life. Miss Device, dressed like her long-dead ancestress; Mrs. Adams, the witch; Joan Solomon, in a dirty torn shift that showed far too much of her ample figure. There were leaves, dark ugly leaves, twisted in her hair. And foremost among them was General Volz himself, dressed in the tall hat and white ruff and buckled shoes worn by the Salem judges. He was smiling.

"We were pretty sure you'd head for here," he said.

They were all smiling. Familiar faces, looking as she had never seen them look. . . . Her mind made the final, mad connection, and without conscious thought she began to count. Seven, eight, nine. Nine of them. And the others, the four others—that made . . .

"Thirteen," she said aloud; and Volz, following her reasoning with an ease that was the final confirmation, nodded his bullet head.

"Thirteen," he agreed. "That's the proper number. Isn't it, Dr. More?"

# Chapter

## 11

THEY TIED HER HANDS AND FEET, SINCE VOLZ WAS DRIVING alone, but they didn't bother to gag her. Kate knew why. The hired chauffeurs had been left at home tonight; but if they had been here, or if Hilary heard her cry out, no one would answer. On Allhallow's Eve the poor ignorant darkies huddled in their shacks, fearing the powers of darkness. . . .

Nuts, Kate thought inelegantly, and gasped as Volz tossed her carelessly into the back seat of the car. The population of the town, black and white, knew enough to stay home tonight, but it was not superstition that kept them in, but a real, tangible fear. Fear of the superior, sophisticated gentry of the town, whose combined wealth and power turned their vicious hobby into an instrument of terror.

Had she been the only blind fool in the whole town? Now that she knew, so many hints and seemingly meaningless incidents fell into place, made horrible sense. But she wouldn't have believed, even if someone had warned her. She hadn't even believed it that afternoon, when Peter had shown her the pattern. The pattern was there, it couldn't be denied, but she had preferred to view it as the result of a suggestion made to a sick mind, carried out with the remorseless, twisted logic of madness. Peter had known the truth. He knew she wouldn't believe him. Peter . . . She turned her head into the slick leather upholstery and stifled a moan. She had failed. And what lay in store for them both was worse even than she had imagined.

Volz's erratic, triumphant driving made even the expensive

car ride uncomfortably; she was jolted and jarred, unable to fend herself off from the hard surfaces against which she was flung. Finally she managed to wedge herself into a corner so that she could see out the window. As she had expected, they were heading for her house. The gates stood open, and Volz drove straight in, stopping by the steps with a jolt that threw her forward.

He left her in the car, and Kate tried to pull herself up. Surely there must be something she could do. . . . She wasn't given time even to think. Volz was back almost at once, and Martin was with him. Between them they carried Peter.

When they reached the car, Volz let his share of the burden drop with a thud and opened the back door.

"Couldn't you have waked him up?" he demanded irritably. "We'll have a hell of time dragging him through the brush."

"Feet in first," Martin ordered. "He'll be waking by the time we get there. I timed the injection carefully. But I don't want him too wide awake. I underestimated his resistance once, and it almost ended in disaster."

"We got her back," Volz grunted, jamming Peter's legs into the car. He stood back while Martin efficiently manipulated the rest of the load in. Kate looked hopefully for some sign of awareness, and found none; Peter slid bonelessly down onto the floor, his head and arms on the seat next to her. His breathing sounded odd.

"Yes, you got her back," Martin said contemptuously. He glanced into the car to make sure all was well; his eyes met Kate's and moved away without a flicker of expression. He slammed the door. "Thanks to me."

They moved around to the front of the car and Kate lost Volz's response. It was evidently acrimonious, for as he took his seat Martin said in a conciliatory tone, "There's no point in quarreling. Certainly not tonight. All's well that ends well."

Volz grunted and started the engine.

Neither man, spoke for the rest of the trip, which was incredibly bumpy; they drove straight across the field onto the bridle path. It was wide enough to take the car, but Volz had to spin the wheel like a top to avoid the worst ruts and holes. Kate twisted frantically and vainly as Peter's head slid off the seat and landed on the floor with a thud. Then she leaned forward, electrified, as he muttered something profane.

He was coming around, but it was too late. The car jolted to a stop, its headlights framing the spot she had expected to see: a scarlet trail of poison ivy winding up a tree trunk, and a broken branch sticking out at an odd angle.

The two men got out, and Martin opened the back door. He prodded Peter with his toe and got a half-intelligible epithet in response.

"How's that for accuracy?" he said in a pleased voice. "He can stand now. We'll have to drag him, but that's easier than carrying."

"We? Who's going to carry her?"

"Untie her feet."

"You fool, she'll bolt as soon as we get into the woods."

"With her hands tied she won't get far."

"She'll try it, though," Volz said glumly. "And I'm sick of chasing her around. We're short on time as it is."

Martin pursed his lips and looked at Kate. She stared back at him, wishing looks could kill.

"You would, wouldn't you," he said meditatively. "Well, let's spell out the obvious, shall we? If you should leave us, I will immediately cut Mr. Stewart's throat. It's a quick way to go, they tell me, but not necessarily painless."

He raised his eyebrows inquiringly, waited for a moment, and then smiled.

"I see we understand one another."

They got Peter on his feet, though he kept insisting he wanted to lie down. The final threat had finished Kate; she felt as if her whole body had gone to sleep, the way a foot does when it is twisted the wrong way for too long. At Martin's command she stumbled docilely off down the path. The two followed, supporting Peter; he was grumbling steadily, and Volz added a stream of curses every time they stumbled, which was fairly often.

As soon as they were out of range of the car's headlights, Martin switched on a flashlight which he held in his free hand. He shone it well in front of Kate's feet, but she was unable to protect herself from low branches, and there were stinging cuts all over her face by the time they reached the glade.

There, on another command, she stopped, and stood watching sluggishly while Martin shone the light around. He finally selected a tall pine almost directly across the clearing from the black stone. They stood Peter up against it. As soon as they let go of him, he started sliding slowly down; his eyes were closed and there was a satisfied smile on his face.

Martin, who was holding the flashlight while Volz did the work, said something uncomplimentary, and Volz propped his unresisting prisoner up again.

"He's still too groggy," he said angrily, and proceeded to remedy the situation by a series of sharp blows across the face.

The cure worked a little too well. Peter's eyes opened, and widened in indignation. He grabbed Volz by the ears and brought his knee up. The blow wasn't as hard as he intended it to be, but it was hard enough to flatten Volz. It happened so quickly, Kate didn't have time to react; she had only taken two steps when Martin's fist came down on the back of Peter's neck. By the time she reached him, he was sprawled face down on the ground, and Martin, the flashlight now in his left hand, said calmly.

"I have a gun, but I don't think I'll need it. All right, you incompetent idiot, get up. Must I do everything?"

Volz got up, but not with much enthusiasm. His face was the color of watered split-pea soup. Kate, who had been feeling frantically for what turned out to be, when her unsteady fingers finally located it, a quite healthy pulse, looked up warily as the general staggered toward them.

"You try that," she said, seeing his foot draw back, "and I'll pull your legs out from under you."

"Leave him alone," Martin said wearily. "We've wasted enough time. Besides, we wouldn't want him to miss the little surprise that's in store for him, would we?"

Volz relaxed, diverted by the thought; and Kate, who knew the sort of thought that diverted him, shivered.

"Try it again," Martin said. "Get a rope around his chest to hold him up, then tie his feet. From behind," he added sarcastically. "I thought you were in the army once."

Volz gave him a sour look but obeyed without comment. He handled Peter circumspectly until he had him securely bound; then he stood back and administered a hard backhanded blow across the face. Peter, who had begun to show a faint interest in the proceedings, subsided again, and Martin grabbed at Kate.

"You take the light," he said coldly. "I'll handle her. Can't you control yourself for a few hours, Harry?"

"I don't like him," Volz said simply. "Supercilious bastard . . . So long as I get a chance later . . ."

"That, as you know, will be the Master's decision."

Volz's reaction was surprising and a little chilling. He stiffened, as if standing at attention, and held the position for several seconds before doing as Martin directed.

That was the end of the conversation. Martin went about his business with his usual efficiency. The tree to which Kate was tied was near Peter's, but not quite near enough for her to touch him. Martin handled her impersonally, as if she were a parcel he was wrapping for the mail. He walked off without so much as a backward glance. Volz followed, carrying the flashlight; for some time Kate could see it, like a giant firefly, bobbing and diminishing along the path. Then it disappeared altogether; and the dark swooped in.

The wind still moaned high in the treetops, but a few stars were visible in the cloudy sky. Something moved furtively in the brush not far away, and Kate wrestled vainly with the ropes. Not that there were dangerous animals in the woods; tales of wolf and bear were still told, but she didn't believe them . . . not really. All the same, it was unnerving to have anything, even a rabbit, approach when you were so helpless. She started when a voice said tentatively, "Kate. Is that you?"

"Yes."

"I was afraid of that. Where are you? I can't see you."

"We're back to back, so to speak. I can't see you either. I wish . . . I wish I could."

"It would help, wouldn't it. I'm sorry; I seem to have missed a good deal this evening. I seem to recall shoving you out the window just before Martin hit me with a mountain or something. I gather you didn't make good your escape?"

"I made it," she said miserably, and in a few sentences recapitulated what had happened.

"Well, don't brood about it," Peter said reasonably. "Thirteen to one is poor odds. . . . Thirteen?"

"Nine of them at the general's. And there are . . . four others."

Silence fell, broken only by the complaint of the wind-driven branches. It didn't seem quite so dark now; Kate's eyes were beginning to adjust. She could see the shapes of the surrounding trees and the menacing bulk of the black stone at the far end of the clearing. She waited for Peter's response with an anxiety which was, under the circumstances, a trifle absurd.

Finally he finished his mental accounting.

"I didn't realize you knew about Tiphaine," he said.

"I didn't think you knew! I was afraid you'd mind, terribly. . . ."

"Why? Oh. It's nice to know my atrocious acting convinced someone. The others must have been laughing up their sleeves the whole time. Tiphaine especially."

The tone in which he spoke the name filled Kate with a reprehensible but very human satisfaction. She said perversely, "I didn't think you could resist her. She's very lovely."

"Fishing for compliments at a time like this? I'll be damned if I'll inflate your ego any further. . . . Oh, there were times when I wondered why I didn't fall in love with her. But I didn't—believe it or not. And when I added up the miscellaneous facts I'd acquired, the conclusion was inescapable."

"It escaped me. Though I've always known there was something wrong about her. Living with her I've seen things—a word, a look, nothing important; but if you'd known Stephan, you'd worry about any child he brought up."

"I did worry. He was obviously serious about his dirty little hobby. Tiphaine had all the earmarks of the convert. Even the change of name, at adolescence, when many of the girls were introduced to the cult. . . ."

"And the name itself."

"Yes, I caught that after I did some reading. And the Folklore Society, the executive committee of the coven. When I think of how they led me by the nose, from the minute I arrived in town, I could kick myself. And I sat there like the sacrificial goat, congratulating myself on my cleverness. . . . I wonder what did go on at those business meetings?"

Kate leaned back against the tree trunk, feeling the rough bark prickle through her shirt and hair. The position wasn't as uncomfortable as it might have been; Martin had tied the ropes tightly enough to prevent escape, but not tightly enough to hurt, unless she moved.

"Peter."

"What?"

"About Mark. I want you to know, before . . . It was an accident, Peter. I didn't mean to."

"I know that."

"How could you know?"

"Because now I know you. MacDonald would have my ears for that remark," he added wryly. "Nailed to his wall. With me still attached."

"Who's MacDonald?"

"My editor."

"Is that what you do?"

"Journalist, yes."

"Journalist? Stewart . . . Is that who you are? I read about you—oh, several years ago. About the trial. They said you were a spy."

"They usually do say that."

"I know you weren't."

"Well, I was, actually. At least I was guilty of conspiracy and aiding a criminal to escape. Unfortunately I was also inept. The escape failed."

"I remember hearing about the execution of the leader."

"I knew Jan at school," Peter said. "That was why MacDonald sent me over there, when we got wind of the revolt being planned. First-hand reports from the rebel camp, that sort of crap. I went—I guess I hoped to talk Jan out of it. We knew it was bound to fail, the Russians have the satellites fast; they can't let any one of them go without losing the rest. Jan knew it, too; but men reach a point of desperation, where nothing matters but the need to act. . . . We almost got out, you know. But Jan had been wounded in the street fighting, he couldn't go fast. I got what I deserved—less, really; they could have shot me. There were times when I wished they had."

The calm, matter-of-fact voice stopped. The tears on Kate's cheeks felt warm in the cold air.

"One of those times must have been when you heard of Mark's death," she said. "Or didn't you find out till after you were released?"

"They told me. They let some letters come through, especially the ones with bad news. The worst of it was that I'd heard from Mark just before I left—one of his hysterical scrawls, full of references to the cold-hearted bitch who'd led him on and broken his heart. The beautiful succubus, La Belle Dame, et cetera. He's my half-brother, that's why our names aren't the same. Younger; I always felt responsible for him, especially after Mother died, even though I knew he was a bloody mess. He was constantly getting into scrapes and having to be bailed out of them, and the scrapes kept getting nastier. That was how he came to the Embassy, in one of those nonessential social jobs; I couldn't think what the hell else to do with him. The letter was typical Mark, full of self-pity and ravings about you. I didn't feel I could take the time to play Miles Standish—or was it the other fellow—not when Jan was in real trouble. So I went east instead of west."

"And you've been blaming yourself ever since."

"I've always blamed myself for everything Mark did. It was Mother, I suppose; isn't Mum the currently popular scapegoat? 'Watch out for Mark, darling, you know he isn't strong. . . . Don't let the big boys hurt Mark, Peter, he's so sensitive. . . . ' She was a very beautiful woman," he added wryly. "It never occurred to me to wonder why two different men had found her impossible to live with."

"No wonder you don't like women."

"You can hardly accuse me of that. . . . Maybe I do. Maybe that's why I was so ready to blame you for what happened to Mark. Transfer of guilt? I hate the superficial psychological jargon we toss around these days."

"You were right to blame me. I'd like to tell you how it happened—"

"I don't want to hear. It's irrelevant."

"Irrelevant? Murder?"

Her voice broke on the word, and when Peter answered, his voice had lost its calm.

"Do you want me to say it, here and now, when we'll probably both be dead before morning? That I'd condone anything you've done, anything you ever will do? If you told me you'd annihilated an entire orphanage, I'd probably just shrug. Oh, God, I've done it again! Always the wrong word . . ."

"I want to tell you about that, too," Kate said softly. "She was so beautiful, Peter. Her eyes were blue—not that dark smoky blue all new babies have, but a lovely clear azure, right from the first day. And bright fair hair, like—like yours. She was beginning to talk; she really was, it wasn't just babbling, she was very precocious. And she was crawling all over the place, puffing—she was so fat—and she—"

The last words were unintelligible even to her. Peter let her cry for a while. Then he said gently, "Can you move, at all? Your hands? Stretch them out?"

Kate found that she could move, though only in one place; by pulling in all her muscles she could slide around the tree trunk inside the ropes. Squinting through the tears she had been holding in for months, she made out the excrescence on the next tree which was Peter. The starlight glinted faintly off his hair. Groping, she felt his fingers meet and close on the tips of hers.

"Feeling better?" he asked.

"Yes." Kate sniffed. "I don't know why I should, but I do."

"Why didn't you marry him? He said he'd asked you."

"After Uncle Stephan died."

"And you inherited how many million dollars. I see."

"It wasn't only that. I guess I was afraid of marrying any-body. I was always a homely girl, and too smart for my own good. But I wasn't smart enough to conceal my brains."

"Why should you?"

Kate sniffed again. She longed desperately for a handker-chief, and a free hand with which to wield it.

"Because men don't like intelligent women," she said in a muffled voice. "And neither do other women."

"I do," Peter said persuasively.

"Oh, you." Kate laughed; it was a choked, hoarse sound, but it was genuine. "You're different."

"Naturally."

"I mean, you believe in yourself. You're sufficiently compe-tent to accept competence in other people without resenting it."

"There you go again."

"Well, it's true. But Mark—it wasn't self-confidence that he lacked, he thought he was entitled to everything in the world." Kate laughed again, bitterly this time. "The truth is that I caught him with Tiphaine one day. I was already pregnant, and he had sworn lifelong devotion to me. So maybe I was just plain jeal-ous, and to hell with the psychological analysis. I threw him out—out of the house, out of my life. I had—the baby. It was kept a secret, of course; Tiphaine knew, and Martin, but they were the only ones.

"This mother-love business isn't a simple reflex, you know; at first the baby was just a duty, a responsibility. I set up an arrangement, with an apartment and a live-in nurse, in Baltimore, and I went up to see her once a week. Then, after a while, I found I was going oftener, and staying longer. . . . I knew I had to have her with me, all the time. And Mark was being intolerable; he'd gone back to Washington, but he was here every weekend, staying with Volz and harassing me. He knew about the baby, but he didn't know where she was—not even Tiphaine knew that. I got so desperate I even considered marrying Mark, just for long enough to give her a name—so she wouldn't have to grow up with that stigma. Then she . . . she got sick. They go so quickly when they're small."

"And you blamed yourself for that."

"Yes, of course. It was foolish—the woman, the nurse, was the best to be had. She loved her, too. But I couldn't . . . I didn't . . ."

"Did Mark know?"

"Not then. I was a little mad, I think; Tiphaine and Martin knew, they went to . . . the funeral with me. Then Mark insisted on meeting me. It was at night. He asked me to marry him again, and mentioned the baby. . . . I told him then, I think I screamed it at him. And he said—do you know what he said?"

"I think I can guess."

"Yes, you knew him, didn't you? You can imagine how I felt. It was like—offering a child a new puppy to replace the one that died. I wanted to kill him. I did. He had a gun; he'd been waving it around, threatening to shoot himself; but I wasn't impressed because I knew Mark would never deprive the world of anything as wonderful as himself. When he said . . . that . . . I flew at him. Somehow the gun went off. I ran; I knew he must be dead, though they didn't tell me so till next day. It was Martin who found him, and Martin who signed the death certificate. The loyal family friend . . . Your hand's all wet. Sticky . . . Peter . . ."

"The general ties a mean knot," he admitted apologetically. "You sure he wasn't in the navy? Kate, darling, you aren't crying about that . . . ? I appreciate your sympathy, but you'd better save it. For later on."

She turned her head. It was a strain on the muscles of her neck and shoulders, but at least she could see him.

"You have a beautiful nose," she said irrelevantly, and heard Peter snort with amusement.

"Sam was right, as always."

"Who is Sam?"

"Friend of mine. A private detective who once lectured me on the foibles of the female. Whom I hired to investigate you. I don't think I'd feel quite so rotten right now if my conscience were clear."

"Don't think about that. My own conscience is a little smudged."

"I'll be damned if I can see why. If there was ever a born murderee, it was Mark. If he hadn't had the gun, you'd have scratched his face, and he'd have slugged you—he would have, you know—and that would have been the end of it. As for the baby—you surely aren't archaic enough to feel guilty about that? Whereas I—"

"No, I'm worse than you, worse than you," Kate said promptly, and heard him chuckle.

"Okay, this is rather pointless, isn't it? Anyway, I've had my punishment. When I realized I love you—"

"When did you?"

"What?"

"Realize."

"Of all the stupid questions to ask at a time like this . . . I don't like to destroy your romantic illusions, but I think the process began the other afternoon, in this very spot."

"It's . . . a little too much, isn't it?" Kate said after a moment. "I'm sorry; I'm trying not to make this any harder for you, but—"

"I'd encourage you to break loose and scream your head off if I thought it would do any good," Peter said harshly. "But there won't be a living soul in these woods tonight except our friends. Do you realize what a reign of terror this group has imposed on the town? The coven has so many ways of exerting pressure; not only superstitious fear—and there's a lot more of that lingering than we like to admit—but purely physical threats. Good God, these people can literally get away with murder—and produce half a dozen impeccable witnesses who would swear they were somewhere else at the time. A doctor has all sorts of chances for skulduggery—drugs, poisons, falsifying postmortem reports . . . Then there's blackmail as a weapon of power. It wouldn't do a certain distinguished Senator much good if his associates knew he spent several nights a year trying to raise the Devil."

"And succeeding," Kate said. "The god is incarnate, you know, in the head of the coven, the Master of—Peter!"

"What? Someone coming?"

"No, I just remembered something. Maybe you didn't hear it. Volz was knocking you around, and when Martin made him stop, he said something about getting his chance later."

"Thanks. That makes me feel a lot better."

"That's not the point. Martin answered that any such decision would have to be up to the Master."

"Well, naturally," Peter agreed; she heard leaves rustle as he shifted his feet, and knew he was still trying to free himself. "Can't have the rank and file making such important decisions. Discipline must be maintained, even if . . . Wait a minute, I see what you're driving at. I thought Martin was the chief devil."

"So did I. Martin or Volz. Could it be the Senator?"

"Some covens," Peter said, in a different voice, "had a woman leader."

"La Reine du Sabbat," Kate murmured.

"Or the Queen of Elfhame. Scottish custom, if I remember your book correctly."

"Peter, if it's Tiphaine, I don't think I can stand it."

"I know. She's not responsible, Kate. Your esteemed uncle had years to make her what she is."

"Think of her as mad," Kate said bitterly. "That will help. . . . Look, it's getting lighter. The moon must be rising."

They watched in silence as the pale half-orb swam into sight through the tossing boughs. It was on the wane, and gave little light, but to their dark-accustomed eyes the change was considerable. The shape of the glade was clear now, with the black stone standing out like an incarnate threat.

"Running water, and the stone, and the clearing in the woods," Kate muttered. "The classic features of the Sabbath meeting place; and I never saw it. That's why you were here today."

"Yes, I hoped to find concrete evidence of what I suspected; I knew I could never convince you without something definite, I was having a hard enough time believing it myself. But I found nothing. Apparently they don't use this place very often."

"Four times a year. If they go by the book."

"Allhallows, May Eve, Candlemas, and Lammas Eve. I've

done my homework, you see. What do you suppose they're going to do tonight?"

"There are all sorts of variants," Kate said. "From a Black Mass, with defilement of the Christian sacraments, to a good old-fashioned orgy, á la fertility cult. The original witch covens tended toward the latter variety, but I expect sophisticates like Martin, who've read the books, have added their own touches."

"Added is about right. The original cult must go back a long way."

"Why?"

"Miss Device's family history is a little bit coincidental, don't you think? And this clearing must have been planned, especially the stone. It's been there for centuries, I could tell that much. I have a feeling, though, that the coven didn't amount to much until the New People arrived and gave it a shot in the arm."

"People like the general. He could contribute such nice— Peter . . ."

"What's wrong?"

"Look. There."

It was dim at first, only a twinkle like that of a fallen star caught among the trees; but the star shone red. A few minutes later she heard the voices.

"They're coming," she said.

"Kate." His voice was rough, no longer pretending. "They'll probably untie us—you, at least—at some point. To arrange the . . . tableau. . . ."

The light was brighter now, and the voices louder. They rose and fell in a strange stiff rhythm that had not yet taken on a tune.

"If they do," Peter went on, "try to make a break for it. Bite, kick—"

"I'm awfully stiff," Kate said, watching the light. Torches?

"I know. But try. Don't head for the path, go into the woods. If they kill you, it will at least be a more dignified way of dying."

"All right." It didn't seem to matter, now.

Torches, yes. The head of the procession came into view; they had to go single file along the narrow path. The torches burned high and fiercely, giving off a dark smoke which writhed and broke in the wind. One by one they came, stepping

in rhythm to the odd, jerky tune. It was a dance tune, but the
tune had been ancient when the flames of the Inquisition destroyed the reasoning world.

One by one they came, the same eldritch crew she had seen
in the stableyard. If they had seemed nightmare creatures there,
they were worse now, in the wild wind-tossed clearing, under a
flickering moon—visions of a madman's fancy, products of
delirium. The weaving line moved out into the center of the
glade, before the stone, and each figure flung the torch it carried
into a heap of fuel. It blazed up with a roar, sending a column
of red flame soaring.

Kate felt Peter's nails boring into her hand. They were cir-
cling the fire now, still to the same weird tune; some had produced musical instruments, small drums and pipes and—good
heavens, Miss Device's violin. . . .

"And the Hags and Sorcerers do howl and vary their hellish
cries high and low counterfeiting a kind of villainous music.
They also dance at the sound of Viols and other instruments,
which are brought thither by those that were skilled to play
upon them."

All by the book—how thoroughly they had done their research. Or was it from minds like these that the material in the
books had come? From Miss Device, jerking and stamping, her
face rapt under the stiff white cap; from Mrs. Adams, whose
coarse gray locks flew as she gyrated wildly? Widdershins
around the fire—against the sun, the Devil's direction.

And that tune, that queer jigging tune; she had heard something like it before, in a concert of medieval dances; the melody
formless, the rhythm irregular; no ending, no resolution, only
an endless repetition. The rhythm lacked the syncopated sensu-
ality of good dance music; it was monotonous, almost prim. Yet
after a time the queer beat got into the listener's blood. . . . Kate
jerked herself erect, shivering, as she felt her knees and bent
arms beginning to twitch.

The circle widened so that the dancers passed within a few
feet of the prisoners; but only one paid them any heed—Volz,
whose eyes glinted whitely at Peter each time he went by. The
faces were terrible in their set absorption; all eyes, except those
of the general, seemed to be looking at something invisible to
normal sight. Their skins had an odd cast, dusky and greasy, as
if they had been streaked with oily soot. . . .

"The fatte of young children, the blood of a flitter mouse, solanum somniferum, and oleum. They stampe all these together and then they rubbe all parts of their bodys exceedinglie . . . by this means in a moonlight night they seem to be carried in the air. . . ."

The witches' flying ointment. It contained other ingredients beside the ghastly mess Scot had mentioned. Belladonna and aconite, hemlock . . . delirium-inducing drugs, when absorbed through a cut or open sore. That was how the medieval witches had "flown" to the Sabbath, in the delirious visions of the drug. By the book; again, by the book. Kate cursed her inconvenient memory. She was remembering other parts of the ceremony.

Tiphaine was not among the dancers. Kate had mentally braced herself for her cousin's appearance—in what *outré* costume, for God's sake, and in what role? A few dancers were so masked and robed as to be unidentifiable, but she would have known Tiphaine · by her size, and her grace. The Master, of course, would make his appearance later, on the platform which had been prepared to receive his presence three hundred years before.

The music stopped; not with a resolution, with a dying failure on a minor chord. The dancers dropped to the ground and lay still.

How long the girl had been there Kate did not know; the slender figure had been masked by the central fire. Now she moved out away from the rock against which she had been leaning. She seemed to walk above the ground, not on it; her slim bare feet—bare, on such a night—scarcely pressed the dry leaves. She wore a costume similar to Joan's, but on her the effect was different; the slender dryad's body shone whitely through the tatters of the scanty tunic. The dark leaves twisted in her hair looked as if they had grown there. She was perfectly at ease, attuned to the fantasy of the coven as she had never been to the real world. The Queen of Elfhame; la Reine du Sabbat; the witch girl, baptized in the Old Religion and raised in its tenets.

Kate heard Peter's voice catch in a gasp that sounded suspiciously like one of terror; her own heart was pounding. This was the closest she had ever come to the reality of black magic. The rest had been stage devices, human perversities, or neuroses; but if Tiphaine had been born in 1610, she would have gone to the stake singing, and cried the praises of her Dark Lord while the flames licked up to meet the flame of her hair.

The girl turned, lifting her arms; and the whole foul crew leaped up, with a wild scream of welcome and adoration. On top of the black stone stood a solitary figure.

It was not his own skin he was wearing, though the garment fit as snugly; no human flesh ever gleamed with that dull scaly luster or gave such a hint of dark coarseness. The hands were like paws; when he raised them in response to the greeting of his worshipers, the sharpened claws glittered in the firelight. The monstrous head was partly in shadow, but the features were not, could not be, human. There was a snout, and a draggle of dark coarse hair, and pointed ears like those of a goat. The head turned, in a lordly survey, and the second face came into view—another set of opposing features on the back of the head. The two-headed god, Janus of the Romans . . .

Peter's hand moved, in a gesture so savage that it twisted Kate's wrist. She cried out; but the pain brought her out of her horrified trance. She saw the poised figure atop the stone for what it was: not a hairy Fiend, but a man wearing a close-fitting garment of leather that covered his entire body, even to the hands. The glitter of those claws suggested a modern improvement on the ancient costume described by so many writers— metal, perhaps. And the head, of course, was masked; the goat-satyr face attributed to the fertility god, the double face found in some of the cults. It was, she told herself with deliber- ate emphasis, a damned effective outfit, and the young man who wore it suited it well. He must be young; his body was slight, but built like that of an athlete.

The howling circle was in movement again; no music now, only wild shrieks of adoration. As each worshiper moved to a position directly in front of the stone, he turned and bent back, lifting one foot. Another part of the old ritual; the more per- verse form of worship was impractical with the devil up there on his throne. Kate's inconvenient memory was bothering her again—this time with a part of the ritual which she had tried desperately to forget.

"Witches confessing that the devil lies with them, and withal complaining of his tedious and offensive coldness . . ." The fertility rites, and the marriage of the God . . . "There ap- peared a great Black Goat with a Candle between his

Horns. . . . He had carnal knowledge of her which was with great pain. . . . A meikle, black, roch man, werie cold; and I fand his nature als cold within me as spring well water. . . . He is abler for us in that way than any man can be, onlie he was heavie lyk a malt sek; a hudge nature, verie cold, as yce." The hard leather covering of the body; Margaret Murray's reference to the phallic cults of Egypt and Greece . . . She heard someone breathing in harsh, choking gasps, and thought it was she herself. Then she turned to look at Peter. His face was frozen in a spasm of horror and his wide eyes were fixed on the slight, posturing figure on the stone.

As Kate looked back, the leather-clad form flexed its knees and jumped, landing lightly on its feet. He was in splendid physical condition; the movement had looked like flying. But it was a pedestrian stroll that brought the weird figure across the glade toward them. The worshipers fell back before him, with the same archaic, backward bow. Tiphaine followed, two paces in the rear, like a priestess following the sacramental objects. As the figure circled the fire, Kate got a better look at the mask. It was a beautiful piece of work, a clever mingling of goat and human. The straggling beard and muzzled mouth were animal; the eyes, shining out from under heavy coarse brows, were those of a man.

It was the sight of those eyes that gave Kate her first clue, and she felt her face freeze in the same incredulous horror that still held Peter rigid. Pacing slowly, the bizarre shape came toward them and stopped. The clawed hand fumbled at the throat, and the mask slipped up, and off.

The face was Timmy's face. But the thick fair hair, tumbled by the removal of the mask, was not Timmy's. The easy athlete's walk had not been Timmy's shambling stride. The eyes, bright and intelligent . . .

Again the clawed hand lifted; this time, with a very human "Damn!" the man stripped off the awkward glove, and raised his hand to the livid face. The whole fiery birthmark peeled off; and Kate saw before her the face which ought to have been crumbling to dust for almost a year. Mark's face.

# Chapter

## 12

HE DIDN'T LOOK A DAY OLDER.

The blue eyes narrowed with amusement as they met hers; the mouth was smiling. He was as handsome as ever, almost too handsome . . . as ever . . .

Kate wasn't aware that she was fainting until she heard Peter's voice, repeating her name. She shook her head, blinking through the gray fog that blanketed her mind, looking, not at the beautiful smiling face in front of her, but at Peter.

Under the ruddy firelight that gave his face a false flush, he was white as paper. The shock had driven the blood from his face, but not from his brain; he knew what she must be thinking.

"He's real, Kate. You didn't kill him. Don't start imagining. . . . Kate!"

"I'm all right," she muttered.

"What," Mark said, "no tender welcome for the dead come back to life?"

That voice—the one that had haunted her for months. No wonder Timmy never spoke.

"I expected more reaction," Mark went on cheerfully. "My fond brother and my—I've always liked the word 'paramour,' haven't you, Kate? So much more refined and Elizabethan than the other terms. . . . But I understand that in this, as in so many of my other specialties, my big brother has surpassed me."

"Blanks," Kate said. "Blanks in the gun."

"Red paint and all the rest," Mark agreed. "Martin was lurking, unseen, in order to bear you away if you overcame your squeamishness and started to investigate the corpse. But you fled, like a nice timid female."

"Why? Why did you do it?"

"Money," Mark said, with an air of pointing out the obvious. "What else? Oh, there were other reasons. Tiphaine has never liked you very much, darling. When Stephan died intestate—and I'm sure he did it deliberately, the old devil—her dislike ripened into something deeper. As for me, it hurts my feelings to be rejected. I've enjoyed watching you squirm."

His gloved hand lifted; the steel claws pricked Kate's cheek. Peter said something unintelligible, and moved his head. Mark turned toward him.

"I've hated you all my life," he said calmly. "It's quite natural; any psychologist could explain it to you. Gratitude is a fiction; the normal return for favors rendered is resentment. Only imagine, dear brother, how profound my resentment of you! All I ever needed to do was yell for help, and there you were, panting with zeal, ready to bail me out. Only—the last time I yelled for help you didn't come."

"You must have known why."

"Oh, yes, I knew; I read the newspapers." Mark chuckled. "I thought of you often. Prisons in Communist countries aren't awfully comfortable, I'm told. But I thought you'd turn up sooner or later; that uncomfortable conscience of yours. And you were stupid enough to use your own name when you booked your room. Not that I blame you," he added condescendingly. "You thought I was dead, and assumed no one else would recognize the name. Little did you know that we were all ready and waiting for you."

There were beads of perspiration on Peter's forehead; they reflected the firelight like drops of blood.

"I can't get you out of this mess unless you release us," he said.

"I don't need you to get me out of it," Mark snapped. "I didn't really need you when I wrote that letter. This"—his misshapen hand swept out to include the circle of costumed figures—"this is stronger than you ever could be. And I'm its head, Peter. I'm the head devil. The Master."

Tiphaine bowed her head.

Kate looked at her cousin. Tiphaine's eyes were fixed on Mark; they were rapt with a blasphemous devotion. Her fervor was genuine. Couldn't she see that Mark was using her, and the coven, for his own ends?

Kate missed Peter's next comment as her eyes moved from Tiphaine to the other members of the coven. The ceremony was proceeding. Next on the agenda was the ceremo-nial meal, and if she had been watching the proceedings from some safe, hidden spot, the activity would have moved her to sick amusement. Most of the Sabbath meals, as described by medieval participants, consisted of ordinary food—meat and bread and wine. She herself had expressed doubt, in her book, about the legends of cannibalism and noxious beverages. And this spoiled crowd—perhaps later, when their frenzy had increased, they might be capable of consuming human flesh or urine, or bread made of flour from unspeakable sources. Now they were setting out what appeared to be a conventional picnic supper. Kate's diaphragm contracted as she watched Miss Device fussily weighing down the corners of the white cloth with wine bottles. Red wine. Naturally . . . And what an elegant little supper it was—*foie gras* and caviar and imported cheeses, crusty French bread. . . . Kate suppressed a rising tide of nausea. She hadn't eaten since breakfast, but she wasn't hungry.

Most of the hampers and baskets had been emptied of their contents now; only one large basket still remained, on the ground by the stone. Some special delicacy, perhaps, for dessert. They weren't going to unpack it now, they were waiting for their chief to join them. Mrs. Adams daintily plucked a few dried leaves from the damask picnic cloth; her streaming gray hair fell across her cheeks and chin, leaving the sharp nose in silhouette. Everything was ready. But Mark couldn't tear himself away; he was enjoying this.

"I succeeded old Stephan," he was saying as Kate turned her attention back to the conversation. "He and I hit it off right from the start. It was rather a slap in the face for Martin; he'd been fancying himself as heir apparent. But Stephan knew that for Martin the coven was only a means to an end. For the rest of us, it's an end in itself."

He turned to smile at Tiphaine, and Kate burst out, "For the

rest of them, maybe, but not for you. Money, power, control,
that's what you want. You asked me to marry you because of the
money. When that failed, you staged your own murder so you
could blackmail me."

"You have such a simple mind," Mark said fondly. The steel
claw touched her cheek again, and pricked a little deeper. "Do
you think you were my only problem? I owed a good deal of
money, dear, not only locally, but to some threatening gentlemen in New York. Not to mention the irate fathers of certain
damsels . . . Without Peter to rescue me from myself, my peccadilloes tended to pile up. Since I could disappear, and make
money on the deal, as they say here . . . Timmy was no loss.
And he was so splendidly easy to imitate."

"And we thought someone was using Timmy," Kate muttered.

"But you were perfectly correct."

The fire soared and crackled, sending red flames licking at
the lower branches. Kate wondered how they kept the dry
leaves from catching. The whole clearing would go up like a
torch if the fire got out of hand.

"Being Timmy did limit me, though," Mark went on
blithely. "I couldn't get in and out of costume quickly, so I had
to rely on my voice to remind you of past events. Peter was
more effective; I got a lot of innocent amusement out of watching his performances and recalling our boyhood days, when we
sent off for occult literature and tried to conjure up demons in
the schoolroom. Yes, he was very useful—until the night when
he interfered with me at the séance." Mark lifted a casual hand
toward his brother's face, and Peter jerked back, too late. Blood
began streaming down his face, and Mark giggled.

"Reflexes a little slow," he said in a voice which was higher
than his normal tones. "I don't imagine you're feeling too well,
are you? Had a bad day altogether. Well, it won't be long now. I
promised the general a few minutes of fun, but don't worry,
there isn't too much he can do. We don't want any odd marks
which would be hard to explain in a postmortem."

"What are you going to do with us?" Kate hated to give him
the satisfaction of asking, but she couldn't help it.

"It ought to interest you. These people have kept the ritual
amazingly pure—in the scholarly sense, that is. No Black
Mass. So you don't need to worry about being stretched out
naked on the altar, or anything crude of that sort."

"Thanks," Kate said.

"Sarcastic as ever." Mark threw his head back, laughing, and caught at the mask as it slipped backward. He readjusted it on top of his head, where it formed a fantastic frame for his young face. "We have to consider the practical problem, you see. When the two of you are found tomorrow, it must appear to be an ordinary murder and suicide. Martin has considerable influence in these matters, but we don't want to take any chances, in case your lawyer gets sticky about the will."

"I see."

"But we can still kill two birds with one stone. Tonight is the night of the Passion—a far older ceremony than the Christian imitation, only two thousand years ago. The god must die, as nature dies, so that life can be reborn in the spring."

"Every seven years," Kate said.

"That's right; you're the authority on fertility cults, aren't you?" His smile was broad and carefree. "But they do it every year, here. A local refinement."

"But you're the—god," Peter said. He was only an amateur at this, Kate remembered; his early religious training had left its imprint, under the layers of adult skepticism, and his disgust showed in face and voice. It annoyed Mark; he made another lunge with his clawed hand, and Peter flinched.

"I'm the god," Mark said.

Then Kate saw what really drove him, under the superficial vices of avarice and cruelty. She looked away, unable to endure the sight of either brother; Peter's sick helplessness was as painful as Mark's madness.

"But naturally," Mark went on in his normal voice, "I don't die. Impractical. And so permanent . . . No, we have the substitute procedure, and a very nice one it is, too. Can you imagine a more appropriate substitute? Tiphaine tried earlier today, but she's not much good with the bow, poor dear. It was a bit premature, actually. All your fault," he added, turning to Kate. "That idiotic song, and your suggestion, gave her the idea."

"But you can't," Kate gasped. "No one will believe . . . Why should I kill Peter? Or is it the other way around?"

"No, no, you had it right the first time. I think, you know, that they will believe it—once Peter's real identity gets out, which it will. People are already talking about my 'accidental death,' you know. . . . I needn't spell it out, not for a woman of your intellectual attainments."

"And Martin will reluctantly testify that I've been going slowly insane for months," Kate said slowly.

"With Tiphaine and the Schmidts to back him up, I don't see how it can fail," Mark said cheerfully. His eyes moved from Kate's face down to her feet and back again. "There are, of course, certain preliminary ceremonies," he said.

Tiphaine glided forward. Kate thought spitefully that her face had lost some of its unearthly concentration. She was human enough to be jealous.

"They are waiting," she said, touching Mark on the shoulder.

"I'll bet they are," Peter said. "Expecially the old spinsters like Miss Device, and that bored, overweight wench, whatever her name is. . . . How far do your duties extend, Mark? I never did believe those stories of yours."

"Peter," Kate said warningly; but Mark wasn't annoyed.

"I delegate some duties," he said, grinning; and the leering goat's head perched on his brow echoed the expression. "The ritual marriage is consummated with the Queen of the Sabbath." He held out his hand to Tiphaine, and she took it, with a grave inclination of her head. "And," Mark added negligently, "with an occasional carefully selected and honored visitor."

This time Tiphaine's annoyance was plainer, and Mark saw it. Still holding her hand, he pulled the mask down into position.

"*A bientôt!*" he said, and, leading his lady by the hand, started back toward the rock pedestal.

With the incarnate god presiding, the ritual supper got underway. It included a few refinements not ordinarily seen at picnics. The climax of the rite was yet to come, but the participants had already shed several layers of civilized behavior. Volz wallowed like the pig he resembled, cramming food into his mouth and drinking his wine directly from the bottle. As the meal proceeded and the bottles were emptied, Kate was reminded, not so much of the witchcraft reports, as of lurid tales of Roman banquets. Sprawled on the ground, the members were paired, two by two. Perhaps the activities wouldn't have been so obscene if she hadn't known these people so well, especially the older, more respected citizens. . . . Ironic, how she could read and write about practices like these with a cool scholarly detachment, and yet turn sick at the actual sight. The wine was flowing freely, not only into individual mouths, but from mouth to mouth and onto the already stained costumes. But Kate knew it was not the wine which brought the red flush to Miss Device's sallow cheeks, nor the wild glitter into the Senator's eyes. Volz poured the dregs of his fourth bottle down the front of Joan's inadequate bodice, and bent forward. Kate closed her eyes.

She heard Peter swear, fluently, and without lowering his voice; she heard the leaves in the dark wood rustle as some four-footed creature crept through the night. Remembering her earlier fear of nocturnal animals, she could have smiled. Then lesser sounds were drowned as the music began again.

It was faster and louder now. The dance was different too, though it was just as ancient; the dancers paired off, locking elbows, back to back.

The crackle of dried leaves came again, so close now that it was audible even over the music—if the cacophonous din could be called music. Kate forgot her major preoccupation in momentary wonder. They were at the very edge of the clearing; only darkness lay behind them, darkness and the tangled brush. But surely no forest animal would approach so close.

Then came a sound that almost took her breath away by its very normalcy, in the midst of nightmare. The sounds of a soft, human voice.

"Don't turn, don't talk. Don't look surprised."

For the life of her—and it might have been just that—Kate couldn't repress a start and a gasp. Luckily the others were too concerned with their own activities to notice. Peter was more controlled. His profile, outlined against the dark foliage, remained immobile.

"Jackson," he said, on a long, sighing breath.

"Yes, it's me. Don't let your arms fall when I cut these ropes. Move 'em a little, get circulation back."

Kate kept her eyes fixed on Peter's face, fighting the urge to crane her neck and look back. She knew, by the twist of his mouth, when his arms were freed. Then she felt Hilary's big, warm hands on hers, and the ropes fell away. He held her wrists, taking some of the strain off her numbed arms, rubbing them to get the blood flowing freely. After a few minutes his hands moved to her ankles.

"Kate?" Peter spoke without turning his head.

"Yes, all right. I'm free now."

"Good. Jackson, get the hell out of here."

"I'm staying."

"For God's sake—as soon as we make our break, they'll be buzzing like flies, all over the woods. I'll give you five minutes' start."

Five minutes? Kate wondered whether they had five more minutes—or whether five minutes would be long enough to restore limbs numbed by cold and confinement. Flexing her fingers, trying to stamp her feet without letting the dried leaves rustle, she was still caught by the ghastly fascination of the rite of the Sabbath. Her scholar's instinct, so long dormant, was not dead; if she survived—what a book she could make out of this!

Peter and Hilary were arguing in whispers which were becoming dangerously shrill. She turned her head to expostulate. Then she heard what Hilary was saying.

"I'm not going anywhere. And neither are you."

Staring straight ahead, hands still behind him, Peter said softly. "We're going, all right. Through you, if we must."

"Why the hell do you think I came? To save you?" Hilary's emotion was so intense that words failed him; he stuttered wildly for a second before he could go on. "Look over there, look—to the right of the stone, on the ground. That's what I came for. And you'll help me, or I'll kill you myself."

It took Kate's incredulous eyes some time to locate the object he indicated. Her mind fought the dawning knowledge as her eyes denied the proof of it. By the stone . . . the basket she had noticed at the beginning of the meal. Only it wasn't a basket. It was made of some plastic material, with metal supports to hold it upright, and attachments by which it could be fastened to the seat of a car. She had bought one like it to take . . . to take the baby . . .

Her stomach rebelled in a surge of nausea so violent it almost bent her over. It was only her imagination, she couldn't have heard it over the screams of the dancers: the high, thin wail that seemed to come from the carrier by the stone.

"Impossible," Peter whispered. "Not even these—how could they? Where did they get it?"

Kate didn't have to wait for Hilary's explanation.

"The Foundling Home. Some of them are on the board. Miss Device does volunteer work in the office. Falsifying records . . . Most of the babies are illegitimate, unwanted. . . . Peter!"

He didn't hear her. He didn't have to; there was no need for discussion of ends, only of means.

"Is it yours?" he asked, and Hilary answered simply, "I don't know. Does it matter?"

"No." Peter began to shiver, violently and uncontrollably. "Get over there, through the trees, to the nearest cover. When you see me step out and raise my arms, grab the basket and run."

"What are you going to do?" Hilary asked.

"What the hell can I do? Dance, sing, do card tricks. Anything to attract attention. I suppose it would be too much to expect you to have a weapon?"

They were speaking in near normal tones; the frenzied howling had risen to a pitch that made whispering unnecessary. The dancers had abandoned any attempt at rhythm. Miss Device had torn off her cap and was plucking at the collar of her dress.

Kate's hands were clenched so tightly that her nails pierced the skin of her palms, but she didn't feel the pain. That would be the time, when the dancers were locked in the embrace which was the culmination of the rite. They would be blind and deaf to anything else. They were nearing the climax now. But would the sacrifice come first? Each time one of the reeling figures neared the stone, and the pitiful little object beside it, Kate's breath stopped.

She had almost forgotten Peter's question, it took Hilary so long to answer it.

"The general's rifle," he said briefly. "Here."

Peter's right side was the one farthest away; she didn't see his arm move, but she could tell, by his face, when his fingers touched the weapon.

"Maybe you'd better keep it," he said reluctantly.

"Can't handle a rifle and the basket."

"Hurry," Kate said. "It can't be long now. Hurry."

Hilary didn't waste breath in answering; she heard the same cautious rustle of leaves which had heralded his approach. Peter said, out of the corner of his mouth, "This doesn't include you. As soon as I move, you run. Straight back, avoid the path."

"If you think I'm going to leave that child . . . and you . . ."

"What are you planning to do, throw stones? If Jackson and I fail, you're our last hope."

He took her silence for agreement. Kate saw no point in arguing; she knew she wasn't going to go. Stones, yes, if that was all she could do. She had left him once before, not knowing whether she would see him alive again; once in a lifetime was once too much, she couldn't do it twice. And the baby . . . Under the impetus of a fear which was not for her own person, her brain began to work more clearly. She would run, but not toward freedom—around the clearing, following Hilary. If any one of the mob defied the threat of the rifle, to pursue the boy and his burden, she might be able to help.

Was Hilary in position yet? She strained her eyes through the smoke and the flames toward a glossy-leaved holly which was the nearest point of concealment. It was a good twenty feet away from the basket, and there was nothing between except flat ground and fallen leaves. There was no sign of Hilary, not even a movement of the jagged green leaves. But there wouldn't be—not until Peter stepped out in full view of the frenzied group and the cold-eyed spectator atop the rock. He had a gun, yes; but what good would that be against a pack of maddened animals?

She looked at Peter. He stood as he had been standing for hours, slightly slumped, his head bowed. It would have taken a close examination to see that he was no longer bound. Hilary had reknotted the most visible rope, the one that circled his chest, so that a quick movement would release it. What was he waiting for?

Miss Device was the first to go. She collapsed onto the ground, writhing and tearing at her clothing; her face was distorted almost out of recognition, and from her squared mouth came an animal scream. The ghoul-figure at her side—good God, was it Will Schmidt?—dropped down beside her. As if a signal had been given, the others followed; it was a contagious mania, a communicable madness, like the dancing crazes of the Middle Ages or the blood lust that moves a lynch mob. Within moments the glade was littered with moving bodies. The effect was too much, even for someone who had known what to expect; Kate turned her head away. Now, surely, was the time for them to move.

Peter stirred, and she tensed—if further tension was possible. She had been standing poised for flight for what seemed an eternity. But the gesture or word she was waiting for did not come. He didn't even look at her. He was staring straight ahead, his head lifted; the blank pallor of his face and the intensity of his gaze made him look drugged or entranced. Then Kate realized what he saw, and why he had not moved.

High on his black throne, the masked figure surveyed his devotees. Tiphaine was clinging to him shamelessly, but he made no response. The goat's mask held its frozen leer; Kate sensed that, behind it, Mark was also smiling. This was the supreme moment for him, not the sexual release the others sought. There had always been something mechanical about his lovemaking, skilled as it was. Watching other people lose the control he never lost gave him a sense of superiority; and his triumph was intensified by the fact that his brother was a witness to it. One part of his awareness had been, and still was, focused on Peter. And there it seemed likely to remain. The mating of the god was not part of the communal orgy.

Peter realized this too; Kate looked back at him in time to meet his eyes. They were as empty of expression as was the rest of his face, and his lips barely moved when he spoke.

"Now. Move, damn it; I won't until you do."

She had been ready for so long, her hands braced against the tree trunk to give that one additional burst of speed; now, at the word of command, she couldn't move. The seconds stretched out impossibly as she stood, staring at him with an intensity that made her eyes ache. When she finally forced herself into motion, it was like pulling against something that stretched and held, and hurt when it broke.

She crashed blindly through the undergrowth parallel to the clearing with no clear notion of what she was doing. The crack of a branch across her head stung her into awareness, and she stopped. She was panting as if she had run for miles.

The first thing she noticed was the silence. Now that she was still, the only thing she could hear was the pounding of her heart and the agonized wheeze of her breathing. From the glade, to her left, came no sound at all except the voiceless roar of the fire. She was only a few feet away from the edge of the clearing; the fire glow shone weirdly through the tangled vines and bushes, throwing distorted leaping shadows along the ground. But no sound; no sound at all. Arms up before her face, Kate plunged through a matted curtain of something that was probably poison ivy, and then she saw what had happened.

It had seemed to her that she had been thrashing about in the bushes for long minutes, but no more than seconds could have passed since she darted out of the clearing. It had taken Hilary the same length of time to cover the longer, though not entangled, distance between his hiding place and the rock. He was the first person she noticed, partly because he was the only one in motion; head down, arms extended, he was within a few paces of his goal.

The Witches' Sabbath—an oil, in full color, frozen now into two-dimensional horror. The sprawled, pallid bodies were still; here and there a blank white face lifted blindly. Mark, atop the rock, looked like a statue out of one of the more esoteric museums—an institution specializing in anthropological curiosities. From her new vantage point Kate could see both faces of the monstrous mask; it looked doubly horrifying atop the slender, poised body.

Kate took it all in in a single, panoramic sweep of vision; then she saw Peter, and for one blissfully simple moment she forgot everything else in an upsurge of primitive female admiration.

She couldn't see his face; it was hidden by the stock of the gun and by his raised arm. The marks of the ropes on his wrist were only too visible; in the strange light they looked like ragged black lines, and the flesh around them was swollen and dark. But the finger curled around the trigger of the rifle was as steady as steel, and the muzzle pointed unwaveringly at its target—Mark.

Hilary reached the basket, scooped it up in both arms, and whirled around. One of the panting glassy-eyed figures on the ground heaved itself to its knees with an animal snarl. It was Volz; it would be, Kate thought. Peter's voice echoed emphatically through the empty night:

"Don't move, Volz, or I'll take care of your sacrifice for you."

"Stop," Mark said clearly.

Volz dropped down to his hands and knees.

Hilary had almost reached the edge of the clearing. Kate knew he was running as he had never run before, but he seemed to be moving in slow motion, like a defective film. The clumsy size of the basket hampered him; why didn't he take the child out? He could carry it in one arm and have the other free. . . . Then she realized that the baby might be strapped down. He was almost there; he was going to make it. . . . She had come to think of the glade as danger, the dark woods as safety, but Hilary wouldn't be safe until he reached town; they could still overtake him in the woods with his awkward burden, unless Peter could detain them. How long could he hold them? And how were she and Peter going to get away after Hilary had gone? For the first time in hours she allowed herself the luxury of speculating on the possibility of her own survival.

Hilary was not more than three feet away from the trees when it happened. How long the man had been there, Kate didn't know; he seemed to materialize out of the night, like one of the dark spirits the coven worshiped. She reproached herself bitterly for her fastidiousness; if she had concentrated on the full glories of the final orgy, she would have realized that the paired couples came out evenly. Too evenly. There were thirteen members of the coven. One of them had slipped away earlier.

She might have anticipated his identity even if she hadn't recognized him, tall and lean and confident, wearing a particularly gruesome costume—that of a phosphorescent skeleton, realistically articulated, painted on black cloth. His mask, a cowl-like head covering, was thrown back over his shoulders for better visibility.

He extended one foot and Hilary went sprawling. The basket flew out of his hands and landed, on its side, several feet beyond his outflung, clutching hands. Kate heard the cry clearly this time, and it was the worst moment of a day which had not been precisely pleasant.

Hilary's reflexes were normally superb; tonight they were superhuman. He was up again, staggering but deadly, at once. He turned on Martin, fists clenched, and rocked to a halt. Martin had stepped back. He had a gun. Not a rifle, a hand weapon of some kind. Kate couldn't see it clearly, but Hilary could. His broad shoulders sagged and his face went gray.

"Martin!" Peter's voice rang out. "Drop it or I'll shoot—him."

He couldn't say the name. Kate wondered if he would be able to carry out his threat; and she wondered whether Martin had noticed the almost imperceptible hesitation.

"Go ahead," Martin said.

"I mean it."

Peter's finger contracted. He meant it, all right, but that didn't mean he would enjoy it. Kate wished passionately that she had the gun. She would have cheerfully rid the world of Mark, even without the additional reward of sparing Peter the sin of fratricide.

"Go ahead," Martin repeated. He laughed aloud; the merry, confident sound made the hair of Kate's neck bristle. "I'd planned to kill him myself; I'd be delighted to have you save me the trouble."

Mark had been a silent, interested spectator. Now, knowing that he was immune for at least the length of time it took Peter to figure out his next move, he turned, shoving Tiphaine out of the way with a careless brutality that sent her sprawling. He pushed the mask up off his face.

"What the hell are you doing, Martin?"

"Completing the sacrifice," Martin said coolly. "You never should have been the head. You cheated me out of my rights. Now I'm taking them back. The others don't give a damn, they'll follow whoever's in control. Go on, Stewart; kill him. When you do, I'll dispose of this interfering young bastard."

Peter stood motionless, his finger still on the trigger. Kate knew he was gripped by the same sick awareness of failure that turned her knees to water. Clearly Peter knew how to handle a gun; but the two vital targets were too widely separated to be covered simultaneously. If he shot Mark, Martin would kill Hilary, and the threat Peter had held over the rest of the coven would be canceled.

She knew she couldn't reach Martin without his hearing her; there were too many dried, fragile objects underfoot, and the glade was too quiet. Once again she heard the thin, wailing cry, like that of some small animal caught in a trap. She turned, in an instinctive response that made her forget her logic.

The crash of the rifle sounded like a bomb in the stillness. Kate's hands flew to her ears; she turned dazed eyes toward the Devil's Pulpit, expecting to see Mark sway and fall. But Mark stood firm on his feet, as surprised as she was.

Martin was down, flat on the ground; Peter had fired at him, not at Mark. His hands were empty, but his arms were moving, groping like separately animated, detached limbs, for the gun he had dropped. Hilary, on hands and knees, was scrabbling wildly among the leaves.

The rifle went off again, and Kate spun around. Peter had fired at Volz, at close range, and missed. The two men stood braced, arms raised, struggling for the weapon. Volz was an obscene, half-naked troglodyte, but the muscles in his squat arms and shoulders were well developed, and Peter had reached the end of his strength. He went over backward, landing with a thud that knocked most of the breath out of him; the rest of it came out in a grunt as Volz's stocky body fell across him. The rifle went flying; and Kate, after an agonized appraisal of the situation, dived for it.

As her fingers closed over the smooth, silkily polished wood of the stock, it occurred to her that she didn't have the faintest idea how to fire it. The thought was fleeting; she bounded to her feet, raising the weapon in the only way that was comprehensible to her then. The butt came crashing down on the back of Volz's round head with a noise that would recur to her, in dreams, for some years to come. At the time it didn't bother her in the slightest. The general slumped to one side, his hands sliding off Peter's throat, and Kate saw Peter staring up at her. His eyes were wide and unblinking; and for a second her overworked heart stopped. Then blood from the reopened cut on his forehead trickled down into one eye, and he blinked. He staggered to his feet and reached for the gun.

In the brief seconds which had elapsed, Hilary's situation had deteriorated. He had the gun, and Martin lay motionless, dead or unconscious, but another danger was creeping up on him from behind as he stood staring down at the doctor.

Mark had vanished from the rock earlier; Kate had noted it subconsciously, thinking it was typical of Mark; he had a well-developed sense of self-preservation. She had underestimated him. To save his position of power he would take a risk, so long as it wasn't too big a risk.

Kate let out a yell of warning, and Peter threw the rifle to his shoulder. Hilary whirled. He handled the pistol awkwardly, as if he had never used one before; but at that range he didn't have to be experienced. Mark was diving at him when he pulled the trigger. The slim, darkly gleaming figure fell like a broken toy, arms and legs sprawling awkwardly.

Peter lowered the rifle; his arm moved stiffly, all in one piece, like a stick of wood. Hilary looked wildly from the huddled body at his feet, to the gun in his hand, to Peter. Then he dropped the gun, and ran. Kate heard his crashing, invisible progress stop momentarily and then go on; he had collected what he had come to get.

Then, and only then, did she remember the others. Miss Device, Senator Blankenhagen of Alabama, Mrs. Adams . . . But when she turned to look for them, they were gone. The fire burned low in the center of a quiet forest glade, empty except for the crumpled dead, and herself, and Peter.

"They've faded away," Peter said, interpreting her look. His voice was flat. "Respectability triumphs after all."

He put the rifle carefully down on the ground, moving like a tired old man, and walked slowly across the glade. Kate followed.

"Looks like the last scene of Hamlet, doesn't it?" There was no amusement in Peter's voice, or face. Going down on one knee, he extended his hand and rolled the still body over onto its back.

Mark had been shot through the center of the forehead—an astonishing shot for an inexperienced marksman. It was a small, neat hole, so neat that it looked unreal, like a painted caste mark, or symbol of the cult. The mask had dropped away in his fall; the tumbled fair hair, so much like Peter's, gleamed golden in the dying firelight. His face looked very young. He was smiling slightly. Lucifer might have appeared in such a form to those who envisioned him as the fallen angel, the morning star; the prince—of darkness, perhaps—but princely nonetheless. "Godlike shapes and forms, excelling human, princely dignities . . ."

She was not moved to mourn for him, though; relief was the strongest emotion she was conscious of feeling. Peter's face was utterly devoid of expression. After a while he stood up. With the tip of his shoe, gently but finally, he turned the body over again so that the beautiful face and staring eyes were hidden. There was some sign of emotion in his face now; but it was an emotion which twisted his mouth into a wry shape, and the bitterness in his voice, when he spoke, transformed the gracious words into a sardonic epitaph.

" 'And flocks of angels sing thee to thy rest.' But, do you know—I have my doubts."

Kate reached out for him, but she was too late. He fell like a log, face down among the crackling leaves.

# Chapter

## 13

IN THE DEAD LIGHT OF A GRAY DAWN, THE GLADE LOOKED FOR-
lorn and unreal. Kate shivered in the bitter air. The wind had
died, leaving swollen gray clouds huddling in the sky. It felt
like winter.

The neat brown-and-tan uniforms of the state troopers
looked out of place. As they moved about, talking in low
voices, she saw one hard young face after another change from
cautious incredulity to consternation. They hadn't believed any
of the story when they first heard it, even though it came from
three separate, hitherto respectable, sources. They believed it
now.

Kate wrapped her arms around her body and tried to keep
her teeth from chattering. She had warm, clean clothes, but her
body ached from lack of sleep and she felt slimy and unclean. A
long hot bath . . . She turned the idea over in her mind, luxuri-
ously and longingly. Later, maybe. Later there would be time
for other things. But first the explanations had to be made. The
dead had to be buried.

And the living had to be tended. She looked anxiously at
Peter. He was seemingly quite composed as he stood talking to
the lieutenant in charge. Someone's borrowed overcoat, several
inches too long, was thrown over his shoulders, and his left arm
was in a sling. Now that his face was comparatively clean, its
pallor was more evident, and the assorted bruises stood out like
the stains of corruption.

Kate wondered when he was going to break down. His collapse earlier that night had been temporary; she had gotten him on his feet without too much trouble, and he had walked unaided down the path to the bridle trail. But he walked like a somnambulist, and she knew that he was only partially aware of what he was doing. He was only responding because it was easier than being nagged.

Mentally she was in much the same condition, too numbed by successive shocks to think of anything except the immediate need. And that need was simple. Escape. Get away. Abandon the whole hideous mess, and find a quiet corner to hide in.

The night was dark, with only starlight to guide them. Kate turned automatically into the wider expanse of the bridle path and had taken several dragging steps before she saw the faint light glinting off the chrome trim of a dark bulk in the middle of the path. It was Volz's car. How the others had come, and gone, she did not stop to wonder. This vehicle's owner would never claim it.

She got Peter into the car, where he sat slumped and staring, and found, as she ought to have expected, that the keys were not in the ignition. They would be in Volz's pocket. A shudder ran through her at the thought of retracing her steps and searching for them. She would rather walk, impossible as that prospect now seemed. Then it occurred to her that Hilary might have an extra key—some people kept one in one of those little cases under the hood. Wearily she dragged herself out from under the wheel and—found it.

She was back in the car, inserting the key into the ignition, when the long-delayed reaction struck. She fell forward against the wheel, hands clenched around the slippery plastic, and felt the heavy circle shiver with the spasms of her body.

At her side Peter stirred and reached out for her. She transferred her frantic grip from the steering wheel to his shoulders, and went on shivering. It was a much more satisfactory position, and the slow, rhythmic thud of Peter's heart under her right ear was the most satisfactory sound she had ever heard, all the more so because there had been moments when she never expected to hear it again.

As the shivering subsided, she realized that she was clinging like a vine and clutching like a limpet, and making disgusting, feeble noises. It wasn't fair; he had undergone just as great an emotional shock as she, and had taken considerably more physical punishment. No, it wasn't fair . . . but it felt absolutely heavenly. . . . Her mind wandered off into thoughts she would have been ashamed to say aloud; and because Milton had been on her mind ("Better to reign in Hell than serve in Heaven,") she was reminded of the maddening words he had put into the mouth of Eve.

" 'God is thy law; thou mine; to know no more is woman's happiest knowledge and her praise,' " she muttered.

" 'He for God only, she for God in him,' " Peter agreed, in his normal voice. "What brought that on? It's the last sentiment I ever expected to hear from you."

"You might know a man wrote it. Oh, God, I'm so tired."

"Not surprising."

"How are you?"

"Tired."

"Am I hurting you?"

"Your head," said Peter literally, "seems to be right on top of that hole in my back. No, don't move. I guess it's worth it."

"We've got to move. We can't stay here all night."

"Let go of me, then."

"I can't. I'm afraid to. I'm afraid I'm dreaming, and that if I wake up you'll be gone."

"Don't start," Peter said harshly. "If either one of us begins with that sort of thing, we'll be babbling for hours. Do you want me to drive?"

Kate pushed herself upright, and his arms fell away; but they lingered, in passing, long enough to take any possible sting from his last speech.

"No, I'd better drive."

After a few minutes she wished she had let him take the wheel. He might be in poorer physical condition, but he couldn't possibly have done worse, even in his sleep. She felt sure she was hitting every rut and hole in the path; they were both jolted around like ice cubes in a cocktail shaker. The path across the field wasn't much better, but at last she bumped the car onto the highway and pressed down on the gas pedal. Peter roused himself and asked, "Where are we going?"

"I don't know," Kate said blankly, lifting her foot.

"Your friendly local constable won't believe a word of this. Where's the nearest state-police barracks?"

"Will they believe it?"

"They will when they see what's back there," Peter said grimly, and relapsed into silence.

It was a drive of fifteen or twenty miles, and it took Kate a full forty minutes. She drove like someone who has been drinking, not enough to make him drunk, just enough to be unreliable and yet to be aware of his unreliability. She parked the car, illegally, by the steps of the barracks, and turned to look at Peter. The brief interlude of darkness and silence was over. Now she would have to relive those moments in retelling them. He returned her look of panic with a faint smile and a shrug.

"Take a deep breath," he said, and opened the car door.

As soon as they went through the door, Kate knew that the way had been paved for them. The sound of a baby yelling burst out at them like a siren. At any other time she would have laughed at the look on the face of the young trooper who was holding the squawling bundle over his shoulder.

"A bachelor, obviously," said Kate, holding out her arms.

The young man's professional cool had abandoned him; he didn't ask who she was, or blink at her fantastic appearance. He dropped the bundle into her arms as if it had been red hot, and wiped his brow on his sleeve.

"It won't stop yelling," he explained nervously. "What's the matter with it?"

"Wet, hungry, and sleepy," Kate said. She bounced the bundle experimentally and the yells subsided, though they did not die away completely. "It isn't hurt. It couldn't make that much noise if it were. It isn't hurt. . . . ." She sat down abruptly in the chair the trooper had vacated, clutching the baby tightly. It responded with an ungrateful squawl, and Kate started to rock back and forth.

"I can't do anything about any of those things," the trooper said unhappily.

"You must have something I could tear up for a diaper. Don't you men sleep here? An old sheet, pillowcase, something."

"Oh. I guess so." The boy's face brightened at the prospect

of handing over his job to a suitable female expert. He turned and caught sight of Peter, who was watching him with amusement; and his face hardened into older lines.

"What happened to you? And the lady—she's been in an accident, or something, too."

"Or something. It's a long story," Peter said. "Take us to your leader, or whatever you call him."

"There's somebody with him now. If you'll tell me—"

"I think we'd better join them," Peter said, gently but inexorably. "It's all part of the same—accident."

"What shall I do with this baby?" Kate turned the unfortunate infant around. "It's a cute baby," she said pensively.

"How can you tell? All I can see is its mouth—wide open. Hell," the trooper said wildly, "bring it along. The lieutenant's going out of his mind now. What's one more baby?"

They found Hilary sitting beside the lieutenant's desk. There were no bright lights; but the air of disbelief was thick. Hilary looked up, startled, at their entrance, and his face broke into a broad white smile of sheer relief that made him look even younger than his eighteen years.

"Man," he said emphatically, "am I ever glad to see you!"

Kate didn't blame the lieutenant for being unhappy. He was a wiry little man, older by some twenty years than many of the men under him, and the remnants of what had been a fine head of sandy hair were standing straight up by the end of the story. He didn't believe it, and he said as much, with amplification.

Peter, who had narrated the tale in a concise, unemphatic manner—with only two small evasions of the truth—made no verbal rebuttal. He simply held out his hands. Some of the swelling had gone down, but the effect was still convincing. Kate couldn't imagine how he had managed to hold onto the rifle, much less get his finger around the trigger.

The lieutenant breathed twice through his nose. "Better put something on those wrists," he said, after a moment. "You, too, miss—er—Doctor. You look as if you could stand a little first aid yourself."

"What I need is a bath," Kate said vigorously, "and I don't

think there's time for that now. And Peter doesn't need any first-aid nonsense either, what he needs is a doctor; that wound in his back ought to be looked at, I don't know what was on the point of that arrow, maybe poison, even, and—"

"Poison? Arrow?" The lieutenant's face turned red. "Lady. Please don't say anything else. We'll go out to the woods, where you said, and have a look. I can't be any fairer than that, can I?"

"I'm going to take Dr. More home first," Peter said. "She needs warmer clothing. We'll meet you there."

"And for pity's sake," Kate added, transferring the bundle from one aching shoulder to the other, "Let me do something with this baby!"

The lieutenant knew a woman in town who would take care of the baby temporarily. Kate watched it depart, still howling, over the arm of the trooper who had been designated for this task. She was already forming vague plans for the child; such a dramatic beginning to its life merited consideration, if not atonement. Besides, it had provided the only light touch, and a badly needed one, in the whole horrible affair.

Hilary Jackson, who had listened to Peter's version of the happening with magnificent composure, was not so easy to dispose of. Peter insisted that he be sent home, and the lieutenant was equally determined to keep him. Hilary broke the deadlock himself. He not only had no objection to being detained; he would, he remarked, feel a hell of a lot better with some good thick bars between him and the outside world. Bars, he pointed out, kept people out in addition to keeping them in.

Peter nodded thoughtfully.

"You've got a definite point. For the next few hours, at least. I wish I could emulate you."

"Yeah," Hilary said unemphatically.

The two men contemplated one another in silence for a moment, Hilary looking down from his magnificent height. They shook hands in frowning silence, and Peter turned on his heel and marched out.

Men, Kate thought disgustedly. She held out her hand.

"He might at least have said 'Thanks,'" she said. "Hilary . . . later, when this is finished—"

"Forget it." He grinned, suddenly and charmingly, and the

big hand tightened around hers so vigorously that she barely repressed a squeal of pain. "You didn't do so badly yourself," he said.


Now, as she stood shivering in the cold light of the glade, she tried to concentrate on memories like that, and not on the things that lay, broken and abandoned, on the ground. The lieutenant was converted; one look at Mark's grotesque mask, and the tattered remnants of the other costumes, was enough. Watching his face, which had lost much of its normal ruddy color, Kate wished passionately that she could remain where she was, detached, an observer. But she had to know what was going to happen. And she had to be near Peter when he spoke of his brother.

"I just can't believe it," the lieutenant was saying, as she approached. "The most influential people in the whole damn town . . . Damn it, Stewart, I can't arrest people like the Senator, not on this charge. Witchcraft! I think they repealed the law a few years back."

"I don't give a damn what you do," Peter said wearily. "You'll need legal advice, I suppose. . . . But Dr. More is not without influence herself, you know. At the very least these people must be made to resign from any positions of responsibility they now hold."

"Particularly Miss Device and the Foundling Home," Kate said.

"But people got killed," the lieutenant said helplessly. "I still haven't got that straight. Who the hell killed who?"

"I'm the only available arrestee," Peter said calmly. "I shot Martin. Delightful thought," he added.

"He did it to save the baby," Kate said. "And Hilary."

"Yeah, the Jackson kid." The lieutenant scratched his head. "How does he come into this?"

"He's the hero," Peter said. Only Kate, who had, in some odd way, memorized his every gesture and expression, observed the slight narrowing of his eyes. "He saved us, and the child."

"Yeah," the lieutenant muttered, "and brought the rifle?"

Kate, who had never played poker, barely repressed an exclamation. She still had an intellectual's contempt for nonprofessionals; she had to fight that, it led her into dangerous errors—such as assuming that the lieutenant's bovine face concealed a brain of the same caliber.

"He brought the rifle," Peter agreed. "And gave it to me."

"Then your prints will be on it?"

"They already are on it," Peter said impatiently. "I've admitted killing Martin. What the hell are you trying to prove?"

"The facts. Only the facts. So you killed Martin. That would be after he shot the other guy—your—brother, you say?"

"Can't you leave him alone?" Kate exploded. "He's hurt and sick and he's had a terrible shock. We told you what happened. And if you think he lied about something, you're right." Peter turned on her, his face forbidding, but Kate rushed on. "He didn't kill the general, I did; I bashed his head in with the butt of that gun. You'll find my prints on it too. I did it to keep him from strangling Peter, but I would have done it anyhow, he needed killing as much as Martin did, and if you think I'm ashamed of it you're crazy, I'll stand right up and tell any judge and jury all about it, and furthermore—"

Peter relaxed, his lips twitching, and the lieutenant literally threw up his hands.

"Okay, okay, okay! Take it easy, will you, Doc?"

"And don't call me Doc!"

"Sorry. Look, Doc—I mean, Miss More. I'm not trying to railroad anybody. I just want to find out what happened. I knew there was something fishy; after all these years I've got so I can smell a lie. So now I know. So he was trying to protect you. That's nice. But stupid."

"And superfluous," Peter murmured. "She doesn't need protecting."

"You're so right," the lieutenant agreed.

They exchanged a superior, masculine look, and Kate watched them tolerantly. Under her calm facade her brain was racing.

Peter's comment had been literally true; he wouldn't insult her by such an idiotic lie. He was trying to protect someone, but not out of quixotic gallantry. Even if he was acquitted, Hilary Jackson would be irreparably damaged by being tried on a murder charge. And he wasn't in the clear yet. Neither she nor Peter had been in any condition the night before to remember the one, indisputable piece of evidence which could bring Hilary before a jury.

She forced her eyes from the one tolerable object in the clearing—Peter's face—and glanced around.

One of the troopers had found the rifle immediately; it lay by Volz's body, where Peter had dropped it, and after the lieutenant had examined it, it had been stowed away as part of the evidence. The other gun had not yet been found. They hadn't really gotten around to looking for it yet, being preoccupied with the human remains, and it was probably buried deep in drifted leaves. She knew approximately where it must be— about six feet from the huddled shape of Mark's body. Somehow she must force herself to go over there. And she would have to hurry. One of the troopers was kneeling by Mark, his hands questing through the leaves.

While she was still thinking, Peter acted.

"Lieutenant. Before you take him away . . . may I . . . ?"

"Huh?" The lieutenant looked from Mark's body to Peter's averted face and blinked. "Sure," he said awkwardly. "Al, come over here."

Peter had also mentally marked the spot; probably neither of them would ever forget the details of that night. When his dragging steps had brought him to the site, he stumbled and dropped to one knee. Still kneeling, he covered his eyes with one hand; the other trailed limply at his side, the fingers moving nervously.

Kate saw the young man, Al, turn his head away. He must be new at the job. But Peter's pose and bowed head were genuine enough to bring a quick sting of tears to her own eyes.

When Peter got to his feet, amid a respectful silence, there was something in his right hand. He looked at it dazedly, and held it out toward the lieutenant.

"Here's the gun," he said.

The lieutenant yelped and leaped forward.

"Damn it to hell! Don't you know better than to pick up evidence?"

"Sorry; wasn't I supposed to?" Peter meekly surrendered the weapon.

The lieutenant's reply was heated. When his wrath died

down, he gave Peter a look in which annoyance, respect, and a faint amusement were mingled.

"Okay, Stewart, that's all. Get the hell out of here before you mess anything else up. I don't need you any longer. Nor Miss More."

"Thank you," Peter said gravely.

"I'll want to see you, probably later today." The lieutenant sighed; he looked not like a policeman but like a tired, middle-aged man with too many worries. "God, this is going to be a mess. . . . Where will you be?"

Peter hesitated.

"Baltimore," he said, after a moment. "I'll call you when we've found a hotel."

"Why Baltimore?" Kate asked.

"Do you want to go back to your place?"

"No. No, I don't."

"Nor is the Middleburg Inn a happy choice," Peter pointed out. "We need to get away from Middleburg, Lieutenant. We'll let you know."

They walked side by side toward the path. In deference to Peter's frowning abstraction Kate didn't take his arm, though she wanted desperately to touch him. She knew what was coming, and knew that he hated it as much as she did. Sooner or later the question would have to be asked, but she couldn't bring herself to ask it.

They had taken Volz's car; it was still parked at the end of the path, and Kate got a sadistic, if illogical, satisfaction when she thought of the beating it had taken in the last twenty-four hours.

Peter had taken over the driving as soon as they left the police barracks. She had questioned the wisdom of his driving with one arm and had received a stare of such silent outrage that she hadn't raised the point again. This time, when he was behind the wheel, instead of starting the car, he turned to face her.

"Tiphaine is at the house," he said. "That's why I don't want you to go back there. You can buy a toothbrush in Baltimore."

"Is she—"

"Alive? Not altogether."

"Peter, tell me. I can't stand euphemisms, not now."

"Schizophrenia, I guess that's the technical term. She's

completely withdrawn; sits, moves, stands on order, but does nothing by herself. She was well on the way before, Kate; last night she went right on over the edge."

"I see."

"Not much else to say, is there?" His arm over the back of the seat, Peter made no move to touch her. "I've seen cases like hers before. The chance of recovery is not very good."

"I know. . . . What happened to her last night? I forgot about her. Isn't that awful. . . . ?"

"So did I. She must have gone into shock when Mark was killed. The police found her this morning, curled up like a worm, beside him."

"That's why you insisted on stopping at the house before we came out here."

"I spoke to the lieutenant before we left, asked him to get her out of the way before we got here. I didn't know what we'd find, whether she'd be alive, or dead or . . . But I didn't want you to see her. They got her away, through the woods, before we arrived."

He waited for a moment. Kate said nothing, only sat staring down at the hands which lay lax on her knee. Peter started the car. When they were back on the highway, he said, "In a sense she's the most tragic figure of all. I know how you must be feeling. . . . If that foul uncle of yours hadn't gotten his hands on her . . ."

"I don't know," Kate said dully. "I just don't know any longer. What about Mark? You turned out all right. . . . Don't sympathize with me, Peter. It's just as bad for you as it is for me."

"Worse for you," Peter said, his eyes on the road. "It's not my world which has fallen to pieces. Will you want to stay on here, do you think?"

"I don't know . . ."

"It's not all that different from the rest of the world, you know. Human beings are the one thing you can't run away from, and they're pretty much alike." He gave a short laugh. "Full of advice, aren't I? I'm sorry, I don't really mean to sound so smug and omniscient. If you don't want to go to Baltimore . . ."

"You have no idea," Kate said, staring straight ahead, "how wonderful it is to have someone tell me what to do. But it won't last," she added wearily. "I'm not the frail female type. I'm bossy, and arrogant, and conceited; I think I'm smarter than most people, so I don't take advice very well. . . ."

Peter put his foot down on the brake. The car slid to a stop on the shoulder of the road, and he turned to face her.

"I'll risk it," he said.